Peter Campbell Scarlett

A Memoir of the Right Honourable James,

first Lord Abinger, chief baron of Her Majesty's Court of Exchequer, including a

fragment of his autobiography and selections from his correspondence and

speeches

Peter Campbell Scarlett

A Memoir of the Right Honourable James,
first Lord Abinger, chief baron of Her Majesty's Court of Exchequer, including a fragment of his autobiography and selections from his correspondence and speeches

ISBN/EAN: 9783337012182

Printed in Europe, USA, Canada, Australia, Japan

Cover: Foto ©Raphael Reischuk / pixelio.de

More available books at **www.hansebooks.com**

JAMES, FIRST LORD ABINGER

LONDON : PRINTED BY
SPOTTISWOODE AND CO., NEW-STREET SQUARE
AND PARLIAMENT STREET

A MEMOIR

OF

THE RIGHT HONOURABLE

JAMES, FIRST LORD ABINGER

CHIEF BARON OF
HER MAJESTY'S COURT OF EXCHEQUER

INCLUDING A FRAGMENT OF HIS AUTOBIOGRAPHY AND
SELECTIONS FROM HIS CORRESPONDENCE
AND SPEECHES

BY THE HON.

PETER CAMPBELL SCARLETT, C.B.

With a Portrait

LONDON
JOHN ·MURRAY, ALBEMARLE STREET
1877

TO MY NEPHEW

WILLIAM FREDERIC, THIRD LORD ABINGER

COLONEL IN COMMAND OF HER MAJESTY'S SCOTS FUSILIER GUARDS

AND TO MY SON

CAPTAIN LEOPOLD SCARLETT

BROTHER OFFICERS IN THE SAME DISTINGUISHED CORPS

𝕴 𝕯𝖊𝖉𝖎𝖈𝖆𝖙𝖊 𝖙𝖍𝖎𝖘 𝕸𝖊𝖒𝖔𝖎𝖗

OF

THEIR GRANDFATHER

JAMES, FIRST LORD ABINGER

P. CAMPBELL SCARLETT

CONTENTS.

a

INTRODUCTION

B

CHAPTER I.

IMPERFECT AND UNFINISHED MEMOIR LEFT BY LORD
ABINGER—MY INABILITY TO WRITE HIS LIFE AND
CAREER AT THE BAR.

MY FATHER, James Scarlett, first Lord Abinger, began too
late in life to compose his autobiography. At the time of
his death the narrative embraced only his youthful days, and
the commencement of his career at the Bar. He alludes in
it to his subsequent success, but the fragment I now venture to
publish, as a filial tribute to his memory, fails to do him justice.
So far as it goes it will, I hope, not be found uninteresting,
and I will endeavour to add some extracts from his correspondence at various periods, and from his speeches which may
serve to revive the recollection of a distinguished man, not
yet wholly forgotten. My own professional engagements in
the Diplomatic Service obliged me to leave England at an
early age, thus depriving me of opportunities I might otherwise
have had of personally observing and appreciating the talents
and ability which rendered my father so conspicuous in Westminster Hall. Had I followed the profession of the Law, for
which I was at one time intended, I might myself have undertaken to complete the history of his life, a task for which I am
now incompetent. I regret this the more, as his own MS. does
not include the most important period of his career, which was
after he entered Parliament. His remarks about Pitt, Fox,
Erskine, and other celebrated contemporaries, his observations
concerning his own practice in Courts of Law, and the comparison drawn between Parliamentary and forensic oratory
will, I imagine, be especially interesting to the legal profession;

but the short narrative he has left does not touch upon that portion of his life during which he was brought more into personal contact and greater intimacy with many eminent and illustrious men, and I regret to think how much matter is wanting to interest the general reader.

It will be seen in this memoir to what causes he attributed his great success at the Bar. It was certainly not owing to patronage or favour, but chiefly to his own ability and acuteness, his untiring industry, the liberal education he had received, and his unsparing labour to acquire a thorough mastery of his profession. No one, I believe, among the barristers of his day, showed greater learning at Common Law or obtained more influence with judges and juries in the Courts in which he practised. Very few have shown the tact and talent he always displayed. He possessed some personal advantages which rendered these powers more effective. A fine intelligent countenance, the tone and bearing of a gentleman, combined with energy and animation. He rarely indulged in declamation, but, avoiding exaggeration, addressed himself rather to the reason and judgment than to the passions and prejudices of his audience. The result of which was that the Bench, the Bar, and the public felt they had to deal with an honourable man who inspired confidence by his truth and honesty.

When he was raised to the Bench he was always clear, logical, impartial, and humane. Some of his charges to grand juries, although wholly unprepared, were both able and eloquent. One will be found among the papers I propose to publish, which was so much approved of at the time, that a deputation of magistrates at Leicester, headed by Lord Charles Manners, publicly expressed to him the obligation it had laid them under. This occurred at a time of great excitement caused by agricultural outrages, and it is the more impressed on my memory as I happened to be present on the occasion.

CHAPTER II.

THE reasons which induced my father to leave Jamaica are
stated by himself in his memoir.

Through my grandfather's liberality, he had ample means
for his maintenance at college in England. He was at first
desirous of adopting the navy as his profession, but was persuaded finally to prefer the law, and with a view thereto, he
was entered a student at the Inner Temple, and at the age
of sixteen a fellow commoner at Trinity College, Cambridge.

The fact of his being entered at the University as a fellow
commoner prevented him from seeking academical honours,
at that time open only to pensioners and sizars.

In those days, noblemen and fellow commoners were
restricted to honorary degrees; but as my father had dili-
gently studied mathematics and classics with a tutor before
his arrival in this country, and for his age was well instructed
in both, more justice would have been done to his abilities
had he gone up to Cambridge as a pensioner. Although he
had not the advantages offered by Eton and Harrow, where

at an early age friendships are often made, and sometimes not forgotten, my father was, as I have heard him say, as a fellow commoner at once thrown into the society of many undergraduates of rank and family, some of whom in after life were among his most intimate friends. Among these, I may venture to name a most enduring friendship with Prince William, afterwards his Royal Highness the Duke of Gloucester, whose affectionate attachment lasted during life.

Through H.R.H. he had the honor of becoming personally acquainted with many other members of the Royal family, from whom he often received proofs of consideration and favour for which he had reason to be justly proud and grateful.

It is hardly necessary to inform my older readers that my father became, very early in life, attached to the Whig party. In politics, he was what would now be called a Liberal Conservative. The old Whigs, at the present day, are not, I imagine, to be differently described, whatever nomenclature may be in fashion. Until driven into opposition by Lord Russell's celebrated Reform Bill, he never deserted the Whig flag. But to that extreme measure he was entirely and conscientiously opposed. Nor was he alone in opposition to a party with which he had always acted, and from which it then caused him great pain to separate. Abercromby and Lord Rosslyn abandoned their political friends on that occasion, and many others it will be remembered, who voted for the Bill, joined afterwards in opposing the Liberal Cabinets which succeeded Lord Grey, although they had, perhaps not without reluctance, given their support to that measure.

The late Lord Derby, Sir Francis Burdett, and even Lord Brougham were afterwards in the Conservative ranks.

Before the time of the Reform Bill, my father had taken office under Canning with the full approbation of the Whig party. It was also with the approval of that party generally that he first took office, under the Duke of Wellington, as Attorney-General.

It has been supposed, with what truth I do not know, that after the Duke had brought in and passed the measure for relieving the Roman Catholics from their disabilities, he would have had the support of the most influential members of the Whig party if he had broken off his connection with the Ultra-Tories, and that some of the leading Whigs, if invited to form part of the Duke's Government, would not at that period have refused to join it. That my father earnestly desired it, I have no doubt.

Under such a coalition a more moderate measure of reform might have satisfied the country, and more gradual and well considered changes would have rendered the Bill 'the whole Bill and nothing but the Bill' as unnecessary, as it seemed to many at the time to be fatally dangerous. To the admission however into his Cabinet of a more liberal element the Duke was hopelessly averse. The hue and cry of the country in favour of reform, he appeared entirely to disregard. The transfer of the franchise to large cities, at the sacrifice of the close boroughs, he believed to be a direct attack on the landed interests ; and to such changes then considered necessary he was opposed, on the ground that after they were made the future government of the Crown would be not more difficult merely, but impracticable. It was at this juncture that the Whigs joined with their more radical allies to turn out the Duke, whose resistance to all reform made his resignation of power a matter of public necessity. The Whigs were triumphant, and the extreme measure they advocated was a natural consequence of the overwhelming force of public opinion, which they had not a little helped when out of office to produce, and the fruits of which at first appeared in some degree to justify the fears and prophecies of their predecessors.

Before these events occurred, all the members of the Canning party, including my father, had ceased to support the Duke's Government, and were no longer in office.

Now that this Bill was brought in he had to consider what line he should adopt. He was expected by his old Whig friends to support it in Parliament ; but, however attached personally to Lord Grey, the great chief of the party with which he had been so long politically connected, he felt that he could not conscientiously take that side on this occasion.

Although by no means opposed to what he considered

desirable and necessary reforms, to the abolition of many
of the close boroughs and the enfranchisement of large
cities, he was absolutely opposed to so sweeping a change.
It involved, he thought, a dangerous separation of power
from property, and was so democratic in principle as to
be no other than a violent attack upon the Constitution,
utterly uncalled for and unnecessary. Nor could he persuade
himself that such alterations might be made in the measure
when in Committee as would render it less dangerous.
Such being the view he took, and grieved though he was to
abandon his party, he determined to take his seat on the
opposition benches. With this object he resigned the Whig
borough of Malton, and accepted from his friend Earl Lonsdale
the offer of Cockermouth, for which he was elected, and he
both spoke and voted against the Reform Bill.

I need hardly remind all my readers how society was torn
by party violence engendered by the Bill. This apple of
discord broke up old friendships, and severed many ties of
ancient standing. New alliances were formed, and each of
the contending factions dubbed its opponent the enemy of his
country, whilst truth and candour were sometimes sacrificed
in the passion and fury of debate.

Looking back to that period of storm, now happily sub-
sided, and which I hope may never return, I cannot help
regretting that my father did not confine his public life at that
period to the precincts of Westminster Hall. Why should he
have thrown himself into the midst of an arena, a prey to
needless spite and rancour, at a time when those who doubted
the merits of the Reform Bill, the patriotism of mobs and
even the legislative wisdom of Birmingham and Manchester,
were treated with virtuous indignation or overwhelmed with
abuse ?

Certainly, had he lived to these times, he would have found
very little difference of opinion between so-called Conservatives
and modern Liberals. Differences of opinion there are, but
chiefly about details, and none are so irreconcilable as to em-
bitter social existence by political enmity.

The Whigs for a time, under such great leaders as Earl
Grey, Lord John Russell, and their Chancellor Brougham,

enjoyed in a reformed Parliament the breezes of popularity; but the Conservative opposition, led by the Duke and Peel, gradually gained strength, and notwithstanding the extinction of the close boroughs, chiefly on the Tory side, they at last defeated the Reform Government and returned to office.

It was on that occasion, in 1834, that my father accepted the offer made to him of the post of Chief Baron, vacated by Lord Lyndhurst.

He had before this event resigned his seat at Cockermouth, and contested sucessfully the borough of Norwich, for which he sat in Parliament.

To hold the office of Chief Baron he was of course obliged to vacate his seat at Norwich, and he was then raised to the Bench and accepted a Peerage.

He desired to be called to the House of Lords by the title of Abinger, and orders were given to make out the patent in that name; but his constituents at Norwich wished him to take the name of their city. The title of Norwich was then held by the Duke of Gordon, who had no successor, and His Grace was so good as to approve of this title being transferred to Sir James Scarlett. However the patent of Abinger was ready, and instead of altering it, he introduced into his coat of arms the Castle of Norwich, out of compliment to the electors, and the original title thought of was retained.

I may mention here, that in the early part of this century, when I had attained my fifth year, Abinger Hall became the property of my father by purchase. I still cherish these early recollections of the place. It was not a large property, and there were afterwards debates in the family as to the prudence of laying out much money upon it; but my father was delighted with everything, and ended by nearly rebuilding the house.

At that period of his life his activity both of mind and body was remarkable. As to the latter, whether walking or on horseback, he was indefatigible. Generally during term time, after the summer vacation, he rode on a Saturday all the way from London to Abinger, sending forward a horse to Epsom, and on the Monday following he returned in the same way to town in time for his court at 9. A.M. where he went through his ordinary labour at the Bar for the rest of the day without exhibiting any sign of fatigue, his health and vigour being then quite marvellous.

During these short visits to the country he often entertained numerous guests; and from his high spirits, lively conversation, and acquaintance with literature, he was an agreeable host, and at all times in his family circle a most agreeable companion.

One of his favourite walks was to a farm he had in his own hands, to which he was fond of taking his friends, who were sometimes diverted if not edified by the quaint manners of a Methodist bailiff and his wife, both much attached to him notwithstanding their rather over-pious contempt for the outer world illustrated by quotations from Scripture, of which they made free use on these occasions.

I believe both Royston and his wife were really honest folks, though the husband's want of memory exhibited in the following anecdote may look a little suspicious. When General Sir Edward Kerrison and another friend were staying at Abinger they had heard my father complain of the numerous bills sent into him, the contents of which he was quite unable to verify, adding that he trusted much more in the honesty of tradesmen and servants than to his own knowledge and recollection of the accuracy of the numerous bills presented for his payment. Sir Edward proposed to me and several others to put my father's faith in such bills to an immediate proof. He accordingly drew up on a long sheet of paper a very tradesmanlike account of repairing furniture and moving cabinets and tables about the house dated at some time back, and supposed to come from some cabinetmaker at Dorking or Guildford, the amount being above 20*l.* This was put into an envelope and directed to him, and left on the table of his study. My father, after a time having seen the bill, adverted to his previous conversation, and to our amusement informed us that here was another instance of a bill just come in about which he had not the most remote recollection. Somebody suggested that perhaps Royston would know, who happened to be near at hand, and was summoned to be questioned. He looked steadily at the bill and went over the items, and then said in a deliberate voice that he had no doubt it must be right. He could recollect some furniture being repaired and moved about that date, he thought. This was too much for us, and we burst out laughing. My father was released from any anxiety about the genuineness of the bill, and Royston retired in confusion to be more accurate, it was hoped, in future.

From the time he left College, my father became intimate with Sir Samuel Romilly, who afterwards lived with Lady Romilly and his family at Tanhurst, about four miles from Abinger. The frequent intercourse between the two families at that time was a great enjoyment, and the rides to Tanhurst, with the fine view over the whole county of Sussex from Leith Hill and its neighbourhood, were a constant delight to him.

Abinger Hall is no longer in the family, but the present Lord Abinger and myself are still landlords to some extent in the parishes of Abinger, Wotton, and Ockley.

My father had estates also in Sussex and Dorsetshire, which have been sold.

My elder brother became a Scotch proprietor, and Inverlochy Castle, in Inverness-shire, is settled on the peerage.

CHAPTER III.[1]

THE ORIGIN AND GENEALOGY OF THE SCARLETTS.

AN interesting and curious book, 'The Norman People,' published last year (1875), thus alludes to the early origin and name of ' Scarlett.'

'" Scarlett" from Carlat or Escarlat (Aquitaine). Bernard was Viscount of Carlat, 932. (Anselme II. 695, &c.) From him descended Richard, Gilbert, and Raymond, joint Viscounts of Carlat, who appear to have accompanied the Conqueror, 1066. From the first descended Hugh, the Viscount, d. before 1159, who had Hugh de Carlat, Count of Rhodes, 1199.'

'In 1195, the Hospitallers had land in York, the gift of Hugh Scarlet or Carlat, and at the same time occur William Scarlett in Somerset and Kent, Gilbert Scarlett in Middlesex. Mon. ii. 540 (R. C. R.) The family thenceforth appears in several parts of England. It still bears the lion rampant of the Viscounts of Carlat. Hence the eminent Chief Baron Scarlett, Lord Abinger.'

Whatever importance may be attached to the above authority, it is certain that the Scarletts have always borne the same coat of arms, Chequy Or and Gules with the lion rampant, which I am informed denotes in Heraldry, a military career. The name also in former times was spelt Carlat.

The crest was originally, but, of course, of later date than the shield, a Doric or Tuscan column supported by lions,

---

[1] This Chapter is intended only as a family record for my own relations, and has no interest for the general reader.

rampant.   In more modern times lions' paws only have been used on the crest.

Antiquarians assert that the name was in existence in Greece and Italy before it denoted a colour.

There is a Greek family of the name of Scarlatto at this day, which word does not signify in Greece a colour, and the word scarlet as a colour was unknown to the ancient Greeks, though so often used as a translation of πορφύρεος or purple in the modern versions of the New Testament.   In fact, the family is older than the colour.   I am not aware of any family of a different name bearing the same arms or crest.   I have seen the Doric column with two lions as supporters over the gateway at Mycene, and it is possible some ancestor may have taken the idea of the crest now used from that device.   Soon after the Conquest, the Scarletts were undoubtedly large landowners in Kent, and down to the sixteenth and seventeenth centuries they had landed estates in Norfolk, Suffolk, Shropshire, York, and Sussex.   Although these families seem to be extinct in those counties, the pedigrees of some of them are to be found at the British Museum and at the Heralds' College.   My father was aware that he was of ancient descent, but he cared little for the study of genealogy.   He always believed that he was descended from a family of that name in the eastern counties. All these families bore the arms and crest used by my family at this date, and may have been related to each other ; but it is now well ascertained that my father's immediate descent was from a branch settled in Sussex, which emigrated in the reign of Charles II. to Jamaica.

At an early period the Sussex Scarletts were settled near Eastbourne and Pevensea.

According to the investigations of the Archæological Society of Sussex, one of the name was a Baron of the Cinque Ports at Pevensea in the reign of Edward III.   Possibly the same person might have been Governour of Rochester Castle, as about the same time one of the name was Governour of the castle, and related by marriage to Lord Broke of Cobham, who succeeded him there as Governour.

There are indications from a search made in the parish

register at Trinity Church, Allhallows Barking, with which locality near the Tower of London it appears that the family of Scarlett in Sussex was connected, that they were probably descended from Thomas Scarlett, Armiger, who fought at Agincourt. The name of this gentleman is on the Agincourt Roll. He brought three archers with him into the field, and a Patent is preserved at the Rolls Office in Chancery Lane, signed by Henry V. at Touque in Normandy, promoting him for his gratuitous services to an office 'in Aulâ Regis.'

My father was undoubtedly descended from another soldier, who distinguished himself at that battle. Namely, Richard Waller, celebrated for having on that occasion made prisoner the Duke of Orleans, of whom he had charge for seventeen years, at his residence, near Groombridge, in Kent. The descent is traced through Elizabeth Waller, who married Sir John Lawrence, the father of the Lord President of Cromwell's Council.

The President married Amy Peyton, the daughter of Sir John Peyton, Bart., a descendant of Malet, a friend and follower of the Conqueror, from whom the present Sir Alexander Malet is descended. The names, both of the President and his father are mentioned in Milton's Sonnet :—

'Lawrence, of virtuous father, virtuous son.'

In later times one of the Jamaica Lawrences was a rich proprietor in England—I mean Miss Lawrence, of Studley Park, now the property of Lord Ripon. My earliest recollection is being taken there by my father and mother, on a visit.

The history of our family in Sussex is well ascertained as follows :—

Benjamin Scarlett, supposed to have been the eldest son of Francis Scarlett, M.A., Vicar of Sherborne, in Dorsetshire, owned, in the reign of James I., several estates and manors in Sussex and in Kent. By wills of the family, copies of which are in my possession, Benjamin's eldest son, by a first marriage, was Captain Francis Scarlett. This son he disinherited ; and the estates in England were left to another son Thomas, his eldest born of a second marriage with Mary

Kenward, of Raynham, in Kent. After his father's death, Francis endeavoured to recover possession of the property as heir-at-law, alleging that his father's will could not be found. After various suits before the first Lord Clarendon in Chancery, it turned out that the will had been burnt at St. Paul's Church, during the fire of London, where wills were then deposited ; but an authenticated copy of the will was produced in Court, and admitted as valid. Francis was deprived of the English estates, but remained in possession of 1,000 acres of land, on the River Wagwater, in the Island of Jamaica, where both he and his brothers had obtained grants of land soon after the island was taken from the Spaniards.

Francis died without issue, leaving by his will all his estates in Jamaica to his nephew William, the eldest son of his half-brother Thomas.

Francis Scarlett was the first of the name, I believe, who resided in the island, and he was a member of the first Legislative Assembly in Jamaica.

His nephew William, a student at the Middle Temple, had been called to the Bar before he inherited his uncle's estates, but he then left England to take possession of them, having previously married.

From that ancestor we are lineally descended.

On looking over the register of names at the Inner Temple, I discovered those of Benjamin and Francis, father and son, who were entered there as students. The next name on the list, although the dates are so far apart, is my father's.

I will relate here a story taken out of the family papers of the late Sir Thomas Maryon Wilson, whose ancestor, in the reign of Charles II., was owner of Compton Place, near Eastbourne, now the property of the Duke of Devonshire, as it has reference to Francis Scarlett.

A younger son of the first Baronet was kidnapped in London by pirates, taken on board a vessel in the Thames, and carried off to Jamaica. He was there taken to the estate of a lady in the Island and sold to her as a slave. He managed to make this circumstance known to the Governor of Jamaica, and as Francis Scarlett was then in the island, and known to the

Wilson family at Eastbourne, he was deputed to use his efforts to release young Wilson from bondage. Upon his arrival on the estate he found that Wilson was not treated as a slave, but that the lady, whose name I do not remember, had become much attached to him, and was very unwilling that he should leave her. After great difficulty, however, Captain Francis Scarlett was successful in his negotiations, and having released the disenchanted slave from the wiles of Calypso he transferred him to the Governor's protection until he could be sent back to his family and friends in England. If I am not mistaken he succeeded afterwards to the Baronetcy.

But to return to William Scarlett, the nephew of the Captain. From that epoch William and his descendants resided chiefly in Jamaica. They were wealthy people, and were connected with many of the best families there. The north side of the island was colonised in a great measure by the Lawrences, and the Scarletts were also considerable land-owners.

My great-grandfather, James Scarlett, was a large proprietor near Montego Bay, married, as it appears by my father's memoirs, to a relation of the General Wolfe who fell at Quebec. He had four sons, William, James, Charles, and my grandfather, Robert Scarlett. He had also numerous daughters, one of whom, Christiana, married the son of Sir John Gordon, of Earlston, a baronet of ancient lineage in Scotland.

My eldest uncle, Philip Anglin Scarlett, inherited from my grandfather the estate of Cambridge, in St. James. My grandfather's third son, Robert, took an M.D. degree at Edinburgh, and inherited Duckett's Spring and the estate of Success, in the same parish; but my father and his youngest brother, William Anglin, afterwards Chief Justice of the Island, declined to be landed proprietors in Jamaica, and in consequence escaped the common ruin which followed upon the sudden liberation of the slaves. My father came to England in 1785.

Several years after my father left the University of Cambridge he was married to my mother, the daughter of Peter Campbell, Esq., of Kilmory, in Argyllshire, who had also large West Indian estates. Mr. Campbell was a lineal descendant of the distinguished family of Auchenbreck. His ancestor, Sir Duncan Campbell, was killed at the Battle of Inverlochy, fighting at the head of his clan. My grandfather Campbell also married a Campbell of Auchenbreck, his first cousin. He had three sons, Peter, Colin, and Archibald. The two last died early. His only sister married Mr. Yorke, of Beverley and Richmond, in Yorkshire. My uncle, Peter Campbell, the surviving son, was a fellow commoner with my father at Trinity College. It was owing to their intimacy that my father made my mother's acquintance. His marriage did not take place until seven years later, after an engagement for that time, her father being averse to the marriage until my father's success at the Bar gave him the prospect of a better income. I propose to make a few extracts from his letters to her, which have been kept. My mother lived often at Richmond with the Yorkes, and also at Tittenhanger, with her grandmother.

My uncle, Peter Campbell, inherited Kilmory, an old family property, in Argyllshire, with the estates of his father in Jamaica, Holland and Fish River, which last, as he died without a male heir, were sold to Mr. Gladstone, the father of the late Minister. Kilmory, inherited by his two daughters, is now the property of Sir John Orde, Bart., who married the eldest.

My mother died in 1829. Later in life my father married the widow of the Rev. Henry Ridley, a sister of Mr. Lee Steere, of Jayes, near Ockley, the present Member for the Western Division of Surrey.

AUTOBIOGRAPHY

CHAPTER IV.

HIS BIRTH AND EARLY EDUCATION IN JAMAICA.

I WAS born in the Island of Jamaica on the 13th day of December, 1769. Having left that country at the age of fifteen, and having at no time taken an interest in genealogy, I can give but little account of my father's family. My father's ancestors, I have heard, had some estates in Suffolk and Essex in the reign of Charles II. How long they had been settled in Jamaica is entirely unknown to me. My grandfather, James Scarlett, married the daughter of a West Indian proprietor. I have heard my father say that she was related to the family of General Wolfe who fell at Quebec.

He had fourteen children who survived him, and during his lifetime he divided among them his numerous estates.

One of my earliest recollections is that I was taken by my father to see him shortly before his death. My mother's maiden name was Anglin. Her father, Colonel Philip Anglin, died long before I was born. He possessed considerable property in the island, which descended to the eldest of two sons. The second was a clergyman. They were both highly educated and accomplished men.

My grandmother Anglin's maiden name was Lawrence. She was the great grand-daughter of Henry Lawrence, the Lord President of Oliver Cromwell's council when he became Dictator. As it was during the usurpation that Jamaica was taken from the Spaniards, it was probably owing to his political connection that his family became amongst the most early and extensive proprietors in the new colony, where they took refuge on the restoration. A very considerable part of the northern side of the island was, within the last century, exclusively possessed by the Lawrences—the brothers of my grandmother—who were five or six in number ; each of whom derived entirely from his father an ample fortune in excellent sugar plantations, which their descendants, for the most part, have not had the good fortune to keep.

My grandmother, Anglin, was living when I left the island. She was an excellent old lady, very cheerful in her conversation, and beloved by numerous families to whom she was related. Among my first recollections is that of reading the Psalter and the Bible to my mother. She had a very happy art of teaching her children to read when they were too young to retain in their memory any traces of the process she adopted. I acknowledge with gratitude the early lessons I received from her, inculcating a high tone of moral and religious feeling, which has never ceased to influence my habits and my conduct.

It is but justice to her to state, that though surrounded by slaves, I was brought up with an abhorrence of the slave trade, and the system of slavery which is the necessary consequence of it. Be it known, notwithstanding the confident allegations of several journalists to the contrary, that I was never at any school.

Both my parents were sensible of the corruption of morals incident to that unhappy state of society where slavery exists. They resolved to separate their children, as much as possible, from an intercourse either with slaves, or with those who were in daily familiarity with slaves. My mother, in particular, was so careful to keep us from that contamination, that she never allowed us to associate with any person whose dialect was touched with the broken English of slaves ; and according to my recollection ours was one of the very few families, if not the only one, in which the language and accent of the nursery was wholly uncorrupted.

I had a brother older than myself, two younger brothers and a sister. As long as I can recollect anything, I recollect a tutor being in the house, to whose care we were assigned the greater part of the day. The first we had was a Scotchman. He remained with us four years, when my father provided for him in some other way. He was succeeded by an Englishman, a man of great good nature and some talent, but not so great a proficient in Greek as I wish he had been, though he professed to make it an essential part of our studies. At the age of fourteen I was emancipated from him, if with no other useful acquirement, at least with a passion for knowledge and a capacity for application not common at so early a period of life. During the last two or three years of his residence, my father allowed two or three of my mother's nephews to have the benefit of his tuition. They came to our school-room, and remained during certain hours of the day. Little prizes and great approbation were destined for him who made the best exercises, and passed the best examinations in any department of our studies. My ardour was insatiable. I soon acquired the superiority, and maintained it over my competitors. As an example of my eagerness, I will relate one circumstance that has continued to retain some influence to the present day. It was the practice, once in a week, to try the proficiency of the pupils in arithmetic by setting problems to be solved in writing. My elder brother, Philip, wrote much better and quicker than I could, and by this advantage at the first he surpassed me. I fell upon the expedient of working the problem in my head without writing the process, merely putting down the result. By this device I not only secured the prize, but acquired a facility of making calculations without notes, which I found of great use in my subsequent studies at Cambridge, and which to a great degree I still possess. From fourteen to fifteen I passed not in idleness, but with no other director of my studies than my father. He was, however, much engaged in looking after his property in different parts of the island; in his duty as a magistrate, and from the year 1776 to 1783 in attention to a regiment of Yeomanry Cavalry, of which he was the colonel, which at all times during the war with America was required to be in a state of preparation for service, and upon several occasions, when the island was threatened with invasion with the combined fleets of France and Spain, was stationed with other troops at points remote from his residence.

Nevertheless, he did not neglect his part in my education.

Whenever he was at home, he found time to read himself, and to make me read to him, from his favourite authors. These were chiefly Pope, Addison, and Swift. Swift's prose in particular he delighted in, considering it as a model of simplicity, perspicuity, and force; and I owe to his lessons an early taste I still retain for the genius and manner of writing of the Dean of St. Patrick.

My only sister, for whom I had a great affection, possessed an understanding of no ordinary vigour, with good knowledge, and a highly cultivated taste. The different merits of these authors were the subject of frequent conversations and discussions between us, but I own I did not feel so much as I have done since the delicacy of Addison's humour and the sweetness of his style. Certain it is, that at an age, when very few boys have read much of either, I was deeply imbued both with Addison and Swift, and most of the works of the latter were fixed in my memory.

At the age of fourteen I was very tall, and I presume was supposed to know as much as my tutor could teach, for about that time he quitted the family for a school my father had established at Montego Bay, the first, I believe, that had been known in that part of the island.

The residence of my family had been transferred, I think in the year 1776, to a large house which my father had purchased near that town, and which I remember as the only one within my limited experience in my own country where there was a fine garden, arranged very much in the English style. It was surrounded by a thick well-trimmed fence of planted trees, bearing an acid fruit somewhat smaller than the lemon, and called there a lime, with a perennial profusion of blossoms and flowers, resembling in appearance and odour those of the orange. Instead of with box, the beds of flowers and vegetables were lined with the pomegranate, kept low by constant trimming without prejudice to the fruit, and much resembling box.

Soon after my tutor had left us, my father announced to me his intention of sending me to Oxford, preparatory to a course of study for the Bar. I had entertained a boyish predilection for the navy, but this soon yielded to his authority, and the advantages he set before me as the result of practising at the Bar in Jamaica, where his influence and connections at that time were of considerable importance. He was on terms of intimacy with many of the lawyers, and the most eminent were his particular friends. From these he procured plans of study for me, and promises of future countenance and protection. I embraced, with satisfaction, the opportunity of seeing more of the world, and of visiting that blessed land which the inhabitants of the West Indies and of America, and even those who had never seen it, were then accustomed to call home.

Accordingly, my father, having very carefully made all his arrangements, took the opportunity of one of my uncle's making a voyage to England to send me under his care.

On the first day of June, 1785, I set sail from Jamaica, and arrived in London on the first of August following.

The events which occurred during my childhood out of my domestic connections were not of any interest except three. One of these was the calamity which befell the island, of a great hurricane in 1780. The other two were threatened invasions of the island by the combined fleets of France and Spain ; first under d'Estaing, and then in 1782 under Count de Grasse.

These events were deeply impressed on my youthful mind. The storm was, for a few hours, so violent as to induce my father, who was happily at home, to remove his whole family, together with some visitors, from the mansion to a low building erected in the garden, where he kept his books and papers. There the whole family passed the night, for the most part agonised with fears, which my father endeavoured, by a cheerful and encouraging tone, to dispel. In the morning the sun rose upon a scene of desolation and disaster I can never forget. Many houses in the town had disappeared, and all, except our own, which escaped, bore marks of the violence they had sustained. All the vessels in the roads were on shore. Many large trees were rooted up, and upon those which remained not a leaf was to be seen. The sudden change from perennial foliage and verdure to leafless forest and dreary pastures presented a horrid likeness of winter scenery in a northern climate. But the power of the sun in a few days restored their foliage to the trees, and to the pastures their verdure. So great, however, had been the destruction of everything on which the subsistence of the inhabitants depended that the dread of famine soon followed the traces of the storm. Immediate measures were taken to procure food by importation, and it was not until this began to arrive that either the slaves or their masters were relieved from deepest anxiety. .

The other two events to which I have alluded were of the same character. Each excited great alarm, but with these were mingled great enthusiasm, and a most determined spirit of resistance. Every other object was sacrificed to the means of defence, and there seemed but one feeling which pervaded the black as well as the white population, that the enemy were to be opposed by every practicable means, to the last extremity.

Happily the dispersion of the Continental fleets on both occasions left us nothing to remember but our courage, our loyalty, and the glory of the British navy.

Upon the last of these occasions, which was in 1782, the ardour for defending our country prevailed to so great a degree as to descend to boys of my age.

I was instructed in the military exercise, to march, to fire, and perform the usual evolutions; and was ready to have taken my part with others in the battle or the flight, as the occasion might require.

Shortly after my arrival in London, I was admitted a student in the Inner Temple under the auspices of a relation of mine who was a student of Lincoln's Inn, who thought the proper consequence of my manly appearance was to add one year to my age in the memorandum of my admission. The same thing occurred, I suppose for the same reason, upon my admission as a fellow commoner at Trinity College, Cambridge, a few weeks after. Circumstances, which are not worth relating, had induced me to abandon the arrangements made by my father for placing me at Oriel College, Oxford, under the special care of Dr. Eveleigh, the President.

In the month of November, 1785—in my sixteenth year—
I commenced my residence at Trinity College. Here a new
world was opened to me ; a scene of life which no part of my
past experience could have led me to anticipate.

Accustomed from my infancy to live in my father's house,
under the care of the most tender and affectionate of mothers,
surrounded by a large family at home, and mixing, when
allowed, with numerous relations and friends, who were ever
studious to show me all kindness and attachment, I found
myself transferred at once to a society consisting of various
ranks, classes, and orders, altogether strange to me ; and among
the whole mass of whom, I not only had no friend, but could
not even claim an acquaintance. I was my own master too,
my own order upon my father's agent in London commanded money without any limit but my own discretion,
and I was accountable to no one on this side of the Atlantic
for my conduct, or for the use of the confidence reposed
in me.

When I reflected on my own position, young and unpro-
tected as I was, I could not but feel astonished at that
confidence. I recalled to mind, however, various expressions
and occasions, from which I had reason to infer that this confidence was founded on the good opinion entertained of me
by my own family, and in particular by my parents ; and my
first resolution was upon no account to afford them cause to
change it. It was true that there were connections and
relations in England to whose care I might have been
addressed, but I was neither required nor requested to call
upon any one of them ; and with the exception of my uncle,
who had left England before I went to reside at college, there
was no individual who possessed any right to control me.

CHAPTER V.

COMMENCEMENT OF HIS LIFE AT TRINITY COLLEGE, CAMBRIDGE.

UNDER these circumstances of no little peril I boldly placed myself under the direction of my own prudence, determined to make myself acquainted with the character of the society in which I was placed, and to take no step even in the way of education till I had gathered some information to govern my judgment. In the meantime the novelty of the scene, the variety of the characters, and the manner in which I was at once admitted amongst the gay and fashionable of the under-graduates of my own College, as well as of some others, made my time pass very agreeably with the cares or allurements of study. I had indeed twice ventured to attend the lectures of the tutors. The head tutor was to lecture on Classics, and the 15th Satire of Juvenal was announced as the task, but what was my surprise to find that the worthy man con-sumed the hour in vain endeavours to explain the rules of the College and the hieroglyphics in which it was then the fashion to write the weekly butter bills. On the following day I attended the Mathematical tutor, who gave lectures in Euclid. I had prepared myself for that by some previous reading, and believe that I should have succeeded in the first four propositions, but when I had in a very satisfactory manner shown that I could, from a given point draw a straight line equal to a given straight line as well as Euclid himself, the wicked tutor maliciously proposed to me to do the problem over again by fixing the given point in the given straight line. This unforeseen case, of which there is not a word in the book (and which, by the by, a good-natured tutor would have shown and not set to me) entirely routed my very small force of. Mathematics and drove me away from those lectures, with a resolution to take refuge under the acknowledged licence of a fellow commoner, to abstain from all lectures.

In this I was kept in countenance by the noblemen and members of my own order, not one of whom, though the class was numerous, had even shown himself at the lecture of the College tutor.

I dedicated the remainder of this, my first term, to gaiety and the most agreeable society I could find amongst the undergraduates.

At Christmas I had engaged myself to visit a family at Tittenhanger Park, near St. Alban's, the property of the Earl of Hardwick. There I first met the lady to whom, after an attachment of nearly seven years, I was married. Her mother died in her infancy. She at that time lived with her grandmother, Mrs. Campbell, an old lady of excellent understanding, fascinating manners, and great hospitality. I experienced from the whole family the greatest kindness, and though I was then but sixteen, and the lady somewhat younger, she inspired me during that visit with a serious and lasting passion, which had a decided influence on my future life and conduct.

I returned to College with a determination to apply myself with all possible diligence to my studies, and to obtain as early as possible that state of independence which might enable me to command the consent of my father, as well as of hers, to a union that was the leading object of all my wishes. My first care was to select a tutor. The choice was not happy. The gentleman had recently taken a respectable degree, and was recommended to me by a College friend, the brother of the lady to whom I have alluded. The tutor was a worthy man, and had at least the merit of perspicuity in his mode of conveying what he knew, but his knowledge was not profound in anything, nor was his industry equal to that of his pupil. Before the end of the year I had exhausted all his stores, and found myself in want of a more efficient guide in my studies. But delicacy towards this gentleman, and a just regard for his amiable qualities, forbade the step which I anxiously wished, but had not the firmness to take. The consequence was that the ardour of my progress in the regular channels of Classics and Mathematics being checked, I wasted my industry and energies on a vast amount of desultory reading, without plan or method. I attended no lectures that year, but I had gained from my tutor all the knowledge that the lectures of my own year could have given me, and I determined that, in the November term of 1786, I would attend the lectures of the year above me, trusting to my own industry and good fortune to be able to prepare myself for a proceeding at that time not very usual.

An event happened in the course of that year which may be worth relating, as it had a considerable influence on my future life. Soon after my return to College after the Christmas vacation, whilst I was hard at work with my tutor, I received a visit from a body of gentlemen, of which Mr. Dundas, the late Earl of Zetland, took the lead. They came to announce to me the honour they had done me of electing me to fill up a vacancy in the True Blue Club, made by the secession of Lord Belgrave, afterwards Marquis of Westminster, who had recently taken his degree. Of the eleven gentlemen who waited upon me the greater part were in the habit of living with me on the most familiar terms, and I need not say that this mark of their preference was deeply felt and freely acknowledged at the interview. I was told, however, that the announcement of my election would speedily arrive in a more formal manner, but that they had resolved to make the communication in person that they might have the satisfaction of informing me that it had been unanimous.

When they took their leave I began, with my tutor, to reflect how far my being a member of the True Blue Club was consistent with the resolution I had formed of severe application to study. The club was of very ancient establishment. It was confined to undergraduates of Trinity College to the number of twelve, and, according to its regular constitution, these were to consist of equal portions of noblemen, fellow commoners, and pensioners. But as they were self-elected their discretion was not fettered by this restriction, if circumstances or the character of the individuals indicated the advantage of a deviation from it.

They consisted, in one sense, of the *élite* of the society of undergraduates. Rank, fortune, but above all, agreeable manners and a social disposition, were the passports to admission. But whatever was the original object of the institution, it had, as was represented to me, been long considered as a mere drinking club, whose business it was to meet at stated periods at Newmarket and at Cambridge, and dine together with abundant festivity.

Nevertheless it was in high estimation, and no one had hitherto ventured to decline the honour of being adopted as a member.

CHAPTER VI.

THE TRUE BLUE CLUB—HIS FRIENDSHIP WITH BAYNES.

IT so happened that at that time I was particularly averse to wine. I made every practicable shift to avoid it, no easy matter for one who lived in society, where it was so much the fashion to drink, that I found myself under the necessity of refusing the invitation of a gentleman who made it a condition that each guest should drink two bottles of wine. The aversion might, no doubt, be conquered by habit, but what was I to gain by this discipline? So far as the habits of the club could have an influence over my habits, they would be prejudicial to my studies, and to the seclusion which, on account of those studies I meditated for a time at least, from the gaiety and hilarity which were ever tempting me to neglect them. Besides, there was some expense attending an uniform which the members wore at the dinners and anniversaries which engaged their attention. For these reasons, with the approbation of my tutor, I returned an answer to the written annunciation of election, declining in the most civil terms I could invent for the purpose.

When I reflect upon this conduct, I must own that I am more struck by the courage than the wisdom it displayed. It happened that after the first coldness, the natural consequence of such a measure, had worn off, I had the good fortune to live upon the former terms of kindness with all those whose fellowship I had rejected, and of some of them I may venture to say that I possessed and retained the friendship to the end of their lives. Amongst these it gives me satisfaction to mention the late Lord Zetland, and Sir George Robinson ; but the effect of my refusal, or rather my election, was to raise some discontent amongst those to whose title to be chosen there could be no exception, and who were much above my standing at College. Amongst these were Lord Grey of Groby, Lord Stamford, Henry and Charles Leicester, the brothers of Sir John Leicester, afterwards Lord de Tabley, who afterwards married Lady Susan Murray ; Mr. St. George, an Irish gentleman; Sir Edward Smith, a Yorkshire Baronet ; and some other fellow commoners. So much were they affected by this supposed slight, and by my example, that several of them, when afterwards elected, declined the honour as I had done ; but certainly not for the same reason.

But the most useful consequence to me which resulted from it, was that it drew towards me the attention of the resident Masters of Arts, and Fellows of the College.

They became disposed to cultivate my acquaintance, admitted me to their society, and gave me opportunities of improvement, which I could not have found elsewhere, not even in the True Blue Club. I own that I was flattered by their attention, and found no difficulty in relaxing my habits of association with the gay and jovial portion of the University amongst whom I had hitherto lived with more pleasure than profit.

To those who are acquainted with the noble institution of Trinity College, it is needless to say that very few persons can be admitted as fellows of that society but such as are most distinguished for their learning and accomplishments. I indulge a pleasing and grateful recollection of Lambert, Jones, Waddington, Hailstone, and Lax, names of high note in the University at that time, and with whom I was permitted to cultivate an intimacy highly honourable and useful to me, which terminated only with their lives.

To the same cause I owed the friendship of John Baynes, which had an important influence on my life and conduct. He was a Fellow of the College who at the age of eighteen had taken the degree of second Wrangler, and had won the first mathematical prize, and the first classical medal. He possessed a very pleasing countenance, courteous manners, a fine temper, brilliant but good natural wit. These, added to his solid acquirements of learning, made him the delight of his friends. His conversation was always lively and entertaining. He appeared to take an interest in everything that excited the interest of those who conversed with him, and had in a high degree that rare and charming facility and tact which places a man at once on a level with his company, and at the same time preserves their respect. He had distinguished himself by a speech made at the Yorkshire Association, at the head of which was Mr. Wyvil, which association had, at the last election, brought Mr. Wilberforce into Parliament. At the time to which I am alluding, he was in the habit of coming occasionally to College to visit his friends; his residence being in London, where he was established as a special pleader, in considerable practice. I was introduced to him at one of those visits in the year 1786, after dinner, as we stood round the fire, just before returning to the combination room.

The next day he honoured me with a visit, proposed a walk together in the gardens behind the colleges, and before we parted, invited himself to drink tea with me in the evening. I was too much delighted with my guest to decline the proposal.

At the evening interview he asked many questions about my reading, made some trial of my depth in mathematics; amongst other things that he in the kindest manner recommended, earnestly insisted upon my rising early in the morning. He told me that he always rose at five, and if he had anything serious to do worked till ten, and generally found himself at leisure for amusement, exercise, or light reading the rest of the day. He proposed, therefore, whilst he remained in College to call me up at that hour; not for hard reading, but to enjoy the freshness of the morning in spring. The next morning he found me up at the hour proposed. We had a long walk, and this was repeated every day whilst he remained at College. During this visit he had so entirely gained my confidence, that he became acquainted with the whole of my little history, and fathomed the very bottom of my heart. In one of those conversations he perceived that my vanity was flattered by his attentions, upon which he said :—'Do you know the reason of my desire to be introduced to you ? It was the report I had heard that you had declined to be a member of the True Blue Club. This was so singular in a young fellow commoner, that I concluded there must be something very unusual about you, which I wished to find out ; and now I must tell you, that having found nothing of the sort I am much more suprised than ever at the step you took, which had I known you at the time I should not have advised. You expose youself to the resentment and perhaps to the malice of persons whom it was your interest to cultivate, and whom you may chance to encounter hereafter, in various turns of your life. A man should never make an enemy of another if he can avoid it, even at the expense of some personal inconvenience to himself. However, the step cannot now be recalled, and you must now endeavour as far as you can, by your manners, to mitigate the feelings you have excited in that party, whilst you cultivate the good opinion of the fellows and the studious part of the society, which after all is the best. In short, you must become a reading man, and be content to undergo, from your former friends, some bantering in that character, by way of revenge for your neglect of them. But be sure you let this be the only weak place they find in you.'

Before he left college we had become sworn friends. He made me promise to visit him whenever I went to town to keep my terms, and to write to him once a week, giving an account of my progress. In return he promised to write to me whenever I wished for his advice upon any subject, and desired me, without scruple, to consult him as I would my own brother. These engagements were faithfully kept on both sides. He paid several visits to Cambridge, during which he devoted much of his time to me. He pointed out several works of history and metaphysics which he enjoined me to read preparatory to the study of the law. It was upon his earnest entreaties I learned the French language. From him I received many useful hints in my Classical studies, and I retain to this day several of his letters which prove his anxiety and the pains he took to assist me.

It was upon one of my visits to town to keep a term in the Inner Temple that he introduced me to the celebrated Richard

Porson.   He had mentioned various particulars of that extraordinary man, one of which was the capacity he had for drinking, and his indifference about the liquor.   He said he had
known him drink at one sitting sixteen cups of tea.   It happened that one Saturday evening I was drinking tea at
Baynes's chambers in Gray's Inn, after which we had agreed
to go to the Opera.   There was a rap at the door, which
induced him to go out of the room to desire the servant to
deny him, but finding the visitor to be Porson, he brought him
into the room and introduced him to me.   He then led him
into a great variety of entertaining conversation, exhibiting
his vast memory and sarcastic wit, during which he plied him
with tea until he had filled up the measure of sixteen cups,
upon which the party broke up, Porson declining to accompany us to the Opera.

That I may finish at once this history of Mr. Baynes, I
may add that our intercourse continued as I have described
it till his death, which happened in the month of August 1788.
In the early part of that year he had proposed to me an excursion in the summer to the West Riding of Yorkshire.

His friend Romilly was to be of the party.   We were to
take up our residence at a house which belonged to Baynes, at
Embsay Kirk, near Skipton.

In one of his letters which I retain he says, 'I have known
many quick men and diligent men, but I never knew any who
combined so much quickness and diligence as Romilly.   You
will find him a most extraordinary person, and a most valuable acquaintance.'

Mr. Romilly had been called to the Bar that year, as well
as I recollect, and was expected to return from the Midland
Circuit some day in August.   That no time should be lost, it
was arranged by Baynes that I should come to town a day or
two before, and occupy some chambers that he provided for
me in Gray's Inn.   When I arrived I received at his door a
note to express his concern that he could not see me on account
of an indisposition which he hoped to get rid of in a day or
two, and to say that his servant would direct me to the chambers he had procured,   Shortly after I had retired there I
was waited upon by Dr. Blackburn, one of the physicians, for

there were two in attendance upon him.   From him I learned that my friend had been attacked with a fever of a serious kind which made it advisable that he should be kept perfectly quiet, that he had made the doctor promise to see me every day during his confinement, and to communicate his hope that I should not be anxious about his health.   The second day, however, after my arrival in town I had the inexpressible grief to hear that he had breathed his last, having made his will the day before his death, sitting up in bed, with his own hand, and charged Dr. Blackburn with his kindest remembrance of me.   In that will he left all his law books and books of historical and legal antiquity which Romilly did not already possess, to that gentleman, and all the remainder, together with his Latin and Greek classics, and all his French and Italian books to me, and in particular the works of Rousseau which he recommended me to read. This passage in his will referred to a conversation with me, in which he had pressed me to learn French without delay, assuring me that the beauty and eloquence of Rousseau's style were sufficient reasons for acquiring a knowledge of the language in which his works were written.   In this he was quite correct.   Rousseau is undoubtedly the most eloquent of modern writers, although I cannot but think that the most beautiful of his compositions exhibit occasionally something of that morbid sensibility under which he laboured.

CHAPTER VII.

HIS STUDIES AT CAMBRIDGE—ACQUAINTANCE WITH PORSON.

IMMEDIATELY upon hearing of my friend's death, I removed my quarters from Gray's Inn.

Two days afterwards, Romilly, having returned to town, called at my lodgings and addressed a charming note to me, expressing his hope that the calamity we both deplored might not prevent the cultivation of that acquaintance and those kind feelings which it was the warmest wish of his deceased friend to bring about between us. My heart was too full not to respond to this proposal. We met in tears, and from that hour until his death I ever found him a firm, constant, and most valuable friend. But I shall have to say more of him hereafter.

The encouragement and advice given to me by Baynes improved my disposition for study, and I believe that very few men exceeded me in the physical powers of application, or in the number of hours devoted to reading. I attended lectures with the year above me, by the help of which, with my own application, I made considerable proficiency in Mathematics and Natural Philosophy. I laboured assiduously to make up my deficiency in Classics. I cannot boast of much progress in Greek, but I acquired great facility in the composition of Latin, and eagerly devoured the writers of the Augustine age, more especially Cicero, many of whose orations I translated into English; and when I had nearly forgotten the original, back into Latin, by way of exercise. I became familiar with all his works, and my relish for them has never ceased.

I read also in French the works of Racine, Boileau, Montesquieu, Rollin's history, and Belles Lettres, Bossuet, and many others; amongst which was the elegant work of Beausobre on the history of Monachism which I read with Porson, with whom I became very intimate, and who allowed me to be his teacher in the French grammar. He was undoubtedly the most perfect Classic scholar of the age, whose memory retained all that he had read, and whose facility of quotations, and felicity of application would hardly be credited by those who did not witness them. I have known him repeat the whole poem of 'The Rape of the Lock,' referring, as he went on to similar passages in Classical writers, which he supposed Pope to have imitated. Upon one occasion when he was upon a visit to the College, he resolved to say nothing for a week which was not to be found in 'Shakspeare,' and he astonished those who lived with him by his readiness in answering in the very words of his author the most trivial as well as the most grave questions that were put to him.

He had an extraordinary facility in writing verses, in which the composition, whether in English or Latin, was perfect, but they were chiefly satirical, and suited only for the entertainment of the passing moment. With the exception of his letters to Archdeacon Travis upon the controversy of the three witnesses, in which he has shown the greatest critical acumen, and some editions of single Greek plays, he has left no monument of his vast genius and acquirements. From the time of our first acquaintance until my marriage, I lived very much with him, and found him a perpetual source of entertainment and instruction. I thought his great memory operated to the prejudice of his judgment. He remembered so exactly what he had read, that he seemed never to think for himself, nor to find it necessary to employ reflection in order to work out his own ideas. He was very poor. After his fellowship expired, he had not for many years more than 40*l.* a year, the salary of his Greek professorship, to live upon, to which may be added the right to rooms and commons in Trinity College. Yet he was too proud to be obliged to any one, or even to write for emolument. He spurned anything like patronage or protection, and would not have changed his fustian breeches and worsted stockings to visit a Prince. His letters to Travis were not published until after I had left Cambridge; and the preface which contains a just and ingenious criticism upon the style of Gibbon was written at one sitting at my chambers in the Temple.

CHAPTER VIII.

KEEPS AN ACT.

As I had acquired the reputation of a hard-reading man, Mr. Jones, the tutor, whose lectures I attended in mathematics, and who was always particularly kind and obliging to me, proposed that I should keep an Act in the Schools. This was a very unusual step in a fellow commoner, and, I believe at that time, had but one example. I complied, however, with his wish. The two mathematical subjects I chose were the first and seventh sections of Newton's Principia. The moral subject was the Paradox of Rousseau, for which he gained the prize at the Academy of Dijon, against the Art and Sciences. After I had formed my resolution I commenced an assiduous attendance in the schools, and was too happy to find that I readily understood the arguments brought forward, and detected their fallacy. I did not compose my Latin thesis upon the third subject till the evening preceding the day I was to keep my Act. I have not preserved it, but I received many compliments upon it afterwards from those who heard it. I had never seen during my attendance in the schools any Master of Arts present, except the Moderator who presided. The gallery appropriated to the Masters of Arts had always been empty. When I entered upon my task what was my astonishment to find it filled with great wigs and black gowns. Masters of Colleges, Professors, Doctors, and Masters of Arts overwhelmed me with dismay. I managed, however, to get through my thesis with a tremulous voice, and was in hopes to recover sufficient firmness to justify in some degrees the great expectation that had apparently been formed of me. But I was doomed to be disappointed. My treacherous opponent had called upon me, a few minutes before we entered the schools, to request I would admit his first proposition, assuring me that the fallacy did not lie in *that*, although, if I put him to prove it, he might be puzzled by a long fluxional process which the proof involved. Nothing doubting his candour I conceded without hesitation his first position—but I soon found it impossible to dispute the others which followed. The Moderator, however, suspecting the truth, desired him to go back to his minor and prove it, in the process of which the fallacy appeared. The Moderator then admonished him of the impropriety of advancing an argument of that nature, of which the fallacy could only be detected by a long demonstration.

The second argument I easily disposed of, but so much time had been consumed by this demonstration and the lecture upon it that the hour arrived which had been fixed for a Congregation in the Senate House, which the Moderator was obliged to attend. He therefore put an end to the Act, giving me a very long honour which I was conscious I did not deserve. My friend, Jones, however, was not discouraged. He urged me to go into the Senate House, and strive for an honour, when I took my degree. He said he had no doubt I should be a high Wrangler, and he offered to prepare me in whatever I should think myself deficient for the examination. But here the desire I had formed for an early establishment in life overcame my vanity. I had been admitted, and had commenced my residence at a period of the year which went for nothing with reference to the time of taking a Bachelor's degree. In order to gratify his wish I should have been obliged to remain at College until the year 1790, whereas I could take my Bachelor's degree in 1789. As I was precluded from sitting for a fellowship I thought the delay of six months too great a sacrifice to the empty honour of a high degree. I therefore became Bachelor of Arts in June 1789, and transferred my residence to the Temple, in London, contriving, however, for the two following years occasional visits to Cambridge.

During my residence at College, upon the occasion of the election of Mr. Hailstone to the Woodwardian Professorship, which drew great numbers of the Masters of Arts together, I had the honour of being introduced to Mr. Pitt and Mr. Perceval. The latter was kind enough to renew his acquaintance with me in town. He was a friend of Romilly, and went the same circuit with him. This circumstance brought us more frequently together. We became intimate, and continued so until his death. With regard to Mr. Pitt, chance threw me in his way upon certain public occasions, but I had no opportunity of being better known to him.

I began, however, to take an interest in politics about the time of the Regency question, when the state of the King's health was a subject of deep interest to the nation. I, for the first time, read the parliamentary debates with eagerness, and took a warm part on the side of Mr. Pitt in his difference with Mr. Fox on the right of the Prince of Wales to be Regent. From this period commenced my attention to political affairs. I never ceased to read the debates in Parliament, or to attend, after my removal to town, the discussions of important questions in the House of Commons, till my professional avocations made the sacrifice of time to that amusement impossible.

I had opportunities of hearing Mr. Pitt, Fox, and Sheridan, Burke, and Grey, who were then the leading speakers in the House of Commons, upon almost every important topic that occurred for several years. I was present also at many of the sittings of the House of Lords on the trial of Mr. Hastings, and heard the entire reply of Mr. Burke, which occupied two hours each day for eight consecutive days.

CHAPTER IX.

LEAVES COLLEGE—SPECIAL PLEADER'S OFFICE.

UPON my first coming to settle in town I had recourse to my friend Romilly's advice to govern me in my study of the law. He recommended that I should read Blackstone's Commentaries, Coke upon Littleton, and the leading cases under each head in Connyer's Digest, which I should continue in my own manuscript as to cases published since the last edition of that work, and thus make myself acquainted with the terms and principles of the science before I encountered the jargon of a Special Pleader's Office. I was already familiar with Cicero's Offices, with Paley's 'Moral Philosophy,' with Locke, with Montesquieu ' Sur l'Esprit des Loix,' and with some portions of Grotius ' De Jure Belli atque Pacis.' But I was not initiated into any of the technical language or principles of the law of England.

I followed the advice of Romilly with great assiduity and a determination to conquer all difficulties, and in the course of a year I had reason to be satisfied with my progress. With Blackstone's Commentaries I was delighted. After all the criticisms of Bentham in his work called ' A Fragment on Government,' some of which are more plausible than just, that work combines with the most profound learning and reflection a perspicuity and polished elegance of style which give life, grace, and interest to the driest subjects, and excite fresh pleasure, and admiration upon each perusal. Indeed it can only be estimated justly by those, who come to read it a second time, after a more general acquaintance with the science of which it treats. Connyer's digest and the cases I must own, I at first found very hard of digestion, but after some study bestowed upon the cases and arguments in the reports, I found much entertainment and exercise of the intellect in reading the modern cases. As I grew more familiar with the principles which I gathered up as I went along I became bolder, and after reading the statement of the case and the arguments of the counsel on both sides with great attention, I laid aside the book and endeavoured to apply my own store of knowledge to solve the question, by giving judgment on the case. Sometimes I wrote down the opinion I had formed, but more frequently was contented with thinking over the arguments, and coming to the conclusion which I thought just, before I read the opinion of the judges. At the commencement of this practice I found myself very inadequate, and that my presumption was often rebuked by the learning and wisdom of the judges. After some perseverance, however, I was delighted to find that I made progress, and that the practice was not only a source of entertainment, but afforded me the best means of judging of the proficiency I had made in my studies. At length I was overjoyed to find that I was right in the majority of instances, and what might have been a source of vanity to me, I generally found that I had hit upon the same system of reasoning as Mr. Justice Buller had adopted in his judgment. This of course gave me a high idea of that learned judge's superiority in legal learning and acuteness.

The practice has been of great use in giving me the early habit of reflecting upon the principles and rules of the law, and applying them to new cases by my own reading ; and I may here observe, what a long course of experience has taught me, that the lawyers least to be depended upon are those who are in constant pursuit of cases in point to govern their judgment, and who, therefore, seldom have sufficient knowledge of the principles to judge for themselves.

But to return to my studies. When I reported to Romilly that I felt myself strong enough for a special pleader's office, and upon his examination of me, had his sanction, I became in the course of the year 1790 a pupil of Mr. George Wood, afterwards a Baron of the Exchequer. Amongst his pupils, at that time, were Mr. Lushington, an intimate friend of mine, who was afterwards a judge at Ceylon, and having resigned that office was appointed Master of the Crown Office under his uncle Lord Ellenborough ; Mr. Trench, since Lord Clancarty, who had been a fellow commoner of St. John's, and one of my acquaintance in the University; and Mr. Sturges Bourne, who was afterwards Secretary of State for the Home Department under Mr. Canning's Administration, a gentleman of distinguished talent and polished manners. I had not been long in the office before Mr. Wood discovered that I had some proficiency, and understood more of the business than a mere tyro.

He did not take much trouble with his pupils, but left them to learn, by the alterations he made in their drafts, the rules and principles of the science. I soon found, however, that he had acquired some confidence in me. He sent me the difficult cases to deal with, and occasionally, when I had no precedent exactly in point and took my own course, he would send for me into his own chamber, and explain why he made certain alterations, and refer me to cases where I might find a principle though not an exact precedent. The facility and confidence I had acquired by my previous reading enabled me to dispatch the business put into my hands more rapidly than my colleagues ; and I believe I may say with truth that after I had been three months in the office, the greater part of the whole business was done by myself.

CHAPTER X.

CALLED TO THE BAR.

I WAS anxious to come to the Bar with a view to the one object I have before mentioned,[1] and having kept most of my terms in the Temple whilst I was at College, and the remainder by the month of June 1791, I was then called to the Bar, some months before the year of my pupilage expired. From that time, though I continued to do all the work sent to me by Mr. Wood, I ceased to visit his office, and surrendered my place to George Canning, with whom I then formed a slight acquaintance, little imagining that I should one day become his intimate friend and zealous supporter. I will not anticipate what I have to say respecting that amiable and highly gifted man.

When I was called to the Bar the question was whether I should return to Jamaica immediately, where I was next to certain of all the success that influence and connection could give me, or whether I should endeavour to gain some experience at the English Bar before I quitted it. Here I had recourse to my counsellor, Romilly. He said, ' I think you are likely to get a great deal of business at the Bar here, and at all events as you are so young and have time before you, it would be well if you added some little experience to your stock of knowledge before you start in competition with men older than yourself.' I thought his opinion reasonable, and I prepared my father by the best arguments I could for my remaining in England, at least a year, if not two years longer. The next question was the choice of a circuit. Professional connections I had none. I did not know an attorney by

---

[1] His marriage with Miss Louisa Henrietta Campbell, of Kilmory, in Argyllshire.

sight, with the exception of two or three whom I had seen occasionally in Wood's office, but whose names were altogether unknown to me.   I was in the habit of visiting the family of Sir John Smith, of Sidling, in Dorsetshire.   He pressed me very earnestly to choose the western circuit.   He said he had the misfortune to have four causes of his own at issue for the next circuit, and that he would direct the junior briefs to be placed in my hands.   Perhaps this offer ought to have determined my choice.   But I had two reasons for wishing to see Yorkshire.   One was the attachment of my friend Baynes to his native county, which had given it an imaginary charm for me. The other was a promise I had made to my tutor, Mr. Redshaw, to visit him at Richmond in that county, where he resided, and where, moreover, Baynes had been educated at the school of Mr. Temple, at that time much celebrated, as it has been since under Mr. Tate.   These were my reasons for preferring the northern circuit.   My first circuit produced nothing but two or three accidental briefs which fell to me as the junior, and one other which was due to my industry in Wood's office.   It was a very complicated case, in which I had been trusted to draw the pleadings.   As soon as I arrived in Carlisle, a brief was brought to me, with a statement that the agent had been instructed to seek some special pleader on the circuit who could give assistance to Mr. Wood in the cause, and that he had returned for answer that no one could do it better than the gentleman who had prepared the pleadings under Mr. Wood's inspection.   I entertained some doubts whether this was a legitimate mode of acquiring business, but these were soon removed by my old master Wood, who upon my representing them to him, said that nothing could be more honourable to me.

Upon this occasion I made my *debut* at Carlisle, and here it may be said was laid the foundation of my reputation. Some questions having arisen in the course of the trial upon the construction of the pleadings, it fell to my lot to explain them, which I had the good fortune to do to the satisfaction of the judge, and to receive from Mr. Law,-afterwards Lord Ellenborough, who was on the other side, a very flattering compliment.

The circuit went off very agreeably. I had no cause to complain of my reception, or of my failure, for I had set out from town without the least expectation or hope of business. The next circuit took me only to York and Lancaster. It was the practice then for one judge only to take the spring circuit, the more northern counties being omitted. I there had a good opportunity of witnessing the knowledge and quickness of Mr. Justice Buller. There were eighty-six causes to be tried at York, one of which was a boundary cause that lasted sixteen hours, thirty-six at Lancaster, and forty to fifty prisoners at each place; but Mr. Justice Buller concluded the whole Circuit in three weeks. It was not the fashion of the Bar to make long speeches, or to occupy any time in resisting the opinion of the judge once declared.

Upon my returning to town and consulting Romilly, he earnestly recommended that I should go to see some sessions in the northern counties. I was recommended to the Lancashire sessions, that is to say to Preston, Wigan, and Manchester, which I attended for the first time in the summer of 1792 ; and to this I ascribed my success in the profession. The business was so great, that when in a few years I came to be the decided leader at these places, the profits of these sessions were as great to me as those of the Home Circuit to Mr. Garrow, or Sergeant Best, and I found the immediate effect of that connection between these places and the assizes in Lancashire in the quantity of business which poured in upon me then, and which from that time to the year 1827 continued a source of abundant profit to me.

My third circuit, in the summer of 1792, gave me courage to make a further struggle for success in this county. More especially at the October sessions I found that I was really gaining ground.

CHAPTER XI.

ON the 22nd day of that month, in the same year (1792), I was married to Miss Louise Henrietta Campbell, the third daughter of Peter Campbell, Esq., of Kilmory, in Argyllshire. She had been the object of my early and constant attachment, and had from my first acquaintance with her exercised a strong influence over my conduct.

Her children, for whom these memories are intended, lived to witness her sweet disposition, her divine temper, and consummate discretion. I lived with her in uninterrupted comfort and happiness from the time of our marriage to the month of March, 1829, and have lived ever since to lament her loss.

Upon this event of my marriage I made up my mind to remain in England, and try my fortune, at least as long as my father was willing to continue the very liberal allowance he had hitherto made me. He had left this matter very much to my own discretion, and I had not abused his confidence. But upon my marriage I determined on no account to exceed what I had taken from him before, and to this resolution I could the more easily adhere as my professional income was gradually increasing. In the year 1798, when my father died, it actually exceeded my expenditure, and has done so from that period to the time of my quitting the Bar. I must, however, own that my expenses have grown with my income (though they have never exceeded it) in so great a proportion, that what I shall leave at my death will fall far short of the accumulations of many who have not experienced half the course of prosperity that has fallen to my lot.

Upon my marriage, I was under the necessity to narrow very much the circle of my acquaintance. I, for some years, avoided the society I had lived in, and became an obscure plodding lawyer, seeking by severe industry no other reputation or fame than that which was to break out upon me in Westminster Hall. It was not until the year 1800 that I found myself in a condition to re-emerge into the world, and to travel out of the circle of the law. I had great reason, however, to be gratified by my position in those circles. Perceval, Erskine, Romilly, Dallas, Jekyll, Lens, and George Wilson, with some others, who were considered amongst the *élite* of the law, were my intimate friends, and continued so to the last. I should have been too happy to include Lord Ellenborough amongst them, but though he was leader of the Northern Circuit, and we were always on terms of civility, and he was in every way worthy of being cultivated, there was something of an imperious temper about him, which I could never very well submit to during our occasional contests at the Bar, and I fancied for some years after he came to the Bench that he carried with him some recollection of the resistance I had now and then exhibited. This might have been mere imagination on my part, for I must do him the justice to own that in the latter period of his life, when I was the most successful competitor before him, I had great reason to be satisfied with the kindness of his manner, and with his apparent estimation of me. But of all the friends whom I cultivated in the profession of the law I must put Romilly the foremost. From the death of Baynes he evidently transferred to me some portion of the attachment which Baynes had possessed. He was a man of reserved habits, and cold demeanour ; but under that exterior were covered the warmest heart and most generous emotions. When excited by controversy, his temper was too easily provoked, and his opponent felt that he was very intolerant, and sometimes too severe upon bad reasoning. As a speaker, though he was often led by the force of his feelings into something like declamation, yet he was not successful in affecting the passions. He did not persuade by his rhetoric, but convinced by his logic. His reasoning was acute, and perspicuous. His sagacity in detecting, and his felicity in exposing, the sophistry of his antagonist, were amongst the first of his oratorical merits. These made him always happy and terrible in reply. His application to study, and his quickness in understanding what he studied, were never surpassed. His reading of all sorts was immense. I never met with any man who was so universally acquainted with ancient and modern literature and history. In the midst of his immense business he found time to read every book that had any real value. Even upon the subject of the last new romance he was the best man to consult. There was something extraordinary in his facility of reading which enabled him to wade through a book in an hour, which would have occupied most men a day. He did not stop at words, or sentences, but took in almost a page at a glance. I have known him read a new work as fast as the leaves could be cut open. I have understood that Mr. Fox had the same facility. Smithson Tenant, the celebrated philosopher and chemist, possessed it in a high degree. He was very fond of books of travels and voyages, and very familiar with them ; and I have several times known him extract from a quarto of modern travels, in a single morning, all that was new, or not to be found in former writers.

Nor does this faculty seem so surprising, when it is considered that a musician reads by a glance of the eye the notes in their several divisions of musical lines, one containing the base, and the other the treble of the accompaniments, and the third the melody for the voice ; and to these combined movements of the mind he adds that of the fingers of both hands at the same moment on the instrument. This operation is extended still further when the same music contains the music in parts for several instruments. The leading player ought to know, by a single glance of the eye, what notes any other player is to sound and what rests he is to make.

But to return to Romilly. In mixed company, he was more a listener than a talker. The conversation which he most relished was of a literary character. He had a great ambition to write a good style, and nothing gave him more pleasure than the society of a person who was disposed to review with him the style of different authors, and to compare them. I have spent hours with him in this occupation.　He maintained that there did not exist as yet, in England, the model of a style.　That no two people agreed what author should be preferred before the rest, nor did anyone deny that the author he most admired was far from perfection ; whereas, in the French language, nobody hesitated to place Voltaire at the head in all sorts of composition, except that which was calculated to excite passion, in which nobody approached Rousseau.

His admiration of Rousseau was pushed almost to enthusiasm, and to a certain extent, at one time, affected his judgment with a bias in favour of the principles and character of the writer.

I had read the whole of his works, with a profound admiration of his style ; but I thought his reasoning, though full of ingenuity, was not always convincing, and that his mind was not perfectly sound.　Romilly, after much resistance, finally came to this opinion.　He admitted to me, that the character and weakness of Rousseau were justly described by Baron Grimm, in his correspondence, a book of great entertainment, and remarkable for plain common sense, free from all delusion.

Romilly was a great walker.　It was our constant habit to walk together for some hours every day, when the weather would permit, immediately after the Court rose, which in those times was generally about two o'clock.　He had then but little occupation, and he passed many of his evenings at my house the first two or three years of my marriage.　It was in one of these walks that he made known to me his wish to become an author.　He had published a small work, some years before, on the Criminal Law, without his name.　He did not think the style good enough to republish it.　But he had composed two volumes on the same subject, which he submitted to my inspection.　I thought that the composition of them was not such as to give him reputation as a writer, and the part he took being at that time unpopular, I advised him not to publish that work.　We projected several works to be published between us.　One was a new edition of Blackstone's Commentaries ; but when we had made some prepara-

tion for this, we found that Mr. Christian had publicly
announced the same project, in which he privately sought our
assistance. It was then proposed that we should write a
history of the influence of particular laws upon morals,
manners, and wealth of nations. The idea was suggested by
the perusal of Lord Bacon's ' History of the Life of Henry VII.'
This work, as far as Romilly might have taken a part in
it, would have been curious and useful. We had made some
progress, but as both care and time were necessary to its
completion, it happened that the increase of professional calls
upon each of us made it impossible to continue the work.

It was in the earlier part of my residence in town that he
proposed to me to translate into English several letters he
had received from Dumont, in the year 1789-90 ; giving a
very lively history of the progress of the French Revolution.

He had made me acquainted with Dumont whilst I was
at college, and it was impossible to know him without admiring his wit and his genius. The letters in question exhibited
both in a high degree, combined with a vigorous and animated style. Romilly had translated two or three of them
himself.

He had also written several essays, on different subjects,
in the shape of letters. It was his plan that these essays
should be translated by Dumont into French ; and that the
work should be published in both languages. It was a great
amusement to me to translate Dumont's letters, and Romilly
submitted all his own essays to my correction before they
were sent to the press. They were, for the most part, beauti-
fully written.

There was one, however, on the subject of Reform in Parliament. His wishes on the question went beyond mine. I was a
reformer to a moderate extent, but always entertained a belief
that a Democratic Assembly in the place of the House of
Commons must necessarily lead to the destruction of the
Monarchy. Upon reading his essays, and another upon heri-
ditary nobility, I added in the shape of a note to the letter,
what I intended to represent as the necessary consequences
of his system of Reform, the dissolution of the Monarchy
and the establishment of a Republic. As we had often

discussed Swift's style among others, I attempted in this note an imitation of it. What was my astonishment when the work was published to find my note also in print.

When I expostulated with him, on the possible consequences of the writer being supposed really to recommend a Republic, he replied, ' There is no fear of that ; the note is too well written for any body to doubt it being an irony.'

The work was published under the title of 'Letters of Harry Greenvelt.' But shortly after it issued from the press, commenced those violent passages in the French Revolution which disgusted and terrified most of those who had been friendly to it, and Romilly, without hesitation, committed to the flames every copy that had not been sold, with the exception of one which his executors sent to me. He did not think proper, even by an anonymous work, to give any apparent sanction to what was passing in France, or to encourage in any degree the spirit of dissatisfaction that began to appear in England.

This incident should have been buried with me in the grave had not some allusion to it appeared in the memoirs of Sir Samuel Romilly published by his sons. That circumstance, combined with the sending of his copy to me by his executors, induces me to think that he must have left some memorial of it ; and as I am aware that several copies of the work have got into circulation, I am anxious if it ever should be published again with his name, that the world should know, that the essays written by him were mere sketches for his own amusement—experiments upon style— and are not to be taken as the true representation of his sentiments. At the same time it is fair to own that he, as well as many other thinking men, were at the first breaking out of the French Revolution inclined to favour it, and to a certain extent to adopt some of the abstractions which were the fashion in Paris.

CHAPTER XII.

PITT—BURKE—FOX.

I WAS in the gallery of the House of Commons in the year 1791, when Mr. Pitt opened his Budget, and well remember that even he spoke of the Revolution in France as a happy event for that country and for the world, as it would probably result in the establishment of a free Government for the benefit of the nation, and of a more moderate system of policy for the benefit of the world, instead of the restless and ambitious despotism of the Bourbons, who had been the disturbers of the peace of Europe for the last century. The mistake made by this great man may surely excuse the errors of many others on the same subject. I may say that the principles of the Revolution had more or less pervaded this nation, and that, had it not been for the wisdom and eloquence of Burke, who published his thoughts on the French Revolution about this time, we should have gone near to follow the example. Even the alarm he sounded had not its full effect till the succession of sanguinary measures, and the tyranny of those who were called the people over a popular Assembly, which followed each other in rapid succession, filled every mind with horror and disgust. For myself, I confess, that I at one time hoped and believed that the dissolution of the despotism in France, effected at first without bloodshed or apparent struggle, would be a fortunate event for mankind. But experience soon cured me of this delusion, and more mature reflection satisfied me that the band of patriot Whigs who joined Mr. Pitt, and encouraged him to make war, were the saviours of their country. Perhaps the war was too hastily begun. Certainly it was for some years neither happily or wisely conducted, but I am convinced it was impossible to have avoided it, or to have terminated it so long as the spirit of Jacobinism governed the French Councils, or was embodied or enthroned in its child and champion Buonaparte. It may be supposed, however, that the French Revolution and the war gave rise to very bitter dissentions and strong party feelings. The rights of man, the equality of men, the authority and power of numbers against property, natural justice, at all times most acceptable topics of declamation with the multitude, were inculcated with considerable zeal and talent among the lower orders of the people, and did not want for partizans amongst some very distinguished persons. But the vigour of the Government, and the great majority in both Houses of Parliament which supported it, arrested the progress of these opinions, till such time as the events of the war, and the conduct of the *soi-disant* lovers of liberty in France had opened the eyes of this nation to the folly of French theories, and the danger of risking the overthrow of the British Constitution by adopting them in this country. I thought, however, that in some instances the prosecutions and the punishment of political offenders were more severe than necessary, and that there was too much of intolerance amongst those in power for the opinions of those who opposed them in Parliament. I was much in the habit of attending the debates, and was so charmed with the eloquence of Mr. Fox that I conceived a great partiality for him and the little party that fought under his banner, and who, for some years, comprised all the good speakers in the House of Commons, with the exception of Mr. Pitt, who was, in his own way, quite unrivalled. With a tall and commanding figure, a graceful action, a most sonorous and perfect voice, he spoke with the same deliberation and fluency as if he were reading a book. There was never a moment's hesitation for a word ; the emphasis was always correct and beautiful, because it served to render the longest sentences intelligible. His language was always vigorous and perspicuous, occasionally sarcastic, sometimes animated and elegant, but never passionate. He aimed only at the understanding, and seemed to disdain all arts but the art of reasoning in pure language and never-failing taste. He possessed a rare and curious felicity in covering the weak parts of his argument, and exhibiting the strongest parts in the clearest light. He spoke with boldness, and without previous study or composition, yet there was no instance of his uttering an indiscreet sentiment or unguarded expression.

Mr. Windham said of him, that his speeches were like perfect State papers, and Mr. Burke, who never liked him, said his style was the very tiptop of mediocrity. Certainly it did not exhibit the brilliant and laboured ornaments of Burke, nor the vehement and passionate tirades of Mr. Fox, who was himself often hurried away, by the force of his feelings, into a lofty strain of passionate declamation, mixed with invective and argument, almost worthy of Demosthenes. Whereas Pitt appeared never to lose the command of himself, nor to allow the force of any sentiment to overpower his reason. Fox, on the other hand, had an ungainly person, a shrill voice, an embarrassed manner, and considerable hesitation when he first began ; but if he wanted the grace, the fluency, the voice, and commanding manner of Pitt, he possesssed in a high degree that which Pitt wanted, passionate emotions in himself, and the power of rousing them in his audience, and using them for the purpose of enforcing his argument. He began in an hesitating manner, repeating his words with an apparent difficulty in finding the right words, confused sentences, all of which continued for some minutes till he grew warm with his argument. Then all hesitation left him, his voice became deep, powerful, and impassioned, and when he had worked himself into a clear and vigorous perception of his argument he poured out torrents of reasoning in beautiful language, mixed with emotions of disdain, anger, resentment, and contempt, which he made it impossible not to share with him. In the meantime all the personal defects were forgotten, and he had so the art of captivating the attention, that you forgot the man entirely and thought only of the subject.

The effect produced on me by these two great orators was this, that I could not help admiring Pitt, and believing Fox. I compared them to Virgil and Homer. In reading the first, the polished elegance and beauty of his manner make you think always of the man. But the rapid succession of events, and the simplicity and energy with which they are related by Homer, make you forget the author and think only of the Greeks and Trojans.

CHAPTER XIII.

BURKE—SHERIDAN—GREY.

WHILST I am on this subject I will speak of Burke, Sheridan, and Grey.

The first, though full of genius, imagination, and learning, was never a successful debater. His manner and action were sufficiently graceful, but his style was too didactic, and his topics too general to affect the passions, or to excite a continued interest in the audience.

He declaimed with great elegance and beauty, but more in the manner of a teacher than an orator. His speeches, like his other works, are treasures of wisdom, lofty sentiments, polished taste, and brilliant ornament. But to feel and do justice to their merits, meditation and reflection are necessary. These, however, are more than an assembly has time to bestow on a speaker. To produce an immediate effect his argument must either be upon the surface, or be short, perspicuous, and made to bear manifestly on the point in dispute, his images must be striking, his manner earnest, his style simple, clear, free from all involution, and above all he should never dwell on abstract or general position, but exhibit his sentiments as much as possible in a concrete form. Cicero, who was master of every sort of eloquence, furnishes me with many examples to illustrate what I mean.

Sheridan was always a most agreeable speaker. His wit was brilliant, his voice charming, his action elegant, and his argument lively and acute. But he never appeared to investigate his subject to the bottom. He seemed rather to delight in playing about the surface and gathering topics of pleasantry and sarcasm to amuse. He was supposed to have bestowed much previous thought and labour upon the shining parts of his speeches. His most celebrated performance was in the debate upon the impeachment of Mr. Hastings. I did not hear it, but it received the highest encomiums from Mr. Pitt, and Mr. Fox said he would rather have made that speech, than any he had ever heard or spoken. This was high praise ; and if Sheridan's industry had equalled his genius and talents, he would have been second to none of his age in the art of public speaking.

Grey's style was polished and perspicuous, his sentiments lofty, his manners full of dignity, and though he did not approach the highest excellencies of his competitors, there was a never-failing common sense and sagacity that distinguished his speeches, and marked a very high order of intellect.

I forbear to say more of him now, as I shall have occasion to mention his name in connection with some of the important events of my life. For several years I was in the habit of passing the whole period of the Newcastle Assizes at a house where he also was a visitor. I cannot look back upon those days without remembering how much they were enlivened by his society, and the pleasure and sincerity with which I endeavoured to cultivate his esteem.

CHAPTER XIV.

EARLY LIFE AT THE BAR.

To return from this digression to my own life as a lawyer, I have to say that, urged by the prospect of an increasing family, as well as by the ambition which has never ceased to govern me, I devoted myself with increasing application to the duties of my profession. By Romilly's advice, I resolved to try my fortune in England. I adjourned from year to year the return to my own country, and always with the approbation of my father. His allowance to me was liberal, and I depended chiefly upon it, during the first few years after my marriage, for the expenses of my family.

In the month of October, 1798, he died. It happened that this was the first year when the income I derived from my profession was sufficient to defray the whole of my expenses. From that year to the period of my quitting the Bar I never spent the whole of my income in any one year. I attended the Lancashire Sessions and very soon had great success there. I may ascribe to the practice I was obliged to adopt at Manchester the great facility with which I was able to conduct the mass of business that afterwards passed through my hands, on the Circuit, and at Westminster and at Guildhall. The counsel were accustomed to arrive late in the evening before the sessions, the attorneys on the next day. The magistrates commenced their business at half-past eleven. It was only during the few hours that elapsed from eight to that time that I had to prepare the day's work. It sometimes occurred that I had fifteen or twenty briefs in settlement cases, which were always taken the first day. To make myself master of the points in each by reading them was impossible. As to the law and the decided authorities I came well prepared, and required no study. The mode then which I adopted to obtain the facts was to interrogate the attorney when he came with his brief what was the fact in his own case on which he mainly relied. Next what he supposed his adversary's case to depend upon. Having made a short note of his statement on the back of the brief, I proceeded to discuss the appeal without further instruction or meditation, and I believe I may safely say that I did not read one brief in ten in the most important cases in which I was concerned at quarter sessions.

In like manner, when I began to lead causes in the superior Courts, it was my practice to enquire of my junior counsel what were the points in the cause on both sides, and to make a minute of those on the back of the brief. Instead of doing this, which I always found successful in practice, had I attempted to read masses of paper delivered in each case, I am certain that I should not have had time to read one in five, applying the whole period of my absence from Court to that duty alone. Undoubtedly the case would be very different at present. The number of causes tried in a day seldom amount to half a dozen of all sorts on an average. But Lord Kenyon and Mr. Justice Buller disposed with ease of twenty-six in a day, and Lord Ellenborough's average was twenty. I do not pretend to assign the causes of this difference, though the fact is unquestionable that the labour of the sittings, though much shorter, was more severe in those times whilst it lasted, than it has ever been since.

My success in town kept pace with my progress at the sessions. There was a description of business in the scope of my profession which by the year 1802 was not at my command. And though I did not leave the sessions for four years afterwards, not liking to give up the certainty for the speculation, I became satisfied that I should have more than doubled my income if I had given them up in 1802.

In the year 1799 Mr. Chambers, a gentleman of the highest eminence and popularity on the Northern Circuit, being promoted to the Bench, a silk gown was given to Mr. James Allen Parke of the same Circuit, who was afterwards a Judge of the Court of Common Pleas. Upon that occasion Mr.

Law, who was counsel with me upon some Bill depending in the House of Lords, desired to know why I had not applied for a silk gown, for, said he, 'Your business on the Circuit gives you a much better title than Parke's does to him.' I replied that I had not thought of it, the sessions being too important to me at that time. I only mention this to show what was the opinion of the leader of the Northern Circuit in the year 1799 as to my pretensions, and for the purpose of remarking that I never did obtain that promotion till the year 1816, for many years before which I was leading almost every cause on the Northern Circuit, and dividing the lead of Guildhall and Westminster with Garrow and Parke.

It may be asked, what was the reason of this delay? I can assign no other reason for Lord Eldon not giving it to me than the supposition that I was attached to the Whigs.

Why the Whigs did not give it to me whilst they were in office in 1806 and 1807, is more difficult to guess. They knew that I wished for it, they thought I desired it, and they bestowed the honour on several gentlemen both at the Common Law and Equity Bar who certainly had nothing like my pretensions.

The riddle, if it be worth solving, must be solved by posterity. But certain it is, in this the first and best opportunity they had of serving me, they did not think fit to do so. They were satisfied with my attachment, and did not wish for my gratitude. Not a week after they had quitted office Lord Erskine called upon me to express his sorrow that I had been passed over, assured me that it was his intention if he had remained longer in office to have done me justice, admitted to the fullest extent my claims, and urged me without delay to apply to his successor, and to Lord Ellenborough to second my application for immediate promotion. To say the truth, I believe it was not Lord Erskine's fault. And now that I am come to the period of his legal life, I cannot forbear to pause awhile upon his memory.

CHAPTER XV.

LORD ERSKINE.

HE was not without his faults as a man. They were the faults of imprudence and of ill regulated passions. But no man was more beloved by those who knew him intimately.

His manners were courteous and obliging. His conversation full of spirit and gaiety. His imagination had something fantastic about it, that made him a constant source of amusement. His good temper was imperturbable. His spirits were lively, his disposition for frolic and fun in private society so extraordinary that to those who were strangers to him it was impossible to believe that he was the celebrated Mr. Erskine or anything else but a schoolboy broken loose for the holidays. The animation of the society in which he moved, the most welcome guest in every company. That he might not appear in this view altogether without a fault, it was observed by his severe critics that he made his conversation turn too much on himself, and that personal vanity was visible in the most brilliant of his exhibitions. There may be some truth in this criticism, but it ought to be qualified by this remark, that the admiration of his talent was so great and so universal, that it was difficult to find a subject of conversation more interesting or more acceptable to himself, and that if the false and offensive arrogance of undue applause be properly called vanity, the just consciousness of merit and superiority ought to be distinguished by some other name, more especially when it is perfectly remote, as it ever was in him from every approach to insolence, ill nature, or the disparagement of others. Such was Erskine in society. As an advocate no language can exaggerate his merits. Cautious, wary, astute, clear in his discernment, and almost infallible in his judgment, no point that could really serve his client was unobserved, no topic that could advance his cause omitted. His examination of witnesses was always pointed, brief, and perfectly gentlemanlike. His manners towards his antagonist, and his mode of speaking of him, always courteous.

His opening speeches short, lively, and characterised by a gay sort of pleasantry, that it made it always amusing to hear him.

I recollect to have heard the late Mr. Justice Chambers say that a day at Nisi Prius was very dull unless Erskine was engaged in it, but he always made it entertaining by his wit and imagination, yet during the whole conduct of the cause nothing was more remarkable to those who listened than his discretion in selecting the points and facts as they arose, and applying them for the benefit of his client, in so much that Sheridan used to say of him, 'Erskine in his gown and wig has the wisdom of an angel, but the moment he puts them off he is nothing but a schoolboy.'

In his reply, though abounding with eloquence and ornament, no topic was admitted that did not bear directly upon the verdict.

He was perspicuous, rapid, vehement, and never failed of success if the case was doubtful. He was the favourite of every jury, and I might add of every judge before whom he was in the habit of practising. His style was always elegant and correct.

It is very faithfully represented in his public speeches, and in the work called 'Armada' which he published after he had quitted the seals. It appears to me as a style for oratory to approach more nearly to perfection than any other. Besides the merit of perspicuity, correctness, and ornament, it has a music and rhythm altogether peculiar to it, and which gives it even in reading a singular grace and energy. But from his tongue, accompanied by his impassioned tones, the beautiful modulation of his voice, and the vehemence of his emphasis, it was quite irresistible. The very sound of his voice had a charm about it which invited you to listen. In fine, he imparted to his audience all his emotions. He was the only orator within my knowledge who possessed the real power of pathos, who could excite the passions, and make the sympathies of his audience subservient to his purpose. This no doubt was the effect of the combination of all his powers. To his parts as an orator he added those of a consummate actor. His eye, his countenance, the action of his limbs and body were full of expression, elegance and dignity. They combined to enforce the passions which his language was exciting. I am satisfied that if one who had not understood the language had merely seen his action and heard the various tones and modulations of his voice, he could not but have experienced considerable pleasure and excitement from the exhibition.

Possessing these rare qualities, it may be asked how it happened that Erskine had comparatively so little success in the House of Commons?

Certain it is that neither Mr. Pitt, nor Mr. Fox, nor Mr. Sheridan, nor one who was inferior to none who preceded him, Mr. Canning, ever excited a tear in my eye or a strong movement of passion in the House of Commons. Whereas I have known the whole audience dissolved in tears at a speech of Erskine's and many eager to press around him, and as it were to kiss the hem of his garment. My opinion is that if Erskine had in early life made the House of Commons his arena for oratory, if he had bent his mind on politics and bestowed his studies on the best mode of speaking in that assembly he would have taken incomparably the first rank. I have in another place observed upon the difference in the styles of speaking for the bar or senate.

I think there are very satisfactory reasons why a habit long cultivated at the former and attended with great success should render the exhibitions of the speaker in Parliament, few and occasional as they can only be whilst he remains at the bar, less successful than might be expected.

The forensic orator is instructed beforehand by a specific statement of facts. He comes prepared to discuss a precise question upon which the issue is joined between the parties. His duty is to make such use of his facts and of the topics which his own imagination may suggest as will lead to the conviction of the jury in favour of his client.

His sole object ought to be to persuade those twelve men to come to a specific conclusion. He may declaim, and be as amusing as he can upon collateral topics, but they will not in the least help him to his object, even though the judge should not interrupt him, nor will they command long the attention of the jury, who are ever anxious to see their way clear before them and to lay aside mere topics of amusement. In short, his business is to carry conviction to an audience who are to adopt or reject a specific proposition upon oath.

How different is the object and the duty of the parliamentary speaker.

He addresses an assembly of which the majority have already decided the vote. He does not expect to bring conviction to any individual amongst them. There is to be no movement, and no act done in consequence of his speech or of the debate. The object is to flatter and encourage his own party, and to hold the opposite party or their measures up to contempt and sarcasm. He is therefore not called upon to apply himself to the subject of nominal discussion, for any other purpose than that of connecting it with such topics of praise or blame as he may think fit to introduce. His chief object must be to command the attention of his hearers, and this is not to be done so well by any efforts upon their reason or their knowledge respecting the question before them, as by the dexterous handling of any extraneous matter that he can make the subject of praise or blame.

There is no method more common or more exciting than that of selecting some individual, and exposing him to ridicule, or sarcasm, or contempt. In short the character of the eloquence of the House of Commons is that which is termed by the ancient rhetoricians '*demonstration.*' It is convenient in praise or blame. The chief figure is exaggeration. It is like scene painting which is to have its effect at a distance. It is not for the assembly, but the gallery, and the newspapers. Hence it appears to me that if two orators of equal parts had each taken one of these two lines, and by usage acquired great facility and reputation, neither would find it easy on changing his line to fall at once into the habits and discipline required to ensure him a successful comparison with the other.

It was very truly said of Mr. Fox when he was one of the managers of the impeachment of Hastings that he argued several points of law and of evidence which occurred with great ability and ingenuity, insomuch that old Mr. Justice Willes asked one of the Lords the name of that promising young man.   But in truth it will be found on referring to the short-hand writer's notes, that there was mixed with his ingenuity more of declamation than would have been tolerated at the Bar, and which though it contributed to the amusement of the House by exposing the defendant's counsel to some ridicule, had not the slightest effect upon the judgment of the House, nor on the merit of the argument.   But though I admit that Erskine's success in the House of Commons was not equal to his reputation at the bar, for in that he surpassed all other men, I am far from conceding that he had not very great success.

I have heard him several times, when he spoke second only to Pitt and Fox, and commanded the profoundest attention. What can be expected from a lawyer in great practice, who has not time for the exigencies of his own profession.   Mr. Burke used to say 'The best that the lawyers bring us in this House is but the rinsing of their empty bottles.'

I can say myself that though I received many compliments upon my first speech in Parliament, and though I was not conscious of any deficiency of talent for debate, I found it im-possible to pursue my profession consistently with the appli-cation to parliamentary subjects which was essential to my pretending to any lead in the House of Commons.

I have endeavoured to do justice to Lord Erskine, with whom in my professional life I formed an intimacy, which never ceased while he lived, and which was ever a source of pleasure to me. He was taken from the Bar to the Woolsack. He had never been accustomed to the Court of Chancery, and his very rapid success at the Bar of the King's Bench naturally directed all his attention to that Court alone, over which he would have unquestionably have presided with great applause. But even on the Woolsack, the profession were struck by his great facility.

He had not thirteen months' experience in the office of Chancellor, and it ought to be remarked to his credit that no one of his decrees was ever reversed.

CHAPTER XVI.

HIS PROFESSIONAL PROGRESS.

TO RETURN to my own story. I quitted the sessions in 1807, and shortly afterwards found myself in the command of every variety of business. The Court of King's Bench, the Court of Exchequer, the Privy Council, the two Houses of Parliament, and even the Court of Chancery seemed disposed to open their doors to me ; not to mention elections and cases of compensation under Acts of Parliament.

Unable to resist solicitations which flattered my vanity and increased my means, I for some time went the round of these varieties, till, by the advice of my friend Plummer, I finally resolved to adhere to the Court of King's Bench and the Northern Circuit. He was, at the time he so advised me, at the head of what was called parliamentary business, and had the decided lead of the Exchequer. He assured me, however, that the King's Bench and the Northern Circuit were worth more than all the rest put together—in point of profit—and would with more certainty lead to greater things, if anything could be deemed greater in the profession.

Partly from his advice, and partly from the inconvenience I felt in being drawn so many different ways, I at length declined all business but in the Court of King's Bench and on my own Circuit.

In consequence of Lord Erskine's advice, which I have already mentioned, and with the approbation of Lord Ellenborough, I applied to Lord Eldon for a silk gown by letter, to which no answer was returned from 1807 till 1816. In the meantime I worked hard in my vocation, and found before long that even under the covering of a stuff gown I was becoming a favourite on both the scenes to which I confined my appearance. I had fairly divided the lead with the silk gowns in the King's Bench and upon the Northern Circuit, and frequently declined special retainers upon other Circuits. It would indeed have been a losing concern to have quitted any place on the Northern Circuit for such an object, and therefore, excepting on three occasions to Northampton, and the like number to Lincoln, which I could take without losing a day at York, I rejected all applications, and they were numerous, to attend other Circuits on special retainers.

One of the instances on which I went to Northampton was in the year 1813, when Lord Lyndhurst, then Mr. Serjeant Copley, had made his first appearance there with his coif. I was retained in two causes, one of which could only be tried, the other was made a remanet by the judge. Upon the next Circuit, which was in the spring of 1814, I found my attendance at Northampton would interfere with my business at the Guildhall, and having signified this to Lord Exeter's solicitor, for his Lordship was my client, he requested me to recommend him to some other gentleman whom he should retain, as the leaders on the Midland Circuit were retained on the other side. I mentioned Serjeant Copley as a gentleman whom I believed to possess considerable talent, and moreover added that I would undertake for his success in the cause, which was not indeed of any difficulty. The solicitor took a day or two to consider of it, and then informed me that as the matter in difference was of great importance to Lord Exeter he could not think himself justified in placing his Lordship's interest in the hands of a gentleman so little known in the profession as Serjeant Copley. I mention this to show the position in which I then stood in reference to that gentleman, who in a few years afterwards was Attorney-General, Master of the Rolls, and in 1827 Lord Chancellor, whilst I was still plodding at the Bar. I shall have occasion to speak of him again.

At length, a few days before the commencement of the Circuit in March 1816, whilst I was conducting a cause before Lord Ellenborough, at Guildhall, I received a note from Lord

Eldon, to say that a patent of King's Counsel was ready for me, and that he would receive me to take the oaths that day at Lincoln's Inn Hall.   I had become almost indifferent to the honour, but on communicating the note to Lord Ellenborough, he desired that I would go immediately, and made some arrangement of the business to suit my convenience. This step was at the time so entirely unexpected that I had made no provision of either wig or robe.   I was obliged, therefore to finish the Guildhall sittings in my stuff gown, and to adjourn my appearance in silk until I arrived at York.

In the course of that year Garrow, who was then Attorney-General, became a Baron of the Exchequer. Parke had before become a Judge of the Common Pleas ; Gibbs, a Chief Baron ; Topping soon after quitted the profession.   I was therefore placed by business, if not by rank, at the head of the King's Bench Bar and the Northern Circuit, and I remained so, without interruption, from that time to the year 1827, when I became Attorney-General, witnessing in the meantime some of my juniors, but who had never been my competitors, promoted to professional honours and offices.   Indeed I may say from the year 1816 to the close of 1834, when I was appointed Chief Baron, I had a longer series of success than has ever fallen to the lot of any other man in the law ; and if my economy and prudence had equalled my good fortune, I think none of my predecessors in that line would have laid such a foundation for his posterity.   But though I have never spent the whole of my professional income since the year 1798, I am sorry to say that I have saved but little of it ; and so much of that comparatively little has been invested in land, and that so injudiciously, that what I leave behind me will scarcely be worth having.

CHAPTER XVII.

ON PUBLIC SPEAKING.

WHEN I contemplate my own success in life, and compare it with the specimens which posterity may possibly find here and there of my performances at the Bar, I am at a loss to reconcile the effect of my labours with the very indifferent appearance I shall make as a speaker. It is true that my style of speaking was rapid, and my voice rather weak, and I conclude it was difficult for the shorthand writers to follow me correctly. Indeed, I may say that I have often, on reading Mr. Gurney's notes, been surprised to find my grammar and language much more accurate than I should have imagined from the representation of the newspapers, and even from the notes of any other artist in stenography which has fallen under my view. But there is something in the contrast to which I have alluded a great deal deeper, and perhaps the investigation may not be without interest. It appears to me, then, that he who seeks great reputation with the public as a speaker, must not only compose his speeches, at least, as far as regards the ornamental part, but must ingraft upon the topics that belong to his cause certain generalities in morals, politics, or philosophy, which will give scope to declamation, rhetoric, and ornament to polished phrases and well-turned sentences; to epigram, humour, and sarcasm. These are the passages which delight the general audience, and make the speech, when published, agreeable to the reader. But they are not the passages which carry conviction to the mind, or advance the real merits of the cause with those who are to decide it. He who looks to this purpose only must never lose sight of any important fact or argument that properly belongs to or arises out of the cause. He must show that his mind is busied about nothing else. He must be always working upon the concrete, and pointing to his conclusion.   He must disdain all jest, ornament, or sarcasm, that does not fall directly in his way and seem to be so unavoidable that it must strike everybody who thinks of the facts.   He must not look for a peg to hang anything upon, be it ever so precious or so fine.   He must rouse in the minds of the judges or the jury all the excitement which he feels about the cause himself, and about nothing but the cause ; and to that he must stick closely, and upon that reason so vehemently and so conclusively, that the greater part of the audience will not understand him, and those who read his speech afterwards will not be able to comprehend it, without having present to their memories all the facts and all the history of the cause.

Mr. Fox used to say that a speech which read well was a bad speech. This, perhaps, was carrying the point too far. But it is true that a speech which reads well is not, therefore, an effective speech for the purpose. Look at the speech of Sir James Mackintosh for Peltier, who ought to have been acquitted.   Look at the most beautiful published speeches of Burke, who was nevertheless called the dinner-bell of the House of Commons.

Again, composing a speech, or parts of a speech, beforehand is productive of this bad effect, that the composition does not appear to arise out of the cause, or that the cause is sometimes distorted in some parts to fit the composition. There may be much to admire, but nothing to excite or animate. The attention of the speaker, too, is necessarily drawn aside from the contemplation of the matters immediately before him, to the care of remembering his composition, of making the cause appear suitable to it, and of delivering it with a theatrical air and emphasis, the only mode of making a composition delivered from memory appear natural.   He is not warmed by the fire which blazes near him, but by a heat reflected from a distant lamp.   Instead of rousing he checks the animation of those whom he is to convince, and makes them think of the advocate and not of the cause.   When I entered on the first practical duties of my profession, I was prepared, by probably more than the common course of study, with the usual theories in the art of public speaking. I borrowed a hint from Mr. Hume's ' Essays upon Eloquence,' and composed an elaborate speech which I got by heart. When I had delivered the first two sentences, I began to think that they did not naturally arise out of the facts of the case, and that the elegance and refinement of my composition would detect the previous labour. This alarmed me, caused me to hesitate, to forget the whole of my lesson, and forced me to plunge at once into the topic of the moment. From that time I not only renounced previous composition, but scarcely ever in thinking over the subject I was to speak upon cloathed a thought with words, certainly with no words that I ever remembered afterwards, and I never found a want of words when I had thoughts or arguments to utter. *Provisam rem, verba sequentur.* I made it my business to know and remember the principal facts, to lay the unimportant wholly out of memory, to open the case, if for the plaintiff, and when I expected evidence for the defendant, in the shortest and plainest manner, with no other object than to make the jury comprehend the evidence which they would shortly hear.

I very seldom thought it necessary to make any anticipation of the defendant's case. It is, indeed, oftentimes dangerous to do so, as it leads the judge and jury to seek for support to it in the plaintiff's evidence. I found from experience, as well as theory, that the most essential part of speaking is to make yourself understood. For this purpose it is absolutely necessary that the Court and jury should know as early as possible *de quâ re agitur.* It was my habit, therefore, to state in the simplest form that the truth and the case would admit the proposition of which I maintained the affirmative and the defendant's counsel the negative, and then, without reasoning upon them, the leading facts in support of my assertion. Thus it has often happened to me to open a cause in five minutes, which would have occupied a speaker at the Bar of the present day from half an hour to three-quarters of an hour or more. Moreover, I made it a rule in general rather to understate than overstate facts I expected to prove. For what-

ever strikes the mind of a juror, as the result of his own observation and discovery, makes always the strongest impression
upon him, and the case in which the proof falls much below the
statement is supposed for that very reason not to be proved at
all.   As the evidence proceeded I bestowed much too anxious
attention upon it to take a note.   I treasured up the facts in
my memory, and arranged them in such a way as I thought
would lead most distinctly to the conclusion I desired. My mind
underwent the same process during the defendant's case.   I
learned by much experience that the most useful duty of an
advocate is the examination of witnesses, and that much more
mischief than benefit generally results from cross-examination.
I therefore rarely allowed that duty to be performed by my
colleagues.   I cross-examined in general very little, and more
with a view to enforce and illustrate the facts I meant to rely
upon.than to affect the witness's credit, for the most part a
vain attempt.   By the time the defendant's case was closed
the topics for reply were arranged in my mind.   I had sifted
the material facts from the chaff, and held them fast in my
memory, stored in their proper places.   I had observed the
facts that appeared to make the most impression upon the
jury either for or against me.   My reply was in general short,
vehement, perspicuous, and directly to the point.   Very often,
when the impression of the jury and sometimes of the judge
has been against me on the conclusion of the defendant's
case, I have had the good fortune to bring them entirely to
adopt my conclusions.   Whenever I observed this impression,
but thought myself entitled to the verdict, I made it the rule
to treat the impression as very natural and reasonable, to
acknowledge that there were circumstances which presented
great difficulties and doubts, to invite a candid and temperate
investigation of all the important topics that belonged to the
case, and to express rather a hope than a confident opinion
upon a deliberate and calm investigation I should be able to
satisfy the Court and jury that the plaintiff was entitled to the
verdict.   I then avoided all appearance of confidence, and
endeavoured to place the reasoning on my part in the clearest
and strongest view, and to weaken that of my adversary ; to
show that the facts for the plaintiff could lead naturally but

to one conclusion, while those of the defendant might be accounted for on other hypotheses, and when I thought I had gained my point I left it to the candour and good sense of the jury to draw their own. This course seems to me not to be the result of any consummate art, but the plain and natural course which common sense would dictate. At the same time it must be observed, that he who would adopt it can only expect success when it is known that he can discriminate between a sound and a hopeless case, and that his judgment is sufficiently strong to overcome the bias of the advocate and the importunity of the client, and to make him at once surrender a case that cannot, and ought not to be sustained. But, although the practice I have mentioned was eminently successful with me, in many instances, both with juries and with Committees of the House of Commons, I have known advocates of great reputation pursue a very different line from want of judgment or influence of temper. With them the discovery that the judge and jury had formed an impression against them, seemed rather to awaken their resentment, and to provoke their vengeance, or to induce a stronger confirmation of their own opinions, and to make them more stubborn and obstinate in maintaining them, and to oppose the prejudices of the judge or jury, or both, as wholly void of all rational foundation. The natural consequence of treating the opinion of a man as unreasonable is to set him upon finding reason to support it, and I hardly know an instance of this practice being successful with a jury, though it may in some cases be so with a judge, who is or aims to be above passion and prejudice. Of course, when I expected no evidence for the defendant I took a longer view of the subject at the outset. But even here my endeavour was to awaken the feelings I wished to excite by way of influencing the damages, or leading to the desired conclusion, by a temperate and candid appeal to the justice and discernment of the jury, and then to make so moderate a statement of the facts as I was sure would be exceeded and appear stronger by the evidence. No error is more fatal to an advocate, or more common, than exaggeration. In Parliament the practice is often successful. But in the trial of causes, the evidence is sure, first or last, to furnish a measure by which to examine the statement and the advocate who, either in his opening or reply, exaggerates the importance of his facts, is sure to be suspected either of a defect in judgment or an excess of zeal which obscures his intellect, or, which is worse than all, of a design to impose on the jury.

CHAPTER XVIII.

CAUSE OF HIS SUCCESS AT THE BAR.

FROM these remarks, it will appear that my success did not in the least depend on those tirades of declamation which make the reputation of a speaker. Nor in the most considerable and difficult cases in which I have carried the verdict can any one who reads the printed speech either take any interest in it or even understand it without reading over and understanding the whole of the evidence. I never made a speech with a view to my own reputation, nor for any other object but to serve my client. The general audience, therefore, which crowded to hear popular speakers took little interest in my performances. But the judge and the jury, on the contrary, gave me their profound attention, and I believe I may say that no advocate in my time possessed a greater influence with them. Upon this subject, perhaps, I may be excused for relating an anecdote which is an illustration of it. On the Northern Circuit at certain periods there used to be a grand supper, at which all the members were assembled, and the expenses of which were paid by fines and congratulations that resulted in contributions to which the principal leaders were subject. These were introduced, in general, in a ceremonious speech, by one of the body who bore the office of Attorney-General of the Circuit. Upon the occasion to which I allude, the present Lord Chief Justice Tindal held that office. I was leader of the Circuit both in rank and business. He introduced my name for the purpose of a congratulation, by stating that his friend Mr. Scarlett had for many years been employing his genius in the invention of a machine which he had brought to perfection. The operation, the whole Circuit were in the habit of witnessing, with astonishment at his success. He, the Attorney-General, had at length discovered the secret, which was no other than a machine which he dexterously contrived to keep out of sight, but by virtue of which he produced a surprising effect upon the head of the judge. 'You have all noticed, gentlemen, that when my learned friend addresses the Court he produces on the judge's head a motion angular to the horizon like this,' he then made a movement of his head which signified a nod of approbation. When he had carried his motion by a unanimous vote of congratulation, he proceeded to another leader of the Circuit, a gentleman of more popular and of much higher reputation as a speaker than myself. He said, 'this gentleman as you all know, has for years been devoting his illustrious talents to surpass Mr. Scarlett. This he endeavours to accomplish by various means, and amongst other by imitating his example in the invention of a machine to operate on the head of the judge. In this he has at length, after much labour and study, succeeded. But you have observed that the motion he produces is of a different character. It is parallel to the horizon, in this fashion,' he then moved his head in a manner denoting dissent. The contrast and the joke occasioned much laughter, in which the gentlemen last alluded to most heartily joined, his good nature being not less remarkable than his talents.

My machine, however, consisted in nothing more than the study to avoid laying down any propositions that were not evident, or that could not be supported by plausible argument ; to make no misstatement or exaggeration of the facts, and, above all, not to combat with warmth any matter advanced by the judge, nor indeed to oppose at all but where I was satisfied I could alter his opinion by the most inoffensive reasoning. The heads of the jury were not less sensible of my machine. I had some tact in discovering what they thought.

I avoided every topic that I observed make an unfavourable impression upon them, and when I discovered the strings that vibrated in their bosoms, I often by a single touch on the true cord, in the course of my address or sometimes in an incidental remark on the evidence as it was given, saw that I

had carried the verdict. I recollect that so early in my career
as 1809 I was junior counsel for the sitting member upon an
election petition. The case was one of very great interest
from many exaggerated and false accounts that had been
published before the meeting of Parliament. The petitioner
was a strong supporter of Ministers, and the great majority of
the Committee was formed of persons actually in office, or of
his own partizans. I soon perceived both from the petitioner's
evidence and the manner in which it was received, that to
retain the seat was hopeless, and that even to avoid seating
the petitioner was a task of considerable difficulty. My leader
was a learned Serjeant, who opened his case for the sitting
member something too high. The evidence, however, on both
sides satisfied me that the true conclusion was to make it a
void election, but that to lead the Committee to that conclusion required very exact and close reasoning on the
evidence. I determined to try my powers. It was the first
Election Committee on which I was concerned. I began my
address by stating that I should add nothing to the arguments
of my leader in support of the seat, because I felt that if he
had not satisfied them upon that point, it would be vain for
me to attempt it. I should therefore confine myself strictly
to the question whether the petitioner had established a right
to the seat, or whether it was a void election, and though I
did not disguise to myself the difficulties that lay in my way
even upon that question, I entertained a strong hope that if
they would honour me with their attention whilst I brought
before them such parts of the evidence on both sides as
appeared to me material, it would be in my power to convince
them that they ought to take the same view of the case which
induced me to entertain that hope ; the more especially as I
did not doubt that much of the prejudice that had been
excited, and which gave so strong an interest in the case, had
already been dispelled by the evidence.

Confining their attention to a single point, I omitted all
facts that might be doubted, selected those only which
could not be disputed, and made my remarks as concisely and
as perspicuously as I was able to do. In the course of the
first half hour I found that the majority of the Committee

were listening to me with the most profound attention, which was preserved to the end of a speech of two hours and a half, much the shortest that had been delivered.   The result was that the Committee came to the conclusion I had desired, namely, that the election was void, by a small majority, in which I considered it a great enhancement of my victory to find the nominee of the petitioner.   This nominee was no other than Mr. Bond the King's Counsel, and at that time Judge Advocate.   A friend of mine, who took an interest in my success, asked this gentleman afterwards how Scarlett had acquitted himself.   He replied 'he made a very masterly dissection of the evidence, and certainly convinced me.'   There was the whole secret, to make a masterly dissection of evidence when the cause depended on a correct judgment of the facts.   I could mention many more instances of the same sort, but forbear.   It must be remembered, however, that a dissection of evidence to be masterly must be short as well as acute ; frequent repetition of the same facts or arguments not only fatigues the attention, but weakens their force by awakening a suspicion that the speaker feels that he has made no progress by stating them, and that there is little else in the case.   After all, I mean by this dissertation no more than to have it understood that the successful speaker in the practical concerns of life, whether in the Senate or at the Bar does not depend on long speeches or beautiful composition, or splendid ornaments, or flourishes of rhetoric, which assume the appearance of reasoning but neither warm the heart or enlighten the understanding. I have known more than one admired orator, who never convinced or persuaded anybody by his magnificent orations. Yet the audience were amused and delighted.   They hung upon his sentences and his accents with the same sort of interest and feeling as if they had been witnessing the steps of a dancer on the tight rope, whose prodigious agility and narrow escapes from falling fill the spectator with pleasure and astonishment.

CHAPTER XIX.

I HAVE mentioned that Erskine was the only orator I had ever known who had real pathos and could move his audience to tears.

I am persuaded that this was owing to his retaining the power of articulation and modulation when under the influence, apparently at least, of great emotion. I have observed that the greatest of all actresses, Mrs. Siddons, had the same power of perfect articulation, and giving effect to the beauties of the poet, when she was sobbing and in tears. With respect to myself, I have often been so strongly moved that I have felt myself capable of doing great things in exciting passion if I had been able to command my voice. But I never could attempt to express any strong emotion of any kind without bursting into tears, and then my voice became wholly inaudible and inarticulate, and it was a considerable time before I could recover the use of my tongue.

Hence I have at all times in speaking endeavoured to subdue strong emotions, when they were rising, to the 'temperatum genus dicendi.' The maxim of Horace, therefore, ' Si vis me flere dolendum primum ipsi tibi,' though it may be properly applied to writers, appears to me not to be just with regard to speakers.

Indeed I am much inclined to think that passion is best acted and expressed in words by those who do not feel it, but by the gift of nature or the labour of art possess the faculty of representing it.

As few men, at least of any common eminence, have remained at the Bar so long as myself, I had the opportunity

of comparing myself in practice with a greater number of
leaders than it has ever fallen to any other individual to
encounter.

In my early progress, the society which I chiefly cultivated
consisted of Perceval, Romilly, Dallas, George Wilson, Serjeant Lens, sometimes Erskine, and more rarely Law.   These
were amongst the *élite* of the profession in the Common Law.
Between the first three of these and myself there was a constant
communication of remarks and criticism upon the performances
and talents of the most eminent leaders of that day.   I have now
a small note-book containing Perceval's remarks on several of
them.   He said of Law, 'he has great strength which he puts
forth on occasions too trivial to require it.   He wields a huge
two-handed sword to extricate a fly from a spider's web.'   The
remark was just.   Lord Ellenborough had great talents, but at
the Bar he always seemed disposed to carry his point by force.
He had happy talent for ridicule, and was not sparing in the
use of it.   All his great speeches were in many parts composed.   He always assumed a high tone, and seemed to
disdain his adversary.   His speech for Mr. Hastings has very
great merit.   But the high talents and authority of the managers did not permit him to treat them with the same contempt
as he appears always to bestow on his opponents when he had
a fair opportunity. He was a well grounded lawyer, an honourable man, and a most lively and agreeable companion.

He carried his love of sarcasm, which was very useful to him
at the Bar, rather too far upon the Bench, but withal he was
an excellent judge.   Before him I soon found it necessary
to allow him the merit of discovering the best parts of my
case.   It was the turn of his mind to set himself in opposition
to the advocate who addressed him, and to endeavour to
refute him as he went along.   But when upon hearing the
evidence he found more important facts than had been urged
in his speech, his sagacity in discovering what had escaped
the counsel achieved a triumph which, to a certain extent,
flattered his vanity and gave him something like the interest
of a parent in the cause.   His mind was naturally suspicious
of fraud.   But it was never quite safe to undertake to prove
it to him, by stating all the facts and arguing upon them at

length.   During the whole of that process his ingenuity was employed in diluting the facts, and refuting the arguments. The safest course with him, was so to state the case as not to appear to rely strongly upon the presumption of fraud, and to keep back the facts that chiefly tended to prove it.

When these facts came out in evidence they never failed to produce all the effect which they deserved to have.   I may add here with regard to his successor, Lord Tenterden, that his turn of mind was exactly opposite.   He was remarkably candid, and followed the speaker implicitly, receiving easily the impression sought to be raised.   It was necessary with him, therefore, to follow a different course.   The fraud was to be fully detailed, and enforced by argument and observation.   He was a most worthy man, a sound lawyer, and a good scholar.   But he had not the talents of a leader. Indeed I believe, he had never more than two special jury causes in his life, before he came to the Bench.

These were two cases of *Quo warranto* respecting the Borough of Pembroke, moved and advised upon by me, but which I had declined though much solicited to take upon the Oxford Circuit, at the cost of giving up any portion of the Northern.   Though much my superior in age he was my junior at the Bar, and as such I often found his assistance very useful at Nisi Pius, not in the examination of witnesses, but in the caution of his temper and the soundness of his judgment.   His elevation to the situation of Chief Justice was owing to the supposed unfitness at that time of any other of the lawyers, official or connected with the Ministry, for that place.   Indeed, I am well informed that it was the opinion of the Government that I was the most proper person to have been appointed to it ; and nothing would have prevented the offer of it to me, but the notion that it was not proper to confer such a dignity upon a man attached to the Opposition.   It is impossible to say what the temptation might have effected, had so flattering an offer been made to me.   I know it was the opinion of Lord Grey, declared to me himself, that it was most unreasonable to make the party attachment of any man the ground of exclusion from a judicial situation.   I cannot say that I altogether agreed with his Lordship in that opinion, nor did he act upon that opinion afterwards. But of this I am certain, that if I had been placed in that situation it would have been the worse for me by at least 5,000*l.* a year, from the year 1818 to the year 1835. A remarkable incident occurred a few days after Abbott's appointment. I met Lord Liverpool, the First Minister, at dinner at a private party. He took me aside and asked me, with apparent anxiety in his looks, what I thought of the appointment. I made answer that he was a competent lawyer, and I made no doubt that he would give satisfaction. Satisfaction, however, he did not give at first.

Those who remembered Kenyon and Ellenborough could not fail to compare him with them. They tried causes at the rate of twenty to twenty-five a day. The very last day that Lord Ellenborough sat at Guildhall, when he was labouring under great infirmity and weakness, he tried seventeen defended causes, whereas during the week before the three Puisne Judges, who sat for him alternately at the same place, Bailey tried seven, Abbott five, and Holroyd three, a day. Abbott was greatly hurt at that difference. He made no secret of his mortification to me, and by way of remedy he fell upon the most extraordinary project of sitting to a very late hour every night. I had warned him of the impossibility of sustaining his resolution, even with reference to his own health, not to mention the discomfiture of the Bar, who besides being exposed to the same peril, had no time left to read their briefs and attend consultations. The scheme was soon found intolerable, and a succession of three or four late nights so affected the vigour of all parties that he was obliged to give it up. He then resorted to the plan of resuming his sittings after the Circuit, and devoting the whole of the vacations with the exception of a few days to the labours of his cause paper. And this continued to the great annoyance of all branches of the profession, till it was determined, by a Bill which I brought into Parliament in the year 1830, to limit the sittings to a certain number of days of each term. But as the younger part of the profession recollect no other judge with whom to compare Abbott except his immediate comtemporaries, and as his own powers increased and improved by practice, during the last seven years of his time his reputation increased, and he must be allowed, before he died, to have made an efficient judge. In some important particulars he could not be excelled; caution, candour, patience, impartiality, and a strict sense of duty. He would have been more effective if he had entertained a more just confidence in his own judgment; but he had not vigour to resist the pertinacity of the Bar, nor to rescue the jury from an eloquent and forcible reply, which sometimes carried the day against the justice of the case. I always felt a very great regard and respect for him. In the year 1827, when Mr. Canning was First Minister, and I was his Attorney-General, he consulted me upon the subject of raising the Chief Justice to the Peerage. I had no hesitation in recommending the measure strongly as a customary mark of respect to the dignity of his station, and a very acceptable compliment to the profession. Accordingly when he took his seat in the House of Peers he was attended by all the Judges, and the whole Bar of his Court.

Lord Tenterden however, was never a leader of causes. I return, therefore, to that class of whom next to Erskine and Ellenborough, Gibbs took his rank in the opinion of the Bar, though not of the public.

CHAPTER XX.

GIBBS—PERCEVAL—SIR ARTHUR PIGOT—LORD ELDON—
MITFORD—SIR THOMAS PLUMMER.

GIBBS was very acute, very ingenious, and well grounded in the
law.   But he had no knowledge out of the Statutes, the year
books, and the reporters, excepting what he brought with him
from the sixth form at Eton.   He was very far from being
an agreeable and persuasive speaker, and there was an asperity
in his countenance and manner that was very repulsive.
Nothing but his sterling knowledge of the law and his acute
reasoning would have raised him to any eminence.   He was
laborious and ambitious, and his success was at least equal to
his merits.   He was the best good man with the worst natural
face.   Perceval's remark upon him was that 'Gibbs' nose
would take out an iron mould.'

Garrow, an eloquent scolder with a fine voice and most
distinct articulation, a great flow of words, considerable quickness in catching the meaning of a witness, and great abilities
in addressing juries in ordinary cases, without education,
without taste, and without law, acquired and maintained a high
reputation with the public, but none in the profession.   He
had a theatrical manner of doing everything, and that which an
ordinary junior at the Bar would have done with simplicity,
without effort and without applause, Garrow gave importance
to by an affected arrangement, an appearance of a difficulty
overcome, and withal a certain tone or manner that made the
vulgar suppose the thing could not have been done but by
the greatest talent and genius.   Perhaps there never was an
instance of a man whose fame stood at once so high with the
public and so low with the Bar.   He was not much known in

private life, but I believe he was kind-hearted, generous and humane.

Dallas was a man of excellent understanding, and an elegant and graceful speaker. His practice was confined to the Parliamentary and Privy Council. He made a respectable Chief Justice of the Common Pleas, and lost none of his reputation in that post.

Parke was a good-natured man, very civil to everybody, and did his business very well, in a plain way, without any pretensions, or any profound merit.

Of my friend Perceval I have the most pleasing recollections. He was a most perfect gentleman in all points, with a benevolence that knew no bounds, of lively conversation, and most amiable manners, of a sound and vigorous intellect, capable of adorning any station in the profession of the law, from his learning in that department as well as his general acquirements.

He quitted the Court of King's Bench on being made Solicitor-General in the year 1801. His progress had not been equal to his talents in that Court, but I am persuaded that had he remained there his merit would very soon have become known by the public as it was acknowledged by the Bar, with whom he was a general favourite. He became Attorney-General when Lord Ellenborough was appointed to the Bench, and continued to practise in the Court of Chancery after he resigned that office in 1806, on the advent of the Whigs. Upon their retreat in 1807 he quitted the profession and accepted the office of Chancellor of the Exchequer, in which he continued till he perished by the hands of an assassin in 1812. 'Multis ille bonis flebilis occidit.' No man was more beloved. Politics were always his passion, and when he was fairly plunged into the arena of debate, he showed himself capable of great things.

He was an excellent debater, and had a great facility in gathering the topics of debate from the speeches of those who had gone before him. He continued his intimacy with me to the day of his death, and I may say with confidence that no one of his former friends or acquaintances found the least change in his manner or conduct after he quitted the Bar. If ever there was an honest man with a pure heart Perceval was the man.

I might mention many other individuals at the Bar who were at some period of my long career contemporary with me, but I confine myself to those who attained some eminent distinction.

Amongst those not before enumerated, was Sir Arthur Pigot, the Attorney-General of the Whigs. He was a man of great modesty of manner, good temper, sound judgment, and competent learning, but a speaker somewhat dull and lengthy. From the time of my acquaintance with him his practice was confined to Parliamentary Committees, by no means a good school for the Courts of Justice.

Sir John Scott, afterwards Lord Eldon. It is hardly necessary to say anything of a man who was Chancellor for twenty-five years, with a short interval. He was a consummate lawyer, of great quickness of apprehension, but of very slow decision. The character of his mind was that of great discrimination. He saw very shadowy distinctions and differences which perplexed him, more than was useful, with doubts, and made him hesitate so long before he gave his judgments, that the delays of the Court of Chancery became more than usually oppressive to suitors and a subject for clamour in Parliament. As a speaker he was elaborate and ingenious, and possessed a turn for grave humour that sometimes relieved his tedious discourses. When he was Chief Justice of the Common Pleas, he investigated every case to the bottom, considered every argument advanced by counsel, and every other topic besides, that the cause suggested: laid the whole of them before the jury in an elaborate and full summing-up which presented more points and more subtle distinctions and more ingenious hypotheses than men accustomed to such discussions were able to deal with, and finally after an admirable lecture for a student at law, puzzled and confounded the jury, and made it often uncertain on what ground they pronounced their verdict. This habit was not the result of his practice in the Courts of Equity. He had been for some years a very successful leader on the Northern Circuit, where he was much esteemed and beloved.

He was in private society always acceptable and agreeable, and so much conciliated the Bar by the kindness of his manner, that no man in his own Court ever joined in the clamour that was often raised against him by the Opposition in the House of Commons.

Mitford, who was Solicitor-General under him, and afterwards Lord Redesdale and Chancellor of Ireland, was not a pleasing speaker, but an excellent Equity lawyer and much relied upon for his judgment. He was rather disposed to seize upon the broad principles on which the case before him ought to be decided, than to seek for distinctions to make the decision doubtful.

I must not omit to mention my friend Sir Thomas Plummer, who served successively the offices of Solicitor and Attorney General, Vice Chancellor, and Master of the Rolls. He was a laborious advocate, and certainly possessed considerable merit, but in all his performances there was conspicuous more rough force which bordered on coarseness than of refinement or elegance. He had recourse occasionally to every style of speaking, but his success was not first-rate in any. I applied to him with a slight alteration a passage from Johnson's epitaph on Goldsmith: ' Nullum fere *dicendi* genus quod non tetegit, nullum tetigit quod ornavit ;' and this was true of Plummer's speeches as the original most undoubtedly is of Goldsmith's writings.

MEMOIR OF LORD ABINGER.

CHAPTER XXI.

THE last chapter abruptly terminates my father's biography, written by himself, and I regret how little I have to add from his private letters and correspondence, to interest the reader.

The first extract I make is from a letter to my mother in 1796, when he was a young man at the Bar. It is dated from Lancaster, on the Northern Circuit, and may prove a consolation to briefless barristers by encouraging them to persevere in the hope of attaining success.

'Lancaster, Aug. 8, 1796.

'My dearest Louise,—I wrote to you the day before yesterday. I have barely time to tell you that I am well and that I have received your letter of the 3rd. My hurry, however, does not proceed from business, but from having delayed writing until the last moment. Would you believe it? here at Lancaster, where I have been accustomed to receive upwards of 60l., I have not yet had a single brief, and do not know of one which I am likely to have! I told you there were others more fortunate in their friends than I am. But do not be uneasy, my dearest, we can but go to Jamaica at last. I shall be happy anywhere where you are with me and happy.'

Again, in another letter from Lancaster, on a subsequent circuit, he writes to her that his state of purse determined him to relinquish his previous intention of returning to town during the circuit to see herself and the children :—

'If I should have fortitude enough to consult my head more than my heart, I shall go from hence to Mr. Thomas

Yorke, at Hatton Place' (instead of returning to London), 'and,' he adds, ' I have had the usual proportion of business here, and have, I believe, less reason to be dissatisfied than some greater men, but the whole is a poor thing, and I am 20 guineas, at least, short of last circuit. I have unsuccessfully defended two poor men from Liverpool for libels. But I am told that I have lost no reputation by my efforts. I attacked the judge with great boldness in the *second*, and exposed, in a manner that I will tell you of, his partial conduct and weakness of judgment in the first. The business has excited some interest. I do not know of any person on this circuit who has ventured on such an imprudence (if it be one) as to avow, with such candour as I did, contempt for the flimsiness of his reasoning and indignation at the oppression of his conduct towards a defendant. It may do me good or harm. I leave that matter to fortune. I have no time for more.   J. S.'

The following letter was written to my mother some years later, when he had already become eminent at the Bar and in much greater business. It is dated from Stackpole, Lord Cawdor's, during an election contest at Pembroke :—

'Stackpole, May 20, 1807.

' I wrote to you yesterday from Pembroke. To-day I have been too much engaged to write until this moment, when everybody has retired to bed, and finding in my bedroom a proper supply of materials for writing, I sit down to devote to you my last waking hour. I informed you yesterday that I was to take up my head-quarters here, about four miles from Pembroke. Lord Cawdor is a man of excellent manners and cultivated mind. He is perfectly obliging and kind in his attention to me, and I have every reason to be satisfied with my reception here. I rise at six in the morning, and go with Lord Kensington to Pembroke at seven. Everybody rises early in Wales. We return to a late dinner here, after making all necessary arrangement at Pembroke. We polled to-day about six hundred men, and I hope from the progress we make that the election will not last beyond the week. The majority is nineteen against us to-day, but our party are quite confident of success.   As soon as I see a chance of finishing I shall let you know.   But I fear I shall be delayed for horses on my return.   Lord Cawdor's house is magnificent.   The whole country is very fine, but, being within a mile of the sea, there is rather a want of wood in the neighbourhood.   The soil, however, is the best possible for a house, being limestone, which is hard and dry in all weathers.   There is a magnificent piece of water, and a farmyard and piggery fit for a parlour. Lady Cawdor is not here, which I very much regret, as you know I like female parties better than male.   The library is excellent, and there are some good pictures, though I have not had time yet to examine them.   The town of Pembroke has nothing in itself worthy of remark, but close upon it are the remains of an ancient castle, which must have been amongst the largest in the kingdom,   The space it occupies very much exceeds that of Richmond.[1]   Some of the towers are in very good preservation, as well as the external wall.   The water from Milford Haven flows up to the foundations.   Underneath the castle is a curious and lofty cavern, of great dimensions every way, but with a narrow entrance.   With respect to the country, I must wait till I see you to give you an account of it.   It is not to be compared to the Lakes, but it is very fine.   I hope to hear that Wyndham and Tierney will dine with us on Saturday.   If I find, from any unforeseen cause, that I cannot be in time, I will write to the Duke of Gloucester; but, at present, I have no fear about it, therefore you may make all necessary preparations.   I hope to hear from you to-morrow.   I am quite well and anxious for some repose.   Adieu.   Ever, &c.

'J. S.'

From his college days, during all the Duke of Gloucester's life, His Royal Highness had always shown the warmest friendship for my father, and after the Duke's marriage with Her Royal Highness the Princess Mary, he was still a favourite at Bagshot Park, as will be apparent from the following letter from the Duke, in 1821.

---

[1] In Yorkshire.

'Bagshot Park, Sep. 27, 1821.

'My dear Scarlett,—It is, I assure you, a very great disappointment to me to find that I shall not have the satisfaction of seeing you here next Saturday, but I think you are perfectly right in not delaying your trip to Paris, and I hope you will have fine weather, pass a pleasant time there, and find Mrs. Campbell quite well.' (His daughter.)

'On the 19th of next month I am going into Hampshire for about a week, but I shall certainly be at home on Saturday, the 27th, and on the Monday following (the 29th) I propose setting out on my shooting excursion, which will occupy me until near Christmas. Therefore, as you mention your intention of returning to England by the 24th, I am very anxious that you should do the Duchess and myself the pleasure of coming to us on Saturday the 27th of October. I hope this arrangement will suit you. It will be a great mortification to me not to see you till Christmas, and a great satisfaction to have the earliest opportunity after you come back from Paris of enjoying your society here, and of talking over the many extraordinary and important events that have occurred since we met, and those that are likely to happen before we are much older, as well as to assure you in person that, with the truest attachment and esteem, I am ever, my dear Scarlett, most sincerely yours.

(Signed)   'WILLIAM FREDERICK.

'The Duchess desires her kindest compliments, and I must request of you to make my best wishes acceptable to Mrs. Scarlett.'

CHAPTER XXII.

DURING the long interval from 1807 to 1822 I have no private letters from my father in my possession which can throw any light on that important part of his life. The greater part of that time and until a much later period, when he quitted the Bar for the Bench, he had been not only leader of the Northern Circuit but also at the head of his branch of the profession both at Westminster and Guildhall, and I may even say *facile princeps* and as a barrister far above all his competitors.

As a relaxation from the increasing nature of his professional occupations in term time, he passed generally the short intervals from laborious work after his circuits at Abinger Hall. There he entered fully into the enjoyment of literary pursuits, and delighted in his frequent rides about this charming country, sometimes in the company of visitors and the society of old friends, to whom it gave him the greatest pleasure to dedicate his leisure moments.

Being short-sighted, he had no passion for field sports, but often enjoyed a day's fishing in a stream, called the Tillingbourne, which runs through the property on its way to Guildford and Weybridge.

In 1816, after the peace, he went with my mother and some members of the family to Paris, but was obliged to return on account of a fit of illness which he always ascribed to the waters of the Seine. In those days, without railroads or steamers, the journey to Paris was thought a great undertaking. I recollect, when a boy at Pearson's school at East Sheen, hearing with great interest of their passage across from Dover in a packet which started at 3 P.M. and could not get beyond Beachy Head all night, notwithstanding the insane efforts of a French passenger, who spent the greater part of the night in blowing up the flapping sails with a huge pair of bellows in the full belief that he was abridging the tedious voyage.

In 1819 my father promised to visit my uncle Robert Scarlett at his residence, the Château de Feuillasse, near Geneva. It was the year before I went to Eton, and in July my mother and my eldest brother, my two sisters, and myself preceded my father to the same destination. After the circuit my father set out to join us with my brother James in a French cabriolet, which he had bought of Quilliac at Calais on his first visit to the Continent.

It was an excellent carriage on French roads, and much easier with its two wheels and good springs on the French *pavé* than a four-wheeled carriage, but the drivers in England could never understand that the horse in the shafts was not in the centre, and there was always a risk of collision in turning corners or meeting another carriage. I believe it was the first carriage of the kind ever brought to England, and I dare say the last.

My uncle was acquainted with all the principal characters and distinguished men then residing at Geneva, who were often at his château, and to whom my father was introduced, which enabled him often to air the French he had learnt. He knew the language well grammatically and wrote it without difficulty, but he had never mastered the pronunciation, which he had failed to acquire at Cambridge from the French priest who gave him lessons.

In 1823 I accompanied my father and eldest brother to Italy. On our way through Switzerland we passed several agreeable days with the Duc and Duchess de Broglie at Coppet. Sismondi the historian, Lord Harrowby, and several other distinguished men were invited there to dinner during our visit. The political topic of interest I recollect was the occupation of Spain by the French army under the Duc d'Angoulême. The Duc de Broglie was at that time opposed to the policy of the Bourbons, but he had not then taken an active part in public life, though he afterwards occupied so conspicuous a political position both in Paris and in London. The Duchesse de Broglie's brother, Auguste de Staël, was also at Coppet. He and my eldest brother had been previously well acquainted, and on a subsequent occasion he joined us at Paris and accompanied us to England and to Abinger.

The Duc de Broglie and his brother-in-law, like other enlightened Frenchmen of that epoch, took a warm interest in the political events shadowing out a more liberal policy in England by the entrance of George Canning and Huskisson and Peel into the counsels of the King. In illustration of the feeling which prevailed a few years later in France amongst the best educated men in favour of a freer Government both in France and in England, I will transcribe here a letter from de Staël to my brother. It is in English :—

‘Paris, May 31, 1827.

‘My dear Robert,—Though I have not written to your excellent father, you will do me the justice to think that I have not waited to this hour to congratulate myself as well as every friend of reason and liberty on the happy change which has taken place in your politics. His name was to me a pledge that the whole negotiation would be conducted with wisdom and discernment, as well as with generosity.

‘This appears to me the beginning of an end in the political history of England, and will I trust be followed by more important consequences than are now contemplated by some of those who are prevailed upon to concur in the change. Be prudent at home and firm in your foreign policy. Encourage by every means in your power the progress of the middle classes. Increase their weight and influence. Patronise the London University. Be favourable to every measure for the improvement of the colonies, and the *gradual* abolition of slavery. First because it is just and wise, and secondly because if you don't you will have against you the powerful interest of the religious party. Give independence to Greece. Let Don Pedro return and unite Spain and Portugal under a free Government. Favour the progress of rational liberty in France. Oppose the Jesuitic influence by the most important step you can take against them, viz. Catholic Emancipation, and you shall have my benison. All this can be effected without the fear of a serious war, provided you speak out and act with decision. Our wretched Government is sure to be humble if you are firm, but the idea that England would submit to anything rather than go to war certainly deprives her of a great portion of the influence which she ought to have abroad. *Dixi.* Am I not a very impudent fellow? Now that I have given you my sentiments, give me yours. Give my kindest regards to your father, and believe me,

'Most truly yours,   'A. DE STAËL.'

In 1822 a vacancy occurred in the University at Cambridge, for which my father was solicited to stand, and on that occasion Lord Fitzwilliam wrote to him to encourage him to become a candidate.

Lord Fitzwilliam's letter is as follows :—

'Wentworth, October 28, 1822.

'My dear Scarlett,—Don't consider your connection with Peterborough as an obstacle to the acceptance of Cambridge. The representation of the University is a high dignity, suited to your character and reputation, and whilst it does honor to you, you will do honor to the University. Should it succeed, all is well, if not, we must take measures for retaining you at Peterborough.

'I need say no more, than to assure you of the extent of esteem of   'Truly yours,

'W. F.'

Lord Grey also wrote to him in similar terms, but finally my father remained member for Peterborough. His reputation at this period was greater than ever, as his laborious life at the Bar most amply testified. King George IV. had the highest opinion of his talents, and he became a still greater favourite with his Majesty after he had declined mixing himself up with the trial of Queen Caroline, in which he was urged to take a part. It was between 1820 and 1830 that so many important trials took place in the King's Bench, in which he played a conspicuous part. I may instance that of Hunt for sedition, Sir Francis Burdett for libel, the abduction of Miss Turner, the heiress in Lancashire, and at a later period the riots at Bristol, and his defence of the magistrates, who were violently assailed for their conduct. On most of these occasions my father was eminently successful. In proof of the King's partiality I insert here a letter from Lord Lyndhurst, with my father's reply.

'George Street, Saturday.

'My dear Scarlett,—The King is anxious that a Commission should issue for the purpose of inquiring into the practice and course of proceeding in the Courts of the Duchy and County Palatine of Lancashire, and he wishes *much* that you should be at the head of the Commission.   His Majesty has honoured me with a letter upon the subject, containing the following passage :—" The King *most earnestly* desires that Sir James Scarlett be prevailed upon to place himself at the head of this Commission.   The King feels himself personally obliged to Sir James Scarlett for the manner and conduct pursued by him in the late trial of the Duchy of Cornwall. The King has the greatest confidence in this gentleman."   I hope you will allow me to inform his Majesty that you will accept the appointment in compliance with his Majesty's wishes.   ' Ever faithfully yours,

'LYNDHURST.'

'New Street: Saturday Night, Jan. 10, 1829.

'My dear Lord Chancellor,—I have received your letter of this morning communicating the very gracious and gratifying terms in which his Majesty has condescended to mention my name, and to signify his desire that I should be placed at the head of a Commission for inquiring into the proceedings of the several Courts of the Duchy and County Palatine of Lancaster.

'Your Lordship is well aware of the incessant labours which absorb my time.   Nevertheless, relying upon assistance I shall doubtless receive in conducting the inquiry, I consider it my duty cheerfully to submit myself with all zeal and devotion to his Majesty's pleasure.

'I beg to assure your Lordship that I am deeply penetrated by the kind and gracious manner in which the King has deigned to accept and to notice my very humble services, and it will ever be my pride and happiness to merit the continuance of his Majesty's confidence.

'I am, my dear Lord,

' Ever faithfully yours,

'J. SCARLETT.'

CHAPTER XXIII.

TRAVELLING ABROAD — FALSE REPORT — LETTER FROM
LORD LANSDOWNE—MR. CANNING.

THAT the time had arrived to initiate a more liberal policy
suggested itself to most enlightened minds both in England
and France, and such a course was as much in harmony with
my father's ideas and wishes as it was with those of the Duc
de Broglie and of Mons. de Staël.

It must be owned, however, that the reforms in contemplation when they took place in England were not all satisfactorily
accomplished. The sudden liberation of the slaves ruined
most of the West India planters, and notwithstanding de
Staël's hopes and wishes the intrigues if not influence of the
Jesuits remained on the ascendant, and they seem still to
exercise in this country more influence than at the period to
which I have referred. But to return to our travels. After
three agreeable days at Coppet we went to Lauzanne, where
my father visited with great interest the scenes amongst
which Gibbon composed his great history of the 'Decline and
Fall of the Roman Empire.' From thence we crossed over
the Simplon, tired to death of the tedious posting road up the
Valais to Brigg in a hot sun, a journey by rail now of a few
hours only; from thence we proceeded through Parma and
Bologna to Florence. On our return we went to Spezzia,
Venice, Genoa, and Milan and Turin, over Mont Cenis. The
present road over the mountain pass from Spezzia to Chiavari
was not then finished. My sister, Mrs. Campbell, and her
husband, the late Lord Chancellor, were also travelling in Italy
at that time, and a few days after in this pass they were in
some difficulty and danger from an inundation, which we
escaped. The road was partly along the bed of a torrent,

which became so violent from a continued storm that their carriage had to be dragged up the bank by men with ropes, and they were glad to pass a night in the house of a hospitable priest, out of reach of the raging flood.

In the following year, when an undergraduate at Trinity College, Cambridge, during the Spring Circuit, news was brought me by several College friends that my father had suddenly died at York ; in confirmation of which they showed me a paragraph to that effect in one of the leading morning papers. My first thought in my grief at this report, the truth of which I could not then doubt, was to hasten to my mother at Abinger Hall. As all the public conveyances had already departed from Cambridge, I ordered a chaise and posted up to London, to my father's house in New Street. The house next door was the residence of Mr. Abercrombie, the first Lord Dunfermline, who hearing of my arrival sent for me and informed me that the evening papers contradicted the report of the death, and that there was every reason to suppose it was a very unpardonable invention. Overjoyed with this contradiction, I posted down the following day to Abinger and found that my mother had only just learnt by the previous arrival of other members of the family that there was no foundation for the report. Indeed I believe she had a letter from my father stating that he had been indisposed but was quite recovered, and at work as usual. It was true that he had on one day from an attack of illness absented himself from court. A cause in which he was engaged of some importance was called on and postponed, and some one had inserted the report of his death in a York newspaper, whether as a joke, or to endeavour to induce the parties to accept a compromise owing to the supposed death of a leading counsel in the case, never transpired. The result of the report was that my eldest brother and Campbell both left their circuits, and my brother James his regiment in Ireland, to arrive as I had done as fast as we could to console my mother.

In the year 1822 (if I recollect right, after the death of Lord Castlereagh) there were reports that the King was inclined to enlist Mr. Canning in his service with Peel, and that some of the leading Whigs would take office.

My father had seen Lord Lansdowne's name mentioned
in a London newspaper as one of those to whom office had
been offered, to whom he must have written at the time, as
I find the following letter in reply from Lord Lansdowne,
dated :—

'Bowood, Aug. 23, 1822.

'Dear Scarlett,—The London papers have disposed of me
without my consent. I left town with the intention of spending
some months here, and occupying myself with my private
concerns, which unfortunately, like those of most landed
proprietors, require a good deal of attention under present
circumstances. Nothing has since occurred to alter my
resolutions. I must, however, thank you sincerely for your
letter, and assure you that there is no person whose opinion
upon public matters, and more especially at critical moments
(such as the present must in many points of view be considered) I am more desirous of learning than yours, knowing
as I do that it is given with the best intentions towards the
public, and towards myself personally with the kindest.

'I suspect from what I hear, that no offer, or at least none
that he can accept, will be made to Canning. That overtures
(sincere or not is another question) may be made to some of
the Opposition is very possible, considering the evidently embarrassed state of the Government, and the necessity of either
recomposing it or having a colourable case for the public
against those who might be represented as unwilling to assist
the public service, but I confess my own opinion is, after all
the negotiations and intrigues which would precede such an
arrangement, Peel will be recognised as leader, and an attempt
made to maintain an administration upon the old high
principles. It will be a poor consolation for all the mischief
which must inevitably attend such an experiment, that it will
place parties and their principles in a more distinct view before
the public, and clear the ground for a warfare which cannot
fail to be violent and probably injurious to the public interests.
I direct this to London, concluding that your circuit is by this
time terminated.

'Lord and Lady Holland are coming here shortly (the
second week in September, I believe), and I wish we could

prevail upon you to come and meet them; at that or any other time it would give us the greatest pleasure to see you; and I remain,   Very sincerely yours,

(Signed)   'LANSDOWNE.'

Shortly after this Mr. Canning had accepted the appointment of Governor-General of India, but the King was anxious that he should take the seals of the Foreign Office instead, and he remained at home. He had made my father a promise to pay him a visit at Abinger, and I find among his papers the following letter from Mr. Canning, dated :—

'Foreign Office, October 11, 1822.

'My dear Sir,—This is only to confirm my engagement and that of Lord Howard, and to state our intention to be at Abinger Hall to-morrow long before the hour you prescribe.

'I do not venture to avail myself of your kind proposal to meet us at Leatherhead, because I could not promise to be there between two and three. There is always a conspiracy of importune visitations against one on the morning of one's going into the country. We will however be with you as early as we can.   (Signed)   'GEO. CANNING.'

'P.S.—Since this was written I have conceived better hopes of getting away in tolerably good time to-morrow, and the sun having come out with a promise of finer weather, I have agreed with Lord Howard to set out soon after twelve so as to reach Leatherhead before three. (Four horses you say would bring me sooner, but what would Mr. Hume say to four horses, for a beggarly Secretary of State, whom you have amerced of 10 p. c. because his salary is already about half large enough for his situation?) If you meet us there with a spare horse, as you propose, I shall be most happy to mount him. Howard sends his own; but I, having reckoned upon riding elephants for the rest of my life, am not yet provided with one.'

I recollect well this visit, as I was with my father at the time; we took a long ride the following day up Leith Hill, and through Pasture Woods to Holmbury. Mr. Canning was mounted on a horse of my father's, nearly of a size to remind him of the rides he had anticipated on the backs of elephants in India.

CHAPTER XXIV.

DEATH OF MR. CANNING — EASTERN QUESTION — MR.
HUSKISSON—H.R.H. DUKE OF GLOUCESTER—MY FATHER
RESIGNS.

IN 1827, Mr. Canning was called upon by George IV.,
on the death of Lord Liverpool, to form a new Administration, and my father then for the first time accepted the
office of Attorney-General, after many expressions of regret
on the part of his friend, the new First Lord of the Treasury,
that it was not in his power to offer him a seat on the Woolsack, that post being occupied by Lord Lyndhurst.

He accepted office with the sanction of Lords Grey and Fitzwilliam and of the leading members of the Opposition, who approved in a great measure of Mr. Canning's political opinions,
and entertained high hopes that his talents and liberal ideas
would be at last appreciated by the King, and prepare the way
for removing those prejudices and scruples in the Royal mind
which were opposed to the removal of the Roman Catholic
disabilities, and to all changes or modifications of the constitution.   These hopes, for a time only, were destined to be
disappointed by the premature death of Mr. Canning, which
occurred during the same year.

He had had, during his political career as Foreign Minister, sufficient time to lay the foundation of freedom in the
British colonies, and to ensure the future independence of
Greece.   He shone with a brilliant light over the embryo of
reforms in England, and just at the period when the full
power of his genius was acknowledged by every Sovereign
and Government throughout the world, England was suddenly
deprived of one of her greatest Statesmen.

Perhaps if he had lived a little longer, his influence might
have persuaded the Sultan to abandon a useless and cruel

war against the Greeks without that injury to Turkish prestige which was inflicted by the defeat at Navarino. This was one in the first series of telling blows levelled at the Ottoman power in modern times, an immediate consequence of the well-known alliance of France and England with Russia for the independence of Greece ; Russia especially re-joicing in joining hands with England in a philhellenic movement, not so much it was thought for the sake of Greece, as to damage Turkey. It is curious to trace from that period the downward path of the Turkish Empire, arrested for a moment by the Crimean War, but now pursuing the path of decadence at a more rapid pace than ever.

The Duke of Wellington called the battle of Navarino 'an untoward event.' It appeared so at the time for Turkey, but it led to the emancipation of a Christian country, and one of great classical renown, that had long groaned under her oppressive yoke.

Turkey is rapidly declining in public estimation. At the time I write, however inexcusable be the Servian War, the conduct of the Turkish irregular troops has justly excited the animosity of the whole Christian race against the Porte, whose Government, though unable to excuse or palliate such atrocities, has, nevertheless, thought fit to decorate its perpe-trators. But to suppose that her Majesty's Government is in any way to blame for events which could not have been fore-seen nor prevented, is a senseless proceeding which no party feeling can reasonably justify. It appears to me that a ground of party attack has been selected, unsustained by facts, often insincere, and most unwisely persisted in.

The Eastern question has been influenced for the last fifty years by a traditional policy for the maintenance of Turkey, the result of treaties, and binding equally on Whigs and Tories.

To expect that this policy should be abandoned at once, on account of these lamentable excesses, and that the British nation should be committed to a war of vengeance and extirpa-tion of the Mahomedan race, may meet with the approbation of some professed Christians, but not with the sanction of those who have British interests, as well as the cause of humanity to protect. But may not the time have at last arrived for counselling or compelling the Turks to establish the independence of all the Sclavonic race ? The Turkish race is decreasing rapidly, whilst the Christian race as rapidly increases, and this will lead naturally to the subversion of Turkish supremacy in the East. By wise concessions granted now, the Turks may continue to reign at Constantinople, with a better title to the sufferance of Europe, after the emancipation of these provinces. I have often regretted that the influence of my old and respected chief, Lord Stratford de Redcliffe, was set aside in Turkey at so early a period. His knowledge and just appreciation of both Turks and Russians, and his uniformly wise counsels to the Porte, might have prevented the present complications. I do not intend, however, to disparage the merits of his successors at Constantinople, nor do I think that, under the circumstances, any other Ambassador could have done his duty more efficiently than Sir Henry Elliot.

But to return to a former period. Lord Goodrich succeeded Mr. Canning as Prime Minister. Shortly after this, Lord Lansdowne, who was a member of this new Cabinet, sent in his resignation, and Lord Goodrich was succeeded by the Duke of Wellington, then holding the office of Commander-in-Chief.

My father was invited by the King and the Duke to remain as Attorney-General. Previously a correspondence had taken place between my father and Lord Milton on this subject. Lord Milton thought that there was no occasion for the resignation of the Attorney-General if he was allowed to vote with his old friends the Whigs on questions which were certain to place them in opposition to the Government. Before deciding, my father was desirous of knowing if Huskisson was to form part of the Duke's Cabinet, and addressed to him the following letter. The *brouillon* does not give the date :—

'My dear Huskisson,—As you are the only one of the late Ministers from whom I have had any communication since the dissolution of Lord Goodrich's Administration, as public opinion assigns to you a place in the new Cabinet, and as I must consider you as the true representative of Mr. Canning's principles in Parliament, I am induced by these motives to solicit from you some information for my own government in case a proposal should be made to me, as possibly it may, to retain my office of Attorney-General.

'I accepted this office under Mr. Canning, prompted by a sincere personal attachment to him, and by a conviction that his policy, under the existing circumstances of the country, made it the duty of every public man to support him. It is true that I took this step at a moment when it was doubtful whether any of those with whom I had acted in Parliament would ultimately become members of the Government, but it was, nevertheless, with the sanction of such among them whose judgment and friendship I most highly valued.

'I am not insensible to the reproach that would be cast upon me, if through refinement, as it might be called, of party honour, I should disappoint those expectations of the public, and of my own profession, which in the immediate state of things naturally grow out of my connection with the Government. Be this as it may I cannot bring myself even to entertain the proposition should it be made to me of retaining my office without the assurance not only that you form an essential part of the new Government, but that the policy, both foreign and domestic, of Mr. Canning are to be supported, more especially with regard to the real neutrality of the Government upon that great and unhappy subject of Ireland so long as it remains unsettled. This neutrality was the professed maxim, but certainly not the practical result of Lord Liverpool's Administration.

'Perhaps I am giving you needless trouble, but as there is no time to be lost, I can only say that if there should be any desire for my services, an assurance of the kind I have mentioned would, I am persuaded, be the only condition on which I could venture to hope or even to ask for the concurrence of my friends in my acquiescence.

'I am ever, my dear Huskisson,
'Yours truly,
(Signed)   'J. SCARLETT.'

To the above letter he received from Mr. Huskisson the following reply :—

' *Private.*   ' Somerset Place, January 22, 1828.

'My dear Scarlett,—I certainly am very anxious to be permitted to propose to you, and that you should feel at liberty to accept the proposal, to remain in your present office. I will say nothing of my private wishes only, because I look to the far greater importance of the arrangement on public grounds.

' Among the latter, I justly reckon what you state to be due to the expectations of the profession on these occasions ; looking as I do to the interest which the public have in everything which contributes to uphold and honour distinction and eminence, either at the Bar or upon the Bench.

' From political considerations, I need not say that your continuance in office will be very gratifying to myself; and I am happy to be assured by the Duke of Wellington that he is very desirous to have the benefit of your assistance ; although, from circumstance, I am not now at liberty to confirm to you that feeling on his part, by making to you a distinct proposal.

' Should I be authorised to make one (and I trust that I soon shall) I hope that I shall be able, at the same time, to satisfy your mind as to the general policy and character of the Administration ; as I should be mortified to find that you deemed insufficient the explanations and assurances which have been given to me and my colleagues in the late Cabinet in these respects.

' As you particularly advert to Ireland, I will only say that nothing can be more pointed and direct than the language of the Duke of Wellington in respect to a *real neutrality*, in reference to the Catholic Question in the Administration of that country.

' It is his very earnest wish (a wish I hope not likely to be disappointed) that W. Lamb should continue in his present office, Hart Lord Chancellor, and that Lord Anglesey should be Lord Lieutenant, as intended before the late change at home.

' Believe me, dear Scarlett,
                    ' Yours very truly,
          (Signed)   ' W. HUSKISSON.'

He could not do less than consult so kind a friend, and of long standing, as his Royal Highness the Duke of Gloucester, on this occasion.   I have not by me a copy of the letter he wrote to the Duke, but I venture to transcribe the Duke's reply, showing how deep an interest his Royal Highness was good enough to take in all that concerned his old College friend.

‘ Private.   ‘Lulworth Castle, January 23, 1828. ’

‘ My dear Scarlett,—I had not till late yesterday evening the pleasure of receiving your letter of the 20th and the first thing I do this morning is to sit down and answer it, which I confess I feel considerable difficulty in doing.   The warmest and the most intimate friendship has subsisted between us for forty years.   You will therefore, I am sure, do me the justice to believe that I am as tenacious of your honour, and as anxious about your interest as I could possibly be about my own ; I perfectly enter into the extreme delicacy of your position, and fully feel the force of all you state to me, and I wish I was in town at this moment, as on the spot one can learn more exactly the truth and the reality of what is passing, and in conversation one can enter into so many particulars which cannot be brought into the compass of a letter.   I am so completely in the dark in regard to what has occurred, and in such total ignorance respecting the cause of the last Administration being broken up, and the principle upon which the present extraordinary compound has been amalgamated, that I must hesitate about giving any opinion.   I take it for granted that Lord Lansdowne will consider himself bound to state to his friends all that has passed, why he is out of office, and why he has separated from Lord Dudley and Huskisson, with whom I was taught to believe he was in the same boat ; and I attribute his silence to his conceiving it a proper delicacy not to make such a communication till he has actually resigned the Seals, but I shall be much surprised if I do not soon receive a full and detailed explanation from him.   I likewise trust that Lord Dudley and Huskisson will explain why they separate from him, and upon what principle the new Government is formed which enables them to remain in whilst he goes out.   This separation I deeply lament and it greatly surprises me, as I was assured that they were in "the same boat." These are the very words of one of the three to me. Under these circumstances, and at the distance I am from you, I can only advise your having, previous to your finally determining what you are to do, an explanation with Lord Lansdowne and Huskisson, and entering with them both fully into your situation, and into every part of all the late trans actions. You then will be much better able to judge what is right to be done, and I am satisfied, my dear Scarlett, that whatever you decide upon will be the proper thing, and that on this occasion, as in every event of your past life, you will be guided by honour, integrity, and sound sense, and that you will merely ask yourself what is right to be done. Pray let me hear from you as soon as possible, as I shall be all anxiety till I know what step you take.

'On Monday I wrote to Spring Rice, and stated to him that I expected Lord Lansdowne would explain everything fully to his friends.

' Ever with the sincerest attachment and the highest esteem,

' My dear Scarlett, most truly yours,

(Signed)   'WILLIAM FREDERICK.'

The course my father took was to send in his resignation, for although he felt great confidence in the Duke of Wellington, he thought under the circumstances that his own plain duty was to resume his seat in the House of Commons amongst his former friends the Whigs, with whose sanction he had taken office, and who approved, generally, at that time of his leaving it.

From the time he quitted office until he resumed it again under the Duke of Wellington, my father's professional labours were greater than ever. He did not attend, as before, the Northern Circuit, but visited on special retainers every part of England and Wales, and was during the Assizes in different counties, carried about from one end of England to another, over thousands of miles, as fast as four horses could take him.

CHAPTER XXV.

CORRESPONDENCE — SPEECH AT MALTON — FURTHER
CORRESPONDENCE.

I RECEIVED the following letters from my father when I was
at Paris. The first is in 1828, shortly after my appointment
there as an attaché to the Embassy. It contains good
advice to a young diplomatist :—

'New Street: 12 o'clock, Monday night.

'I am more pleased than surprised to learn that you
received so much kind treatment from the English. Lord
Darnley was good enough to call upon me, at eight one
morning, to speak of you, which he did in handsome terms.
I wish, however, you would circulate more among the French.
If you are ever to be Ambassador yourself you will find great
advantage from knowing all who make a figure in the French
Court at present. You must, of course, be very easy with
them, and say *nothing* in the best manner, but you should
show a desire to cultivate them. Have you called on
Broglie? Do not omit it by any means. You ought to be
introduced at Court, and get well acquainted with the Ministers and the leading Members of the Assemblies. Your
position makes this easy if you take any pains about it.
Inquire always the history of persons you may be introduced
to, that you may avoid blunders and take more interest about
them. I expect France, for the whole of your time, to play a
considerable part in the politics of Europe. You should
study her diplomacy, and find out now what are the leading
objects of her policy as well as what would be her most probable object in a future war. Depend upon it this is not to
be known by talking to Englishmen. You should also make
yourself well known to all the Foreign Missions, and strive to

I

learn the object of each. These are the rudiments of a great Ambassador, a very uncommon character in our country.

' I have little to say to you on English politics, except that I have at length reason to believe that the Field Marshal really intends to do something decisive for the Catholics. If this be so, I shall be ready to forget all " untoward events," and support his Government *de bon cœur*. The Kentish meeting is disastrous, but I hope not fatal. I should think nothing of it, except that folly is ever catching, and that the greatest absurdities are always the most popular. The King is better, but feeble from his last illness. Duke of Clarence better. This is all the news. You seem to have forgotten Cottu.[1] You will do well to cultivate him, as he will bring you amongst the men of business who have always the most influence in affairs. I think I have had the honour of meeting Madame de Bourke, but I would not swear it.

' You must excuse me for not performing your commissions for Lady Blessington ; I am too busy, and Blessington can get the books she wants without troubling you or me. Give my love to her, however, if she will have it. I am grateful to them both for their attention to you. Have you got a house for Burdett ? I left Robert at Ábinger. He has taken to hunting, and is very fond of his horse. Adieu.

(Signed)   ' J. SCARLETT.'

' P.S.—If you get into the circulation I wish you to do, you would often have to give the Ambassador information he may find important for his Court.   Adieu.'

The following letter was written before the French Ordinances were dreamt of in London, and when French political affairs did not wear a threatening aspect or fortel the sudden dissolution of Charles X. and his dynasty.

' New Street: Dec. 18, 1823.

' The enclosed letter is from the Duke of Gloucester on his business. He has requested me to write to you upon the subject, and to say that he will thank you to pay the money which he encloses to the individual himself (some

---

[1] A clever legitimist lawyer, an old acquaintance of my father.

charity) and to obtain his receipt for it, which you must forward to the Duke. I trust you will accomplish this mission to the letter, and enclose the receipt in a note from yourself to the Duke without delay. You know he is very particular in matters of business.

'There is no news here, at least of an authentic character. Nobody is certain what is intended or what he himself will do, and I do not believe there are ten men in the House of Commons who would pledge themselves to any party or individual. Those who are in place excepted.

'I think affairs look well in France. You have never mentioned in any letter whether you have seen the Duc and Duchess de Broglie. Are not my friends good company?

'Your dear mother is much as she was, certainly there is no improvement. If there be any change, I think she is more feeble. Do not allude to this in your letters. She is cheerful, and I dare say will write to you soon.

'Ever Yrs.

'J. SCARLETT.'

Undated, a little later.

' Thank Mr. Okey for his pamphlet, the reading of which I must put off *ad Græcas Calendas*. I am quite well. I wish the King were so, but we are in great alarm about him. I have not seen the bulletin of to-day. Louy' (my sister) ' hears from or sees the Duchess (Gloucester) every day, who is in great distress. I think a few days will decide this melancholy question. It would be happy for the nation if the event be favourable, though I have no reason to suppose that any change of men or measures would follow the disaster we dread, but a new Parliament, and a question of Regency which must come on may perplex and give rise to new factions. Remember me to the Rendleshams! I shall be happy to find them at Paris, should I get there this summer. Which is the best time, July, August, or September? The Duke, I hear, was pleased with your letter. I have no time for more.

'Yrs. affect.

'J. S.'

I 2

In the following year, 1829, my father accepted office again as Attorney-General, with the general consent of the Whig party, excepting only the Duke of Gloucester, as the following hasty letter will show.

Undated.

' I have but a moment to tell you that I was sworn in and had my patent last Tuesday *omnium consensu*, excepting only the Duke of Gloucester, who was sadly displeased. I hope it will end well, however. I am quite alone, R. and S. being at Ashted. I go to Abinger for two holidays to-morrow, and shall be in town again on Tuesday. In great haste.

' Yr.

' J. S.'

It will be observed that he says he is alone. This was after my mother's death. She died so suddenly that I was not able to reach England to see her before the event occurred. I joined him and the other members of my family after the funeral at Abinger, in great affliction.

It was the year following that he took office again as I have stated. The Duke of Wellington had emancipated the Roman Catholics and repealed the Corporation and Test Acts. The Whigs hoped he would go further in reform, and my father, who had always been in favour of a moderate Reform Bill, entertained a hope that the King's hostility to a reform in Parliament might be overcome, and the Duke would get rid of the ultra Tories and fill up the gap with a greater infusion of the Whig element in the Cabinet.

In the following letter my father, whilst Attorney-General, alludes to the prosecutions he had undertaken in defence of the Government against the libels in the Press, with which, in consequence, he became unpopular :—

' Bagshot Park : Jan. 4, 1830.

' You will see all that I know about the libels in the papers, but will not read all I said. My speeches are not agreeable to the Press, or entitled to be faithfully and fully retailed. They all join to abuse me, but I know I have done my duty, and am not afraid. The liberty of the Press does not consist in the power of publishing slander with *impunity* any more than the liberty of using your hands implies the power or the right to assault your neighbours with impunity. This is a mistake which the gentlemen of the Press too often make. The liberty of the Press means nothing more than the right to publish without a previous censorship.'

In the same letter he describes very clearly the meaning of the par of exchange to a novice in such matters.

' The par of exchange is when you give exactly the same quantity of gold in one country for that which you are to receive in another. Thus the English sovereign, a pound, is worth in French money as much as would be equal, in gold to nearly twenty-five francs—not quite. When there is more money owing by France to England than by England to France, then a bill upon France is easier to get in England than a bill in France upon England. This makes bills in France upon England a little dearer, and *vice versâ*, and then the exchange is said to be in favour of England by the small additional price you pay for the bill above what is the exact equivalent in gold. This is the only explanation I can give you. When the gold was driven out of England and nothing but bank notes remained, they fell in value, and a bill drawn in France for 40*l.* upon England, would have been worth fifty in bank notes. The exchange was in favour of France nominally, but yet to find the true amount of it and on which side the real exchange lay, you ought to ascertain how much gold, of a given standard of fineness, 40*l.* would buy in France, and how much 50 would buy in England, and the difference would show the real exchange. I have no news for you except that I have a bad cold and cough. I hope I shall not sit near the Duchess to-day, as I fear to molest her with my barking. I shall be in Town on Wednesday and hope to find a letter from you.

(Signed) ' J. SCARLETT.'

' June 22, 1830.

' I owe you two letters. I had rather have news of yourself than of Naples and Sicily. I think the present Government (French) is fast going to ruin, and I am not sure that the English will last long.   It seems as if the Liberals would not know how to use their power.

'I was much gratified yesterday to meet my old acquaintance, Lord Clarendon, in the street, near Westminster.   He turned back and walked with me for half an hour, between the King's Bench and the House of Commons, to tell me how much he was pleased with you, and what good advice he had given you.   He is now about writing a long letter to you, and he intends to send you a book if he can find it.   He is an excellent man, and much esteemed by those who know him.   I was particularly pleased with his remark that he found in you a certain deference for old age which he does not remark in the careless and self-sufficient manners of these times.   I have always had this feeling myself, and am glad to find it remarked in you.

'The state of the King is precarious, but he exhibits such wonderful strength that the people begin to think that his life may be prolonged.   He appears to recover from the most alarming crisis, and to surprise those who see him by his energy.   This is what I hear from the Duke of W. in substance.   The bulletin yesterday was bad, but I make no doubt we shall hear to-day that he is better.   I am worn out in the House of Commons.   Two and three o'clock every night have become the habitual hours of breaking up, and yet nothing is done, or next to nothing.

'Can you be spared any time this summer?

(Signed)   'J. SCARLETT.'

My father had at this time given up the seat of Peterborough, and at Lord Fitzwilliam's request came in for Malton, but the Whigs could wait no longer for liberal measures and a hoped-for modification of the Duke's Cabinet, to which modification he had not assented.   Soon after the King's death they united with the Radicals to turn him out, and brought in their famous Reform Bill.

The following letter is dated in 1830, before the crisis in France :—

'July 13th.

'I am inclined to agree with Broglie about France. I think the crisis is coming for a new dynasty, and perhaps a war, owing to the madness of the Liberals.

'My spirits are not good, I own. This is not owing to politics, but to the dull life I lead. I almost dread going to Abinger.

'I speculate on a special retainer to Winchester, then a journey into Yorkshire, to be elected at Malton, then into Somersetshire to Wells, before I sit down to repine at Abinger. Robert is now on his way to Guildford, where he went yesterday to a public dinner. I am going to the King's funeral on Thursday. The next week the festivities commence with a levee on the 21st. I have not yet seen His Majesty.

'I have seen nothing of Cradock, nor of the letter you promised to send me, which I should like much to see. In September I am to make a journey for a few days to Portsmouth. If you come thereabouts you will go with me, but I will join you at Paris if possible.

'Adieu.

'J. S.'

'Monday Night, July 29, 1830.

'I am two letters in your debt, that by the courier of to-day brought the news which was in all the papers of yesterday. By the way, I find that is generally the case. The newspaper messengers are quicker than yours by at least a day.

Charles X. has cast his die. Weak men often take bold measures. He must either restore despotism or retire himself. He has no alternative. He may succeed for a time if he can depend on his army, but I should think the habit of contemplating the forms of free government was too strong in France to make success possible for long. I think I see work for our Major, and leisure for your Excellency near at hand.

Now for home affairs. Our King is very popular and very active. The grass does not grow under his feet. His health must be vigorous to endure what he goes through, and I heartily wish him long life. He has been driving out and working incessantly. I shall be elected for Malton next week, but expect to resign my seat soon after Parliament meets.

I suspect your Chief keeps a grand secret under his affected surprise. The project was shadowed out on the Stock Exchange some days ago. I imagine Paris will be too hot for my temperate politics just now ; I must therefore be content with passing a few weeks at Abinger as early as I can, then to Wales for a few days, back to the King's birthday the 21st, again at Abinger until October, except one visit to Portsmouth on business. Will your Excellency join me any part of that time ? I heard from the Duchess of Gloucester to day of a report in town of an attempt to assassinate Prince P—— in Paris. Your next courier will bring the news !'

My father's political opinions may be gathered from his speech at the Malton election, of which I have made an extract.

' From the earliest period I have been taught to revere the British Constitution. Both experience and reflection have convinced me that the form of Government we possess, taking it altogether, is the best that the world has ever known for the security of the greatest degree of liberty, the development of genius, and the protection of industry and property. My attachment, however, has never been that of a blind prejudice which can see no fault, and tolerate no improvement, and I make no scruple to avow that I am disposed to adopt any well considered reform that in my judgment is not calculated to affect the stability of the throne, or the just and useful authority of either House of Parliament, whilst it promises the suppression of abuse or any increase to the well being of the people. At the same time experience and reflection have also taught me this caution, that it is very easy to discover the defects of any human institutions, none of which can be perfect, but very difficult to find remedies for them. I therefore place no confidence in those who seek popularity by declaiming against our institutions, an easy task to the ignorant and a beaten road to vulgar fame, nor in those who without education or knowledge offer the crude remedies suggested by their own imaginations. But I am ready to receive, and to deliberate upon the plans of the temperate and the wise, whose object is not to destroy but to sustain the main edifice.

'From my earliest years I have imbibed a horror of slavery which is not to be extinguished, and it affords me pleasure to reflect, that I was if not the first, yet among the first of the undergraduates of the University of Cambridge who put his name down to a subscription for the abolition of the slave trade. No efforts shall be wanting on my part to the accomplishment of that great measure in which this country took the glorious lead. Nor shall I ever be backward in adopting such means as may be consistent with safety to the unhappy objects of it, of putting an end to colonial slavery.

'With respect to legal reforms, I hope I may venture to appeal, for my sentiments, to the part I took in the last session of Parliament by introducing and supporting against much clamour and much resistance one of the most important measures connected with this subject that has ever received the sanction of Parliament in our times. The habits of my profession, though I admit their natural influence, have not prevailed to exclude from my view the defects in our administration of justice, nor the desire to remove them. The work is begun, but not yet accomplished. Much remains to be done, and I am happy to think that I speak the sentiments of the Government with which I am connected as well as my own, when I express my hope and belief that the attention of Parliament will be duly bestowed upon this important branch of Reform.

'Gentlemen, I have further to say that I am a zealous advocate of retrenchment, and economy in the public service. None of the votes which I have given in Parliament have been given with more pleasure than those which had that object in view. You are aware that his Majesty's present Ministers have done much upon this head. I feel confident that they are disposed to do as much more as is possible, consistently with the honour and safety of the nation, and to that extent whether in or out of office they shall have my cordial co-operation.

'Upon the subject of parliamentary reform I have very few words to say. I am not insensible to the defects of our present system of representation, but it has also some very great advantages, and I am free to confess that none of the sweeping and systematic plans of reform that have been hitherto submitted to Parliament, appear to me calculated at once to preserve the advantages and remove the defects. But I am not therefore unwilling to bestow due attention upon any plausible scheme that may be suggested, and there is one particular in which I think a specific reform would be highly useful, as it would be a restoration of the House of Commons to that proportion between the Constituent and representative bodies which once existed, but which time and accident have destroyed. I mean the transfer of the elective franchise from those towns which population and trade have abandoned to the great towns, which have risen into wealth and consequence since the union with Scotland, and which are still without representation. Whether this could be done by one general measure or gradually as the occasion of a corrupt exercise of the franchise may occur, is a question of great consideration upon which there is much difference of opinion. Certainly it is not desirable to increase the number of members in the House of Commons, perhaps already too large, nor to make great alterations too suddenly, and experience has shown that the opportunities will not be long in occurring in which the transfer may be made with justice and with good example.

' Under this persuasion I have, as well in the case of East Retford as in the other cases that have occurred since I have been in Parliament, voted for the transfer of the right from Boroughs convicted of corruption to great towns.

' But, gentlemen, there is one point connected with this subject on which I wish explicitly to declare my sentiments. I never will consent to any plan of reform that has for its object the separation of power from property in this country. The House of Commons is doubtless, from our free institutions and from its important privilege of holding the purse, the chief seat of power in the legislature. Any attempt to exercise that power at the will of numbers only unaffected by the influence of property has a tendency to destroy the constitution without putting anything better in its place. For you may rely upon this truth, that be the form of Government what it may, power will have property sooner or later. The union between them is indispensable to the stability of any government whatever. The measure which separates them must introduce perpetual disorder and struggle in the state until they are again united. These disorders and struggles would be of no advantage to liberty which might perish in the conflict. For who shall tell whether the reunion between these two great elements of civil society, property and political power, may not take place in a form more odious and more mischievous than that in which they were united before. In a military despotism, for example, where property follows the sword, or in a system of universal corruption whereby a people like the ancient Romans flattered, debased, and demoralised, become at last an easy prey to ambition and tyranny.'

'August 6, 1830.

'I thank you for your letters and the accompaniments which I have received down to the 2nd. I have been trembling for you and I think your Ambassador ought to let his hotel be a barrack for all his corps. At this moment I suppose the King will do all he can to annoy his *ci-devant* subjects. He has had a set of egregious fools and ignoramuses about him. I fear the worst and dare not tell you what it is. I hope our King will take a decisive line, and that "*vous autres Parisiens*" will not force us from our propriety. I came to town from Malton this morning. All well at present. Campbell is returned for Stafford, I fear at great expense. He is indebted to nobody but himself for it. I am going to Abinger to-morrow, and hope to meet M. and J. there. I have not been so lucky as to encounter his Majesty anywhere but at the levee, and you know the bore of fighting one's way to that honour.

'Cottu is here a fugitive, I have a note from him. I shall see him if I can before I leave town.'

The Reform Bill brought in by Lord John Russell was the cause of my father's separation from the Whig party.

His first speech in opposition to the measure was highly praised for its good constitutional arguments against it though condemned by the *Times* and the radical prints.

He wrote to me after he had spoken :—

'I have made my speech which met with more attention than the *Times* represents. You must take your account of it from others. I called the next day on Lord Milton to tender my seat, but he had left town and I therefore sent it to him by post. I expect his answer to-morrow, and conclude that on Monday I shall be out. I shall endeavour to console myself for a few days in the next week at Abinger.

'The game is however I fear up with the Constitution. You must not state to any person, however, that I express a strong opinion upon it, as I made a moderate speech without any party feeling. There must be some sort of con-vulsion I fear, whatever happens. I think there will be a dissolution during the Easter recess. The present Parliament will not answer the purpose. Your friend Cradock was ill and could not vote. Although I am full of uneasiness about our home affairs, I have a deeper interest in what is passing and is to come at Paris because you are there and my thoughts are always with you. You must know everybody and lead a stirring life. You may, perhaps, be but a short time at your post, for war is not improbable, which makes it more expedient that you should learn and know all about the present actors on that scene. You have the *volto sciolto* which a diploma-tist should have, but have not yet acquired the *pensieri stretti* which I recommend as most essential at this crisis. Neither a republican or a liberal nor a Charles X. man nor Orleans man should know your sentiments about their affairs.

'The French are always too glad to communicate their own, and ready to dispense with your sentiments. You must therefore be a good hearer.'

'Abinger Hall: Aug. 9, 1830.

'I hope to hear from you by every courier. Your news is always interesting, though I generally find it in the papers the day before I get your letter. I sincerely hope that everything may end well, but my fear is that the Duc d'Orleans will only serve Messrs. les Liberaux for a time, and that the genius and talents of the Press will not be satisfied without a return to the happy times of 1789. Not that I believe that any indi-vidual wishes for a renewal of those horrors, but that I do not perceive amongst the French any attachment to any civil institution of sufficient force to overrule the vanity of those who think that they can form the best of Governments and the enthusiasm of those who think that human nature is capable of being influenced by the sole dictates of reason. This vanity and enthusiasm create a difficulty almost invincible in the formation of a new political society. Men are prompted to act, not by reason but by passion, and it is happy for them when their passions have some sensible object in their institutions to which they are attracted. Such is the case with us in England at present, though I am sorry to say that many of the irresponsible ministers of the Press are doing their best to destroy our prejudices in favour of our English forms of liberty. But in France the only attachment is to something ideal which they have never yet tried. To some imaginary boon concealed under the general terms of "la liberté! *la gloire de la patrie, le bonheur des hommes, l'égalité &c.*"

'I am therefore the more anxious to learn exactly what turn affairs take with you. I presume and I hope that our Government will be perfectly quiescent, unless some outrage forces them to defence, but I do not see how they can at present give any instructions to their Ambassador.'

'Monsieur Cottu has taken an alarm which I imagine was unnecessary, and has placed himself with me at present. As he has done nothing but publish unpopular opinions, it would be very inconsistent with the freedom for which the French are contending to persecute him. But as he was not at Paris and only heard of the commotions, he thought he might as well make a visit to England of a few days, and here he is. I dare say my reception of him will be set down to the account of my aristocratic opinions, but the duties of hospitality to a stranger who flies from persecution are sacred. I hope he will be able to return in a few days. If you can, without at all committing your official character, open a communication with Madame Cottu and facilitate her correspondence with him, I shall be glad, but run no risk of any kind.' 'J. S.'

'Wales: Aug. 18, 1830.

'I do not like your news the worse for it being forestalled, because I seldom read the papers, and I never know whether they speak the truth. On your intelligence I can rely. I accept the *abonnement* of the papers you mention during my stay at Abinger, for there alone I can read them. If I did not expect a visit from the Duke and Duchess of Gloucester next month I would go to Paris to fetch you, for to say the truth, I covet some of that fine weather that you enjoy on the Boulevards in the evening, whilst we are endeavouring to mitigate the severity of the summer by hovering round a fire. Except one week of warm and fine weather, which was the memorable week of your revolution, we have had rain and fires every day, and I am now writing almost with my knees in the grate at ten at night. Do you mean that I should apply to Lord Aberdeen for your leave.

'I shall be at Abinger on Sunday next, and shall know by then of the Duke's visit.

'I presume our Ambassador can receive no instructions till the French Court has made its new character known to us. I hope we are not to stick on the tail of the Holy Alliance. If we do I know who will soon go to the wall. Look at the elections for Devon, Cambridge, Suffolk, Yorkshire. Public opinion was never so decided against the Tories, though I think it is in favour of the Duke of Wellington and Sir Robert Peel. I can give you no better news than the *Times.* Cottu left on Sunday, and I hope he is on his way back. Whether his opinions on French affairs be right or wrong I cannot decide. He expects and fears a republic, a war, and a military government. Time, which proves all opinions, will show. I am here on a cause which I shall easily win to-morrow, and then I intend to pay a short visit to Lord Lansdowne at Bowood. I have invited myself.

'Ever, &c.,

'J. S.'

The next letter was written after he had resigned his seat at Malton the following year :—

'New Street: March 29th.

'By this time you will probably have read my funeral dirge in the *Times*.   The only paper which does not make nonsense of it.   I have been pressed to publish it, and perhaps you will before long have a copy.   I, in due form, departed my life in the House of Commons on Saturday, and I believe that the last obsequies were performed upon me yesterday evening, by a motion for a new Writ.   Lord M—— had left town early on Wednesday morning, so that I could not see him.   I wrote, however, to Milton and received the answer on Saturday, to show me that his will was to be done in the House of Commons as it was in Malton. It is far from clear that there will be a dissolution, or that the Bill will pass.   I am glad Lord G—— inquires after me. Pray remember me to him, and tell him I have taken leave of Parliament, where I have never yet been in a desirable position between a party-seat and moderate opinions.   Moreover that I have lost my seat by an adherence to the same opinions upon which I came into Parliament, upon the question of Reform, which opinions have never varied or been concealed.

'I shall go to Abinger for a few days, and perhaps to Erlwood, but an engagement of business, which I have for the 11th, will prevent my joining you at Paris.

(Signed)   'J. SCARLETT.'

The following letter was written evidently before he had any idea of being again in Parliament, after resigning his seat for Malton.   There is no date :—

'New Street: Thursday night.

'I have to thank you for two letters, and I hope to have another to-morrow if it has not gone to Abinger, from whence I came to-day.   I hope next week to send you a copy of my speech.   It is but the substance, for I could not recollect the whole.   We dined at Guildford on Monday with the Bailiff. As the occasion led to it I again let fly and I suppose I spoke with some effect, for Lord King who was there spoke handsomely of my address, and told me privately that he agreed with some parts of it.

'I had a very kind letter from the Duke of Wellington this morning, regretting the loss of my seat. More persecution from the Whigs. The old lie about my having applied to Lord F. for a seat is revived and published in the *Sun* of Monday week, though I only saw it to-day. And I hear that I am much abused for not having resigned before the second reading, as if my long letter, which you copied, was not a sufficient tender if Lord Milton had then chosen to accept it.

'His answer, in fact, gave me full liberty to have kept the seat after voting, as I liked, and it was nothing but an excess of delicacy on my part, combined with a wish to quit a seat which exposed me to constant envy from some quarter or another, that induced me to tender my resignation a second time. Pray find some opportunity of explaining this to Lord Granville.

'I am not able to give you further information of the chance of success for this measure. I believe the only people who are competent judges, and calm judges at the same time, are frightened into it.

'There is a talk of further intimidation for the committee. I am sure, however, if the Bill passes as it is, the greatest confusion must follow.

'I have taken possession of my new fields, and next year shall be in a large park.

'I have seen nobody since I came to town but your friend Brydges at the University Club. They say he is mad. His manners are very singular for a parson, it must be owned.

'I shall send you a speech for Guizot, and for Broglie, and for Dupin, and for your Ambassador. That will be enough, I conclude. We are all run mad about reform. Adieu.

'Ever yours,

'J. S.'

'Friday, April 15, 1831.

'I received yesterday your letter of the 11th. I cannot send you a copy of my speech, though I expected it would have been ready by to-day. It is accompanied by a letter to Lord Milton.

'The Bill does not seem to flourish quite so much in the

House as it did, and it is said by many persons that most thinking men are against it.

'You will see what Hunt has said in the House about the millions who do not think. Those who are for it are the Radicals—the Ultra Whigs, and a certain active and restless class that belong to every free government and that love the excitement which attends any change. They have persuaded the people that it will give them cheap bread, abundant work, and exemption from taxes. If these consequences were not expected, the rabble at a public meeting would not be so vociferous for it. I ought to add to the supporters the vast class of journalists whose importance will be increased by it.

'Nevertheless I fear it will be carried. Fear will make men vote for it who actually disapprove of it. Amongst the placemen themselves, they do not scruple to avow that it is a rash and foolish measure. Yet, I suppose, it will pass with some modifications which will not mend it. I have no news to tell you, being now out of the world.

'The Duke of Gloucester has been very ill, but is much better. I saw him yesterday, and the dear Duchess, who is all goodness. This is the first day of term, and I am going to the Lord Chancellor's, not so much by way of compliment as to further your friend Rendlesham's affair, which the Chancellor has made his own. We are altogether in a strange disjointed state. I am not upon the whole sorry to be out of Parliament at this moment.

'Ever yours affectionately,

'J. S.'

CHAPTER XXVI.

CORRESPONDENCE WITH LORD HOLLAND.

ON the back of a copy of a letter to Lord Holland, in my father's handwriting, are these words :—

'Copy of my letter to Lord Holland, 24th of April, 1831, in reply to his. Parliament was just dissolved, and as I was informed by his letter that the Reform Bill was the vital question of the Whig party, I accepted the offer of a seat in the new Parliament from my old and excellent friend, Lord Lonsdale, that I might, in the most authentic manner, signify that I had quitted the Whig party.'

This letter is a justification of his political conduct in separating himself from the Whigs, on account of their Reform Bill, in reply to a letter from Lord Holland.

Here is an extract of Lord Holland's letter and my father's reply :—

'Holland House, Monday morning, April 24.

'Dear Scarlett,—In the first place I must express my hopes that the story of my servants, that you had a fall from your horse is not true, and if it is that their subsequent conclusion may be true also, and that you were unhurt. Pray answer this, for they alarmed us about you.

'I mentioned to Lord Grey the substance of our conversation. He disclaimed, I assure you, as strongly, as warmly, and as eagerly as I could do the notice, or as we both and indeed all should call it, the imputation of the sort of proscription and exclusion, which at the commencement of our conversation you seemed to me to apprehend. Believe me, there is nothing of the kind—on the contrary, there is good will and sincere wishes, if it were practicable, to see our old relations of political attachment renewed, and you and our party, whether in Government or not, on the same footing with one another as before.   There is nothing but regret that the difference on a question so vital to us as the Reform Bill, exclusive of the yet higher consideration of its importance, renders anything like *political* concert, co-operation, and confidence immediately impracticable.   For unfortunately the contest on that point continues, and is likely to absorb for a time all other considerations in Parliament and in the country.   When that great business is over it would, I am sure, be both a credit and a comfort to us if we should find ourselves once more politically connected with the great leader of the Bar, and with an old political associate as well as an invariable personal friend.   Your claims in the event of such a connection would naturally be such as your station in the profession would command from your political and personal friends ; and I think I may safely appeal to your own knowledge of the individuals to judge whether it is likely that any unpleasant recollection of past transactions would weigh a straw with such minds as Lord Grey's, the Lord Chancellor's, or those with whom they would consult and act on such an occasion.

'At all events, you will allow an old and sincere friend to subscribe himself ever truly and unalterably yours,

(Signed)   ' HOLLAND.'

' *Private.*   New Street, Monday night, April 24.

' My dear Lord Holland,—It is true that I had an unlucky fall yesterday near the Duke of Wellington's gate, I was taken into his house for a little time till I recovered from the shock, when I was brought home in a hackney coach.   I was condemned to the pain of being cupped and imprisoned in my chamber the rest of the day, which enabled me to appear in Court this morning without any other detriment than the remains of a broken head.

' The only real annoyance resulting from the accident was, that it prevented me riding after your carriage to entreat you to say nothing of what had passed between us, and to give me

K 2

another opportunity of speaking with you.   It did not occur to me till I was half-way to town, that our short colloquium at your carriage window must have left an impression on your mind that I wished some communication to be made with Lord Grey.   The intention you expressed of writing to me in the evening had not at the first struck me so forcibly as it did upon subsequent reflection, when I perceived from the whole tone of the conversation that my proposal to make certain inquiries of you as a personal friend had assumed the air of a wish to ascertain the sentiments and views of others, as to some very undefined objects of future consideration.

'In truth, I had no other object than to ascertain from you individually whether the feeling which I supposed to exist towards me in certain quarters had not originated in some misconception which it might be in my power to remove ; and without asking for explanation, much less for pledges, to which I could have no right, to lay before you as a private and personal friend an exact view of my own situation and duties.   The great kindness with which both you and Lady Holland received me, I was afraid had encouraged me to say more than I ought to have said without the opportunity of a fuller explanation on my part of my motives.   Your letter, though it affords me great satisfaction in the sentiments it expresses both on your own part and the part of Lord Grey, yet proves to me that I was unlucky in being arrested in my way to remove the impression I had left on your mind.

' I hope the following statement may convince you that I am not likely to make the hope or the fear of anything personal to myself the rule of my conduct.

' Upon the peace of Amiens in 1801, my friend Perceval proposed to me a seat in Parliament, that I might support the Addington Government.   His pretext was that Mr. Fox and his party having declared themselves for peace, I had a fair opportunity of taking such a part in Parliament, consistent with my party attachments, as would open the way to immediate advancement in professional honours.   I declined his proposal, because he could not assure me that upon any other subject besides the peace Mr. Addington's Government was likely to be conducted upon Mr. Fox's principles.   Again, in

the year 1813 the choice of one of two seats was offered me
if I would consent to support the Government, which would
have led to the immediate consequence of office. I refused.
Again, in 1816 just before Gifford was made Solicitor-General,
I was assured by a person now living and whose word I did
not doubt, that if I would only permit him to say that I
would accept that office, he knew the offer would be made
to me immediately, and that it would be made with express
permission to make it known to my friends that it was
intended merely as a step to the situation of Lord Ellenborough, who was anxious then to resign if a fit successor
were then in office. It was moreover stated that as long as a
doubt remained of my acceptance it was resolved not to make
me an offer. I refused to remove the doubt by any declaration
on my part. Shortly before the general election in 1826
Mr. Canning earnestly pressed me to quit Parliament. Upon
that event he assured me that the King was desirous that I
should have the first judicial office that fell vacant and that I
thought worth my acceptance, if I would but quit the ranks
of opposition in Parliament. Out of compliment to him I
took a day to consider his suggestion, and then refused to
abandon my seat for any such object. I have now in my
possession a letter from him upon the appointment of Copley
to the Rolls, referring to this conversation and expressing his
regret. You are aware that when I accepted office under him
the following year, it was in conjunction with other members
of the Whig party, and with the general support of all except
Lord Grey. Finally in 1828 upon the accession of the Duke
of Wellington, I declined that office, though I was pressed by
several of Canning's friends, and by several messages from the
King to continue.

'These particulars, though I never boasted of them, nor
alluded to them in the House of Commons, nor indeed even
threw them together before, I hope may be considered as
proofs that neither the hope nor the offer of high places could
tempt me to abandon my friends or my principles.

'After the abolition of the Corporation and Test Act,
and the emáncipation of the Catholics, I certainly thought
that all grounds of party difference had ceased to exist, and I

avow that I should have felt no scruple in joining the Duke of Wellington upon principle. It happened, however, that at the time he made me the offer, domestic calamity had greatly indisposed me for public life ; and in the then temper of my mind I should certainly have declined it, had I not been encouraged, and I may say pressed to accept it by many of my political friends, and emphatically by Lord FitzWilliam and Lord Grey. Whilst in office I studiously avoided all occasions (and they were not wanting) of personal controversy with any member of the Whig party, and anxiously sought to bring about that union which till the last moment I did not despair of seeing accomplished. I considered myself as only obeying their impulse in accepting office, and rather than have broken with them would at any time have resigned it, upon a suggestion that such a step was expected from me. No hint of the sort was ever given.

Nevertheless when the Government was changed, I was dismissed from office, *sans phrase.* I was not desirous of continuing in office. But I freely own that I did expect from a Cabinet composed, with one exception only, of my personal friends, some explanation or some kind words at parting. They could not consider me, after the station I had occupied, and if I am not too vain, in the station I continued to occupy, as a mere hanger on upon a Ministry, subject to the mandate of a Treasury note. I declined however to enter into any engagement to oppose the Government. On public grounds I was anxious for its permanence and its success. But what was the impression produced on the members of my own profession when they contemplated the situation of one to whom they had long ascribed the first place amongst them, and of whom it had been their habits to think for twenty years that his unfortunate party attachments alone had kept him from the highest stations ? There were two opinions. One that I was most scandalously treated, the other that it was the immediate intention to make some arrangements to remove me from the Bar. It had long been the general wish, that as the Court of Exchequer was thrown open to general practice (as it was by my Bill last year) I should be placed there for the purpose of making the Court effective. The report of the Commissioners of the Common Law had pointed me out for this purpose by a description that could not be misunderstood, and there was a sort of combination to overcome my reluctance to accept that office by the force of public opinion.   I certainly should not have accepted it ; the office would have been more laborious to me than to any other individual by the business that would have followed me there, and I should have lost half my income without gaining any repose.   But I pray you to contemplate for a moment the situation in which I was placed, by *not having had an opportunity of refusing it.*   In the first place, there had been found no objection to appoint the late Solicitor-General for Ireland to a high judicial station.   There was no contamination therefore in the contact with the late Adminis-tration.   In the next place, one of the Duke of Wellington's Cabinet or even his Chancellor being appointed to the Court of Exchequer was a proof that the closest connection with him was no ground of exclusion from the new Government.   What then could be inferred regarding me, except that upon some personal ground I was deemed unworthy ?   Or what conclu-sion could I form, but that some influence was at work to degrade me in public estimation, and to make the Government itself a party to the holy work of the press in trampling on me ?   I must pray you, my dear Lord, to consider these matters with calmness and attention, and if you entertain those sentiments of me which it has long been my anxious wish to cultivate, judge whether the universal feeling that I have been both abandoned and abused is wholly without foundation ?

'Notwithstanding I have never till now suffered any complaint to escape me, though I have not felt the less deeply and bitterly how much I have had occasion to deplore my connection with the Whigs.   It was far from my intention to join any party to oppose the Government.   It was my deter-mination to have resigned my seat and to have abandoned all public life, whenever I found I could not maintain my neutral-ity.   Nor would it cost me much to quit a profession to which I have perhaps been too long attached.   I could not see much to approve of in some of the new measures, but I waited for the promised reform, as an opportunity for showing that I was actuated by principle alone.   I anxiously hoped, and indeed believed, that it would be of such a character as to justify me in giving it a zealous support with which I should have taken my leave of Parliament for ever.   You will not however doubt my sincerity, when I say that the measure far exceeds the limits, which in my conscience I think prudent or safe.   I have found myself upon principle bound to oppose it.   Thus I am committed against the Government in spite of myself.   I collect from your letter of to-day, as well as your conversation yesterday that the question of this Bill and nothing but this Bill is now the only but vital party question left.   It is with pain and regret that I view as an inevitable consequence my opposition to the Government whilst that question is depending.

‘After unburdening my mind on these matters to you, it was my intention to have mentioned yesterday that several offers have been made to me, for the new Parliament, in terms the most handsome, expressly excluding all pledges both regarding men and measures.   I cannot refuse to perform what I think a public duty, though it may be attended with the same sort of sacrifices which I have so often made.   They are of little importance in my eyes.   But there is one thing of the last importance, which is my honour and character.   I am most anxious that my motives should not be misunderstood or misrepresented.   I am too proud to make resentment a motive of public conduct, and perhaps I am too calm to be long susceptible of that feeling.   But I wish to avoid all just ground of reproach for inconsistency.   With this view alone I entreat you to bestow three minutes on my letter to Lord Milton appended to the publication of my speech, which I desired Mr. Murray to send you.   You will see what my sentiments on Reform were in 1829, and that I made no compromise of them on joining the Government.

‘I would also request your attention to the enclosed extract from the *Sun* newspaper of 28th March.   This is a specimen of the mode in which I am assailed under the colours of an old associate.   It is plain that the writer means to hold himself out as a member of the Fox Club, and as having some intelligence with Lord Milton.   I enclose you, therefore, the answers of Lord Milton and myself, published without the least concert, in a following number of that paper. With whom originated the report which these letters contradict I have never been able to trace. All I know is that the first person in whose possession I found the slander, and that very soon after it was hatched, was your Lord Chancellor, but I do not believe he gave any credit or currency to it.

'I anxiously hope the time may come when party feelings may give way to a sense of justice. But I know that these feelings, always intolerant, are likely to be carried to the highest pitch of intolerance. The great question of your Bill engenders more than the ordinary passions to which political differences give rise. It involves much more than a mere change of power from one set of men to another, or even a mere change of the measures of Government. On your side three parties may be considered as engaged. One, and I make no doubt the largest, consists of those who honestly think the Constitution will be preserved without being impaired by it. Another, of those who view it as a step to a Republican form of Government, which from principle and through ignorance they prefer. The last, of those who naturally love the excitement of strong passions, who find their enjoyment in political agitation, and look with pleasure upon the agonies of a party whom they hope to extinguish. On the other side are embraced two classes. One, who fear the destruction of those blessings and advantages which are admitted to be peculiar to our Constitution, *bad as it is*. This, I doubt not, is the largest but most silent class. The other consists of the Tory party, who are struggling for the continuance of their existence as a party in Parliament from which they see in the success of this measure their inevitable expulsion. Here, then, are sufficient materials for explosion. And it must be admitted that if that smallest of all the parties who love to live in agitation, have had any influence in the measure, whatever its other merits may be, they at least have accomplished the object of shaking the State to its foundations, and awakening almost every passion that can influence and divide a nation against itself. In these jarrings and conflicts men who are moderate, like myself, are pressed between the contending factions, and generally persecuted by both. Neutrality is, therefore, no longer safe.

' I anxiously hope that if this measure does pass it may
answer your expectations.   I doubt not it will pass by the
force of that *very* popular influence upon the House of Commons—the alleged weakness of which is the great pretext for
it.   And I hope the time may come when the feeling to which
it gives rise may subside.   Sure I am that the time can never
come on this side the grave when I shall cease to entertain
for you those sentiments of esteem, admiration, and affection,
which during the greatest part of my life have been interwoven
with all my habits and opinions.

' Ever yours,

(Signed)   ' J. S.'

CHAPTER XXVII.

CORRESPONDENCE WITH LORD MILTON, ETC.

I SHALL devote this chapter to a correspondence between my father and Lord Milton regarding the Reform Bill, prefaced by an explanation written by himself.

It was reported that Lord Milton had requested him to give up Malton, before his first speech in Parliament against the measure. This was not the case, but immediately after the speeeh he lost no time in resigning the borough, for which he had become a member by Earl Fitzwilliam's wish and sanction, after he joined the Duke of Wellington's Government.

The correspondence commences in 1829, when my father first took office under the Duke of Wellington. It was resumed again in 1830, and the last letters were in the year following. The correspondence is prefaced by his own memorandum.

After the passing of the Catholic question, and some time before the Duke of Wellington communicated to me His Majesty's desire that I should accept the office of Attorney-General, which I had resigned upon His Grace first becoming Prime Minister, I had been apprised of the sentiments of Lord Grey, of Lord Fitzwilliam, and of many other individuals of the Whig party, that I ought to accept the office if it should then be proposed to me. I understood it to be the general wish of the party that the offer should be made to me. And I afterwards learned that Lord Fitzwilliam had gone so far as to communicate his wish to the Duke of Wellington. When I received the Duke's proposal, the seat for the University of Cambridge was vacant, by the promotion of Lord Chief Justice Tindal, and I was informed that, if disposed to try my interest there, the Government would support me. Lord Fitzwilliam was not then in town ; but I proceeded immediately from the Duke of Wellington to Lord Milton, to communicate to him what had passed. His Lorship was aware of his father's wishes upon the subject, and expressed his own approbation of my accepting office. His words were, ' When it was proposed to you to continue in office last year, I said, No, but now I say, Yes.' But it was his express desire that I should not change my seat for Peterborough. He said he would support me for that place, but not for Cambridge. In consequence of this conversation, I informed the Duke of Wellington, whom I was appointed to see on the following day, that I was requested to keep my seat for Peterborough, of which he approved, and my acceptance of office was then finally arranged. In the course of the same evening I received a letter from Lord Milton, of which the following is a copy :—

' Grosvenor Place, May 28, 1829.

' Dear Scarlett,—It is very difficult, at least to me, to think at the moment of everything that ought to be considered, and this has been the case with our last night's conversation. Only, however, in one particular point, but that point of sufficient importance to induce me to write to you.

' Governments in general, and I suspect the Duke of Wellington's is no exception, are not very favourable to parliamentary reform. Now, as you have always been, and as I have for many years been, a very ardent supporter of that question, would it not be very desirable that you should have some explanation with the Duke on that point ? My father, it is true, does not care much about it, but both you and I are, with his acquiescence, pledged to it past all retreat, so that I confess I feel very anxious there should be no misunderstanding on that head, and that the Duke should know beforehand that whenever it is brought forward in the general or in detail, you will expect to be at liberty to support it ; for you know it would not be dealing fairly by the question if we were to shut our eyes to the possibility of an Administration calling upon their Attorney-General, either to oppose, or to absent himself from the question, both of which courses would, in my judgment, be inconsistent with the position in which we stand towards it.

'I have taxed my memory for anything else and can recollect nothing, except the Libel Act of 1819,[1] but it is a minor point.

'Yours very faithfully,

'MILTON.'

As this letter appeared to me to treat the subject of parliamentary reform too generally, I thought it right to state my sentiments upon it explicitly in writing, not only that Lord Milton might know them exactly, but that I might in case he concurred with me, have something specific to lay before the Duke of Wellington, as to the length to which I should be disposed to go upon that question. I therefore returned an answer, of which the following is a copy :—

'May 29, 1829.

'My dear Lord Milton,—I wish I had received your letter about parliamentary reform before I saw the Duke of Wellington yesterday. I will, however, find some opportunity of speaking to him on the subject. In the meantime you are aware that I have not been asked to abandon any principle or pledge as the condition of office.

' I wish, however, in order to prevent all misconception, to put in writing those opinions upon parliamentary reform which I entertain, and beyond which I should be very unwilling practically to go.

' I think I once mentioned to you a letter I had written to Canning upon the subject of a speech he made some years ago at Liverpool, in which he described parliamentary reform as the supposed panacea for all manner of grievances, and compared the reformers to persons who ascribed some magical force to particular signs—as if, for example, the sign of the Red Lion should be thought to afford a refuge from all calamities. Some would have a large Red Lion, others a small

---

[1] This Act was repealed the last session.

one.   I wrote to him that, notwithstanding his joke, I was
for a small Red Lion.   I must say then that I have never yet
heard proposed any uniform system of election which I could
prefer to the present.   And I am greatly inclined to doubt
whether any uniform system could under any circumstances
be desirable.   The House of Commons, constituted as it is,
affords a voice and a hearing to every class of opinions in the
country, and above all to the minority ; which notwithstanding
the paradoxical length to which the late Mr. Wyndham pushed
that argument, does in general comprise the best informed
and most intelligent of the community.   Whereas, a uniform
system of election would tend to confine the representation to
the majority, and would exclude many classes, unless the
scale of qualification descended so low as to approach universal
suffrage, which would then lead to another objection, which is,
that I can never approve of any system of representation that
takes from property the power and influence necessary to
protect it.   I hold it as a maxim, that any Government which
tends to separate property from constitutional power must be
liable to perpetual revolutions.   For power will seek property
and always find it.   The separation is a source of perpetual
agitation till they unite.   Now it must be owned that the
mode in which property and power are combined in our present
system presents many anomalies and many specious objections.
But I am not sure that the disguised and irregular mode in
which that connection now exists is not more useful and less
odious, upon the whole, than a more obvious and systematic
connection would be.   At all events, I think it would not be
worth the while to substitute an untried system, upon mere
grounds of theoretical advantage, for providing the same connection in another form.   Can the reason of man make any
thing perfect ?   Does not the most perfect form of organized
matter, the work of the most consummate artist, exhibit
unsightly parts which are as essential to its functions as the
most beautiful ?   What more can be effected in the conflict
of human passions and interests, than a compromise of what
is desirable with what is possible ?   Subject then to these
grand exceptions, I am a reformer of the small Red Lion.
That is to say, I am an advocate for all the gradual improve-

ments in the *present* system which occasion may suggest, more especially for every fair opportunity of diverting the representation from the small towns which do not require it to the large towns which loudly cry for it, and which undoubtedly would (but for the union with Scotland) long since have had it by virtue of the King's prerogative.

'Now I shall always be desirous and hope I shall be permitted to take my own line, either upon any particular occasion which may give rise to the proposal for such a change, or in support of any general measure which may appear to me *fitted for and confined to that object.* These are my sentiments, in which I shall have more confidence if I find them agreeable to yours.

'Ever yours truly,

'J. S.'

To which I received the following reply :—

'Grosvenor Place, Friday night.

'Dear Scarlett,—Our notions of Reform are not very unlike. Indeed, I may say that they are very similar.   To disconnect property from power must, as you say, lead to confusion. *My Red Lion is therefore about the same size as yours* ; but my anxiety is not so much about the *size* of the Lion, as about the *good will* of the house. The truth is that I am not a Reformer, because I am or have been in opposition (for I was in Parliament, and therefore in opposition, as a very young person, many years before I was converted), but because the experience I have had of the House of Commons this Session as much as any other, has convinced me of its necessity to the ultimate preservation of the Constitution.

'All I have to beg therefore is that we shall still be favoured with your custom, and that you will continue to put up at the Red Lion instead of the Blue Boar.

'Yours most faithfully,

'MILTON.'

Towards the close of the last Parliament I had a communication from Lord Milton, through Lord Dundas, of his intention to resign his claim, at the next general election, to represent the county of York—that in such case, it would be naturally expected that he should represent Peterborough, with which place he was so much connected—that he imagined I was the more likely person of the two then representatives of Peterborough to procure a seat elsewhere ; on which account alone it was suggested to me that I should make the vacancy. In a very friendly conversation, which I afterwards had with Lord Milton upon the subject, I fully ascertained that it was not from any dissatisfaction with me, nor from the then state of parties in the House of Commons, nor from any political feeling whatever that the suggestion was made to me. He assured me that he had no other motive than that above mentioned. And he stated that the matter was unknown to his father, to whom he did not wish to mention it till all arrangements were finally completed, but that he had made the communication of his wishes thus early to me for my convenience.

In consequence of this I avoided making the slightest allusion to the subject to my Lord Fitzwilliam, although I continued to receive from him the same kindness, and to be treated with the same confidence as ever.

Before Parliament was dissolved both their Lordships had left town and were at Milton ; no other communication had passed between me and either of them, directly or indirectly, upon the subject when I received from Lord Fitzwilliam the following letter :—

'Milton, 12th July.

'My dear Scarlett,—Allow me to make a proposal to you to represent, at the next general election, the Borough of Malton in Yorkshire, instead of that of Peterborough, for reasons which I wish not now to explain. I am convinced it will be more convenient, and therefore make the proposal.

'Ever yours most truly,

'W. Fitzwilliam.'

I could only conclude from this letter that in consequence of some unexpected vacancy having occurred at Malton the offer had been made me in concert with Lord Milton. I had no hesitation of course in accepting it, and I wrote to Lord

Milton by the same post to express the pleasure with which I contemplated the continuance of a connection of which I was very proud, and to request from him instructions what steps I should take on the dissolution with a view to Malton. Afterwards, on the same day, I declined another seat which had been offered to me in the most flattering and friendly manner, from another quarter.

Parliament was dissolved the following week.

On the 26th July I received from Lord Milton the following letter :—

'Wentworth, July 25, 1830.

'Dear Scarlett,—Our Sessions have been going on this week, which of course brought me in contact with Maude, from whom I learned that you were in some uncertainty about the election at Malton.

'Mr. Allen, our agent there, was informed above a week ago that you were to stand, so I hope you will find no difficulty when you go thither, which the people will expect you to do. They are a numerous body almost all engaged in some employment or other, scarcely any living upon private fortunes, of whom you had so many among your Peterborough constituents. In writing upon this occasion, however, I must say that there are two points upon which, notwithstanding the adjunct to your name, I must earnestly beg that you will continue to support any *general* propositions that may be made or any details that are not manifestly absurd. The two questions I allude to are Parliamentary Reform and the Corn Laws. On the former, I consider that if not actually engaged *as a party* there are scarcely any of the Whigs who are not agreed to support the general proposition and some measures of detail—such as John Russell's *motion about Leeds, Birmingham, and Manchester*.

'On the latter I individually feel particularly earnest, and I think you agree with me in deeming the present system impolitic and perhaps unjust.

'If I were not to press those two points, I feel that the public might suspect that we were not thoroughly sincere in our professions upon them, and as I know I am sincere I

L

think I have a claim to make such stipulations as will secure me from suspicion, and tend to promote objects to which I attach great importance.

'Yours very faithfully,

'MILTON.'

The measure of parliamentary reform specified in this letter precisely agrees with that to which my letter of May 29, 1829, had pledged me. Upon the Corn Laws, now for the first time introduced, my opinions were in perfect accordance with those of Lord Milton, which he well knew. His Lordship also well knew that I did not enter the House of Commons as a political adventurer or a tool of party, and that I was not disposed upon any question involving a principle of great importance to the public interest to vote against my own opinion, either from personal interest or from party feeling. I considered his letter therefore, notwithstanding this new stipulation about the Corn Laws, as perfectly consistent with my accepting a seat for Malton. But it so happened that by the same post I received a very friendly but a very extraordinary letter from Mr. Brougham, dated at Scarthing Moor, in which he expostulated with me for accepting a seat from Lord Fitzwilliam, and stated that it was the subject of much conversation in town, and was supposed to be without Lord Milton's concurrence, obscurely hinting that I had applied to Lord Fitzwilliam for the seat. I thought it proper immediately to enclose that letter to Lord Milton with a copy of my answer, in which I entered into a full detail of all that had passed upon the subject and stated the course I should take of laying his letter before Lord Milton.

In my letter to Lord Milton of which I kept no copy, I stated that if Mr. Brougham's letter contained his Lordship's sentiments, though I might have some cause to complain that they had not come to me from himself, and at an earlier period, yet it was not then too late to decline the offer which had been made to me and which he knew I had never suggested.

I received an answer by the return of post from Lord Milton which was perfectly satisfactory to me. As it contains remarks upon other individuals it would be improper to annex a copy, but so far as relates to the subject in question his Lordship confirms the statement made in my reply to Mr. Brougham, entirely acquits me of the insinuation of having applied to his father for a seat, and expresses his satisfaction under all the circumstances that I should represent Malton.

He does me the justice further to say that he knows my general principles are in favour of liberty, and is satisfied that if principles of a different character should display themselves in overt acts of the Government with which I was connected, those principles of mine would induce me to resign my office.

My former conduct and my communications with his Lordship must have fully satisfied him not only of the truth of that observation, but also of this, that I really valued the friendship and connection with Lord Fitzwilliam and his family at a higher price than any office, and that to preserve the former it would at no time have been irksome to me to have given up the office I then held. I have further to add that Mr. Brougham, by his reply to my letter and subsequently at a personal interview he had with me at York, admitted the entire misapprehension under which his first letter had been written, and engaged to do me justice by a correct statement of the facts to several distinguished persons whom he conceived to have been misinformed on the subject.

I proceeded to Malton the beginning of August, where I was received with every mark of pleasure and enthusiasm. Lord Fitzwilliam was at that time in Ireland. Lord Milton was however with his family at Milton, where I passed a day on my return from Malton, and was received by him and them with the same kind and grateful welcome which I had ever experienced.

The events which took place soon after the meeting of the new Parliament are well known. A correspondence of the most friendly character had taken place between Lord Milton and myself, upon the subject of these events, but which had no relation to Reform in Parliament, or to Malton, or to the matter in question in this narrative. I was not apprised of his arrival in town till the day when Lord John Russell opened the heads of his Bill in the House of Commons. I called upon him the following day, Wednesday, when we entered upon the subject, and had some conversation upon parts of the measure, which was interrupted by the arrival of other visitors, when I took my leave. The discussion commenced on Thursday in the House of Commons. On Friday evening, the 4th of March, I mentioned to Lord John Russell the difficulty I found in supporting the whole of his Bill, and my concern at that circumstance ; he requèsted me not to form any conclusive opinion till I had given it further consideration, and had seen the Bill.

However, on the following Sunday I received this note from Lord Milton : —

'Grosvenor Place, Saturday night, 5th March, 1831.

'Dear Scarlett,—It is but fair to apprise you of what I am told this evening, that the world are again taking your name in vain, and putting it about that you intend to vote against the Reform Bill. That the Reform Bill is not perfect (as what great measure is) may be true, and perhaps you have made some remarks to that effect, upon which this foolish story has been hung up, but after all it is a measure so infinitely superior to what the most sanguine, and at the same time, the most moderate reformers could have hoped to see, that I am sure one ought to help it on with all one's strength ; and even if you fail of amending it to your liking in the committee, probably it will be right to be content, and support its passing, even though it should not be freed from those objections which you and I entertain to some parts of it.

'Yours, very faithfully,

'MILTON.'

On the same night I addressed a long letter to Lord Milton, which I find has been mentioned in an abusive letter, published in the *Sun* newspaper of March 18th, with the signature 'Co-Radical.' As my letter consisted chiefly of the grounds on which I objected to the Bill, it is not necessary to state the whole of it, but the following extracts will sufficiently show the object of it.

'Sunday night, 6th March, 1831.

'My dear Lord Milton,—In answer to your note, I think myself bound to state the opinion I have formed upon the leading parts of the proposed measure of Reform; an opinion not hastily formed, but upon much and anxious consideration, and with a very earnest desire to find reasons for approving rather than condemning the measure.'

After stating the objections at some length—

'You had my sentiments upon this subject in a letter addressed to you when I last accepted office. Lest you should have destroyed, what indeed was not worth keeping, I send you with this, a copy of that letter, which I preserved myself, only that I might in compliance with your desire, lay my sentiments upon the subject in the most precise form before the Duke of Wellington and Sir R. Peel. I claimed from them the privilege of acting consistently with these sentiments whilst in office, and that privilege I exercised.[1]   I could not carry my attachment so far as to support this Bill, unless it should come out of committee with many more alterations in it than I can hope it will be permitted to receive, if it should ever find its way there.

' You, and you only, are now in possession of my opinions. I think you will find them consistent with those expressed in my former letter, of which the copy is enclosed. From your short reply which is now before me, I concluded that our sentiments were very similar. I am certain you will not expect me to act inconsistently with my own conscientious judgment. If the Bill does not come out in a very different shape from the committee, I cannot support it. The parliamentary connection between us may therefore probably terminate, but I wish to assure you that my sincere attachment to your Lordship and your family, and my pride in the friendship with which you have honoured me, can never cease.

' I remain &c., &c.'

The letter, a copy of which was enclosed in the foregoing, .

---

[1] I voted against the Government upon the East Retford Bill. The only other occasion when Reform was the subject of a vote was upon Lord John Russell's motion, upon which occasion I was obliged to leave the House on urgent official business. But it was my intention to have voted for his motion.

is the letter of May 29, 1829, set forth in the early part of this statement.

My letter was despatched to his Lordship on Monday, March 7. I certainly considered and intended it as a tender of my resignation, in case the advance which appeared to me to have occurred in his opinions upon the subject of Reform should lead him to think that my adherence to the opinions I had so distinctly stated in May 1829 was a sufficient ground for putting an end to the connection between me and the Borough of Malton. It was not however till Thursday, March 11, that I received the following answer :—

'Grosvenor Place, Wednesday night.

'Dear Scarlett,—I am sorry you think the Red Lion too large, but as I have no ambition to play the part of Procrustes you need not apprehend any attempts on my part to stretch your swallow to the dimensions of my own. Your arguments however appear to me to be adverse to Reform altogether, or at least to be in favour of a lion hardly powerful enough to kill a mouse.

'Yours very faithfully,

'MILTON.'

Judging that this letter indicated no wish on the part of Lord Milton to put an end to the connection between us, despairing from all the information I could obtain of the intentions of Government, of seeing the Bill materially altered in the committee, and thinking it incumbent on me not to shrink from expressing my opinion in public, I spoke and voted against the second reading.

The reasons for my subsequent resignation belong to myself alone. It was my own act, and neither requested nor suggested by Lord Milton.

J. S.

CHAPTER XXVIII.

CORRESPONDENCE.

IN the following letter addressed to me, my father alludes to the fall from his horse, and to the offers of a seat in Parliament made to him about that time by Lord Lonsdale and others, and gives his opinion of the political aspect of affairs.

'New Street, Monday night, May 2, 1831.

' I received at 4 o'clock to-day your letter of April 29, containing the ugly dream about me which I hope for your sake will not be realised. My fall from The General was a bagatelle. It was owing to the groom bringing the other horse so near me as I was going to mount that I could not get my leg between. At the same time the collision of the horses caused a stick which I had in my right hand across the saddle to crack with some noise. This made my horse plunge whilst one leg was in the stirrup and the other half-way over his back, in the middle of the street opposite the Duke of Wellington's, where I had been calling. I was taken into his house a little stunned by the fall, but recovered in a few minutes and was brought home in a hack. I believe nothing was the matter but a little scratch on the head. However Bransby Cooper advised cupping. Next day I was quite well. Now for politics. I had on Saturday the handsomest offer from Lord Lonsdale expressly without any pledges as to men or measures. The next day, Sunday, I had the same sort of offer from Mr. Baring in the most flattering terms. In the meantime the ground at Cambridge had been taken, and if I ever had any chance I should have been too late. Indeed without the circulation of my two speeches which I never thought of, I could hope for nothing.   I hesitated between Baring and Lord Lonsdale, but as the latter required no trouble and was a more declared adhesion of party I thought it best to close with it.

'I had written a letter to Lord Holland to state my grievances against the Whigs and the necessity I was under in being in opposition to them upon this measure, that notwithstanding the usage I had received I should be disposed to a neutrality; but that upon this great measure, which must shake the State to its foundations and excite every passion that can inflame and divide a nation, neutrality was not safe, and that those were lucky who could take the side of their conscience.   I shall now take my part firmly in Parliament and meet my fate, as I have hitherto done, without dismay.   The Bill or something like it must be carried.   I doubt if this was the original intention, but the Ministers have excited a tumult which is still raging, and which if it continues much longer will force them to the ballot and universal suffrage.   These indeed are the necessary consequences of the measure at no great distance of time, for as the people will find neither bread nor work more abundant than before, there will still be a cry, and the press has learnt the secret of its power over the Government.   I am very much mistaken if the reformed Parliament is not in the power of the editors.

' Robert could not have come in for Guildford unless he had agreed to vote for the Bill.   Before I spoke it was offered to me if I would vote for the Bill, but I refused upon these terms.   Baring Wall had been turned out, and old Mangles and a young officer, a brother of Norton, are returned.   They cannot keep it, and I must have my eye upon it next time.   I was returned for Cockermouth on Saturday without leaving town or any expense.

' The Whigs will keep the Government for some time; indeed, their Bill is intended to crush the Tory party in Parliament, and it will succeed.   But the party will exist in the country, and, if it becomes factious, I think the Whigs will be very intolerant, and very unpopular before long.   They are destitute, at least, if I may judge by their measures, of real wisdom and discretion.   Broglie was at Court on Wednesday last, but has not made any sign to me, nor Rocca either. They are with the Whigs I imagine, and will not think me worth notice. Campbell has been elected for Stafford. He and Mary came to town yesterday. He will do the Whigs good service, and I shall not be surprised to see him Chief Justice.

'I must beg you to be very cautious in stating your opinions. Your success now depends on your own interest. The Whigs are more likely to forget their friends than tolerate their enemies, but I hope the sins of the father may not be visited on the children.

'The closing part of your letter is full of comfort. Be .assured that neither fortune nor honours would be of any value in my eyes with reference to myself only, and if my children are contented to see me a private gentleman I shall have nothing to regret on my own account. When the world is more at peace we may yet make a tour into Italy and see the Campidoglio and Coliseum.

'I have had with me to-night a Monsr. de la Charimotte, an eminent French merchant, settled long in London. He tells me that the number of travellers on the Continent is reduced, as to amount, almost to nothing in the way of commerce; that he is now not called upon to make any remittances to the Continent, whereas, before the Revolution, he often sent 25,000*l*. a month to take up the bankers' bills changed by travellers there from England. I do not think any part of the world is now safe from the Vistula to the Po. Here is a long letter, and now as it is time for me to sleep, I bid you adieu.

'Yours, &c.

'J. S.'

The next letter, I imagine, was written some months later, but the date of the month or year is not given.

'Tuesday, 25th.

'I would not have you, for the present, think of anything but the business before you. The world is in a very unsettled state, and I am sure that for the next six months no princes, potentates, Ministers, nor man, can decide what he ought to do. The great experiment of the Reform Bill in·England remains to be tried.

'Here is a pretty question you must make yourself master of. To wit: What is the distinction between Piracy and Legitimate War? Again, What does the law of nations demand should be done by a nation before it commences hostilities? Again, If there be any rule on the subject, what are the excepted cases in which a nation may be justified in departing from that rule? Now these are all questions that belong to diplomacy. They also partake of law. And they have the advantage of being questions of present interest. For authority you must look into Grotius "De Jure Belli et Pacis," Vatel "Sur le Droit des Gens," and the references they will give you. You may as well also look into the first chapter and book of Livy, where you will find the laws which the Romans laid down for the commencement of a war. These questions have nothing to do with the causes of war, for the causes of war may be found in the weakness of one Government or the insolence of another, or the love of conquest, or the caprice of a Minister, or in the necessity he is under of throwing his nation into war to keep his own power.

'But all wars, except in extraordinary cases, ought to be commenced with certain restrictions, which humanity and good sense require to be imposed upon the folly or fury of mankind. I believe I once mentioned to you a little work of the Abbè Mally, "Sur le Droit Publique de l'Europe." It is not of much value, but you will find a reference to many treaties in it. I shall not ask your application of these questions to the present crisis until you are master of them.

'You have by this time seen the Rendleshams. Offer my regards to my Lady. She will, I am sure, be very kind to you, and you will assist her in whatever is in your power. She left this last Friday. We expect a dissolution on Monday. Campbell is Solicitor-General. So he may join the Whigs in abusing me as soon as he pleases. That will be a part of the duty demanded of him if he should be returned to the House of Commons. Adieu.

'Ever,

'J. S.'

At the end of the following letter my father alludes to Norwich, for which he was invited to stand in the event of an expected dissolution of Parliament. For this borough he came in triumphantly, and it was the cause of increased hostility to him on the part of the Whigs whose ranks he had so recently deserted.

During the short time he was seated for Cockermouth he took no part against the Whig Government, but his election for Norwich by a large Conservative majority rendered his new position in opposition to them more conspicuous.

'Nov. 22, 1831.

'I rob the night of half an hour rather than disappoint you of a letter by the next Courier. I received your last of the 19th. You seemed to think that I was reproaching you for extravagance, and that it was necessary you should justify yourself. Nothing was farther from my thoughts. I wished that we should both look at the true aspect of our situation. I have nothing to complain of in your conduct and expenses. I know that you have never intended to be extravagant, and the proof of my confidence is that I have given you no limit, and I am equally persuaded that I may always rely upon your prudence. I would rather make any sacrifice myself than allow you to want, or to think that I begrudged you anything that I could afford you. Our fortune has indeed been unlucky. But we must not judge by events. Had poor Canning lived, and he was as likely to live in 1825 as I was, your success was certain. That you are now without interest is not your fault, and I hope it is not mine. I have lost friends and perhaps made enemies, but I protest my conscience is clear of offence, and I know of no reason in the world why I should be abandoned by those who once made such strong professions of kindness to me, and considered me entitled, in spite of adverse politics, to the honours of the profession. I am doing my best, however, to prove that I still continue to deserve what I never shall attain. The newspapers do not report me, but I assure you that at no period of my life have I been more engaged in business, and, if I may believe what the Puisne Judges say, at none have I been more distinguished by the manner of doing it. Your friends, the Rendleshams, left town to-day for Paris. Lady R. and Arthur and his wife dined with me *en famille* on Tuesday, and I dined with them yesterday (no one else) at Hawarden's.

'Robert is at Norwich. I hope all will go right there. I shall know in a few days. The General Election will take place in the first week in December. I imagine the Government will precipitate it on account of the Dutch War, into which they have either bungled themselves, or been led by the address of the French. I own I am surprised at the influence of France, and can only account for it on the principle which is laid down in the "Tale of the Tub" (which you ought to read) where Jack, the Calvinist, lays it down as a rule that he will do everything just by the rule of contrary to what his brother Peter (the Papist) had done when he was in power. All the maxims of our foreign policy, as well as of domestic, are the reverse of what they were ; and even the law of nations is no longer regarded. For instead of declaring war before you begin hostilities we begin hostilities and declare that we are at peace at the same time. We are knocking down the Dutch in pure affection and kindness. I heard a great Whig who lives much with the Ministers, say on Saturday, that it was a war of mere petulance; because the Dutchman was not willing to obey orders, and so had offended the temper of the British Cabinet. Government should have no temper, no passions. If they act from resentment or anger they are sure to do wrong, let the subject be what it may. I see no difference between the Minister who makes it the object of his power to please a mistress, or one who employs it to gratify his pride or satisfy his vengeance. I would banish anger, and love too, from the Cabinet if I could.

'If I should get into Parliament and abuse the Whigs very much, they will perhaps propose to do something for me. I never got anything from their friendship.

'You say Lansdowne asked you after me—at which I am surprised. The Hollands have shown no symptoms of their knowing that I am in existence, nor any one connected with them.

'I am quite well, and very much yours affectionately,

'J. S.'

CHAPTER XXIX.

AFTER my father's election for Norwich he was threatened with a petition. He writes :—

'I have no fears about myself at Norwich except for the expense I may be put to in resisting an attack which can never prevail but from the grossest perjury. The disappointed party is full of rage, and they are appealing to the populace for subscriptions to turn me out. They will next appeal to them for evidence. The fact is that my success at Norwich is rather owing to the absence of that profuse bribery which, for many years, secured it as Mr. Gurney's borough. It is said that on this occasion he would not spend more money than Kerr would spend on his part, and this being much less than usual they had not the same influence as heretofore. I am sure that my election has cost me much less than any election has ever yet cost Mr. Gurney or Mr. Grant. So much for Norwich.

'I called lately on Lady Holland, but was refused admittance. A note from her afterwards excused herself because she was engaged with Pozzo.

'I have no news for you. I meet your former Chief Stuart sometimes. He is good natured and clever, but his manners are more plain than those of a Courtier. I have not fallen in with my Lady. I am very little in society, *hors de* Whiggery, and am not courting much of new people, though I must own that the Conservatives are more attentive and civil to me than ever the Whigs were. I would not go to Brighton this winter, as I did not care to make any *affiche*

of myself at the Pavilion.   I believe the King thinks kindly
of me.   I have been twice to Bagshot.   The Duchess is at
Brighton, better but not strong.   The Duke is visiting at
Belvoir Castle and some other places.

'J. S.'

I find a letter dated after the meeting of the next Parliament :—

'New Street, Feb. 11.

'I enclose a note to Lady R.   I have in that stated my
opinion of the new Parliament.[1]   It consists of more editors
of papers, shopkeepers, obscure barristers, and attorneys,
than any former Parliament.   I think the Ministers will get
through no business.   About one hundred determined Radicals are enough to stop all the business of the House, and
if they get the mob with them, as is natural, the Ministers
must let them rule.   I have not spoken for three reasons.
First, because I do not stand firm whilst threatened with a
petition ; secondly, because I do not wish to support or
oppose the Government ; and lastly, because I cannot get a
seat in the House.   All the opposition bench, on which I
used to find a seat, has been seized by O'Connell, Cobbett,
and sundry new men who will hardly allow Sir Robert Peel
to find a corner on it.   The troubles are but beginning.   The
House is so eager to do something popular that no man
among the multitudes who have yet spoken has alluded to
Foreign Affairs, except Sir Robert Peel, who did so very
slightly, and found it the only part of an excellent and
statesmanlike speech that was not received with any appearance of interest in the House.   Holland and Portugal might
disappear from the world without exciting the feelings or
care of a single shopkeeper or attorney amongst us.

'Sir Francis Burdett has offered me a stout horse, which
I am going to try to-day.   He is ugly behind, but seems
well made before.

'Adieu.   'J. S.'

[1] This was the Parliament elected before the Reform Bill was passed.

CHAPTER XXX.

CORRESPONDENCE.

ON account of illness at Paris I had obtained leave of absence to travel, and the following letters from my father were written to me at that time :—

'New Street, May 31, 12 at night.

'I have had your letter from Utrecht, and have just been informed by Scott that he has heard from you at Cologne. I despatch this, therefore, that you may receive it at Frankfort. By the way, I fear you run too hastily through the towns. There is a picture by Rubens in the cathedral at Cologne worth seeing.

'You ask for political news. I can tell you none that is cheering. We are to have all the three Bills without amendment. The King and the Lords have both fallen beneath the despotism of a reforming House of Commons and the political unions. I see no cheerful faces but those of Whigs, who love place, and are in a fool's paradise, or of those of Radicals who already foretaste the joys of their Republic, and those happy times when the poor may tax and govern the rich. The symptoms of revolution are daily growing stronger. As to change, I see no possibility of anything but change, until the first crisis comes. The King can keep no Ministers against the press and the reformed Parliament. But the next change will not be to the Conservative party.

'I am glad to find you can write so much better, and anxiously hope for your speedy recovery. Do not let your prospects in diplomacy affect your mind ; everybody's prospect is bad.   Pray give my most humble duty to the Landgravine.   Say that I think the Duchess of Gloucester is really better, though her illness has been very severe.

'Adieu, my dear son ; remember that in taking care of yourself you are showing your tenderness for me.

'Ever yours.

'J. S.'

After the Reform Parliament met, the Whigs became unpopular, and a great Conservative reaction was evidently not far off.

My father writes to me :—

'I promised you an account of the Lord Mayor's dinner. It was much crowded, badly arranged, badly served, worse attended, and so far as the rude feasting was concerned much inferior to what I have seen there.   The seats were scrambled for ; though I had a place secured, and a card put into the plate, I was ousted, and indebted for a seat to the good nature of a Radical ex-sheriff at the lower end of the table. But these are trifles.   The Ministers came in a great body. The Chancellor, Lansdowne, Melbourne, Althorpe, Lord John Russell, Stanley, Auckland, and some of inferior note.   On the other side there were no eminent persons, unless you choose to place Wetherall, and Sugden, and me in that number.

'First toast, the King (in silence) and a song.   2. The Queen ; universal cheering from all quarters, and for two or three minutes in a marked way.   3. The Lord High Chancellor of England.   At all the upper part of the hall silence. The same at all the lower, except eight or ten voices in one corner at the lowest end, which sounded a few faint notes of applause.   A speech, flat, short, not connected, and received in same manner as the toast.   4. His Majesty's Ministers ; a dead silence.   Speech from Lord Lansdowne ; not heard. No cheers from any quarter.   5. Army and Navy ; nothing remarkable.   6. The Duke of Wellington ; universal shouts of applause, reiterated at different times from all quarters. Everybody but the Ministers standing.   Hats waving.   Hands uplifted, more frequent, more loud, more marked, than the applause for the Queen.   After this nothing was heard.

'I forgot to mention Captain Ross, whose health was drank after the Duke of Wellington's, and who spoke but was not heard.   It was all over by a quarter to nine, because the Chancellor wanted to get away to Brighton.

'J. S.'

Shortly after my return to Paris I was appointed paid Attaché at Rio de Janeiro.   The Duke of Gloucester, who had blamed my father at first for joining the Duke of Wellington, notwithstanding the acquiescence of his Whig friends, had become, soon after the Reform Bill was brought in, as great a Conservative as my father.   I went to take leave of His Royal Highness at Gloucester House before my departure, and learnt that he did not expect the Whig Government to last.   I never saw the Duke again.   His death occurred in 1834, before my return.   I find among my father's papers an account of the Duke's death, by Sir Henry Halford, which I venture to insert :—

'A kindred spirit to that of King George III. has lately left us, and has been received, we hope, into the mansions of the blessed.

'The Duke of Gloucester's disease was seated in the liver, and involved the stomach in so much irritability as incapacitated it for receiving the smallest supply of nourishment. His powers failed therefore, and were unequal to the accomplishment of those efforts by which his enfeebled constitution attempted to disengage itself from the malady, and to terminate it.

'As the brain was not affected, his mind was left at liberty to indulge its natural propensity to look into futurity, and to anticipate the fatal issue of the struggle of the body with the disease.

'With a hope then full of immortality, and with an entire confidence in the promises of the Gospel, the Duke easily detached himself from this world, and felt no dismay in entering

M

upon the life to come. Never in all my converse with the dying did I remark more calm resignation, more deliberate courage, or a warmer piety. The pain of separation was their's only who hung over his sick bed ; to every one of whom, and to those also who were dear to him at a distance he bequeathed his blessing, leaving to us all the rich inheritance of his example.

'Upon the Duke of Gloucester's merit as a soldier, it becomes not me to descant. But as a specimen of that bravery which belongs so remarkably to the House of Brunswick, I have it from the highest authority, that when the brigade which he commanded in Holland, early in the revolutionary war, was drawn up before the enemy, and could not restrain its fire until it might be given with the best effect, the Duke, that he might prevent the effects of their impulse to engage, stepped forth before his soldiers, and interposing himself between his own troops and the enemy, walked deliberately between the two armies.

' Of his conduct in civil life, let the University of Cambridge bear testimony to the prudence and to the spirit with which he defended their privileges in Parliaments as its Chancellor. His memory will be cherished by that learned body long, I am convinced, and with a most respectful attachment.

' His private virtues, which gave a grace and a dignity to his interior and domestic habits, were proclaimed " trumpet tongued," by his steady personal friendships, by his humane attention to the poor in the neighbourhood of his residence, and by his patronage and protection of a thousand charitable institutions, and were recognised and assured by the manner of his departure from life ; for in the spirit of his prayers, " He died the death of the righteous and his last end was like their's "--distinguished by every pious sentiment that could indicate a conscious hope of salvation in his Redeemer, and overflowing with every kindly and generous affection for the welfare of those whom he loved and was leaving behind him.'

During my absence of one year from England in 1835, the Duke of Wellington had taken office for a short time and was now out again. My father had accepted a Peerage and become Chief Baron.

The reply to a letter I wrote to him to announce my arrival at Falmouth, was as follows. He was at the time doing duty as Judge of Assize in Lancashire :—

'Liverpool, Aug 20, 1835.

'I received your welcome letter from Falmouth yesterday, as I was going to a sumptuous dinner with the Mayor and Corporation in their magnificent Town Hall. I need not say how much more delightful your letter was than the banquet. I find my progress here very slow, and I see no chance of my taking leave before this day week at the soonest. Mind, I do not wish to put the least constraint on your inclinations, but only to mention, for your information, that if you should be disposed to visit Liverpool I can receive you in a great house here and lodge you superbly, and can give you a place back to town in my great coach, by the romantics of Buxton, Bakewell, and Matlock. But in case you do not join me I shall hasten to town, where probably the House of Lords may detain me for a few days.

'The weather here is delightful, but very boiling. That is to say, we are boiled in our own juices. Such an unbroken continuance of serene weather is so rare in the north, that I ascribe it to your approach, which, like that of Halcyon, always brings beautiful days. I believe Campbell is at Chester, and that he is to be here in a cause next week. You will find party running higher than ever. The Whigs grow more unpopular every day out of doors. This town is an example, that almost every decent and respectable man that once supported them has abandoned them. Their only party consists of a few of their ancient orators, and the rabble that were accustomed to follow them. As the party in town live with each other exclusively, they are deceived with a notion that all the world think as they do. You will observe that even some of the very Peers created by Lord Grey begin to abandon them ; but such is their infatuation that they will not believe in the very small and contemptible minority which supports them, or they are determined to throw still more power into that minority in order that they may be better supported. Such is the only object of their Corporation Bill, by which they seek to sacrifice rights, franchises, and property to the accomplishment of their desire of adding forty or fifty members more to their own party, as if the great object of the Government, and what they call reform was only to secure the power of one party in the State ; that party having confessedly the Army, Navy, Church, wealth, Aristocracy, and intelligence of the country against it. This is a short sketch of the state of parties just now.

'The Conservatives are making the best struggle they can to support the Monarchy and the Church, because they think them essential to good Government and the safety of property. The Whigs and Radicals are striving to destroy these, not because the Whigs differ on that opinion, but because they cannot get them on their side. The more powerful party of the Radicals, to whom the Whigs have now openly attached themselves, are more honest, as they openly avow their design against the Monarchy and Church upon principle.

'J. S.'

During the long vacation in the following year, I accompanied my father again to the Continent, but we had not time to travel farther south than Switzerland. We went to Brussels, and had the honour of dining with the King of the Belgians. At Schlangenbad we met Admiral Digby and his daughter, formerly Lady Ellenborough, still in wonderful beauty. She had recently married a second time, and was travelling with her father and husband. We entered Switzerland at Bâle and proceeded to Berne and Thun. Whilst walking along the high street of the latter town my father pointed out to me a young officer in the uniform of the Swiss artillery. It was Louis Napoleon, who little thought perhaps at that time of the extraordinary career which destiny had in store for him. We visited Grindelwald, and lingered until the last moment in the Oberland. The weather being fine, my father seemed thoroughly to enjoy this holiday trip.

During our absence from England he received a note from the Chancellor, Lord Brougham, inviting him to Brougham Hall.

'Brougham, Aug. 13, 1836.

'My dear Lord Abinger,—I perceive by to-day's Yorkshire papers, that you have passed through Doncaster on your way to the north, and I trouble you with this to say that I hope and trust no unhappy difference in politics will prevent you from making use of this place as an inn, if it suits your convenience, on your way back. You will find me, what I fear you will regard as very *destructive* in my principles, but always ready to do you the most ample justice (as I ever have been), knowing few men indeed who have made greater sacrifices to their principles.

'Believe me, ever truly yours,
'H. B.'

'P.S.—I direct this through London, as the newspapers do not say where you are going.'

To which he replied :—

'Berne, Suisse, Sept. 16, 1836.

'Dear Lord Brougham,—I received your letter here this morning. The Yorkshire papers were mistaken in sending me to Doncaster. I have been wandering in Germany and Switzerland for the last month.

'Though not in a position which enables me to take advantage of your invitation to Brougham, I am not the less bound to acknowledge your civility, and assure you that I am as far as I have ever been from allowing mere differences in political opinions to affect my conduct or feelings towards individuals. I have never thought that the union of party ought to be the sole test of merit, or the exclusive bond of friendship. In many important points even of principle in politics, and of party attachment I differed from no person more than from the late Mr. Perceval, yet there was none for whom I entertained greater personal kindness or on whose friendship I could more surely have relied.

'You say that few men have made greater sacrifices to principle than I have. It is true that I have on more than one occasion preferred political consistency and the esteem of a party to place or power. But I pretend to no merit on that account. The emoluments of office would not have added to my income, and I have ever spurned the dictates of personal interest and ambition when opposed to a sense of duty or of propriety. The only sacrifice that I found it painful to make was my connection with the Whigs, when I ascertained that with them the Reform Bill was the criterion of party. Then indeed with the opinion I entertained of that measure I thought it my duty, postponing all personal considerations, to prefer the interests of my country to all claims of party, and to make the most public demonstration in my power of my adherence to the Conservative, instead of the destructive party; these being the only two parties into which the nation at that time was and still continues to be substantially and for all practical purposes divided.

'I must say, therefore, that I am sorry to learn from your note that I am still to rank you as a destructive. I was not without a hope that, having done so much more in that line than you ever contemplated when I acted with you in politics, you might have been satisfied with the past, and that your country might at length have had the advantage of your great talents and eloquence in the struggle that awaits every institution on which the monarchy depends.

'Yours truly,

'ABINGER.'

It will be in the recollection of many that Lord Brougham when out of office afterwards became much more Conservative in his ideas, and gave more support to the Conservatives when again in power than to his old friends the Whigs.

CHAPTER XXXI.

FROM the time I returned from South America until my father's death in 1844, when I was restored on promotion to my diplomatic duties, I lived at home with my father and acted for a time as his Marshal and Associate when he went the circuit as Judge of Assize.

The disturbances all over England caused by political agitators produced a destructive feeling amongst some of the lowest classes against every institution in the land and a desire for the compulsory division of property. This species of popular madness was illustrated in several places by the burning of stacks and farm buildings and other outrages.

The charge to the Grand Jury of Leicestershire in 1839, to which I have alluded in Chapter II., was necessarily of a political character, because the cases under consideration, which were tried by a Special Commission, were eminently political. It will be seen that the charge in question met with the approval of Lord John Russell, though in opposition at that period to the Government in office.

Two other charges of a similar character were delivered by my father in Cheshire and Lancashire, at a subsequent time, relating to Chartist outrages, which were equally effective. My father sent them afterwards to the Duke of Wellington, accompanied by a letter, of which I have made an extract, and transcribe at the same time the three charges.

When I see the widely spread and organised tyranny of trades unions and strikes, now so common, destroying individual liberty, and driving away skilful hands, which cannot be replaced, from the British labour market, I cannot help thinking that the more reflecting public, if they peruse again these charges, will be struck with the remarkable forewarnings which appear prophetically in them respecting the ill-advised combinations of workmen to which the present period is unhappily too much subjected.

' New Street, Feb. 25, 1843.

' My dear Duke of Wellington,—I beg permission to lay before you the charges which I delivered to the Grand Juries of Cheshire and Lancashire, upon the late Special Commission. They are accompanied by one which was delivered to the Grand Jury of Leicestershire in 1839, and which I have printed with the others for two reasons : one, that it is far more political than they are ; the other, that Lord John Russell expressed to me his high approbation of it in very flattering terms, shortly after my return from the circuit. It appeared to me, when I was sent on a Special Commission to try offences highly dangerous to the public safety, and which assumed the character of conspiracies for a political object, that it was my duty to set forth in the face of the country the mischievous consequences of these crimes, and to dissipate, as far as I could, the delusions under which the industrious classes had been impelled to commit them. It certainly never entered into my imagination that a judge who endeavoured to show the advantages of a limited Monarchy, with a House of Peers and House of Commons such as we have, above those which involved the heterogeneous elements of a King, a House of Peers, *and a pure democratic assembly* elected by *vote by ballot* and universal suffrage, and, moreover, without any qualification in property, would be considered as introducing politics into his charge or his sentences.

' If the conspiracy had been by Socialists for the abolition of all religion, or by traitors who avowedly aimed at the subversion of the Monarchy, it might as well be said that the judge who maintained that an established religion was essential to the prosperity and safety of the State in the one case, or that the existence of the Monarchy was of the highest public utility on the other, was to blame for introducing politics into his charges. I am perfectly ready to concede that a judge is highly criminal who admits the influence of party connections or party attachments upon his judicial conduct or language. But upon the recent occasions, if I had been the most determined of modern Whigs, which I assuredly am not, or felt a strong bias, which I certainly do not, in favour of the late Government, I should have thought it my duty to hold the very same language.

'I am, &c.,

(Signed)   'ABINGER.'

CHARGES BY LORD ABINGER.

LEICESTER SUMMER ASSIZES, 1839.

'GENTLEMEN OF THE GRAND JURY,—There is nothing, for the most part, in the calendar which calls for remark. The offences, with the exception of one, are of ordinary occurrence, and your own experience at the quarter sessions will, doubtless, enable you to deal with them without any suggestion from me. But to one case I am desirous of drawing your attention, from a peculiar circumstance connected with it. It is a capital offence—and the principal witness in support of the charge appears to be an infant under the age of five years. If you should think, on an examination of the case, that the evidence of that infant is not essential to establish the charge, you will, of course, find the bill. But if the charge cannot be proved without the testimony of that child, whose tender years make her incapable of understanding the obligation of an oath, and probably of giving any distinct account of the transaction, I would beg to caution you against relying upon communications which she is alleged to have made to others. If she cannot be a witness herself, from want of sufficient intelligence, neither can what she has said to others be received as testimony. And however revolting the offence may be to your feelings, and however strong and laudable your desire that it should not pass unpunished, I am sure you will agree with me that the general rules of evidence, which are established for the safety of us all, ought not to be violated in order to arrive at justice in a particular case. And of what avail would it be to put the prisoner on his trial, if the result must necessarily be, that he must be acquitted by reason of the incapacity of the only witness who could prove a case against him, and which witness, therefore, it would be my duty to reject ?

'Gentlemen, it has not been my habit, upon occasions like the present, to travel out of the immediate objects for which grand juries are assembled, but I should not discharge the duty of the station in which I am placed if I abstained from calling your attention to some observations on the momentous crisis which appears to be approaching—if, indeed, we are not already involved in it. I have not received any information that your county has yet been visited by the calamity which has disturbed several parts of the kingdom, and which in some instances has been displayed in seditious riots, and in the burning and destruction of property by tumultuous assemblies of the people. But the nature of your population, and your contiguity to the county where those disastrous events have occurred, make it more than probable that this county also may be afflicted by the same scourge, unless every precaution that the law allows is taken to resist it, and unless those precautions are seconded by the spirit and energy of gentlemen of your rank and station acting in unison with the masses of the population which, I have no doubt, are well affected to the laws and constitution of their country. I am further led to advert to this subject by a paper which has lately been put into my hands, called " The Address of the Northern Political Union to the Middling Classes." It is composed with great eloquence and ability, and very dexterously employs those topics which at all times, and under every form of government, are adapted to inflame the minds of the labouring classes against those who have property and who employ them—representing that riches are the fruits of labour, and therefrom deducing a consequence, very captivating to the labourer, that he who produces wealth ought to enjoy it. There is no form of government under which it would be difficult to persuade him who is destined to ride on the box, that it would be more just and expedient that he should change places with his master, and ride in the coach.   Moreover, this address, after painting in strong colours the advantages of a government by the people, and referring to the republic of America and the republics of the ancient world, first invites the middle classes to join the labouring class in effecting that revolution upon which they are, at all hazards, determined; and in case of their refusal, denounces them as the victims of that universal conflagration and ruin through which they mean to wade to their object.

'Gentlemen, I must say that no Government nor any form of civil society can long be safe where such papers are permitted to be circulated with impunity—to excite the poor against the rich—to encourage the destruction of that capital which alone can set labour in motion, and afford employment to the industrious; to hold out a delusive theory to the multitude; to excite in them a notion that they, the mass, who in the due course of nature must be *governed*, ought by right to be the governors, and to usurp, by violence and bloodshed, that dominion which they could not wield for a moment without destruction to themselves as well as to their employers.   They propose to do nothing less than to pull down the monarchy, to destroy the aristocracy, and to set up in place of our present constitution some visionary commonwealth, formed upon their own fanciful theories.

'Gentlemen, I will venture to say that no Government, that no form of civil polity, was ever constituted by a theory, to last a day; I will go further, and say, that no constitution of civil government was ever mended by a theory.   It is practice and experience alone that give wisdom, and furnish a rule and a principle for mending what may appear defective in the political constitution of a people.   The proper objects of all social unions are the security of property and the security of person.   But for those objects why should men submit to any restraint upon their natural liberty?   It is because, in a state of nature, the person as well as the possessions of each individual are ever at the mercy of the strongest, that the union and organisation of numbers become necessary to restrain the hand of violence, and to make the protection of each individual the common cause of all. The numerical strength of a people should therefore be so organised that it may ever be directed to the protection of property and of persons. The attempt to govern, by placing political power in the hands of the multitude, is an attempt to subvert the very foundations of civil society. Power and property, the two great elements of the political edifice, must be united in order to give it stability; for if the property has not the power, the power will obtain the property, and there must be a perpetual convulsion and struggle till they are combined: the attempt, therefore, can only be followed by plunder and bloodshed. But if you could suppose, that by one universal agrarian law the whole territory were equally apportioned amongst the nation, so that each was doomed to earn his own subsistence by digging with his own spade, what would this be but a scheme of universal pauperism and misery, without capital, without power to resist internal violence or foreign invasion, the direct road to slavery and despotism : the best government, therefore, is that which more effectually in practice provides for the two objects, the security of property and the security of personal liberty.

' Gentlemen, I have read and have meditated as much upon these topics as most men of the present age, and I will venture to assert, with the most perfect confidence, that the history of nations, whether ancient or modern, furnishes no example of any government which so effectually provides for and secures these two great objects as the Government of these realms. I put aside all theories of the constitution as set forth by writers,—they are vain, and have sometimes led to mischief ; but I desire to point out to your consideration those matters which form the practice and habits of our social union, and which I am sure you will recognise, though they are not noticed, much less made the subject of panegyric, by any theoretical writer. I say, then, that under the forms of a limited monarchy, limited by the very institutions which support it, the people of this country have enjoyed greater practical liberty of person and security for property than were ever afforded by any republic whatever. In effect, the constitution of this country may be considered as formed of a number of small republics, gradually increasing in extent and importance till they are combined under the great authorities of the State, at the head of which the monarch is placed. By the action and reaction of these upon each other, the force of the democracy on the one hand, and of the monarch on the other, either of which, if unchecked in its progress, would, like a mighty torrent, overwhelm the land, is broken into a number of small and circuitous channels, which whilst they refresh and invigorate the soil, cannot waste or destroy it. Look for example to a parish, where all matters of local interest are governed by a vestry consisting of the inhabitants. They repair their own roads; they provide for their own poor; for their clergyman; appoint their own officers; and, in general, without any interference of the Government, have the superintendence of all their own local interests. From a parish, ascend to the divisions of a county, where the inhabitants are assembled four times a year, at quarter sessions, for the purpose of taking part in the administration of justice—the grand juries are formed of the people of that district—so the petty juries—presided over by the gentlemen who act as justices of the peace. These, you see, are instances of the administration of justice, the most important function of a Government, in the hands of the people themselves. Again, if you ascend to the counties at large, twice in the year are assembled the principal gentlemen of the county, to meet the judges, and to render the most important assistance in the administration of justice. No man can be put upon his trial for any offence without their previous sanction, after a full inquiry by themselves into the circumstances of his case; nor can he be finally condemned without the intervention of another jury assembled at the same place and time, consisting of his equals, and who have no interest or wish but to do impartial justice: add to this the exercise and superintendence of the general police of the county by the principal gentlemen in rank, station, and property, who perform the important duties of magistrates, without pay, and without intervention of the Government, except when they find occasion to seek advice or assistance. Finally, the Parliament, formed by the representatives of the people, the hereditary Nobility, the heads of the Church, and the Crown—without the concurrence of all which estates no law can be made and no tax imposed.

'Thus the people are in a constant state of healthy agitation in the performance of all those functions which in other states are generally vested exclusively in the Government. The result of all this has been the security of property, the encouragement of industry, the advancement of prosperity, with a greater degree of personal and individual liberty than was ever enjoyed by any other people.

'Gentlemen, this is not the work of any theory; our usages have grown up by time, been improved by experience, and have become grafted into the habits and affections of the people. I agree with the great statesman of the last age, Mr. Edmund Burke, who says there is no such thing as liberty in the abstract. It cannot result from a single law, nor even from the will of the people. It must be bound up with and form part of the customs and usages which distinguish one nation from another. The liberty of an Englishman, therefore, is English liberty. No true Englishman can be attached to any other sort of liberty. The most perfect system of laws in theory, as well as the most perfect forms of Government which the philosopher can devise, are of no force, unless they have been rendered by usage congenial to the feelings and manners of the people. " *Quid leges sine moribus !* " says the poet, who speaks only the language of truth in saying that laws avail nothing unless founded upon the habits and usages of a nation.

'Gentlemen, entertaining these opinions, I cannot do better on this occasion than borrow from Her Majesty's proclamation which has just been read to you, the precept which she has thereby commanded me as one of her judges to inculcate, which is, that I should exhort you to follow that example which Her Majesty informs you she is determined to set to her people, of discountenancing all vice, immorality, and impiety, and generally all those persons who by their conduct and character are disturbers of the public peace; and on the other hand to give countenance and encouragement to those only who show by their conduct a disposition to fulfil the duties of religion and support the authority of the law.

Indeed, I will venture to say that if every gentleman would strictly adhere in his own sphere, and within the circle of his own influence, to the injunctions contained in Her Majesty's proclamation, the necessity for providing gaols and new systems of prison discipline would be greatly diminished.

'Gentlemen, I have been induced to address these topics to you because I cannot but feel that under the circumstances in which we are placed our chief reliance for the preservation of all our happy institutions depends upon the spirit, the zeal, and the energy of the gentry of England in animating, and by their example encouraging that part of the population which is well affected to resist the machinations and the violence of those who have declared war against their country.'

CHESHIRE SPECIAL COMMISSION, 1842.

'GENTLEMEN OF THE GRAND JURY,—You are assembled at this unusual season to discharge a very painful, but a very important duty. A due regard for the public safety makes it essential that all tumultuous and unlawful assemblies of the people should be put down by force, if necessary, and punished with the utmost rigour of the law. At the same time we cannot reflect on the occurrences which have recently taken place in the manufacturing districts without mixed emotions of compassion, and, if I may say so, indignation : compassion for the weakness and ignorance of those deluded multitudes who imagined they could effect the purposes they had in view by force and violence, and who, as they never fail to do, must become the victims of their own delusion, and suffer misery and privation, and many of them punishment ; indignation at the artful contrivances of those who, to serve their own private objects and their own political ends, promoted and excited the delusion of the industrious classes, by addressing to their minds deceitful arguments, unfounded in reason or in sense, and then endeavoured to take advantage of the delusion they had caused, in order that they might thereby carry into effect their own objects.

'I need hardly remind you that it is one of the evils incident to a nation of great manufacturing and commercial prosperity, that it should occasionally be subject to great reverses. It is the nature and habit of industry and enterprise, to keep full the channels of supply, sometimes to overflowing ; and whenever a check to the demand occurs, there must follow for a while a suspension of employment, a diminution in the price of manufactured produce and in the wages of labour, and very often, unhappily, distress and misery of the manufacturing classes. The history of our own country furnishes examples of this kind. A bad harvest either at home or abroad ; the blockade of foreign ports with which we are accustomed to traffic ; a war with a nation which takes a large quantity of our manufactured goods ; the disturbance of friendly relations between this and other nations, with which we have commercial intercourse ; the uncertainty of the laws which affect trade and commerce ; sometimes the public agitation of the great questions or principles on which commerce depends ; sometimes even the opinion that the Government is not wise enough to propose nor strong enough to carry important measures for the maintenance and advancement of the public weal : all these are circumstances which tend to paralyse industry and the enterprise of commercial men; and at the same time to suspend all those advantages which the country was before gaining from a prosperous condition of trade and commerce. It would be easy, if necessary, to trace many, if not all, of these causes which have in succession or combination produced that distress we have lately witnessed.

'I stated just now that we cannot view without emotions of compassion the situation of the industrious classes, who, not having a competent knowledge to form a judgment of their own as to the principles or the rights of property, or upon the questions in which their own prosperity is involved, imagine that they can by force and violence dictate terms to their masters, and thereby rescue themselves from a degree of privation and discomfort, against which no government, however it might be formed, and no law, whatever might be its provisions, could effectually secure them. Nevertheless you will find many in that situation of life to which I have just alluded, and with that infirmity of judgment which I have just described, whose passions are most easily inflamed when subjects are touched on relating to their own means of subsistence, and their state of discomfort, induced by crafty persons, who excite and mislead them, to imagine that they are themselves the fittest persons to govern, and that they ought to have an equal, if not a superior share, in the conduct of the government and in the making of laws. I am afraid that the manufacturing classes have been of late the dupes of this sort of persuasion; and you will find in the occurrences which have called you together, sundry examples of this delusion. You will find that there is a society of persons who go by the name of Chartists, and who, if they have not excited or fomented those outrages which will be brought under your notice, have nevertheless taken advantage of them for their own purposes, have endeavoured to prevent the unfortunate people from returning to their work, and sought so to direct them that they might, by the suspension of all labour, be conducive to the attainment of political objects. And what is the object of the Charter which these men are seeking? What are the points of the Charter? Annual Parliaments, universal suffrage, and vote by ballot. Yes, gentlemen, you will find by the evidence which will be produced before you, that it has been inculcated upon many misguided persons that the sovereign remedy for all abuses, and the only means of putting themselves in possession of such a share of power as would enable them to vindicate their own rights, and secure themselves against oppression, is by the enactment of what they call the People's Charter.

' In what a strange situation this country would be placed, if those who had no property were to possess a preponderating voice in the making of the laws! These unhappy men do not consider that the first objects of civilised society are the establishment and preservation of property, and the security of person. What, then, would be the state of any country, if multitudes were to make the laws for regulating property, or were permitted to employ physical force to restrain individuals from employing their own labour, according to their own judgment, for procuring their subsistence? The foundations of civilised society may be considered to consist in the protection of property and the security of person; and if these two objects were abandoned, society must be dissolved.

N

What a strange effect, then, would the establishment of a system of universal suffrage produce; for under it every man, though possessing no property, would have a voice in the choice of the representation of the people ! The necessary consequences of this system would be, that those who have no property would make laws for those who have property, and the destruction of the monarchy and aristocracy must necessarily ensue.

'I do not pretend to judge the motives of those individuals who entertain such views as I have been alluding to, but they seem to forget that it is impossible to establish a perfectly democratic representative assembly, in the formation of which every man in the country should have a voice, without eventually destroying the monarchy and the influence of property, and leading to the creation of a form of government which would become in the end an odious tyranny. Such is the history of all attempts to establish a democracy in countries where a government consisting of mixed elements formerly existed.

'There is a country which cannot be spoken of without respect and attachment, as emanating from ourselves, I allude to America, from which you may collect what security for property is afforded by a pure republic. In the different states of America there are pure democratic associations elected by universal suffrage and vote by ballot ; and some of these states have recently exhibited the regard paid to property by democratic assemblies, by having protested against paying the public creditor, and disregarded their own obligation to obey their own law made for his security. If such a system of democracy were established in England, the first consequence would be, that the security of property would be removed ; the public creditor and all commercial accumulations would be destroyed ; and, finally, if it were not the first object aimed at, would follow the destruction of property in land. There would be an universal agrarian law. The formation of such a government in a country like this must work universal ruin and distress ; and after inflicting the most bitter of all tyranny, that of a democratic assembly, would terminate in a despotism. But it appears that persons entertaining a design to establish such a form of government have taken advantage of an occasional depression of the commerce and manufactures of the country, and the privations which the labouring classes are suffering, for the purpose of encouraging them to resist their masters, and to abstain from labour, telling them that this was the only means within their reach, by which they could obtain the accomplishment of their favourite charter. I am glad to be informed, gentlemen, that on some portions of the multitudes to which such topics were addressed, they failed to have any effect. There was a certain feeling of common sense, and a remaining attachment to the institutions of the country, which forbade many to listen to the voice of these Chartists. Nevertheless, gentlemen, you will find by the evidence which will be produced before you, that great pains were taken to inculcate these doctrines on the minds of the people and to encourage them by the force which belongs to assembled multitudes to carry them into effect. In the cases which will come before you, gentlemen, you may find persons preaching these doctrines. I am desirous not to be understood as stating that the mere holding of any abstract opinion on political subjects is an offence ; but if those persons who entertain such doctrines as I have alluded to endeavour to enforce them by popular tumult, they must be guilty of a grave offence. If you should find, too, cases satisfactorily proved, where persons have used efforts to prevail on the labouring people not to return to work, or have resorted to measures of tumult and disorder in order to carry into effect their favourite objects, there can be no doubt that such persons are justly liable to punishment ; and you, gentlemen, will doubtless feel it due to your country to bring them before this Court.

' There is another class of offenders who will be brought before you, namely, those who joined in assemblies of the people, the object of which was by force to turn others out of employment, or prevent them from continuing at work. This is a species of tyranny quite intolerable. What right has any man to dictate to another at what price he should labour? If the party who labours, or the party employing, is dissatisfied with the terms of the contract, they have nothing to do but to put an end to the contract. I am afraid, for I believe the law has been altered in this respect, that even the combination of a number of workmen for the purpose of dictating terms to masters has ceased to be an indictable offence in itself. But, though this is not an indictable offence, so long as the combination be conducted in a peaceable and quiet manner, yet if they attempt to force others to join them by terror or intimidation, they are guilty of one of the most daring and outrageous acts of tyranny.

'What would be said if a government differently constituted from our own, and acting by direct force on the people, if the powers of such a government were exercised in a similar manner, in order that the workmen might not continue at their labour? Would it not be described as an insupportable tyranny, and as forming a just ground for insurrection? Yet you will find that these unhappy men were not content with exercising the privileges which the law allowed them, of agreeing amongst themselves not to work without a certain rate of remuneration, but they attempted by force to compel others to quit their labour. When a case of this kind comes before you, gentlemen; when you find attempts made by tumult, riot, and force, to detach the labourer from his occupation, you will consider them offences of an aggravated character, and in such cases I would recommend you to find the bills.

'The third class of offences is in its nature not so aggravated, and yet is not to be passed over, namely, where persons have joined in a tumultuous crowd, engaged in some illegal design. You may say, and justly, that though a vast number of persons might assemble together, a few only might be engaged in any criminal design. Still, as the criminal design could only be effected by the terror which a multitude inspires, any man who joins the mob, becomes one of the persons countenancing and furthering the illegal end. If, therefore, a crowd tumultuously collect together, creating alarm to the neighbourhood in which it assembles, and assuming a character dangerous to the public peace, every person who joins it becomes an implicated party, and is by law guilty of riot, though the party accused may have done nothing more than merely brought to the mob the sanction of his personal presence. I do not mean to say that a man might not be in a mob innocently; for a person going home might find it necessary to pass by the place where the mob was assembled, or he might go into the mob for the purpose of inducing another not to join it, or to prevent excess. There might be innocent motives which brought a man in the midst of a mob ; but as by his presence he increased the multitude, the amount of which occasioned terror, it lies upon him to prove his innocence, and to show whether his presence there was voluntary or otherwise. I mention this as a case of simple riot ; and if you find persons joining assemblies which had illegal objects in view, or which conducted themselves in a tumultuous and riotous manner, you must bring them before this Court ; for if they have any excuse which may operate in their defence, they have no means of producing it before you. The finding of a true bill against them will be justified by the evidence of a *primâ facie* case against them ; and if that case be proved against them, the *onus probandi* as to their innocence will afterwards be thrown upon them.

'From the information laid before me, I believe that I have now described the general character of the cases which will be submitted to your consideration ; but there are two other cases which I ought to mention. I have stated that where a crowd assembled and acted illegally, those facts determined the character of the assembly to be unlawful. You will find that in some cases attempts have been made to extort money or provisions, and whenever the parties so acting have succeeded in their design through the aid of terror and force, they have been guilty of the offence of robbery. This will probably form a class of the cases which will come before you. Gentlemen, you are aware that if any assembly of persons begin to demolish and pull down any building, that act constitutes a felony. Whether any cases amounting to this offence will come before you, I am not sufficiently informed to say, but I have reason to think that some of the cases may take that shape. All the different classes of offences which I have mentioned will probably come under your consideration. If you find any persons fomenting disturbance, or endeavouring to work out their own particular views by creating a suspension of labour, ruinous not only to the parties themselves, but also to the country, and by forcibly compelling others to cease labour, they are liable to heavy punishment. If you find others seeking to obtain by intimidation money or provisions, or engaged in pulling down buildings, these offenders would come under a different class, but they would deserve your serious attention. I believe I have now described the character of the different offences, and I am not aware that I could add anything which might direct your inquiries. Still I shall be very happy to give you, if needful, every assistance in my power to facilitate your investigations. Nevertheless, I do not think it probable that gentlemen of your experience and knowledge will require any further information.

'I cannot conclude without repeating my expression of compassion for the unhappy people who have acted under the delusion I have referred to. But, gentlemen, the law takes no account of such delusions ; and if a man commits guilty acts, he must be prepared to submit to the consequences of his conduct. It is true that the poorer classes of the country have been suffering from great privations ; and I may allude to this subject, as it is matter of notoriety, and has formed matter of public discussion ; but it is very singular that the time chosen to break out was a period when a more settled commercial policy had been adopted, when every person expected a revival of manufacturing prosperity, and when, I believe, every person felt there was existing a salient point from which commercial prosperity might take its start. It is singular that this should be the moment chosen to foment these disturbances ; and the country has suffered in consequence a suspension of that prosperity which might confidently have been anticipated, and of which, I trust, it is not too late to hope for the return.'

LANCASHIRE SPECIAL COMMISSION, 1842.

'GENTLEMEN OF THE GRAND JURY,—It is with unaffected pain that I address you on the present occasion. You are aware of the disastrous state to which this great country was reduced for several weeks of the present summer. You are aware that lawless and riotous multitudes of persons assembled in various manufacturing towns of the county have proceeded to create disturbances and excite terror and alarm in the minds of Her Majesty's peaceable subjects, and have by violence prevented workmen from following their daily occupations. It is impossible that such a course of lawless violence could long endure; indeed, it would itself perish by its own infirmity, but along with it, if not speedily checked, must perish the industry and prosperity of the working classes. It becomes, therefore, the duty of the Government to put down such unlawful and tumultuous assemblies, to preserve the peace and property of the subjects of the realm, and to punish by the rigour of the law all persons engaged in these unlawful offences.

' You are aware, gentlemen, that occasional reverses in the tide of prosperity in a manufacturing and commercial nation must occur, and that when they occur they must produce, to a greater or less extent, much distress and privation among the labouring classes. I presume that the state of the country for some months, if not for some years back, may be traced to some of these checks in the tide of commercial and manufacturing prosperity.

' Much has been said of the privations to which the working classes have been reduced, and I make no doubt that they are considerable ; for it cannot be denied that many of the usual channels of trade have been interrupted, and that there was existing a general feeling of despondency among commercial men as to the advantage of engaging in commercial enterprises, the result of which was attended with great uncertainty; but I am bound to say from the experience I have acquired as to the history of this insurrection in a neighbouring county, that that distress has been greatly exaggerated. It does not appear from any evidence which I have hitherto seen or read, that the parties engaged in these excesses either complained of the high price of provisions, or the wages of labour.

' What gave rise to the immediate occurrence which was the commencement of these transactions has not at present been ascertained. Whether it was owing to the imprudence or indiscretion of any master manufacturers, whether it originated in the schemes of any persons, who considered that a general turn-out would tend to the advancement of their own political objects, or whether, when the disturbances commenced they were not checked so early as might have been done by greater activity on the part of the magistrates,— all these are circumstances at present left in obscurity, and which can be developed by time alone. But it is certain from the information to which I have referred, that the insurrection of the labouring classes does not seem to have originated in any spontaneous feeling (if I may so express myself) respecting their privations or the high price of provisions. They all seemed to be sensible that the rate of wages in this country must depend on the price of provisions ; and I think it is evident that they thought that those who promised them an increase of wages by a diminution of the price of corn were not persons to be trusted. It appears certain, however, that when once these riots began, when the people were formed into bodies to turn out by force industrious men pursuing their occupations in other places, there did arise a disposition among many persons, and those possessing considerable power and some talent, to make use of this insurrection, to foment, perpetuate it, and direct it to political objects.

'It seems that a society of persons, who are recognised by the title of Chartists, mixed themselves up with the unhappy class of the community who were deluded into this sort of insurrection ; and having more intelligence than they, but deeper designs, instead of employing that intelligence to point out to their unhappy victims the delusion under which they were acting, to show them that all attempts of workmen to rise against their masters and to dictate the rate of wages have terminated, must and ever will terminate, in the distress of the workmen themselves, instead of telling the persons engaged in these disturbances that their conduct would probably make their condition worse, have endeavoured to persuade them that the true remedy for all their grievances was the adoption of what they call the Charter, which appears to be principally aimed at a larger reform of Parliament than has already been adopted ; and in defiance of the promises, and no doubt the sincere hopes, of those eminent persons who introduced and carried the late reform of Parliament, that it was to be a final, efficacious, and satisfactory measure of reform ; these infatuated persons, for they also must be infatuated, have formed an opinion, grounded on what foundations I know not, that a representation created by universal suffrage and vote by ballot, together with the payment of wages to members of Parliament, would be a panacea for all evils, and endeavoured to inculcate these doctrines on the assembled multitudes they addressed, and to persuade them that to perpetuate the insurrection against their masters, and to make it universal, was the best means of getting the Charter. They mixed up with their orations many affected recommendations to peace and order; but, gentlemen, you will find these recommendations always accompanied by false and exaggerated statements of the general feeling of the country. The people were told that all England was in arms; that Scotland was pouring forth hundreds of thousands of men; that Ireland was coming to the battle; and that the men of Birmingham, to the number of 100,000, armed with steel, and fearless of the force of the military, were ready to join them and carry the day. These are circumstances which plainly show that these parties endeavoured to delude the multitudes they addressed with the notion that their force was becoming irresistible, and that they might effect their objects, by alarming the Legislature, or by imposing restraint even on the Sovereign.

'I must say, gentlemen, if these conspiracies, having such purposes in view, had been made the subject of prosecutions for high treason, the consequences might have been serious, indeed, to the parties concerned. I am at a loss to know what distinction there is between a conspiracy to subvert the Government, and impose force and restraint on all the branches of the Legislature, on purpose to have a particular measure passed into law, and the crime of high treason. By the ancient law of this country, the crime of high treason is technically limited to imagining or compassing the death of the Sovereign, or to levying war on the Sovereign; but the judges have, from the earliest times, considered that a conspiracy to levy war, and to employ force to restrain the will of the Sovereign, an overt act of high treason; and, if satisfactorily proved, sufficient to justify a jury, when combined with the intention of really imposing restraint on the Sovereign, in finding it to be high treason. I do not understand that the Government intend to push the indictments to that extent, and these people owe it to the lenity of the Government that they are not placed in a position hazardous to their lives.

'Gentlemen, you will have laid before you indictments for conspiracies to excite the people to insurrection; to endeavour to prevail on those who were not at work to continue the state of suspended labour; to compel those at work to quit their avocations, and to persevere in a lawless course of violence, until their favourite Charter should be carried. If bills of this kind shall be laid before you, gentlemen, and you feel satisfied by the evidence adduced, that though the great mass of the people might not actually have been disposed to take part in conspiracies to effect that object, yet there were persons among them who were active instruments in persuading them so to act, you will be justified in finding the charge of conspiracy against these parties. But, independent of this charge, you may find other cases of conspiracy to prevent the working classes performing their labour; in other words, to turn out the workmen from the different mills, and by the force of terror and intimidation to compel not only the workmen in mills, but every class of labourers, navigators, workmen in canals, hatters, &c., to quit their employment, in order that they might assist in the grand scheme of obtaining the Charter.

'A conspiracy for the purpose of turning out workmen, and the agreeing together to effect that purpose, are in themselves criminal; and if such cases shall be brought before you and the parties indicted are satisfactorily proved to have participated in the acts I have described, they are by the law of the land guilty of the crime of conspiracy, and you will be justified in putting them on their trial. Another class of offences, which, though not equal in magnitude to those I have just referred to, is yet very dangerous, and must be punished when satisfactorily proved, is that of simple riot. An unlawful assembly is an assembly collected together for some illegal object; and in case it exhibits by its acts and conduct some improper design, or excites alarm among the well-disposed subjects of the Queen, it is a riotous assembly; and all persons forming part of such assemblies, and countenancing by their presence their objects, must be taken, unless they can show that they were present innocently and honestly, as participators in a misdemeanour.

'A greal deal has been said at different times, as to what should be considered an unlawful assembly; and, I am sorry to say, that what has taken place in this county has given rise to discussion on the point, both in courts of law and in Parliament. But one thing is clear, that an assembly consisting of such multitudes as to make all discussion and debate ridiculous and a farce never can be assembled for the purpose of deliberate and calm discussion. Will any person in his senses say that when a man assembles together 3,000 or 4,000 individuals, he does so to form a deliberate assembly, to discuss speculative points either of law or government? Such a profession would carry with it its own refutation? If, therefore, an assembly consist of such multitudes as to render all notion of serious debate impossible; or if you find that at such an assembly all attempts at debate are put down, and that the only object of the parties is to hear one side, the meeting ceases to be an assembly for deliberation, and cannot protect itself under that pretension. Again, assemblies of such magnitude, without a president, or any one empowered and able to restrain and dissolve them, must lead, as every one will see, to alarm and terror, and to the disturbance of the peace. Such assemblies are in themselves unlawful; and if their conduct occasions a breach of the peace, they are riotous. If you, gentlemen, find individuals among those assemblies who, by their conduct, manifest intentions of violence and mischief, and proceed to the extent of committing outrages on property, and preventing the free employment of labour, those men are rioters in the worse sense of the word. It will be your duty to find bills against all persons proved to be concerned in such proceedings.

'I believe, gentlemen, you will have laid before you some cases of violent and inflammatory speeches. Of course you will exercise your own judgment as to whether the speeches made the subject of charge were uttered with a view of inflaming the people, and of a nature to produce disturbance. It is for you to say whether the speeches had a tendency to excite sedition, disaffection, and insurrection; and, if you think so, I have no doubt you will feel it to be your duty to put the parties on trial.

'There is another case, I understand, likely to come before you, namely, the charge of publishing a seditious libel. Whether or not it will come before you I am not certain; but I am informed that it will, and if so, you will have an opportunity of seeing what the libel is. It purports to be an exhortation from the Council of the Chartists to all the labouring classes to continue in the state of suspended labour till the Charter is carried. It professes peace and order, but it reminds the people that they were governed by laws to which they were not parties, and endeavours to persuade those who read it that they can obtain no real security for their rights, or protection for their labour, except by means of an organic change in the constitution of the country. You will form your own judgment of this paper. I have had an opportunity of seeing it, and I must say that the impression made on my mind is, that the paper is full of danger, and that at the particular season when it was published it might have tended to consequences very different from what such a document would produce if published at an ordinary time; for when a paper of this kind is addressed to multitudes already assembled in a lawless manner, with their passions excited, and with an opinion that their force is sufficient to carry their object, you can easily conclude that such an exhortation, made at such a time, would be far more dangerous, and therefore far more criminal, than if published under ordinary circumstances. It seems that the statement made in this paper, and made use of by many who addressed the assembled multitudes, is, that they wished to procure "a fair day's wages for a fair day's labour;" and they argue that nothing will ensure this result, except the giving to the labouring population an equal, if not a preponderating, voice in the Legislature of the country. For this purpose they propose those changes which I have before referred to, the adoption of the principles of the Charter; that is to say, they desire that the labouring classes, who have no property should make laws for those who have property; that the labouring classes, who have shown by their recent conduct that they will exercise a tyranny over their fellow-labourers, should make laws for the protection of labour. These persons never take into consideration that the very object of law and civilised society is the protection of property from the outrages of one or more individuals, and the protection of person from the violence of those who attack it. They show by the example of their own conduct, by the violation of the law by which they live, how little calculated they are to compose a Legislature like that which they aim at as the result of the Charter. The consequence of the success of their endeavours would be, not a reform of Parliament, but a subversion of the Government; because everybody who reflects on such things, knows that the establishment of any popular assembly entirely devoted to democratic principles, and elected by persons the vast majority of whom possess no property, but live by means of manual labour, would be inconsistent with the existence of the monarchy and the aristocracy. Its first aim would be the destruction of property and the overthrow of the throne, and the result would be the creation of a tyranny so intolerable, that the very persons who assisted in establishing it would be the first to put it down; and out of the confusion which would ensue, would possibly result a military despotism.

'You will excuse me for using this language to gentlemen of your description; but I cannot help expressing my deep concern, that some of the persons who propagate these doctrines appear to have talent enough to know the consequences to which they must lead, and yet persevere in attempting to delude the people for some private objects of their own, perhaps in the hope of acquiring some consequence for themselves, or actuated by malice against the success of those who have left them at a distance in the competition of honourable industry.

'Who can say, in the county of Lancaster, that labour wants protection from the law; that working men, even of the lowest description, if they possess diligence, talents, and application, may not arrive at the highest honours of the state? How many examples are there of persons who, in a class of society not superior to many of those who form the objects of the present prosecutions, have acquired by their talents and frugality, fortunes, honours, and distinctions, under the fair fabric of the British constitution, which these unhappy men are desirous to destroy, a constitution the only one in the world which, as is known from repeated examples, properly protects labour; which gives the poor man, if his talents are but exercised with diligence, sense, and frugality, an opportunity of rising to independence and fortune? And yet there are individuals reckless enough to hazard all that they enjoy under such a constitution, and claim that labourers should have a greater influence than heretofore in the formation of the law.

'Gentlemen, by the law of England labour is protected. Labour is the commodity of the poor man, and ought to be protected; and I believe that the law of England is so framed, that it furnishes a remedy against any oppression on the part of the master towards the labourer. The law does not restrain any man from quitting his master at the termination of his contract, if he feels dissatisfied with his wages, or with the mode of conducting his employment; but leaves him at perfect liberty to make such engagements as he thinks fit, and to quit his employment when the term of his labour is at an end. Therefore there is no restraint by law on labour. But if the object of these parties is to put a restraint on the masters, and to make laws for the employment of capital, to what a state, if this purpose were accomplished, would those who possess capital be reduced! If the holders of capital are not to be allowed to employ it according to their own judgment, and according to the information they receive as to the state of the foreign and home markets, and various other matters, but are to be compelled to lay it out according to the limited views which the labourers take of their own interests, this would at once destroy capital which employs labour, and the result would be, when capital should be destroyed, that all would be reduced to an equality, and become labourers. What would the unhappy labourers gain by this state of things? The market for labour is, like other markets, supplied cheaper when an abundance exists; and if all men should be reduced to the state of labourers, what would be the price of labour? I fear very trifling indeed. Therefore the delusion on which these men have acted, when once explained is very obvious, and I am surprised that men of common sense should be so deceived; but there is reason to fear that some of those who inculcate these doctrines on the industrious classes are themselves conscious of the mischief which must ensue from their accomplishment; and if they should be detected, they deserve condign punishment.

'Gentlemen, I will not detain you longer; the bills will be immediately laid before you, and you will find them of the character I have described.'

I was much diverted on another occasion during the Midland Circuit, whilst he was acting as Criminal Judge at Warwick.

I must preface the story by observing 'that there was formerly a great diversity of intellect amongst gentlemen of the common jury, especially in Warwickshire, or perhaps at that time thick heads were more common there than elsewhere. A ruffian was in the dock charged with a theft. The counsel for the prosecution made a very short story of it. The man in broad daylight entered a shop in Warwick, and was seen by a shopboy to unfasten a coat from a peg and run down the street with it. The shopboy followed him in a moment, found him in possession of the coat, and gave him in charge to the police. This was the case. The Chief Baron turned to the jury and said, 'Gentlemen, the story is so clear I need not trouble you with summing up. You may retire and consider your verdict. After ten minutes absence the foreman appeared with his colleagues and said, 'My Lord, we say he is not guilty.' My father then turned to the prisoner and said, ' Prisoner, take care not to place yourself in the dock again for a similar offence; you may not always be so fortunate as to find a Warwickshire jury to try you. You may go, but remember.'

My father, soon after he became Chief Baron, was grievously affected with a complaint near the right eye, for which malady he was attended chiefly by Bransby Cooper. He wore a large shade over the eye, and on account of his health now seldom attended the House of Lords or entered into general society.

He was, nevertheless, as assiduous as ever in all his legal duties, and never a day absent from the Court of Exchequer,

over which he presided for the transaction of business. At
that time too the Court of Exchequer had an Equity Jurisdiction, which made its proceedings additionally onerous.
This sort of business, less interesting than a Nisi Pius Court
to the public, was of special interest to the Chief Baron, who
had not forgotten his early studies in Equity law, and liked
to apply the acuteness of his mind particularly to that subject ;
and his decisions, I believe, generally gave great satisfaction.

I may mention here, in reference to a subject in which
my father took great interest, that after my return from
South America, I published with some notes I had taken of
my rapid journey, a project for the establishment of a Steam
Navigation Company in the Pacific. Whilst in Valparaiso,
I made the acquaintance of Mr. William Wheelwright, of
the United States. He had made this scheme his particular
study, and the advantage of steam navigation in the voyage
going South from Panama, in the teeth of a strong head
wind, were so obvious that no one could doubt its success.
In consequence I promised to use my humble efforts to second
his views. On my return to England, my father appeared
equally struck with the advantage of steam for this voyage,
so ably advocated by Mr. Wheelwright. A Company was
formed under this gentleman's auspices, for which my father
assisted in obtaining a Royal Charter. By dint of perseverance, great impediments and difficulties were removed.
The Spanish authorities on the Pacific Coast granted a
right of monopoly for a given number of years, and the
Company became very successful, both as a means of
transport and as a remunerative undertaking. It has since
greatly extended the field of its operations, and has become
most flourishing. To the end of his life, Mr. Wheelwright
gratefully acknowledged my father's assistance, and was
pleased to associate my name also with his good fortune,
ascribing it to our joint intervention.

CHAPTER XXXII.

ANECDOTES—REMARKS ON SIR JAMES MACKINTOSH.

I HAVE it on Lord Chelmsford's authority that the Duke of Wellington said of my father: 'When Scarlett is addressing a jury there are thirteen jurymen.' This is both characteristic of the influence he exercised when addressing juries and of the Duke's terse manner of expressing himself.

His amiable character in private life is thus referred to in Adolphus's recollections. He says: 'On the circuit I dined with him at Abinger, a very beautiful country seat, near Guildford. He was surrounded with grandchildren, and a most interesting sight it was to see those little creatures climbing on his knees and shoulders to share his caresses. Their innocent and interesting looks, with his fine and beautiful countenance and benignant smile, produced an effect which, without exaggeration, might be termed sublime.'

I will not vouch for the accuracy of the following anecdote in detail, but give it as I received it at second hand.

Mr. Justice Patteson related the following story of my father's dexterity in the conduct of a cause, the ends of justice being attained by a theatrical display of incredulity which deceived both Brougham and Parke, the counsel on the other side. My father with Patteson as junior counsel were for the defendant. He told Patteson that he would manage to make Brougham produce in evidence a written instrument the withholding of which, on account of the insufficiency of the stamp was essential for the success of his case. That on Patteson observing that even if he could throw Brougham off his guard he would not be so successful with Parke, my father answered that he would try. And

o

he then conducted the case with such consummate dexterity, pretending to disbelieve the existence of the document referred to, that Brougham and Parke resolved to produce it, not being aware that my father had any suspicion of its invalidity. Patteson described the air of extreme surprise and mortification of my father on its production by Brougham, with a flourish of trumpets about the 'non-existence of which document his learned friend had reckoned on so confidently.' Patteson went on to say that the way in which my father asked to look at the instrument and his assumed astonishment at the discovery of the insufficiency of the stamp were a masterpiece of acting.

I am indebted to my friend and neighbour, Mr. Evelyn, of Wotton, for an anecdote relating to my father. It is as follows :—

'I remember my late uncle, Mr. Francis Massey Dawson, speaking of Mr. Scarlett as a barrister. My uncle was also a barrister, and used to be on the same circuit with Scarlett.

'Mr. Dawson corroborated the universal testimony in regard to the marvellous power of Mr. Scarlett in conciliating juries; that he used to catch the eye of a particular juryman, and speak as if he and the jury were on the best of terms and were ill-used by the rest of the world. Unfortunately I have forgotten most of the anecdotes related by Mr. Dawson.

'On one occasion an action was brought for the abatement of a nuisance, and Mr. Scarlett was employed for the defence. He began his cross-examination of a lady, the plaintiff's witness, by enquiring tenderly about her domestic relations, her children, their illnesses. The lady became confidential, and appeared flattered by the kind interest taken in her. The judge interfered with a remark about the irrelevancy of this. Mr. Scarlett begged to be allowed to proceed, and on the conclusion of the cross-examination he said, "My Lord, that is my case." He had shown, on the witness's testimony, that she had brought up a numerous and healthy progeny in the vicinity of the alleged nuisance.

'The jury, amused as well as convinced, gave a verdict for the defendant.'

The next anecdote was sent to me by a lady :—

Sir Walter Scott promised a friend that he would write a book for his benefit. The friend died before the promise was fulfilled, and his executors insisted that Sir Walter should write a book for the benefit of the widow and children of the deceased. This Sir Walter refused to do. The executors sought the advice of Mr. Scarlett, who having listened to their case, said : ' Let us suppose the position to be reversed ; if Sir Walter Scott had died, should you have required his executors to write a book for the benefit of your clients ?' 'Oh, no!' exclaimed the executors, convinced at once that they had no case against Sir Walter Scott.

Amongst my father's papers I have found the *brouillon* of a letter he sent to Mr. Mackintosh, when the latter was writing the life of Sir James Mackintosh, his father. As it contains some remarks illustrative of the character of that distinguished man, it may not be out of place to mention them in this memoir. The whole letter *in extenso* will be found already published in Sir James Mackintosh's Life. I will therefore only extract a portion of the letter.

When I was a very young man I accompanied my father to Ware, on our way down to the North of England, not to see the famous bed of Ware, but to breakfast with Sir James Mackintosh, who resided near that town. His agreeable and amiable manners I recollect made an impression upon me at that time, and I had frequent opportunities in after years of listening to his conversation. The breakfast on that occasion was rendered more remarkable by the presence of Lord John Russell then a distinguished member of Parliament and a rising politician.

SIR JAMES MACKINTOSH.

' In the more unmixed circles of his society almost every subject of letters and metaphysics was freely discussed, and in every discussion Mackintosh bore an eminent part, not only for knowledge and acuteness, but for a spirit of candour and a love of truth which were ever in him paramount to the desire of victory. His learning, various and extensive, was not confined to ancient authors, or those of the English language, in which he was deeply read, but embraced a great portion of foreign literature, more especially German and French. With the latter he was particularly conversant, and enjoyed amongst the philosophers and men of letters of that nation a distinguished reputation. His facility in the French language was proved by a remarkable instance before he went to India. A cause between two Frenchmen had been referred to arbitration. He was counsel for the plaintiff. The defendant, a noble emigrant, pleaded his own cause in person. When the parties were assembled before the arbitrators the defendant complained of the hardship to which he was exposed from his imperfect knowledge of English when he had to combat a gentleman of such extraordinary talents as appeared for his opponent. Mr. Mackintosh, to accommodate him, without further preparation made his speech and conducted the whole controversy in French with a facility and elegance that were applauded by all who heard him.

' The author whom he always appeared to me to prefer above all others, was Cicero. He was familiar with every par. of his writings, and retained in his memory most of the passages which he thought distinguished by any peculiar merit. He considered him the greatest master of morals and philosophy, and his works the most universal magazine of wisdom and eloquence. He thought that if Demosthenes equalled him in force and vehemence of passion, he was far from approaching him in variety, grace, urbanity, imagination, or knowledge. The delight he took in this author, if we may trust the judgment of Quintilian, proved the perfection of his taste—" Ille se profecisse sciat cui Cicero valde placebit."

' He had chosen the Norfolk circuit, which did not offer a very extensive field to his exertions. His progress in the profession of the law, at his commencement, was not equal to his just pretensions. He was desirous of devoting a portion of his time and abundant knowledge to giving public lectures on the law of nature and nations. For this purpose he applied to the Society of Lincoln's Inn for the use of their Hall. Here, again, he was encountered by political prejudice. Difficulties were suggested and objections urged of a formal nature against such an appropriation of the Hall. But the real objection was the apprehension of the doctrines he might teach.   Mr. Perceval once more became his friend, and used his influence with such of the Benchers as were known to him, to set them right and subdue their scruples.   While the negotiation was depending, however, he composed the preliminary lecture: a sort of prospectus of the whole design and of the principles of the lecturer.   Having submitted the manuscript to some of his most intimate friends, he was advised to publish it without delay as the best means he could adopt to secure the approbation of the public and obtain the consent of the Benchers to his application.   The effect produced by this publication surpassed our most sanguine hopes.   It was received with unmixed applause by all parties, and most highly valued by those who were the best judges.   The style was, in simplicity and elegance, a great improvement upon that of the "Vindiciæ Gallicæ," which bore too evident marks that the author had, in his early studies, been captivated by the vigour of Doctor Johnson.   His more mature taste had relished the sweetness and delicacy of Addison and the richness of Burke.   I am disposed to consider this essay as the most perfect of all his writings.

'The late Doctor Currie of Liverpool, himself a great example as well as a great master in the art of composition, in a letter to me on the subject of Mr. Mackintosh's literary attainments, expressed his opinion that this essay had placed him at the head of the writers of the present age.   Every body became anxious to hear the lectures which were announced with so much elegance, learning, and reverence for truth.   The difficulties of the Benchers of Lincoln's Inn vanished, and their Hall was never more honoured than by the use which they readily permitted him to make of it.   Here he delivered a course of lectures to the most learned and polite audience which the metropolis could afford.   Not students only, who sought instruction as a duty, but peers, members of Parliament, eminent judges, the gravest lawyers, and the most distinguished men of letters crowded to hear and admire him.   Here, with little preparation and, for the most part, without previous composition, he poured out the abundance of his stores in the most perspicuous and elegant diction, with a facility and a force of argument and illustration that could not be surpassed. Maintaining all the principles which induced him to take a liberal view of the theories of Government and society, he nevertheless thought it the duty of a teacher of morals and politics to inculcate rules and not exceptions ; and to prove that it was not the great business of life to seek out the occasions and cherish the means of resistance to authority, much less to preach up discontent, as a merit, and sedition, as a duty. He satisfied his friends and conciliated his opponents in politics, by aiming his flight above all party questions and temporary topics, and laying the great foundations of society, and government, and law on the wants and principles of human nature. . . . But though these lectures added so greatly to his fame, the popularity they gave him, and the habits of life they produced, were not so favourable to his progress at the Bar. To descend from knowledge to rudiments is ever an irksome task, and it was not to be expected that one who possessed so complete a mastery over the great rules and principles of all legal science should readily condescend to the daily drudgery necessary to the technical parts of practice in the legal profession, and not very consistent with the allurements offered by a command of society and a peculiar facility both of receiving and giving pleasure in it. Nevertheless it is certain that he might have accomplished whatever his taste had led him to desire in the profession of the law. He had become too well known not to be well encouraged, and it seemed to depend upon himself what degree of success he should attain, and in what particular line. He confined his practice chiefly to the business of Parliament as most suitable to his tastes and habits, and made rapid advances in that department. During the short peace of Amiens and the administration of Mr. Addington, he was called upon to defend Monsieur Pelletier, the editor of a French journal published in London, who was prosecuted by Government for a libel upon Buonaparte, then First Consul of France. The defence has been published. Considered as a treatise, it is a masterpiece of eloquence and reason. Some, however, who most esteemed the author, thought that the manner was too didactic, that the style had borrowed something from the habits of the lecturer, and that it wanted the compression and force that were desirable in forensic performances. Whatever might be its defects in these particulars, in my judgment its merit in others surpassed the powers of any other advocate. Monsieur Pelletier was convicted, but the war which soon followed rescued him from punishment.

'It was during this peace that Mr. Mackintosh visited Paris. His reception there and his success in society were as remarkable as in England. The First Consul expressed a strong desire to see him. He was accordingly introduced, but by some accident Buonaparte had mistaken for him Mr. W. Falkland, and had paid that gentleman many compliments upon his reputation as a writer, and particularly as the author of the "Vindiciæ Gallicæ." Mr. W. Falkland, not being much accustomed to speak French, found it impossible to undeceive him, and was obliged to accept the civilities intended for Mr. Mackintosh, whose conversation with the great Captain was confined to such trifling questions as are necessarily current at all Courts. One of those questions, which I believe was proposed to him as well as to Mr. Erskine, was, whether he had ever been Lord Mayor of London. The mistake was afterwards a subject of much pleasantry with both the gentlemen who had been the subject of it.

'The administration of Mr. Addington, and the hollow truce, miscalled a peace, which accompanied it, had to a certain extent and for a certain time softened the asperity of political parties in England. During this period the office of Recorder of Bombay was proposed to Mr. Mackintosh by the Minister in the most flattering terms.

'He returned to this country in 1811, after an absence of nine years, and found his friend Mr. Perceval at the head of public affairs. I had before learned from that Minister himself his wish to have the benefit of Sir James Mackintosh's assistance and to place him in some eminent office worthy of his talents and reputation. I expressed my doubt whether he could be induced to accept any political office in the existing state of parties, but I was not fully aware, till the day of Mr. Perceval's death, that the proposal had actually been made and rejected The circumstances will be thought worthy of narration by those who take an interest in the history and character of Sir James Mackintosh. My excellent and much valued friend, the late Lord Cawdor, made some communication to me on the subject of the representation of the county of Nairn, in Scotland, in which his family and connections had an influence that would be important at the next general election. I ventured to suggest to him Sir J. Mackintosh as one who would do most honour to his lordship's interests, and who could not fail of being acceptable to that county, as the seat of his birth and family.

'Sir James Mackintosh shortly afterwards proceeded to Cawdor Castle where he passed a portion of the ensuing summer in cultivating the interest which he represented in the next Parliament. From the time of his arrival in this country he had devoted much labour to the investigation of historical documents and papers with a view to a great work which was expected from him. His anxiety to search for the truth, and to leave no source of intelligence that came within his reach unexplored, gave him but little leisure for the task of composition. The superadded occupation of Parliament unfortunately contributed to that disappointment which has been experienced by his friends and the public. He soon took a leading part in the debates of the House of Commons, and it is enough to say that he lost nothing of his reputation by his performances there. If, however, I may be allowed to express an opinion on that subject, I should say that the House of Commons was not the theatre where the happiest efforts of his eloquence could either be made or appreciated. Whatever may be the advantages derived from the division of political men into parties, it is obvious that it must have an important influence upon the character of the debates in that assembly. The result of each discussion, and even the exact numerical division being, upon most important questions, known beforehand, the speakers do not aim so much at conviction as to give satisfaction to their respective parties, and to make the strongest case for the public. Hence a talent for exaggeration, for sarcasm, for giving a dexterous turn to the events of a debate, is more popular, and perhaps more useful, than the knowledge which can impart light or the candour which seeks only for justice and truth. It is the main object of each party to vindicate itself, or to expose the antagonist party to indignation and contempt. Hence, the most successful speaker, that is, he who is heard with the greatest pleasure, very often is one who abandons the point in debate altogether and singles out from the adversary some victim whom he may torture by ridicule or reproach, or lays hold of some popular party topic either to point the public indignation against his opponents, or to flatter the passions of his adherents. Many of the speeches are not, in effect, addressed to the supposed audience but to the people, and consequently, like scene painting which is to be viewed at a distance and by unskilful eyes, are more remarkable for the boldness of the figures and the vivacity of the colouring than for nature or truth. It is not the *genus deliberativum*,[1] but the *genus demonstrativum* of eloquence that is most successful in the House of Commons. The highest praise of Sir James Mackintosh is that he was, by disposition and nature, the advocate of truth. His eloquence and his powers were best fitted for that temperate sort of discussion which, admitting every ornament of diction and illustration that can please the taste or the imagination, still addresses itself to the judgment and makes the passions themselves captives to reason. He could not, without being easily foiled or surpassed, attempt that strain of invective and vituperation of all manner of things and persons which is sometimes so eminently successful in debate, not by the fascination of its charms but by the force of terror, and which though it may open the way to station and fortune, never either produces conviction or leaves a sensation of pleasure behind. The mildness of his temper, the correctness of his judgment, the abundance of his knowledge, and the perfection of his taste, all combined to make him averse to the pursuit of applause, either by inflicting pain upon others or by sacrificing truth and good feeling to the coarse appetite of the vulgar. It cannot be denied that whenever the nature of the subject and the disposition of the House were favourable to his qualities as a speaker, he exhibited specimens of eloquence that were of the highest order and elicited the most unqualified applause.

[1] The *genus deliberativum* is for the Senate; the *genus demonstrativum* is conversant in praise and blame.—Cicero, *De Inventione.*

'It is not my desire to speak of this illustrious man as a politician, much less as a party man. His merit and his pretensions have placed him, and will maintain him with posterity, in a position far above those who were engaged in the strife of party and the contentions for power. His genius and his talents will shed a lustre over the age in which he lived, when his more fortunate competitors for temporary objects are forgotten. As an elegant writer, a consummate master of metaphysics and moral philosophy, as a profound historian, as an accomplished orator, he will be known to all future times. The charms of his conversation, the pleasure and the instruction which were found in his society can be appreciated by contemporaries only, who enjoyed the opportunity of intercourse with him. They alone can bear testimony to that urbanity of manner and that sweetness of temper which mitigated the awe inspired by the superiority of his mind and the profoundness of his knowledge, and made the approach to him not only safe but delightful, which conciliated confidence and softened the emotions of envy ; of that passion he was himself altogether unconscious and incapable. His greatest pleasure was to find cause for encomium in others, and to draw merit from obscurity. He loved truth for its own sake, and exercised his mighty power in dialectics, not for his own reputation but for the investigation of truth.

'But I have been betrayed by the subject further than I intended. The memory of departed excellence, "like the sound of distant music, is pleasing though mournful to the soul." Even this melancholy tribute in awakening recollections of the past is not without its charm. One thing only is wanting to make it a source of consolation and even of pleasure, that he could but be conscious of the genuine affection and pious feeling with which it is paid.'

CHAPTER XXXIII.

EXTRACT FROM FOSS'S 'LIVES OF THE JUDGES.'

IN Foss's 'Lives of the Judges,' I find the following remarks about 'James Scarlett' of which I have made an extract.

Speaking of him after he had joined the Northern Circuit and Lancaster Sessions he says, 'For nearly a quarter of a century he was doomed to remain as a junior counsel undecorated by a silk gown. But long before that period had elapsed his extraordinary merits and intellectual powers were appreciated both on the circuit and in the Courts at Westminster.

'His extensive legal knowledge, his steady attention to the work before him, his quiet management and prudent judgment in the conduct of his case, soon inspired clients with entire confidence in his advice; and while yet in a stuff gown it was no uncommon thing to see him entrusted with a leading brief. In his arguments *in banco* he was remarkable for his ingenuity and acuteness, and for the peculiar power he had of extricating the point in dispute from the involvements that surrounded it. It was considered that he had too great an influence over the judges, and it was said of him that he had invented a machine by a secret use of which he could always make the head of a judge nod assent to his proposition.

'This striking success rendered it impossible any longer to refuse him the accustomed distinction, and in 1816 he was called within the Bar as King's counsel. From that time for the next eighteen years, he enjoyed such an ascendency in the Courts, that it became an actual race between litigants which should secure his services in the impending contest, and the loser felt that one of his best chances of success was snatched from him.   His influence over juries was wonderful ; some called it magical.   It was not obtained by any extraordinary eloquence, for he seemed carefully to avoid rhetorical flourishes, but it was produced by laying before them in clear and simple language such a well digested exposition of the case of his client as made it appear that he himself was satisfied of its justice, and that they had no choice but to endorse his opinion by their verdict.   There was no apparent effort in his argument, no violent expression in his address, no attempt at brilliant periods, but the impression was effected by an easy gentlemanly and colloquial appeal to their understanding, perhaps in some degree heightened by his handsome person, his musical voice, and pleasing countenance.   Yet when occasion demanded it, neither energy nor eloquence were wanting. Coleridge in his " Table Talk" (June 29, 1833) says, "I think Sir James Scarlett's speech for the defendant, in the late action of Cobbett *v. The Times*, for a libel, worthy of the best ages of Greece or Rome, though to be sure some of his remarks could not have been very palatable to his clients."   Whether the case was trifling or important, he took the same pains for his client, and seemed to be equally interested in the result. One of his greatest merits was that when he was engaged in a cause his services might always be relied upon.   He disdained to adopt the vicious practice of some barristers, then far too common, of wandering about from court to court, and taking contemporaneous briefs in all, to the damage of those whose retainers and even whose briefs they had accepted ; and many has been the time when Mr. Scarlett, deserted by those employed in the same cause, has borne the brunt of a long day's investigation sole and unaided.   He occasionally expressed his indignation at what he deemed dishonesty in practice or conduct with great severity, and soon after he became King's counsel an action was brought against him for a lashing animadversion he had administered to an attorney at the York Assizes.   A verdict was given in his favour, which was afterwards confirmed by the full court in London.

' With the accession of King William IV. came the triumph of the Whigs, and the consequent removal of Sir James, who from his first entrance into office had been gradually approaching those conservative but liberal principles which for the whole remainder of his life he consistently maintained. His permanent change of opinion was no doubt confirmed by the coldness, and what he deemed the ingratitude of the Whig party, who forgot that he accepted office at their request, or at least with their approbation.'

Foss further states that his reputation as a judge did not equal his fame as an advocate, and that he had too much the habit of deciding which of the two parties was in the right and arguing in his favour, while juries who had been accustomed to be led by his pleadings as a counsel refused to submit to his dictation as a judge. Probably the ends of justice would have been always attained if the juries had listened to his advice when on the Bench as much as when he pleaded before them as counsel, and I have heard it said that very rarely, whether at common law or in equity, has there been a reversal of his decision as judge.

CHAPTER XXXIV.

SPEECH AGAINST COBBETT.

I have found amongst my father's papers the trial, published in 1819, of Wright *v.* Clement.

The case was a libel, the author of which was the celebrated Mr. Cobbett.

I here give a portion of the opening speech. I have before alluded, on Foss's authority, to the praise bestowed on the oration by Coleridge the poet, who was present at the trial.

' Gentlemen, this last charge terminates the attack in this publication. So that Mr. Wright calls on you to say what damages you will give for a publication which holds him out to the world as a person guilty of almost every crime—the writer stating that he intends to take a fit opportunity of so holding him up to the public—and in compliance with the promise, performing it in the way you have just heard. He demands damages for the publication of a paper charging him with fabrication, with fraud, almost with murder, and with forging every man's hand of whom he had seen the writing—a publication charging him with forging Mr. Cobbett's name in order to obtain money from Mr. Bosville—a capital felony!—and lastly, accusing him of being a spy. Gentlemen, are men to be exposed to this species of warfare? Giving Mr. Cobbett credit for great reach and variety of intellect—for consummate skill as a dialectician—for so perfect a mastery of his weapon, which is language, that whichever side he takes, his dexterity gives him the appearance of advantage even over the opponent who has justice on his side— there is yet one peculiarity, which (if I may venture upon a remark that has the air of criticism upon so eminent a writer,)

qualifies his style, and robs it of unmixed praise. There is a
certain coarseness of feeling, a spice of *blackguardism*, which
pervades his compositions, and which, though it renders them
less acceptable to circles of the highest polish, makes more
formidable his power over the vulgar mind.

'Upon the present occasion, he is not the publisher of the
libel before you ; but whoever is the publisher, is justly
chargeable in a civil action with all the injurious consequences
that may result from it. It seems extraordinary that a libel
of this description should come from the pen of any man
engaged in literary pursuits, one who pretends to have
culled the flowers that strew the paths of learning, and boasts
of pursuing those studies which tend to soften and civilise
mankind. Suppose the fact that Mr. Cobbett had conceived
Mr. Wright to have wronged him, that in the accounts between them Mr. Wright had not made him all the retribution he
ought, though the fact is the other way, is he, for that reason, to charge his adversary with every species of fraud ?   If
the cultivation of the mind is a blessing, it is because it purifies
the passions, represses the barbarous and bitter feelings which
pervade the savage breast, and renders them incapable of injuring
society. If, therefore, in answering a man whom you suppose
to have done you wrong, you falsely and maliciously charge
him with felony, and the basest of all conduct, that of being a
spy, if you are capable of doing this, you are still a savage, and
are capable of fighting with poisoned weapons, a practice unknown to civilised nations. It is the effect of uncultivated
nature, still influenced by all the barbarous passions. But it
is the saying of an illustrious writer, a profound master of
human wisdom, *Corruptio optimi, pessima*, the power of language and the perfection of reason, unless bottomed in morality
and a true sense of the rights and duties of mankind, and I
may add of the lights of religion, become not a blessing but the
greatest curse. For the man who, with those talents, can use
them uncontrolled by moral feelings, disdaining the ties that
bind men together in social intercourse, looking only to the
gratification of his own interest or his own malignity, and wholly
disregarding whether his object is attained by the ruin of
individuals or of nations, such a man affords a proof that the

corruption of the best things becomes the worst. If high talents are accompanied, as Providence intended they should be, by elevated sentiments of private and public duty, they will surely lead men to sacrifice their petty enmities and pitiful resentments to the good of their country. But when the highest powers of reason are found in the possession of one who wields them only for the purpose of personal revenge or private gain, he hardly deserves the character of a man. He may be something more or less. He may be in intellect an angel, but he surely is a fallen angel.

'The plaintiff, gentlemen, will lay the case before you. The greater part is contained in the publication itself, the other parts will be supplied by witnesses. Then the question will be, what damages you ought to give. No man ever came into a Court more dexterously or foully libelled than the plaintiff has been by Mr. Cobbett. He even calls persons from the dead to asperse him. We cannot call Mr. Bosville or Mr. Howell as witnesses to contradict these posthumous slanders. The author of the libel writes it in America, where he was safe in his person. Nothing could have been more cowardly or dishonourable. I call upon you to vindicate the feelings and character of a most meritorious man, and to show that you know how to value the blessings of a free press by restraining its licentiousness. I consider an attack of this kind, if it can be made with impunity, as most injurious to the vital interests of Englishmen, embodied as I think they are with the freedom of the press. I consider that the best mode of preserving the liberty of the press is to show that when a man is thus assailed a jury will give him redress ; for how can we sit down in security if juries refuse to give reparation for such injuries ? It would be better to blot the art of writing out of the history of mankind than to permit that one man shall, by its means, destroy the character and happiness of another. And this, gentlemen, will be the case unless the injured party can successfully seek at your hands a liberal redress. From you the plaintiff seeks that redress ; and I am confident he will not have sought it in vain.'

CHAPTER XXXV.

FINAL CHAPTER—DEATH OF LORD ABINGER, MORAL AND
RELIGIOUS·CHARACTER OF HIS MIND. ·

IT was in the year 1844, on the 26th of April, the day
after my appointment by Lord Aberdeen as Secretary of
Legation at Florence, that a letter reached me in London to
announce the Chief Baron's sudden illness at Bury St. Edmunds. On that evening their guests, the Magistrates of
Suffolk, had only just sat down to dinner with the Judges at
their lodgings, the former residence of the late Sir John
Walsham. On taking his seat my father complained of
giddiness, got up and walked to his own bedroom, followed by
my cousin, Mr. James Williams Scarlett, then his marshal, who
had observed his sudden departure. He was found immediately after speechless, but possessing his mental powers. He
never spoke again. On my arrival, the following day, I put
into his hands Lord Aberdeen's note about my appointment
to Florence, which he looked at with great attention. This
was, I believe, the last act of his consciousness.

Few men have ever had a more laborious, active and distinguished career at the Bar. A conscientious adherence to
the Whigs in early life and their long exclusion from power
deprived him of the honours which usually follow much
sooner the professional exertions of great lawyers.

He took leave of the Whigs at a time when by supporting
them he would have rendered such honours easy of attainment from the party with which he had acted for so many
years.

His honours were derived from the other side, from the
Duke of Wellington and Sir Robert Peel; nevertheless, I hope

P

that the Whigs or at least their descendants have by this time forgiven him for voting against their Reform Bill, as to the merits of which there was then so little unanimity of opinion among the wisest and best educated classes.

As he appeared to be in his ordinary good health to the day of his mortal seizure, my father's death at Bury St. Edmonds, during the spring assizes in 1844, was a very unexpected event. On that day he had charged the Grand Jury of Suffolk, and summed up in several cases. He may be said to have died in harness, in the midst of his judicial duties.

He lived long enough to see his eldest daughter, Lady Stratheden, elevated to the Peerage, his son-in-law, her husband, successively Attorney General, Chancellor of Ireland, and a Cabinet Minister. He might have seen him, had he lived longer, Lord Chief Justice, and Lord High Chancellor of England ; and his own younger son, James York Scarlett, become a distinguished Cavalry General in the Crimean war, Governor of Portsmouth, Adjutant General, Commander of Her Majesty's Military Forces at Aldershot, and a Knight Grand Cross of the Bath.

I may here record also, that his grandson, William Frederick, who represents the dignity of his Peerage, distinguished himself in the Crimea, and has now the honour to command Her Majesty's Scots Fusilier Guards, being at the same time a faithful supporter of his grandfather's Conservative principles in the House of Lords. It is time to end as I began. I lament the scarcity of material, and my own inability to illustrate the life of James, first Lord Abinger. But let me linger a moment on the memory of his great qualities and social adornments. His wit, his pleasant humour, his agreeable conversation, the melodious tones of his voice, his great intellectual capacity, his well stored mind and powerful memory, his love of literature, both prose and poetry, including French and Italian, rendered him at all times delightful and interesting to his family and friends.

In his Autobiography he dwells on the religious education given him by his mother, which regulated his whole life. It led him to the study of Theology and Christianity. I recollect to have heard him say, that independently of moral conviction, there was sufficient circumstantial evidence of the truths of Christianity to convince any twelve unprejudiced and enlightened jurymen. This was his remarkable legal view of the question. He believed implicitly in a merciful and over-ruling Providence. His rectitude of mind was at all times exemplary. He might have taken for his motto *Integer vitæ, scelerisque purus.* No one had a keener sense of moral duty and honour. With these virtues, could he be otherwise than the kindest parent and friend ?

APPENDIX

PREFACE *to* APPENDIX.

———◦◦———

A FEW prefatory words to the Appendix may not be considered superfluous. I desire to direct attention to some extracts of Lord Abinger's speeches, and to the proceedings at important trials, on three different occasions. The first is a trial of the King *versus* Hunt, for riot and sedition ; the second is a motion for a new trial in the case of Sir Francis Burdett, who was imprisoned for a libel on the Government; the last is a trial of the Mayor and Corporation of Bristol, for neglect of duty during serious riots in that city in the year 1832.

In regard to the first and last of these trials, the magistracy and the military had difficult duties to perform. In the case of the trial of Hunt, a charge made by the yeomanry of Manchester against the mob, and an endeavour to quell an incipient rebellion by force, was regarded by many of the Opposition in Parliament, including Sir Francis Burdett, as a heinous offence against the rights of the people. During the riots at Bristol, the Mayor and the officers in command of the troops feared to incur the necessary responsibility, and the houses and inhabitants of Bristol were exposed to great risk.

It is to be hoped that, in these days of public virtue and reform, when neither the '*populus ardor prava jubentium*,' or the '*vultus instantis tyranni*,' can afflict society, no opportunity will ever again occur to render the action of troops a necessity.

The proceedings on a motion for a new trial in the case of

Sir Francis Burdett, will doubtless be passed over unnoticed by the general reader, although, on account of the circumstances and the distinguished Baronet concerned, the interest it created at the time was intense. A connection of my family by marriage, the Rev. William Thursby, listened to the speeches in court on this occasion for five hours, his attention so riveted by the learning and acuteness displayed by both judges and counsel that he had no idea of the passage of time.

To the learned and the curious I especially recommend the perusal of the Appendix.

APPENDIX.

THE KING *v.* HUNT AND OTHERS.[1]

THE indictment was opened by *Mr. Littledale.*

Mr. Scarlett.—May it please your Lordship :—

Gentlemen of the Jury,

You have heard from my learned friend, who has opened this indictment, the nature of the prosecution against the individuals who are now called upon to take their trial. Gentlemen, it is impossible, it would indeed be affectation, to disguise that this prosecution arises out of a transaction that has much agitated the public mind ; not, indeed, from any peculiar difficulty or importance that belongs to the consideration of the case in point of law, but that it chances to have been combined with events of great political importance, that have excited a deep, and I may say, a proper interest in the public. It is, therefore, to be presumed, that hardly any one of you, gentlemen, to whom I have now the honour to address myself, can be a total stranger to them. Most of these events will be partially the subject of discussion to-day. At the same time, I feel a perfect confidence, in addressing myself to gentlemen of your description, that you will consider it a duty you owe, both to your own character in this county, to the defendants who are to take their trial, and to the public on whose behalf you are to administer justice, to dismiss from your minds all impressions favourable or unfavourable to any side of the question ; and, so far as it lies in your power, to forget every previous conception you may have formed upon the subject, waiting only till you hear the evidence in the cause, and deciding by that evidence alone.

For my part, I must commence by stating my peculiar satisfaction, that this cause comes to be tried before a Special Jury of the county of York. Nothing should be further from the wish of any person who

[1] The trial of the King *v.* Hunt, for sedition and riot at Manchester, caused considerable interest at the time. My father conducted the prosecution. It was in the year 1820.

conducts a public prosecution on public grounds, than that he should have a jury to try the cause that could by possibility be affected by any local or any personal prejudice. And if I were to choose a tribunal, the most enlightened and the most impartial, I know of none that I should prefer to an enlightened jury of the gentlemen of this county, who have ever maintained a high reputation for a sense of public duty and of private honour. On the part, therefore, of the public, as well as on the part of the defendants, I, for one, feel perfectly satisfied and well contented that that course has been taken which gives me an opportunity of addressing you who, to a certain extent, must be strangers to all personal feelings ; who can have no local fears or local prejudices ; and who will, therefore, receive no impression, except from the just and legitimate evidence in the cause.

You are aware that the charge arises out of transactions which took place in the month of August last, in the county of Lancaster. The defendants are charged with taking part to concert a meeting at Manchester, the object of which was to inspire alarm and terror into his Majesty's peaceable subjects. That is a short definition of the nature of the offence with which they are charged to-day. The circumstances and details, previous to the meeting, will be offered in evidence, and will reflect light upon the motives of those who took part in the transaction. Those who appear before you now, as defendants, are singled out as being amongst the leaders who assembled at that meeting, and who, therefore, if any purpose inconsistent with the law was either contemplated originally, or conceived in its progress, are the principal offenders.

Gentlemen, with respect to public meetings, it may be necessary that I should say a few words, and few they shall be, in the outset, as to my conception, under correction of his Lordship, of what constitutes a legal meeting in this country. It is undoubtedly the privilege of the people of England, stating the proposition broadly and in an unqualified manner, to meet to consider of public grievances, and to seek the lawful means of redress. But the meetings of that description known to the constitution, and known to the practice of former ages, have been meetings either of counties or of towns, of corporations, of particular districts, or of particular classes of individuals united by one common interest in the pursuit of one common object, as, for example, if a particular trade be affected by a particular law, no question those who are engaged in that trade have been accustomed to meet, and have a right to meet, to discuss that grievance, and to obtain the lawful means of redress. If a particular class of individuals, resident in any place, are affected by any private or public grievance, they may assemble in like manner, and for the same purposes. The inhabitants of a county assembled by the Lord Lieutenant of the county, or the Sheriff, or otherwise, as the case may be, may have to consider a grievance affecting their particular interests, or the public at large. It has been the practice, and is sanctioned by the constitution, that they should so assemble, to present any petition to the Throne, or to either House of Parliament. But I never yet heard it stated by any lawyer, and I trust I never shall hear it decided by any judge, that it is a part, or ever was a part, of the law and constitution of this land, that any individuals, be they who they may, should have a right to assemble all the people of England in one place, there to discuss public grievances, or the nature of the constitution, and to come to resolutions for the purpose of obtaining redress or alteration. I will tell you, shortly and plainly, why that never can be the law of any country. No man can deny that the great physical force of every community lies in the mass of the people when assembled. Those who maintain the most popular principles of government and constitutional law, and who admit or contend that all power and all right are derived from resolutions of the people at large, and who refer back to some distant period when they suppose the people to have so assembled to frame the great groundwork of the constitution, they, above all others, must be obliged to contend, that when the people do assemble in a mass, supposing all ranks, and all degrees, and all numbers, were to be assembled in one vast plain, I say, those who contend for such principles, and those who admit them, must also admit, as a consequence, that when the people are so assembled, all the constitutional powers they had before devolved upon the functionaries established by themselves, must, for the moment, cease and be resolved into the original mass. It would follow, therefore, that if you could suppose the case of all the individuals in this land assembled in one vast plain, with a determined purpose to consider of public affairs, and to take into contemplation such measures as they might promulgate for the general relief, or for an alteration in their system of polity, it must be admitted by those who contend that all power and right are derived from the people, that the people must then resume their original functions, and that the Government would be dissolved. Hence it follows, beyond all contradiction, that vast masses of persons assembling under no specific character, under no constituted authority, not called by any public functionary, but upon their own individual free will and choice, or by the call of some demagogue, who may exercise a temporary influence over their minds, but has no right to exercise an influence over their actions, connected with no peculiar trade, affected by no peculiar interest, but taking into their most comprehensive scope all the great principles that support the fabric of the constitution, that persons so assembled, by such means, in such a manner, and with such objects, never can be a lawful assembly by the constitution or law of any country on the face of the earth, save, perhaps, one only : if you can suppose a case, of which, indeed, modern times furnish no example, if you could suppose the case of a perfect republic, like that which the history of antiquity tells us existed at Athens, where 30,000 free citizens, who formed the whole State, had a right to meet on public affairs, and resolve on immediate measures affecting their interests.   That is, indeed, a case where the government itself, by the constitution, lay with the people at large ; and, therefore, such a meeting would be a constitutional meeting.   I know of no other case in which it could be supported.   But even there, that I may not be supposed to touch the point too lightly, it is well known that under the constitution of Athens, free as it was with respect to the citizens who exercised the powers of government, the greater part of the inhabitants, being consigned to unrelenting slavery, were admitted to no part in the public councils.

Gentlemen, these are all the remarks I shall offer to you at present for the purpose of pointing your attention to the character of the meeting which you are now to consider.   Taking it at the outset as a principle not contested by me, that the people of England, in the mode in which I have represented it to you, have had, by the practice and usage of our ancestors, a right to meet, and which right I trust no seditious movements, no factious disturbances, no alarms affecting the minds of moderate men will endanger, but that we may, when the troubles are past, resume those rights for which our ancestors have fought and bled, and hand them down unimpaired to our posterity.

Gentlemen, the defendants upon this record it is fit I should describe to you, before I enter into a discussion of the part which they took in the meeting which is the subject of your consideration. Of Mr. Hunt it is unnecessary I should say anything, because his name has appeared too much of late, connected with these transactions, to leave a doubt upon the mind of any man, that you must have heard and known what are his description and character : the others are more obscure, and, therefore, I must state to you who they are, upon whom we make the charge to-day of being persons assembling and inviting others to assemble, to disturb the public peace, and to accomplish those objects which are suggested upon this record.   Mr. Knight, I understand, was formerly in trade, but of late years his occupation has been that of an itinerate orator, going from place to place to harangue at public meetings. Mr. Joseph Johnson is a brushmaker in or near Manchester, and, I rather believe, is a person in the habit of attending such meetings. Of Mr. Saxton, one of the defendants, the description I have is, that he is in some way connected with the office of a newspaper in Manchester, called the *Observer*. Mr. Moorhouse is a coachmaster, resident in Stockport. Mr. Joseph Healey is an apothecary. Mr. Samuel Bamford is a weaver, at Middleton. Mr. Robert Jones is also a weaver. George Swift is a shoemaker, at Manchester ; and Robert Wild lives at Staley Bridge, near Ashton-under-Line : these persons, in the progress of the evidence, you will find to be connected by most unquestionable testimony in some sort of design. You will have to say whether it was the design charged upon them or not. In order to show the parts they severally took, it will not be necessary that I should detail to you, in the outset, all the respective acts of each. It will be sufficient to give you the outline ; the parts will be filled up, I trust, to your satisfaction, by the evidence.

To commence then with Mr. Hunt. It appears that some time in the month of July, of the last year, a meeting had taken place in London, at Smithfield, by whom assembled, or for what purpose, is needless to inquire; but that certainly filled the metropolis with considerable alarm. At that meeting certain resolutions were passed, the object of which was (as far as I can collect the object from resolutions, I admit, somewhat cautiously worded) to inculcate upon the people of England that the time was come when some extraordinary and unprecedented measure was to be taken. In fact, the body there assembled appeared to assume to themselves a right to form a provisional government, and at once to disfranchise all those in whom, by the established constitution and laws, were then vested the public powers. It appears that Mr. Hunt was the party proposing these resolutions, amongst which were two, inviting and recommending to the people of England to consider that they were not bound to obey any laws made by the present Parliament as it is now constituted, but that, for some reasons which the persons there assembled must, in their enlightened wisdom, have discovered, it was fit that they should obey no laws and pay no taxes until they had such a Parliament as they thought it was their right to have.

Gentlemen, I allude to the transactions of this meeting, at which, whenever it is necessary, I shall fix Mr. Hunt as the principal leader, for the purpose only of pointing out to your attention what was the probable cause of his being invited, as I understand he says he was to attend the meeting at Manchester. One of the effects probably of this London meeting was that other meetings were held, to which, as they form no part of this discussion of to-day, I shall allude only as matter of history. One took place at Birmingham ; and it appears that, on the 9th of August, a meeting was projected to be held of the people at Manchester for the purpose of considering public grievances, and the mode of obtaining parliamentary reform, and also for the purpose of electing a representative to be returned by themselves to sit in Parliament, a measure that no man can for a moment contend is anything short of the highest misdemeanour that can be committed by any British subject ; renouncing at once the authority of the King himself, by whose sanction alone, in the earliest times of his constitution, unlimited to a great extent as the prerogative of the Crown then was, could any person return a member to Parliament. It is well known to those acquainted with the history of the constitution that parliaments were assembled at that time only at the pleasure of the Crown, and that, by a rare concurrence of happy accidents, by degrees the prerogative of the Crown has been defined, qualified and restrained, so as at present to compel the calling of lawful Parliaments.

It appears that on the 8th day of August, Mr. Hunt arrived in the neighbourhood of Manchester. You will find him at Bullock-Smithy, nine miles from Manchester, and three from Stockport. He was there met by Moorhouse, one of the defendants, who conducted him into the town of Stockport ; he was there joined by Johnson ; three of the parties, therefore, are there assembled : whether he was immediately joined by Johnson, and whether he was joined at Stockport by Moorhouse, or met in the road, are circumstances of no importance : but you will find him there on the 8th. In the course of the 9th they make a progress towards Manchester, accompanied by Sir Charles Wolseley, and another person whose name does not now occur to me. Arriving at Manchester, he learned, as I shall prove by the language of Mr. Hunt, and by placards fixed up in the town, that this meeting, of which notice had been given, had been prohibited by the magistrates, who had stuck up placards in the town, representing to the people that the meeting they were invited to was highly illegal. It appears that Mr. Hunt was grievously disappointed at that prohibition, or rather at the willingness of those with whom he associated to submit to it : for you will find him making, in different parts of his progress through Manchester, harangues to the populace, in which he represented, in very indecorous terms, the magistrates who had issued that handbill, in number nine, as nine tailors, using opprobrious expressions, and telling the people, with some sort of reproach of those who had given way, that he thought their object was legal, that he thought they were acting with too much submission in yielding to the suggestions of those placed in authority over them, and that therefore he invited them to meet him on the 16th day of August.

Now, gentlemen, here you have, probably, in the obedience of the persons residing in the neighbourhood of Manchester, or in the habit they had formed of looking with some respect to the public authorities, some reason to think that, when the magistrates, who, from the peculiar situation of the town of Manchester, are the sole authorities called upon to administer the law in that town and neighbourhood, there being no corporation in Manchester, you have, I say, in their habitual submission, and their connection with the place, a sort of security that they were disposed, in the first instance, to yield to the suggestions of the magistrates. But when Mr. Hunt came down, who had been attending other meetings, who had been, if I may so say, the hero of the populace elsewhere, he told them the time was come when the law was to be set at defiance, and when it was fit to deride, in the face of the populace, the persons set by the law over them ; he, therefore, gave notice that a meeting would be held on the 16th day of August, in the town of Manchester, in defiance of the magistrates.

Having transacted that business, and given that notice in Manchester, from which you may infer, as I think, reasonably, that he and the other defendants with whom I have connected him, projected and resolved that that meeting, which they agreed should not take place on the 9th, should take place on the 16th, Mr. Hunt proceeded to the house of Mr. Johnson, near the town of Manchester ; I understand it is called Smedley Cottage. There Mr. Hunt remained from the 9th. Whilst he resided there, I will show you that he received a visit from Mr. Knight, another of the defendants ; and as Mr. Hunt had a sort of popular reputation in the town of Manchester, which is not very difficult to be acquired by any man who chooses to assemble a mob and utter the language of sedition, in that neighbourhood he proceeded to mature the plan of the meeting. In the meantime, the magistrates had received intelligence that came to them partly by way of suggestions, upon which it was extremely difficult to act, there being no possibility of obtaining consistent and clear evidence, that certain movements were taking place at the dead hour of the night, in the neighbourhood of the various towns surrounding the vast population of Manchester, to the distance of five, six, or ten miles, of a nature quite unprecedented, difficult to be proved, and dangerous to be approached. It was their duty, they thought (and undoubtedly everybody will agree with them), to take precautions, lest this meeting of the inhabitants of Manchester, to be assembled and presided

over by a perfect stranger, who had no local interest nor any connection in trade with the place, should be attended with those incon-
veniences which too often attend such meetings, and they took precautions accordingly. But on the morning of the 15th, or, I
should rather say, on the night of the 14th (and I beg your attention to this fact), it appears that two persons who had gone from
Manchester to a place called White Moss, observed a considerable
number of persons there to be going through military evolutions, and
to be training in such a way that no person accustomed to view
troops could doubt the object. The curiosity of those persons was
excited, and they approached too nearly to the scene of action to
escape observation. They were, in consequence, pursued by the
men, and were beaten most cruelly; and one, a special constable of
the town of Manchester, who appeared to be known, in order to save
his life, was forced to fall upon his knees, and abjure his allegiance
to his King; this man's name was Murray. The event took place on
the approach of the morning of the 15th of August, which was Sunday.
This perhaps threw some light—

Mr. Hunt.—I must ask the counsel how he means to connect
this with the charge made against myself and the other defendants.

Mr. Justice Bayley.—I presume he will connect this; if not, the
observation I shall make upon it is, that it is producing a prejudice
by collateral circumstances.

Mr. Scarlett.—My Lord, I trust your Lordship will prevent
my being interrupted in this way. I conceive I am perfectly
regular.

Mr. Justice Bayley.—I must take it for granted that Mr. Scarlett,
who is conducting this cause for the Crown, as to every fact of which
he is apprised, and as to every fact of which I am entirely ignorant,
will not, for his own sake, introduce anything which he does not
conscientiously think is evidence, and which he does not mean hereafter to lay in evidence before the jury for their consideration. The
court must give credit to the counsel in that respect, because they
know the rule, and, I am satisfied, would not intentionally deviate
from it. And if from any circumstance they did, I dare say advantage would result to the defendants, and not to the Crown, from the
circumstance.

Mr. Hunt.—I feel very happy under your Lordship's protection.

Mr. Scarlett.—Gentlemen of the Jury, I have been too long used
to practise in this and other places, to be deterred by the interruption, however designed, from the main object of my address, and I
am too much conversant with the rules of my profession intentionally
to deviate in my statement from the proof I have to offer. I will

inform that gentleman that I do expect, by the evidence, to affect him deeply and criminally with the circumstances I am now stating. On the morning of the 15th, this extraordinary event occurred, which appeared to throw some light on those obscure movements which were reported to be taking place in the different parts of the neighbourhood of Manchester, and of this county.

Gentlemen, those who are clothed with authority in the county of Lancaster, the magistrates residing within that district, having received an intimation that this public meeting was intended, and that a gentleman from London had preached to the populace his dissatisfaction at their submission to the orders of the magistrates, and that he had declared his intention to hold a public meeting on the 16th, thought it their duty to take the ordinary precautions, which it is the duty of magistrates to take on all vast assemblies of the common people held for any objects whatever. But I must now open to you a scene which I will venture to say, in the whole history of public meetings which have taken place in this land of ours, has no example. What was this? A meeting of the town of Manchester? Why that was what it imported to be because, although I do not mean to say that Mr. Hunt, in the notice he gave, was so extremely definite as to exclude from the cavil of objection the possibility of introducing persons who were strangers to the town of Manchester, yet as the notice was given in Manchester, as it was given to the people of Manchester, the natural interpretation and the supposition was, that it was to be a meeting of the inhabitants of the town of Manchester. But I will tell you what took place early in the morning of the 16th ; and for the purpose of describing it to you, I shall beg of you to cast your eyes upon this map. There is no occasion for minute objects to be specified to you. This is the position of the town of Manchester ; a town, I believe, second only to London in its population, in this kingdom ; combining a population still greater, if you embrace the neighbourhood of Manchester, the parish consisting, I think, of no less than four-and-twenty townships, the greatest part of which are, to a degree beyond any other part of the kingdom, populous, and that population consisting of the laborious and industrious classes of the community, not of persons possessing very considerable property, although there is no doubt much wealth in the aggregate ; but the greater proportion of the population consisting of the laborious classes. This population, from the nature of it, makes it necessary to observe more than usual precautions, when they are assembled together for no definite object. On the morning of the 16th, it appeared that from various places, at the distance of ten to twelve miles from the town of Manchester, considerable bodies of men were forming in military order, assembled with banners, with ensigns, which, by and by, I will describe to you, and approaching the town of Manchester with all the forms of an invading army, save only that they had no cannon. For example, from the town of Rochdale, which is twelve miles from Manchester ; from Saddleworth, which lies in Yorkshire ; Lees, a place on the borders of the two counties ; Oldham, at eight miles from Manchester, lying on the Yorkshire side ; Royton, Middleton, and various other places, that will be named to you in the evidence, surrounding the town of Manchester : from every point of the compass, you will find there were assemblies in large bodies, having all the appearance, except that they wanted the uniform, and had not the fire-arms, of regular soldiers.

At an early hour of the 16th, at the town of Middleton, Mr. Bamford was seen assembling a party in military order, a body of about 2,000 men ; and though they had no uniform, you will find that he had the method of knowing how to make them perform their evolutions together—for he formed them in a regular square, then he addressed them, and delivered to each, who appeared to take the station of officers, leaves of laurel to designate them. There he waited till he was joined by a body of about 2,000 men, marching from Rochdale to unite with the Middleton force. I believe you will find from Oldham or that neighbourhood, Mr. Healey, another of the defendants, proceeding in the same form—I am not prepared to say that he assumed the command of the body ; but he marched with it, and was singing before it a song of triumph, as if he anticipated something glorious from the result of that day. From other parts of the neighbourhood you will find the town of Manchester inclosed by the force moving by every high-road that approached it. These movements were taking place up to the period of eleven o'clock.

As they approached the town, one of the bodies, in which I shall prove to you were numbers of those who had been seen training at the White Moss, passed the house of Murray the constable, whose name I have mentioned, who had been beaten on the morning of the day before, and who had been made to abjure his allegiance—the man was then lying in his bed from the bruises he had received. They stopped opposite his house, evidently pointing to their object ; they made a huzza, when halted, and evidently exhibited tokens, which the witness will describe to you, that they recollected the proceedings of the anterior day, and that their object was either to hail this man in order to confirm him in the abjuration which had been extorted from him, or, if they suspected him to have given information, to make him understand what might be the result of their vengeance. I should tell you these bodies marched with banners and with ensigns; I reserve, however, the opportunity of describing them to a later period of my address.

At eleven o'clock it appears that Mr. Hunt and his party were preparing to enter the town. From the residence of Mr. Johnson, he came in a carriage, I believe an open hackney carriage, and I shall prove, though I cannot state the precise period at which each individual was taken up, that he, and Johnson, and Moorhouse, and Knight, were, at different periods of that day, seen in the carriage, approaching the place where the multitude was to assemble. Mr. Hunt appeared with a triumphant band; the Middleton division and the Rochdale division had united, and served as his guard into the town; he came at the head of four or five thousand men, with increasing numbers, as an army is generally accompanied by stragglers, advancing into the town of Manchester. As he entered the town, the first object that arrested his attention was the Star Inn, in Dean's Gate, at which place the magistrates were then assembled; I beg pardon, I am told the first place was the house of Mr. Murray. Mr. Hunt, when he came opposite to Mr. Murray's house, assumed the command of the party; he stood up in his carriage, and by signal with his hat and his voice, commanded them as he thought fit. A halt was made opposite the house of Mr. Murray, the individual to whom I have referred; and there the same tokens were repeated of admonition to Murray, either in good or in bad part, whichever you please. From thence Mr. Hunt proceeded through Dean's Gate, and passing the Star Inn, where the magistrates were assembled on one of the most arduous and delicate duties on which they had ever assembled, he commanded those attending upon him to halt, and there, by hisses and groans, the magistrates were hailed. This, no doubt, was an admonition to those assembled with him, in what manner he proposed or required they should treat the persons invested with legal authority. He then advanced by the police office, where the constables were assembled, and which was their head-quarters. There the same ceremony took place: hisses and groans for the constables, and then Mr. Hunt proceeded with this vast body to the place of meeting. This place of meeting had been arranged previously by the other defendants, whose names I have not yet connected with the party. I have mentioned Bamford, Healey, Johnson, and Knight.

You shall now hear what was passing while these forces were assembling at St. Peter's Area in the town of Manchester. It appears that Mr. Jones, Mr. Saxton, Mr. Swift, and Mr. Wild, all the remaining defendants, whom I have not yet connected with any particular fact, were engaged in preparing the hustings and the mob

- Q

for the appearance of Mr. Hunt. I will not go through the particulars, but you will hear that the magistrates had directed that from the house where they proposed assembling, a line of constables should be formed to a cart which was to be the hustings. When the persons whom I have named to you found that the constables approached so near the hustings as to form an immediate line of communication, and that the mob had assembled to such an extent as to enable them to have a sufficient party to surround the hustings, they directed the hustings to be removed about fifteen yards from where the line of constables ended; and then the mob, I beg pardon, I hope I give no offence, the persons there assembled were directed to form a thick body to surround the hustings, and to guard them from any except their friends. Speeches were made by different persons; one by Jones, whom you will find addressing them, and telling them that it was the desire of the committee (it seems therefore there was a committee formed to arrange all this) that they would take their stations near the hustings; and that when Mr. Hunt approached with his body, they should make an opening to admit him and his party through, and then close their ranks, and take special care not to admit any but friends; for their enemies were at hand. These speeches were made by some of the defendants; and they were all seen, more or less, making arrangements about the hustings.

Now, gentlemen, to describe to you the parties assembled, and in what manner they were formed. You will find many of them had large sticks, which they shouldered, and which they brandished in their approach to the town, as they met persons to whom they thought it proper to express their meaning; that they had all ensigns or banners; that they came four abreast or six abreast as their leaders directed; and that they advanced with a firm step, with all the regularity of troops who had been instructed to march; that when they arrived at the place where the church of St. Peter stood, the words of command were given; that they made their evolutions and wheeled off in order, with the exactitude of persons accustomed to military discipline, and you will find that each troop took up its ground as it arrived, under the direction of its leader; that Mr. Healey marched to meet one body, and brought it in with full military forms; that their evolutions were perfect, and that everything had the appearance of previous habit and military discipline. Then came Mr. Hunt, with the largest and most formidable of all these bands, consisting of more than 4,000 men; he approached in triumph, and took his place on the hustings, those along with him either going upon the hustings or remaining in the carriage.

Now, gentlemen, a word or two about the banners. Upon some of these banners you will find were inscribed these words : ' Equal representation or death.' What was the object of that banner I pray you to consider, as men free from all prejudice ; but taking for granted, as I know I safely may do, that you are men who at least would wish for no violent revolution, and that you would desire nothing should be effected but by legal means, I ask you to lay your hands upon your hearts and say what can be the design, or what the object of a flag that exhibited to the people there assembled, '*Equal representation or death*?' We are not assembled here to enter into an inquiry whether the representation of the House of Commons be the best possible representation that can exist. Many wise, many patriotic men have differed in their sentiments upon that subject, and for their differences every wise and patriotic man must feel a due indulgence. But there is no one man who desires to stand by the law and the constitution, whatever his wishes and his hopes may be of improving the constitution, in any branch of it, that would not resist, to any extremity, a forcible violation of that sacred fabric. Whether equal representation be your motto or not, equal representation or *death* is by no means equivocal. ' We will have equal representation, or death shall ensue !' Are the mob to be informed, who I should think (with all deference to those who have a better opinion of their judgment) would be more usefully employed in pursuing their avocations, than by indulging in speculative opinions, for which their education does not always fit them, are they to be informed that equal representation is either so inherent a right, or is so useful (for no right can be justified but by utility), that it is to be purchased at the hazard of death? Is it not then saying (though no man would have the courage to say it by his lips), ' Those who assemble you here consider equal representation as the *sine quâ non* of your existence ; and advise you rather to perish than fail to procure it ?'

Now we come to another of the flags, ' No Corn Laws.' Upon that subject, gentlemen, a word or two. We come not here to discuss whether the laws passed by the legislature, on the subject of corn, were wise or pernicious. I have my opinions upon that subject; it is neither fit nor decorous I should state them to you here. But this I know, that though the most wise of mankind, though the most consummate of Legislatures, may sometimes pass an unwise law, it would be a most dangerous thing to provoke or to permit the populace to resist that law, and to dictate to the Legislature. I will suppose that every one of you, gentlemen, may be as inimical to the corn law as every one of that unhappy populace could themselves be. Yet you must agree with me, that to a mob of 60,000 persons then assembled, and when I say 60,000, I speak in moderation; for some of the defendants have themselves represented them to be 15,000, but to a mob of 60,000, consisting in a great measure of those who were subject to great privation and distress, there could not be a more inflammatory and dangerous exhibition, than to present to them in all parts of this field, that there should be no more corn laws; this was not a declaration to soothe any particular party amongst them, it was a declaration to the whole mob there assembled. What object could it have but to inflame them? and *that* on a topic of which they were not competent to judge, and I think I may say upon which those who instructed them were not competent to instruct them, what object could it have but to inflame their minds?

We come to the next, 'Annual Parliaments.' There are men in the kingdom, I make no doubt, respectable and honourable, who think annual Parliaments would be very useful. But is there any man who thinks that annual Parliaments ought to be carried by violence, as the *sine quâ non* of existence? Let them meet and declare their sentiments in petitions, but are they to hold that up as a thing they demand? that is the point to be considered. If you submit to the Legislature by argument and by reasoning, what you think a proper alteration, no man can complain; but are you to dictate and declare what you will have, and to say we must have this, or we will have death?

Then we come to another inscription, 'Universal Suffrage and Elections by Ballot;' these are the three terms, on the subject of Parliamentary Reform, which formed either the ground or the pretext, I should rather say the pretext, for calling these vast assemblies. For having had an opportunity of seeing the gentleman, who conducts his own defence, in other places, and being willing to admit that he possesses talents far above those of the orators who often attend public meetings of this kind, I cannot but think that he is aware that these three terms taken together, *Annual Parliaments, Universal Suffrage,* and *Elections by Ballot,* import a total subversion of the constitution. But be it or be it not so, so long as it remains *sub judice,* what right has he to say, 'I call upon you to require those three things, and to be content with nothing less?'

Gentlemen, it is not fit nor is it safe that on the subject of public grievances the mob should dictate to the Legislature. Let the people assembled inform the Legislature by their wisdom, if they think that they, the cotton spinners and weavers, and other trades and artizans of this kingdom, who earn their subsistence by the labour of their hands, are enabled to give information to Parliament on subjects interesting to them. But let not demagogues come and teach them to be contented with nothing less than that which they demand by those ensigns. And for this reason, that mobs are too apt when they get hold of a favourite idea, inculcated upon them by those whose talents they respect, to resolve all which they regret into that which they are taught to consider as a grievance ; and they are at length led to believe that the removal of that grievance, and that alone, would operate as an effectual panacea for the cure of every evil they feel. This has been admirably illustrated by the celebrated painter, Mr. Hogarth ; you all know that on the change of the calendar, for the purpose of making it consist with a more perfect computation of time, it was necessary to make an alteration by which eleven days appeared to be suppressed. Would you believe that there were mobs in the neighbourhood of the Court, composed of ignorant persons who actually thought that the Legislature was doing them injury by taking away those eleven days, as it deprived them of eleven days of their existence ? Whether a Mr. Hunt existed in that day to preach to them, or a Mr. Johnson, I know not, but the mixed passions of the mob are well explained by the engraving of Mr. Hogarth, which represented them throwing up their hats, and crying out, ‘Give us back our eleven days ;’ and for aught I know, those who now preached these doctrines to the populace, as essential to the recovery of their supposed lost rights, may lead them to the same excess of absurdity and violence, and finally to their own ruin, by urging them to demand that which it is not in their power even to explain or comprehend.

Gentlemen, I have not done with the banners : ‘ Let us die like men, and not be sold like slaves.’ Who, I should be glad to know, had been selling the people of Manchester? Who had been selling the people of Rochdale? Who had been selling the people of Saddleworth? Who had been selling the people of Lees? Who had been selling the people of Oldham, and of other places, divisions from which went to Manchester that day? I have not yet heard that any body had sold them, but this was the mode of representation adopted, when a man was not found with courage enough to say so absurd a thing from the hustings,—to hold it up on a flag, where it might make a deep impression on the whole multitude. But the matter does not rest there ; for one of the staves which held up the flag ended with a spike, the top of which was painted red, to make it the more conspicuous. I leave you to guess what was the object of that. Another had painted on it a dagger. God forbid the time should ever come, or that I should ever witness it, when any man shall have the courage, shall dare at an assembled meeting of the people of any form, or of any description, to preach to them in open language, that a dagger is the instrument by which their supposed lost rights are to be recovered. But I am afraid, gentlemen, that though no man has the courage and the audacity openly to preach that sentiment to an assembled mob, the time is come when there are persons who have a lurking design to insinuate to the mob in this way that the dagger is an instrument they may use. I ask you, as honest men assembled in this place, whether this does explain to your satisfaction the object of that banner, lifted up in the presence of 60,000 persons, and representing a dagger painted upon it. A dagger has not been the instrument that Englishmen have been accustomed to use, and I hope that those who conceive that our rights are lost, and do us the favour to endeavour to recover them for us, will not teach us to use the dagger as the means for effecting this object. I know that the moment the common people have such a notion, you may bid adieu, not only to constitution, to monarchy, and to the House of Commons, but to all safety and all hope of preserving this happy empire, with any practical or moderate degree of liberty.

Gentlemen, this was the form in which this multitude was assembled, this is the progress it made to the place of its rendezvous, these were the people assembled appearing to take their different parts, and to conduct and originate it. What was this meeting? Was it a meeting of the town of Manchester? No. What was it? A meeting of the county of Lancaster? No. Was it a meeting of a particular trade? No. Who assembled it; who presided at it? Was it any man connected with the county, or having an interest in the town? No. Why was it assembled? What was its object? Gentlemen, these are questions which must be left for you to decide; but this I know, you cannot fail to feel that the effect of that meeting, whatever might be the secret object of those who took a part in it, was to inspire alarm in the minds of his Majesty's subjects. Will any man tell me that the vast population of Manchester, comprising a prodigious abundance of wealth, and a vast proportion of property, would feel no alarm at finding the shoemakers, the weavers, and the journeymen of all descriptions, approaching to the number of 60,000, to invade the town? Can any man doubt that that meeting was calculated to excite the greatest alarm in every mind? What more is necessary to make it illegal? No lawyer can doubt, for the law has defined that any meeting, even for a legal object, with such an array as to inspire terror and alarm in his Majesty's subjects, is an illegal meeting. No man can doubt that, but, good God! does it require law books to tell us that ? Why have laws at all, if it be not to prevent the rude hand of violence and force from injuring the property and destroying the peace of the well-disposed of society ? But, in God's name, if we are to be told that in every town in England a mob may at pleasure approach and take possession of the town, we had better put an end to all laws, and consider ourselves as in our original state of nature, and say that force must be met by force. Nor is it possible, as you will see, gentlemen, that this can be tolerated, unless every town is guarded by such an increase of military force as no good subject, and no man who wishes to preserve the constitution and the laws, would ever desire to see prevail in this country. For it is quite clear that the ordinary means which the civil power possesses cannot control such a meeting. What can a limited number of constables and peace officers do with such a multitude ?

Gentlemen, I hasten to conclude my address. The magistrates, finding that the numbers assembled in this manner, and that they continued to approach in this alarming order, and not knowing to what limit this proceeding extended—whether persons from Birmingham and Coventry might not be coming—whether this might not be made a rendezvous for the whole kingdom, seeing that it was not a meeting of the town of Manchester, and was not attended by the inhabitants of that place, nor headed by a man who had any local connection with the town—the magistrates felt it their duty not to allow such a meeting to take place ; and being informed by the oaths of many persons of the town, that they felt that alarm which might be expected, they thought it necessary to issue a warrant to arrest the individuals who appeared to take the lead. Some of the individuals were then arrested, and there my case terminates ; for in what passed afterwards, whether in good or in bad part, of course, those individuals can have no share.

Gentlemen, the defendants are charged with having conspired to assemble this meeting, and with having gone to it with seditious banners and ensigns, in order to inflame the public mind. It is charged to be an illegal meeting, and they are charged with having taken part in it. I am not answerable for any defect in the evidence, but I have no reason to doubt that the case will be proved much more fully than I have stated it. If it is so proved, I can have no doubt that your verdict will be in the way I seek. I do implore you to give your attention to everything which can be urged for the defendants. It is a great benefit of the law that the poorest and meanest shall be heard ; but I implore you, when you have heard all that they shall say to you, to consider the real character of and the effect to be produced by this public meeting, and the part taken by these several defendants, in relation to it.

REPLY.

Mr. Scarlett.—May it please your Lordship :—

Gentlemen of the Jury,

The period is at length arrived when it becomes my duty to address you upon this tedious, though very important case, but you may be assured that neither for your sake nor for my own shall I be disposed to add more to the consumption of time which this case has already occasioned, than I feel to be necessary, and demanded by my imperious duty.

Gentlemen, I am sure that when I address you, I hardly need do more than remind you that a counsel, in discharging his duty in a cause, is not to be considered as carrying about him any personal views or wishes, but that he is a minister of justice, entitled and obliged to do his duty ; and that in the course of the conduct which he pursues, and the observations which he makes, it is neither candid nor decent to impute to him personal motives, much less improper motives, when he does that only which his conscience dictates and his duty demands. I introduce my reply to you by that observation, because, in the course of my address to you, I shall find it my duty with boldness to unmask the hypocrisy of the defence you have heard, and to endeavour to satisfy your minds, as I trust I shall do, to your absolute conviction, that four-fifths of all the mass of evidence by which his Lordship and you have been persecuted, had no more to do with the real issue that you have to decide, and the points legitimately to be discussed in this cause, than any other transaction of any other meeting that these or any other gentlemen have hitherto held. To do this, it will be my duty to make some comments upon the speeches that have been delivered to you, and to show you the manner, and temper, and the tone in which this defence has been conducted; that you may have to pronounce, upon your solemn conviction whether it is a defence of the conduct of these parties accused upon the record, or whether it is an attempt, by insult, by persecution, by intimidation, and by menace, to do that in a court of justice which has been attempted, and with too much success, in the town of Manchester. Melancholy will be that day, and fatal the result, if the spirit of intimidation, that disposition to disorder, that scorn and defiance of all legal authority which, unhappily for the times we live in, prevail too much out of doors, and are too much encouraged by men whose talents might destine them to worthier purposes, should ever find their way into a court of justice, and when that court shall be transformed into a hustings, and your verdict be asked by the popular voice, instead of being asked, influenced, and sanctioned by the law of the land, which you are sworn to administer. I hope not to live to see that day, but if I do, as far as depends upon my humble powers, feeling, as I ever have felt, a deep and solemn conviction, that all that is dear in liberty, in life and in property, depends upon the reverence that is paid to the administration of the law—I say, that until that fatal day arrives, I will, as far as my humble talents enable me, struggle to the utmost to prevent its approach. I therefore crave your indulgence, as I know I shall have his Lordship's, while I proceed fearlessly, without any apprehension of popular clamour, which upon this subject I should despise myself if I did not despise, to make the comments which my duty obliges me to make, and to call upon you to come to that conclusion which, it appears to my mind, the law and your consciences demand.

In the early part of an address made to you by one of the defendants[1] you were told that he had made an application to his Lordship to give him an hour more ; that he was labouring under great infirmity of body, as well as anxiety of mind, and I was pointed out in these terms,—' It was unfeelingly opposed by that man.' Gentlemen, you shall learn, by one trait, the faith, the candour, and the honesty of this defence. The application was made to his Lordship, not upon the ground that the defendant was unwell, but because he had a vast amount of evidence to wade through, and therefore only he demanded a further indulgence. I reminded his Lordship, that only three witnesses had been examined upon the Monday, and that the whole of Sunday had been a day of leisure to that gentleman ; that was all I said ; but the following day you were told by him that I was an unfeeling man, because I refused to give my assent to an application founded upon his debility of constitution ! And this is to go forth to the public. I take leave to say, that knowing nothing of Mr. Hunt out of this cause, if he, or any one of the defendants, had made an application to his Lordship, upon that ground, I appeal to all those who have known me, whether I am the man that could for a moment have resisted it ? But I thought the

---

[1] Hunt.

application was made, and I think so still, not upon any such ground; but with views, probably, to obtain a reinforcement of that audience which his Lordship has found so much difficulty to keep in control, during the progress of this cause.

The next remark in that extraordinary defence is also personal to myself. Because I had the honour to state to you, that I, as an individual felt highly gratified that this important cause was to be tried by a jury of this county, without prejudice and without fear, he chooses to insinuate that I uttered a sentiment that was foreign to my heart, because, says he, 'When I made an application to remove the trial from Lancaster, that gentleman had a retainer, a brief, and a fee, and did his utmost to oppose it.' He knows this statement to be untrue, but he has ventured to make it that it might go forth to the public, and perhaps operate upon some of your minds to destroy the influence he might suppose I possessed, notwithstanding my humble and retired character, upon the minds of a special jury of the county of York. Gentlemen, you shall have the truth. He made an application, upon the last day of the term, at least, he came prepared with an application in proper form, only upon the last day of the term, to change the venue. I knew nothing of it until I came into court in the morning,—I was absolutely ignorant that the court was occupied on such a subject. I took my seat in court, and then found that the court was anxious to assist him in putting (which the want of skill in those who advised him, probably, had not enabled him to do) his affidavit into proper form; and I found my honourable and learned friends the Attorney and Solicitor General resisting it, upon this ground, and this ground alone, that they had a strong apprehension that the only object was that of delay; and that all the defendants upon the record might not be brought to enter into proper recognizances, so as to take their trial at the present assizes. I say not one word upon the subject. I never opened my lips nor uttered a syllable till the court had given their judgment, and then only my private friends knew my sentiments, and they know that what is stated by this gentleman in court, to insinuate that I uttered a sentiment foreign to my heart, has no foundation but in his own imagination, or in his desire to mislead you. And I must do those learned persons, whom I have mentioned, the justice to state that after they had discharged their duty, in taking the opinion of the court on those defects of form, and this difficulty of proceeding which had been thrown in their way, so far were they from desiring to avoid the tribunal which this gentleman has adopted, that they have actually given that to him which he had not the candour to

state, further time to enter into those recognizances ; and even at
this day you are now trying by a record which, by the leave of the
court, is brought down by the Crown, the defendants having forfeited
their recognizances, and entered no record for trial.

Mr. Hunt.—My Lord——

Mr. Justice Bayley.—Your record was sent down too late.

Mr. Hunt.—They gave us notice they should bring down the
record.

Mr. Justice Bayley.—Do not interrupt.

Mr Scarlett.—You shall judge from this of the candour of the
defence. The next is a statement also intended to reflect on my
character—(I hope I have sustained a character in this county too
long to apprehend its being affected by such statements), that in the
Court of King's Bench, I forsooth was at one time solicitous to hold
a brief, as the phrase was, for this gentleman. If Mr. Hunt, or those
who advise him, had ever been desirous of bringing before the Court
of King's Bench the conduct of the magistrates, the conduct of the
constables, or the conduct of the yeomanry of Manchester, upon that
unhappy day, I will venture to say that no legal impediment would ever
have been thrown in his way, that no avenue of justice would have
been stopped to him, and that there is not one man in the whole profession of the law, from the highest down to the lowest, that would not
have felt it his duty to render him, as we do in every case, all professional assistance. But he thought fit to come into court himself,
daring that which he knew the constitution and the law would not
permit, to be himself the mover of an information, which he had
applied to no counsel to move for him, and having ventured to state
in the face of the Court of King's Bench, as an apology for his conduct, that no counsel would do it for him.

Mr. Hunt.—I beg your Lordship's pardon, but as this is a misstatement, I hope I may correct it. I did not know that I had no right,
but as soon as I was informed, I applied to the Attorney-General,
and the learned counsel knows that.

Mr. Scarlett.—The learned counsel does not know it, and does
not believe it. He came into the Court of King's Bench, as he says
now, and I will concede that he thought he might make the motion,
when the court told him he could not make such a motion, that as a
public prosecutor he had no right to appear in a court of justice, in
the characters of those to whom the court has confided that province ; he then stated to the court that he could get no counsel to
do it. I thought it due to the character of the bar——

Mr. Hunt.—My Lord, I must beg to interpose, when facts are
stated, which are not upon the record, which are not correct. Your

Lordship will recollect you told me I could not move it myself, and that I came into court the next day, and stated that I had applied to the Attorney-General, and offered his letter, and stated myself ready to make affidavit of it, and Mr. Scarlett knows that.

Mr. Scarlett.—I thought it due to the English bar to relieve them from the aspersion, and I said, I believed there was not a gentleman practising in that court, who would refuse a retainer, a gentleman *practising in that court*, for if it was made to the Attorney-General, it was an application founded in impertinence, Mr. Hunt knowing that he does not practise in that court, and that nothing but official duty would bring him into that court for the purpose of applying for any information. So much for the third head.

With respect to the fourth, which was an application against the under sheriff of this county, his Lordship having already disposed of that, I shall say nothing, except that probably it was his intention to hold you out as a packed jury, as persons selected by the hand of power, to find a verdict against him : for it seems he has the misfortune to be at enmity with all sheriffs, with all magistrates, with all juries, with all administrations, with every House of Commons, and every House of Lords, and, I might almost venture to say, with every king.

Another topic was, that I had introduced into my speech, for the purpose of exciting a prejudice against him, things of my own imagination or invention. Why, if the lord of the manor of Glastonbury[1] had imbibed from the clergyman with whom he has lived, and the lords of manors and the squires with whom he associates, the spirit and candour of persons in that situation, he would have thought it due in courtesy, to suppose that if I had misstated anything respecting a dagger on a banner, it might have arisen from the instructions in my brief, and not from a tortured imagination. But no ! he comes with his charge, as if it was not *he* upon *his* trial, but the prosecutors on *their* trial, and therefore, I am to be charged with inventing facts of my own imagination, to prejudice him. Look, gentlemen, at the good sense and justice of such a remark. Am I so bad a tactician (he has two or three times used the phrase) as not to know that it would, in the result, be injurious to my cause, to suppose or invent a fact, that my witnesses might belie it ? But in my own vindication I will read to you from my brief the very passage: 'On another banner was inscribed, "No Corn Laws," and the figure of a dagger painted upon it.' I had interpreted this, as I presume any one of you would have done, that it was painted red upon the banner ; but when the

---

[1] Mr. Hunt stated that he was lord of the manor of Glastonbury.

witnesses were called to explain this, two of them spoke of its being, not painted upon the banner, but the termination of the staff, to which the banner was annexed, there being one with a pike, and another with a dagger, both of which were painted red. That is the evidence, and it does not strike me that it makes any important difference. But the dagger was a term introduced for the purpose of making a tragic termination to a tragic speech, to give it a good handsome finish, and to catch the applause of the multitude.

Gentlemen, the next was this : I was charged with endeavouring to make a witness say that Mr. Carlile was attending that meeting. I was charged in terms which, that I may not misstate, I will read from the note of the gentleman's speech what he said upon that subject. It seems, then, that the object is so entirely to persecute this gentleman, that there is no fiction, that there is no calumny which I and those who bring forward this prosecution are not ready and desirous to heap upon him ; that we insinuate, by endeavouring to hitch the name of Carlile into this cause as a party attending that meeting, that, forsooth, he is not only hostile to the throne, but to the sacred dignity of religion. And the gentleman, who amidst his varied talents does not seem to want the aid of a rhetorical tear, seasonably sheds a tear of regret and mortification that he should be suspected of an association with this Carlile, or ' of having said or done aught that could reflect upon the power of the throne or the sacred dignity of religion ; he, on the contrary, if Carlile was not suffering for his temerity in a way that makes it indecent to make comments upon a man suffering in that situation, would freely give his opinion about that person, and about the wrong he has done to the cause of religion.' Oh, no, he had no meeting with Carlile ! it is insinuated to calumniate him, to prejudice the cause ; he knows nothing of Carlile, at least to his honour, and God forbid that he should be accused of associating with him ! Gentlemen, it sometimes happens that we cannot prove the things which are stated to us. I purposely made no mention of Carlile. Yet one witness we called did mention that in the coach, at the hustings, there was a man they called Carlile. Upon this alone is hitched this hypocritical cant, for the purpose of making you believe that he is the victim of misrepresentation. What has he proved by his own witnesses ? Have *we* wrongfully associated him with Carlile ? Have *we* insinuated what was false ? Have *we* brought a witness to swear that by conjecture, by implication, which has no foundation in truth ? Mr. Hunt has produced a witness, and one of the most respectable of those he has produced, a young gentleman of the name of Tyas, who actually proves that Carlile was in the coach with him ; and one of the defendants has done us the favour to read that which I will by and by bring back to your recollection, an invitation to Carlile to attend that meeting, together with Hunt, as two of the principal personages of that important assembly; and, accordingly, we find Carlile coming in the same carriage with him.

Gentlemen, I come now to a part of his speech which I will admit has a great relation to the subject, and of which I admit he made, for the purpose of his address to you, by no means an uncandid or an improper use. Because I perceived at the moment, and I could not fail from the nature of this cause long ago to perceive, that, in this county, and probably to a great degree in the public mind, the transactions of that day which are not the subject of legitimate evidence at this time, will be the objects of much greater interest and much greater importance than the result of the present trial. And therefore I do not blame Mr. Hunt, and that he has done it fairly I will freely admit, for appealing to you in the way he did, that I did not call the magistrates or the constables. But it becomes me to explain why I did not, and that will give you a clue to the whole of the preposterous defence which is attempted to be set up by his evidence and will show you what legal application it has to the question in hand.

Gentlemen, whether the magistrates, who acted upon that occasion in a way, and from motives that have not yet been explained to you, acted discreetly or indiscreetly, lawfully or unlawfully; whether the constables, in the opinion they formed and the representations that they made, were justified in their consciences or by the truth of the fact; whether the yeomanry after they had surrounded those hustings (and I meant not to enter into that) acted rightly or wrongly, has no more to do with the inquiry you have to make in this cause, than whether Mr. Hunt is the lord of the manor of Glastonbury, or whether the respectable Mr. Widmore the squire, and Mr. Hutchings the parson, visited him at Middleton Cottage. But first let me say, gentlemen, why I did not call the magistrates; the magistrates were in attendance, the constables were in attendance, though the opinion I have stated to you is that which I formed, and which the Law Officers of his Majesty had also formed; we did not know what opinion the learned judge might entertain upon the trial; and, therefore, we thought it our duty to have those persons present. But I forbore in my opening address to you one word as to what passed after the cavalry advanced, because I waited to hear his Lordship's opinion upon that subject. What I expected did take place. My Lord confirmed the opinion we had formed, that *that* inquiry had nothing to do with this; and, therefore, as I well knew that that inquiry was one of great public and anxious solicitude, one, I admit, (for why should I

deny it?) in which this gentleman has an interest, and for aught I
know may think he has a duty to perform, one which may still be
brought in some criminal shape before the public, if any person
chooses so to bring it, why should I lend myself to this purpose for
or against those persons, when the inquiry could only disturb and
draw you from the present subject of your investigation? I know if
you were sitting here to try the conduct of the cavalry, or the magistrates, you would be trying a much more interesting question to some
persons than that which is before you. Should I then have done my
duty if I had not refrained from observations on that which, being of
deeper interest, though unconnected, must have distracted your attention, and might have done injustice, and have mixed up in the public
mind much more important questions? Gentlemen, that is my
apology, if apology can be required, that is my justification, for not
calling the magistrates, and not opening the case upon that subject.
And you have seen, from the anxious pains his Lordship has taken
to preclude the inquiries which this gentleman and his assistant were
perpetually urging to be made upon that subject, that he concurs with
me in opinion. Whatever previous sentiments, therefore, you may
have formed upon the subject of the dispersion of that meeting, and
whether the magistrates acted rightly or wrongly, upon which for the
purpose of this cause no man has a right to pronounce an opinion,
whatever be your opinions upon that subject, your verdict upon this
cause ought not to receive the slightest influence from those opinions.
I will tell you in what way this cause is to be tried, in which I am
satisfied I must have his Lordship's confirmation: the charges upon
this record are to be treated exactly in the same manner, and the
question before you to be tried in exactly the same manner, as if no
magistrate, and no constable, and no yeoman had appeared upon that
field. If the meeting was unlawfully assembled, if in its form, in its
concretion, in its object, you have reason to believe, as I trust you
will, before I sit down, that the meeting was an illegal meeting, and
had the objects specified upon this record, the question is exactly the
same as if the meeting had gone through all its regular forms and
ceremonies, and had dispersed of itself. Whether the magistrates, or
those with whom they acted, might or might not have dreaded the
consequences that might have resulted from such a tumultuous crowd,
orderly at the first, proceeding with peace, and with the words of
peace in the mouths of their leaders; what might have been the result of the shades of evening falling upon them, is quite another
thing. The motives of those who assembled it, and what their conduct was, are wholly foreign from that question. Now I trust you
concur with me, that, except as a mere circumstance, the question is

exactly the same as if no yeoman had appeared. I admit that the circumstance of the yeomen appearing, of an assault made upon them, and an insult offered, is a circumstance to denote, but not conclusively the one way or the other, what the object of the meeting might be. But it is no part of the facts to be tried, whether the yeomanry drew their swords and cut the crowd, or whether the crowd resisted, and threw brickbats and stones at them. That inquiry I have kept back from you, that the true question might not be mixed up with it. For the original formation of the meeting, and the object of those who assembled it, cannot depend upon what the result was. Although one of the arguments of the law, one of the reasons, in the wisdom of the law, for prohibiting such meetings, is, that whatever such a meeting may be at the beginning, no man can answer for the result ; for who is the man that can command, by merely holding up his finger, 80,000 men ? Will the law or the constitution permit any individual to have that power? Is it safe, is it reasonable, that any one subject in this kingdom of England shall assume to himself the power of governing a multitude of fifty or sixty thousand persons at his pleasure? And do you think Mr. Hunt would be a less dangerous person to this community if he could indeed, as he more than insinuates, successfully organise and keep in discipline 50,000 men, whom he could carry about like a wild beast with a muzzle, saying, ' I can keep him at peace or let him loose at my pleasure?' Should we all enjoy, with peace and tranquillity, our liberties, if that were so? He may dream of the powers of his eloquence; he may think he is that person pictured by the poet, who in the midst of a violent commotion of the people, when arms are furnished by their fury, and when stones and other missiles begin to fly, upon merely erecting himself to speak, would soothe the passions of the multitude, and make them listen with the utmost attention and silence to his commands. *Ille regit dictis animos et pectora mulcet.* He is mistaken if he dreams that he is that person ; nor, if there is any one who possesses that power, ought he to be allowed an opportunity of exercising it in this country.

Now, gentlemen, having disposed of this head of the observations of the defendants, and having shown you how little the conduct of the yeomanry or the magistrates had to do with the original formation and objects of this assembly, I beg leave to ask how have the last four days been occupied ? They have been occupied in precisely repeating those facts which every one of my witnesses on cross-examination swore, with the exception of two or three little circumstances, which, in trying a cause of this importance, were absolutely immaterial. For in a crowd of sixty, eighty, or a hundred thousand people, it is not to be supposed a man is perjured who in some particular part of it swears that he saw or heard an expression or action which another man, in another part, did not see or hear. Is a gentleman perjured because, when the crowd turn round upon the military and fix their eyes upon them, he says, ' I considered it as a defiance,' particularly when it is accompanied by a great shout? Good God! is a man to be considered guilty of perjury because he puts a different interpretation upon that conduct from what another does? Or is a man to be considered as perjured because he swears that there was a groaning in one corner, which another did not hear? I put it to your candour: he has called fifty-six or fifty-seven witnesses; might not he equally have called five thousand? Did you ever hear of a mob of any description, of which individual members might not be called, until the judge or jury were put to death by langour in hearing they had no improper motive? I will undertake to say, that of the mob who, upon the same day when it is said this gentleman held a meeting in the Spa Fields, attacked the gunsmiths' shops, proceeded to the Tower, and did that for which certain persons were put upon their trial for high treason, you might have called three hundred who would have sworn to the same thing. Is that the way to try such a cause? Did my case deny that they advanced in due order, or that when carriages came they made way for them? On the contrary, my first witness stated Mr. Bamford's speech the same in matter, and almost in form, as their own witnesses did. Again, my witnesses, in general, informed you that Mr. Hunt stated that their enemies were to be put down if they disturbed the peace of the meeting; and yet you have been for four days hearing the same thing. I read in a speech said to be made by this gentleman; I do not say it was made; but in a newspaper before you it was, perhaps, said as a pleasantry, but it appears to have approached to verification,

Mr. Hunt.—I submit here, without meaning to interrupt the learned counsel, that that paper is not in evidence.

Mr. Scarlett.—It is in evidence, certainly, as far as the resolutions go.

Mr. Hunt.—Does your Lordship think that it is evidence as far as the resolutions go?

Mr. Scarlett.—I beg I may not be interrupted, except by your Lordship—not by the defendant.

Mr. Hunt.—I submit whether the learned counsel may speak in reply to that which is not in evidence.

Mr Justice Bayley.—Certainly not.

Mr. Scarlett.—Gentlemen, I beg to know upon what principle it is that the defendant attempts to dictate in this court.

R

Mr. Justice Bayley.—No, he is not dictating ; he is objecting that that which you are about to cite is not in evidence.

Mr. Scarlett.—If the gentleman will hear what I am about to cite he may then object. *He* read part of several speeches, which his Lordship permitted, and I will read, as part of my speech, the mode in which the authorities may be put down and trampled upon.

Mr. Hunt.—What I object to is to the counsel reading it as mine.

Mr. Justice Bayley.—He has a right to read from a newspaper that which he thinks fit.

Mr. Hunt.—But not saying it is my speech.

Mr. Justice Bayley.—No.

Mr. Scarlett.—Gentlemen, I will not say it is Mr. Hunt's speech, for I do not mean to detract from its authority, but I will read it for the purpose of showing the mode of resisting the law, and which has been exemplified by what has taken place in this cause.

Mr. Hunt.—My Lord——

Mr. Justice Bayley.—Mr. Hunt, I have heard your objection, and have been of opinion Mr. Scarlett is at liberty to read that as a part of his speech.

Mr. Hunt.—What I have read were general propositions.

Mr. Justice Bayley.—I do not know at present what this is; if I find anything improper I will immediately stop it.

Mr. Scarlett.—Gentlemen, I hope it will not be supposed I am desirous of clothing anything I say in this cause with the authority of Mr. Hunt; far from it. But if I find a sentiment well expressed in a newspaper, I am at liberty to read it as a part of my speech, and to show how that has been exemplified which I state to you. I state to you that any man that is charged with assembling a mob improperly, and with addressing them with the intention to excite disaffection among them, may say: 'This is the mode in which I will defend myself: if I should be taken and subjected to such a charge, let them bring their witnesses, let me bring their spies and their informers. I see before me 50,000 men, all of whom will be my witnesses; I have but to call "thirty a-day" (fifteen are enough, I think), and then the trial will last three years, and let us see what judge and jury will stand it.' And so here this gentleman might have called, instead of his fifty-four witnesses, five thousand four hundred who would have proved exactly the same facts. No doubt he might. If anybody expected any of the multitude assembled would come here and confess they intended that which was improper, the expectation was vain. His Lordship has tried persons for riots and for disorderly meetings.

Mr. Justice Bayley.—No, never.

Mr. Scarlett.—I thought his Lordship had, but I have witnessed many such trials, and no person has ever come forward to say, ' I went to it as a disorderly meeting.' But, I say, if out of the four thousand from one place, and three thousand from another, and two thousand five hundred from a third, Mr. Hunt, instead of calling forty had called four thousand, who had every one of them proved that he would not have gone if he had expected disturbance, that he would not have taken his wife or his daughter with him, I say it would be trifling with the cause to make it depend upon such evidence, as I will by and by demonstrate, when I come to the real grounds on which this prosecution stands. But I will tell you whom he has not called, witnesses I did expect to see, not one of whom have been called before you, which shows, I think, that this defence has *some dexterity* about it, if it is not founded altogether upon craft. You have heard it reiterated over and over again, until at last I was surfeited with it, that there were seven hundred respectable house-holders of Manchester who signed the requisition for this meeting. Has not the doctor,[1] when he made his defence, put in the very paper? from which I expected that he of course would call some of those respectable persons. Mr. Hunt has added one to them, but he puts the one in the wrong place, for he puts it before the seven hundred, and calls them seventeen hundred ; where are they? Have you seen any of them? Does Mr. Hunt think you are to be caught by such chaff as that; because you see their names in a newspaper you are to believe in their existence? No, no, depend upon it that the whole is a fabrication founded in the shallowest craft, *or* they are not called because he has a legal adviser who has found that he dare not call them, because no one of them would dare stand a cross-examination as to the real object of that meeting. I beg you to consider that, when a man is put on an important trial, in which no expense has been spared for him, in which there has been no pains spared (for there is not a witness put by me into the box who has not had the last twenty-five years of his life scrutinised by the defendants), if any one of those persons could have been called to stand the fire of a cross-examination, do you not believe they would have been called. What are we trying? whether a meeting held at Manchester was a lawful meeting, or whether under the circumstances it was not a meeting calculated to inspire alarm and terror in the people of Manchester. We are told by the defendants that seven hundred of the inhabitants signed a requisition to call it. But they do not bring any one such person before you. I have kept a separate list of the Manchester people called, and I do not find one that signed that paper. That is

[1] Healey.

R 2

one head of negative evidence, if you please, upon the part of Mr. Hunt, and you shall see by and by what use I make of it when I comment further upon his defence.

Now let us proceed to another. It was an important part of my case, which for these four days, perhaps, you have forgotten, and which, if the trial had lasted twenty-four days longer, would have been consigned to perfect oblivion by you and the public, and by his Lordship too, till he came to read over his note, that for a time before the 9th of August, and between that and the 16th, there were trainings of the people in the neighbourhood of Manchester; a circumstance which, in my humble judgment, you will decide was alone and by itself calculated to create in the minds of the magistrates a certain degree of alarm respecting the motives of the persons so drilling, and the conduct of those so drilled. Yet no one man is called by Mr. Hunt who took part in that drilling.

Mr. Johnson.—He does not know them.

Mr. Scarlett.—Gentlemen, the unparalleled effrontery of this defence is equal to its craft. I will expose both, and the interruptions shall not prevent me. Has he called any one who took a part in that drilling to prove that the sole object was the regular marching of the people to Manchester, and that they had no further design? No, gentlemen, in the course of a long, tedious, and tiresome defence, worked up with infinite care, on which no expense has been spared, and there has been no want of a previous investigation of the evidence, upon that important head which I consider to give a form and a character to this assembly, which in my own judgment damns the defence, not one of these individuals has dared to present before you any one man who drilled at any one of the places, nay, not even to contradict Mr. Chadwick, whose testimony I shall by and by bring to your recollection. What do you think of the integrity of this defence? Of the impudence of it you long ago formed an opinion. But when you are trying whether a meeting was legal, of 80,000 persons assembled at Manchester, not of Manchester people, for it was not proved, even by his own witnesses, that any Manchester body marched and took up a position there, but of people marching in regular procession from various parts of the country into Manchester, and taking possession of one place, manifesting to every man of common sense a previous combination and design, even his own witnesses dare not deny that those circumstances manifested a previous discipline; no man is called to prove why they were disciplined; but it is left to the same conjecture as that on which I rested it at the outset of the cause, in the absence of such evidence as he does not dare to call. So much then for the integrity of the defence.

But it seems Mr. Bamford, as to whom I will say, in candour to him, that no man laments more than I do that that individual should have exposed himself to such a situation; for his defence undoubtedly was conducted with simplicity, with reverence to the Court, and with that degree of talent that does him high credit, and which makes me wish he had kept company more fitted to his talent and his just expectations, Mr. Bamford says, and Johnson, and Mr. Hunt, and the Doctor have repeated, that they consider certain measures as their political rights. Mr. Bamford says, that they consider annual Parliaments and universal suffrage as the political rights of the people. Mr. Johnson has said the same thing, though he has had the candour to admit that many honest men think otherwise. (I only hope that neither all the honest men that think otherwise, nor the men that think with Mr. Johnson, will deem it lawful to frighten other men out of their opinions.) Mr. Hunt says, in making his defence, that which of course he could not disavow, as a reformer, 'in every sense in which you will interpret the word, consistently of course with the rules and principles of law;' '*we think that universal suffrage and annual Parliaments are the rights of the people.*' Gentlemen, I said in my opening, and I repeat, that this is not the tribunal before which the question of parliamentary reform can be considered upon its merits. Whatever your opinions may be upon that subject, or whatever mine may be, is a matter of no sort of importance to this cause. But this I will say, that if any man forms an opinion, that any particular measure of parliamentary reform is essential to the welfare and prosperity of the people, if he is of that opinion honestly, yet, I say, if he attempts to inculcate that opinion as a measure to be dictated to Parliament, as a measure that the people must insist upon, or be contented with nothing, I say, that that man is not only guilty of a violation of the law, but that he is the greatest practical enemy to reform that can exist in the country. Annual Parliaments and universal suffrage the political rights of the people! Surely nothing can be more vague, nothing more absurd. The political rights of the people are those resulting to them from the constitution of the body politic, as framed by law. Unless the law gave them, they could not exist as political rights. But I will not quarrel about a term. They mean, perhaps, that they are so essential, in their judgment, to the proper constitution of the representative body that they think they are the rights the people ought to insist upon. As to what Mr. Hunt says, that they are natural rights, a man might as well say he had a natural right to a King or to a House of Commons. In what book of Nature do you find a King or a House of Commons? How can either be a natural right? But I will suppose it an opinion which honest men may entertain, that annual Parliaments and universal suffrage are essential to the prosperity of the country, an opinion that cannot be founded on any reference to our past history : for at no period have such rights ever existed, as you all know. The institution of the House of Commons was an emanation, in the early periods of our history, from the power of the Crown. By degrees it has become that which it now is, a body existing between the King and the people, as well poised as any body of that kind ever was ; gradually it has acquired its present constitution, and it may possibly yet admit of greater improvement, unless the rude hand of violence should interfere and bring us back to despotism. But at no time were there ever annual Parliaments and universal suffrage ; and *they* misinterpret the Act, '*that Parliaments should be held annually, or oftener if occasion may be,*' who consider that Act as countenancing such an idea. And how were the members at first nominated? Those for the counties, one by the King and the other by the Sheriff ; and for the towns, they were named by the bailiff of the lord to whom the town belonged. It was by degrees that the popular privilege has been enlarged to its present state. To say that you will begin again, and undo all that system which has been a work of time, enlarged by slow degrees (and nothing ever lasted long that was suddenly performed), that you will destroy the fabric altogether, naturally sets the mind of every man who values the country and its institutions against the parties who hold such language, and insist upon their particular measure as a *sine quâ non*, as to which, they say, we will be content with nothing unless you do this.

If a man has a right to go to a public meeting and say, 'I am of opinion that annual Parliaments, universal suffrage, and vote by ballot are essential to the safety of the commonwealth, and that we, the people, must insist upon them or perish in the contest,' he has equally a right to say that he thinks there ought to be no representative body at all. 'I am of opinion that the formation of the House of Commons, which interposes a body between the people and the throne, is a violation of natural right, and that all men have a right to vote upon the laws that govern them, and that they ought not to delegate men to do what they may do for themselves. Let the law be proposed in each parish, and let the parishioners decide it.' He has a right to go to a meeting and say, ' *Universal suffrage for every law, or death.*' That is just as consistent with the law, and just as consistent with the evidence of that respectable gentleman, Mr. Hindmarsh, who carries his toleration (which I value as much as any man) to men preaching up to the multitude anything which they approve. Suppose that Mr. Bamford should be of opinion, or that Mr. Hunt should by and by persuade him that he has such opinions (I do not say that he has), that the immortal memory of Thomas Paine is the greatest glory of the British nation, that we ought to rally round that revered name, and that neither king nor religion should remain amongst us, has he not the same right to put upon his banner 'Republic or Death'? It is just as conformable to the law. A man may, if he pleases, give his private and speculative opinions, and state what he thinks about one form of government as superior to another. But no government under which men live can tolerate the attempt to alter the very constitution and frame of the government, by urging a mob to insist that there is one thing wanting which they will have, or be content with nothing.

Gentlemen, the season may arrive when the great mass of the population of England, unless the verdicts of juries are interposed between them and their destruction, may be persuaded by Mr. Carlile that, as republicanism is the best form of government, so deism is the best religion ; or, perhaps, they may go a step farther, and say that religion is a fabrication of the priesthood to gull mankind ; that it is nothing but a fiction. If Mr. Carlile does indeed think that man is born to perish like the beast of the field ; that that which distinguishes him from the brute creation is not the divine inflation of an immortal spirit, but accidental organisation ; that the frame of the universe was not the work of an Almighty hand, but a fortuitous event ; that the heavenly bodies, those bright constellations which you cannot contemplate without emotions of reverence and wonder in their solemn march through the heavens, move without order or arrangement ; that the story of salvation is a fable, Christianity an imposture, the Bible itself a fabrication by the rich to keep down the poor, and the consolations of a future life mere inventions, in order to reconcile the people to a state of existence which is a deprivation of their rights in the present world ; supposing all this should be really felt by Carlile, shall he be allowed to put it on a banner, and to preach it to the multitude? Gentlemen, these observations may be considered, perhaps, as bringing the question of religion into a cause which is connected more with politics ; but that is not a just inference from my remark. Even the events of this trial have been such as to prove that the observations I make are not unconnected with the cause. I should be glad to ask any honourable man who now hears me to lay his hand upon his heart and to say what, in his honest opinion, was the motive of those who invited Mr. Carlile to be present at that meeting. Mr. Carlile was a tinman originally, as it is said, and has been for two or three years a bookseller, now proved to have been established in a shop called, I think, 'the Temple of Reason, and the office of the Republican and the Deist.' Mr. Carlile was known to have been under an indictment for selling blasphemous and seditious works. Who invited him to that meeting? What was the fame of him that spread at Manchester, and that brought him to that place? Who recommended him? What was his merit? Can Mr. Hunt explain to us what made him worthy of riding in the carriage with the lord of the manor of Glastonbury, and the cultivator of five thousand acres? What made him a fit person to be invited to attend that meeting? I ask of you, gentlemen, to lay your hands upon your hearts and say (as no one of the seven hundred has been called to tell you) what, in your opinion, was the motive of inviting that man, if it were not for the purpose of giving countenance to his proceedings, and to show that those who assembled that meeting applauded his conduct and his principles? Good God! to what a state are we reduced! A man, without the least tincture of learning, has discovered, I presume by the mere force of his natural genius, that there is no God, and thinks fit to publish that discovery for the benefit of mankind! This man, who understands neither his own language nor any other, is invited to attend a meeting at Manchester, and would have been returned perhaps the colleague of Mr. Hunt, as a representative for that very town of Manchester, if that meeting had gone to the final termination contemplated by those who had called it together, and who are put forward as inhabitants of Manchester, though none of them dare to come into this court and to avow the reasons why Mr. Carlile was invited. I ask you, if I do unjustly in calling upon you to form the inference that his merits, as I have described them, proved to have been known by the witnesses called for the defendant, were the real grounds of this invitation? Then, gentlemen, I can tell all those who think that the administration of justice may be frustrated by calling thirty witnesses a day, I will tell them that, which is no secret to them, probably they will find another most effectual way to frustrate the ends of justice, in the doctrines that are preached by Mr. Carlile, and tolerated by Mr. Hunt. If these doctrines should once find their way amongst the common people, and take that deep root which some persons wish them to do, in God's name what becomes of the sanctity of an oath? What becomes of the credit due to human testimony, or what witness that comes from such a quarter, can be trusted to speak the truth upon his oath, if that is the mode by which the wickedest man in the county, the most daring demagogue, may defend himself; if once he is allowed to urge the common people on to that pass, that they take their religion from a tinman, and their politics from Mr. Hunt?

Now, gentlemen, having disposed of these observations upon the nature and character of the defence, I proceed to recall your minds to the real subjects of discussion in this cause, what it is you are to try, and what to determine ; and I venture to say, unless I deceive myself more than ever I was deceived, that I am as much entitled to your verdict upon the parts of the case upon which I now claim it, as I ever was to any verdict in a court of justice. What are the charges upon this record ? You will exercise a discrimination between the one and the other, when it becomes necessary to distinguish them. We charge conspiracy to assemble a meeting in the town of Manchester, for the purpose of exciting disaffection and discontent. We charge a conspiracy to assemble a meeting, in a formidable and menacing manner. We charge a meeting held unlawfully for the purpose of exciting discontent and disaffection to his Majesty's Government. We charge an unlawful meeting, held in a formidable and menacing manner. These are the substance, I do not travel through the words, of the charges ; but these are the substance. Now let us see what is the evidence. Let me bring you back to the recollection of those early parts of the case, which to this moment have received no contradiction, but the strongest confirmation ; and let me ask you, whether any man living, whose mind is not biased by prejudice, can entertain a doubt upon that subject ? Here you have, just upon the eve of the prorogation of Parliament, a meeting taking place in Smithfield ; at that meeting one of these defendants presides, having before been to Manchester, and held a public meeting there ; at that meeting, at Smithfield, he proposes and he passes resolutions which have been read to you in evidence, and which he himself hands to Mr. Fitzpatrick, the last witness that is examined; which resolutions I did not in the outset read to you, because I was not at that time satisfied that I might have been able to have traced them to his hands. Much of what passed in public, and much that you know as private individuals, you cannot judiciously know in a court of justice, and therefore I forebore to state them ; but I stated the general character of them. Mr. Hunt has been pleased to say, more than once, in his cross-examination of my witnesses, and, in the re-examination of his own witnesses, to repeat his opinion upon the subject, that because those resolutions were passed at Smithfield, and no bad consequences followed, that is, no heads were broken, and no houses burnt, therefore it was legal to pass them. I deny that; I say that it was highly criminal ; and that the people were deluded by those who had the most criminal and traitorous designs against the Government ; of which these resolutions will satisfy any man who reads them. You will see in a moment whether a reform in Parliament, or the destruction of the whole fabric and constitution of government, was the real object of those resolutions. Let us read them ; ' Resolved, that every person born in Great Britain and Ireland, is by inherent right free,' a resolution which no man can deny, nay, I will say there never was a country, in ancient or modern times, in which there was more freedom. If any gentleman will examine the pages of ancient or modern history, he will find no country in which individual liberty was more protected, than in the land in which we live. And let me tell you the present trial is an exemplification of it. What country before ever exhibited such a spectacle, except our own country on other occasions? that defendants accused of a seditious attack on the Government shall be brought here by the weight and authority of the country, and be admitted to urge their own defence before a most learned and impartial judge, and have full liberty to bring forward all matters, some relevant, and some irrelevant, in their defence before a jury of the people. It is well known that in Rome, if any man was supposed to meditate a change of the government, the consuls were at liberty to put him to death ; that a dictator might be created who had the absolute power of life and death over every citizen. What country in the world is there as to which it may be more truly said that the protection of liberty and the administration of the law are absolutely vested in the people themselves? That resolution, therefore, is true.

Let us see, then, whether the subsequent resolutions are proper deductions from this : ' That for the protection of the life, the liberty, and the property of every member in a free state, it is expedient and essential that a Code of Laws should be established, and an executive administration thereof provided.' Now why the resolution 'that a Code of Laws should be established, and an executive administration provided,' in this country ? Is there not an executive administration provided ? You will see the subsequent one explains this, and you will see that the object was not to make such a code of laws, nor to provide for an administration of them. Let us see then: ' That as life, liberty, and property are equally dear to every man, whatever may be his rank, condition, or attainments, it follows of necessity that every man in a free state is equally entitled to a voice in the enactment of such laws and their provisional administration :' pray mind that, gentlemen—their ' *provisional administration.*'

Now comes the third resolution, which is to declare what is to take place : ' That every man is free ; that there ought to be a Code of Laws established, and an executive administration thereof provided, and that every man, whatever be his rank, condition, or attainments, is equally entitled to a voice in the enactment of such laws, and their provisional administration.' Why provisional ? I will tell you why. It is only to be a provisional government till such time as the people have framed another, with Mr. Hunt at their head : that is the object of it. But to go a step further in this resolution, compounded with a degree of folly equalled only by its audacity : ' That, as life, liberty, and property are equally dear to every man, whatever may be his rank, condition, or attainments, it follows of necessity that every man in a free state is equally entitled to a voice in the enactment of such laws and their provisional administration.' So that an idiot, a man who has had the misfortune once to be a lunatic, and who may be twitted with it in a court of justice,[1] and, therefore, be held out as incompetent to be a witness against Mr. Hunt, because he has had a malady which ought to entitle him to commiseration, may yet take a share in the making of laws ; a man who is by his daily labour prevented from giving his attention to these subjects is to have the same voice as a man who is by his habits of life fitted for entering upon them. ' That to support the just expenses attendant upon a due administration of the law, a proportionate contribution from every member of the community ought to be equally levied.' I take occasion to state here that there were some of these that Mr. Fitzpatrick said were applauded by the public. I think this was not quite so palatable, for I see no mark of cheers. ' That the rights of all being equal, no freeman in Great Britain or Ireland ought to be taxed without his previous admission to a participation of universal right. That this universal right may be exercised in the choice of representatives to be fairly and freely nominated or chosen by the voices or votes of the largest proportion of the whole members of the State ; that the persons who at present compose the British House of Commons have not been fairly or freely nominated or chosen by the voices or votes of the largest proportion of the members of the State.' Now that proposition is, in a certain sense, undoubtedly true ; not in the seditious sense in which these persons use it, for the purpose of enforcing upon the people that that House of Commons ought to be trampled upon and scorned. ' Therefore, *that* any laws which may hereafter be enacted, or any tax which may be imposed by the British House of Commons.' The House of Commons is of that plastic nature that it is capable of remedying its own defects ; but the way to do that is not to represent to the people that the House of Commons is defective, and therefore ought to be abolished. The further words, I think, show the intention of the whole. ' Therefore, that *any laws which may hereafter be enacted, or any taxes which may be imposed by the British House of Commons*, ought not in equity to be considered obligatory upon those who are unjustly excluded from giving their

---

[1] One of the witnesses for the prosecution was cross-examined as to this concerning himself.

voices or their votes in the choice of representatives.' So that every
one is to be told that, in equity, the laws ought not to oblige him,
and that, in equity, he is not bound to pay the taxes.

'That from and after the 1st day of January, 1820, we cannot
conscientiously consider ourselves as bound in equity by any future
enactments which may be made by any persons styling themselves
our representatives, other than those who shall be fully, freely, and
fairly chosen by the voices or votes of the largest proportion of the
members of the State. That, with a view to accelerate the choice of
legal and just representatives of the whole people, we will cause
books to be forthwith opened in the different parishes of this metropolis, for the enrolment of the names and residence of every man of
mature age and sound mind resident therein, so as to enable him to
give his vote when lawfully required so to do. That an humble
address be presented to the Prince Regent, requesting that he will be
graciously pleased to issue his writs to the sheriffs and other returning officers of the different counties and cities of this empire, to cause
representatives to be chosen agreeable to the foregoing resolutions,
and to assemble in Parliament in January next.'

Let us here pause for a moment. A resolution is proposed and
passed, that the House of Commons and the House of Lords shall
be wholly removed from all functions of legislation ; that the existing
session of Parliament is a nullity, and the throne is invited by a
petition, which is treason in itself, to summon a Parliament to sit in
January next, at the very period when Parliament is sitting, a few
days before the Prince Regent goes down to prorogue the Parliament.
These daring and traitorous resolutions are passed, and Mr. Hunt's
is the hand that has the audacity to offer them to a multitude of
eighteen or twenty thousand men. Gentlemen, I say with boldness
that in no period of the history of this country did an attempt so
daring pass so long unpunished. Now see for what they travel down
to Manchester. Here is a representation made by the press to the
people of England : they are told that these resolutions are passed by
a meeting of great multitudes of persons ; to be sure, Mr. Fitzpatrick
has told you how they passed. Were they the subject of deliberation ? Did those persons, many very honest and serious persons,
know what they were ? No, they came ready printed out of Mr.
Hunt's pocket, or the pockets of those who attended him, framed by
some secret committee, framed by those who had a desire to impose
upon the multitude, and proposed and passed *by the mass*, though
heard by a few, and a few only who could hear them. Then what
was done ? It was represented in the newspapers as if a vast meeting
of the metropolis had passed these resolutions, and called upon the

people in all parts of the kingdom to join them in the attempt to subvert the authority of Parliament. Mark the progress. We have heard, and had the right to give it in evidence, that it was known at Manchester that an election had taken place elsewhere, of a legislatorial attorney to sit in Parliament. The Prince Regent, as everybody knows, had, in his speech to Parliament, intimated the state of the country, and expressed his opinion of the necessity of using prompt measures to put down that spirit, urged by demagogues to their own destruction. At Birmingham an election takes place, almost in the spirit of these resolutions ; and then at Manchester a meeting is announced for the 9th of August, with Henry Hunt, Esq., in the chair, by an advertisement, which I will read as it was printed in the newspaper, and as it was placarded about the streets of Manchester ; in the very same newspaper in which these resolutions are published in the town of Manchester, to give information to all those who watch the proceedings of Mr. Hunt, and take an interest in his progress through the country, in the same paper in which is announced the meeting of the 9th of August, these resolutions are made public, in order that the public, and those who attend that meeting, may know precisely what it is that the City of London has acted upon, and may, if they think proper, follow the example—I will read it to you : ' The public are respectfully informed, that a meeting will be held, on Monday the 9th of August, 1819, on the area, near St. Peter's Church, to take into consideration the most speedy and effectual mode of obtaining radical reform in the Commons House of Parliament, being fully convinced that nothing can remove the intolerable evils under which the people of this country have so long and do still groan ; and also to consider the propriety of the unrepresented inhabitants of Manchester electing a person to represent them in Parliament, and the adopting Major Cartwright's Bill. Henry Hunt, Esq., in the chair.' What ! is there no boroughreeve of Manchester ? Is there no magistrate in that place ? Is there no gentleman of property and fortune in the neighbourhood ? Is there no person who has a greater and deeper interest in the commercial and manufacturing interests of Manchester than Mr. Hunt ? No, ' Henry Hunt, Esq., in the chair ; ' ' Major Cartwright,' ' Sir Charles Wolseley,' who had already passed through his election, ' Mr. Charles Pearson,' a lawyer, ' Mr. Wooler, and Godfrey Higgins, Esq., have been solicited, and are expected to attend ; ' and you will please to observe this purports to be subscribed by several persons, not one of whom has been called before you in the course of this long trial. And here, gentlemen, begins the head of a topic, which I mean to press upon your conviction—the contempt, the derision, and the abhorrence of all authority, which it was this gentleman's object to inspire in the neighbourhood of Manchester. In order to show that he dared to hold a meeting in Manchester, to consider the election of a member of Parliament, even in the face of the local authorities—what does he dare to do? 'the boroughreeve, magistrates, and constables, are requested to attend.' What is the meaning of that? Are they to preside? Oh no; Mr. Hunt was the chairman. Are they to direct the meeting? Oh dear no; that was arranged by a few persons not called as witnesses; what does that mean? Do you not think it was fabricated in London? It appears that that meeting, being so published and placarded, had excited the attention of the magistrates, and that they thought it their bounden duty, on the best judgment they could form, to publish to the town a placard, directing that all persons should abstain, and abstain *at their peril*, from attending it (an idiom well justified by our language, though it was criticised because not understood by those who are not acquainted with the idiom); but you have it in evidence, that Mr. Hunt comes down from London to Manchester, and he learns, in his way at Coventry—

Mr. Hunt.—I beg to say there is no evidence that I came from London.

Mr. Scarlett.—Very well, gentlemen, then he dropped from the clouds, somewhere in the neighbourhood of Coventry; he takes flight above other men, and his motions are involved in mystery except when he perambulates his manor of Glastonbury with his servant.

Mr. Hunt.—That is not in evidence, my Lord.

Mr. Justice Bayley.—Do not interrupt, Sir.

Mr. Hunt.—It is not in evidence, my Lord.

Mr. Justice Bayley.—How can it be in evidence that you dropped from the clouds.

Mr. Scarlett.—Mark the impertinence of the gentleman; do I state that he came from London (having been there very shortly before) to Coventry? I am not allowed to state that he came from any place! Did he come then from the clouds, or from the earth? What does it signify whence he came? Gentlemen, he learnt at Coventry that this meeting was put off, but he pursued his course; and it is in proof that at Bullock Smithy he was again informed of it. What does he do? He meets Mr. Moorhouse and Mr. Johnson at Stockport. Having there assembled, they come in a sort of procession, not like that to take place on the 16th, into Manchester. Here is a part of the case which I must recall to your recollection; you will find it confirmed by his Lordship's notes, and it puts an end to this gentleman's defence. I ask any man who has a conscience and understanding about him *this*; whether he can say that the object of this man in coming into Manchester was to inspire respect to the local magistrates, or to preach up disaffection, and excite the mob to resistance to those placed in authority over them? What does he do? He makes a speech to the persons assembled, many of whom he had brought from Stockport, and he tells them, what? There are witnesses who speak to it, some of them using expressions different from those used by others, which is quite natural in the statement of a speech. They state, and the very servant who accompanied Mr. Hunt, and gave him a character as a witness, was not asked to contradict it, that he addressed the people in some such way as this : that he was sorry to find they had resolved, in obedience to the magistrates, to postpone the meeting; that the magistrates considered it illegal, but he did not ; that they were no more fit to be magistrates, or no more worthy of being called magistrates, than so many tailors to be called men ; that it wanted nine tailors to make a man, and nine magistrates to make that proclamation, which he treated with contempt and scorn ; and I put it to you whether that was not the object? He regretted that they had resolved to postpone that meeting ; the meeting which was to have been assembled to elect, or consider of the election of, a member to represent them; and he has the audacity to go further, for there is nothing human or divine that is free from his insults. Having by his side, or at least in another carriage, the newly-elected legislatorial attorney for the town of Birmingham, he says that somebody was gone to Liverpool to consult a pettifogging lawyer, to get his opinion whether the meeting to elect another for Manchester was legal or not. So that my friend, Mr. Raincock, a gentleman of the greatest knowledge of his own profession, and who, perhaps more than any other man in this kingdom, possesses a variety of learning and science, is called a pettifogging lawyer, whose opinion, when in opposition to this divine orator, this Demosthenes' of Athens, the people could not, and ought not to, listen to. He says, I am sorry this meeting is put off, but I invite you to come, and to bring with you as many of your friends and neighbours as you can, to the meeting on the 16th. Mark that, gentlemen, we have him here inviting them to come on the 16th ; we have the notice published on that very day that the meeting is to take place on the 16th. The clause for the designation of a representative had been omitted, it is true. No credit, however, is due to Mr. Hunt for that omission, for it was published in the Saturday paper, before he had time to tell them that he would dare to meet the magistrates and face it out with them, and hold that argument for the amusement of his friend, Mr. Moorhouse, who, it seems, was to be a witness in this discussion, which Mr. Hunt invited him to attend, when he would prove they had a right to meet for that precise object.

Then he proceeds, and is for a time at Smedley Cottage ; and please, gentlemen, to mark those who visit him there, what he was doing there, how he passed his time with this brushmaker at the place called Smedley Cottage, from the 9th of August to the 16th. It appears, indeed, that he once went to Manchester, and made a ridiculous bravado before the magistrates, that he was ready to surrender to them if they had a warrant, when he had done no act in the County of Lancaster, except showing the disposition by which he was actuated. There is no secret evidence of what he was doing during that time, but I think I can show you by one thing what occupied him : he remains there till the 16th ; and now that I may not misrepresent him, I will read from his own speech the extract of the letter which he read to you, which he caused to be published to the inhabitants of Manchester at that period, a letter, gentlemen, the whole of which I have not the means of reading to you in evidence, because the witnesses did not recollect it. He put it into the hands of Mr. Grundy, his witness, who said, that was the letter he saw ; but Mr. Hunt had the prudence not to read the whole of it ; and when I attempted to supply the deficiency, by proving it was placarded in the streets, he very seasonably interposed, and I cannot deny it, dexterously, to prevent me. I have, therefore, taken from the short-hand writer's notes a part of it, the only part he chose to read ; and now let us judge what prompted him to give the advice he did. We have proved in evidence, that, previous to the 9th, reports were received in the town of Manchester that the lower orders of persons in the neighbourhood were drilling in different places, that a great apprehension existed of the object of such midnight movements ; we have proved that just before the 16th a particular event took place, which I shall, by and by, recall more pointedly to your recollection. Do you think Mr. Hunt was ignorant of all this ? Do you not think it probable that a consultation was held whether this was a seasonable time to come armed to a meeting ? Do you not think the advice to come without arms might be connected with the object of a more dexterous use of that physical force ? If so, perhaps it will point out as clearly as daylight, how much more sagacity was shown in preventing than in encouraging a display of arms till he could bring his men to battle in more perfect order. This is the advice given by him in a letter addressed to the inhabitants of Manchester. It is a long letter ; one part of it you have in evidence. I wanted to read you the whole of it, and I fully expected he intended to read

it, when he put it into Mr. Grundy's hand, or I should have called
his Lordship's attention to it that it might be put upon his note. But
Mr. Hunt, in his address to you, stated it thus: 'I suppose this
might have been brought against me to show that I did not invite
them.' Speaking of the meeting which had been called, 'I said,
come then, my friends to the meeting, on Monday, *armed with no
other weapon but that of a self-approving conscience.*' Who told him
they were coming armed with weapons? Who suggested the propriety of that advice? Was it Johnson that told him? Was it
Knight that told him? Who informed him? Can any one of you,
gentlemen, (I speak to you as gentlemen and men of honour) doubt
that he had secret consultations during this period, and that when he
hesitated whether he should attend the meeting or not, and told his
friend Mr. Grundy that he wished to go back to town, can you doubt
that he felt that the common people, encouraged by his resolutions
in London, inflamed by what had passed in other places, and ripe
almost for the very consummation of their wishes, were precipitating
themselves too eagerly for his object, that they were likely to come
armed to the spot, that he had not, at that time, courage to meet
them in that posture, and that he wished to give them to understand that they must come without arms; but not liking to disclose
that which, if stated in open language, might have convicted him of
fear, then and therefore he put in these more cautious words, '*armed
with no other weapon than a self-approving conscience?*' Let us com-
bine this with other evidence in the cause. Some witnesses have
been called by Mr. Bamford, in his defence, who have proved that
on the very morning of the 16th, as they approached Manchester,
they heard it said by their comrades, it had been agreed they were to
go without sticks, and those that had brought sticks left them on the
road, and one gave his to his father-in-law to take home for him.
Had it been agreed that they were to go without sticks? That forms,
I conceive, an important feature in this cause. If, gentlemen, that
was agreed, it must have been agreed in consequence of this letter;
and thus it appears there was one individual amongst these defendants, who combined sensations of fear with the suggestions of
policy, from a desire that the projects at that time existing in the
neighbourhood of Manchester should not burst forth in his presence,
at least until not only that neighbourhood, but possibly all the other
populous districts in the kingdom, should be equally trained and
organised; when, and when only, it would be time to take up arms.
What is the interpretation of this? You have seen the printed paper;
for aught I know, you might have seen the word *armed* put in
italics, to mark it. Now we will go on: 'Come then, my friends, to

S

the meeting, on Monday, *armed* with no other weapon but that of a self-approving conscience ; determined not to suffer yourselves to be irritated or excited.' All this breathes the same feeling ; he was afraid of their irritable state, he was afraid they might break out too soon. It has been the plan of all conspirators to keep their partisans back till they were ready for action. See how some persons in London who, for aught I know, may be disciples in his school, have broken out too soon. It was not safe to come into the field till they could stand the shock ; in the meantime it was his object to preach peace and quietness ; for God's sake do not show your teeth till you are able to bite : 'to be excited by any means whatsoever, to commit any breach of the public peace ; our opponents do not attempt to show that our reasoning is fallacious.' What reasoning is there ? Is there any reasoning in these resolutions, or in Mr. Hunt's speeches ? Is there to be reasoning to eighty thousand persons ? Were those resolutions produced by reasoning, or did they come ready cut, and even printed ; though the rest of the world might suppose the mob had reasoned upon them before they passed them ?—'or that our conclusions are incorrect, by any other argument but the threat of violence, and to put us down by the force of the sword, the bayonet and the cannon. They assert that your leaders,' mark that, gentle-men. Who are their leaders ? Is Carlile one ? Is Mr. Smith of Liverpool one ? All I wish to say of that gentleman is, that he gave his evidence in a manner that relieves him from all imputation. He says, that he declined attending the hustings, and therefore God forbid that I should reflect upon that gentleman, who may be an honourable man, whatever are his opinions on politics. 'They assert that your leaders do nothing but mislead and deceive you, although they well know that the eternal principles of truth and justice are too deeply engraven upon your hearts, and that you are at length, most fortu-nately for them, too well acquainted with your own rights ever again to suffer any man, or any faction, to mislead you. We hereby invite,' do observe the language of this proclamation, addressed to the in-habitants, inviting the boroughreeve, magistrates, and constables to attend,—'We hereby invite the boroughreeve, or any of the nine wise magistrates who signed the proclamation, declaring the meeting to have been held on Monday last illegal, and threatening, at the same time, all those who abstained from going to the said meeting, to come among us on Monday next. If we are wrong, it is their duty, as men, as magistrates, and as Christians, to endeavour to set us right by argument, by reason, and by the mild and irresistible precepts of persuasive truth. We promise them an attentive hearing, and to abide by the result of conviction alone.' So that the magistrates are

invited to come and discuss this thing on the hustings; this is treating them with due respect ! to invite them to this meeting ! Mr.
Hunt is to take the chair, and then they, the magistrates, are to discuss this point with Mr. Johnson, Mr. Bamford, and Mr. Wild, and
Mr. Healey; and Mr. Moorhouse is to be the judge, and to decide
upon the harangue of his own Demosthenes[1]; though it appears, I
think, that Mr. Moorhouse has not yet attained to all the maturity of
intelligence and taste of the Athenian cobbler, who was a celebrated
person in his time. This man has the effrontery to write thus, and
show the people *his* way to treat the authorities. Yes ; and there is
no man who does not know what you meant on that day; you meant
to hold them up to scorn and to ridicule; to show that it depended
upon you, and you only, whether they should be insulted, assaulted,
and trampled upon. You meant to show the extent of influence,
power, and control which you had over this rabble.

Under this invitation, gentlemen, the meeting does take place on
the 16th of August ; and now I beg your attention to the other parts
of this case. I will venture to say, whatever may be the opinion of
any man upon the events of that day, I maintain here, and will maintain everywhere, that if the magistrates had not felt alarm, and had
not taken precautions in the then state of that populous neighbourhood, after the information received by them, and proved to be true,
of the drilling the populace, they would have deserved, every one, to
be dismissed as incapable of discharging their functions. When they
found that, in defiance of their own prohibitions, a man had come
down from London to preside at this meeting, that the people were
arming round Manchester, that they were then directed, by that man,
not to come armed, thereby proving that an armed meeting was
probably in contemplation, were they wrong in assembling a military
force, lest occasion might require it ? Was it not their duty to make
the constables to take their part upon the field to prevent excess, if
excess should take place ?

Now we come to the events of the day preceding, and we shall
see whether Mr. Hunt and his party are, indeed, free from all imputation of what passed upon those occasions. Upon the 15th of
August, at the hour of twelve at night, a young man of the name of
Chadwick sets out from Manchester, having heard, as many others
had heard, that the people were training at a place called White
Moss, about five miles or five miles and a half from Manchester. He
proceeds at that hour to White Moss, he has proved before you that
he saw many persons there marching in different companies, arranged

---

[1] It was proved that Moorhouse had so named Hunt.

in different orders, obeying different leaders, and going through all the accustomed evolutions of military discipline, except that they had no weapons ; and he has proved before you that they not only marched but drew up in line, that they formed in ranks two deep, that the words were made use of, '*make ready, present, fire*,' upon which there was a simultaneous clap of hands. Let any individual lay his hand upon his heart, and consider the effect of this circumstance. Do you believe Mr. Chadwick or not ? If he swears falsely, might not he have been contradicted by a host of witnesses? Might not some of the time which has been wasted, since this cause began, have been spent in calling witnesses to prove that that which he has stated was false? Might not some one person, at least, have been called who had been trained ? No, not one man, in this laboured de- fence, has been called who was engaged in training. Upon this man's testimony not one breath of imputation has been cast but by the mouth of Mr. Hunt. Various witnesses are called, in reply to the evidence, in the progress of this cause, and Mr. Hunt would have had his '*twos*' and his '*threes*' come from Manchester, to contradict him if he could be contradicted. But there is no man who either swears that he is not worthy of credit, or that his story is founded on fiction. But it appears that two witnesses called by us, Heywood and Shaw- cross, are supposed by an ingenious cross-examination to contradict him. Whereas they state they were there only a few minutes. Hey- wood was there at a later period, and does not contradict him. For at the time he was there, the people were marching ; Shawcross also saw them marching, Heywood says he saw them marching. But Chadwick saw them stand in line as well, and you know that the *making ready, presenting*, and *firing*, and so on, is only when they are standing in line. Are you to take it upon Mr. Hunt's and Mr. Bamford's credit, that all this was only to enable them to march the better to Manchester? Who then contradicts Chadwick? No man. Unless, then, you see cause to disbelieve that man on Mr. Hunt's bare assertion, it is your duty to believe him. He proves that from half-past one to six these evolutions were going on by considerable bodies of men, who kept increasing in number ; that finally they compelled every spectator to fall into their ranks, conceiving they were favourable to their plan, but that he himself soon afterwards escaped and got over the hedge, that he saw Murray come there, and saw him pursued with the cry of 'spy'; that also is proved by Murray and by Shawcross :—this innocent training then cannot bear the inspection of a constable ; and when this Mr. Murray, a confectioner at Manchester, goes to see it, he is assaulted, and no man is called to contradict this fact. The fact, then, must be taken to be true ; he is beaten, knocked down, and a consultation held whether they shall murder him because they deem him a spy—a constable! Then they form a circle round him, and they ask him to abjure his allegiance; and the man says he did it under the peril of his life. They administered to him the form of an oath that he would never again acknowledge or act in the name of the King, and having done this, they give him two blows and part with him. The poor man crawls to the next house he can find, he obtains admittance, is conveyed by a post-chaise to Manchester, and is there confined to his bed; that is confirmed by Shawcross, who saw him on the field. Now what happens the next day? You have proof that several of those persons were going to Manchester the next day; Chadwick relates this, that whilst they were assembled, and whilst they were training, a letter came upon the ground stated to have come from Manchester. A communication, therefore, is held with Manchester, at that time. The letter is received by a person who is there, but on opening it, he states there is no name to it, and, therefore, it ought not to be noticed, and the letter is not noticed; and that very individual, mark, who performed these notable transactions on that important night, Chadwick swears that he saw commanding some of the bodies that approached to the field of St. Peter's on the ensuing day. You have other witnesses who prove that some other of those persons were there, but not a man is called by Mr. Hunt from that meeting at White Moss. You have it then in evidence from my witnesses, but I thank the defendants for confirming them in a most important manner, that when the body approached the house of Murray the constable, I do not go through the details, but it was proved by Murray and by two others on my part, that on passing Murray's house there was a cry, and that the crowd passing by, called out 'No White Moss humbug,' and pointed with their fingers and hissed; that is a fact in the cause, mark you, not contradicted.

Mr. Justice Bayley.—I am not quite sure whether that was at the time that Hunt was there.

Mr. Scarlett.—No, not at that time precisely at least. Then come Mr. Hunt's party; now a word about the construction and organisation of that party. We are told that Mr. Hunt came in a carriage, and that he came perfectly innocent of all knowledge of what was to happen, that he had no control over the mob. Do not let Mr. Hunt blow hot and cold; do not let him tell us that he can calm the rising waves of this ocean, and yet that he is not at all answerable for what they do; for that he is, God help him, in his carriage! I deny the assertion; he is the avowed leader, and it is fatal to the cause of justice if you separate him from what was done by the mob. I do not mean to say that he intended they should commit an actual breach of the peace in his sense of the words, but I will tell you what I believe he intended. When his party passed by the house of Murray the constable, Murray and other witnesses tell you that they hissed and groaned, and pointed their fingers to the house. Do you then believe that the head-quarters at Smedley Cottage had no intelligence conveyed to them of what was passing at White Moss, and that Murray the constable had been there; if not, why was not somebody called by the defendant to prove something on that subject? It is proved that he proceeded from those quarters, and by his own evidence, I thank him for it, by the respectable evidence of Mr. Tyas, who got beside him, by the evidence too of a clergyman, a doctor in divinity, who, by his appearance, evidently showed that he wished to state nothing but the truth in the most cautious and candid manner; and I thank Mr. Hunt for calling Mr. Tyas, whom I understand to be a man of character. I have heard to his honour, since I came to this place, that he distinguished himself considerably as a student in the University of Cambridge. He was walking by the side of Mr. Hunt's carriage, and when they came opposite to the Star Inn, which was the place where the magistrates had been on that very morning, the carriage stopped, and the mob hissed and groaned—at what? Was it not at the nine wise magistrates who had been invited to attend the meeting? Was it not a specimen how they would be treated if they attended the meeting? Not many yards farther they came to Back King Street, which leads up to the police-office, and there the carriage stopped again, and the parties hissed and groaned again. What was the object? Was it to show how Mr. Hunt intended to inculcate on the people of Manchester reverence and obedience to the magistrates?

Gentlemen, obedience can never exist long unless it be combined with respect and reverence. Be assured, none of our magistrates can be obeyed or respected when his person, or the institution of magistracy itself, becomes a subject of scorn and ridicule. To hate, to despise, and to obey, is not the nature of man, and Mr. Hunt knows that as well as any man. Well then he advances, and by a road which was not the shortest he might have taken, but to carry on his parade, and his insolent triumph through the streets of Manchester in defiance of all the local authorities; who are those magistrates? are they persons that of necessity are to be considered as inimical to the peace of the town of Manchester? are they, who have character and property at stake, to be considered as persons whose precautions are founded purely on their own mischievous imaginations? I thank Mr. Hunt for proving by Mr. Grundy, one of the few respectable witnesses he has called, that these magistrates consist of the most respectable inhabitants of that vast town and neighbourhood, though they are treated with scorn and derision by the multitude assembled on St. Peter's Field: so much for 'the work of Mr. Hunt.'

It is observed on that important day, that a great variety of bodies, marching with the precision of troops, are advancing into the town of Manchester, not one of the seven hundred supposed inviters to this meeting appearing to be present to welcome them or exhibiting himself here before you. They march from Stockport six miles, from Saddleworth twelve miles, and from a variety of places. Can any man so trifle with his understanding as to doubt that this marching was the result of previous discipline? Look at the evidence of the witness Bamford, that he saw from two to three thousand men training a few days before on Tandle Hills; he did not train with them, no, no man that trained is called, but he saw it done, he heard of it, he went from curiosity, and he saw it in the night time.

Mr. Justice Bayley.—No, not in the night.

Mr. Scarlett.—At six in the morning.

Mr. Justice Bayley.—About seven they came through the village.

Mr. Bamford.—It was between eight and nine they came through, my Lord; the names of the witnesses are Barlow and Dyson.

Mr. Scarlett.—I will turn to the evidence of James Dyson. 'He saw from two to three thousand men drilling on Tandle Hills on a Sunday morning, two or three weeks before: they continued together from six to ten in the morning.' Then he says, he thinks that on the 16th they did not march the nearest way to St. Peter's. I leave that to you, gentlemen; either they trained for no purpose connected with Manchester, or for some purpose connected with Manchester. If they did not train for any purpose connected with Manchester, why does he not call them to say so? If they did train for any purpose connected with Manchester, can you doubt that they would have been called if the purpose was innocent? Their excuse and apology for the thing is an admission of the fact; the fact is admitted by them, that those who came to Manchester were previously trained; they were trained to march, forsooth? Why trained for marching I do not know? But I do not believe the assertion for two reasons: one, that had it been true ten thousand men might have proved it; but no man has proved it; and the other, that I have proved the direct contrary by Chadwick. Then Mr. Barlow says, 'he was at Tandle Hills on the Sunday week before the Manchester meeting; that he went between six and seven in the morning; that the people were drilling in companies, about thirty in each company; that he never counted the companies, but supposes there might be about eighty companies.' That is pretty consistent with the last witness, who says from two to three thousand ; if you multiply eighty by thirty you will find it comes to two thousand four hundred. To be sure, Mr. Bamford has selected those who knew least upon the subject of drilling ; he has selected those who can say the least against him, and the most in his favour. But even these witnesses tell you, that on that morning, before they marched, Mr. Bamford, who came evidently as their leader, formed them into a hollow square. Another witness says he was not the person, but another. Here is the seditious tribune mounted on the rostrum. He preached peace and good order. Why did you do that? Did you expect any tumult? No. Then why were your words so inconsistent with your sentiments? Why did you do that unless you apprehended that which every reasonable man must have apprehended, that you could not expect good order that day? But you preached good order, and what then? Why he gives to each officer the insignia of command—he gives his laurels to them, and orders them to take charge of the company ; and then he is seen waiting for another company, and is heard directing his people to march on, he going at their head, and charging them not to desert their colours, even in the hour of danger. Gentlemen, I admit that Mr. Hunt had taken pains to prevent an actual explosion on that day. What occasion was there to call his witnesses, confirming what I had already proved in that respect? I never made it a part of my case that he intended violence. But I made this a part of my case, that whatever he intended, even his own vanity could not make him believe he could have prevented mischief, upon assembling such a number of men; and that it was highly probable they would have broken out into acts of violence in spite of his intentions.

But he has called some persons to prove that *they* felt no terror and alarm, as if that feeling in others could be brought into question upon this occasion. I have extracted the evidence of all the persons he has called, having an immediate residence in the town of Manchester. I find he has called in number, including good, bad, and indifferent, seventeen: the first of whom is Mr. Scholfield, who certainly gave his testimony, at least, like an amateur, to say nothing more of him, a gentleman who gave his testimony as if he was practising for some future occasion, but knowing nothing of the gentleman I say nothing against him ; what he says is but matter of opinion. The next is Morey Jones, the publican, who keeps the Windmill, in Windmill Street. Another is a caravan driver, who would not have much property to lose ; then we come to John Molineux, a tinplate-worker, who had attended the famous meeting, and the dinner after it, and who there drank, what I am bound to

say, were no disloyal toasts; and, finally, I would select John
Scholfield, the Dissenting minister, whom Mr. Hunt has thought fit
to produce, as a grace to his cause. Gentlemen, this cause is too
important, and my powers are too feeble to pursue by detail all the
features of that man's evidence; but I put it to any one who heard
him, do any one of you believe Mr. Scholfield upon his oath? That
man who cannot tell what he had written in the *Manchester Observer*,
who writes, however, for that seditious paper, a man who pretends
that his articles were not connected with politics, though it turned
out that they contained nothing but politics, when I pressed upon
him in cross-examination. I saw his inconsistency had an influence
upon you, as it must have had upon every man of candour who
heard him. Now I have called to you witnesses, whom I must bring
back to your recollection, as well as the manner of their giving their
testimony, seventeen, equal in number; not only inhabitants, with
the exception of one of the magistrates, Mr. Hulton, not only inhabitants of the town of Manchester, but persons having a deep interest
in the place, many of them respectable persons, taking the office of
special constables; solicitors, personally known to me as men of
honour and character; gentlemen who can have no bias upon their
minds, surely, in this case to tell anything but the truth; and they
swear to you, that the mere assembling of the crowd, independently of
the intentions shown towards insult and violence; that the mode of
assembling the crowd, combined with the circumstance of their
having a foreign leader; a man having no connection with the
place; a man coming to usurp the power of the local authorities;
created alarm in their minds, as well as the acts they committed.
You remember the questions asked upon a celebrated occasion, of
one who, like Mr. Hunt, alleged that he neither felt nor inspired
fear, 'Nihilne te, nocturnum præsidium Palatii, nihil urbis vigiliæ,
nihil timor populi, nihil concursus bonorum omnium, nihil hic munitis-
simus habendi senatus locus, nihil denique horum ora vultusque move-
runt?' Why are these things not to move you? Was not the town
alarmed? Were not the constables placed in activity? Did not the
justices seek protection from the military? Can you doubt that those
who assembled with so much anxiety at the Star Inn, and afterwards
transferred themselves to Buxton's house, under a guard of special
constables, felt the deepest alarm? What was happening? Under a
pretence, which had no existence but in the wicked imaginations of
those who gave it utterance, a meeting was assembled, alleged to be
called by the people of Manchester. Not one of those persons came
forward then to avow such a requisition; or now dares to say that he
asked for any meeting. Instead of that, a meeting is formed by the

band of persons who conspire to produce it, formed by numbers of persons who invade the town of Manchester, who march into the town in regular discipline, under the command of appointed leaders. Mr. Bamford says, 'If I am taken, or any of those called the leaders are taken, do not resist.' I asked the witness whom he called the leaders? He could not tell; but with all these precautions, Mr. Bamford could not prevent some excess. One man says 'We will make a Moscow of the town;' another says, 'Thou hast a good coat on thy back, but I will have as good a one before night;' and a third says, 'We are going to West Houghton Mills.' I do not mean to say these sentiments actuated Mr. Bamford. I say it is the character of a multitude so assembled that individual passions will break out, and that no human force or authority can restrain them when they come to the point of being so influenced by the encouragement of their numbers, and the movement of their passions. I do not give this in evidence as indicating the designs of the leaders, but as indicating correctly the feelings of the mass of people who invaded Manchester, a certain jealousy of the poor against the rich, a most calamitous feeling for the poor, and which it is too easy for a demagogue to excite. But was this to be brought into action? Oh, no! they were only to receive a lecture, and hear a soothing speech, which could not inflame any meeting. You will hear Mr. Hunt begin, 'Good friends, sweet friends, let me not stir you up to any sudden flood of mutiny.' You know a demagogue, in leading on a mob to the greatest violence, begins always with temperate language, 'For God's sake do not let it be supposed I lead you to mischief; I am the friend of good order!' But Mr. Hunt might have effected all the violence and the mischief, though he had not the talents of Antony, in exhibiting before them the garment of the Constitution, and showing how it was stabbed in various places, holding those places up as the work of their enemies. I ask Mr. Hunt to explain, not to practise over again the indecency of interrupting me, but I ask how has he explained, from the beginning of the cause to the end of it, what he intended by that significant expression '*your enemies,*' 'do not let *your enemies* interrupt you?'

In passing, I will say a single word to show the futility of a great part of his evidence. I called a witness to prove that he was so situated that he could see the line of infantry drawn up; he did not say Hunt saw them, but he supposed he did; he saw a disorder in the mob, and he heard the words, 'There are your enemies,' and he thought he heard, 'Get them down, and keep them down.' Every witness of Mr. Hunt proves that he made use of similar expressions, and all the difference is, that this man who saw the soldiers thought they were applied to them ; whereas the others say, and very likely correctly, that they were not applied to them, but to those who might interrupt the meeting. But who were the enemies? Were they the constables? Were they the magistrates? Are you, gentlemen of rank and character and property in this country, trying this cause, to be told that a demagogue shall rise up and tell a multitude that the magistrates and constables are their enemies? Yes ! these are your enemies ; show them that you dare to do that which they say you have no right to do, and show them more, by the organised manner in which you assemble, by the multitudes you bring together, by the determination of your purpose, by the form and character of your meeting, that you have the power to trample them down, but at present are not disposed or ordered to do so. This, gentlemen, was the character of that meeting ; it was a meeting with a menace and an intimidation, to show that Mr. Hunt and his mob had power to destroy Manchester, but that in their good pleasure they meant for the present to save it. Is this law? Is it safe to be allowed to any man to possess such power, whatever might be Mr. Hunt's intentions? I much deplore the calamities that happened that day ; but I give perfect credit to the honour and judgment of that magistrate, who states that if they had permitted that meeting to continue, the town of Manchester might not have been standing the next morning. What does history tell us? Do we not know that Lord George Gordon, in 1780, caused a meeting to assemble for a legal object, to petition against a bill introduced into Parliament, the meeting consisting of ten thousand ; that he preached to them peace and good order ; nay, when he was tried for high treason, his declarations that he meant only peace and good order acquitted him of high treason, as Mr. Hunt would have been acquitted of high treason if he had been charged wth that offence ; but did that acquit him of the fatal consequences of that day? Having preached peace and good order, a proposal is made that they should all attend him to the House of Commons. They did so ; and notwithstanding his popularity, notwithstanding his eloquence, notwithstanding the peace he preached, they broke out into acts of violence ; many of the members were seized, and the metropolis was the scene of violence, conflagration, and outrage for days. And were the magistrates to sit down quietly, and to see eighty thousand persons assembled to hear lectures, I speak only by conjecture what the lectures might be, but to hear the eminent person, Mr. Carlile, held up as an object of reverence, and the local magistrates held up to scorn and contempt, and then to expect, that because the demagogue of the day preached peace and good order, the vast multitude were to return hungry to their homes? I say the man who thinks so does not judge rightly of the constitution of man. Upon that very occasion of Lord George Gordon's mob, the Lord Mayor, who presided in London, was prosecuted for not having taken prompt and effective measures to disperse that multitude before they had committed any act of violence.

Gentlemen, the history of these things is a school in which wise men learn ; but there are some who are too wise to learn, and who consult only their own imagination for the consequences of their imprudent conduct. I say no more, except to vindicate a high-spirited and honourable man [1] from the aspersion cast upon him in this cause, a gentleman of honour and family, and who has been known in his neighbourhood as one of the most humane and charitable men in that quarter of the world. There is not any part of his evidence that is shaken by Mr. Hunt except this (and I meet it fairly in the first place)— he stated that when the cavalry were forming he heard some of the persons in the crowd hissing and groaning. If Mr. Hunt had called twenty men to say they did not hear it, that would not have contradicted him ; but he proves that which all the other witnesses prove, that the people near them turned round, and he combined with the hisses and groans the shouts of the multitude, and thought it a shout of defiance ; one of Mr. Hunt's witnesses says in one sense it was. Then I hope the magistrate may be excused. He says (and Mr. Hunt has taken advantage of my not introducing the subsequent events of that day) he says he saw cudgels brandished, and brickbats and stones in the air ; he will not swear they were thrown at the cavalry, but that he saw them, and that as the cavalry approached the hustings, and formed round the hustings, the crowd closed in upon them. Mr. Hunt may call twenty witnesses to contradict that, but he has called two who prove it, Mr. Tyas and Mr. Dobson, a respectable witness from Liverpool. Mr. Hulton thought that that was done for the purpose of cutting them off (I do not say that it was, but he thought it was), and then he saw an apparent scuffle. All the contradiction to him in Mr. Hunt's evidence is removed, because the closing in upon the cavalry is proved by Dobson and by Tyas. Tyas proves that he saw the constables beating off the crowd, to keep up with the cavalry, and people getting in their way. Then the rest is this, that Mr. Hulton stated he saw the sticks brandished and the stones flying. Now, surely, in the giving an account of the transactions of that day, if a man states a fact which forms part of that account (though I industriously declined pointing his attention to it, wishing his Lordship to stop him when he came to that period at which our inquiry terminated) there is nothing so blameable. I

[1] Mr. Hulton.

think it my duty to vindicate an honourable man. Mr. Hulton has probably confounded the period when the brickbats and sticks were thrown ; he says he thought they were thrown at the military : 'I conceived the military were beaten, and I felt it my duty, in consequence, to order that the cavalry should proceed directly ;' and he says, 'I believe, upon my oath, conscientiously, that it never did enter, until that moment, into the contemplation of the magistrates to disperse that crowd by military force, but they thought it due to their country and to the peace of the town to prevent seditious speeches being made to these people.' Is Mr. Hulton confirmed in this ? I say there was a period when missiles were thrown, and Mr. Hunt has proved it by two witnesses : first, William Nicholson saw sticks and stones after the standards were taken, and another witness says the people did not seem willing to part with their standards ; and then his Lordship says we must not go further : that is the period at which this transaction stops. Mr. Hulton says they did fly ; and so they did fly, but not at the precise moment which Mr. Hulton was supposed to speak of : that is the history of that absurd and pretended contradiction. He has called about twenty witnesses, and asked them with an air of triumph, as if he had trampled Mr. Hulton to the bottom, ' Did you see any rioting ? If there had been any, must you not have seen it ? Is it not manifest if there had been you must have seen it ?' He has put down all my witnesses, that Mr. Orton who actually was locked, Mr. Walker who saw it, and two or three other witnesses who saw it, are all guilty of manifest perjury. Judge, from the witnesses he has called, of the nature of a great part of his case. He has called two witnesses, both of whom prove the fact distinctly. Mr. Dobson from Liverpool, who appears to be a respectable man, who distinctly saw the first line locked, but could not see any farther, from a very distinct reason, because a man cannot see, where there is a close line of gentlemen immediately in front of him, whether the next line are locked or not. We have witnesses to prove, not that Mr. Hunt said it, but that Mr. Swift said, *Lock your arms* ; and Mr. Dobson says, that though he did not hear what the speaker said, it was done immediately after someone addressed them from the hustings. I proved that that was Swift, and I had two respectable witnesses who dictated certain words to Mr. Ellis on the spot. One was Mr. Green, an honourable and respectable man, and the other Mr. Hardman. They both heard the words, and Mr. Ellis wrote them down at the moment ; they heard one of the defendants, Wild, say, ' Keep your ranks close ; it is ordered by the committee that you should form so many yards round the hustings ' (I should be glad know what committee. What member of the committee is called here?), 'because, if you do not, they will pour in their cavalry and all their corruption.' Mr. Green said, very properly, ' I do not say there is much sense in the words, I only swear they were used.' Much sense ! I hope Mr. Wild may by-and-by, from the lesson of this day, turn out to be an honest man ; but God forbid that the country should ever come to that state when the sense of Mr. Wild is to be the guide for this kingdom. I think it is very probable that many of them talked non-sense ; but that is no reason why Mr. Green must be taken not to have spoken the truth. The leaders and Mr. Hunt did not wish to produce any disturbance that day, but they wished to show to their enemies that they could trample upon them when they chose, and that they were inspired with courage to face a military force if opposed to them. If Mr. Hunt can induce his body of patriots to stand forth in the face of a military body, and to pass their resolutions without fear and alarm ; if he can teach them the secret and force of organisation; if he can teach a man that it is not his own individual arm, but that of his neighbour and his neighbour's neighbour, that he may depend upon ; if he shall be able to show them that they are a connected phalanx, then and then only can an explosion take place safely ; and therefore his object was to show that the multitude might be put into such a form, and made to take such a position, and to come with such determined spirit, that if they chose they might, on occasion, make resistance.

Now, gentlemen, I say again that this meeting is not a meeting of the inhabitants of Manchester ; I say it never was so intended. The people of Manchester are à loyal and well-disposed people ; they invite no such meeting. There may be a committee there, for aught I know, who may have corresponded with certain persons, and Mr. John-son may know who they are ; but that seven hundred persons invited such a meeting I do not believe. Seven hundred weavers, perhaps, might be found to swear that they put their names to the paper ; but that seven hundred persons, respectable inhabitants, called upon Mr. Hunt to take the chair at a meeting, I do not believe. You see the effect. From the neighbourhood, from the villages round, there are to be assembled eighty thousand persons. It is said they had women and children with them. My case did not deny that. It has been proved by Mr. Tyas that there were two female reform societies. I do not mean to say that *they* intended open violence that day ; but that Mr. Hunt intended to have a great body of women and children there is likely ! The object was *deliberative*, as one of the witnesses says ! It had a great air of a deliberative assembly. It was intended to determine on the election of a representative, and women were the best persons to engage in that discussion ! But how trifling is this ! Is there ever a mob without women and children? When danger takes place they are crushed and injured. The best thing would be to keep women and children out of it. I believe Mr. Hunt wished them to be there. The story has long harped upon the women and children; but, forsooth, does this great orator come from London to preach to women and children? Are they to adorn him with the palm of eloquence? Are they to form part of his new republic? This is trifling. There were many women and many children in Lord George Gordon's mob, and many were killed. It is no part of my case that they premeditated violence that day; but I will tell you what I think they did premeditate. I say a spirit has long prevailed in this district, where the proportion of poor to the rich is greater than in the neighbourhood of the metropolis, and a disposition to shake off the authority of their superiors. I say, if that disposition is taken advantage of, if Mr. Hunt, and those who act with Mr. Hunt, can extend it, can organise it, can bring it into action simultaneously at such points as he thinks convenient—the Government is at an end. The moment that a system of intimidation takes place, that a multitude can be brought together at a certain point to invade the peace of a town that never invited or expected them; if all the local authorities can be put to fear, and possibly to flight, I say there is an end of the administration of law. We are to be governed by a system of intimidation and violence. You do not want the actual blow; a threat is sufficient; the very holding of such an assembly is sufficient; and I say that by the law of this land, as established by the best authorities, such a meeting is illegal. I will state to his Lordship a passage from Mr. Serjeant Hawkins's ' Pleas of the Crown,' in which he will see this sort of assembly designated and pointed out. He makes a distinction between a riot and an unlawful assembly : a riot must be accompanied by some offer of violence, but an unlawful assembly need not. For example, if persons do assemble armed, though they commit no act of violence, where it is not necessary to assemble armed : ' From hence it seems to follow, that persons riding together on the road with unlawful weapons, or *otherwise assembling together in such a manner as is apt to raise a terror in the people*, though without any offer of violence to any one in respect to either his person or possessions, are not properly guilty of a riot, but only of an unlawful assembly.' Now I ask of you, gentlemen, when you come to deliberate upon your verdict in this cause, and to try amongst yourselves this issue, Was this or not an unlawful assembly? Do you believe that every witness I have called to prove that terror and alarm existed in the town of Manchester is perjured? Do you believe that the witnesses I have called to prove that it was an approach in the form of a military array, though not armed, are perjured? Do you believe that the magistrates felt no alarm when they witnessed what passed on that day and the preceding day? Do you believe that the constables were assembled on a false pretext? Can any man doubt that such a multitude must inspire terror and alarm? Not from their demeanour upon the field, not from their dispositions betrayed by any acts they did, or any expressions they uttered; no, but by their secret organisation, by their mode of marching, by their appearing to be under some secret leader? The very mystery in which that organisation is involved is a proof of the danger, and necessarily excites the mind to alarm and terror. Good God! are we to take the law from Mr. Bamford, that people may train and drill without his Majesty's commission? Yes, if you prove a legitimate object; the master of an academy may have his scholars drilled; the master of a factory, to defend his factory; but if he drills and trains them, and cannot prove, by satisfactory evidence, his object, I say he is guilty of an unlawful act; for no man has a right to usurp the authority of the King, or has a right to train his subjects for any military evolution or purpose but by the King's authority. And when I prove that they are trained to go through all the accustomed evolutions, unless you have evidence to show, by some persons who trained them, that it was for a lawful object, you must believe that it was for an unlawful object; and it was for an unlawful object if it was intended to inspire in the town of Manchester a belief that they had an organisation which might enable them to resist the authority of the magistrates whenever they should so be pleased.

But suppose the populace themselves had no such intention, what shall we say to Mr. Bamford and the numerous leaders, Mr. Wild, who appeared upon the spot, and the Doctor from Oldham? who did not, indeed, appear from his temperance to be in the best predicament or tone of mind to judge upon political questions; if the others advised to peace and good order, I think the Doctor was one who was preached to by Mr. Hunt, for he was already singing the song of triumph, 'Victory, my lads.' The danger lies in the organising a multitude; they obey some secret and unknown authority; that authority wheels them at its pleasure. Mr. Orator Hunt is the person who is to take the occasional command of them. He is invited down by them on account of his great merits and his constitutional principles. Then how do they assemble? I will not be told, without expressing my dissent, that the assembling a multitude of that sort, with banners and the kind of proceedings which took place in that field, is lawful.

Gentlemen, we have had a trifling comparison of these banners with the banners of an election and a benefit club. Why does Mr. Hunt make that comparison? He has been in the habit of addressing men, women, and children till he supposes that everything he says passes for law, and that you are capable of being gulled by his statement, as if these were the same sort of banners as at an election. A man may at an election carry before him a banner 'No corn laws,' if he has supported opinions consistently with a particular line of politics, and the voters support him because he supports those opinions. A gentleman might as well say 'Banners! do not soldiers carry banners?' The argument might go that length, and therefore you are to consider the occasion. I say nothing can be more fatal to all hope of improvement of the constitution of the country, nothing can be more destructive to the common people themselves, than to have it taught and preached up by demagogues, that 'equal representation or death' is that they are to seek; that taxation without representation is tyranny, which implies that the House of Commons are tyrants, as they do not represent the greater portion who have not and cannot have voices in Parliament; though the way is open for every man, by industry, to attain the means of being personally represented; to preach up that they are sold as slaves, which the rev. gentleman thinks may be safely preached up, I say nothing is more dangerous to the safety and prosperity of the kingdom than to permit such doctrines to be preached up.

Gentlemen, I shall never lift up my voice against the animation which a large assembly may give to those who take a lawful part in their deliberations. But the constitution of this multitude was of a totally different character. They were persons who assembled, not to deliberate, but who had before decided; not to discuss, for Mr. Hunt prevents them. No discussion there: he invites them, indeed, to discuss with the magistrates the legality of electing a member. Which of those industrious spinners of cotton or cutters of fustian were the fit persons to discuss that matter or enter into that debate? Are we not trifling if we suppose political subjects are fit matters for the discussion of sixty thousand people? Now I will give in his own language the character of that multitude. Hear his address, and you shall judge from that whether Mr. Hunt did not mean to inspire the magistrates with alarm, whether he did not intend to treat the constables and the local authorities with scorn, whether he did not mean to hold up to scorn all the public functionaries that the law had entrusted; and whether, finally, he did not characterise the multitude by the words spoken to by two of his witnesses, 'a tremenduous meeting?' A tremendous meeting it was, and the

T

consequences indeed have been tremendous. But, for aught I know, they may be still more so if, by your verdict, you say that such a meeting has the sanction of law. Here is a passage in his address: 'For the honour which they had just conferred upon him he returned them his most sincere thanks, and for any services which he either had or might render them, all that he asked was that they would indulge him with a calm and patient attention. It was impossible for him to think that, with the utmost silence, he could make himself heard by every member of the numerous and tremendous meeting which he saw assembled before him;' and I verily believe at that moment there was in his mind a mixture of fear and vanity that was expressed by those two words; 'if those, however, who were near him were not silent, how could it be expected that those who were at a distance could hear what he should say?' (a dead silence now pervaded the multitude). 'It was useless for him to recall to their recollection the proceedings of the last ten days in their town.' Yes, I hope then I may say he was a party to these proceedings, that he knew what had taken place, and that the multitude were all privy to it, except this, that those who had attempted to put them down by the most malignant exertions, had occasioned them to meet that day in tenfold numbers.' Here then are the doctrines inculcated upon this assembly, to whom peace and good order are preached, 'You had a meeting in contemplation on the 9th of August; I came to preside over it; it was to elect a Member of Parliament; the magistrates declared it was illegal; I declare that it was legal. It was put down by the malignant exertions of men who had no honesty nor knew no law; but witness the effect, our numbers are tenfold, and if they should show any design to disperse this meeting, I do not advise you to resist them; no, show your firmness, and I will meet you again with fourfold your present numbers; stand firm, show your determination; do not be alarmed at the appearance of the cavalry; at present you are raw and undisciplined troops, who cannot see a red coat without being alarmed; but learn to practise your manœuvres in the presence of soldiers; then I will by and by meet you with them face to face.' He said, 'they would have perceived that since the old meeting had been put off and the present one called.' (Now I beg you, gentlemen, just as I go along, to remember that Mr. Hunt spent about two hours in cross-examining a most respectable witness from Manchester, Mr. Entwistle, to prove that he could not have made use of the word 'adjourned' or 'postponed,' and his own evidence proves that he made use of both). 'They would have perceived that since the old meeting had been put off and the present one had been called, though their enemies' (Who had put it off? Who had put it down?) The magistrates—were they their enemies? Who can doubt it?—'flattered themselves with having obtained a victory, they show by their conduct that they had sustained a defeat.' And this was followed by long and loud applause; it is a matter of applause that they had defeated their enemies. Whom did he mean to characterise as his enemies? The magistrates. Then followed that which is perfectly consistent with the evidence on both sides. 'That when the cavalry advanced, Hunt and Johnson desired the multitude to give three cheers, to show the military that they were not to be daunted in the discharge of their duty by their unwelcome presence.' Half his witnesses have sworn that the cheer was to welcome them; but Mr. Tyas has shown that he desired the multitude to give three cheers, to show the military that they were not to be daunted in the discharge of their duty by their unwelcome presence. It is quite indifferent whether their presence was welcome or unwelcome, if Mr. Hunt meant to teach his men to stand firm in the presence of the military, welcome or unwelcome.

It has been stated by Mr. Hunt that this meeting was legal, because there had been two or three Acts of Parliament since to prevent similar meetings; and my learned friend Mr. Holt, whose speech has been followed up by so much matter since, that I had quite forgotten it, says there has been an Act of Parliament to prevent meetings within a mile of Palace Yard. Gentlemen, I deny the inference. I say a meeting must be considered under the common law according to the circumstances. The meeting alluded to in that Act, must be taken as a meeting of the inhabitants of the district; but this was a meeting summoned by some secret and unknown committee, pretending to have been called by the inhabitants of Manchester, but not so proved—a meeting not of the town or the county, but of every man who had a real or supposed grievance. Mr. Hunt cries out, 'Come unto me all ye that are heavy laden, and I will lighten your burden, and you shall give to me the crown of laurel and the palm of eloquence.'

Gentlemen, I have, I am afraid, fatigued you too long, by a reply too minute upon many parts of the case. The broad question for you to try is this: Was this a lawful assembly? That is the first proposition which I refer to your judgment and your best consideration. Do you think it was lawful to assemble a multitude in such a form, and with such banners, and with such designs? designs not left only to conjecture. I am sure I shall have his Lordship's confirmation, when I say, that if Mr. Hunt, and those who joined in assembling the multitude, did design to pass such resolutions as those passed in London, that design alone makes such meeting highly illegal, and the attempting it a grave and serious misdemeanour. Has Mr. Hunt, or any of the defendants, brought before you any one person to prove what were the resolutions they meant to pass? Have you any information to this day, what was the real object of that meeting? No; it is left to be inferred from the circumstances, from the mode of assembling this multitude, and the previous suggestions that your own judgment upon the evidence may lead you to form. I call upon you to come to the conclusion that his object was to elect members, as their fellow-countrymen at Birmingham had done, and which was intended on the 9th; or to pass resolutions similar to those passed in Smithfield, and advertised in the Manchester papers a week before. Whichever of these was his object, if you are of opinion he had some such object and some such design, then the meeting was illegal. But whatever his object, if the form and mode of assembling, if the vast numbers, if the organisation, the secret and undiscovered hand that trained and disciplined them—if all these circumstances conspired together to produce alarm and terror in the minds of peaceable men, the meeting was unlawful. This is one question you have to consider.

The next question is the part each took. With respect to Hunt, there can be no question; he is the prime mover in the whole. With respect to Johnson, they are residing together. He proposes Hunt as chairman of the meeting; and there is certain evidence given which is pretended to be contradicted; for that they swear they do not believe Willie on his oath. Yet who swears that he does not believe Slater upon his oath? Johnson comes there by accident on the 6th of August, and finding Willie at the bar (this is the effect of Slater's evidence, as well as Willie's), the conversation turns on the meeting of the 9th, which had been resolved to be put off—'Why,' says Slater to Johnson, 'I understand you and Nicholas Whitworth are to be elected Members for Manchester. You do not suppose they will elect you?—they did not intend to take a townsman; probably, they would take another gentleman to be the Member. You do not think the people at the House of Commons would let you in to be a Member?' 'Oh,' says he, 'you do not know what may happen!' Slater goes out of the room, and the subject of the meeting is carried forward by Willie; and he tells him, in consequence of their having put off the meeting to the 16th, they will bring together a force greater than the magistrates can bring. Slater comes back, and the conversation is renewed with Slater about their going to the House of Commons, and Slater ridicules the idea. Slater is a respectable man; there is no question upon his testimony; he says, as soon as Johnson was gone away, Willie asked who it was, and said, if Nadin had been there he would have taken him up for what he said. That is a strong confirmation of Willie; and Willie and he both concur in this—' Why, you do not suppose the House of Commons would resist if a body was to go with sufficient firmness? I can tell you this,—at the time Horsefall was killed, I knew it as a fact, there was a body of men who had resolved to go to London, and to put every man in the House of Commons to death, or to disperse them, but the subscriptions were not large enough to keep their families while they were away, or in case they had failed. I am persuaded it might have been done ; for when Bellingham killed Perceval, what confusion there was ! Lord Castlereagh scrambling to get out of one window and Mr. Canning out of another, until Bellingham was taken up, and then they all flocked around him.' Thus reminding Mr. Slater of a circumstance, the commemoration of which is no honour to the nation nor to the man who desires to record it in our history with applause, for the purpose of encouraging and teaching other assassins how a Minister may be destroyed.

Who contradicts this ? Two witnesses—one a builder, and another a butcher, who swear they do not believe Mr. Willie upon his oath ; do they state that they do not believe Mr. Slater upon his oath ? No : but I will tell them how Mr. Johnson might have contradicted this : —Willie was sent for by a magistrate,—he was watched in coming back,—Johnson sent out his servant to watch him : he says he came into his shop ; and recollect, gentlemen, that the fact is verified by his own cross-examination ; for he says he put to him questions in the presence of his men: ' Did not you say I had no private conversation with you? and did not I say that you might say what you pleased ? ' What does he say was the reply? 'I told you I would not enter into conversation before so many persons, whom I suspected to be spies, but that if you would go with me into another room, I had no objection to tell you what I said.' ' No, you shall tell it in the presence of these persons, or not at all.' That evidence, combined with these two facts, that Willie was dogged by Johnson, and that there are persons who keep spies and informers in their pay besides those who are charged with it in a public meeting, proves that Johnson might have called those persons to contradict Willie : I say this is be taken as evidence of Johnson's intention not to breed a riot, but to show the magistrates that they could bring such a force together as might resist them.

Then, with respect to Mr. Moorhouse, he appears to me to be a main actor in this design : he comes to hail Hunt's approach ; he takes him to his house ; he makes a speech at Stockport to him ; and he goes to Smedley Cottage on the day of the procession from

Stockport : and that he was in the procession is clear from this, that they waited half an hour for him.

Mr. Barrow.—He did not go to Smedley Cottage.

Mr. Justice Bayley.—I do not recollect that he made a speech for him at Stockport.

Mr. Scarlett.—I do not mean to misrepresent : he made speeches before, perhaps.

Mr. Hunt.—No ; afterwards.

Mr. Scarlett.—He learned to make speeches from what he heard that day, I suppose. But it is proved that Mr. Moorhouse said, ' Bring as many of your friends and neighbours as you can on the 16th.' Then Mr. Moorhouse advances in his carriage, and he takes half an hour to bait and water his horses in a stage of six miles and a half. I ask you whether the object was not to come in with that procession ? He does not take his carriage on the ground. He looks at the main chance ; but he is not like the great orator, the object of his subscription, (we find in the same paper a subscription advertised for the Lord of the Manor of Glastonbury). He arrives ; he goes to seek Mr. Hunt, he finds him just opposite the Exchange ; and he gets into the carriage, and approaches so near that any man, at a distance of thirty or forty yards would mistake him as being there ; and if he was not there it was not through any design of his, he intended to be there, but, having an accident with his finger, he retires to dress it with brandy. It is for you to say whether he did not take an active part in desiring the Stockport people to come, and in approaching the hustings with Mr. Hunt. As to Swift, he addressed the people from the hustings. Wild directed them to retire so many yards, and to link together, lest they should bring in the cavalry and all the corruption ; Jones erected the hustings ; and, finally, Dr. Healey ! The Doctor, it seems, is very indignant that he should be suspected of anything wrong ; for he says, ' Where there is no law, there is no transgression.' It would be very convenient to the Doctor to have no law, or if we could arrive at a period when there shall be no law ; that is the use he makes of St Paul ; and the Doctor, thinking there is no law against men marching as they like, or talking what they like, assumed a more military appearance, perhaps, on that day, than was usual with him ; perhaps his temper was reduced to a greater calmness than it has exhibited here ; and, besides, the Doctor has taken the pains to tell you that he exercised his invention about some part of the inscriptions on the banners : he brought with him a little fac-simile of the flag, and took merit for the having procured it, lest the prosecutor should be so base as not to exhibit the flag when Mr. Hunt had made so much parade about it ; but I produced the original. He has given you a fac simile of a cap of liberty: I would have favoured him with the inspection of the original. These ensigns may be on some occasions well meant. I do not say that they may not, but you have had half an hour's examination about a cap of liberty being innocent. Gentlemen, a cap of liberty has been a revolutionary emblem since the French revolution. The miseries of a revolution under that ensign have changed its designation. It is no longer exhibited as the emblem of liberty, but the mischiefs that have been engendered and perpetrated under it have converted it into a badge of licentiousness.

Gentlemen, with respect to Knight, he was in the carriage with Mr. Hunt, and proceeded with him to the hustings. As to Saxton, I say at once that, as my evidence has only traced him to the hustings, and as he is a reporter, I think it is a fair ground for you to give a verdict in his favour. I should have said earlier in the case, that Mr. Saxton might be acquitted, but I had some faint hope that the editor of this respectable paper, the *Manchester Observer*, of which he is proved to be a reporter, would have been called to prove this fact ; if he had been so called and those seven hundred names which appeared in his paper were not mere moonshine, I would have asked him a few questions. I beg to dismiss Mr. Saxton from your consideration. With respect to the others, I think they are all implicated in the common design.

The first question, gentlemen, is, was the assembly unlawful? If it was, then, were these defendants parties to the design of forming it? I am perfectly at ease when I have discharged my duty upon this important subject. With respect to consequences I fear none, unless it should be established by the verdict of a British jury that such a meeting was lawful. I adjure you to dismiss the subsequent events of the day from your consideration, and to consider the important consequences to your country if you establish such a meeting to be legal. Gentlemen, I know that in a country like this such a meeting must not be tolerated. Those who, under the sanction of a law which gives useful powers to the people, and ought to be esteemed and cherished by them press those powers on to abuse and licentiousness, are the most dangerous enemies of liberty. For men of reflection will say, ' If this is to be practised, better it is to surrender a portion of our rights and of our power than to retain them by the violation of all order, and by trampling on all authority.' So it is that one of the most wise and eloquent historians, when describing how the people of Rome, on the death of Augustus, became willing instruments of the perpetuation of their own slavery, because they recollected the tumults and dangers of former times, says ' *tuta ac præsentia mallent quam vetera, et periculosa* ; ' they submitted rather to the safely of despotism, than they would venture to go back to licentiousness that would put every man into danger, and afford to the evil-minded and turbulent an opportunity of taking away the lives of their countrymen. I trust, by your verdict to-day, that you will save your country from such a peril, for I think when the verdicts of juries support the laws, they do the most essential service ; they prove the laws of the country are equal to the care of their own vindication. But if, from any popular prejudice, from any compassion for persons not before you, from feelings unconnected with this case, you shall be led to find a verdict that this was a lawful assembly, I for one shall hold down my head with sorrow, for I shall feel that the part which very many wise and virtuous men took in a place where there is freedom of debate, in vindicating the sufficiency of the existing law, is a part they might regret. I think the law is sufficient. I trust by your verdict you will say it is sufficient, and that a jury of the country will not permit such a meeting, under such circumstances, to be tolerated by their sanction.

THE KING v. SIR FRANCIS BURDETT, Bart.[1]

REPORT *of the* ARGUMENT *of* Mr. SCARLETT *in the Court of King's Bench at Westminster, on Saturday, the 17th June, and Tuesday, the 20th June, 1820, in support of the motion for a new trial.*

Mr. Scarlett.—My Lords, it is with great reluctance, and not without some embarrassment, that in this stage of the proceedings I offer myself to your notice. Were I at liberty to consult my own personal feelings, I should decline it altogether ; but the professional duty which obliges me in consequence of the application of the honourable defendant, is corroborated by a duty I owe to the public ; for I can assure you, most unequivocally, that in the course of my professional experience I never had entrusted to my humble ability a question which I deemed of such deep and general importance.

If the subject is of importance in itself, the view taken of it, and the view which by possibility may be taken of it, as I tremble to apprehend, from a concurrence on the part of your Lordships in the arguments I have heard advanced, overwhelm me with anxiety and alarm. I certainly did never expect that in this period of our history, after so much consideration of the subject of libel, after fifty years, during which the principles broached this day have slept, I did never expect to hear them revived and pressed by the Counsel for the Crown, with as much zeal and energy as they were ever pressed with in those fatal times which I had hoped we had long survived, and almost forgotten. If the law of libel, if the principles on which that crime depends, are to be drawn from crude notions, founded in an ignorant conception of the nature of the offence, and a strong desire to support arbitrary government, if the doctrines and authorities brought forward to-day have a chance of being received and countenanced by your Lordships, I shall think that the history of

[1] The trial of Sir Francis Burdett for libel, led to his being fined and imprisoned. His high character, noble qualities and social position, added to his great personal popularity, gave unusual interest to the occurrence. A large party in Parliament and numerous friends lent Sir Francis all their support and sympathy, and used their endeavours to obtain his liberation. The accompanying speech, in favour of a motion for a new trial before the judges in banco, was considered at the time a great display of legal acumen and learning.

mankind is destined to go round in a fatal circle, and that it is not
the enjoyment of an hundred years of just government and rational
freedom that can insure the public from a recurrence of those wretched
systems which disgrace the periods from which those doctrines and
authorities are derived.   I am one of those who have felt a degree of
surprise as well as alarm at hearing the doctrine of the law of libel
drawn from those sources which, after the mature consideration of
all the judges, after the most solemn authority that could be given
to the subject, I had thought buried in total oblivion.   I had thought
that the very nature of the crime, the principles on which it depends,
the mischiefs which the punishment is intended to prevent, and all
the mischiefs which occur to a reflecting mind as resulting from the
punishment of it, had been resolved and illustrated by the opinions
of the judges at the time when they stated that the crime of libel
consisted, emphatically, in the publication.   But it seems we are now
to revise those opinions, and to correct them by the principles that prevailed just before and just after the Revolution, at a period when the
decisions of the judges, to a certain degree, were fettered by recent doctrines and authorities, from which they could not immediately, nor until
the public mind was prepared to go along with them, emancipate themselves.   That the cases of the King and Beare, and the King and
Payne, existed as law, I am not disposed to deny; but I will contend,
with conviction on my own mind, that there is no one principle, no
just consideration of the nature of crime and punishment that can
sustain those cases : and I will undertake to satisfy you that the
reasons on which they are founded destroy all their authority ; for
my learned friends must take the cases for good and for bad, and
must not attempt to put on me the authority of a judge, however
great his talents, however revered his name, who does not, on a
question of this nature, appeal to authority, but to the understanding,
and gives the whole of his reasonings ; thereby enabling me to show
that it is founded on fallacious principles.

   I will follow the arrangement of the Attorney-General in considering, first, what is charged in this indictment; next, what is the
effect of the verdict of the jury ; and, lastly, what is the evidence to
support it ; and I shall have deceived myself indeed, if I do not
show, on some of the very authorities stated, and on their own statement of them, that a new trial ought to be granted : for I will show
that this verdict is not supported by evidence, even though I should
admit the principle, which is horrible to state, that the mere writing
without publication is an offence.   What is the charge on the record?
The charge is, that the defendant composed, wrote, and published,
in the county of Leicester, a scandalous and malicious libel, of and

concerning the Government of the realm, and of and concerning the King's troops. I have inverted the order of the words in the information, to make them more perspicuous ; for though it says that he 'at Loughborough, in the county of Leicester, composed, wrote, and published,' it means that he did all and each of those acts in the County of Leicester ; the word published referring as much to the County of Leicester, as the antecedent charges of writing and composing. We are, then, in possession of the charge alleged. What is the verdict ? it is a verdict entirely supporting the charge. If this charge were capable of a division into a minor and major offence, then I should say that the verdict of the jury might have been confined to a distinct and separate branch of the offence ; and if, as my learned friends have contended (and I should not have entered into it except for the serious and earnest manner in which they have contended), that the mere writing is an offence at law ; then I say that they have produced authorities to show that where that is proved, upon a charge combined with publication *not proved*, the jury ought to acquit of the publication, and confine their verdict to the former charge. But it seems convenient to them to take from those cases the parts that suit them, and to reject the remainder. When they state the cases of the King and Beare, the King and Payne, and the King and Knell, are they not aware that they compel the court to this conclusion, that the verdict in this case should only be for writing and composing ? I do not say at present whether the offence charged is or is not an entire and a continuous offence. That question belongs to another division of the argument. If they have succeeded in satisfying you that the writing is *per se*, and without publication, indictable by law, then there being no evidence of publication in Leicestershire, it follows that the verdict ought to have been for writing and composing only, in order to have given the defendant an opportunity of taking the opinion of the court, whether such an offence existed in law. If such a distinction had occurred to the advocates or to the learned judge on the trial (for the distinction did not occur to him), the defendant might have had an opportunity of showing that the intention of publishing might have been an afterthought, or he might in some way have qualified the mention, so as to disconnect it with the act of writing. But I will meet the charge of my learned friends, and trace the fountain higher in our law ; and I hope to show that the whole of that fountain, from which the doctrines of the King and Beare are derived, is an impure and adulterated fountain, and therefore one you cannot safely draw from.

With respect to the civil law it is true that Lord Coke, in his report *de libellis famosis*, referred to the civil law in support of the law of the Star Chamber. I hoped I should live to see the day when the law of the Star Chamber would not, as a matter of course, have been stated as the law of this court. I do not say it has been so stated by your Lordships, but it may be done, if the doctrine we have heard is to prevail. The particular crime of libel is one of which the nature, when it comes to be considered, is referrible to the principles on which all other crimes depend. It has been observed by Mr. Starkie, in his admirable preface on the law of libel, that crimes, which affect the visible property or persons of men, are much more obvious to the understanding than the crime of libel, which is of a more intellectual nature; and, therefore, the law respecting them is much more likely to be founded on just principles in its commencement in the more simple state of society, than those laws which, arising out of a complicated state of society, and relating to a more refined object, call for more refinement in observation, and greater discrimination between the good to be done by enacting penalties, and the mischief to be done by repressing a practice generally useful. You must see that one of the most refined conclusions to which a refined state of society can arrive, is, that a man should have a solid property in his reputation. It is one of the greatest privileges that belong to the nature of man, that he possesses a sensibility to fame and a love of glory, and that the individual, by the combination of opinion and the force of character, begets in his own reputation a property more valuable than the brute materials to which the crude notions of property are first applied. The art of printing, the circulation of written papers, would give rise to a great variety in the degrees of this offence. It was a considerable time before human laws could arrive at the just principles of it, before you could see the extreme danger of pressing your correction so far as to destroy the best source of that reputation, which is the property you mean to sustain; and that, without allowing it to a certain extent to be attacked by libellers who might injure the peace of some parties, you diminish the value of the character of all. It was long after it was the habit in enlightened Rome for every man of respectable rank to be in possession of books, that the crime *de libellis famosis* was known.

Lord Chief Justice.—Cicero says it was to be found in the twelve tables.

Mr. Scarlett.—False accusation ; if a false charge was preferred by a *delator* or representation on the stage.

Lord Chief Justice. —It is a fragment of his fourth Book de Republica, and printed among the fragments. The passage is this : ‘ Nostræ contra duodecim tabulæ cum perpaucas res capite sanxissent, in hanc quoque sanciendam putaverunt, si quis actitavisset sive carmen condidisset, quod infamiam afferret flagitiumve alteri.' He does not understand that as referring to a question of anything like a judicial course of inquiry. Now, Cicero speaks himself : ' Præclare, judiciis enim ac magistratuum disceptationibus legitimis propositam vitam non poetarum ingeniis habere debemus, nec probrum audire, nisi eâ lege ut respondere liceat et judicio defendere ;' which I think shows that it is not on a question with respect to which a person could be called on to consider criminally.

Mr. Scarlett.—What I mean is, that before a written libel was a crime, the art of writing must have been known and common. I believe, though I am not certain, that the first instance of the word *famosus* applied to libel, will be found in Horace, *famosum carmen.* when it was found to injure the opinion and respect in which a man was held, or by which the government was supported, as the character of individuals as well as the security of a government not upheld by brute force are founded on opinion and respect, it became important to punish those who destroyed that opinion and respect by written slander. It seems extraordinary how the word *famosus* was first introduced, unless it had a reference to publication ; the very word has relation to a thing bruited abroad, bottomed in fame. The word *famosus* in the best period of Roman literature had indeed acquired a bad meaning. Cicero uses *famosa* to express a courtesan. ' Ad famosas mater me vetat accedere.' Here it combines the reputation of being public with an actual want of chastity. There is a passage of Horace, ' Si quis mœchus foret, aut sicarius, aut alioqui famosus.' Here *famosus* means notorious, ' alioqui famosus,' or otherwise notorious for some vice. The word *famosus*, in its natural sense refers to notoriety. Unless that notoriety is effected in a libel against the Government by publication, where is the offence? Look then to the principle—unless something is done to stimulate individual revenge or public discontent. If it is done in secret, it wants the very essence of the meaning ' famosus,' by which the civilians describe it. I am not at present aware that any good writer in the Augustan age has used it in an indifferent or a good sense ; but Tacitus uses it for renown, ' famosa urbs ' ; and Suetonius says, ' famosi equi,' by which he means horses that were celebrated for their good qualities, and not infamous. The very essence of the crime, whether against the individual or the public, as well as of the word by which they qualify it, consists in the publication. Other acts may be committed, which in their concoction are criminal and dangerous ; they may imply a crime, as the *crimen falsi ;* the very act of forgery is a crime, it imports a fraud. No bad consequences can follow from declaring that a crime *per se*; forging is a criminal act done, not a thought expressed. We shall, however, by and by return to this subject. The passage the Attorney-General cited will show that the civil law refers to a publication. On the short investigation I have made, I find there is not one authority by the civil law which shows that the crime could exist without a publication ; but if it did, are we to refer for the principles of English law to the civil law, which is often built on a system of casuistry, to torture the consciences of men, and convert their very thoughts into crimes ? Upon a subject new at the time, it was likely and excusable that Lord Coke should refer to it for illustration, where there was a want of authority in his own law, though if he had looked to the statutes and doctrines of our own law in cases of *scandalum magnatum*, he would have found, even there, that the crime consisted in publishing. The passage quoted is this :—'Si quis librum ad infamiam alicujus scripserit, composuerit, ediderit, dolove malo facerit, quo quid eorum fieret.' Observe, the Attorney-General reads as much of the passage as suits his purpose. I do not complain of my learned friend, but I think if he had read the whole of the passage, or of those passages in *pari materiâ* which illustrate it, he would have found that it contained a meaning different from the one he has put upon it. The very words *ad infamiam* import a publication : it must be *ad infamiam;* it cannot be *ad infamiam,* unless his fame is affected by it, and that cannot be done unless it is published. I say it means this ; and this is a clue by which you may well determine the meaning of similar passages, and of several cases which have been cited, and, amongst others, Lamb's case, which I have not considered for the first time to-day, nor for the purpose of this argument only, with a view to reconcile it with just principles : that case also assumes a publication. The judges say, if the man published, then he is guilty ; if he wrote, or contrived, or maliciously published. Let us see the words quoted by Mr. Phillips in his argument : ' Si quis librum *ad infamiam* alicujus pertinentem scripserit, composuerit, dolove malo fecerit, *etiamsi alterius nomine ediderit, vel sine nomine,* et si condemnatus sit, qui id fecit, intestabilis ex lege esse jubetur.' The whole of this is from the Pandects, book 47, title 10, sec. 9. This passage applies only to a case of publication. I submit, also, that Lord Coke in Lamb's case means to say that the actual publisher was guilty, though he was neither the writer nor composer. But assuming the publication, he says this, ' that every man who shall be convicted of a libel in this case either ought to be a contriver of the libel, or a procurer of the contriving of it, or a malicious publisher of it, knowing it to be a libel ; meaning, that if he is the malicious publisher, though neither the author nor contriver, he is guilty of a libel. Now I wish to know if the Attorney-General will take this case as law on all occasions, and to its full extent. It is true that the publisher of a libel must know it to be so before he can be convicted? He must take the case for better and for worse. If you depart from the law supposed to be laid down by an eminent judge in the Star Chamber, shall you do so only to make it more severe? Will he take the alternative? Will he adopt this case as authority that no man shall hereafter be found guilty of publishing a libel unless he knew it to be a libel, and published it maliciously? But this would be contrary to the principles on which both he and his predecessors in office have acted, and contrary to the law as now established; for although I do not mean to say that I do not think it would be better if the law had followed reason in laying down some distinction between the gross negligence which publishes a libel without knowledge, and the guilty knowledge of the publisher, yet I am ready to admit that some punishment may be due even to negligence. Indeed the distinction your Lordships make in the sentences you pass on the author and ignorant publisher show that you are sensible of the difference between the cases, though you consider both as criminal. Does he then mean to contend that the law has improved, in modern times, in making the punishment for libels more severe; and that he will adopt all the severity without any of the relaxation of the ancient doctrine? If the case of Lamb is law, according to the letter of it in one part, in establishing the offence of the mere writer without publication, then it will be authority for the other part, to acquit the unconscious publisher; but in truth it bears no such interpretation as the Attorney-General has put upon it. The case assumes a publication throughout, and then says that the guilty publisher is as amenable as the contriver.

Bayley, J.—Will it interrupt you? Suppose the publisher to publish in one town, and the author to write in another, in which would you indict?

Mr. Scarlett.—That will come to be considered in another part of the argument. I am clear in the principle. If the mere author is guilty, I should say, on principle, he must be guilty of writing in the place where he commits the offence of writing; and if the publication is a distinct offence, it must be indicted in the place where it was committed. I do not, however, come to that at present. If the Attorney-General can treat this as a continuous offence, having its commencement in one place and its consummation in another, and can prove that he has therefore a right to choose his venue in either, *cadit questio.* I hope to satisfy you that it is neither a continuous offence, nor that, if it were, can the venue be chosen at pleasure; that the publication

is a *sine quâ non* of the crime, and makes it indictable in that place
where it is so consummated. I refer you to a very just argument on
the doctrine laid down in Lamb's case. It is in the publication of
Mr. Starkie on the Law of Libel, p. 564, he states these cases. I will
adopt it as part of my argument. 'My Lord Coke goes so far as to
say, that if one find a libel, and would keep himself out of danger,
if it be composed against a private man, the finder may either burn
it or presently deliver it to a magistrate ; but if it concern a magistrate
or other public person, the finder ought presently to deliver it to a
magistrate.' The next case, for aught I know, may be this, that if a
man is in possession of a libel he is criminal; and Lord Coke may
find his authority in the civil law, that if a man finds a libel he must
take it to a magistrate.

Best, J.—The offence was punished capitally.

Lord Chief Justice.—It was punishable more severely anciently.

Mr. Scarlett.—That shows we advance in civilisation and
knowledge. I will now state the passage :—'Si quis famosum
libellum sive domi sive in publico, vel in quocunque loco ignarus offen-
derit, aut discerpat priusquam alter inveniat, aut nulli confiteatur
inventum ; nam quicunque obtulerit inventum certum est reum ex
lege retinendum nisi prodiderit auctorem, nec evasurum pœnas hujus-
modi criminibus constitutas si proditus fuerit cuiquam retulisse quod
legerit ;' which shows that an act of publication of some sort is
necessary. Your Lordships will find he must publish,—'Si quis
famosum libellum ignarus repererit, aut corrumpat priusquam alter
inveniat, aut nulli confiteatur inventum. Si vero non statim easdem
chartulas corruperit vel igne consumpserit, sed earum vim manifestaverit' (what is the meaning of that, but that he shall make it manifest)
'sciat se ut auctorem hujus modi delicti capitali sententiæ subjugan-
dum.' He goes on to take notice of the other cases. My Lord Holt
says, in the case of the King and Beare, that the collecting and tran-
scribing of libels, for the purpose of publishing them, is criminal,
though no publication should ever take place, since men ought not
to be allowed to have such evil instruments in their keeping. But
in another Report of the same case, Salk. 417, the defendant having
been found guilty of writing and collecting certain libels, it was said
that the collecting had been better out of the case, and it is clear
that judgment was given on the ground that the defendant wrote the
original libel ; since, though Lord Holt intimated that the bare
copying a libel was criminal, he said there was no necessity for the
opinion because the defendant had been found guilty of writing the
original. The conclusion drawn by this learned gentleman is, that
as the law is now understood, publication is necessary : the same

opinion has prevailed ever since the case of Entick and Carrington: the same is held by Mr. Holt in his publication; he considers that publication is necessary, and indeed says that printing is publication.

Now I will go to the case of the King and Payne. There being no judgment, I cannot but think it of doubtful authority. It is reported in Carthew, the same book as that in which the King *v.* Beare is reported. It is said to have been tried at Nisi Prius at Bristol. In Modern Reports it is said to have been tried at bar in Westminster by a jury of Bristol. I submit that my learned friend must stand or fall by the whole of his case. If you refer us to the judges, and quote their *dicta*, it is a fair and just argument, and ought to have weight to show that the judges have taken a false view of the subject. Let us hear the judgment of the court. 'The making of a libel is an offence, though never published; and if one dictate and another write, both are guilty of making it. To what purpose should any one write or copy after another but to show his approbation of the contents, and to enable him to keep it in his memory that he may repeat it to others. Now the bare reading of a libel may not be a crime, because a man may be surprised and not understand what he is about to read; yet when one takes it from another and hears it spoken before he writes it, this cannot be by surprise, because he has time to exercise thoughts before he writes; so that it is not a libel by repeating but by writing. If one repeat and another write a libel, and a third approve what is wrote, they are all makers of it; for all persons who concur and show their assent and approbation to do an unlawful act, are guilty; so that murdering a man's reputation by a slanderous libel may be compared to murdering his person; for if several are assisting and encouraging the man in the act, though the stroke was given by one, all are guilty of homicide.' If any man shows his friend an epigram in which there is a reflection on another, and he takes a copy of it to look at for his amusement, he is guilty because he *may* publish it. Nobody ever thought that a man could be guilty of shooting at another by keeping a gun, merely because somebody might take it and charge it. 'If one repeat, and another write, and a third approve, they are all makers.' Now we get a step further. I advise the Attorney-General to lay hold of this; he has now a new class of offenders, those who approve a libel; and he is not without authority if he calls on you to decide it to be law now. I only pray I may not live in a country where such a law prevails. So that murdering a man's reputation by a libel may be compared to murdering his person; for if several are assisting and encouraging a man in the act, though the stroke was given by one, all are guilty of homicide. He likens it to the case of murder. Now how is a man's reputation

U

murdered by a libel never published? If one indites and another writes, and another laughs because it is a humorous thing, they are all indicted by the Attorney-General, and called up for judgment. Why? Because they have murdered a man's reputation : but how is reputation to be affected by keeping the thing close in your closet? Now as to the reasoning in the King *v.* Beare. Without meaning to deny that there were great authorities to support the learned judge, I hope to show you what these authorities were. Here is the verdict ; let us see whether at this time a judgment could be pronounced on such a verdict. The jury found the defendant guilty as to writing and collecting the several libels only, and as to all the residue of the information, not guilty. He is found guilty of the writing and collecting, but the publication is denied, and you find that the verdict does not even convict him of any intention. If a man transcribes and keeps a libel in his closet, the Attorney-General insists that the man is guilty of a crime. Now let us see what Lord Holt says: It is a violation of all the principles of the law. He says : ' It was objected that writing a libel may be a lawful act, as by the clerk who draws the indictment, or by a student who takes notes of it, and so the defendant's might be a lawful writing:' to which the judge said, that the matter, abstractedly considered, is unlawful, therefore the general finding shall be taken to be criminal; and that if the writing was innocent, as in the case objected, there ought to be a special finding of these particulars which distinguish and excuse it. If an action be brought on the statute of maintenance, 'tis sufficient to say *quod manu tenuit,* yet in some circumstances a man may lawfully maintain a suit as an attorney, or a near relation, and so on. Now, unluckily for this reasoning, the words of a statute are always deemed sufficient in a declaration or indictment upon that statute, for the words must receive the same construction on the record as they do on the statute ; and the defendant has the opportunity, when charged by the same words, of insisting upon all the proofs required, and making all defences allowed by the statute ; therefore the parallel is a bad one. The principle is this, and I beg the Attorney-General may stand or fall by it ; if a man should write a libel, or buy it of a bookseller, and keep the libel locked up in his closet, and there it should be found, the *onus probandi*, according to Lord Holt, is cast on him, to show an innocent intention. See the effect of this. Is there any work that any one has in print which does not contain a passage that may be considered a libel on some person or other? See to what fatal consequences this doctrine leads. Lord Coke lays it down that one may be guilty of a libel on those who have gone before him, and it is established by authority which I must ever respect, though I think it a decision humiliating for England, that a man may be indicted for a libel on a foreign prince or government as well as on his own. I will venture to say that there is hardly a book, not excepting the prayer book, that has not in some passage, a libel on the living or the dead, on princes or on governments. Now, suppose a man writes a libel and puts it in his closet, what man living can express or prove his intention but himself? If he keeps it in his own drawer, how is he, a defendant, to come forward and prove his innocence, when the Attorney-General charges him? and yet, according to the doctrine of this great judge, the *onus* is on him. And it is remarkable that he was stepping beyond the authorities of his own day, even in permitting such proof; for it is the first case I believe, about that period, in which it is admitted that a defendant may show an innocent intention by way of defence. What is it this judge says? that the whole principle of the criminal law shall be inverted, and that the *onus probandi* shall be on the defendant, and his guilt presumed: he alone could say whether he wrote for publication; he alone could say whether he was collecting historical anecdotes, meaning that they should be published a century hence, or by his heirs and executors. He says, 'that the jury having found the defendant guilty of writing a libel, he must be taken to be guilty of writing the original, and a copy could not be given in evidence; on the other side, if the copy of a libel be a libel, then the writing of it is a great offence; but that people may not go away with a notion that writing of a copy, though by one that has no colourable authority, is not libelling, the Chief Justice said, that such a copy contained all things necessary to the constitution of a libel, viz. the scandalous matter, and the writing. It has the same pernicious consequence; for it perpetuates the memory of the thing, and some time or other comes to be published.'

It is an assumption. Why is he to assume that it will be published? A man may burn it. The very notes I have in my hand ought, in twenty-four hours, to be burnt; if not, it may be said you have kept this libel in your house, and your executors may publish it. The descendants of Jefferies, Allybone, and Scroggs, whose names may have been mentioned without much respect in these notes, may say they are a libel on their memory. If a man does not confine his notes to his drawer, twenty years hence he may be charged by some person for a libel on his ancestor. But all the cases cited by Lord Holt are either cases of publication, or imply a publication; though I am free to say that the law, as laid down in what I had deemed obsolete or condemned authorities, did seem to justify a contrary position. You shall see those authorities; Lord Holt was not the first who adopted them : see what the judges did a few years before. Where there is a series of authorities coming down in a course of ten or twenty years, no man can say how far judges, who had those authorities before them, without any public reprobation of them in Parliament, might think they were bound to act upon them. How often do your Lordships say, that although you do not approve of a doctrine, yet you are not at liberty to depart from previous decisions and establish your own notions as law.   When I show you that Lord Holt, and the judges with him, had the recollection of recent decisions of all the judges, which no Act of Parliament had rescinded, and no resolution of Parliament had condemned, it will account for their appearing to be bound by them.   I will refer you to a case the Attorney-General may find useful to him : it is in Shower, 2 vol. 456. Dr. Eades, the defendant, was tried at the bar, on an information for commending a book in which were several seditious sentences and clauses, and convicted.   It was moved in arrest of judgment, that here was not a sufficient charge upon him ; for that it was not averred that he either read, or knew these sentences to be therein ; and Vaux's case, and the case of the King *v.* Sir John Ashley, were cited. Another exception was also taken, that amongst the continuances there was a *dies datus* to Sir Samuel Astrey, Clerk of the Crown, whereas the information was in Mr. Attorney's name, and he had joined issue : and therefore *prædicto Samueli Astrey* could not be good, he not being named before.   It was answered that the King was always present, and any one might prosecute for the King : but afterwards in another term, all exceptions were waved ; and upon the defendant's submission, he was fined a hundred pounds.

In the first place, it was tried at bar, in the second year of James II., the reign preceding that in which Lord Holt was Chief Justice.   You see how the law stood then.   Can anyone doubt that the gentleman who paid a hundred pounds must know that he had no chance of escaping, though the charge against him was nothing but commending a book, the offensive passages of which he did not even know?   Upon a solemn trial before all the judges, he is convicted of the crime.   I now come to another.   The Solicitor-General has stated the argument of Mr. Williams, who was counsel, as he says, for most of the persons in the unhappy situation of being accused of state offences.   My learned friend says it was not contended——

Mr. Solicitor-General.—That was an offence of publication.

Mr. Scarlett.—See what he suffered for his independent spirit. It is in the same book, the King *v.* Williams, an information for publishing ' Dangerfield's Narrative.' ' The defendant pleads that by the laws and customs of England, the Speakers of the House of Commons have signed and published the Acts of the House, &c. Mr. Attorney-General demurs. Mr. Jones was beginning to argue, and took some exceptions, as that he does not aver the libel in the information and that in the plea to be the same. Lord Chief Justice : We will not, in such a case, debate the formality of such an idle, insignificant plea; let us hear what they have to say for it. Mr. Pollexfen began : The Court of Parliament——. Lord Chief Justice : Court do you call it ? Can the order of the House of Commons justify this scandalous, infamous, flagitious libel ? Mr. Pollexfen then said : I have no more to say. Lord Chief Justice : Let judgment be entered for the King ; and afterwards Mr. Williams was fined ten thousand pounds, and upon payment of eight thousand of it satisfaction was acknowledged upon record.' We have now a record. Lord Coke says the law is to be found in the records, not in the *obiter dicta* of judges. You have it on the record that this publication was by the Speaker of the House of Commons, by order of that House.

Lord Chief Justice.—These are cases no one would venture to act upon in a court of justice. If they were quoted as authority, you know how every one of us would treat them.

Mr. Scarlett.—I know it well, my Lord; these cases are no authority now, but they were authority for Lord Holt. The King and Paine was a few years afterwards.

Best, J.—The Revolution had taken place in the meantime.

Mr. Scarlett.—Yes ; but the statute of James for licensing the press was in existence after the Revolution. The moment the Licensing Act expired, the judges had to consider a new code of laws ; for while it existed the mode of considering libels was much qualified by its existence ; at least, I have Lord Camden's authority for saying so. I have a right to show that these cases existed shortly before the cases of the King and Beare and the King and Payne. The judgments were never reversed. The judges could not altogether immediately reject them. They might have thought that Jefferies and Scroggs were influenced by the Court, yet that their judgments were not wholly unfounded in law. I will come to what Lord Camden says, and you will see the view he took of it. I heard my learned friend the Solicitor-General say that Lord Camden's judgment was in support of the doctrine of the King and Beare.

Solicitor-General.—I said it did not impugn the doctrine of the King and Beare.

Mr. Scarlett.—I say no man can read this who knows anything of the manner of that learned judge, and not see that there could not be a greater sneer than the way in which he expresses himself about that case.

Lord Chief Justice.—He states a good deal more than the Solicitor-General quoted.

Mr. Scarlett.—It is in the 19th volume of 'Howell's State Trials,' 1070, and in Wilson.[1] He says : 'I cannot help observing that if the Secretary of State was still invested with a power of issuing this warrant, there was no occasion for the application to the judges ; for, though he could not issue the general search warrant, yet upon the least rumour of a libel, he might have done more, and seized every-thing. But that was not thought of, and therefore the judges met and resolved, first, that it was criminal at common law, not only to write public seditious papers and false news, but likewise to publish any news without a licence from the King, though it was true and innocent.'

Upon what occasion did they do this ? You will see that the expiring of the licensing law was a circumstance from which it was conceived, that the change of a system, to which the people had been habituated, might lead to pernicious consequences. It happened that the Licensing Act of Charles had expired, and the King consulted his judges what could be done. There is not one of your Lordships who would not agree with me, that an Act of Parliament to license the press would be a most dangerous and improper thing ; but if we had been brought up under the influence of such a law, and in the habit of respecting it, we should perhaps think that when it came to be abrogated we were approaching to ruin. He says, 'when the Licensing Act expired at the close of King Charles II.'s reign, the twelve judges were assembled at the King's command to discover whether the press might not be as effectually restrained by the common law, as it had been by that statute.'

Lord Chief Justice.—That is in Charles's time. It was renewed in the reign of James.

Mr. Scarlett.—It expired after the Revolution, and was renewed for two or three years in King William's time. Upon the expiration of the Licensing Act, in the reign of Charles II., the twelve judges were assembled to discover whether the press might not be as effectu-ally restrained by the common law. I make no doubt they honestly thought the expiring of this law was a great mischief, and that as all mischiefs have a remedy in the common law, that as the common law has a sort of plastic power which leaves no mischief unremedied, they had a notion that the publication of any news whatever without the king's authority was illegal. They came to this resolution, that it was criminal at common law, not only to write public seditious papers

---

[1] Entinck *v.* Carrington.

and false news, but likewise to publish any news without a licence from the King, though it was true and innocent.

This is not all. On the trial of Harris for a libel, 7th vol. ' Howell's State Trials,' p. 929, Scroggs, C. J. says, ' Because my brethren shall be satisfied with the opinion of all the judges of England what this offence is, which they would insinuate, as if the mere selling of books was no offence, it is not long since that all the judges met by the king's commandment as they did some time before too ; and they both times declared unanimously, " that all persons that do write or print, or sell any pamphlet, that is either scandalous to public or private persons, such books may be seized, and the persons punished by law ; that all books which are scandalous to the Government may be seized ; and all persons so exposing them may be punished ; and further, that all writers of news, though not scandalous, seditious, nor reflective upon the Government or State, yet if they are writers (as there are few others of false news,) they are indictable and punishable upon that account." '

Let us here pause. Upon the trial of individual cases before Scroggs and Jefferies, their obvious political feelings have exposed them to remark and censure, and their judgment ought to be of no authority ; but upon abstract questions, in giving their opinions of the common law, nobody can deny that Jefferies was a man by no means deficient in talent and learning ; the same may be said of Scroggs : when abstract questions were proposed to them without relation to political and individual cases, it would be too much to say that all they laid down was corrupt. At this moment, if any of your Lordships should differ from the opinion of the judges in the House of Lords in 1792 on the law of libel ; if any of you should differ from the judgment of Lord Chief Baron Eyre then delivered, it would nevertheless be somewhat violent to suppose that you would act upon your own judgment in opposition to the law as solemnly laid down by all the judges. You will surely take the law from them as laid down in the abstract, yet on a particular trial a judge may have the infirmity of other men, and be actuated by feelings which may destroy his judgment. I am offering an apology for Lord Holt, and those who acted with him, when they deferred to the opinion of the judges on a great public question, in which there was no view to serve, and when they were called upon to declare the law generally. Will any man say that this is law, which comprehends the principles of the King and Beare, and the King and Payne? Lord Camden goes on : ' It seems the Chief Justice was a little incorrect in his report ; for it should seem as if he meant to punish only the writer of false news.' Sir George Jefferies says—

Lord Chief Justice.—We are obliged to be in another place; if you think you can finish in half an hour we will hear you.

Mr. Scarlett.—I am anxious to finish the argument, but I am afraid I cannot within that time : I feel the subject grows under me.

Further hearing adjourned.

MONDAY, 19TH JUNE, 1820.

Abbott, C. J.—We shall be called upon in an hour to go to the House of Lords. If you think you can within that time conclude what you have further to offer, you may proceed.

Mr. Scarlett.—I doubt whether I shall be able to conclude within the time your Lordship has mentioned, though I am most anxious to do so. I have already exceeded so far the limits which I contemplated, that I dare not pledge myself to finish the remainder of my argument before your Lordships will be obliged to rise. Having had notice at a late hour last night, that you would take this to-day, I had recourse to some notes I had made on the cases cited by the Attorney and Solicitor-General ; and I shall find it necessary to offer remarks on several of them.

Abbott, C. J.—We will hear you to-morrow.

TUESDAY, 20TH JUNE, 1820.

Mr. Scarlett.—My Lords, when last I had the honour of addressing you on this subject, the state of the question was this, whether the cases of the King and Beare, and the King and Payne, were bottomed on any just authority in law : and I was endeavouring to show what I think to be the only colourable authority on which they were founded ; and I had undertaken, according to my humble ability, to show that these authorities rested upon no principle, but that which all mankind had at this time agreed to repudiate. I had alluded to the case of the King and Eades, who was tried for the approbation of a libel, which is mentioned in the King and Payne as a crime ; and I was stating part of Lord Camden's judgment in Entick and Carrington, in which that noble Lord has given a history of the opinions of the judges on the law of libel, from a certain period of the reign of Charles II. I was pressing on your attention that, during a great part of that reign, an Act of Parliament was in existence for licensing the press ; that the judges who lived in those days, when the press was looked upon with greater horror than it has been since, upon the expiration of that Act of Parliament, being assembled by the King, to advise how the mischiefs attendant upon the expiration of the Act might be remedied, resolved that by the common law they might be remedied. Lord Camden states the opinion they gave, and in particular, the opinion of Scroggs at the trial of Harris, for a libel ; that the communication of news without authority of the King was an offence at common law ; that all the judges met by the King's commandment twice, and both times declared unanimously, that all persons who do write, or print, or sell any pamphlet scandalous to public or private persons, such books may be seized and the persons punished by law. So that it was decided by the resolution of all the judges, not on any particular case, but as a general principle of law, that any man who wrote a libel might be punished by law. The same thing is confirmed by Sir George Jefferies, then Recorder of London, and Scroggs, C.J., in the case of Carr, ' Hargrave's State Trials,' vol. 3, in which Scroggs says : ' When, by the King's commandment, we were to give our opinion what was to be done in point of regulation of the press, we did all subscribe that to print or publish any new books or pamphlets of news whatever is illegal ; that it is a manifest intent to a breach of the peace, and they may be proceeded against for an illegal thing. Suppose, now, that this thing is not scandalous, what then ? If there had been no reflection in this book at all, yet it is *illicitè* done, and the author ought to be convicted for it. Here is the authority of all the judges stated by Lord Camden, with all the accuracy and research which distinguished that illustrious and honest man, whom I shall ever consider it an honour and a happiness to have had the opportunity of seeing and hearing, when he filled the office of President of the Council at an advanced age, but still retaining much of the vigour and splendid intelligence with which, in his high judicial station, he had served and enlightened his country. He shows that the opinions of the judges at the times to which he refers were naturally qualified by the practice of the Star Chamber and by the existence of the Licensing Act. He might perhaps have justly added that, the press being introduced into this country by Henry VII., an opinion prevailed that it was part of the prerogative of the King to govern it, and that opinion was not eradicated for many ages. It was not extraordinary that the judges should have conceived, the press being introduced by the King, and the art of printing being by his munificence communicated to his subjects, as is undoubtedly the fact, and he having at first licensed certain persons only to print, that it should still have remained under the King's control, and that therefore, by the common law, the use and the excess of it might be regulated as matter *de prerogativâ regis.* I suggest these matters to show that the opinion of the judges did not want a colour of autho-

rity from the maxims of the times. Now Lord Holt, some years after
the Revolution, with the judges who assisted him, were placed much
in the same predicament as the judges stood in at the expiration
of the Licensing Act in the Reign of Charles II. In the fifth
year of King William's reign the Licensing Act, having been prolonged for a year, had expired. An attempt was made to renew it
in Parliament, but the wisdom and intelligence of Parliament rejected
it. It was therefore not unnatural that Lord Holt and his brethren
should, to a certain extent, feel themselves bound by the authority of
the judges on the like occasion, and conceive that there was some
principle of law that warranted them in the determination they made
in these cases. At the same time, as the very first effect of the Revolution was to bring into odium, and possibly into very just odium, the
opinion of those judges who were most inclined to support arbitrary
power in the antecedent reign, Lord Holt was perhaps willing to refer
to antecedent authorities for the opinions he had imbibed, which
antecedent authorities, I undertake to say, will not bear the interpretation he puts upon them. It would be an unjust inference to suppose
that the mere event of the Revolution put an end at once, as it were by
magic, to all the bad principles and prejudices which prevailed before,
and rendered necessary that event. The Revolution, like the Reformation, undoubtedly gave birth to a spirit of inquiry, and to just
notions of government and law, which it required some ages to
mature. Nobody supposes that when the Reformation took place
the first reformers were at once friends to impartial and unlimited
inquiry; but it introduced that spirit which advanced towards free
inquiry. So with regard to the Revolution. Who can suppose that
that great work was consummated by the great men who saw and
deplored the errors of James II.'s reign, in which they lived, immediately, and that it by magic produced a revolution in the minds of
all men? No; it required ages of moderate and liberal government
to bring to maturity and to develope the maxims of the Revolution,
and to give them their due effect; and therefore I am not surprised
that in their early decisions, or even after some years had elapsed
from that event, the judges, on the subject of libel, should have
borrowed something from the prejudices of their own age, and that
they should not have arrived at that maturity of intelligence and
liberality, and those just conceptions of the advantages of a free press
and the principles on which they are founded, by which, I trust, your
Lordships will be influenced on the present occasion. I shall proceed to show that Lord Holt had no authority for his doctrine but
that of Scroggs and his brethren; that the doctrine of the King *v.*
Eades, which was a prosecution for approving a libel, was the autho-

rity for the King *v.* Payne, in which it is laid down that if a man approves a libel he is guilty. This is one of the cases in point now relied on ; the other is the case of the King *v.* Beare. Happy shall I be if I may become the humble instrument of convincing your Lordships that they are both cases which cannot be too much condemned. The King *v.* Beare was a special verdict, and you remember the terms of it. The charge was that the party had written, made, and collected (with all the malicious intentions that accompany such a charge in an indictment) a number of libels, in which were contained the passages set forth in the information. The jury did not find that he was not guilty of the publishing, but guilty of the other parts of the charge ; what they found was this : ' Quoad scriptionem et collectionem, &c., prout in indictamento supponitur *tantum* culpabilis, et quoad omnia alia præter scriptionem et collectionem, &c., non culpabilis.' You are to look for the law, as Lord Coke says, not to the *obiter dicta* of judges, but to the record. Then let it have the weight of his authority. It is this : it finds the man guilty of the simple fact of writing a libel, and not guilty of any one intention charged.

Lord Chief Justice.—Do you find that in any one of the arguments in the report the point you are putting to us was put, the finding him guilty of the collecting without the intention ? Is there any part of the report that so states it ?

Mr. Scarlett.—Yes, my Lord, the judgment of C. J. Holt proves it. You see what the record is. It acquits him of everything but the simple fact of writing and collecting only. We know, in modern times, that a verdict of publishing only would not be a legitimate verdict ; the word *only* would exclude every part of the charge but the publishing. I will show you that Lord Holt considered the point. It is the very particular point to which his attention is drawn when he makes use of this expression. He says this, and he could only have said it on his mind being drawn to this exact point. He says it is sufficient to find him guilty of writing *only*, because the writing of a libel, unless he shows some innocent intention, is matter of guilt. He states that the *onus* is put upon him, when the fact of writing is proved, to show that his intent was innocent ; and therefore he says the simple verdict, guilty of writing only, is sufficient to warrant a judgment. I do not believe you will find the passage in Carthew. In Salkeld it is more fully given. He says, ' It is objected that writing a libel may be a lawful act, as by the clerk who draws the indictment, or by the student who takes notes of it, and so the defendant's might be a lawful writing ' ; but then, says he, it lies upon him to prove it, for the fact of writing is evidence of guilt ;

and therefore he supposes that the verdict that found him guilty of writing *tantum* justified the Court in passing sentence upon him. If you refer to the case you will find that Lord Holt's mind was drawn to the form of the special verdict, and that he considered that the fact of writing authorised the Court to pass the judgment, on the ground that the act of writing was alone a presumption of guilt, and cast it on the defendant to prove his innocence. He refers to Lord Coke, and we will therefore go through the only cases to be found in Lord Coke applicable to the question. It appears from Lord Coke's expressions, and the illustrations of them to which Lord Holt refers, that Lord Coke never did conceive that a man could be found guilty of writing only, or that anything short of a publication could subject him to a criminal proceeding. I will first take the case *de libellis famosis*, 5 Rep. 125, which consists merely of resolutions : ' The case of Lewis Pickering was for composing and publishing an infamous libel in verse, by which John Archbishop of Canterbury, who was a prelate of singular piety, gravity, and learning, now dead, by descriptions and circumlocutions, and not in express terms, and Richard Archbishop of Canterbury, who now is, were traduced and scandalised, in which these points were resolved : First: Every libel, which is called *famosus libellus seu infamatoria scriptura*, is made either against a private man or against a magistrate or public person. If it be against a private man, it deserves severe punishment ; for although the libel be made against one, yet it excites all those of the same family, kindred, or society, to revenge, and so tends *per consequens* to quarrels and breach of the peace, and may be the cause of shedding of blood, and of great inconvenience. If it be against a magistrate, or other public person, it is a greater offence, for it concerns not only the breach of the peace, but also the scandal of government ; for what greater scandal of government can there be than to have corrupt or wicked Ministers to be appointed and constituted by the King to govern his subjects under him ; and greater imputation to the State cannot be than to suffer such corrupt men to sit in the sacred seat of justice, or to have any meddling or concern in the administration of justice. Second: Although the private man or magistrate be dead at the time of the making of the libel, yet it is punishable ; for in the one case it stirs up others of the same family, blood, or society, to revenge, and to break the peace ; and in the other the libeller traduces and slanders the State and Government, which dies not. Third: A libeller, who is called *famosus defamator*, shall be punished, either by indictment at the common law, or by bill, · if he deny it, or *ore tenus* on his confession.' Then he states that it is not material whether the libel be true, or whether the party against whom it is made be of good or ill fame ; and he gives some general reasoning which does not apply to the question of publication. He mentions several cases. First I pray your attention to the definition, to the nature of the crime, its tendency to excite a breach of the peace. How can it tend to excite a breach of the peace, unless the individual libelled, or some person connected with him, should see it ? The definition of the offence shows that it lies in the publication ; for if the writing is kept in a drawer, it cannot have a tendency to provoke a breach of the peace. It is, indeed, a technical definition more like that of a lawyer who is in the habit of considering all crimes as against the peace, than like that of a legislator : but in truth the crime consists in this, that it attacks that reputation and character which are precious to the owner: and an assault on a man's reputation ought to be as much the subject of restraint as an attack on any other species of property. But the technical definition shows that the party must publish, otherwise he does not put himself in the situation where the definition applies. Lord Coke states how the libel may be *published ;* but there is nothing that shows he meant it to be understood that the bare act of writing was a crime. He says, ' It may be published, 1, *verbis aut cantilenis ;* as where it is maliciously repeated or sung in the presence of others : 2, *traditione,* when the libel, or any copy of it, is delivered over to another, *to scandalise the party. Famosus libellus sine scriptione* may be, 1, *picturis,* as to paint the party in any shameful and ignominious manner : 2, *signis ;* as to fix a gallows, or other reproachful and ignominious signs at the party's door, or elsewhere.' Now, if a man fixed the sign in his own private drawing-room, what evidence would appear of an exhibition so as to found a charge of libel, if nobody saw it but himself? Then it is said that, ' if one finds a libel, and would keep himself out of danger, if it be composed against a private man, the finder either may burn it, or presently deliver it to a magistrate :" that is, only prescribing a moral duty, he does not lay down the law to be so ; and though he refers to the civil law, I have shown that the finder of a libel could not, by that law, be punished for the mere possession of it. Then we come to Lambe's case, 9 Rep. 59, which is the one that Lord Holt relies on, and I am surprised any one could think that case an authority for deciding that the mere writing was a crime. What was the case? ' John Lambe, a proctor of the Ecclesiastical Court, exhibited a bill in the Star Chamber, against William Marsh, Robert Herrison, and many others of the town of Northampton, for *publishing* two libels,' so that the charge was a publication. What was the question ? It was, as you will see in the report, what constituted that sort of publication, which in that particular case, justified a conviction ; that is to say, we have before us many defendants, all charged with a publication, some may be the authors, some the contrivers, some the malicious publishers, others the mere unconscious instruments of other men's malice ; perhaps the printer's boy, the porter who carried the papers to the press, or brought them away in a covered parcel when printed. We wish to know'from the judges, looking at the particular case, which of these parties can be convicted on this charge. What is the resolution of the judges ? I say their opinion implies that a publication is essential. ' It was resolved that every one who shall be convicted *in the said case*, either ought to be a contriver of the libel, or a procurer of the contriving of it, or a *malicious* publisher of it, knowing it to be a libel.' This question might have occurred. There might have been some person who could neither read nor write, who conveyed it to or from the press. This definition would exclude him because he would not be a *malicious* publisher, knowing it to be a libel. Another case might be, that the man who wrote it might not have been the contriver of it, or might not be the hand who, by *traditione*, delivered it to another person to be published. The different parts of the case must be taken together ; when you find that publication was the charge upon all the defendants, and that without publication none could be convicted, the question clearly was, how far the contriver or writer of the libel should in that case be deemed the publisher? It was natural for the judges to say he cannot be a publisher unless he publishes, or writes for publication. I apprehend no man alive can doubt that if a man writes and hands over a libel, with a charge that it shall be put to the press, he is a publisher ; because *qui facit per alium, facit per se* : he who does a thing by the hand of another, is the doer. Then considering with a curious nicety what shall be a publication, he says, ' If one reads a libel, that is no publication of it ; or if he hears it read, it is no publication ; for before he hears or reads it he cannot know it to be a libel.' Here is a little sentence which shows that in the King *v.* Paine, Lord Holt could not rest upon Lord Coke, but could only refer to the King *v.* Eades as his authority, ' or if he hears it read, or reads it and laughs at it, this is no publication.' Now, laughing, I think, implies approbation, and, according to Holt, in the King *v.* Paine, ' where one man indites, another writes, and a third approves of a libel, all are guilty.' What better evidence can you have of a man's approving of a libel than where he laughs at it? And yet this is not a publication, nor, consequently, a ground of prosecution, according to Lambe's case ; for *Lord Coke* there says the contrary ; he says, ' If one hears it and laughs at it, it is no publication ; but if after he has read or heard it, he repeats it, or any part of it in the hearing of others, or after he knows it to be a libel, reads it to others, that is an unlawful publication.' I now come to another part, which is an authority directly against Lord Holt. ' Or if he writes a copy of it, and does not publish it to others, it is no publication.' ˙ Why should he be so anxious to go into every particular of publication, and not say a word about a man being indictable if he wrote it only? Let us here pause a moment. I affirm that a man is not indictable without publication. It is said on the other side, that a man may be indicted because he merely wrote the libel. Now, what is the case of the King *v.* Beare? It is not the case of an original author, but of the transcriber: he had collected libels, transcribed them, and kept them in his house. Now, that is precisely one of the positions in Lambe's case. Lord Coke says : ' Or if he writes a copy of it, and does not publish it to others, it is no publication of libel ; for every one who shall be convicted in this case ought to be the contriver, procurer, or publisher ; but it is great *evidence* that he published, when he, knowing it to be a libel, writes a copy of it, unless he can prove that he delivered it to a magistrate.' Why should Lord Coke be so very anxious to show that the writing was presumptive evidence of publication, and yet not inform posterity that it was of itself a guilty act? It is remarkable that Lord Coke, who was not accustomed to confine the great extent of his knowledge to the precise and single question of the cause, but to advert with learned industry to every branch of the subject, in a manner which has given such authority to his works as to make them text-books as well as reports ; it is remarkable, I say, that he should lay down with so much exactness the presumptive evidence of writing to support a charge of publication, and yet have forgotten to mention that the act of writing alone, without publication, would constitute him guilty. I say, therefore, if you take the case of Lambe, as reported by Lord Coke, there is no part of it that supports Lord Holt's construction of it in the case of the King *v.* Beare, and Lord Holt appears to have thought so himself; for without meaning to insinuate (God forbid I should) anything reflecting on the memory of so great a man, yet he seems to think that Lambe's case, as reported by Lord Coke, did not go to the full length in support of his doctrine. He says it ought to be explained by Moore's account of it. I agree to this, for it is more in my favour. I join issue with him upon the report in Moore. I deny that it is more effectual to support his doctrine. Let us turn to the case in Moore, 813. ' Lambe complained in the Star Chamber against divers, for *publishing* scandalous libels in the town of Northampton ; but none of them were the contrivers, and the libel was concerning the officers and ministers of the Ecclesiastical Court, of which Lambe was the registrar referred to in the libel, by which the Lords think him a party grieved to complain; but where he had inserted in his bill another libel against the knights and gentlemen of the county of Northampton, in which he was not referred to, the Lords discharged all the defendants who were charged with that, because he could not inform of a libel which did not refer to himself when King's Collector. And in the principal case many questions arose which of them were publishers, and what should be said to be publishing a libel.' He shows there that the question was, what should be deemed a publication, and who, *in that case*, should be deemed guilty; and he says it was resolved that the procurer and writer are both contrivers. Second, that the procurers of another to publish a libel and the publisher of the same are both publishers. Third, the reading of a libel, not knowing it to be a libel, is not publishing. Fourth, he who shall write the copy of the libel, by command of his master or father, is not a *publisher*. Fifth, he who laughs when he hears another read the libel, if he does nothing more, is not a publisher. Sixth, he who lends a libel to be copied, he who repeats the libel, or any part of it, or reads the contents of it, or any part of it, knowing it to be a libel, is a publisher; so if one writes the copy, by command of his master or father, he is a publisher; for Coke says, ' Nec domino nec patri in illicitis obediendum est.' Note also that in this case there was a woman accused of being the publisher of this libel, and because, through the infirmity of her sex, she was ignorant whether to speak of the said libel was an offence or not, she was admonished without censure ; for Coke, Chief Justice of the Common Pleas, said, that ' fœminæ sunt imbelles.' You will see in what class he places the fair sex when they are ignorant. He says, ' Fœmina si nescit, clericus miles, et cultor, parcat ei judex et ultor.' In the principal case many cases arise. He shows there that the question was, what should be deemed a publication ; who in that case should be deemed guilty of publishing ; amongst other things, not whether the writer was *ipso facto* guilty, but whether *writing* was evidence of publication, without which there could be no conviction ; and he says, it was resolved, that both contrivers, contrivers of what? of the thing to be published ; therefore, of publication, the man who writes the thing is the contriver ; that the procurer of another to publish a libel, and the publisher himself, are both publishers ; so that the whole question here was, what should be evidence of a publication. If, then, we were looking at the report in Moore, to illustrate the case of Lambe, you would find *à fortiori* no ground to warrant you in saying that the writer of a libel, not published, was punishable by law.

If you will forgive me for a few minutes' digression on this part of the case, I should wish to allude again to what my Lord Chief

Justice was so good as to say, in answer to that part of the argument in which I referred to the civil law ; that by the twelve tables the party *writing* a libel was punishable with death, which, I apprehended, was not the law till the time of the Emperors. I have the work to which your Lordship referred. It was the fragments of Cicero's work De Republica, some of which are preserved by Saint Augustin in his book De Civitate Dei, and some by other writers. Saint Augustin seems to have brought together those passages which have reference to exhibitions on the stage. I imagine that the law of the twelve tables referred to by Cicero had reference to the same subject, namely, to the practice of exhibiting individuals on the stage. ' Nostræ contra duodecim tabulæ cum perpaucas res capite sanxissent, in hanc quoque sanciendam putaverunt, si quis actitavisset sive carmen condidisset, quod infamiam afferret flagitiumve alteri ; præclare, judiciis enim ac magistratuum disceptationibus legitimis propositam vitam non poetarum ingeniis habere debemus, nec probrum audire, nisi eâ lege ut respondere liceat et judicio defendere.' The *probrum audire* refers to the hearing the actor who represents the character attacked by the *malum carmen* of the poet. In one of the fragments of the same work, also preserved by the same author, Saint Augustin, you have, as I conceive, a reference to the poets who composed for representation, ' probris et injuriis poetarum subjectam vitam famamque habere noluerunt capite etiam puniri sancientes *tale carmen* condere si quis auderet.' I apprehend by *tale carmen* is meant such a composition as was actually represented on the stage, and not a mere private, unpublished composition. In order to explain this, some illustration may be found amongst the poets themselves. The laws of the twelve tables were brought by the Decemviri to Rome. It appears that in very early times it was the habit of the rustics at the conclusion of their harvest, to exhibit in a species of rude scenic representation, the history and the characters of individuals under their own names. The same thing had taken place in Greece, and was in both countries the origin of comedy, which was distinguished by the names of the *prisca* and the *vetus comœdia*. It continued in Athens to the time of the thirty tyrants, when a law was introduced by Lamachus to prevent the representation of individual characters upon the stage. Aristophanes furnished examples both of the old and middle comedy, because in some of his plays he represents individuals by name ; in others under feigned names, and employs the chorus for the purpose of satire. This licence continued in Athens, with the modification introduced by Lamachus, till she lost her liberties, under the subjugation of Alexander, when the chorus was silenced,

X

and representations of real life were altogether prohibited.   Then the *nova comœdia* commenced, in which fictitious events were introduced under imaginary characters.   The history of the whole subject is to be found in Horace (in the 2nd Book of his Epistles, i. 139.)

> Agricolæ prisci, fortes, parvoque beati,
> Condita post frumenta, levantes tempore festo
> Corpus, et ipsum animum spe finis dura ferentem,
> Cum sociis operum, pueris, et conjuge fidâ,
> Tellurem porco, Silvanum lacte piabant,
> Floribus et vino Genium, memorem brevis ævi.
> Fescennina per hunc inventa licentia morem
> Versibus alternis opprobria rustica fudit;
> Libertasque recurrentes accepta per annos
> Lusit amabiliter ; donec jam sævus apertam
> In rabiem verti cœpit jocus, et per honestas
> Ire domos impune minax.   Doluêre cruento
> Dente lacessiti : fuit intactis quoque cura
> Conditione super communi :

Now here is the law of the tables referred to :—

> Quin etiam lex,
> Pœnaque latâ, malo quæ nollet carmine quemquam
> Describi.   Vertêre modum formidine fustis,
> Ad bene dicendum delectandumque redacti.

Here, as the commentators say, he alludes to the very law of the twelve tables, by which law, as I contend, the infamy must have been attached and fixed to the individual by representation, which was a publication, the word which Cicero has turned into *actitavisset* is *occentâsset*, which I presume was obsolete, though its meaning is clearly indicated.   The words of the law are these, ' Si quis occentasset malum carmen, sive *condidisset*, quod infamiam faxit flagitiumve alteri, capital esto.'   Observe, it is not *ad infamiam tendens*, but *infamiam faxit*; and so in the interpretation of Cicero, in the fragment quoted, the words are ' quod infamiam *afferret* flagitiumve alteri.' It would seem therefore that the infamy must have attached, the mischief must have occurred, before punishment could be inflicted on the author or actor.   In reference to the practice of introducing upon the stage living characters and private transactions, which were audaciously pursued by the *opprobria rustica* and the *sævus jocus*, into private and honourable houses, the same poet in one of his satires says—

> Eupolis, atque Cratinus, Aristophanesque, Poetæ,
> Atque alii, quorum comœdia prisca virorum est,
> Si quis erat dignus describi, quod malus, aut fur,
> Quod mœchus foret, aut sicarius, aut alioqui
> Famosus, multâ cum libertate notabant.

Mr. Justice Best.—The word *famosus* is mentioned before.

Mr. Scarlett.—I apprehend the word *famosus* there means not merely bad, but a *notoriously* bad character. He is the man who becomes interesting from some notorious vice of his character. The *fama* is bottomed in notoriety and celebrity ; when the same poet speaks of the ' infames scopulos Acroceraunia,' he undoubtedly means not merely rocks that are dangerous, but that are notorious or famous for their danger, as Milton does when, in imitation of this passage he speaks of

> *Infamous* rocks and sandy perilous wilds.

Horace again says—

> Successit vetus his comœdia non sine multa
> Laude ; sed in vitium libertas excidit, et vim
> Dignam lege regi : lex est accepta : chorusque
> Turpiter obticuit, sublato jure nocendi.

This refers to the law of Athens, which was sufficiently severe, being made after she lost her liberty. But to show that the law of *famosus libellus* did not exist in the early times in Rome, I will refer you to Suetonius's History of Augustus. This is the passage respecting Augustus ; it is in Vitâ Augusti, c. 55 : 'Etiam sparsos, de se in curia famosos libellos, nec expavit nec magna cura redarguit. Ac ne requisitis quidem auctoribus id modo censuit, cognoscendum posthac de iis qui libellos aut carmina ad infamiam cujuspiam, sub alieno nomine edant.'

It is remarkable that Augustus, who was very popular, and probably as susceptible of flattery as other elevated personages, if there was already in existence a law to punish libels with death, should not only have prosecuted none of them against himself, but should have introduced another law to subject those only which were anonymous to legal restraint. Tacitus too, in the first book of his annals, says, ' Primus Augustus cognitionem de famosis libellis specie legis ejus (*i.e.* legis majestatis) tractavit, commotus Cassii Severi libidine, quâ viros fœminasque illustres procacibus scriptis diffamaverat.' Again, Suetonius, in his life of a character very different from that of Augustus, namely, his successor Tiberius, has this passage on the subject of libels, cap. 28. He says, ' Adversus convitia malosque rumores, et famosa de se ac suis carmina firmus ac patiens, subinde jactabat in civitate liberâ linguam mentemque liberas esse debere. Et quondam, Senatu cognitionem de ejusmodi criminibus ac reis flagitante, non tantum inquit otii habemus ut implicare nos pluribus negotiis debeamus,' that the senate requested him to punish those who circulated libels against him, to which Tiberius replied, that he should have too much upon his hands if he were to add any care of his own person and reputation to that which he was bound to bestow upon the safety and dignity of the state. The same author says of Julius Cæsar, that he was so regardless of certain *epigrammata famosa* and scurrilous verses that were current against him, that he proposed a reconciliation with one of the authors, and invited the other to sup with him ; notwithstanding the clemency of Cæsar, it is extraordinary that such things should circulate if they were liable to capital punishment. Mr. Justice Blackstone indeed supposes that it was in the time of the Emperor Valentinian that the law to punish libel with death was first made, and he quotes the very passage of Horace—

> Quin etiam lex,
> Pœnaque lata, malo quæ nollet carmine quemquam
> Describi. Vertêre modum formidine fustis—

to show that libellers were originally liable only to flagellation. I apprehend he is certainly mistaken. If I am correct, the law alluded to by this passage of Horace is that of the twelve tables relating only to theatrical representations, and moreover the flagellation by that law was *usque ad mortem.*

I beg pardon for this digression, into which I have been led by a desire to show that the word *famosus* always implied something of notoriety, and that it was not used as an epithet for written compositions in the early periods of the republic of Rome, nor until the circulation of books had become so common as to justify the application of a word denoting what is at least equivalent to the notion of publication in our law. But I am well aware that the law of England requires no illustration, and perhaps can receive none, from the doubtful hints which remain of the early jurisprudence of the ancients.

Having endeavoured to show that there is no authority in the best times of our law for the doctrine of the King *v.* Beare and the King *v.* Payne, but the reverse, I shall proceed to show that the more modern authorities are equally inconsistent with Lord Holt's doctrine in those cases. But I just beg leave to advert to a case cited by the Attorney General from *Ventris,* to show that publication was not necessary ; one would think the authority of the judges in 1792 as good authority as that of Scroggs and his companions in King Charles's reign, and of those judges who before the Revolution determined that a man who approved of a libel was guilty. Your Lordships recollect that when a law respecting libel was introduced by Mr. Fox, and supported by Mr. Erskine in Parliament, the judges were summoned by the House of Peers, and certain questions were put to them. As none of your Lordships were then on the bench, I may without offence to you, and I hope without detracting from the respect due to the judges of that period, say that some of their opinions were affected to a certain degree by the reigning prejudices of the day as to the mode in which the law of libel ought to be interpreted. I think we may see, be it spoken with due reverence for the manes of those eminent men, that the wisest and best of men in the most enlightened times, the freest from all suspicion of political influence, could not help falling under some bias from the judgments and opinions of their immediate predecessors, whose character and learning they revered. I think you will find a reluctance even in those judges to part with the favourite principles held, if not established by Lord Mansfield, namely, that the sole questions for the jury were these. Did the party publish? and are the innuendoes proved as alleged? If so, leave to the court the interpretation of the libel, and the question with what intention it was written. No doubt the meaning of a libel, in like manner as the meaning of every written composition, is matter of law for the judge to decide. But I own it has always appeared to me that Lord Mansfield and the judges who immediately followed him, were led into a fallacy by confounding the meaning of the libel with the intention of the writer, which last is matter of fact for a jury. The meaning is unquestionably one very great, and in general a principal source from whence the intention is to be collected. But it is not the only source. There may be matter *dehors* the written paper to prove an intention inconsistent with the obvious meaning, and which when combined with the meaning so explained by it, may give to the composition altogether a different character. However to the purpose of this argument, I find that the judges had this question put to them, 22 'Howell's State Trials,' p. 300: 'Is a witness placed before a jury on a trial as above by a plaintiff to prove the criminal intentions of the writer, or by the defendant to rebut the imputation, admissible to be heard as a competent witness in such trial before the jury?' The answer is this: 'This question is put so generally that we find it impossible to give a direct answer to it.' It was put by Lord Loughborough, perhaps, as he thought, to place the judges in a difficulty. Do you mean to say that a witness cannot be called at all to give evidence of intention? They give their answer, 'This question is put so generally, that we find it impossible to give a direct answer to it. The criminal intention charged upon the defendant in legal proceedings on libel is generally matter of form, requiring no proof on the part of the prosecutor, and admitting of no proof on the part of the defendant to rebut it. The crime consists in *publishing* a libel ;

a criminal intention in the writer is no part of the definition of the crime of libel at the common law.' ' The *crime consists* in PUBLISHING *a libel !*' Here are the words of ten of the judges ; and we may presume that Lord Kenyon, one of the remainder, concurred with them in opinion, that the crime *consists in publishing a libel.* A criminal intention in the writer is no part of the definition of the crime of libel at the common law.' Good God ! is *the* Attorney General *to take us back to the times of the Revolution ! to the times of Scroggs and Jefferies to learn the law of libel? Need we go beyond the enlightened period when most of us* CAN BEAR LIVING TESTIMONY *to the* INTEGRITY *and learning and high* HONOUR *of the Judges?* Is it in the beginning of the NINETEENTH CENTURY, and above all, when your Lordship sits as CHIEF JUSTICE in THIS COURT, AND MY LEARNED FRIEND IS THE ATTORNEY GENERAL, THAT WE ARE TO DEPRECIATE BY SUCH A COMPARISON, AND THEN TO DEPART FROM THE JUDGMENT, THE SOLEMN OPINION OF THE JUDGES OF 1792? Are they supposed to have departed from the old principles of the common law, and, from an excess of liberality for defendants in libel, to have introduced something new and fictitious, when they made use of those expressions which ought to put this argument to shame? ' The criminal intention of the writer is no part of the crime of libel at common law !' And yet the Attorney General comes into court and says, *I have found* a case on which I pray your judgment, that the WRITER IS HIMSELF A GUILTY PERSON, that you may look at his intention, nay further that YOU MUST PRESUME IT TO BE A GUILTY INTENTION ; AND THAT WITHOUT A PUBLICATION, I MAY ASK FOR A CONVICTION ! ! Here I have the authority of all the judges, at the most learned, enlightened, and intelligent period of our history. For in 1792 the just principles of our law remained, as indeed so far as depended on the character and learning of the judges, they might still have remained unaltered and unshaken by that bitterest of all calamities, the French Revolution, which agitated the minds of men in various ways ; and if it induced some to look with more favour to principles of a popular tendency in England, produced, I hope, not a fatal, but a strong counteracting effect on others, and made them more fearful of leanings and interpretations in favour of popular rights and opinions than the judges in that age, and before that calamitous event, were likely to be. Therefore I consider the year 1792 as the best period in all the history of the law in this country. I do not mean to say for the integrity or the independence of the judges, but because the human mind on the seat of justice was then freest from the popular bias on one side, and from suspicion of any bias towards the Crown on the other. It is the best period to look for the foundations of the criminal law, when it must be admitted that those judges were as incapable, as I know your Lordships to be now incapable, of being influenced either by the *civium ardor prava jubentium*, or by the *vultus instantis tyranni*. They go on to say, ' he who scatters firebrands is *ea ratione* criminal ; but, inasmuch as criminal intention may induce to the proof of the publication of all libels, and inasmuch as the criminal intention is of the substance of the crime of libel in some cases, by statute, cases may be put, where a witness is competent and admissible, to prove the criminal intention on the part of the prosecutor, and to rebut the imputation on the part of the defendant.' I heard the Attorney General say that there was a difference between a private action and a public prosecution. Whether he meant to allude to this, that the question so answered by the judges, containing the word *plaintiff*, applied only to a civil action, I know not. If he meant that, I say in answer, that the judges did not so consider it, for they treated it as a question relating to a criminal proceeding. I should be glad to know, however, whether he has not admitted himself out of court, when he admits that in an action there must be a publication, for that there can be no damage without a publication. If so, then there can be no wrong without a publication. What an extraordinary position to maintain, that an individual when there is no publication shall not be heard to complain of any imaginable wrong, and yet the wrong done is so great by the mere act of writing, that the king shall come forward to prosecute criminally and to punish. It is to me one of the most arbitrary, I mean not in a despotic sense, but most capricious propositions I ever heard, to say that the injury to the individual is nothing, but to Government or to the public everything ; that the individual may be excited to a breach of the peace, is the technical ground of the crime. Even this ground cannot exist without a publication, at least to him. But the better, and the only rational ground, is, that the individual sustains an injury to that which is as dear to his feelings and as necessary to his peace as any other species of property. If the poet says truly that the man 'who steals your purse steals trash,' and yet he shall be punished for the theft, why not he also 'who filches your good name, which not enriches him, but makes you poor indeed'? Is there a man who has a spark of honour in his bosom that would not sooner part with a large portion of his property than with any portion of the honourable character he sustains? And shall it be said that a man shall not have an action when there is no publication, because there is no wrong without publication ; but that the king shall indict for the mere writing, when the individual is neither wronged in his character nor roused in his feelings? I say that the public offence grows out of the private injury to the individual. It arises out of the injury to his name and reputation, which cannot be effected till the writing is published. I had forgot to observe that there was another case stated by Lord Holt, the case of John of Northampton. That is a case too loose to be relied on. He was charged with writing a letter to John Ferrers, one of the King's Privy Council. The authority of that case for my learned friend's would be destroyed at once, if it appeared that the letter had been received. But, upon the report, it appears ambiguous ; therefore it cannot affect the force of my argument. It was before the Privy Council the prosecution took place. He was probably accused by the very person who received the letter—he confessed the charge. Lord Coke does not say that it was an indictment, but that he was charged, and confessed it. If I should say that I wrote a letter to Mr. such a one, you would in common parlance infer that it reached him ; more especially, and *à fortiori*, would you infer this if Mr. such a one charged me with writing it to him, and made it the subject of a prosecution. Therefore, John de Northampton's case must be taken to be a publication, or doubtful, and then of no authority. There is another case of Lord Coke's upon which I must make some observation ; the case of Dr. Edwards *v.* Dr. Wooton, 12. Co. fo. 35, 36: the observation is this. I take it for granted none of your Lordships will differ from me in this, that the doctrines and the jurisdiction of the Star Chamber were pushed as far as they ought to have been. But even there it was a doubt whether the sending a libel to the party libelled was such a publication as gave the Star Chamber jurisdiction. Will any one say that the judges of the Star Chamber imagined that the mere writing was criminal without publication, when they made it a question whether the writing and sending it to the party was so criminal as to give them jurisdiction? In the case of Edwards and Wooton it is stated, that he wrote an infamous, malicious, scandalous, obscene letter, to which he subscribed his name, and this sealed and directed 'To his loving friend, Mr. Edward Speed, this.' And after the said doctor published and dispersed to others a great number of copies of the said letter, and it was resolved that the infamous letter, which in law is a libel, shall be punished, although it was solely writ to the plaintiff, without any other publication. The same author uses the same words in the former case ; he says that John of Northampton was charged with writing a letter to John Ferrers, one of the king's council, which said John confessed the letter to be written with his own proper hand ; so that he probably wrote it, and sent it to the party, which is a species of publication.

Now Mr. Attorney having referred first to cases for the purpose of showing that the writing is alone a crime, afterwards likens the writing a libel to the case of forgery. It is certainly worth consideration. He says, forgery by the common law is criminal, although the party does not publish the forgery. I felt all the effect this argument was calculated to produce. If he will give me leave, before I examine the argument, I will state it with all candour in the strongest way against myself. If a man forges an instrument with an evil intent, and you say that it shall constitute him criminal without publication, why should you not by parity of reasoning admit that if a man writes a libel, the intent of which is evil, he also shall be criminal ? I will give you an answer. If you speak of forgery by the statute law, the answer is, that the statute constitutes and defines the crime. But you say, by the common law forging any instrument with intent to defraud is punishable as a misdemeanour. Then let us see what the definition of the crime is by the common law. First, the instrument must be capable by its nature of affecting the property of the individual to be defrauded. In the next place, it is essential to the crime that there must be an intent to defraud some individual, and that intent must be proved by the prosecutor by some circumstance independent of the writing. The crime is capable of a strict, of a limited, of a precise definition. The party who commits it must contemplate the fraud at the very moment he commits it ; he must therefore contemplate an uttering the forged instrument as true. By every principle of law and of morals he unquestionably must be a base, sordid, and wicked man. In the third place the act is specific and distinct : he must either forge the name of the party, or some false writing that has the name annexed, or alter something already written, to falsify it in such a way as if published to injure another's property ; therefore the nature of the instrument is also capable of exact definition. Fourthly, if you did not punish the man who forged with an intention to defraud, unless he combined an uttering and publication as true, you would leave an offence unpunished which the laws of all civilised countries have branded with the odious name of the *crimen falsi*. A man who forges and utters a false instrument cannot be punished by our law as the *utterer*, unless he utters it *as true*. Therefore a man who forges with intent to defraud, and communicates the instrument to another *as false*, cannot be indicted at all except for the forgery, by the common law. It was necessary to make an Act of Parliament to charge the man who sold a forged bank-note for five shillings, as the putter-off or disposer of it ; because if it appeared he had not forged but only sold the note as a forgery, the law would not reach him ; therefore the man who attempts by the actual fabrication of a false instrument an injury on the property of another may well deserve punishment, because his offence is of a nature specific, definite, and intelligible. Moreover he must be a man devoid of all moral principle, insensible to the most obvious dictates of conscience and justice, incapable of restraint, except by force, and unconscious of all moral fear, except the fear of a witness or a judge. Now let us see what analogy this crime bears to that of libel. Not to mention that according to the King *v.* Beare, the innocent intent is cast upon the defendant to prove ; I own I am at a loss to conceive how it could enter into the mind of any gentleman of sound and generous principles, or endowed with a relish for literature, to suppose that the case and conduct of a man, who, intending to compare the works of genius, should collect, amongst other things, and, if you please, transcribe all the libels of different classes that ever were published, bore, *primâ facie,* any analogy to the case or conduct of him, who with sordid and fraudulent views becomes the forger of a pecuniary instrument, deed, or receipt. Criminal laws are made for the punishment of offenders against the well-being of mankind, but not to limit and cramp the operations of human genius, by which are developed and improved the faculties communicated by providence for the general benefit and prosperity of mankind. I should like to know what definition is yet to be found of a libel, which will exclude the whole contents of any one book of literature, poetry, history, or even of divinity, in our libraries. If the doctrine is to prevail that the mere writing is, *primâ facie,* criminal, I would ask, IS THERE ANY ONE WORK THAT HAS ADORNED THE LITERATURE OF ANY COUNTRY, THAT HAS LASHED THE VICES OF ANY AGE, OR THAT FORMS PART OF THE INTELLECTUAL RICHES OF ANY NATION, THAT MIGHT NOT HAVE BEEN THE SUBJECT OF A CRIMINAL PROSECUTION ? Was not every other line of Pope's Dunciad a libel on some living person? IS NOT ALL HISTORY FULL OF LIBELS ON THE LIVING AND THE DEAD ? If the author possessed at once the candour and the courage which ought to form the character of an historian ; if he is ever fearful of stating what is false but ever bold enough to declare the truth 'ne quid falsi dicere audeat, ne quid veri non audeat,' which is CICERO's definition of an historian—HOW CAN HE WRITE THE HISTORY OF PAST TIMES WITHOUT LIBELLING THE DEAD, OR OF HIS OWN WITHOUT LIBELLING THE LIVING? IS ALL POETRY TO BE COMPOSED BY THE LAUREAT? IS ALL HISTORY IN FUTURE TO CONSIST OF PANEGYRIC? Do we live in an age in which the boldness of invention, the very criterion of genius and liberty, is to be indulged only in vapid effusions of panegyric and praise, the very symptom of the most violent despotism and the most abject degree of degeneracy? of which we have had a signal instance in a neigh-

bouring kingdom, where A GENERAL, MOST ILLUSTRIOUS IN ARMS,
BUT A MOST FATAL INSTRUMENT AGAINST THE LIBERTIES AND
HAPPINESS OF THAT COUNTRY, ASSUMED THE GOVERNMENT, AND
EXERCISED A DOMINION, THE LIKE OF WHICH WAS NEVER KNOWN.
See how all the literature of the country was infected with servility,
how the press teemed with fulsome adulation, AS MUST EVER BE
THE CASE WHERE IT IS PLACED UNDER THE DOMINION OF GOVERN-
MENT. Look at the same principle unfolding itself in the beginning
of the reign of Augustus, and advancing to maturity with the loss of
liberty in Rome, until ALL WE HAVE IS PANEGYRIC UPON THE
LIVING EMPEROR. If, then, the law of libel is to be laid down as
analogous to the law of forgery ; and if the very act of writing is to
be deemed sufficient to call upon the party to answer to a criminal
information, so dangerous will it be to write at all, that I say your
Lordships cannot lay down the rule required of you by the Attorney
General, without imposing fetters on human genius, without repressing the most noble propensities of our nature, and rendering
dangerous the exercise of those faculties with which Providence has
blessed man, only to improve and make more happy the condition of
his being. My Lords, I now close this part of the argument, in
which I have considered the question, whether the simple act of
writing can be the subject of a conviction, according to the authority
of the cases of the King *v.* Payne and the King *v.* Beare. I shall
now proceed to the second part of the argument, in which I shall be
as short as possible. I do not consider it so important as the other.
The Attorney General has stated cases to show the distinction
between the writer and the publisher. He makes an odd use of that
distinction for his argument. First there is the case of the King[1] *v.*
Tutchin ; that was tried before Lord Chief Justice Holt, in the 3rd
of Queen Anne. The defendant was indicted for several letters
published by Mr. How, in the *Observator.* It appears from the
report that the Attorney General pressed the case with a degree of
zeal that the Chief Justice did not quite approve of. The case
was this:—' It appeared that Tutchin lived at Lambeth, and that
How lived in London. There was proof the papers were sent to
Mr. How, for him to print them in London. The counsel pressed
that there was no evidence of writing in London. The Chief Justice
says, ' Now whether he received them from him in London or no,
(but suppose out of London), yet if he received them to print them
in London, that is a publication in London. If they scruple that
matter, it shall be specially found. If they were delivered to be
printed at London, I must leave it to your consideration, whether
you will not find him guilty of publishing them in London; they

[1] *Query*—Queen.

were some of them printed in Fenchurch Street, and others in
Gracechurch Street. He knew where the printer lived; the contract
was made, and he was paid for them. Gentlemen, I must leave it to
you; if you are satisfied that he is guilty of composing and publishing
these papers at London, you are to find him guilty. Then the jury
withdrew, and about a quarter of an hour after returned into court.—
Clerk : Answer to your names, &c. How say you, is John
Tutchin guilty of the charge laid against him, or not guilty?
Foreman : Guilty of composing and publishing. *Lord Chief
Justice :* They appeal from my opinion; they do not find
the writing in London, but they find him guilty of composing and publishing in London; that is, supposing he did
write them out of London, and deliver them, in order to be printed
in London. *Solicitor General :* Do you find that the papers, the
copies of these six *Observators* were delivered to be printed in
London? *Foreman :* Yes; guilty of composing and publishing, but
not of writing. *Solicitor General :* Do you find him guilty of the whole
charge, except the writing? *Foreman :* Yes:' Now let us see the
use the Attorney General makes of this. He says it is a case to show
that if you indict for writing, you must indict in the county where
the work was written, and we could not do otherwise with Sir Francis
Burdett. I say it puts an end to the Attorney General's argument;
he says you could not indict for the writing but where the writing
was Be it so, if the mere writing be indictable; but if it be an authority to show that you must indict for the writing in the county where
the work was written, it is no authority to show you may indict for the
publishing where it was *not* published. Directly the reverse. This
case establishes a distinction between the place of writing and the
place of publishing; and if it be good authority to show, that if a
libel be written in one county and published in another, you can
indict for the writing in that county only where it was written, it is
equally good authority to show that you cannot find the defendant
guilty of publishing in that county where the writing only took place :
because if you cannot find him guilty of writing where he did not
write, it follows that you cannot find him guilty of publishing where
he did not publish. If the position be good for one branch of the
crime, it is equally good for the other; and if, in that case, where,
according to the facts, the writing was in Surrey, and the publication
in London, the defendant had been prosecuted in Surrey, instead of
London, he must have been acquitted of the publishing, and found
guilty of the writing only. Admitting, therefore, as this part of the
argument assumes that there was no publication in Leicestershire, it
follows, from the principle of the case, that the verdict, finding a pub-

lication there, cannot be supported. Next comes the case of King and Knell, in I. Barnardiston, 305 ; it is a Nisi Prius case, where the party is said to have been found guilty of the printing, and acquitted of the publishing. If I remember right, the Attorney General cited this case as belonging to the first head of argument. The reporter does not state any judgment.

Mr. Attorney General.—The history of the times acquaints us that there was a judgment.

Mr. Scarlett.—The *Monthly Chronicle* is the history you allude to. I do not know whether the *Monthly Chronicle* of that day was more correct in reporting proceedings of courts of justice than similar publications of the present.

Best, J.—It may be easily ascertained.

Mr. Scarlett.—I have seen in a brief a statement of a Nisi Prius case on the authority of a newspaper.

Bayley, J.—What is meant by D. L. L. in Mr. Starkie's book ? by D. L. L. to which there is a reference ?

Mr. Starkie.—The digest of the law of libel ; but it was not published then.

Mr. Scarlett.—It may be the *County Chronicle.*

Bayley, J.—Mr. Dealtry's contains the sentence.

Mr. Scarlett.—I did not think Mr. Dealtry was so old as to remember it.

Abbott, C. J.—No, Mr. Scarlett; but he has access to the records.

Mr. Scarlett.—Well, my Lord, be it so ; it is generally thought that the man who prints is a publisher. If he has even a private press he cannot very well print alone. I am bold enough, however, to contend that, nothwithstanding the case in Barnardiston, that if printing be not a publication, the judges in 1792 have declared that it is no crime. I beg pardon for adding here what I omitted in the first head of argument, Lord Chief Baron Comyns' authority to that of the judges in 1792, as great an authority as can be referred to, title 'libel.' His words are, 'Libel is a contumely or reproach *published* to the defamation of the government, of a magistrate, or of a private man.' I need not state that Chief Baron Comyns, when he gives no authority, is understood to give his own opinion, the result of his own researches. But whatever authority the case of King *v.* Knell has to confirm Lord Holt's opinion, which I think is sufficiently impeached, it is an authority to show that if a man is not guilty of publishing, he cannot be found guilty of it, and I need not contend before your Lordships that if a man is not guilty in the county where he is indicted, he cannot be found guilty there.

Now the Attorney General has two other heads of argument : one is, that where several acts constituting an offence take place in different counties, as suppose you consider the act of publication, the consummation, and the writing or printing the contrivance, he contends that where he can show one part was done in one county, and another part in another county, he can indict in either. I say the authorities are against him. I will first look at the authorities. The first case he supposes is the case of a nuisance, mentioned in Hawkins. I wish he had gone into the particulars of that nuisance. I apprehend Hawkins will be found to refer to a case where a nuisance exists in both counties. I have not had time to look at the reference.

Best, J.—The case put by the Solicitor General was that of a windmill ; where the nuisance was in one county, and the public annoyed in another.

Mr. Scarlett.—And what is the nuisance of a windmill, my Lord ?

Best, J.—Why it is a nuisance in frightening horses.

Mr. Scarlett.—That is, my Lord, the imagination of my learned friend ; there is no such case in Hawkins ; there is indeed a windmill on the Brighton Road, which I have often wished was elsewhere; but I never heard that a man, who was imprudent enough to ride a starting horse, had a right to consider every windmill he approached as a nuisance.

Best, J.—There was one in Essex presented as a nuisance.

Mr. Solicitor General.—And in Derby, where in an action considerable damages were given ; but I put it merely as an hypothetical case, when I cited the passage from Hawkins.

Bayley, J.—If you erect a windmill by an old established road, is it not a nuisance ?

Mr. Scarlett.—But unless he can cite the case of a windmill in one county indicted in another, his instance does not apply. Where a windmill in one county is indicted as a nuisance in another, I should like to know how it is to be abated. How is the sheriff to execute out of his own county the judgment *quod prosternatur nocumentum ?* It is true there may be a judgment *in pœnam* against the person, but the other is the legitimate judgment. If a man erects a windmill in *A.*, whereby the king's subjects in *B.* find their lives in danger, I say he must be indicted in *A.* only, for there is no act done by him in the county *B.* I can indeed put a case where an act is done in both counties. I will suppose a man, for the purpose of argument, should stand in the county *A.*, and let off a smoke across the road in the counties *A.* and *B.* so that his act operates immediately on persons passing in both counties, there he may be indicted in either, because he does an act of nuisance in both. Although he stands in one county, the mischief is caused by his own immediate act. In the case of the windmill, the owner is not the immediate cause of the alarm of the horse, he is the remote cause. The immediate cause is the motion of the mill. The nuisance is not effected nor contemplated at the moment of erecting the windmill, but it is the result of it at some future time ; the person who erects the mill therefore can be indicted in the county only where the act of erection took place. I am sure your Lordships would be very much surprised to find a windmill indicted in a county where it does not exist. An erection which is a nuisance is always indicted as being in the parish where it exists, although in numerous instances it operates as a nuisance to neighbouring parishes. Who ever heard of an indictment for a nuisance in St. Martin's in the Fields for a steam-engine in a parish in Surrey? Suppose a man temporarily stops up a stream of water in one county, by which a road in another county is overflowed, and thereby a nuisance created, you may indict where the road is, for there his immediate act is done.

Bayley, J.—I think there is a case somewhere of wrongfully erecting floodgates in one county, whereby passengers were prevented passing the road in another.

Mr. Scarlett.—If the effect was gradually produced by a permanent erection, such as a dam or floodgates, then I conceive that the party may be indicted in the county where that erection exists. If indeed the prosecutor meant to abate the nuisance, he must indict there ; but if the injury done be immediate, where is the difference whether the man comes upon the road and digs a pit there, or stands in a neighbouring county and lets in water upon the road to produce the same effect. I say in that case you may indict in the county where the destroying of the road takes place, for the act of nuisance is immediately done there. If a nuisance be locally situated in two counties, you may indict in either, which is all, as I conceive, that Hawkins means. It was once doubted how a parish which lies in two counties, should be indicted for the non-repair of a road. The point is now settled by the King v. the Inhabitants of Clifton, 5 Term Rep. 502. The next case cited is that of Robson, from Mr. East's Pleas of the Crown. It is a case of embezzlement. The answer to it has already been given by my Lord Chief Justice. It is in principle the same as larceny, where by the common law the goods are considered to be taken in each county where the thief is found with them. The statute respecting embezzlement is merely declaratory of the common law in enacting that the money so embezzled shall be deemed to be feloniously stolen. The conduct of the person in denying the receipt of the money and appropriating it to his own use, is evidence that the original taking was with intent to secrete and embezzle, and so according to the statute to steal. Therefore the prisoner in the case cited by the opinions of some of the judges might be indicted either where he originally took the money, or where he afterwards continued the act of embezzlement. The whole crime is consummated in each county, and the party may be tried in either, for the same reason that an action for an asportation of goods might at all times have been brought in any county where the goods were carried, or the party found in possession of them. This case then, as far as it goes, is an authority in my favour. Next comes the case of Scott *qui tam* against Brest, in the 2d Term Reports, 238. Let us see what that case is :—A gentleman living in London, and having certain estates in Middlesex, made a corrupt contract in London, that Brest should be a receiver of his rents in Middlesex, and should retain, under colour of that agency, a greater sum than the lawful interest of certain money borrowed by him from Brest. The evidence was, that the contract was made in London, the rents received in Middlesex, and the account between the parties settled in London. The account was kept correctly, and when the interest and the agency were settled, Brest gave a draft for the balance. The objection made by Mr. Baldwin before Lord Kenyon at Guildhall, was, that as the receipt of the usurious interest took place where the rent was received, which was in Middlesex, the venue ought to have been laid there, and not in London ; to which it was answered by Mr. Justice Ashurst, that he was quite clear the whole act was consummated in London, because he considered that the interest was in fact not received till the account was settled, for he had not till then a right to keep the money, and he expressly says that it is not necessary to give any opinion, in which county the venue ought to be laid in a case where two facts necessary to constitute an offence occur in different counties. This case therefore is not only from the facts of it, no authority for the position for which it was cited, but is expressly declared by the court which decided it, not to be authority for any such point. With respect to felony, it is admitted that if one of two acts necessary to the consummation of a felony be committed in one county, and the other act in another county, the party is guilty of felony in neither county, but guilty of misprision in both. But the act of misprision must be some act that amounts to a breach of the peace, and not, I apprehend, a mere innocent act. Suppose for example a man should merely buy a stick in one county, I apprehend that except in the case of high treason, where the crime consists in the intention, which may be manifested by an overt act, innocent in itself, the single act of buying a stick, in order to commit a felony, could not be considered as a misprision, or as any offence whatever. Where he is an accessory before the fact, by inciting a man to commit a felony, it is a breach of the peace, as was decided in King *v.* Higgins. The act in its nature must be a criminal act, and indictable as such. The case of an appeal has been cited where the stroke is given in one county and the death in another. It is a sufficient answer to say that in such a case by the common law there could be no indictment of murder, and that though an appeal may terminate in the death of the party, it is considered as a civil remedy, therefore in the nature of an action. I have always thought that in misdemeanours, where all are principals, any act done by any of the parties which made him guilty at all, made him guilty in that place where the crime was consummated ; and if the crime consists in publication, as I now assume the crime of libel to do, I have always taken it to be clear that every man was guilty of the publication who was the contriver or procurer of it in the place where it was made, although he was never himself on the spot. I take it to be clear that a man living in Middlesex, and publishing by an agent in London, is guilty in London. This doctrine has been emphatically applied to the offence of publication. Many of the proprietors of newspapers living in different places the Attorney General has brought forward upon charges of publishing in London and West-minster. I remember an exhibition in this court (which I certainly did not applaud) of sundry proprietors of newspapers, who had retired from business into different and distant parts of the country, some of them retaining a legal interest in the property, only to secure the pensions on which they had retired, who were all brought up in a body, and fined from twenty to twenty-five pounds each for publications of which they had probably never heard, in the metropolis, upon the ground, not obvious at first sight, that wherever the proprietor is, the property gives him an interest, which in the case of libel makes him a guilty publisher in that place where the act of publication is consummated. It is quite new to me to be told that in misdemeanours, which are trespasses, you may lay the venue in a county where no trespass was committed. Suppose the case of breaking windows, he who commands as well as he who breaks is guilty there where the windows are broken. Suppose I, living in Middlesex, send my servant into London to break a man's windows maliciously, can any one doubt, though I gave the command in Middlesex that I must be indicted in London? All parties, who in misdemeanour contribute to one common end, are guilty where that end is effected. If I send my servant to commit an assault in the county *A.*, though I send him from London, and though I give him the stick in London, I am yet liable to be indicted only in the county *A.*, and if (sending a stick to assault another's person) I am indictable only where the assault was committed ; so by parity of reasoning, if I send a libel to assault the reputation of another, am I not indictable there only where the publication took place ? Can my learned friend find an example of a man who was the proprietor being indicted where the publication did not take place ? No case has been stated to show that a misdemeanour can be split into parts, and laid at pleasure in different counties. See the power it would give to the Attorney General. I would suppose a man conceiving libellous matter, to buy the paper, pen and ink, in *A.*, to write the libel in *B.*, to put it in the post in *C.*, and to cause it to be delivered in *D.*, there to be published. Here then would be a most fortunate case for a Government that was wicked enough to desire, or weak enough to expose itself to the suspicion of desiring to multiply its tribunals, in order to find one that was partial, and would serve a particular turn. In such a case, according to the argument, the Attorney General might say, we will split the case, and give the prosecutor the means of choosing the county where he can find the most convenient jury. My Lords, no maxims of law, no practice of the courts of justice, no policy of State, no public convenience, can justify such an option in a prosecutor ; nor would such a power be sought by any wise Government, sensible of the odium and disgust excited in the breast of every honest man by a suspicion of partiality in the administration of criminal justice. Surely the obvious place in which an example of punishment should be given, is the place where the crime was committed by publication.

With respect to the case cited of an action for a libel contained in a letter sent from Hull to Hamburgh, and in which the court refused to change the venue from Hull to London, it should be recollected, that an action for a libel is transitory ; that the publication being in Hamburgh, the only part of the injury which took place in England was in Hull ; and that the court never, except when induced by special circumstances, will allow the venue in a transitory action to be changed elsewhere than to the county where the cause of action really arose, and in that case the only cause of action that existed in England arose at Hull. The case of the King *v.* Brisac and Scott, 4 East, 164, has been mentioned. I cannot see how that is an authority to prove a general proposition, that where any misdemeanour is committed in one county, and there are different parties who contribute to it by different acts in other counties, you may indict in any one of the counties. Before I state the particulars of that case, I beg to point out a distinction. Where a misdemeanour consists of several distinct acts, each of which is a specific offence, no doubt you may indict for each crime in the county where it was committed. For instance, several persons may, be charged with a conspiracy to cheat and defraud a particular man ; the conspiracy, or some proof of it, may exist in one county, the act of cheating and defrauding may be committed by one of the parties in another. If you indict for the cheating and defrauding, you must clearly indict in that county only where the act took place. But——

Best J.—The instances are, that you may indict in either county, as in the case of the King and Bowes.

Mr. Scarlett.—Yes, my Lord, for the *conspiracy.* I was about pursuing that distinction. The case of conspiracy is anomalous ; it stands on its own peculiar foundation. I pray your Lordships' attention to distinguish it from all other crimes. The law respecting conspiracy is severe enough in its nature. It would indeed be unfortunate, if that peculiar crime were to be adopted as an analogy to bestow a new character of severity upon the trial, the punishment or the construction of any other crime. What is conspiracy? It is the agreeing together of a number of individuals, either to do some illegal act, or to do some lawful act by unlawful means, which is, perhaps, much the same thing. Suppose a case where the only evidence of conspiracy was that of a witness, an accomplice, who was present at the act of agreeing together, and that no overt act can be proved; does it not appear manifest that in such a case you could lay the venue in that county only where the act of conspiracy took place? As, for example, if I could produce one of a dozen men who met together and agreed to make that noise[1] near this court, which in defiance of your authority, now interrupts your proceedings, and prevents the possibility of your Lordships hearing me or each other ; though they had never committed the overt act under which I am now labouring most severely, yet upon his evidence they might have been tried in Middlesex, and there only. But mark, the law says that upon a charge of conspiracy you need not prove the particular fact of conspiracy. But upon proof of divers overt acts, all tending to one common end, you may call upon a jury to presume a conspiracy for the accomplishment of that end, though you cannot by evidence exhibit the actual scene of conspiracy in any particular county. Therefore, if you can prove by a number of overt acts distinctly affecting each individual charged, that all must have breathed together one common design, you may prosecute in the county where the overt acts were done, though you cannot assign any place where the parties met together ; because, the crime of conspiracy is a crime which the parties carry about with them wherever they carry their criminal designs into effect. If, indeed the crime be capable of proof in one

---

[1] The works going on in Westminster Hall for the coronation.

particular spot, it ought, undoubtedly, by analogy to the general principles of law, to be indicted in that spot. But if you cannot tell where the parties met together, and conspired, but can only prove that they *must* have consented somewhere, by all their different acts concurring in one common design, you may then bring those acts before a jury in any county where they were done, and allege that those acts were designed, communicated, and breathed, by the parties together in that place. If then the case of conspiracy be an anomalous case, as I think must be conceded to me, it serves only to illustrate the principle of the rule I contend for, by proving the exception to it. Now in the case of the King *v.* Brisac and Scott, the actual conspiracy was at sea, not within the jurisdiction of the common law of England, but it was a conspiracy to do an unlawful act within the dominion of England ; and the criminal purpose was accordingly executed in England. An objection was made that the offence was not triable in England ; and it was urged in argument by the counsel, that the conspiracy, which was the *corpus delicti*, never had place in England. Mr. Justice Grose, in passing sentence upon the defendants, replies to this argument, and refers to the case of the King *v.* Bowes. But observe how he refers to it : ' Conspiracy is a matter of inference, deducted from certain criminal acts of the parties, done in pursuance of an apparent criminal purpose, in common between them, and which hardly ever are confined to one place ; ' and again referring to the case of the King *v.* Bowes and others, he says, ' where no proof of actual conspiracy was attempted to be given in Middlesex, but the conspiracy as against all having been proved, from the community of criminal purpose in different places and counties, the locality required for the purpose of trial was holden to be satisfied by overt acts done by some of them, in prosecution of the conspiracy in the county where the trial was had.' Therefore, your Lordships see he adopts the principle I have been contending for, that where you cannot show precisely where the conspiracy existed, you may infer it from overt acts, and give it a local habitation in the place where those acts demonstrate a community of design. A man may be a conspirator, though not exactly in the place where any overt act was done ; because by a previous concurrence of design and arrangement of measures, he may become a party to the performance of an act by the hands of others in a particular place. For example, men may be engaged in a conspiracy, some in Yorkshire, and some in London : they may communicate by letters only, to forward the object of their conspiracy in London ; they may all be indicted in London where the act was done, of which they were all the guilty instruments, although some of them were never there. This principle is applicable even to cases not amounting to conspiracy. Suppose a man in Leicestershire mixes poison, and sends it by an ignorant man to be administered in Lincolnshire, I say he is liable to be indicted for the administration of the poison in Lincolnshire, where it took place, and not in Leicestershire, where the poison was mixed.

Lord Chief Justice.—Suppose the poison is not administered, where then is he indictable?

Mr. Scarlett.—My Lord, he would then be indictable, if at all, for the unlawfully sending it only, which would be in Leicestershire, where that act took place. If the poison be actually administered, and he be indicted for the administering, as in this case Sir Francis Burdett is indicted for the publishing, then I say, that as in the one case the indictment must be where the administering took place, so in the other must it be where the publication took place.

Holroyd, J.—In the case of Lady Strathmore *v.* Bowes, there was one of the parties in the county of Durham, who had done no act except the receiving the others there. The whole conspiracy was hatched and carried into execution in London.

Mr. Scarlett.—If he had been indicted for the specific act he did, and not for the conspiracy, he must have been indicted in Durham : the case your Lordship puts is not stronger than that of the King *v.* Brisac and Scott.

Best, J.—There everything was prepared ; even the vouchers out of England.

Mr. Scarlett.—Yes, my Lord, but the object of the conspiracy was to commit a fraud in England, where it was consummated; and every act done in furtherance of the conspiracy is evidence of the conspiracy in the place where it is done. Where parties are engaged in a concerted design, which is the case of conspiracy, the act of one is the act of all. If in the present case Sir Francis Burdett, Mr. Brooks, and any other gentleman, had been indicted, not for publishing, but for a conspiracy to publish a libel, and the overt acts done by each respectively had been in different counties ; then the indictment might have been laid as well in Leicestershire, where the act of writing by Sir Francis was done, as in Middlesex, where the act of publication took place. The act of publication in that case would not have been an essential part of the charge, as it is in this case, but only a medium of proof in support of the charge.

I come now to the next position advanced by my learned friends, and it is a very important one. Hitherto I have been contending, that when you indict, not for conspiracy, but for a specific act, you must indict in that county where the act was consummated, although it might have had its inception in some other county. As if a man coming from Scotland to London, should write two lines of a libel at each stage, and, finally, publish it in London; according to their argument he must be indicted for the publication in any of the counties through which he passed; according to mine, he could be indicted in London only. But they go further, and contend that in this case there was evidence of a publication in Leicestershire. If they can contend this successfully, there is an end of all further argument. But by what rule is it, and upon what authority, that they so contend? First they cite a case of the King *v.* Watson, from Mr. Campbell's Reports, of an indictment for a libel, in several letters, written by the defendant to the prosecutor. The letters were proved to be the handwriting of the defendant; but there was no proof that he sent them, except what was derived from the post-mark of Islington, where the defendant lived. It is said that the prosecutor failed in his endeavour to prove the Islington post-mark. Now my learned friends make an extraordinary use of that case. They say, how could it be necessary to give evidence of the post-mark, if it was not clear that putting it in the post would constitute a publication in Middlesex? One would think my learned friends had never practised at Nisi Prius. Everyone knows it is the common course for a learned judge to say—first prove your fact, and then argue the question of law. Lord Ellenborough, above all other judges, was averse to give speculative opinions of law. Before he would determine at Nisi Prius whether putting a letter into the post amounted to a publication of a libel, he would certainly require proof that the letter had been put into the post. The inference to be drawn from the case, therefore, even as they cite it, is, that he gave no opinion upon the subject. To quote that case, as a decision in their favour, shows the state to which they are reduced for authorities. One would suppose, if their position were really well founded, that they might have produced abundance of authority; but, I think, this is the only one they have cited, except the case of sending a challenge by the post, to which I shall advert presently. But, in the meantime, upon reference to this case of the King *v.* Watson, as reported by Mr. Campbell, it will be found by no means to justify the use they make of it. I find no hint from Lord Ellenborough, of the most distant kind, that putting a letter into the post is a publication. He says that where the letter has been put into circulation by the act of the defendant, it must be taken to be published by him in the place in which it was delivered to the person to whom it was addressed. The defendant was, therefore, found guilty of that libel, which was received by the prosecutor in Middlesex; but acquitted of that received by the prosecutor in Berkshire, although the post-mark was proved. And it is worthy of remark, that no suggestion was made at the time that the defendant should be found guilty of the writing, though there was evidence of that in Middlesex. With regard to the challenge, they are correct in saying that it has been held in a case at Nisi Prius, reported by the same author, 2 Camp. 506, that putting the challenge by letter into the post is sufficient to make the party guilty in the county where that act is done. But, I would ask, is a challenge necessarily a libel? It may be the most complimentary composition that a man can write; it may be addressed to one whose character he esteems; it may assign his known character for integrity and honour, as the very cause which, under peculiar circumstances, impels the writer to demand satisfaction. No man would call that a libel ; it is full of compliment and praise. But, as Lord Ellenborough expressly said in that case, though it never reaches its destination, the sender is guilty of a criminal act in breach of the peace. It is not publication that constitutes the offence ; there need not be a publication, and here is the distinction. My friends say it is a publication of a libel to put it into the post, because putting a challenge into the post is criminal. I say, on the other hand, that putting a challenge into the post is criminal, because, in the case of a challenge, publication is not necessary. But that putting a libel into the post is not criminal, because it is not publication, which in libel is necessary. There is no defamation without publication; there is neither injury nor tendency to break the peace. The crime of sending a challenge does not consist in its tendency to break the peace ; but has ever been considered as an actual breach of the peace. The act of writing and sending a challenge is therefore criminal, though the challenge never arrives ; in like manner as the giving a loaded pistol to a man, and desiring him to shoot another, is criminal, though no shot is fired. The act of sending is the crime in the one case and in the other. For if, in the one case, he puts the challenge into his pocket, or in the other the loaded pistol, and changes his purpose of sending it, he has the benefit of the *locus pænitentiæ*, and is not guilty. But if I give a pistol to my servant to shoot another, or a challenge to fight him, and in either case, before he obeys my orders, he is intercepted by a magistrate, and discloses the facts, can any man doubt that I should be indictable for a misdemeanour, though my objects were in neither case accomplished? But in the crime of libel, publication is essential to constitute the offence. If the intention to publish be defeated, the crime is prevented. But it may be said, publication of the challenge is necessary to induce the individual to whom it is addressed to break the peace, as publication of a libel is necessary, before a man's character can be affected by it. To this I answer, that where a guilty intention is clear and unambiguous, as must be his who writes a challenge to another to fight a duel, and where that intention is manifested by an act of immediate dangerous tendency, as by the despatching of the letter, the law may well step in before the further progre_s of the offence and treat what has already passed as criminal. You have an actual intention to fight, you have written and despatched a challenge to another.

Mr. Justice Best.—Can the party be provoked to fight till he reads it?

Mr. Scarlett.—No, my Lord, but the challenger has done all that in him lies.

Mr. Justice Best.—Then you must say the crime arises when he puts the letter into the post, because that is a publishing?

Mr. Scarlett.—No, my Lord, I do not say the crime of sending a challenge arises upon its being put into the post, because that is a publication, but because publication is no part of that crime. If there be any technical analogy between the crime of sending a challenge and that of a libel, it does not at all rest upon the ground of publication being common to both. It is at best but a sophistical analogy resulting from the narrow and technical view of a libel as criminal, because it has a tendency to excite a breach of the peace. A challenge is a direct breach of the peace. Writing a challenge, and manifesting the intention with which it was written, by sending it, is criminal. If my learned friends have established by argument that, in like manner, the mere writing a libel with intent to publish it be criminal, then I admit the force of their conclusion, that the sending the letter is evidence of that intention, and therefore consummates that species of crime, as in the case of a challenge. But we are now upon the question, not whether publication be necessary, for upon this part of the argument the necessity of it is conceded; but what amounts to a publication, and where that publication took place.

Mr. Justice Best.—The delivery to the post is evidence, as they put it, of a publication there. The words that have been cited are, 'ediderit vel manifestaverit.' Now is not the delivery to the post, *edere*, in contradistinction to *manifestare*, which may mean a disclosure of the contents?

Mr. Scarlett.—I can only say that the words *edere* and *manifestare* appear to me in the different passages of the Civil Law which have been cited to mean the same thing, as I think will be found upon a reference to the words which surround them in each passage. But I assume here that the crime of libel is constituted by the publication. If it were not so, publication need not be alleged as part of the charge upon an indictment for libel. It is the constant practice to allege it. Can any case be shown of an indictment or information for a libel that did not charge publication? or of a decision, that putting a libel in the post was evidence of a publication? I say no such case can be shown. On the other hand, I say, that in the case of a challenge, publication is no part of the charge; that it is not usual to aver it in the indictment; and that it is an immaterial circumstance in proof. The evil design manifested by some overt act of a criminal character, and of immediate danger, though arrested before its final object be accomplished, constitutes a crime, as in the case I have before put of sending the loaded pistol; or to put another example, suppose a man intending to communicate to another some fatal disorder, as the plague, despatches it in a parcel by a messenger, who discovers the design, and declines to deliver the parcel; or if the beast, who carries it, is drowned in passing a river, and thus the parcel never arrives; the party is clearly guilty of a misdemeanour. In such a crime the question of communication does not arise any more than the question of publication arises in the crime of sending a challenge. My learned friends tell me that if publication be essential to a libel, the putting a letter into the post was deemed publication of a challenge. I say, if their instance be correct, that putting a letter into the post containing a challenge was deemed a sufficient manifestation of an illegal and dangerous design, to be of itself a criminal act, and punishable by law, without any publication; according to them, if a man puts a letter into the post, and that letter is by any accident burnt in its progress, he is guilty of publication. What then is publication? It is a making public. It is true, the law declares that a communication to one individual is a making public; but neither the law nor common sense can call concealment a publication. It can be no publication to put a seal upon a letter and to put it into the post. It is an act towards a publication I grant; and if the law defines that act as a crime *per se*, of course you may indict for it in the county where it is committed. But that act is in itself a concealment. If you indict a man for a concealment, and call it a publication, in order to make a constructive crime, you not only violate the principle of common sense, but you pervert the plain meaning of words. It is trifling with common sense, and common understanding, to say that a man is guilty of publishing a letter, in the very act of taking the greatest pains to conceal it from every eye, but that of the individual whom he intends to see it. He may intend to publish it, and the putting it into the post may be evidence of that intention; but the intention to do an act, which is not done, does not make that act. The intention to murder is not murder, neither is the intention to fight a fighting, nor the intention to publish, publishing. To manifest an intention of publishing is one thing:

but if no one has seen it, is it not a violation of language to say that it has been published ? Will you say, then, that it shall be deemed a publication in law, when no human being has seen the composition, except the person who composed it ? Surely the argument cannot be called ingenious, which offers so much violence to the understanding, as to contend that the progress towards publication, which may be arrested, and the object of publication thereby defeated, amounts itself to a publication. How absurd would it be to apply the same reasoning to the ordinary acts of life. Suppose a man, having received an invitation, gets into his carriage for the purpose of going to dinner ; the carriage breaks down with him. Has he actually dined ? Is the getting into his carriage, although he never arrives, or does not arrive until the second course is over, sufficient proof of an absolute dining? This instance may appear ludicrous, but it is surely not more absurd than the doctrine that a publication or edition of a work, which is the same thing, for it is a putting forth of it to the public, has taken place at a time when, and at a place where no human eye has seen it, or can have seen it, but that of the composer. The design to do a particular act may be evinced in a thousand various ways, and you may, if you please, declare the design itself, or any of those modes of manifesting it, criminal ; but you cannot, without a violation of language, declare anything short of the final consummation of the design to be equivalent to the accomplishment of it. You may declare the writing of a libel, and the putting it into the post with the intent to publish it, a crime ; but do not call it a publication, in order to make it a crime by construction. Allow me to put this case. I know how it would be decided now, though I am not sure how it would have been decided a hundred and fifty years ago. Suppose Sir Francis Burdett, the very day of putting this letter into the post, had repented of it, had mounted his horse, and made the best of his way to the gentleman to whom it was addressed, to anticipate the arrival of the post. He then says, 'There is a letter coming from me ; I have particular reasons why it should not be opened ; you know my handwriting, when it arrives have the goodness to put it into the fire sealed as it is' : the gentleman puts it into the fire accordingly. Now I ask, is this a publication ?

Mr. Justice Bayley.—You never could have set out the tenor, unless you had seen the libel.

Mr. Scarlett.—Yes, my Lord : for I will suppose in addition, that he afterwards confessed that he did write such a letter ; that he did put it into the post ; and that afterwards, by the means I have mentioned, he caused it to be burnt, or by a bribe to the postmaster, got it back into his possession.

Mr. Justice Best.—I will put you a case :—you seem to consider publication and manifestation of the contents as the same. Now, in the publication of a will or of an award, do you declare the contents ?

Mr. Scarlett.—The publication of a will is a particular act, specified by the statute of frauds, which does not concern a will of personal estate ; a will to pass real estate must be attested by three witnesses, in the presence of the testator, when he signs it, or declares it to be his will. This is the sort of publication required, in order to identify the particular instrument. The contents need not be declared : so of an award. What is called the publication, is no more than the execution, or acknowledgment of the execution, of the particular instrument, in the presence of a witness who can identify it. The act of publication in both cases is confined to the character and identity of the instruments, and therefore need not extend to their contents. Neither the will nor the award is complete till it is communicated by a public act, which specifies the instruments. If I make an award, and then before the time expires, and before any person has seen it, I think fit to make another, the latter when delivered and published would be a good award ; but if I had published the former award by declaring, in the presence of witnesses who could identify it, that it was my act and deed, without any manifestation of the contents, and had delivered it, my authority would have been at an end. The publication, therefore, which the law requires of a will or an award is a communication to others of the nature of the act done, and not of the contents of the instrument. I do not say that a party might not publish a libel by the same words, combined with the delivery of the paper *to be read;* but your Lordships cannot fail to observe, that even in those sorts of publication which are the best defined and the most technical, the law requires a communication to one or more persons of the nature and character of the instrument, in order to consummate a publication. A deed is published by delivery, *as a deed,* and so of a will or an award, the publication of which is a declaration, in the presence of other persons to whom the character of the instrument is made manifest. Yet, supposing a will to contain a recital grossly libellous of another, the publication of it as *a will,* without any disclosure of its contents to the witnesses would, as I most confidently submit, be no publication of the libel.

Mr. Justice Bayley.—Supposing a bookseller wishing to sell a libel and avoid punishment says, I will sell you this libel in a sealed envelope, if you will not break the envelope till you are out of the county, would the publication be in the county where the article was sold, or where the envelope was opened?

Mr. Scarlett.—It is an ingenious case. I am anxious not to prejudice my argument by making an unwary admission.

Mr. Justice Bayley—I throw it out now that it may be considered by and by.

Mr. Scarlett.—I should say, my Lord, that the publication would be in the county where the envelope was meant to be opened. The case, however, might be qualified, by different circumstances. If, for example, the bookseller has some particular criminal view in opening the paper in a particular county, and with that criminal design he constitutes the party to whom he delivers the sealed packet his agent for there publishing it; but, in the meantime, vests the absolute dominion in him by a sale, perhaps the law would hold him responsible for the publication in any county where the party publishing thought fit to open it, or, perhaps, in the county where it was sold; because, by the act of sale, he parts with the right, as well as the dominion, and his actions are in opposition to his words. But I am inclined to think, even in that case, that there would be no publication, except in the place where the purchaser thought fit to open the parcel : he has the power to do the act, but it is not done. Suppose, however, a case more like the present, that I deliver to my servant a sealed packet, with strict injunctions to throw it into the fire, or to carry it across the boundary into another county. If, in the first case, he should lose the parcel, or make it known, by betraying my orders, I should say I was guilty of no publication at all; in the second case, I contend that I should be guilty of the publication in that county only where he had delivered it, in pursuance of my orders. Suppose a bookseller or an author should deliver to an agent, sealed up in a packet to be carried abroad, a work, which he never meant to publish in England, or should send it to the post, addressed to a foreign correspondent, I should say, that though the work was arrested in its progress by another person, and published in England, yet that the person who so despatched it was guilty of no publication. On the other hand, my learned friends, if their argument be consistent, ought to contend that though the work reached its destination, and was published abroad only, yet that the party was guilty of a publication in England, by the mere act of despatching it by an agent, or by the post; a doctrine that may be very convenient for a vindictive government, after the liberty of the press in England has ceased to exist.

The Solicitor General cited the case of the King and Sir Samuel Barnardiston, not, as he was pleased to say, as an authority for any point thereby decided, I presume, because the trial was before Chief Justice Jefferies. The opinions and feelings of that famous person, if I may call him famous in the abstract sense of the word——

Lord Chief Justice.—I suppose you mean '*famosus*'?

Mr. Scarlett.—Yes, my Lord. There is no case in which the
virulence of his zeal, and the prejudice and bitterness of his mind
were more strongly evinced ; but the Solicitor General stated the case
thus : that Mr. Williams was counsel for the defendant ; that he
was a very eminent lawyer of that day, and concerned as counsel for
some of the persons who were prosecuted for State offences ; that the
proof of publication in that case consisted in putting letters into the
post in London, where the trial took place ; and that Mr. Williams
allowed it to pass without objection, conceiving there was no ground
to object. The case is cited, not for the opinion of a judge, whose
authority upon such a point would have no weight, but as a sort of
negative authority for the opinion of a counsel, whose very silence,
dictum à non dicendo, is deemed of sufficient importance to demand
attention in a case that stands so much in need of authority. Unfortunately for the Solicitor General, upon reference to the case, it will
be found that there *was* other evidence of publication, besides that
of putting the letters into the post, and that Mr. Williams *did* press
his objections to the latter head of the evidence with great anxiety
and earnestness, both to the judge and jury, treating the circumstance of a delivery to the post as clearly no publication in London.
The information was for writing several private letters to a friend in the
country, containing the news of the day ; among other things 'that
the Duke of Monmouth was come to town, that it was reported that
he was received into favour—that many persons who had taken part
against him, had now been to pay court to him—that Sir George
Jefferies was said to be very much down in the mouth,'—at which Sir
George seemed to have been greatly affronted ; for he says more
than once in the course of the trial, 'Sir George is not so down in
the mouth, but he will have a word with you, Sir Samuel.' It was
proved by Sir Samuel's own servant, or clerk, that it was his habit,
after he had written his letters to his friends, to give them to him,
the clerk, to copy ; and when they were copied, sometimes the
originals, and sometimes the copies, signed by Sir Samuel, were put
into the post. Some of the letters produced in evidence were the
actual copies in the hand of the clerk, signed and addressed on the
back by Sir Samuel ; one, if not more, was in the hand of Sir Samuel
himself, which the clerk swore that he had copied before it was despatched. Here was clear evidence of a publication to the servant in
London. Mr. Williams appears to have reserved himself very much for
an objection appearing on the record, which, to his great surprise, he
found, when he made his objection *in banc*, had been removed, by an
alteration of the record made since the trial ; and there does appear
some ground for the charge he insinuated that this was done by the

order of the Chief Justice. However, upon the trial he found himself a good deal hampered by the evidence of the servant. He felt that if credit was given to him, the publication in London was sufficiently proved : but that if his credit was destroyed, then the only fact remaining was the evidence of the letter being put into the post. He therefore addressed the jury upon the credit of the witness, and if that was disposed of, upon the want of evidence of publication in London ; and on this part of his argument he expressly states that sending the letters by the post was not a publication in London. I do not find that any other case is cited upon this point.

Mr. Justice Bayley.—There is a case, not in print, which seems to have a bearing on this case. It is the case of the King *v.* Collicott, in 1811. It was for uttering forged stamps, and the question was, whether the uttering was in the county of Middlesex. The party lived in Middlesex, and delivered the stamps there in a parcel to his servant to take to London to send to a customer in Bath. The indictment was in Middlesex ; the majority of the judges, that is seven, were of opinion the uttering was in Middlesex ; the other five differed. All agreed it would be an offence in London, when it got out of the possession of the servant, and they recommended a fresh indictment in London ; upon that he was convicted, and the case was reserved for another point. All the judges were satisfied that it was an uttering in London. I thought it proper, knowing there was such a case, to mention it. It may have an effect upon the ultimate determination of this court : the difference there, in the view the judges took, was as to the delivery, whether it was to a servant, or a carrier ; five judges thought it not out of his possession in Middlesex ; that so long as it was under the care of the servant, it was *quasi* under his own control, and therefore not so completely parted with as when under the care of the carrier.

Mr. Scarlett.—I thank your Lordship for the communication— the case is not in print.

Mr. Justice Bayley.—No, but the gentleman who follows you will probably find it mentioned in the Old Bailey paper ; it was in the sessions of 1811, or February, 1812.

Mr. Scarlett.—That case may probably be found to depend on the particular circumstances, or on the words of the Act of Parliament relating to the uttering of forged stamps, to which I cannot immediately refer. If the Act contains any words making it criminal to put off or dispose of forged stamps, without publishing them as true, as is the case respecting forged bank-notes, then undoubtedly I conceive in the case your Lordship has cited, that the crime might have been committed in Middlesex by a delivery of the stamps to the servant there : though even in that case, as they were sealed up, I should have thought the opinion of the minority of the judges the sounder of the two, that the possession still remained with the master ; and I would venture to apply to them in comparison of their brethren, the proverb, '*ponderantur* non numerantur' ; but if the law respecting the uttering forged stamps requires that the party should utter and publish them as true, then, I must own, I can have no conception how the delivery of the sealed packet to the servant, without any declaration of the contents as true, could be an uttering to him. With respect to the uttering in London by a delivery to the carrier, I can well conceive it to have taken place. If by the previous correspondence with the customer, the prisoner was directed to send true stamps by the carrier, and he under colour of complying with that order, delivered forged stamps to the carrier, I apprehend there would be no difficulty in maintaining that these circumstances amounted to an uttering in London as true ; the previous correspondence amounts to an engagement to deliver true stamps, and the delivery to the carrier in compliance with that engagement is a delivery to the customer, and therefore an uttering to him of a parcel, of the contents of which he is apprised, though not of their fictitious nature.

Mr. Justice Best.—But suppose the stamps were sent sealed up from Middlesex into London by the post.

Mr. Scarlett.—In that case, my Lord, I have no hesitation in saying, that the five judges must have been right that there was no uttering in Middlesex ; and as long as I live I must maintain the authority of their opinion over the seven.

I have but two other arguments to offer upon the subject of publication. Your Lordships know that generally speaking, according to the rules of pleading, you are at liberty to use words upon the record of a precise and understood acceptation, or to substitute for those words their exact legal effect ; that is to say, you may either use a known word or its legal definition. I speak of this as a general rule. I know there are certain exceptions in cases of a highly penal nature, where the law in favour of life, as it is said, demands greater strictness ; as in an indictment for murder, the word *murder* is indispensable, and so possibly of a few other cases. But I am not aware of any case of misdemeanour in which the offence may not be well described by its definition. Now the technical definition of the crime of libel is, that it is an excitement to a breach of the peace by means of a written instrument containing matter injurious to the fame and character of another. Let us suppose first, that the indictment, omitting all words of publication, charged the defendant in the language of this definition, 'that he at such a time and place did unlawfully excite some particular person to commit a breach of the peace by means of a certain written paper containing the matters following,' &c., &c., setting forth words apt for the purpose. I ask then if you would be satisfied with proof that the defendant at the place charged, wrote the paper, that he sealed it, that he there put it into the post, although the person to whom it was addressed never received it? Clearly not, because there is no evidence of an excitement. Excitement is the operation of some act upon the mind of another; and the writing can have no tendency to a breach of the peace, according to the definition, till it begins to operate upon the mind of him whose passions it was intended to provoke. But this is the technical definition of the offence. Take that which I think more enlarged and much more correct. It is an injury done to the feelings, the good fame, and the reputation of another, by means of a written instrument. Let the indictment charge that the defendant did at a certain place injure the feelings or fame of another by means of a certain writing, &c.; upon the same evidence would you not say, if the offence be properly charged in the indictment by that definition, it has not been proved; there must be some other evidence of publication in this place; except some persons saw the paper there, no mischief was done, no crime was committed there? If he merely put it into the post, and nobody ever saw it, no crime has been committed anywhere; the definition shows that the reputation must be affected, or the mind of the individual wounded, and this must be proved to be done in some particular place; whereas if the paper has never been seen by that individual, or any other, neither can his fame have been affected, nor his passions inflamed in any place. The crime is not consummated until some person has seen the paper; that is, until publication.

Bayley, J. –You say it must be seen in the county. Put the case that a man living in England, and taking care never to leave it, writes a scurrilous libel to a man in Scotland, where alone it is published. Is he to be protected from prosecution by the laws of England?

Mr. Scarlett.—I go that length fully, my Lord, and I am not afraid of the consequence of the admission. I think it is quite clear. Surely criminal laws are not made for the protection of persons not living within the kingdom or jurisdiction to which they extend.

Bayley, J.—Then suppose the person libelled comes from Scotland, and commits a breach of the peace in England. Is not that a consequence the libel is likely to produce in England?

Mr. Scarlett.—To show that no argument can be derived from that circumstance, allow me to put the case that both parties being British subjects, are in France, and one of them there writes and publishes a libel on the other, and immediately comes to England, where the other follows to punish him. Is the person who has written and published the libel in France punishable in England?

Best, J.—There the whole offence is out of the jurisdiction of England. You put a case where the libel is written in France; the case put by my brother Bayley is where the letter is written in England.

Mr. Scarlett.—True, my Lord, the case put by the learned judge is for the purpose of the argument called the *reductio ad absurdum.* He says, 'See the consequence that might result from your argument; the peace might be broken in England in consequence of a libel which you say cannot be punished there.' The case I put in answer is for the purpose of the argument *non valet consequentia*, because I say the very same consequence might equally result from a case in which you admit that no crime was committed, or could be punished in England; therefore that consequence is of no avail to show that the crime must be punishable in England. I assume that the laws of every country, and more especially the criminal laws, are made to protect the subjects of that country only. The criminal laws of England are made for the security of his Majesty's liege subjects, and others who may reside within his dominions, and not to protect the reputation or the peace of persons living in foreign countries. By the civil law of England indeed, which is a most liberal law, a man may have an action here for an injury to his person committed abroad, and possibly for a libel published of him in France, but not an indictment. In the act of Union with Ireland, there is a clause expressly enabling the Lord Lieutenant to send Irish subjects to this country in order to make them amenable to the jurisdiction of our criminal courts for offences committed by their means, or by their authority, in this country. Upon this law, Mr. Justice Johnson was sent to this country to be tried for a libel published by him here, though written and transmitted by the post from Ireland. But for this law he must have gone unpunished, unless he had of his own accord come to England. Perhaps as he owed allegiance to the sovereign of the United Kingdom, it might have been held that the offence committed by him by a publication in England was punishable here whenever he could be found here. But there was no law to bring him here for trial but the Act of Union. He was not indicted for putting a letter into the post. The Attorney General of that day, Mr. Perceval, (I speak from personal knowledge of his sentiments) had exercised a very grave consideration of that case; and though the libel was upon the government of Ireland, he thought he was indictable in this country, because it was published here by his authority. But according to the argument of the day he was also guilty in Ireland, because he had put the letters into the post. If this be so, he might be indicted twice for the same offence. In this case it must clearly be admitted, that Sir Francis Burdett was guilty of a publication in Middlesex. Now, suppose your Lordships should pass sentence upon him on this record as it stands, and the Attorney General should file an information against him the next day for publishing the same libel in Middlesex, and he should plead that he had been indicted for the same offence in Leicestershire, and *autrefois* convict, I say the Attorney General would demur.

Mr. Attorney General.—No, no.

Mr. Scarlett.—Very well ; then I will only say that you ought to demur. There is no doubt that a man is guilty and liable to be indicted in respect of each distinct act of publication of the same libel. If what he did in Leicestershire does not amount to a distinct act of publication, he was not guilty there. If it does amount to a distinct act of publication, it is clear there was also a distinct act of publication by his agent in Middlesex. I have already wasted too much time, if I have not satisfied your Lordships that an act which only tends to publication, or which only manifests a design to publish, is not publication, and that this verdict cannot be maintained except upon evidence of a distinct publication consummated in Leicestershire. If the putting the letter into the post be a distinct act of publication in Leicestershire, and not merely an act done towards a publication in Middlesex, then I confidently maintain that it is immaterial to that offence what becomes of the letter afterwards ; the offence is complete, and the party indictable for a publication to the postmaster, I presume, or somebody of legal imagination in that county. It is equally clear that if the letter is afterwards published by the defendant's authority in Middlesex, this is a distinct act of publication to different persons, and in a different place, and therefore the Attorney General would have a right to say you have only shown upon the record that you committed another offence in Leicestershire, for which you have been punished. The matter must appear in a special plea, which would be rather a novelty.

Abbott, C. J.—No novelty. You could introduce an averment that the offence was the same.

Bayley, J.—You would say this ; that the act of publication in Leicestershire was the sending the libel from Leicestershire into Middlesex, and that you were not guilty of any other publication in Middlesex than what arose from the sending in Leicestershire.

Mr. Scarlett.—Then I say the Attorney General could demur. If the argument, on which the publication in Leicestershire must rest, be available, he would say that the act of sending it in the county of Leicester was of itself a publication *there*, and could neither alter nor qualify a subsequent publication in Middlesex. The one, if a publication at all, was a publication of the manuscript ; the other was a publication by the press. In the one information he would be charged with writing and publishing, in the other with printing and publishing. In order to make the plea sensible, you are obliged to assume the very proposition that I contend for, namely, that the sending the letter to Middlesex, to be there published, is only an act done in Leicestershire towards a publication in Middlesex ; that it is part of the *res gestæ* of a publication in Middlesex : whereas, to support this information, you assume that the act done in Leicestershire was a consummated publication in that place. If you admit that the subsequent publication in Middlesex was a necessary part of the proof to sustain this charge of a publication in Leicestershire, then I say you admit that the crime was not complete till the publication in Middlesex, which again is all that I contend for ; because I hope that I have already proved that where the consummation of a misdemeanour takes place (excepting only, and perhaps but apparently, the case of conspiracy) there the indictment must be preferred. The Attorney General would say to such a plea, that an indictment in Leicestershire imported and implied a publication to somebody in that county, and that his information in Middlesex imported, and could only be proved, by a publication *to somebody* in Middlesex.

Bayley, J.—One thing is clear, that upon an indictment for larceny in the county of *A.*, a plea of *autrefois* convict, or *autrefois* acquit, in the county of *B.*, where you had stolen the goods and carried them to *A.*, and that you were not otherwise guilty in *A.* than by carrying the goods there, would be good.

Mr. Scarlett.—That is because the law peculiar to that case has determined that wherever a trespasser carries the goods he has taken by trespass, he continues a trespasser.

Bayley, J.—It is a continuation of the felony.

Mr. Scarlett.—Yes, but it is the same felony committed in each county.

Best, J.—It is a continuation of the same offence.

Mr. Scarlett.—Is the publication in Middlesex a continuation of the publication in Leicestershire? I can only say that I should be very much alarmed if my liberty depended upon the construction the court would put upon such a plea, supposing this case not to have previously occurred. I own the circumstances appear to me to bear no analogy to that of the case of a larceny, by carrying the same goods through different counties. The argument is not *ad idem*. It violates all my

notions of the propriety of language to call the act done in Middlesex
a continuation of the act done in Leicestershire. The acts are not
only distinct but different in their nature, when the effect of each is
considered exclusively, and without reference to the other. The one
is the delivery of a sealed letter to the post, the other is the distribution, by an agent, of printed papers. Has Sir Francis Burdett, by
this admitted publication in Middlesex, continued to do an act
whereof the crime consisted in exciting his Majesty's subjects in
Leicestershire to a breach of the peace? Which of his Majesty's
subjects has been so excited, or which of them did he intend to
excite? Nobody saw it there but himself. Could anybody be
excited who did not see it? Could he intend to excite anybody
whom he did not intend to see it? Surely it is a strange confusion of
ideas to introduce into the criminal law, the principles and maxims
of which ought to be simple and obvious. Can it be anything but
casuistry and sophistry which results in so extraordinary a conclusion,
that an intention to excite the county of Leicester, or an actual
excitement of that county, to a breach of the peace, is to be inferred
from an act, the only effect, the only intention of which, was directly
and exclusively to excite the county of Middlesex? That the crime
was committed in Middlesex, if committed at all, is agreed on all
hands. Then why resort to another county, in order, by a construction which violates the ordinary sense of mankind, to infer a publication, or an excitement to a breach of the peace of his Majesty's
subjects in the county of Leicester, where it is admitted that the
paper never publicly appeared, or was seen by any one individual.

Bayley, J.—He is charged with intending in the county of
Leicester to produce an effect elsewhere, which would naturally be
produced by this libel. If you send a libellous paper, addressed to
the gentlemen of the county of Middlesex, and you remain stationary
in Leicestershire, that may have, and in some instances would have,
the effect of inducing those persons to leave Middlesex, and go down
there, and be guilty of a breach of the peace; that is one way in
which it might endanger the safety of the peace there.

Best, J.—For if it be a seditious libel it may produce a breach of
the peace in any part of the kingdom. I think it is sufficient for a
libel to have a tendency to excite sedition.

Mr. Scarlett.—The question is, what amounts to a publication? If
an intention in Leicestershire to produce an effect elsewhere, combined
with an act of concealing the contents of a letter till it gets elsewhere,
be a specific crime, declare it so. I am only contending that it is
not a publication in Leicestershire. Or if because a seditious libel
may by possibility produce a breach of the peace in any part of the

kingdom, though it has never appeared in more than one part, therefore, the author or publisher may be indicted in all parts, let the law be so declared, openly and intelligibly ; but do not conceal it under a new definition of the word publication. Nothing can have a tendency to excite sedition, that does not in some shape or in some place meet the public eye. I had thought that a man, to be criminal in any place, must do some act in that place which comes within the legal definition of the crime ; and therefore, that if a man be charged with an attempt to excite a breach of the peace in the county of Leicester, you must show that a breach of· the peace was likely to follow in that county : not remotely, circuitously, and by possibility (for then any imaginable act might be indictable), but immediately and directly, as the natural consequence of the act done in that county. The publication of a libel in Middlesex might by its consequences actually excite a breach of the peace in Leicestershire : so might a publication in China ; but neither the one nor the other would therefore be a publication in Leicestershire.

My Lords, I therefore submit that the cases of the King and Beare, and the King and Payne, cannot be considered as authorities ; that they are not, and never were, sustainable on any principle of law or reason : that whatever authority they might have, has been overruled by the unanimous and solemn opinion of the judges; delivered in answer to the questions proposed to them by the House of Lords, in 1792 ; when they declared that the crime of libel consisted in the publication. I submit further that the publication of a libel is an act that it requires no refinement or ingenuity to explain ; that it is obvious to the meanest capacity that it consists in making the libel known to one or more persons. That to put any other signification on the word than its plain and natural import, in order to make it embrace a particular case, is nothing less than by casuistry and construction to pervert, and confound, and mystify plain language : to do which, in defining the nature of crimes and punishments, where the public interest is so much involved, is neither the province of a legislator nor the office of a judge. I say further, that there can be no continuation of this offence, because each act of publication is of itself a simple and consummated offence. It may be committed by a man in person, or by his agent ; but in either case the manifestation of a libel to a third person must be effected before the publication is consummated. I submit that in all cases of misdemeanour, with the exception of conspiracy, and that only apparent, the indictment must be where the offence was consummated : that in the case of libel, the indictment must therefore be where the publication took place : that in this case no publication took place, and no offence was committed in Leicestershire. It has, indeed, been said by the learned judge who tried the information, that it did not appear but that the defendant might have given the letter open. I say the defendant has a right to tell the prosecutor to *prove* that fact, and not to presume it against him. The case of the seven bishops is exact to this point, where the very question was put, and the judge made this answer : Mr. Justice Powell, whose honesty was equal to his law, says : ' My Lord, the contrivance and publication are both matters of fact, and upon issue joined the jurors are judges of the fact as it is laid in the information; but how can they be judges of a matter of fact done in another county ? And it must be presumed, in favour of innocence, not to be done in this county, but in another, except they prove it.' It is as to this particular point, almost the identical case.

Best, J.—This information is in Leicestershire. If it had been in Surrey it would have been the same case.

Mr. Scarlett.—My Lord, it is the same as to this point, which is merely a question of the *onus probandi.* The Attorney General in that case says, ' We can prove they wrote it, and we find it published in Middlesex.' Therefore the proof lies on them to show that it was not their publication. So here it is said, we prove that he wrote it in Leicestershire ; it must have been delivered to somebody there, either opened, which would be a publication there, or sealed ; and it lies upon the defendant to prove it was not delivered open, because we found it open in Middlesex. The facts, though not exactly the same, present exactly the same question. Had this case been then under trial, the question would have been as it is here, how did this paper come out of Sir Francis Burdett's possession into Mr. Bickersteth's ? To which the Attorney General would have answered, the proof lies on the defendants. But the reply of the Chief Justice is, No : the proof lies on your part. In consequence of which they waited for the Lord President, and unless he had appeared and proved that the paper was actually delivered by the bishops in Middlesex, the Chief Justice would have directed an acquittal upon that point. I submit, therefore, in like manner, that the proof how this letter came out of the hands of Sir Francis Burdett in the county of Leicester, into the hands of Mr. Bickersteth in Middlesex, must be adduced by the prosecutor, not by the defendant. But to put this beyond a doubt, the presumption from the facts proved, is, that the letter was not delivered open to Mr. Bickersteth, or delivered to him in person by Sir Francis. It is proved that it was enclosed in an envelope to him, directing him to forward it to Mr. Brooks. A man does not direct another in writing, and at the same time deliver him a message ; the presumption is, that it came by the post. How is it proved that he put it in the post in Leicestershire. He was seen in the county the day it bears date, and your Lordship seems to have acted upon a presumption arising from that.

Best, J.—No, I never acted on that at all.

Mr. Scarlett.—Then why have we been arguing whether putting a letter into the post amounts to a publication? That it is dated in his house I agree is good evidence against him that he wrote it there. But he was seen on horseback passing through a turnpike gate the same day. How near is that gate to the county of Rutland, where his post-town may be, for aught that appears? What right had the jury to presume from the mere facts of his writing the letter at home that day, and his being seen riding on the borders of Leicestershire and Rutlandshire, that he put it into the post in one county more than another, without any evidence of the distance from the post-town of either county? It is a mere presumption drawn from facts perfectly ambiguous. It is quite as consistent with all the facts proved, to suppose that his post-town is in Rutlandshire, and that he carried the letter there. Why is it to be left to conjecture and presumption that he either put the letter into a post-office in Leicestershire, or delivered it open to some private hand there? There is no post-mark on the letter. Mr. Bickersteth, who delivered it to Mr. Brooks, is not called to prove where he received it. Does the proof lie on Sir Francis Burdett? No : you undertake to prove that he published it, as you call it, in Leicestershire, either by delivery to a private hand, or by putting it into the post ; and you have proved neither the one nor the other, but desire the jury to presume one or the other, unless he shows the contrary.

Best, J.—I should tell you, that it was in evidence, that his house was within two or three miles of the county of Rutland.

Mr. Scarlett.—I thank your Lordship. I was aware of this fact, but did not know it had been proved in evidence. Rutlandshire is a small county. It is probable that the post town of the defendant is in that county, and not in Leicestershire. But, supposing this quite equal and indifferent, upon the evidence what right had the jury to presume one more than the other? My learned friends not only assume the law without authority, but they call upon the jury to assume the facts without proof. This is the first time I have ever heard that facts essential to the conviction of a defendant need not be proved against him, but may be presumed unless he negatives them.

Best, J.—Either you or I misunderstand this. I think the result is the other way. Here is a letter written in Leicestershire, and it arrives in London, which proves that it was sent away or parted with by the defendant. You say it is possible he might go into Rutland-shire to put it into the post. I say, then, the presumption is on your part, and if you proved it, there might be something in it. But in the absence of such proof, it is open to us to presume that it was in the county of Leicester.

Mr. Scarlett.—My Lord, my objection is to any gratuitous presump-tion on the subject. Let me put a case. Suppose a man's house lies at equal distances between two post-towns, I say nothing of the county, and it becomes essential, in order to convict him of some offence, to prove that he put a letter into the post at one of those towns in particular, on whom does the *onus probandi* lie? Would it be enough to prove that the letter was probably put into the post at one or the other of those towns, and then call upon the jury to presume that it was put into the particular one you desire, unless he showed the contrary? If you proved that his usual course was to send a letter-bag to one of the towns in particular, I admit you would then have given evidence that would justify a presumption in favour of that particular town, till he rebutted it by contrary proof. But if you give no evidence on the subject, from what is the presumption to be drawn? Can it be said, that if a man is proved to have written a letter in a particular place, but it is ambiguous in what place he put it into the post, that he is called upon to prove the place? But suppose the house, in the county of Leicester, is ten miles from any post-town in that county, and three only from a post-town in Rutland, which way is the presumption then, in the absence of all evidence? There is no magic in the circle of a county, that a man must be bound by a sort of spell always to use a post-town in the county where his house is. The contrary is often the fact : and I never heard there was any presumption of law upon the subject of post-towns, or that a man uses one instead of another, without evidence of his general course.

Holroyd, J.—There is no evidence about the post. The evidence is, that he lived in Leicestershire ; he is proved to have been there on the day of the date, and it is found not sealed in the hands of some other person in another county ; *non constat*, that the publica-tion was in the county where the person has it in his possession. The inference is, that it got out of the possession of Sir Francis Burdett, in the county where he was proved to be. How it got from him does not appear ; that can only be presumed : but is there not presumptive proof that it got out of his hands in the county of Leicester, where he was proved to be.

Mr. Scarlett.—Then it is to be presumed, that because he was seen in the county of Leicester, he was not out of the county on the same day; and this, although he was on horseback within three miles of another county.

Holroyd, J.—How it got from him is within the knowledge of the defendant. In considering what is proof, you are to consider what is within his knowledge, and what is within the knowledge of the prosecutor.

Mr. Scarlett.—With submission, in considering what evidence amounts to a presumption, so as to shift the *onus probandi*, you are to consider not what is within the knowledge of each party, but what it is within the power of each party to prove. Here it was as much within the power of the prosecutor as of the defendant, to show how the letter came from his hands to those of Mr. Bickersteth, because it was in the power of both parties to call Mr. Bickersteth, who was certainly a competent, if not the only witness to prove it. The question then is, whether the evidence adduced, considering what the prosecutor might have added, affords a presumption, or leaves the matter in a perfectly neutral state. If your Lordship is correct in supposing that it does not appear how the letter got out of the hands of Sir Francis Burdett, then I complain, that in the absence of all evidence upon that subject, though it was clearly and easily in the power of the prosecutor to produce it, the jury were called upon to presume that it got out of his hands, first, in the county ; and, secondly, in such a state, and under such circumstances, as amounted to a criminal publication ; that is to say, there being material evidence in the power of the prosecutor, he chooses to omit that evidence altogether, to leave the case ambiguous, and to call upon the jury to presume by way of inference all the facts essential to a conviction, which he purposely declines to prove. Now there is no rule of evidence more certain in principle, or of more safe and universal application in practice, than this, that where a party who is bound to prove a particular fact has in his power a material witness touching that fact, but omits to call that witness, and prefers relying upon a presumption arising from circumstances, the presumption ought to be against the inference he wishes to establish, even though, upon weighing the circumstances, there should appear a slight probability in its favour. But in the present case, independently of the omission of the prosecutor to call Mr. Bickersteth, which I say of itself destroys his right to ask for any presumption of what Mr. Bickersteth could prove, the circumstances actually proved leave the question of the county in a state of perfect indifference and ambiguity; and as to the state of the letter, afford the strongest presumption that it left the defendant sealed, and therefore not published. His house is within three miles of the county of Rutland. He was seen the day the letter bears date going on horseback in that direction. There is no evidence what post-town he uses, or which post-town is nearest to him. Then it is perfectly ambiguous and uncertain whether he carried the letter himself, or in what county he first parted with the possession of it. Again, the letter was in the possession of Mr. Bickersteth, in London, the very day when it would have arrived there in due course of the post, if put into the post at that distance from town the day it was written. There is, then, a reasonable presumption that it came by the post, the ordinary mode of conveying letters. It appears to have been enclosed in a cover, containing written directions to Mr. Bickersteth. Therefore it is probable that the defendant did not deliver it in person to Mr. Bickersteth, and that when he parted with it it was under seal, that being the ordinary mode of transmitting letters accompanied by confidential instructions, by the post or by a servant. Therefore I submit there should be a new trial upon the ground that no publication is proved in the county of Leicester.

There is one other point which I feel it my duty to bring to your Lordships' attention. Upon looking at this information, I find the charge to be that this libel was written of and concerning the King's Government and of and concerning the King's troops. This is the character given to the libel. Your Lordships will not suppose me to be offering anything in vindication of this or any other libel : but there is no evidence given to fix the libel with this character ; and therefore, I say, that if it does not, upon the face of it, appear to be of and concerning the Government and the troops, the defendant ought not to have been convicted. I agree that truth is no justification of a libel; and I shall not contend that the defendant in this case ought to have been allowed to prove the truth by way of justification: but I think it clear that the defendant ought to have had the liberty of explaining the true object and meaning of the libel, or of any ambiguous passage in it, by showing the facts to which it referred. And I go further: I say that the prosecutor was bound to show by evidence that this libel was of and concerning the Government of the realm; because I will show you that the libel from beginning to end contains no one passage which necessarily bears that interpretation.

Lord Chief Justice.—Necessarily !

Mr. Scarlett.—Yes, my Lord. I say necessarily, and not only not necessarily, which it ought to be, but not even probably. If at some future period, when the unhappy transaction at Manchester shall have been forgotten, or known only as a matter of history, any

person should look into this record, with the judgment entered upon
it, to ascertain some point of law, he would naturally suppose that in
order to obtain the verdict the Attorney General must have given some
evidence that the outrage or the act inveighed against in this letter
was not only committed by the King's troops, but in pursuance
of an order of the Government; because I say the libel itself
would afford him no such information. I agree that where words
are plain in their meaning, an innuendo is unnecessary. Nor am I,
for the purpose of this argument, contending that there should have
been an innuendo; because I say that the words 'of and concerning
the Government and the troops,' have all the force of an innuendo,
and require all the proof. 'Gentlemen, on reading the newspapers
this morning, having arrived late yesterday evening, I was filled with
shame, grief, and indignation, at the account of the blood spilt at
Manchester. This, then, is the answer of the Boroughmongers.'
He would be puzzled with this word. He must consult some dictionary or some pamphlet of the present time, to find that this word
in all probability denoted certain persons who had incurred odium
with certain other persons on account of some supposed traffic in
boroughs. But he would clearly find that the Government was not
intended. 'This is the practical proof of our standing in no need of
reform—these the practical blessings of our glorious boroughmonger
domination—this the use of a standing army in time of peace. It
seems our fathers were not such fools as some would make us believe,
in opposing the establishment of a standing army, and sending King
William's Dutch guards out of the country; yet, would to heaven
they had been Dutchmen, or Switzers, or Hessians, or Hanoverians,
or anything rather than Englishmen! What! kill men unarmed and
unresisting? and, gracious God, women too, disfigured, maimed,
trampled upon, and cut down by dragoons!' meaning, says the
information, 'the King's troops.' Observe, it does not say, nor has
it been proved, meaning the troops employed by Government to do
this act. The soldiers, by some improper impulse, may cut down
persons without any order from Government; and a man may
naturally break out into indignation at such conduct, as the effect of
a standing army which breaks through all laws, and in the wantonness
of power cuts down men, women, and children. I think it cannot
truly or decently be presumed that the Government directed them to
act in this manner. Then comes the figure of 'bloody Neroes ripping
up their mothers' wombs,' which can have no allusion to the Government; and then the words 'reign of terror and of blood.' To say
that these words necessarily or probably apply to the Government,
appears to me a very strained construction. The word reign, in that

sense, is used to express the prevailing character of the times, as the reign of folly or of fashion. It has no relation to an act of Government. But I understand the learned Judge who tried the cause, in his charge to the jury, laid some stress upon this expression.

Best, J.—No : I said the words 'standing army' referred to the King's troops, as in the case of the King and Horne, and I told the jury to look at the whole paper, and to collect from that the meaning and application of particular expressions.

Mr. Scarlett.—In the case of the King v. Horne, I have always thought that Lord Mansfield and the Attorney General felt that the case of the Crown required some evidence to show that the facts referred to in the libel had relation to the King's troops at Lexington, and that, therefore, the evidence of the defendant was admitted, of which a dexterous use was afterwards made to supply that deficiency ; but in that case the libel spoke of the troops at Lexington, commanded by an officer of the King. And that case is authority to show that a defendant, in a prosecution for libel, is at liberty to give in evidence facts to explain to what the supposed libel relates. But to proceed with the letter now in question. There is an allusion to the seven bishops. 'When the seven bishops were tried for a libel, the army of James II., then encamped on Hounslow Heath for supporting arbitrary power, gave three cheers on hearing of their acquittal ; the King, startled at the noise, asked, "What's that?" "Nothing, Sir," was the answer, "but the soldiers shouting for the acquittal of the seven bishops." "Do you call that nothing?" said the misgiving tyrant, and shortly after abdicated the Government. 'Tis true, James could not inflict the torture on his soldiers, could not tear the living flesh from their bones with a cat of nine tails, could not flay them alive.' It is said that this passage was written to excite discontent in the soldiers, yet there is no averment nor innuendo on the record, nor any fact in evidence to explain in what way it could so operate. Your Lordships, who know the history of the times, may be aware of some particulars respecting the discipline of the soldiers of the present day, to which this passage may allude. You may be aware of a motion made by Sir Francis Burdett upon this subject in the House of Commons, from which you may possibly form your own conjectures of his intention. But how is the man, who may read this record one hundred years hence, to know any of these things? Surely he must take for granted that to give a libel, which to him will be wholly unintelligible, the meaning and the object imputed to it, evidence of particular facts was adduced to prove that the dragoons and the soldiers here mentioned were the King's troops, that they were employed in some act directed or authorised by the

Government, and that there was something in their state of discipline different from that which existed in the time of James II., to which the last passage alluded, and upon which they were likely to be excited. I beg to be understood that I am not now objecting to the want of an innuendo, or of an inducement upon the record to make the libel intelligible. I am supposing these defects to be supplied by the words *of and concerning*; but my objection is to the want of evidence to prove what were the facts stated or alluded to in this libel, in order that it might appear to a man wholly unacquainted with these facts that the libel was of and concerning the Government and the King's troops. You have no right to supply the deficiency of the record, or of the proof by any facts within your knowledge, in order to give it the meaning, or the object imputed to it. For example, the act of the soldiers alluded to in this libel may have been committed by order of the Government, or by the order of the magistrates, or by the order of the constables, or by the arbitrary violence of the soldiers without any authority, and against the will of Government. The information chooses to adopt the first supposition, by alleging the libel to be of and concerning the Government, which means nothing, unless it means that the transaction, which it was the object of the writer to condemn, was one ordered or sanctioned by the Government. If the fact be otherwise, or if any of the other cases I have put be the true case, the information cannot be supported. Surely, therefore, it was competent to the defendant to prove that the transaction, to which he alluded, was not the act of the Government; that he meant to impute no blame to the Government; that the very newspapers, from which he took the account, imputed none; that, on the contrary, the Government disapproved of it. But it was also, as I confidently submit to your Lordships, absolutely incumbent on the prosecutor to give some evidence that the Government was concerned in that transaction, in such a way as to make it probable at least, if not certain, that the writing did relate to, and was of and concerning the Government of the realm; that if you disconnect your own knowledge or belief of the facts from the intention to be collected from the libel only, that intention will rest *in ambiguo*. I submit, therefore, that there ought to be a new trial upon this distinct ground, that the prosecutor has not made it appear by evidence that the libel is of and concerning the Government, which is one of the most important allegations in the information.

Sir James Scarlett.—May it please your Lordships, Gentlemen of the Jury,

The time is at length arrived when the mayor and the magistrates of Bristol have an opportunity afforded them of stating their case, and proving it by evidence. They have suffered much obloquy, much persecution, much misrepresentation. They feel, and they deeply deplore, the calamity that has befallen their city. They cannot deem it otherwise than a great aggravation of that calamity that they should have been made the subjects of reproach as having occasioned it, and that for a long period. For twelve months, since that calamity befel the city of Bristol, they have been the subjects of an investigation, not by Commissioners appointed by his Majesty, not by the authority of Parliament, but by a private and voluntary Committee, appointed amongst their own townsmen, and formed, however respectable the individuals may be who formed it, which I do not doubt, formed chiefly, if not exclusively, of that party in the town which, from their political feelings, as well as religious differences, have been long opposed to the magistracy of Bristol.

Gentlemen, the administration of justice in that town, the chief authority, is vested in the magistrates; and whether they are right or wrong in entertaining such a feeling, I trust you will think it not an unnatural feeling for them to entertain, that they were subjected to a gross indignity, when they found that a tribunal was formed of their own citizens to sit in judgment upon their conduct, to which tribunal they could not be parties, but as culprits. However, gentlemen, the day is at length arrived. The result of that investigation, in which, I understand, those who instituted it boasted they had received the countenance and support of his Majesty's Government, has produced this information, with various others, filed by my learned friend the Attorney-General; and the mayor of Bristol is now called upon to meet the weight and authority of an accusation by the public prose-

[1] I have made an extract from the trial of the King *v.* Pinney, Mayor of Bristol, for neglect of duty during the riots, containing the speech of Sir James Scarlett for the Defendant on that occasion. The case was tried in the Court of King's Bench, Oct. 27, 1832.

cutor, without having, until he heard the evidence detailed in this court, any opportunity of learning any one particular in which his conduct was condemned.

Gentlemen, the information that you have now to try deals in very general terms. It embraces a period commencing with the Saturday and terminating on the Monday, and the only charge made against the magistrates, except one, is that they did not do their duty. In what particular they failed, what precise.duty was expected from them, or omitted by them, all this they have to learn from the evidence of to-day, having had no intimation, either by the record which you are now trying, or by an opportunity of hearing their accusers face to face, what were the imputations cast upon them.

Gentlemen, you have heard but half the case. You have heard, indeed, a statement which my learned friend has read, addressed by the mayor to my Lord Melbourne, and to Lord Hill, containing a general outline of the proceedings, a statement exclusively made for the purpose of giving a general view of the progress of the riot, and without the least apprehension that those who made it were called upon, at that period, to exculpate themselves from charges of which they were not conscious.

If, gentlemen, I were to endeavour to represent to you the great anxiety I feel in this cause, an anxiety that probably would render me less capable of discharging my duty, you might, perhaps, think that I was using the common art of an advocate to endeavour to bespeak your attention and your benevolence. I am confident, however, that when you look at this case in the whole, in its detail and in its result, you will think it one of the most important cases that ever was brought before this great tribunal, one in which the magistracy and the gentry of England have a deep and an important interest. For I will venture to say that if Mr. Pinney, the mayor of Bristol, could by possibility be convicted by your verdict upon the evidence you have already heard, or upon the topics that the Attorney-General has laid before you, there would be no safety for any magistrate in the Kingdom ; no honesty in the discharge of his duty ; no zeal, no integrity, could save him from the malice and the vengeance of his enemies.

Gentlemen, I shall find it necessary to make some, although but few, observations on the evidence adduced by my learned friend, because, as I must necessarily occupy a large portion of your time in filling up those parts of the case which he has left imperfect, I shall by my evidence, not oppose, but reinforce, many of those statements that his witnesses have made, from which I think, that even now, were it an ordinary case, were it not so deep a trust in which I feel myself bound, not only to vindicate the innocence, but the honour of the gentleman intrusted to my care, I should, upon that evidence alone, confidently expect your acquittal. But you must hear further evidence. Upon the statement of my learned friend, considering the trouble I am afraid I shall have to give you on my part, I shall detain you but a short time. Indeed it would not be necessary for me to call your attention to those statements in my learned friend's speech, which have been contradicted by his evidence. A great many of the facts which he has stated have been already explained, or contradicted and refuted, and to the evidence, therefore, I should refer you, and not to his speech. But there are two or three topics in that speech, which I think myself bound to draw your attention to, because I am persuaded that you will find, upon consideration, that the weakness of my learned friend's evidence has not been supplied by the strength of his argument. Let us hear the propositions made by my learned friend.

He states to you 'that the magistrates had authority,' as undoubtedly they had by law, 'and a duty cast upon them to endeavour to prevent those crimes which result from breaches of the peace.' But, he says, 'that they are invested, by law, with an authority of compelling every man, within the sound of their voice, to take up arms if it be necessary.' Now, gentlemen, do not let us be caught by words. The magistrates are invested with an authority of compelling every man to take up arms, says my learned friend. Now, in one sense, that proposition is true, but not in the sense in which you are called upon to apply it to Mr. Pinney. It is true, that as magistrates they are entitled to call upon every man, when they witness a breach of the peace or a riot, to act in the King's name in assisting them to quell it. But it is not true, that if a man refuses to come he is therefore liable to immediate coercion. If, indeed, the law could invest the magistrate with the force of a giant, with the hundred arms, as well as the strength of Briareus, so that he might, in his own person, compel immediate assistance, my learned friend would be right. But all that the law does, is to make the party who refuses to aid the magistrate, liable to an indictment, and upon the trial of that indictment and his conviction, his punishment must depend. That is the sole process of compulsion. I should be glad to know, whether that power which the law gives, and which can only be enforced by the administration of the law, would enable a magistrate to call upon the population of a town that is determined to resist him, and to make them at a moment, whether they will or not, come to his aid. How could my unfortunate client, Mr. Pinney, whose description you have heard from the witnesses, how could he expect that assistance, or how command it? or, if commanded, how enforce it upon the very evidence you have already heard? Gentlemen, you will please to recollect, therefore, that, though I agree in the proposition of my learned friend, in that sense, that the law makes every man liable to punishment who refuses to aid a magistrate or the Sheriff in keeping the peace, yet that there is no law that can overcome the law of nature, which disables a magistrate, by any personal force that he possesses, from compelling men to assist him whether they will or not.

Now the next proposition of my learned friend, to which I shall call your attention, is one that I can hardly suppose, upon due consideration, he would wish you to consider that he would deliberately support. The proposition is this : he says, 'the law requires every individual magistrate, under such circumstances, to act with vigour, and decision, and resolution, for the protection of the peace ; and in case of any small excess of power, covered by his own good intentions at the time, he need not be afraid of any severe consequences, either of a civil or criminal nature.' Now let us see what that proposition means. The good intentions of a magistrate, his honesty, his zeal may excuse him. In what case, according to my learned friend? In case he commits an excess of severity, and sheds blood unnecessarily? My learned friend is right. If a magistrate is honestly of opinion, and those who act with him concur, that it is necessary to use deadly weapons for the purpose of putting down a mob, and to cause the military to fire upon them, I agree with my learned friend, that although, by and by, it might turn out, upon cooler consideration, that the magistrates might have accomplished their object without that degree of force, yet their good intentions ought to excuse them. But my learned friend has been quite silent on the other part of the proposition. If the magistrates have good intentions, if they wish to avoid shedding blood, and if they err, not in an excess of severity, but an excess of lenity, my learned friend is not the man to say that they could be excused from any severe consequences of a civil or a criminal nature. Gentlemen, I ask at this moment, in the progress of this cause from the beginning to this time, either in the speech of my learned friend or in the evidence, has any improper motive been ascribed to these magistrates? Has any one corrupt intention, any one desire not to do their duty, been either pointed at by the evidence or suggested by my learned friend? Have I not a right to say, that if they have erred, which I do not admit ; have I not a right to say, that if they formed a mistaken judgment ; have I not a right to say, that if they mistook the disposition of the town of Bristol, it was, at least, an innocent misconception that they could not obtain the civil aid of their fellow-citizens to assist in quelling the riots ; have I not a right to say, that they are also entitled to a little consideration, and to be protected from any severe consequences of a criminal nature? My learned friend has not thought proper to give you that part of the alternative. We are to take the law, therefore, to be this, that when an excess of severity takes place, accompanied with good intentions, the magistrate may be excused ; but where error is committed on the side of lenity, though with equally good intentions, whilst my learned friend administers the law, he is not to be excused.

Gentlemen, what is the result of the whole evidence you have been hearing for several days? Do me the favour to consider that you are now sitting calmly, free from all fear, from all alarm, from all agitation, to deliberate upon what was proper to be done in the midst of tumult that might have alarmed any man ; and in the midst of agitations and violence that might have disturbed the coolest judgment. Let me ask you if you would think it, even at this time, supposing the evidence had been of a different character from what it is, and had led more justly to the conclusion my learned friend demands of you ; I ask now, would you say, that because you might be of opinion that, if some other course had been adopted, Bristol might have been saved from conflagration, that, therefore, the magistrates must be guilty? No, gentlemen, you have this advantage of them, you have, in the calm consideration of this question, nothing to molest you ; you have no wives and families to think of; you have not the safety of the citizen to think of; you have not the responsibility of acting with or without the military to think of; you may, therefore, form a judgment. Perhaps you may be of opinion, that if a few lives had been sacrificed upon the Saturday, that if blood had been spilt, the town of Bristol might have been saved ; you may be of that opinion ; it is but a conjecture. But suppose you are right ; are you ready on that account to condemn the magistrates when they acted under the assurance of an officer of his Majesty, that he would undertake for the safety of the town without using that dreadful expedient?

More than that, gentlemen, does any honest man believe that, if the magistrates, upon the evidence of my learned friend, had done that which he says was their duty, and had spilt blood upon the Saturday, and saved Bristol; does any man doubt but that they would have been indicted for murder, and that the Government would not have defended them? That when the magistrates call upon a military man to aid them in clearing the streets, and desire him to use all the means necessary, and he tells them there is no occasion to do more than to ride about amongst the mob, who are good natured, and will disperse presently, 'If you leave them to me, I

will be responsible for the safety of the city;' can any man doubt
that if a magistrate said, 'Sir, I do not ask you to be responsible, I
will be responsible myself; I order you to fire;' can any man doubt
that if a magistrate had done that, and a life had been taken away
by it, though the city had been saved, the magistrate would have
been justly indicted for murder? Would his good intentions have
excused him then? I think they ought, but I have great doubts
whether they would in these times.

Gentlemen, we know the history of that very transaction; a constable who had the imprudence to go out with a pistol, with the best
intentions, I believe a half-pay captain, upon that very Monday
morning, and had the misfortune to kill a person, was indicted, and I
never heard that he was defended by the Government. My learned
friend did not defend him. He was defended at his own expense.
I allude to Captain Lewis's case.

But let us look, gentlemen, at the evidence. I think the whole of
the evidence that my learned friend has given to you may be summed
up in two sentences; and the first is this: that all the efforts of the
magistrates to induce Colonel Brereton to use the military for the
purpose of repressing that riot were ineffectual. And the second is
this: that in consequence of the military refusing to assist in the
suppressing of these riots, the civil force of Bristol also refused to
aid the magistrates. I should be glad to know what they were to
do? On the one hand they were deserted by the military, and on
the other hand they were deserted by their fellow-citizens. That is
the general state of the case; and they are now called upon to be
responsible for the burning of the town. Gentlemen, I say this is
the sum and conclusion of the whole evidence. I admit that it has
been dressed out in parts (by what sort of ingenuity or with what
motive I do not pretend to conjecture), with some ridicule cast upon
the mayor of Bristol, with some attempts to trace him in particular
situations for the mere purpose of exciting ridicule, which will but be
the triumph of a day; for you will find the whole story to be founded
in fabrication and falsehood, supported, if not by perjury, by the
grossest misconception. And then, by a number of negatives which
my learned friends labour to string together, they think to make an
affirmative. Witness after witness is put in the box, and asked, 'Did
you go to the Council House? Had you any directions? Did you
go to the Guildhall? Had you any directions?' So that if a man
goes to the Council House or the Guildhall, and has no directions
from a magistrate, the magistrate must needs be guilty. That is the
conclusion you are desired to come to. Is it not very extraordinary
that my learned friend, in the investigation of a case regarding the

conduct of the magistrates, should not have called before you any one of those persons that could give the best and most detailed account of their conduct? Here is Mr. Burges, their solicitor; here is Mr. Brice; here is my honourable and learned friend Mr. Serjeant Ludlow, whose name has been mentioned by almost every witness. They do not think fit to call them, who can explain everything, but they take the case of the magistrates and divide it into tatters. With respect to the mayor, they first shew him here, then shew him there, then they do not shew him anywhere, but leave you to infer, from the defect of their evidence, that according to the opinion of the last witness but one, Mr. Goss, and the pretended universal report, he was out of Bristol during the Sunday night. That is what my learned friend invites you to believe was the fact, because he cannot prove it.

Mr. Goss is the gentleman that goes to the Council House to make his speech to the magistrates; he goes three or four times, and gives a great deal of trouble, and because his foolish plan is not adopted, and they will not tell him what their plan is, he makes a communication to the Secretary of State for the Home Department, and instils a little of his feeling into that quarter. You will be surprised when I tell you that an inquiry into the state of the arms had taken place by the order of the magistrates on the Sunday, and that arrangements had been made at that time to secure them, though suspended for a while by the mob being in possession of the jail. The number and quantity were ascertained; but the magistrates did not choose to tell everybody, either the description, the quantity, or the place of deposit. Upon that very Monday the arms were sent away, not to the float, but to the jail. When the possession of the jail was recovered by Major Mackworth, the arms were there secured. Why should they tell Mr. Goss? Why should every speechmaking gentleman that goes for the purpose of bullying the magistrates be informed where they deposited the arms, or where they intended to deposit them? He goes to make his proposition. He proposes, like a military man, to distribute the town into posts, to put arms into the hands of persons that might be trusted; it was not very easy to find, at those moments, such persons perhaps; and then to let them go forth and sweep the town; and then he says, at all events let the arms be secured; and Alderman Daniel, who, I understand, is a gentleman of high respectability and honour, now above seventy years of age, says, 'Oh! Mr. Goss, I think we had better throw them into the float.' He protested against that; he says, 'You cannot be in earnest.' The Alderman was not in earnest, but he was desirous of putting off the importunities of Mr. Goss, who was molesting the magistrates then engaged in important transactions, with his silly plans and impertinent curiosity.

Again you are told that the magistrates did not form a plan. So that when the military had deserted them, it was inherent in the very office of a magistrate, he was bound by law to be possessed of the knowledge of an engineer, and by a sort of magic to perceive in himself an innate skill and cunning to defend a town, and to arrange and organise the population in half an hour, so as to secure it from conflagration ! Why, if the magistrates were a little taken aback upon that desertion; if, with an unwilling population, they did not know how to proceed; if, when they summoned together the whole population only two hundred came ; if, when those two hundred came they refused to act without the military; and if, when they bade them adjourn and bring more of their neighbours, a smaller number still came ; if all these things happened to them, and still they were not able to devise a plan for defending the town, perhaps you will think that the crime is not, at least in a moral point of view, of any great magnitude.

But, gentlemen, I speak in general of the evidence. Let us come to some of the details ; I earnestly hope that you have the evidence in your memories, and that you do not refer to any other source to obtain an amended recollection of it.

A gentleman was called only two days ago, a most respectable gentleman, Mr. Roberts, who appeared to me to be a man of great intelligence, as well as great moderation. He stated that he was a minister of a Baptist chapel, that he had a very large congregation, and from his habits had much intercourse with the lower orders of people at Bristol. That gentleman gave his evidence in a way that satisfied me that he is a man of conscience and honour, though I never heard of his name before he came into this Court. You will remember that he suggested, first of all, that he should attempt to go to the people in Queen Square, and endeavour, by conciliation, as he probably might know many of them, who would respect his injunctions, to prevail upon them to go home.

Now my learned friend turned the magistrates' accepting this order into ridicule. He says, they thought by a speech to put the rioters down. They thought no such thing. But look at their position. At the very time the gentleman made that proposal they were abandoned by the military, a part of the population refused to act without the military, and another party refused to act if the military came back. Mr. Roberts makes a proposition to the mayor with the utmost good faith and candour. Mr. Pinney goes and states it to the magistrates, and, as Mr. Pinney appears to have known him as a respectable man, it was adopted. A party go with him. Was a party of magistrates to go? My learned friend insinuates that the magistrates were afraid of accompanying Mr. Roberts. With a view to that insinuation I asked a particular question. You will recollect that when Mr. Roberts went to the square he saw the soldiers,—he called to one of them, and mentioned to him that he came with the magistrates' authority in order to use some efforts, and wished him to make an opening through the Square, the soldier refused to do it.

Mr. Roberts.—The Captain.

Sir James Scarlett.—I asked him this question :—' When you mentioned the authority of the magistrates, was it your intention that this should be known to the multitude, or only privately to the soldiers?' He said, 'Privately to the soldiers, because my intention was to go as of my own accord, and not to appear authorised by the magistrates.' That answer speaks of itself that it was no part of the proposition that a magistrate should accompany him, because he would then have lost the benefit of all that he intended to do ; what he did would have been supposed to have been a scheme of the magistrates, and Mr. Roberts's speech would have passed for nothing. Mr. Roberts further stated, that he came back and suggested to the magistrates what he thought might be advisable to adopt. Nothing was said to him. He got no answer. Oh! what a crime! that was emphatic! The question was put to him with great solemnity, ' You received no answer?' 'No, no answer.' 'Your proposition was not accepted?' 'Not accepted.' And so it was left that he made a reasonable proposition, and the worthy gentleman received no answer. Gentlemen, you will please to recollect that the magistrates must, with common sense, have felt it a duty to keep back, as long as possible, from the knowledge of the population that they could not have military aid; but Mr. Roberts said, most candidly, ' Though I do think still that my plan would have been efficient, I ascertained afterwards, but not that day, that the magistrates could not carry it into effect, because the 14th Light Dragoons had been sent out of the town,—and Colonel Brereton refused that the 3rd Dragoons should act.'

When Mr. Roberts stated that which only came out in cross-examination (for observe it was left to me in cross-examination to bring that fact out), I ventured to put to Mr. Roberts this question : —'From what you saw of the state of Bristol at that period, you seemed to be satisfied that military force was necessary; in your judgment, was there any disposition evinced by the population of Bristol to give the magistrates any civil aid?' Now I will give you his answer in terms : his answer was: 'I was astonished at the infatuated apathy of the inhabitants of Bristol when their town was about to be burnt under their eyes.'

Now, gentlemen, I hope you will remember that evidence, and all the evidence, and that you will not refresh your memory by referring to the newspapers for it. For see how this is represented in an exceedingly popular and distinguished journal, which circulates throughout England and throughout the world. The answer given to that question here is this: 'I had a strong impression of the dangerous consequences of the infatuated apathy of the *civic authorities*, in permitting the city to be occupied and ravaged by the mob !!' So that the evidence is directly perverted: the impression it was intended to make by that gentleman absolutely defeated, and a counter·and opposite impression raised in its stead; and that has gone throughout England.

That representation is, that the civil authorities, that is, the magistrates, were in a perfect state of apathy, but the witness's expression was that the population of Bristol was in a state of apathy.

We have also another important circumstance appearing upon that respectable gentleman's testimony. At a late hour upon the Sunday, when this was passing between him and the magistrates, he has given a candid description of what he saw in the square, and you observe that he makes the number of persons engaged in plunder, and those engaged in supporting them, much larger than any of the witnesses do. That gentleman's evidence clearly shews that at that period the magistrates were deserted; that nobody would act with them. He goes to the Commercial Rooms, and finds multitudes of gentlemen there assembled with apparent unconcern; and as an additional reason to satisfy him of the apathy of the people, there was in the Commercial Rooms a notice which has not been proved to you, except incidentally, which I will prove to you was universal, to all the inhabitants of the town to assemble in aid of the magistrates.

Gentlemen, I have now mentioned Mr. Roberts, who is the minister of a dissenting congregation, a gentleman of great respectability; and I of course mean to say nothing in the least disparaging of any religious sect whatsoever, and least of all of one that has so respectable a head. But I must observe, and I call it to your attention, that the greater part of the witnesses examined have been either Catholics or Dissenters from the Church of England. I do not mean on that account to impugn their respectibility, but you may easily conceive that in the local political differences of a great corporate town, the party that support the civil authorities in general will not consist of that description of persons.

The next witness I shall advert to is Mr. Edgeworth, a Roman

Catholic priest, who gave his evidence with a good deal of unction ; I will just call your attention to one part of it. Mr. Edgeworth received a notice on the Sunday, requesting that his congregation might be called upon by him to assemble at the Guildhall, and do their best to aid the magistrates. Mr. Edgeworth went himself. I am not sure, but I believe, that he did not read the notice to them ; but certainly none of his congregation went with him. Mr. Edgeworth then relates what passed upon the Monday. Mr. Edgeworth on the Monday made an offer to the magistrates that he could raise them two hundred men that he could depend upon ; and it is made criminal in the magistrates that one of them said, ' Oh, they are Irishmen, and they will drink ;' he said, ' Oh, I can depend on them.' Now, I ask any one of you, gentlemen, why Mr. Edgeworth did not offer that aid upon the Sunday? Sunday was the critical day. This took place upon the Monday, when the riot was completely subdued ; and you hear that upon the Monday an account had been spread throughout Bristol that the rioters had begun to fire, not Corporation property only, which is in Queen Square (for be it known to you that every house that was burnt there belonged to the Corporation), but that other property was in danger ; and when the people found that their apathy might lead to such consequences as might affect individuals, they then began to attend to the precept that had been issued the night before, and assembled in the churches, and by ten o'clock on the Monday morning there was a considerable force of the population ready to attend the magistrates? What signifies his two hundred Irish Catholics at that time? Very good men I dare say ; they would have been important on the Sunday ; yet that witness, who, as I say, has given his evidence with an unction, by which I mean that he has given his evidence clearly prejudiced against the magistrates, does not profess to tell you why he did not make the proposition on the Sunday.

Another thing you find proved by my learned friend's witnesses, and you will take for granted, gentlemen, whilst the question is in suspense that the evidence called by the prosecutors will not be disposed to represent the colouring of the thing too much in favour of the defendant ; but yet you have, from those very witnesses, an account of the shouts of the multitudes upon the first assembling of the mob before the Mansion House. Why, gentlemen, to be sure only a few persons were engaged in the actual work of destruction. You do not require one thousand men to set a house on fire or to plunder it ; but if a thousand men look on and support twenty whilst they make the plunder, then you require a force equal to remove one thousand men. Now, gentlemen, what is the evidence my learned friend has given by various of his witnesses? not by all; some have denied it; that when the military came in the first instance there were shouts of 'The King and Reform;' that when the Mansion House was perishing in flames there were shouts from the multitude, shouts from persons spread in different parts of the crowd, and that no one in the crowd, consisting of many thousands of men as well as women, laid hold of any man that shouted and said 'Sir, I will take you to a magistrate.' Even upon their own evidence, there never was so conclusive a case of the apathy that Mr. Roberts speaks of, that when the citizens of Bristol, to the number of ten thousand, saw their Mansion House falling in the midst of the flames, the shouts were general, and the cry was, 'It's only Corporation property.'

This is evident upon the very statement these men make. You will observe a question I put to many of them: 'If the rioters were so few that so small a number of persons were sufficient to quell them, how came you not to step forward, and how came not some of the bystanders to step forward?' No answer is given, 'I did not find anybody to assist me; I would not go alone.' Can it be thought, if the Mayor of Bristol had the talent to make an immediate organisation of a multitude in order to quell the mob, that there were none of those ten thousand that had the same talents? Why should not the persons present have said, 'It is abominable to permit this outrage. The constables are overpowered, they are driven in by only one or two hundred fellows of rabble; come forward, let us go and disperse them?' Why, if one hundred and fifty gentlemen amongst that mob of ten thousand (for I call them a mob if they support the mob) had come forward to aid the constables, all the mischief might have been remedied. But they would not go forward; they protected the rioters by their countenance, their presence, and their shouts, and they had an object in doing so.

Then, gentlemen, Mr. Townsend is called, you remember the discharged servant of Mr. Lax, and upon Townsend's evidence you are first desired to infer that the Mayor made a ridiculous escape. Now, what will you think when I prove to you, by three or four respectable and honourable witnesses, that there is not a word of truth in that story? He has been contradicted already by the very next witness; for the next witness called was a servant of Mr. Leman, who lived next door to the Mansion House, and over whose house the escape took place, and that servant tells you he saw Townsend assisting the gentlemen, and that Major Mackworth was with the Mayor at the time; but Townsend has sworn that nobody was with him; he has taken upon himself to swear that Major Mackworth was not with him, but that three women servants were, and he has placed him in the larder near the men's water-closet in order to give an air of ridicule which may spread the story over the United Kingdom.

Gentlemen, that witness is unworthy of belief. He has stated three things which I shall entirely contradict. He has stated that he introduced Colonel Brereton to the magistrates, that he went up-stairs into the drawing-room, that he found no magistrate there (which is another crime), and that the Sheriff came from behind a bed in the state-room, I know nothing of the Sheriff, because he is not a party before you, and that he went upstairs and found the magistrates in the bedroom. Now, what do you think of my proving to you that two magistrates were down in the hall and received Colonel Brereton, and that this man never introduced him at all? Again, he stated that he was at Mr. Sheriff Lax's in the night when the mayor called with Mr. Daniel the surgeon, and the mayor inquired for Mr. Lax; and then that Mr. Daniel made use of a signifi-cant expression, which he will not distinctly swear to, but swears to his understanding that they told him they were going to Mr. Fripp's, but desired him to be cautious not to tell any one. Now the absurdity of the story is manifest upon the face of it, because why should they tell *him* if they wished nobody to know it? but what will you think when I prove to demonstration, that at the time the Mayor called at Sheriff Lax's, he had no contemplation of going to Mr. Fripp's, though he was obliged to go there afterwards, for a reason I will explain? Mr. Townsend, therefore, will be flatly con-tradicted.

Now, then, gentlemen, we come to another witness, Mr. Waring, a Quaker, a gentleman who has the honour of corresponding with my learned friend, the Attorney-General. I did not ask him whether he corresponded with Lord Melbourne. I had heard by accident that he was a correspondent of my learned friend's, and therefore I put the question. Mr. Waring is not quite pleased with the magistrates, because they did not adopt his suggestion. You see that the wit-nesses laid hold of by my learned friend, who prove that the magis-trates gave no directions and had no plan, are persons chiefly who had a plan of their own. Now what was *his* plan? A most ingenious one. I hope you will remember my cross-examination of Mr. Waring, I do not mean to say anything against him. I know that the Quakers are exceedingly cautious in giving their evidence ; so much so, that I hardly ever, in cross-examination, got a direct answer from any of them. It is no disparagement, but the fact is so ; men have peculiar habits, and as part of a Quaker's religion is not to take off his hat, so another part is that when he is cross-examined he does not give an immediate and direct answer ; that is owing to great deliberation. You will remember that in his examination by my learned friend, he very reluctantly gave it out by a sort of insinuation, ' I thought that an effigy was proper to be burned ; I had it in my mind that if an effigy was burned it might as well be Sir Charles Wetherell's.' The witness did not state it distinctly, but it was quite plain to every one's mind that his impression was, that he recommended that an effigy should be burned of Sir C. Wetherell ; but I wanted him to bring it out plainly, because I have witnesses to prove it, and you will observe that it rests now in his evidence thus—that if he did not say it, it must be manifest to every one that he meant it.

Now think of a grave Quaker coming to make the proposition that to quell the mob, the magistrates of Bristol should burn their own Recorder in effigy ! And really, upon this record, I do not know that that is not a crime that will be urged against them ; for there is nothing distinctly charged upon the record. If my learned friend had put upon the record, that whereas there was a riot at Bristol, that whereas the Gaol was burned, that whereas the Bridewell was burned, that whereas the Mansion House was burned; whereupon a suggestion was made to them that, to prevent these riots, they ought to burn Sir Sir C. Wetherell in effigy, but that they maliciously, knowingly, and against their duty, refused so to do, I should have known how to meet that charge. But it comes upon us here, upon this general record, where everything may be brought into evidence against the Mayor, without any previous notice. I must own that I never did expect to hear in this criminal proceeding such evidence produced by the Crown, with a view to criminate the defendants; and I must own that I should have thought the magistrates the most contemptible and wretched of mankind if they could have ventured to stoop to burn the Recorder in effigy in order to quell the mob. I presume, if the Recorder had been actually in the town, the Quaker might have gone a step further. It is said that in a certain place where mobs govern, that is to say, in Constantinople, for no country is free where the mob governs, sometimes the Grand Seignior is obliged to chuck out the chief minister to the mob to appease them; and if the Recorder himself had been at Bristol, Mr. Waring might probably have suggested, ' Surely, gentlemen, you cannot do better than to throw the Recorder out amongst them, that will amuse them, and when they get hold of him, they will be entirely contented and satisfied ; they will pull him to pieces in fine style, and then you will have appeased all the tumultuous vengeance of the Reformers against Sir Charles Wetherell.' There was another man who did say he wished that had been done. He says, ' I certainly did very often say that it was a pity they had not thrown Sir Charles Wetherell into the river, rather than all this confusion should have taken place at Bristol.' That was another of their witnesses.

Gentlemen, by this sort of testimony my learned friend has supported his case ; and what is remarkable, until you had it from the witnesses, and until you had it from the statement made by the Mayor to Lord Melbourne, in the letter my learned friend has read, no allusion was made by my learned friend, the Attorney-General, to the state of Bristol at the time. I heard his speech, it was a speech of great eloquence and expression, and calculated, till met and contradicted by his evidence, to produce a great impression against the defendant ; but in that speech there is not the least allusion to the excited state of Bristol at the time.

Gentlemen, I must proceed, therefore, to take that task upon myself, and I do assure you that, in describing the state of Bristol at the moment when these agitations took place, I wish that I had the powers and the eloquence of my learned friend to raise in your minds an adequate idea both of the activity and the alacrity of those who took part in the riots, and the apathy and indifference of those who viewed them.

Gentlemen, it was not Bristol alone that was agitated, but other parts of the country. The magistrates do not complain, and never did complain, that they had not sufficient aid of military force. I make no doubt that they had as much as could be conveniently spared ; for the military were in requisition in various parts of the kingdom. Neither am I instructed to insinuate that Colonel B., if he committed any error of judgment, is on that account to be condemned. That gentleman acted under a fearful responsibility ; I have no doubt that he was under the impression that, if he had caused a man to be put to death, expecting as he did that the town would be secured without that calamity, he must have felt that he acted under responsibility which, in these times, would be fearful indeed ; and therefore I would not be too harsh in blaming him. It has been stated already by some of the witnesses, or if not, it will appear by the evidence I shall produce, that Colonel Brereton, actually in conference with the magistrates, stated his case to them thus: he said, ' Gentlemen, the force that I have is not sufficient to keep the peace of the town, considering that the inhabitants will not come forward to obey your call, that they will not come in sufficient numbers, and that they will not consent with activity to support you ; it will therefore be quite in vain to expect that the use of the military will accomplish the object. What you have to do, therefore, is to gain time ; send in all directions for reinforcements (and you will find that they were sent for), and by to-morrow (that is Monday) you will have probably a sufficient force collected, and then I will undertake to suppress the riots ; but in the meantime we can do nothing.' Now although I might differ in judgment from Colonel Brereton, and although I might agree with some of the witnesses, that if he had employed the military at that time, he might have succeeded without more force, yet I by no means desire that any impression of that sort should be formed against him ; he might act honestly, and he certainly was in a situation to judge for himself.

But, gentlemen, to the case of the magistrates, need I remind you that the country generally, at that period, was in a state of great agitation ? The very important measure that was depending in Parliament, and which had been disposed of at that time by the House of Lords, had produced a crisis of extreme agitation in the country. Do not understand me as meaning to say one word against that measure ; it is the law of the land ; and it never has been, and never shall be, my practice, as long as I maintain my position in this Court, to discuss the merits of any law before a jury or before judges. You are bound to execute the law as you find it, and have no right to exercise a judgment upon its merits. Therefore all I shall say of that most important measure is this, that I sincerely hope, and earnestly pray, that it may accomplish the great objects which I am quite sure many of those who introduced it intended to attain by it. No man in this Court, no man in this kingdom, would be more happy than I should be, or more grateful to its authors, if it is found in the result to secure the authority of the Sovereign, to maintain the privileges of the Peers, and to give us a House of Commons containing all the elements of wisdom and moderation. I shall be most happy if it produces those effects, which I have no doubt are their intentions, and I shall be grateful to the authors of it. I think, and always have thought, that true liberty in this country can only exist under a constitutional monarchy ; that a constitutional monarchy can only be sustained by an hereditary peerage, and an hereditary peerage by wisdom and moderation in the House of Commons, in order to prevent their taking the executive government into their own hands, which, if they ever do, they will first destroy the Crown and the Peers, and become themselves the most odious tyrants of the people.

On these accounts I shall be most happy, and feel a degree of gratitude I cannot express, if these great and important blessings are secured by that measure. If our Empire abroad is properly sustained; if foreign nations are taught to respect us, as no doubt every man wishes they should; if the union with Ireland should be consolidated, and the affections of the colonies conciliated, I shall be still more

happy to witness these results, and therefore I say nothing against
that measure. But I may be allowed, historically, to recall to your
recollection the means taken to enforce it, and the state of the
country at the time it was depending. I impute blame to no man.
Every man has a right, as long as he does not violate the rules of
law, to take his own course to advance any public measure he thinks
fit. But this I think must be conceded to me, that the state of
excitement in the country generally on that great cause of Reform
had very nearly brought this Government, I mean the Monarchy, to
dissolution, and sapped the foundations of civil society in this
country.

Gentlemen, it cannot be denied, whatever were the merits of this
important measure, that at least a very great number, if not the
majority, of the wealthiest and most intelligent classes of the community were against it; whether they were very wrong or very right
I care nothing, I only state the fact. Now, as these classes of the
community had for ages generally exercised a great, if not the chief,
influence in the state, it was natural that the numerical mass of the
nation, with whom the measure was undoubtedly of the greatest
popularity, should feel a hostility to those classes in which they found
their only opponents. The opposition made by those classes of course
was made in Parliament, because they are not accustomed to assemble
multitudes, or to mix with them. It became therefore necessary, it
became therefore expedient, or at least was thought to be so by men
who were friends to the measure, to use all means in their power for
the purpose of exciting the feelings of the people, I am sorry to say
against these very classes, and thus to operate on Parliament. On
that account magistrates were defamed; libels were published, without
number or check, against almost every person that had rank or wealth
in the country; a system of persecution against them was adopted;
and in most places a matrix was industriously formed for those seeds
of turbulence and discontent which flourish in a very high degree
even without the aid of cultivation. Bristol was one of those places,
and I am not surprised at what we have seen of the occurrences at
that place, because, unhappily, from what has passed in this Court
heretofore, as well as the evidence in this cause, we have witnessed
that in Bristol there did exist great local differences.

You will recollect that the distinguished part taken by Sir Charles
Wetherell in Parliament, which is the alleged cause of the immediate
riots at Bristol, involved him not only as an opponent of the measure
but as an advocate of Corporations; and Corporations were a subject
of attack; all the Corporations in the kingdom were the subject of
attack. There was hardly a printer in any provincial town that had

not something to publish against Corporations. All the magistrates were attacked. The effect of this was, that in the agitation necessary to subdue the supposed indisposition of Parliament towards the measure, the very foundations of all authority were loosened; all respect and reverence for the magistrates were gone, and therefore there was no magistrate in the kingdom, I will venture to say, not even the high and venerable magistrates before you, who possessed at that time the influence that they ought to possess, and do possess in a sounder state of the community.

Under these circumstances, and with that state of excitement, the period came when it was necessary to deliver the jail at Bristol. You must know that the delivery of the jail at Bristol cannot be effected without the Recorder. He is by their constitution an essential person to be present at the trial of prisoners. It was formerly the practice at Bristol to deliver the jail once a year; but of late years, in consequence of the complaint of the citizens, and the just complaint, that it was too long a period to detain prisoners in custody, the Corporation had adopted the practice of holding the assizes twice in the year. The month of October was one of the general periods. There were sixteen prisoners in the jail, all of them detained for capital offences. Other smaller offences may be tried without the Recorder; but there happened at that time to be sixteen capital offences; his presence therefore was necessary.

Now, what did Mr. Pinney and the magistrates of Bristol do? I should inform you that Mr. Pinney had been Mayor of Bristol only two or three weeks, this being the first time that he was elected; he had never served the office before, and was also new to the magistracy; for it was by virtue of his mayoralty that he became a magistrate. They had a consultation upon the subject; they were aware that in the town of Bristol there existed a great sensation against Sir Charles Wetherell; perhaps they were not aware, certainly not, that the prejudice, the hatred against the magistracy itself, would be carried to the extent of a desire to see their property burned and plundered; but they were aware that there was no part of the country in which a more angry feeling prevailed than at Bristol; that at Bristol the feeling for reform was very general, and in fact, universal; that this feeling might break out in some demonstrations against Sir Charles Wetherell; and they considered whether they could, with propriety, postpone the jail delivery. They had on the one hand to consider that, if they postponed it of their own authority, they were open to the reproach of keeping men in jail for a considerable time: I make no doubt they would have heard of it in various places, that they had assumed too much authority. On the other hand, if they held the Session at the usual time, in the month of October, they exposed the town of Bristol to some chance of agitation and riot.

Under these circumstances they felt, and in my opinion they felt justly, that it did not become them to undertake the responsibility; that unless they could have the sanction of the Secretary of State, who might be able to say in Parliament, if any attack were made upon them for postponing the jail delivery, that it was done by his sanction, they could not undertake it. They sent a deputation to town, consisting of one of their number, together with one of the sheriffs (a gentleman who sits before me) who were first to consult Sir Charles Wetherell, whether he thought, in point of law, it was necessary to hold the jail delivery with the Recorder; upon which Sir Charles Wetherell could not give any other opinion than that it was necessary. Sir Charles Wetherell did not like himself to undertake the responsibility of putting it off; he said, 'I think it ought to be held; you had much better go to the Secretary of State.' They then stated their case to Lord Melbourne. Lord Melbourne said, 'I quite agree that it ought to be held, and with the usual forms.' The magistrates were anxious that he should see Sir Charles Wetherell; they have stated that in the case which has been read to you to-day. He did see him; the conversation was renewed, and the result was, that my Lord Melbourne was decidedly of opinion that they ought not to postpone the jail delivery. He said, 'If you want troops, you shall have them;' the number, of course, he could not specify; that was to depend upon arrangements at the Horse Guards, 'but upon this condition, that you do not use them but in the last extremity;' of course it was not their desire to do so.

When they returned to Bristol, they were desirous of using every expedient to ensure a safe reception for Sir Charles Wetherell. They thought that in doing that, when they had once conducted him to the Guildhall, and brought him to the Mansion House, the popular ebullition would have passed away, and that everything would have been tranquil. They were aware that the reformers felt that it was proper to make some demonstration, that there was no reaction in the town; but they thought that might be done sufficiently by the attacks and insults made upon him upon his approach; and that if they defended him from these, they would then have done all that their duty required. They had no contemplation that there existed that degree of apathy in the town, which the result has proved did exist, or that there existed so violent a party who would come forward to plunder and to burn, and to make reform the pretext for it. That Bristol contained an angry population; that its neighbourhood was occupied very much by persons of the working classes, they were aware; but they thought that those persons would be contented when they had made a demonstration of their feelings, and retire.

They then applied to the under-sheriff, Mr. Hare, a very intelligent and honourable gentleman, and said, ' It is your business to see the Recorder safe in the town ; what number of constables do you think will be necessary? how many officers have you ?' He stated the officers he had, and his opinion (and no man was a better judge at that moment, for you must not judge by the event afterwards), that three hundred constables would be sufficient ; and he was then told that he had the authority of the magistrates to say, that he should get that number at least, that he should organise them, and arrange them to attend Sir Charles Wetherell upon his coming into the town. Mr. Hare applied to the chief constables of each district, and you heard from one of them who has been called, that the chief constables and the various petty constables under them, amounted altogether to about one hundred.   Mr. Hare was of opinion that they ought to treble the number, and therefore he said, ' In each ward you will contrive to get as many persons as you can to serve as special constables, but the magistrates have authorised me to say, in case you cannot get a sufficient number, to treble your present number by voluntary service; you must hire such men as you can depend upon to make up the deficiency.'   Accordingly, 119 were hired, whom the magistrates paid.   They formed about 315 or 320 constables altogether ; and Mr. Hare will tell you he was perfectly satisfied, and that he told the magistrates the number was sufficient.

They took the precaution of meeting Sir Charles Wetherell at a short distance from the town, instead of going to the usual place, which was two miles further.   They likewise desired him to approach the town early in the morning, the usual hour being the middle of the day, and they thought by that means to avoid the presence of a great multitude.   With these precautions he was introduced.   That sort of agitation took place that was expected ; but the constables were formed to protect the carriage, and you heard from the statement of one of them, that he was conducted in safety to the Guildhall.   While he was in the Guildhall, some demonstrations of riot took place, some even in the court itself made demonstrations of anger to Sir Charles Wetherell ; and I believe that Sir Charles Wetherell desired, that if anybody interrupted the proceedings, he should be brought to him to be committed.   Nobody, however, was brought.   The Mayor then received him at the Mansion House.

But I should first tell you (for I am now going to relate the con-

B B

duct of the Mayor) that he was up at seven o'clock in the morning. He went to the Council House ; he saw the marshalling of the constables ; received from the sheriff the plan he had made of marshalling them. When they were all assembled at the Council House the Mayor made them a speech, exhorting them to temperance in their conduct, and to firmness at the same time, and to do all they could to avoid provoking the multitude. That speech he made to them at eight o'clock, and he then returned to the Mansion House and dressed himself ; the ceremony is to receive the Recorder in full dress, to put on his buckles, and his silk stockings, and a dress coat ; and then he went to the Guildhall to wait the coming of the Recorder.

After they had finished the opening of the Sessions at the Guildhall, they came to the Mansion House. At that place the usual ceremony is for the magistrates that do not attend at the Guildhall to meet the Recorder. All the magistrates met that were able to come ; I believe there was one in a distant part of England. When they met the Recorder there were certain demonstrations of riot. Boys and men had been throwing stones at the Recorder during his progress. Some of those boys and men were discovered, and the constables attempted to take them up. That caused some struggles between the constables and them. The constables have been accused of using rather too much violence to provoke the mob. Some of the persons assembled thought so. However, there was no serious demonstration except the hootings and the crying out against Sir Charles Wetherell, and shouting, 'The King and Reform !' 'The King and Reform !' Of course Sir Charles Wetherell could not take that cry as any objection to him personally. It did not put his person in danger. But in consequence of the multitude continuing, the Mansion House was protected by the constables. The magistrates held a consultation whether they should go to church the following day, the Sunday, with the Recorder, as had been usual ; and they thought, seeing there was a very angry feeling in the town, that it might be more expedient that the Recorder should not go to church in state on the Sunday. Being a day when most of the population were idle, those who were ill-disposed would find an opportunity of insulting him and disturbing the peace, and therefore they proposed that he should not go to church until Monday, and that from the church he should go directly to the Guildhall. There was no idea at that time that any violence would be committed like that which afterwards occurred. However, as that letter of the Mayor describes, the multitude continued to increase ; they threw stones at the windows and broke them. I will not repeat what that letter has stated. They made an impression upon the Mansion House itself; some of them got in and began to do mischief.

At that moment a deliberation was held whether it was not proper to send for the military. Now that was a question of very great importance. There were at that time some two or three hundred constables about the Mansion House, who had been out from seven o'clock in the morning. It was their duty to remain there till discharged; but nobody had apprehended that it was necessary they should remain the whole night at the Mansion House at that period. Gentlemen, I must tell you frankly that my learned friend Mr. Serjeant Ludlow did think it was proper to send for the military. The magistrates applied to Sir Charles Wetherell, and he thought it was not. You heard from a witness who was examined the first day, that he went to the magistrates and suggested that the military should be sent for, when Sir Charles Wetherell stated in a very emphatic manner (you will recollect how he described him putting his hands into his breeches' pockets) 'Sir, I am of opinion that there is not a sufficient case to justify the magistrates in sending for the military.' It was a question of discretion; it was a question upon which judgments might differ; and Sir Charles Wetherell, who was undoubtedly not deficient in courage or in prudence, did think it was not necessary. But very shortly afterwards, the mob continuing to increase, the Mayor went out in his full dress, which he had had no opportunity during the day of changing. He was necessarily engaged during the whole day. There was to have been a dinner at the Mansion House for the Recorder; the magistrates and others who had assembled to meet him had not quitted the house. The Mayor went out and addressed the mob, impressing upon them the impropriety of their conduct, entreating them to disperse; and when he saw, as he did, great numbers of decent-looking persons assembled, and appearing to cheer the mob, he expected of course that his address would have some influence upon that description of persons. He implored them to disperse, and said that ' he should be exceedingly sorry to take any measures of force, but that he should be obliged to do that unless they would disperse.' He could not, however, prevail upon them; upon which a further deliberation was held as to what should be done, and it was then agreed by everybody that it was time to read the Riot Act, and send for the military. The military were sent for; and while the messenger went, the mob increased in fury and in violence.

Gentlemen, was this a time for the sheriff to order out the Posse Comitatus, or for the magistrates to go out and get every man to come and assist? The life of every man in the house was in danger; the mob had forced the Mansion House door, and had begun to plunder the lower apartments ; they had brought combustibles into the house to burn it. Sir Charles Wetherell was advised, as it was conceived he was the object of the fury of the mob, to quit the place because his life was in danger; and I thank my learned friend for not filing an information against him, because he certainly did abscond. If it be any crime in a magistrate to avoid the danger of an infuriated mob, Sir Charles Wetherell ought to be thankful to my learned friend for not having indicted him, for he too is a magistrate. But there was no crime in the one any more than the other. He was advised to quit the place ; the mob forced their way in ; the drawing-room windows were broken. The magistrates had been in the drawing-room. Some of them retired to the bed-rooms upstairs, that they might have a better view of what was passing ; and some went higher still, in order by throwing down tiles to check the mob. The opinion of the majority was that they ought not to do so, that such ammunition would be soon exhausted, and not effectual while it lasted. The Mayor, while that was passing, and from first to last, was not backward in exposing himself to personal danger, and in fact he surprised even those who knew him, by his activity, his personal exertion, and his zeal. He went down and received Colonel Brereton at the risk of his life. That is the first lie I give to Mr. Townsend's evidence. Now, gentlemen, let me ask here, is it to be gravely urged by my learned friend, the Attorney-General, that the magistrates are to be prosecuted because when an infuriated mob break into the lower part of the Mansion House, and break the windows of the drawing-room, they take refuge upstairs in the bed-room ? That is the argument. Of the variety of witnesses he has called, not one has told you that the magistrates there (six or seven or more in number, some of them very old men) if they had gone out bodily could have checked the riot. Nor am I aware of any law that compels a magistrate to do so ; he is to read the Riot Act, but not to play at fisty-cuffs with the mob. Where is it to be found, in what law book, that a magistrate is to put himself at the head of the constables or the military, and make a charge upon the mob? Whoever states that, states a proposition new in this land. A magistrate may do it ; there may be circumstances where he or any other individual ought to do it perhaps ; but the law does not make him criminal for not doing it. It is no part of his necessary duty to place himself with or without arms at the head of a body of constables ; his duty is to make arrangements, and to employ others to put an end to the riots, but not to use violence with his own hands.

When Colonel Brereton arrived with the 3rd Dragoon Guards, something had occurred regarding that regiment of which I do not know the history, but which made the mob well disposed towards them. Colonel Brereton was not the officer of that regiment; he was a colonel upon half-pay; and if he had no other duty to perform he would not have had any command at all there; but being upon duty in the recruiting service it was his province to take the command of whatever subordinate officers came within his district, and therefore the other regiments sent into the neighbourhood, which were ordered into Bristol, were placed under the command of Colonel Brereton. A squadron of the 14th Light Dragoons came in; but they were not so well received as the 3rd Dragoon Guards. As these last approached, I shall prove to you that they were received with cheers; that there were hurrahs for the 'King and Reform;' they were approaching the soldiers and shaking hands with them, which might have satisfied Colonel Brereton himself that he could not have relied upon the 3rd Dragoon Guards. Colonel Brereton went out and saw the state of things, and gave it as his opinion that there was no reason for the soldiers to do anything but to ride about the square and the streets. The magistrates differed in opinion from Colonel Brereton; they were of opinion that it would have been easy to make use of the soldiers to disperse the mob. The constables stated that they were not sufficient for that purpose, that they were worn out with fatigue. The constables had been there from seven in the morning till four or five in the evening; they had had no refreshment nor repose. Neither magistrate or constable at that period had had any rest or refreshment. But the Colonel was of opinion it was sufficient for the soldiers to parade the streets, and guard the Mansion House and the Palace; that the mob were a good-natured mob, and would disperse. He went out a second time, and came in again and said his arm was tired with shaking hands with them, and that they would disperse of themselves. Others thought differently; that as the troops were shown they ought to have been used, and the mob immediately dispersed. He said to the magistrates, 'Do you order me?' The answer was, 'Yes, we give you orders to clear the streets.' He replied, 'Do you order me to fire?' The answer was, 'Yes, if it is necessary; you are to do what is necessary.' But were the magistrates to order him to fire at all events? The opinion was given to him that it was necessary for him to clear the streets by the sabre at least, and force the mob out of Queen Square; and he said this: 'Gentlemen, be at your ease, there is no occasion for it; I undertake on my own responsibility for the safety and peace of the town this night.' At that time some of the dragoons were brought in wounded, and some of the constables also. Sergeant Ludlow said to him, 'It is odd you should say the mob are good-humoured, when these persons have been wounded by them.' Meantime a party of the 14th Light Dragoons had attacked the mob, and driven them down to the bottom of the square, but from whence they escaped into the market. An officer came in to say that the mob were pelting the soldiers with stones, from the positions they had taken; that they had put out the lights, and that it was necessary to have some of the constables to detect them and drive them out; and a constable present offered that with twenty-five men he would go with the officer, and find out the parties assailing them; but Colonel Brereton said, ' It is not necessary; I have been among them, and it is not necessary; let the 14th Dragoons go to their quarters, I will parade the streets, and be responsible for the safety of the city to-night.'

Gentlemen, at this period are you ready to say that the magistrates were guilty of any crime? It is not from the record, but from the speech of the Attorney-General, and from the evidence, that I collect what the charge is; he says it was their duty to order the soldiers to fire, and not to throw the responsibility upon them. I beg to tell my learned friend that I think no man in England would entertain that opinion. When the military officer had given his opinion, and undertaken to secure the peace of the town, and that the mob should disperse; if the magistrates had ordered him to fire, they would have been guilty of murder; and Colonel Brereton, if he had fired, would perhaps have been guilty of murder also; because if he was of opinion the thing was not necessary, he was not bound to obey the orders of the magistrates. But he undertook that the town should not be exposed to disturbance; and if he had fired, or the magistrates had ordered him to fire, and death had ensued, they would have been guilty of murder; and sure I am that with the then feeling in Bristol, and the feeling throughout the country, they would not have been protected. I do not think that innocence of intention would have saved them from prosecution or from being removed from their situations as magistrates.

But now, gentlemen, advert to the period of the night towards ten or eleven o'clock; the mob had began to subside, and Colonel Brereton was a true prophet. At twelve, or soon after, the town was in perfect quiet; the man was right. Up to twelve o'clock, is there anything to show, Colonel Brereton being right in his prediction, that they would have been justified in firing upon the mob that night? What do the magistrates do? My duty now is only to detail to you Mr. Pinney's conduct. Colonel Brereton having informed them that the town was perfectly quiet, and that they were in safety, he added, ' I shall leave a few soldiers to protect the Mansion House, and retire myself; but I shall be ready to attend your orders if anything further takes place to require my presence.' But this Mayor, who is accused of neglect, and two aldermen who remained with him, sat up the whole of the night. It was agreed among the aldermen that they should meet at the Guildhall, the next day, at ten. Sir Charles Wetherell had retired from the town. A gentleman was sent to convey him away in secrecy, that his departure might not be molested. Placards were then posted about the town to notify that he was gone. It was agreed that the magistrates would meet at ten o'clock in the morning, to concert whether any further measures were necessary, which would depend upon the transactions that took place in the course of the night. The Mayor and two aldermen sat up the whole night. Major Mackworth, a gentleman of high character and honour, and one of the staff of Lord Hill, happening to be in the town, came, as you have heard, to tender his assistance; he was at the Mansion House, and I shall call him as a witness. He will prove that, in the course of the evening, himself and the Mayor did marshal the constables. Major Mackworth supposes that he suggested it. Two other gentlemen claimed the merit of it ; but however, the Mayor was advised to marshal the constables ; and you have heard the fact from one of the witnesses for the Crown, that he was put at the head of twenty-five men, and ordered to protect the east corner of the Mansion House, and prevent any attack of the mob upon that part ; that others were stationed in other positions, in order, by a combined operation, to suppress any violence ; and you further heard from him that he had not been there long when, happening to turn himself round, he was deserted by all but five of his men ! The Mayor had ordered him twenty-five, and only five were left; he had no means, therefore, of doing what he had been directed to do. That is the evidence. I admit that the Mayor is to make provision to get constables together ; but if those constables choose to go away, is the Mayor responsible? Some of the magistrates quitted Bristol ; some of them resided in the city ; and some of them in the neighbourhood. Some were magistrates of the county of Gloucester ; some of them resided at Clifton, which is not within the city of Bristol. The Town Clerk's residence was in Clifton. Mr. Pinney himself had recently arrived from the West Indies, and was recently married. It was not necessary for him to procure a residence immediately ; being elected Mayor for that year, he had the Mansion House, and he remained in the Mansion House. But from that period you will see it was in such a state that he could not go to bed. One of the witnesses said that Mr. Sheriff Lax went to bed there ; whether that was so, we do not know ; but the beds were devoted to some wounded people who had been brought in, and the Mayor and some of the magistrates sat up all night. Major Mackworth agreed to come, and did come to the Mansion House early in the morning, While he was there, some of the military who had been left, six or seven of them, having retired from the Mansion House, the mob assembled together again very suddenly, and renewed their attack. That will be described to you by Major Mackworth. The attack was renewed with so much violence, that not the Mayor only, but this gentleman, thought every man's life was in danger; but notwithstanding that, I shall prove to you that the Mayor expressed his determination not to leave the house. But when Major Mackworth said, 'I give you my authority as a military officer, that you ought to leave it; and if I give you my opinion that the post is no longer tenable, surely you may quit it;' the Mayor, with Major Mackworth and two other gentlemen, accordingly left it and made their escape in this way, which is contrary to the evidence of Mr. Townsend. The larder, and other places in the Mansion House, you have heard spoken of; but you are not to suppose that the Mayor was intimately acquainted with every part of the Mansion House, or that he went peeping and prying about it. The mode in which they escaped was this: they got through a window on the staircase, and descended upon some leads adjoining the house, and from thence descended by a ladder upon Mr. Leman's premises, and were lifted up by the same ladder on to the next house, and four or five of them escaped together: at least there were Major Mackworth, the Mayor, and Mr. Gibbons; there were three at least, if not five, who escaped in that way. The mob were in multitudes, then increasing, before the Mansion House. They had renewed their attack, and forced through the barricades made by the beds which had been put to the lower windows, and Major Mackworth and the Mayor were obliged to crouch down below the parapet, so as not to show that they were escaping, and they so continued till they got to the Custom House, and there they escaped.

Gentlemen, my learned friend leaves the Mayor without any history of what he was doing after that period. I beg you to pause, however, and ask yourselves, can you find any cause to blame the Mayor up to that period? Was he wrong in not ordering the military to fire in the night? Could he then have assembled more constables? Would they have come? Was not the riot quelled? Was it renewed with his privity and concurrence? Was not he justified in escaping to save his life? If he was, I have him in safety till seven or eight o'clock in the morning. My learned friend's evidence takes him up at a subsequent period. A witness has proved that he went to the Mansion House early in the morning, and saw Alderman Hilhouse; and that Alderman Hilhouse and himself afterwards saw the Mayor. My learned friend does not give you any explanation of that transaction. It will be my duty to supply the omission. I will prove to you that the Mayor went about in the original dress which he had worn on the day of the procession. He had not had time to change his clothes. He was in his silk stockings and thin shoes, walking about the streets towards Colonel Brereton's office; and in his way he knocked at the door of many houses, inviting every person to come and join him, stating the riot at the Mansion House, and calling upon them upon his authority as Mayor, in the King's name, to aid in restoring peace. No one joined him. He proceeded to Colonel Brereton himself, and stated that the Mansion House was attacked and the mob assembled again, and required immediate assistance. He met Mr. Alderman Hilhouse in his way, and returned with him to the Mansion House. The troops were brought out, and he followed them with Colonel Brereton. I do not recollect whether Colonel Brereton was there, but the Mayor actually came with them himself in the morning, and Mr. Alderman Hilhouse read the Riot Act. The Mayor and the troops came together, and for a time the tumult was quelled.

Gentlemen, recollect that I told you that the Mayor had made an arrangement to meet the magistrates next morning, at ten o'clock, and had ordered hand-bills to be circulated, stating the absence of Sir Charles Wetherell; here is one of them: ' Mansion House, October 30th, 1831;' they were printed that night; it is in these terms:

It is with feelings of the deepest regret, that the magistrates deem it their duty to call for the immediate aid and co-operation of their fellow-citizens, to allay the great state of excitement now disturbing the inhabitants.

The delivery of the jail has been abandoned, and Sir Charles Wetherell, the Recorder, left the city for London last night.

CHAS. PINNEY, Mayor.

This was dated from the Mansion House; it was agreed that Sir Charles Wetherell going away should be published early on the following day, and this was distributed about the town: ' Sir Charles Wetherell left Bristol at twelve o'clock last night.' This very act of notifying his departure proves that the opinion of the magistrates 'at the time was, as it was the opinion of one of the persons already examined, that Sir Charles Wetherell was the main object towards which the enmity of the mob was directed, and that his being withdrawn, the riot would be quelled. They were in hopes that would be the case. The renewal of the riot at the Mansion House did not confirm that opinion. Many persons tore down these handbills; they were torn down as fast as they were stuck up. The Mayor accordingly went to the Mansion House at ten o'clock, and this was agreed upon, that they should issue immediately notices to call upon the citizens to assemble to aid the magistrates. Now, gentlemen, I pray your attention to this part of the case, because I have some facts to state to you, that seem to me to put an end to the case for the prose-cution. I am now upon Mr. Pinney's case; I do not enter into the case of the other magistrates; their time will come. They issued this: 'The Riot Act has been read three times; all persons tumul-tously assembling are guilty of capital felony; by order of the Mayor.' They then issued what has been read already: 'The magistrates most earnestly entreat the assistance of their fellow-citizens to restore the peace of the city by assembling immediately at the Guildhall; Sunday morning, half-past ten o'clock.' This was carried and left at every door; it was printed during the Sunday, and is dated Sunday morning; it was left at the houses of the inhabi-tants. I will call to you the witness who left it at every door, and you will see how many that produced. But that was not all; the magistrates issued this further notice. Only one person has been yet called who got this notice; for my learned friend, though he has called witnesses from Baptists' chapels, and Dissenting chapels, and from Lady Huntingdon's chapels, and Quakers' chapels, has only called one churchwarden. This was the notice that was distri-buted at each of the churches:

> The magistrates feel it their duty earnestly to request that you will adopt immediate measures to assemble your parishioners in your church in order that they may be formed into a constabulary force in aid of the civil power, for the protection of the city and its inhabitants, and as you form, to proceed to the Guildhall immediately.
>
> C. PINNEY, Mayor.

Now, pray what does my learned friend expect the Mayor to have done? Was he to go himself to each church? Must he have gone to as many houses as he could? Was he to go and drag men out of their beds and say, 'You shall go with me?' He had not the power to do so. But what was the result of this notice? One churchwarden has been called alone who got this notice, Mr. Quinton. Mr. Quin-ton, upon receiving a notice which was not read to you, but which I will prove to be this notice, immediately assembled as many of the parishioners as he could, and he found he could muster seventy. Did they form and proceed to the Guildhall? No; he went himself; he saw the magistrates; he said, 'I have received your notice, and I have come in obedience to it, and I find I can muster seventy of my parishioners who are willing to serve, but they require to have arms; upon which the Mayor, or the Town Clerk, he does not know which, said, we could not authorise the use of arms;

every man is justified in using arms to defend himself, but the
use of firearms to disperse a mob cannot be authorised.' One
of my learned friends thought he meant staves, 'Had you
any staves?' 'Yes; we had staves in the parish, but we
meant fire-arms.' I presume one of the charges against the Mayor is,
that he did not order the use of fire-arms. My learned friend will
excuse me for making these presumptions; I do not find anything
specific upon the record; I only collect the charges from the evidence. I say the Mayor had no right to do it; and if he had, it
would have been very imprudent to do it. But you will have the
opinion of military men upon that subject. Now, in the first place,
among the 70 men, how many of them are you sure may not join the
mob? In the second place, suppose they do not join the mob, how
can you tell that these 70 men, if you give them arms, supposing you
have fire-arms to give them, will be so trained as not in a moment of
panic to shoot each other; or if they do not shoot each other, how
do you know when they go out and charge the mob, that instead of
keeping in compact order as soldiers would do, they may not open
their ranks and thus let in the mob to take their arms away from
them? The better opinion has always been, that it is a most dangerous thing to attempt to quell a mob by fire-arms in the hands of
persons not acquainted with the use of them, or accustomed to act
together. In a case of extreme necessity, you may be excused for
resorting to them; and if I saw Westminster Hall on fire, and Westminster Abbey plundered, if I could turn one of the cannon in the
park against the plunderers, I own I should not wait for the order of
a magistrate; and I should hope to be excused, although I spilt
some patriot's blood in saving them; but I am not to be hanged,
drawn and quartered for not doing it. But that would be nothing
compared to putting fire-arms into the hands of an undisciplined
rabble. I should like to know with certainty, before I took such a
step, that I did not run the risk of spilling innocent blood instead of
the guilty, by the mob getting possession of the arms from the
constables. What was the answer? Without fire-arms they will not
go. Here you have a distinct notice from 70 men, who were ready
to go with fire-arms, but a small portion of the parish you will observe,
that they would not act without them. Have no inquiries been
made of other parishes? Have the prosecutors brought forward this
charge without inquiring of other parishes what effect that notice
produced? Is it credible? Is a prosecution by the Attorney-
General brought into this place against the magistrates, whose protection ought to be the object of every wise Government—is it a part
of his case to impute crimes to them, and make general charges

without laying before you the history of any inquiries he has made in other parishes, to know what other people were willing to do ? The history of this cause, up to this date, answers the question. But I will tell you what you have ascertained. With all the labour and pains taken by administering leading questions : 'Did not great numbers assemble ? ' 'Were there not more than 200 ? ' you have not been able to find that all the pains the magistrates took up to that hour of the morning, produced a meeting exceeding 200 persons. What is the population of Bristol ? It must possess a population of 30,000 able-bodied men ; considering the occupations in Bristol, and the number of persons required for different trades, 30,000 might have been found in Bristol. But 200 men are the utmost amount my learned friends give you as the result of all the pains of the magistrates to collect them. They dropped a notice at every door, and delivered one at every church, calling upon persons to form themselves into bodies, and thus formed to assemble at the Guildhall. That was the way to preserve the peace of the town. If in every parish 70 or 80 men had been formed, and headed by the churchwarden or chief constable, they would have been enough to put the mob to the rout. You have one officer who says that his people will not go unless they are armed, and you have only 200 people assembled. The Mayor is at the Guildhall ; Colonel Brereton has ordered in the 3rd Dragoons again to protect the Mansion House, and the 14th Light Dragoons to come in. The 14th Light Dragoons the night before had unhappily fired and shot a man. Upon retiring to their quarters they were assailed by stones, and a random shot had killed a man in the dark. This had caused an irritation in the minds of the people, and Colonel Brereton said it was unsafe for them to stay. Colonel Brereton came to the magistrates, and told them he must send the 14th Dragoons away. They were alarmed ; they said, 'With the present disposition of the mob, and the indisposition of the people to come and assist us, you cannot intend to do that.' He said, 'yes ; they must go away ; ' he had ordered them to their quarters ; they were pursued by the mob with missiles, and they were obliged to fire in their own defence ; and when they got into their barracks they were obliged to barricade their doors. I am not sure whether Colonel Brereton was wrong ; things were coming to a crisis ; and let me state to you from a book in great circulation, some little matter upon this subject. These transactions happened on the 30th of October last, and about the 30th October preceding, this book was published, being the 'Edinburgh Review,' a work of very extraordinary merit, and under high patronage— a book that is circulated in all good societies, and read by every officer in the army who pretends to know any thing, and very much read by the mechanics in their institutes, and worthy to be read by every one. No one can deny that it was edited with considerable ability. I am about to read sentiments of this reviewer, to show how magistrates and military officers were put upon their guard. It is an article professing to give an account of the three glorious days of July in Paris, and it is entitled, ' The late Revolution in France ; ' and I find in it these words :

' Several lessons have been taught in the *University of Paris,* which will not soon be forgotten. The soldiers of other countries have taken a degree there. It will be an honour to them, for it will make them remember they are citizens. It will be an advantage to them, for it will keep them from being exemplarily punished, and without any delay by their fellow citizens. The lesson which all armies have learnt is, first, that their duty is not to butcher their fellow subjects at a tyrant's command, in order to save a priest's favour, or a minister's place. Next, that if in breach of their duty they lend themselves to the treasonable plots of courtiers, they are rushing upon their own certain destruction. For a lesson has also been taught to the citizens of all great towns, that the soldiery cannot succeed in enslaving them by force of arms. A well-inhabited street is a fortress which no troops can take if the inhabitants be true to themselves, provided there be other streets near requiring a like attack from the military. Far be it from us to suspect the gallant soldiery of other countries of showing less patriotism, less humanity than those of France lately displayed, but the example is encouraging to the virtuous portion of the army.'

Now this work (continued the learned counsel) is read by every body, and admired by all who read it. What impressions must this passage make upon the minds of military men ? Colonel Brereton thought the 14th Light Dragoons would be sacrificed. The 3rd Dragoons had learnt their lesson ; they had taken their degree ; and he doubted whether he could compel them to fire if he ordered it. How did he know in this state of things if the 14th Dragoons came in, that the citizens had not also taken their lesson in this university, and were ready to sacrifice them ? He thought they had, because it is proved over and over again, that he stated his firm opinion that they would be sacrificed, every man, if they returned to the town. Now, whether Colonel Brereton was right in that opinion or not, it proves this, that the force of the mob was very great, and that it required a great force to repel them. Then having sent them to their quarters, and having witnessed the scene that passed, he comes to the magistrates during the period of time when some of those 200 persons had not dispersed, and Colonel Brereton says, ' I must send them out of the town ; they are gone to their quarters, but I must send them out of the town.' 'Good God ! you will not do any such thing,' says the Town Clerk ; 'you must not do it.' You will subject the town to a conflagration,' says the Mayor. 'I must do it,' says Colonel Brereton, 'or every man will be sacrificed.' 'You do not intend it ?' 'Yes ; I will do it on my own responsibility.' 'Then the magistrates do not divide the responsibility with you ; you do it on your own responsibility.' My learned friend says that a magistrate has the power of compelling any man within the sound of his voice to assist him ; but he does not mean to say they could do that with Colonel Brereton, and lay hold of him. Colonel Brereton then inquired what places there were near to which the 14th Dragoons could be sent ? The magistrates said, 'If we point out the nearest places, recollect we do not divide the responsibility with you ; there is Brislington, you may order them there ; but we do not authorise you to take them away.' But he ordered them away ; and the magistrates, finding that all their notices had brought together only 200 persons, and those not formed and not armed with staves, stated to them that their assistance was not sufficient ; 'let us advise you each to go home, and come here again at half-past three o'clock ; speak to as many of your neighbours as possible, and get them to come forward with you, and come at half-past three, and let us see what we can then do.' My learned friend's case turns upon this great sophistry, as if the magistrates were to make them a plan to operate with ; but what signifies a plan without the materials to work upon ? The magistrates had already stated the plan they meant to adopt : 'Come with your men formed to the Guildhall.' That was not done. Then what were they to do ? The constables who had been out the night before, had, for the most part, retired to refresh themselves; some were wounded and bleeding ; and some few remained with the magistrates to give them assistance, but they were not adequate to suppress this mob.

What happened at half-past three ? You have it in evidence by the prosecutor himself, that instead of coming in increased numbers, with all the supposed activity they were to use to increase their numbers, not more than one hundred and fifty came. Observe in what a destitute state these magistrates were left. Can you suggest any better means by which they could invite persons to come forward to aid them ? Can you tell how they could make the inhabitants come forward, and disregard all private motives, all local prejudices, and all personal danger, to save the town ? No ; at that time nobody speculated upon any danger to property, except to the Mansion House and the Corporation property. But I must return to my narration, and pursue the Mayor. You have heard repeated ques-

tions put, 'Did you see the Mayor? Did you go to the Guildhall
doors? Were they fast?' You should be aware, gentlemen, that
the Guildhall doors are never opened but upon the accustomed sessions
of the magistrates, and there is a regular known private entrance to
the Council Chamber, as well as to the Guildhall, and a person was
stationed at a proper place to tell the people where they might get
access to the magistrates. I will prove that after this meeting the
Mayor, who had passed the night without going to bed, was still in
his holiday clothes, except a frock coat for which he had changed his
dress coat ; and his brother magistrates said, 'You had better take
some repose ;' he refused. The magistrates said, 'You must do it ;
we must compel you ; you can do nothing ; the people will not come
forward to help us, and we must wait to see what occurs at three
o'clock ; if you get but an hour's sleep it will be of service to you.'
Only think of that short dedication to necessary repose being tortured into a crime. The only specific charge in this information is
that he absented himself from his post ; so that a magistrate is to
go without food and sleep while a mob is raging, however long, in
the town ! He went, compelled by a sort of gentle violence, for
an hour to the White Lion, where they ordered a room to be prepared ; the city solicitor, Mr. Burges, went over the way, for it is
in the same street, to direct them to get a fire for him and a bed
ready, as he wanted some repose. Gentlemen, during that hour,
while the Mayor was in that place to which I have now traced
him, first from the Mansion House in the morning, and then from
the Guildhall, it was in that hour, between one and two o'clock,
that intelligence came to the other magistrates that the Bridewell
was in danger. Now here I must correct what was a mistake in
that letter to Lord Melbourne which has been read ; the date was
given eleven o'clock. That was a mistake in the fair copy; I have the
person here who wrote the letter ; it was between one and two o'clock;
it ought to have been one instead of eleven in the letter, but it stands
now eleven. It was about one o'clock that the magistrates received
intimation that the mob were going to the Bridewell; Mr. Burges
immediately went over to the Mayor, who had not been in bed any
part of the time; he went into the room and found the little man
with his coat off, and apparently in the act of shaving. I cannot call
him before you, but from what Mr. Burges saw, he had no reason to
suppose he had lain on the bed ; he had been shaving and washing his
hands, with the intention of coming back again when called for. He
put on his coat immediately, and went back again to the Guildhall.
Then comes the deliberation what shall we do about the Bridewell?
They had received information that the mob were hurrying off to the

Bridewell in considerable numbers. Does the witness understate the numbers? People see differently according to the views they take; but I complain of no man, who, when a town is in a state of riot, does not see things with the same eyes as other people. I have known very honourable persons who witnessed a riot, in a court of justice give very opposite accounts of the same transaction. He returned, and was told of this event. They had not a sufficient force at the Guildhall to go to the Bridewell. They applied to Colonel Brereton, and Colonel Brereton said his men could not stir. It was in vain to go without them. He was asked, 'Why cannot you order them out?' He answered, 'Their horses are so tired they cannot raise one heel after another.' 'Will you consent that we shall find other horses for you?' This is a part of the case which my learned friend has partly proved. Mr. Protheroe has been called, who went to two repositories to find horses, and found none. I shall prove by another person that he went and found forty horses. Brereton was told he might have fresh horses; Colonel Brereton said, 'Are they trained horses? The troop cannot use them unless they are.' Then he was asked, 'Will your men go dismounted, and we will endeavour to afford the best assistance we can?' To which the Colonel replied, 'Who ever heard of cavalry acting dismounted? It is impossible.' While this was passing, the Bridewell was captured. You have heard, in point of fact, that its gates were assailed by a mob; that they carried hammers and instruments of great force and violence; and they actually broke the gates, and I believe took them off their hinges. Mr. Roberts has told you that they went in compact order; I forget what he said as to the number, but he said that they went as if they were organised, and had a leader; that a dense multitude immediately followed them. Did the multitude join them? Perhaps not; but the multitude was very formidable; they looked on and countenanced them, and gave protection by their presence. The next object was the jail. The Mayor was still at the Guildhall, and the moment accounts were received from the jail, they despatched a messenger again for Colonel Brereton; and you have it in evidence that two of the magistrates did go, accompanied by forty people. The jailer came to ask what was to be done, and you have an account given you, that it was said, 'You may discharge your prisoners, we will give you no directions;' that is the evidence at present. Were they wrong upon that? The information does not charge that as an offence; but it depended upon his judgment, if the mob were satisfied with the prisoners being discharged; you will not say, if he could save the place from being burnt, that to release them was wrong. But I will prove the fact, that two of the magistrates did go, and that they sent for the troops, and told them at their peril to come instantly. You have accounts in the paper which Mr. Dealtry has read to you of the appearance of dense multitudes; they forced their way through as well as they could; they were attacked, and one was severely wounded; the mob was entirely overpowering; they could not penetrate it. They could, however, see the troops come and go over the bridge into the island near the jail, and the mob begin to fly; when, to their great surprise, presently the mob came back,. the soldiers went away, and left the mob to do as they pleased. I will prove to you by persons who heard it, that the military were cheered and hailed by the mob as soon as they were found to be the 3rd Dragoon Guards, who had taken their degree at the university of Paris. It was nothing but 'the King and Reform.' The officers paraded the troops for a moment ; and seeing that the mob had likewise taken their degree, they marched back again, and left them to do as they pleased. What were the magistrates to do? Who assisted them? What parishes were ready with their forces? What Quaker or Catholic Priest, or Dissenting Minister, was ready. with his flock, with their staves upon their shoulders, to aid them? None. These calamities took place in a period almost as short as that in which I have stated them to you. You know when once a mob breaks into a place, their work is done immediately ; they burnt the jailer's house, but not the jail ; I presume the jail presented some difficulties; the jail was secure from the flames, but they let out the prisoners.

Gentlemen, the next place was the Bishop's Palace. But what had become of the Mayor in the mean time? I do not go over the history of the meeting at the Guildhall. You find that Colonel Brereton refused to bring in the military again ; and you find that very singular circumstance which is opened as a charge against the magistrates, namely, that Mr. Isaac Cooke, a solicitor of Bristol, goes to the magistrates, and makes an attack upon them for not employing the military in putting down the riots. Were they guilty of that? Mr. Isaac Cooke tells them he was ready to go if he could but get ten or twelve soldiers to cover him ; that he would go and get some men to accompany him ; he says, he knows, from prior transactions, the angry nature of a Bristol riot, and that the mob were not to be put down without military. Then what happened? Could the magistrates give him military aid? They said they could not give it. Then Mr. Cooke grew angry, turned round, and said, ' I will go and take care of my own property.' Here is a distinct refusal by a man of property in the town ; he is an honourable man, I am sure, if he is the person I have known in the profession ; he ought to have known all the law which the Attorney-General has been giving you, and a little more too, but he will not assist the magistrates if they will not give him that which they have not the power to give, namely, the military aid? Is not that conclusive evidence in the cause? Here is a respectable man and his fifty friends, who will not give any aid without the military, which they could not have. The magistrates cannot sow dragons' teeth in a moment, and let them grow up and use them to fight. Mr. Cooke could not have his military men, and the magistrates shall not have the civil men. Does my learned friend mean to say that they ought to have gone out themselves? 'Yes, says the Attorney-General, 'if ten men would go with them, they ought to go out.' I say that they ought not, if by going out, there is, every probability of those ten men and themselves being sacrificed. But the magistrates *did* go. The Mayor himself did not go to the jail ; he is not a very good man to see in a crowd when he walks ; and it is one of his crimes that he never mounted a horse in his life ; he did not know it was a crime before ; he did not go with them, but two other magistrates did go to the jail. After that effort was made, there was a respite for a short time. The Mansion House was not then in flames ; there were a few troops put to guard it ; they were guarding the front, and when they were told the mob were breaking into the back, they said their station was the front, and they would not quit it. You have heard that the soldiers stationed at the front were sufficient to protect that part, but the moment a dragoon moved from his post, some of the rioters opened one of the cellars ; the men then got into the cellars, and the soldiers had no objection to share the wine with them ; they drank wine with the mob, and were hand and glove with them. Nay, one of the witnesses has said, 'When I went and found the troops and the mob were hand and glove together, I thought it was of no use for me to stay there.' But no conflagration had taken place at that time, except at the Bridewell and the jailer's house. The Mayor was advised, and the magistrates, that it was proper to send an express to Lord Melbourne. In the course of the morning they had been writing in all directions wherever they heard there were troops, even at Gloucester, forty miles off ; wherever they heard there was a yeomanry corps there was a messenger despatched ; and I believe there was a very considerable sum of money paid that day for expresses at the post office to go in all directions. But they thought it their duty to send an express to the Secretary of State, and it was thought fit that, before it was sent off, Colonel Brereton should be aware of what they wrote. For though they differed in opinion with Colonel Brereton as to the military, they were not prepared to say that their own judgment was the best ; they might

think him the best judge whether the 14th Dragoons would be sacrificed or not. They informed Lord Melbourne of the state of things,
and two magistrates went to Colonel Brereton's office close to the
Palace, the windows look into the Palace Court, to read this letter
to him. They wanted also to see him, to arrange with him to
provide for the troops that might come in, in the course of the
evening, by the Mayor's orders. Two of the magistrates went to
Colonel Brereton ; not the Mayor, he did not arrive with them, for be
it known to you that Serjeant Platts and the Irish gentleman who
have been called, are mistaken in their story. One of them was
drunk at the time; how he got his liquor I do not know, but I will
prove to you that he had been drinking with the mob. One of the
magistrates inquired for Colonel Brereton, he was told he was at
dinner; and as they were writing a letter, they said 'You need not go
to him now, he will not be long absent.' While they were there, the
Mayor, the Town Clerk, and Mr. Burges joined them ; they all had
the common object of making some arrangement with Colonel
Brereton as to what could be done. A letter to Lord Melbourne
was written by Mr. Fripp, and signed by the Mayor. Colonel Brereton
came in and the letter was read to him. But the immediate cause
that took the Mayor to Colonel Brereton's, combined with others,
was this : a report had come to the Guildhall that the mob intended
to go to the Quay, and set fire to the ships in the harbour. The
harbour is so situated that, if the ships were set fire to, the whole
town must have been in a conflagration. It surrounds, or runs
through, nearly the whole of the town; and the ships are mixed up
with the streets and the population. A report coming of that sort,
they went to concert with Colonel Brereton how the mischief could
be prevented. Mr. Alderman Fripp was to read the letter to Colonel
Brereton, and, if he approved of it, it was to be sent off immediately.
The Mayor arrived, and the whole of the story you have heard, as to
any enquiry about the means of escape, is utterly untrue as regards
that period ; the witness is confounding it with another period later
in the night. There was no occasion to escape then ; there was no
alarm. Colonel Brereton sent a sentinel to ascertain what direction
the mob were taking ; that is true, and I believe it did happen that,
just before or just after the Mayor went in, a report came that the
mob were going to move towards the Palace. But the Mayor went
away in perfect calmness ; the magistrates had done their duty; they
had arranged the letter, and Mr. Burges carried it to the post office,
and Serjeant Dinidge went with him, and he told him he heard the
mob crying out, 'Down with the Bishops.' I beg your pardon I have
fallen into a little inaccuracy here; there had been some men going

towards the Palace, and he asked who they were; he said, only some
of the mob. I am mistaken about the hour when 'Down with the
Bishops' was cried, and I am much obliged to the gentleman for
correcting me. I understood it took place at a later hour of the
night. But the Mayor went away in perfect calmness, and returned
to the Council House. The adjournment to the Council House, as
you have heard, had been made as to a place of last resort, as a
matter of desperation. They found that the civil force would not
come to assist them, and the military had been withdrawn, and a speech
made by Mr. Serjeant Ludlow has been introduced in Mr. Roberts' evidence. I am sure, if Mr. Roberts could explain it, he would tell you that
he never put the explanation upon that speech which the Counsel for
the Crown has done. Mr. Serjeant Ludlow expressed no personal
fear; but he said, 'As we find it impossible to decide upon anything,'
(not that the magistrates were unwilling, but that they had not the
means of concocting any plan) 'it is time to consult for our own
safety (that is, of the Mayor himself and the magistrates). What is the
fortress? Shall it be the Guildhall, or the Council House?' The
Council House contains the Corporation muniments; and of course
that was the place chosen, and the few persons who remained, were at
the Council House; and therefore it was from the Council House that
the Mayor went to Colonel Brereton. Upon his return he went
upstairs; and whilst he was upstairs, Alderman Camplin came. He
had not been out for some days; but he came out in consequence of
the disturbances. He is the brother-in-law of Dr. Gray, the Bishop
of Bristol. Dr. Alderman Camplin being there, and hearing the
report that the Palace was likely to be attacked, and that the Mansion
House was then in flames, proposed that a party should go to the rescue
of one or the other. You have heard the evidence upon that subject,
'Shall we go to the Mansion House, now burning, or to the Palace
not yet on fire?' The cry was, 'To the Palace'; and forty or fifty were
ready to go, and Alderman Camplin issued out, when there was a cry
that the Mayor was coming down; and immediately some persons
said, 'We will go with the Mayor;' the Mayor said, 'We will go with
you,' and returned upstairs, I believe for his hat, or some other
momentary purpose. Only think, gentlemen, of the evidence which
has been given upon that subject. The prosecutors know that the
Mayor *did* go, and they leave it to you to imagine and receive an impression, as if he had skulked away! He asked Mr. Serjeant Ludlow,
'Have you any objection to go with me?' 'No,' said Mr. Serjeant
Ludlow, and he goes, and thirty or forty people go with them. I will
prove that he called upon every person he met, and Mr. Serjeant
Ludlow called upon them in the King's name to assist the Mayor in

putting down the riots. Instead of accession, however, the party diminished as they got to the Palace. The Mayor had before then arranged with Colonel Brereton, that he must draw out some troops to the Palace. Mr. Alderman Camplin's party arrived just when the troops had driven the mob away, and his party went in ; the entrance was entirely clear ; he wished to preserve the interior of the Palace ; he went to a neighbouring house and got a light, and went into the Palace, where some of the mob were taken prisoners. I will prove some extraordinary facts upon this part of the case. The military were in the yard ; and in one or two instances, when one of the Bishop's own servants had taken hold of a man who was plundering the property, a soldier forced him to let go his prize. He then took hold of a second man, who had got some of his master's plate ; he told the soldier, 'It is my master's plate.' 'Let him go,' said the soldier, 'or I will cut you down with my sabre.' That was the use the 3rd Dragoons made of their force ; they had taken their degree in the University of Paris ; and I do not attempt to conceal from you, that the persons who went to suppress the mob were as much afraid of the soldiers as they were of the mob. Such is the consequence of giving useful lessons to the soldiery ! The immediate plunderers, you observe, who had got into the house, were some of them taken prisoners, and carried down to the yard ; the military forced the people to let them go ! A party of the persons who accompanied Mr. Alderman Camplin, as I proved by some of their witnesses, staid in the Palace from twenty minutes to half an hour, to rummage about for the rioters. I shall call some who will prove that they put out the fire in several places ; and when they were coming down stairs, to their astonishment, they heard the cry, 'The mob is coming again, and the troops are gone.'

Gentlemen, just before that period the Mayor arrived with his party. When he came to the Palace gate, there was a gentleman of the name of Bulwer ; I have not the honour of knowing him, but I understand he is a respectable man, and of considerable personal courage. He had joined the Mayor in his progress. Mr. Bulwer ran before and found his way into the Palace gates ; but when the Mayor arrived with his party, which was not more than fifteen, he was informed that the troops had surrounded the mob ; that they were now in possession of them ; that the rioters were surrounded by the troops, and that he could not go in without passing through the troops and the mob. There was no occasion for the Mayor to do that ; the object was accomplished, and he said to Mr. Serjeant Ludlow, 'The best thing is to go to Colonel Brereton's office,' which looks on the yard. Gentlemen, you should be aware that Colonel Brereton's office consists of two rooms. The back room has a bow-window, which opens upon the place where the soldiers were, so that if you opened the window you might take hold of the horses' tails. The Mayor and Mr. Serjeant Ludlow went to this place. They were told that the mob were all secured when they got in ; that very Sergeant who was examined said, 'They are all encompassed ; they are all altogether, taken like rats in a trap. I will show them to you if you will come into the back room ;' and one of the gentlemen went in, and sure enough saw some of the military forming a kind of circle near the entrance of the Palace, and appearing to have some persons inclosed. It was quite dark at this time, and in a few moments an immense shout was heard of persons approaching, and another shout, 'The mob is coming in increased numbers,' and the gentlemen in the front part of the house, who had gone upstairs, descended to ascertain what it was, and as they came out of the front door of Colonel Brereton's office they found that the military had deserted the prisoners and the Palace, and were riding past the door in very good order ; in the meantime the mob shouting and hurraing, and coming with increased force to attack the Palace.

Gentlemen, what has become of the Mayor? You will find that eight or ten persons, descending from Colonel Brereton's, were obliged to run for their lives. One of them received a violent contusion, and some of his teeth were knocked out of his jaw. I am, however, pursuing the Mayor. He made his way towards the Council House; Mr. Serjeant Ludlow did not know what had become of him ; the Serjeant and Mr. Burges were together, but they all had escaped without looking after one another, as rapidly as they could, on seeing the troops pass by, and that the mob were coming in greater numbers. The Mayor was in College Green, when Mr. Daniel, a surgeon in the town, got hold of him. He knew him, and begged of him to take his arm. The Mayor was very much fatigued and exhausted ; he had had no food or sleep since Saturday morning. Mr. Daniel said, 'Where are you going?' 'I am going to the Council House.' 'Do not think of it ; you cannot force your way through the mobs ; there is one before you and another behind you.' Mr. Daniel knew he had no residence except the Mansion House, which was burnt, and having passed two sleepless nights, he said, 'Where will you go?' The Mayor said, I think Sheriff Lax does not live far from here.' Mr. Daniel said, 'What is the use of your going?' I do not pretend to use the words, but they are the substance, 'unless you receive reinforcements of military? The town is gone. You had better go to Clifton with me ; it is only half a mile off.' 'No,' says the Mayor, 'I will not leave the city.' It is hard that a man is, twelve months afterwards, to have it thrown in his teeth that it was the universal report that he had passed the night out of the city. He said, 'Where will you go?' He said, 'Take me to Sheriff Lax's; perhaps he will receive me.' He had been told he could not go to the Council House with any safety. Why should he go there? The only use was to assist in defending it. Of what use could he be if the Chamberlain was left with a body of sixty people who were ready to stand by him to defend the Corporation muniments? The Mayor went to Mr. Sheriff Lax's, and there he saw that fellow Townsend; and I will prove that Townsend was asked if Mr. Lax was within; that Townsend said Mr. Lax was out of town and his family; that there was no one in the house. At that time there was no notion of the Mayor going to Mr. Fripp's; the Mayor was not even acquainted with Mr. Fripp, but Mr. Daniel said to him, 'My partner, Mr. Granger, I have no doubt, will receive you;. let us go to his house.' He took the Mayor to Mr. Granger's house, and the Mayor was admitted; the Mayor went upstairs, and desired to have a messenger to communicate where he was, and while he was in the act of writing to make that communication, Mr. Granger came in to Mr. Daniel, and said, 'I am extremely sorry, but my wife is in a very delicate state of health (I believe she was about to lie in or something of that kind), and she is alarmed at the Mayor being here; if the mob find out where he is, they will destroy the house, and my wife will quit the house if the Mayor stays; do not put it upon me to turn a gentleman out of the house; ask him to leave it; if you do not, I must do it.' Mr. Daniel reasoned with him; he said, 'I am very sorry for it, but Mrs. Granger is in such a situation that it may cost her her life.' Mr. Daniel was obliged to go and tell the Mayor 'Mrs. Granger is in such a state that she is afraid of your staying here,' and they left the house, without the Mayor of Bristol knowing where he was to put his head; upon which the Mayor said, 'Does not Mr. Daniel Fripp live near this in Berkeley Square? I dare say his brother, Alderman Fripp, will be at his house, and I wish you would conduct me there, if you know him.' He said he knew him very well; and that was the origin and cause of the Mayor going to Berkeley Square, which was only a few doors off. Mr. Fripp did receive them, and Mr. Alderman Fripp was there; it was a late hour at night. What did the Mayor do? I will prove that in his way to Mr. Fripp's he met two persons, and charged them to go to the Council House to inform the magistrates that he was gone to Mr. Fripp's; whether they went or not I do not know, but he charged them to go, and when he got into the house the first thing he did was to set about making communications of where he was; he sent to the Council House, but I believe nowhere else at that time.

Gentlemen, I am now going to open another event to you which makes part of the tragedy. The Mayor had sent, in the course of the day, a letter to Captain Codrington; he is a young gentleman, the son of Sir Bethel Codrington. The Mayor had learnt, as the witness has told you, that there was a corps of yeomanry at Dodington, twelve miles off, commanded by Captain Codrington. The Mayor immediately wrote to him, as he did to all other military stations. The witness told you that Captain Codrington desired him to go to Tetbury to hasten another troop, and Captain Codrington took immediate measures to collect his own troop. The witness upon returning, as he went faster than the troop, passed them on the road, arrived before them, and went to the Council House. He says he found no magistrate there; but recollect he did not go into the Council Chamber. He went to Queen Square; he came back again, and found Mr. Alderman Hilhouse. He knew where the Mayor was, and he being informed that Captain Codrington was coming, and it might be necessary to provide billets for the troops, Mr. Alderman Hilhouse went to Mr. Fripp's, where the Mayor was, in order to get these billets. Mr. Serjeant Ludlow also had reached the Mayor's residence. He was driven away on the dispersion at the Palace; he went through the mob with Mr. Burges, with some difficulty and danger; went to Clifton to look after his family, and after his return soon learnt where the Mayor was, and went to him.

Gentlemen, I am reminded of a circumstance by my learned friend, and I am grateful to any one in this important case for suggesting any facts that may escape me. Mr. Serjeant Ludlow and his companion, in their escape, passed by two constables with staves. These men actually threw down their staves, and said, ' This is the second time we have been deserted by the military, and we will not make any further attempt.' Mr. Serjeant Ludlow arrived at the Mayor's at the time Mr. Alderman Hilhouse was there, or found him there; I beg pardon, Mr. Alderman Hilhouse sent Mr. Brice up to get the billets, and it was then that the Mayor wrote the letter, dated twelve o'clock at night, which is supposed to come from a man who wished to conceal his residence. He dates it at ' Mr. Daniel Fripp's, No. 30 Berkeley Square, Sunday night, 30th October, 1831. The Mayor of Bristol begs leave to inform Colonel Brereton that if he should have occasion for the orders of a magistrate, either the Mayor or some other magistrate will be found at No. 30 Berkeley Square, Mr. Daniel Fripp's, the second house on the right hand, on turning into the square from Park Street.' Colonel Brereton therefore had a distinct and full communication where the Mayor was. This communication is made to Colonel Brereton in consequence of Lieutenant Macclesfield calling at the Council House and requesting to see a magistrate. Colonel B. was gone out when a call was made at the staff station to inform him as above ; there had been a call made upon him to inform him of it; he was out, and therefore the Mayor wrote that letter, that it might be sent to him under his hand ; and at the same time billets were sent for this troop of Captain Codrington's : that is to say, blank billets were signed by the Mayor, with directions to fill them up as emergency might require.

Gentlemen, this makes it necessary for me to introduce to you the episode about Captain Codrington's corps. It is alleged as a crime that the Mayor was not there to read the Riot Act or go with the corps. I should inform you that on the previous evening, when the Mayor had sent despatches to obtain the assistance of the military, he had provided quarters for them ; he had got Fisher's and Leigh's repositories, and as many other places as could be furnished. Colonel Brereton knew it, and was a party to it. Having sent away the 14th Light Dragoons from Fisher's livery stables, those stables were empty ; and when Captain Codrington arrived, who has stated nothing in evidence but what is consistent with truth, as far as he knows, he tells you that his communication was with Colonel Brereton, and he says he did not leave Bristol till half-past twelve o'clock. Colonel Brereton knew that quarters were provided, and that letter was delivered to his officer at his chamber door, and you cannot doubt that when he got up to receive Captain Codrington he got the letter. But more than that, some person had gone down to Fisher's to apprise them that the troops were coming in. It was thought very odd that the troops should come in; that Queen Square was blazing, and that the troops, instead of being led to the scene of riot by Brereton, should want billets. It was supposed that they would immediately commence action, and therefore it was that the Mayor sent that letter to Colonel Brereton, that he might employ them immediately. Captain Codrington said, 'As we could not be employed we had better have quarters,' and they went to Fisher's, and this sort of misapprehension takes place. I will call Mr. Fisher, and he will prove the orders he received : that Colonel Brereton came to him and told him that the yeomanry were coming, and that he lighted up all the stables. He stated to Colonel Brereton, 'I do not know that I can give them a single stall for every one, but I can provide a stall for every two, as the light Dragoons had before;' and he was actually lighting up the stalls with candles at the time that he was informed that Colonel Brereton had told Captain Codrington

he might go away with his troops.　Is the Mayor to blame for that?
Did he not provide quarters and send billets?　But my learned friend
said, ' He ought to have been there himself.'　If he had been out of
bed five nights, what signifies it to the tender-hearted Attorney-
General?　He ought to have gone with them; he is bound *ex officio*
to ride like a cavalier, and he ought to have headed the corps.　I
deny the position *in toto*, and I deny the law.　I say the moment
that Captain Codrington came into the place he was bound to take
his orders from Colonel Brereton, who was the superior officer,
and he was told to do what he did, to go and report himself
to Colonel Brereton.　He says, at the Council House he was told to
go and report himself to Colonel Brereton, which he did, and Colonel
Brereton was to receive orders from the Mayor.　I have already read
to you the Mayor's orders: ' The Mayor of Bristol desires Colonel
Brereton to consider himself fully authorised to take whatever
steps, and give whatever orders he, as the military commander of the
troops in this city, may think fit, to restore and preserve, as far as
possible, the public peace.　The Riot Act has been read three times
to-day.　Colonel Brereton will have the goodness to consider this
order to apply not only to the troops at present under his command,
but to any which may subsequently arrive in the city.'

Now, gentlemen, I cannot call this unhappy man from his grave.
I do not wish to cast imputations upon him.　I can see many, many
considerations to excuse him.　I cannot believe that Colonel Brereton felt any pleasure in seeing Queen Square in flames; it is unnatural to suppose it.　I cannot conceive that he wanted gallantry or
courage; and when he told Capt. Warrington it was of no use to go
to Queen Square, he must have had some impression that even with
that accession of strength the mob would have made head against
him.

That is the only thing which, in candour, I can suppose.　You
cannot imagine that Colonel Brereton enjoyed the spectacle, which,
as an honourable man, he would have been glad to put an end to.

Gentlemen, I have now brought you to twelve o'clock, when the
Mayor is at Mr. Fripp's.　Did he go to bed there?　He remained
the whole of the night sitting up with Mr. Fripp, ready to receive any
communications; and some communications he did receive.　You
have another letter written at three o'clock in the morning, addressed
by him ' To Colonel Brereton, or the Commanding Officer of his
Majesty's troops, Bristol.　Sir, I direct you, as commanding officer
of his Majesty's troops, to take the most vigorous, effective, and
decisive means in your power to quell the existing riot, and prevent
further destruction of property.'　I admit a military officer, who comes

in to assist the civil power in dispersing a mob, is entitled to ask protection of the civil magistrate's authority to justify him in acting ; but it does not follow that the civil magistrate is bound to go with him to every place. The usual course is to ask for a letter, in case he should be indicted, that he may show that he was authorised by the civil power. What could you expect this man to do ? If any one of you happen to be a magistrate, consider your own case. Ought you to have a horse ready saddled at the door, and to have mounted every time you heard that a corps was arrived ? Was he bound to be at the Council House ? That was a place of refuge in case of siege. The Council House would naturally be expected to be besieged, and not wholly to escape. Suppose he had escaped from the Council House, is he to be indicted for that ? I deny it. But he could not get back to the Council House ; he informed the persons at the Council House and the persons at the Guildhall where he was, I do not mean those who had no interest in knowing it ; and that was all he could be expected to do. I shall call Mr. Daniel Fripp before you, and he will tell you that the statement he made to the witness Mr. Goldney, that he was not to tell where the Mayor was, was not done at the mayor's suggestion, or with his knowledge or consent. I can easily conceive that Mr. Fripp did not wish it to be generally known where the Mayor was, for the same reason that Mr. Granger turned him out of his house. The very circumstance of the Mayor being there threw Mrs. Fripp into fits. She thought the house was in danger of being attacked, as the magistrates were the object of attack, as well as the property of the Corporation.

Gentlemen, the Mayor remained there, and you find him next at the Council House ; he arrived there the next morning at five or six. Information is brought to him by a witness who happened to be in the square by five or six o'clock in the morning that the rioters were seen to be exhausted. Many of them had perished in the flames ; many were drunk ; and at that period of the morning their force was so considerably decreased that they were no longer formidable. They had burned nothing but Corporation property at that time, for the whole of Queen Square belongs to the Corporation. But an apprehension was entertained by the persons who witnessed the deeds done that they might go further ; they therefore received no further countenance from those who had stood by applauding the destruction of the Corporation property ; they began to fear for themselves, and they went home. Information was given to the Mayor, and he sent to Colonel Brereton, and desired him to go out with the troops. Major Mackworth also came, and he will state to you that he represented that the thing might be done, and

Colonel Brereton and he went together ; and before Major Beckwith arrived, Major Mackworth and Colonel Brereton had been in the square and charged the rioters several times. I will prove that Colonel Brereton was unwilling to charge, and that Major Mackworth said to the troops, ' I command you to charge, and Colonel Brereton will not object to it ; ' and the result was that the square was cleared before Major Beckwith arrived. He did his duty when he arrived, and did his best to accomplish what had been begun by the others in clearing the streets.

But, gentlemen, a word about Major Beckwith. A conversation is brought in to criminate the Mayor. This is too much. He speaks with two magistrates ; he knew the Mayor from his being short, and he knew the tall Mr. Hilhouse ; but he only knew those two. How can he undertake to say that all the magistrates said that they could not ride and would not ride ? I do not mean to suppose that Major Beckwith is capable of stating anything he does not believe to be strictly true ; but he might have confounded later conversations with other men. The truth is, that some of them never were on horseback in their lives. But Major Beckwith received what was sufficient to act upon, he received a written letter ; and I must ask, whether it is a crime, if a military man goes to a magistrate and says, ' I am ready to suppress the riot, will you ride with me ? ' ' No, I cannot.' ' Will you give me a letter ? ' ' Yes, with pleasure.' Is the magistrate indictable for not riding ? Do not let us try this case by making a sort of omnium gatherum of the whole information ; let us come to precise points, and I say that no man of common candour, or that has any knowledge of the law, can for a moment pretend that a man is to be indicted because he refuses to ride with the military. If the military officer is content to act upon the authority of the Mayor, he gives him that which is sufficient. Now it is said that the reason alleged was, that they had property, there might be some conversation about property, they were unpopular in the town ; and if they were to show themselves, they might be exposed to danger ; but you have it in proof, that the magistrates did show themselves, and did expose themselves to danger. Mr. Alderman Savage went ; the Mayor went ; Mr. Alderman Hilhouse went ; and Mr. Alderman Camplin went. It might be true that the magistrates might feel that, and the conversation might have taken place, are we to expose our own property to be burned ? A conversation of that kind might occur ; but I believe no one of the magistrates would have made that a reason for shrinking from his duty.

Gentlemen, you have now had the history of this case. My learned friend the Attorney-General in his opening, was pleased to remind you of the prosecution of the Mayor of London in 1781. The riots were in 1780, and the prosecutions in March, 1781 ; he is mistaken in one fact, which I do not wonder at, because the note at the end of the record is a mistake.   Mr. Kennet, the Mayor, was tried in March, 1781 ; he did not die till May, 1782 ; he was not therefore brought up for judgment on account of his death.   But I have a report of that case, and what were the facts in Kennet's case?   The Mayor of London had been informed at the Mansion House that the mob were burning the Roman Catholic houses in Moorfields ; he had sent for a body of military from the Tower ; he was pressed to go and accompany them ; when he went to Moorfields with this body he witnessed the conflagration ; but before he went he had asked the messenger whether he was a Catholic ; he said he was ; the Mayor said, ' I thought so,' and he delayed to go for a considerable time ; when he did go he was desired by the officer of the company to read the Riot Act, which he refused ; he was pressed by several people and refused.   He saw the houses burning before his eyes and would not authorise the military to act, and he gave as a reason for it, that they were only burning the property of the persons they thought their enemies, and when they had done that they would be satisfied.   Lord Beauchamp, who had the command at the Tower, went himself upon the ground ; he had sent the troops, and was a witness against the Mayor ; he asked him why he would not read the Riot Act?   He refused, and stated the same thing as he had stated before.   Lord Beauchamp said, ' I will report you to the House of Commons ; ' and when he was indicted what was he charged with ? He was charged with this, that ' Whereas there had been a riot and the mob were burning houses, and whereas the Lord Mayor had notice of it, and whereas it was his bounden duty then and there to read the proclamation contained in the Act, commonly called the Riot Act (which commands the magistrates to repair to the place and read the proclamation), that he, having notice of this duty, and being requested to perform it, that he maliciously, wilfully, and knowingly refused to do it.'   That is a specific charge.   There is also a general charge in the indictment, and that is made a precedent for the one before you ; it is a general charge contained in a distinct count, as we call it, that he then and there neglected to exercise the powers vested in him by law.   But the whole scene of his delinquency was accomplished in an hour.   What is the situation in which the present Mayor of Bristol is placed?   Here is a charge of forty-eight hours ; the town was under riot and confusion, and the jail, Bridewell, and Palace were burned, and a variety of houses in the square, and there is no particular thing charged which he was called upon to do.   It is not charged that he was called upon to go to the Palace, or to read the Riot Act, and that he refused. He is called upon to defend himself against a variety of charges which the Attorney-General may make in his reply, and this is to be the result of this ingenious mode of preparing an information, that it is just possible to get a verdict without any concurrence of opinion in any two jurymen, and I will tell how. We begin at eight o'clock on the Saturday morning, when they sally out to meet the Recorder, and we do not close till Monday; that is, a period of about forty-eight hours; it embraces the whole of Saturday, the whole of Sunday, and Sunday night. I will suppose that any one gentleman amongst you should be of opinion that upon such a particular event the Mayor did not do quite right, but that the eleven others do not agree with him; and that another should be of opinion that in another particular he did not do right, no one agrees with him; and there may be twelve different opinions upon twelve different subjects, upon which twelve separate individuals may form a notion that the Mayor did not do quite right, though there are not twelve who concur in that opinion as to any one act; and the Attorney-General, by that sort of net, hopes to catch a verdict. But I hope your good sense and justice will prevent it; I hope you will think, one and all, that there is no one point upon which the Mayor can be justly impugned; but I do think, and I distinctly complain of it, that this is the hardest prosecution that ever was instituted for the purpose of running down and degrading the magistracy. This general charge is made to cover forty-six or forty-eight different events, without any intimation being given as to what particular charge it was intended to urge; and if ever there was a net made to catch innocence, if ever the proceedings of a court of justice were calculated and arranged to catch men not guilty, this is an expedient to do it. I should have expected, in common candour, as an enquiry had been going forward, conducted by the enemies of the magistrates, and as they had no opportunity of knowing upon what particular point the charge was intended to be pressed; I should have expected when they came to see the information, they would have found a specific matter in the shape of a charge, whereas all that you find is nothing but a statement that for forty-eight hours they did not do their duty.

Gentlemen, one of the benefits of a free Government, and one of the blessings of freedom is, that by the administration of the criminal law innocence is protected by certain rules; one of the objects of those rules is, to obtain a degree of certainty in the charge made, that the man who has to meet it may apply a certain defence. The law therefore at one time required, and I hope it will continue to require, that all criminal charges should be aptly made, so that the person to defend himself may know what he is to meet; but if an Attorney-General is to say that for forty-eight hours the town was in confusion and riot, and then to make a general charge that the magistrate did not do his duty, the whole object of criminal justice is eluded and defeated; and those rules, instead of being found protections to guard innocence, are made snares to entrap it.

Now, this obliges me again to make a short summary of this case. What is the particular period that my learned friend fixes upon to say that the Mayor of Bristol was guilty? He is charged with being absent from his post. Where ought his post to have been? Has the Attorney-General assigned it? Ought he to have been at the Mansion House? Was he bound to stay there when it was burnt? Was he bound to stay at the Guildhall? He was there the greater part of the day. Was it criminal for him to go for one hour to wash his hands and shave himself? Is that to be his ruin? Does my learned friend intend to say that? If he does he had better say so in his reply, and I call upon him to do so. If he means to say that the Mayor was guilty of a crime for reposing one hour, let him say so, that you and I may know what the law of the land is to be.

Then it is said he did not go to the Palace, that he ought to have put himself at the head of the constables and have gone to the Palace. He did go, but he was not bound to go. It is also said he was not to be found afterwards; and Mr. Goss actually thought he was not in the town. Is a magistrate bound to keep his seat constantly at the Council House or the Guildhall? Colonel Brereton went to bed; he never disturbed his repose. But the Mayor did not go to bed, he was at Mr. Fripp's, and they had notice of it; Mr. Goldney and Mr. Harris, their witnesses, knew it. It is proved that they knew it; when he went there they had learned it, and so did other people who wanted to find him. But is it necessary that every officious gentleman, who had nothing but his own tittle-tattle to make known to the magistrates, whether the burning of an effigy or assembling the people with arms, should know where the Mayor was to be found? I want to know, where does my learned friend mean to put his finger when he comes to his reply, which will be able and powerful, no doubt; but you will not be satisfied unless he lays his hand upon some particular point, and satisfies you that there guilt took place. Is it because the Mayor did not call upon the military to fire? He has stated it, but he could not mean to maintain it. He could not call out the *posse comitatus* in the night; that force is not to be moved so easily as my learned friend supposes, nor is it to be moved more than the Mayor could move the constables. The Sheriff is authorised to call upon every man to aid him ; and if he does not choose to do so, the King can only indict him ; the Sheriff cannot flog him, and force him to do it. There is a case, but the case hardly ever occurs, and I believe it never occurred before, where he may call out the *posse comitatus*, and that is to be done by precept ; they are obliged to be served upon the inhabitants, so that it is a long time about the doing of it. The magistrates had arranged with the Sheriffs, and called upon them to aid them when they met on Sunday. The magistrates had no authority ; the people would not obey them, though the town was delivered to the flames. The magistrates consulted with the Sheriffs, and it was their duty, and not the duty of the magistrates, to take measures to call out the *posse comitatus* ; and the Under-Sheriff was employed the great part of Sunday evening and the night issuing these precepts, and by ten o'clock on Monday morning there was an assembly of multitudes of people. Two causes contributed to that : the Sheriff's injunction under penalty for disobedience ; and the conviction of the inhabitants that the Corporation property was not the only property in danger, which induced them to come forward at ten o'clock, by which time on the Monday they were arranged as a constabulary force, in aid of the civil authority of the town. If it is a crime that it was not done before it is not the crime of the justices ; it was the Sheriff's duty to do it ; he may do it as conservator of the peace ; it could not have been done in four hours, and if they had begun it at ten o'clock on Sunday morning, it could not have been effected before Queen Square was burnt. But you will hear the tremendous shouts of applause that were uttered when the Corporation property was firing ; the shouts of 'The King and Reform,' and ' Down with the Bishops,' and you may readily judge for yourselves whether the magistrates could, without a considerable force of constables, quell such a mob ; and when you find that the constables could not be found, and the inhabitants would not join them, I leave it to your candour to say whether you can find this gentleman guilty. Can you suppose that the magistrates of Bristol had not the greatest interest in protecting the safety of their town ? As Corporators their property was in danger ; they are the greatest sufferers, at all events ; but whatever your judgment is, they will have this self-gratulation, that they never did by word or deed excite these rioters. If the property of the Corporation was sacrificed and condemned to the flames, and the inhabitants were content to witness it with shouts of applause, it was not the Mayor and magistrates that published declarations against corporations and against magistrates. They are not guilty of any endeavour to decry the magistrates, and to alienate the minds of the people from those whom the law has vested with power. If the Custom House and Excise Office were burnt, and the population of Bristol exulted in the conflagration as in a triumph obtained over *tax-eaters*, the Corporation of Bristol never, by act, word, or deed, to their knowledge, took any means to inflame the minds of the people against the national creditor, and to treat those who live upon the interest of the public funds as public malefactors. They had never declaimed against taxes ; they had never declared that no Government could be good that would support taxes ; they had never taken that part which, unhappily, many of their townspeople, not the respectable part, I' hope, but many had taken ; they had not said that they would not pay the taxes unless they had measures of their own ; no meeting was held at Bristol where a magistrate declared that the people should not pay taxes unless a particular measure was carried. If the Bishop felt, and amongst the individuals composing that pious and reverend body he is one of the most respectable and amiable ; if he had the mortification to feel that amongst the population of Bristol a considerable multitude derived satisfaction from pulling down and burning his Palace, at least the magistrates were no parties to that excitement. No, gentlemen, they did not advise the Bishops to 'put their houses in order.' Do not charge upon them, for God's sake, the result, the necessary, I cannot call it the innocent, but the unintentional result of that agitation, those speeches, and those declamations, and those perpetual firings from the press, that excited the people of England to think that the Bishops were interested oppressors, that their magistrates were tyrants, and deserved to be crucified ; and that every institution of the country ought to be suspended to carry a favourite measure.

This was the state of Bristol ! What could these ten magistrates do to resist it ? All I ask is that they shall not be made the victims of that excitement. I condemn nobody ; I blame nobody ; but I declare to God that if it were possible to conceive the magistrates of Bristol would be convicted, upon this evidence, of any defect of duty or any abandonment of their posts to prevent what has taken place, I declare before God and heaven that this country would no longer be the land of liberty.

Gentlemen, I beg pardon for having troubled you so long. I felt the great importance of the trust committed to my charge, and I thought it my duty fearlessly to defend the magistrates ; I feel they have been persecuted where they ought to have been protected ; they have done their duty, and exposed to peril their wives and families, and their fortunes and their lives. Their reward is that they are sacrificed to some sentiment prevailing in their town, that it is time to put down the Corporation of Bristol.

Gentlemen, this is the first step towards that end ; there are nine other informations to be tried after you have disposed of this. I trouble you no longer ; but, with your Lordships' permission, to-morrow you shall hear the evidence I have to offer; and I do assure you most honestly that I shall be surprised if it does not go much beyond the statement I have made to you.

THE accompanying PEDIGREE, the chief part of which was given to me by the Rev. Robert Grignon, a nephew of Chief Baron Abinger, contains the descent, the greater portion verified by the Heralds Office, of the Eastbourne family of Scarlett, and a pedigree of the descent of Lord Abinger, through the Lawrences, from Malet, Gernon, Peyton, and Waller. It also shows the connection between the first of the name after the Conquest, and the descent of Hugh Scarlett in Yorkshire from his ancestors, the De Carlats of Rodés, in Aquitaine.[1]

It may interest those who bear the name and arms to look at Anselme's scarce and valuable work on French and Norman noblesse. It therein appears that the second branch of the Counts of Rodés were Viscounts of Carlat, from a town and castle in Aquitaine. Their shield was *or* with a lion rampant *gules*, which were the colours of the family of De Carlat. Écarlate ; Anglicè, scarlet.

The arms of the Scarletts in England are also *or* and *gules*, but in cheque, with the lion rampant.

There was a distinguished Ghibelline family at Florence in the middle ages called Scarlatti, whose supporters were lions rampant, but in other respects their shield is different. I was informed that before they settled in the Val d'Elsa, in Tuscany, they probably came from the other side of the Alps. They might have been a branch from Aquitaine. Their arms, carved in stone, are still to be seen in a street 'oltre Arno,' and a castle goes by their name near Empoli.

The crest of the English Scarletts in very early times was a Doric or Tuscan column supported by lions rampant. The later families had assigned to them the same Doric column with lion's paws.

The word and colour '*écarlate*' is probably derived from the name of the family De Carlat, which bore that colour on their coat armour. The Counts of Rodés were the same family, and bore the same arms. The word Rodez is said to be derived from the Greek word ῥόδον.

---

[1] With reference to the genealogical history of the family, I am under great obligation to my cousins James William Scarlett and the Rev. Robert Grignon. I have also to thank Mr. Stuart A. Moore and his assistant at the Rolls' Office, both celebrated investigators of ancient records, and likewise several gentlemen connected with the Heralds' Office and the British Museum.

LONDON : PRINTED BY
SPOTTISWOODE AND CO., NEW-STREET SQUARE
AND PARLIAMENT STREET

50A, ALBEMARLE STREET, LONDON,
January, 1876.

MR. MURRAY'S

GENERAL LIST OF WORKS.

ALBERT (THE) MEMORIAL. A Descriptive and Illustrated
Account of the National Monument erected to the PRINCE CONSORT
at Kensington. Illustrated by Engravings of its Architecture, Decora-
tions, Sculptured Groups, Statues, Mosaics, Metalwork, &c. With
Descriptive Text. By DOYNE C. BELL. With 24 Plates. Folio. 12*l*.12*s*.

———— (PRINCE) SPEECHES AND ADDRESSES with an Introduction, giving some outline of his Character. With Portrait. 8vo.
10*s*. 6*d*.; or *Popular Edition*, fcap. 8vo. 1*s*.

ALBERT DÜRER; his Life and Works. By DR. THAUSING,
Keeper of Archduke Albert's Art Collection at Vienna. Translated
from the German. With Portrait Illustrations. Medium 8vo.
[*In the Press*.

ABBOTT'S (REV. J.) Memoirs of a Church of England Missionary
in the North American Colonies. Post 8vo. 2*s*.

ABERCROMBIE'S (JOHN) Enquiries concerning the Intellectual
Powers and the Investigation of Truth. Fcap. 8vo 3*s*. 6*d*.

———————————— Philosophy of the Moral Feelings. Fcap. 8vo.
2*s*. 6*d*.

ACLAND'S (REV. CHARLES) Popular Account of the Manners and
Customs of India. Post 8vo. 2*s*.

ÆSOP'S FABLES. A New Version. With Historical Preface.
By Rev. THOMAS JAMES. With 100 Woodcuts, by TENNIEL and WOLF.
Post 8vo. 2*s*. 6*d*.

AGRICULTURAL (ROYAL) JOURNAL. (*Published half yearly*.)

AIDS TO FAITH: a Series of Theological Essays. 8vo. 9*s*.

CONTENTS.

Miracles	DEAN MANSEL.
Evidences of Christianity	BISHOP FITZGERALD.
Prophecy & Mosaic Record of Creation	DR. McCAUL.
Ideology and Subscription	CANON COOK.
The Pentateuch	CANON RAWLINSON.
Inspiration	BISHOP HAROLD BROWNE.
Death of Christ	ARCHBISHOP THOMSON.
Scripture and its Interpretation	BISHOP ELLICOTT.

AMBER-WITCH (THE). A most interesting Trial for Witchcraft. Translated by LADY DUFF GORDON. Post 8vo. 2*s*.

ARMY LIST (THE). *Published Monthly by Authority*.

ARTHUR'S (LITTLE) History of England. By LADY CALLCOTT.
New Edition, continued to 1872. With 36 Woodcuts. Fcap. 8vo. 1*s*. 6*d*.

AUSTIN'S (JOHN) LECTURES ON GENERAL JURISPRUDENCE; or, the
Philosophy of Positive Law. Edited by ROBERT CAMPBELL. 2 Vols.
8vo. 32*s*.

———————— STUDENT'S EDITION, compiled from the above work.
Post 8vo. 12*s*.

ARNOLD'S (THOS.) Ecclesiastical and Secular Architecture of
Scotland : The Abbeys, Churches, Castles, and Mansions. With Illustrations. Medium 8vo. [*In Preparation*.

B

ADMIRALTY PUBLICATIONS; Issued by direction of the Lords Commissioners of the Admiralty:—

A MANUAL OF SCIENTIFIC ENQUIRY, for the Use of Travellers. *Fourth Edition.* Edited by ROBERT MAIN, M.A. Woodcuts. Post 8vo. 3s. 6d.

GREENWICH ASTRONOMICAL OBSERVATIONS 1841 to 1846, and 1847 to 1871. Royal 4to. 20s. each.

MAGNETICAL AND METEOROLOGICAL OBSERVATIONS. 1840 to 1847. Royal 4to. 20s. each.

APPENDICES TO OBSERVATIONS.

    1837. Logarithms of Sines and Cosines in Time. 3s.
    1842. Catalogue of 1439 Stars, from Observations made in 1836 to 1841. 4s.
    1845. Longitude of Valentia (Chronometrical). 3s.
    1847. Description of Altazimuth. 3s.
         Twelve Years' Catalogue of Stars, from Observations made in 1836 to 1847. 4s.
         Description of Photographic Apparatus. 2s.
    1851. Maskelyne's Ledger of Stars. 3s.
    1852. I. Description of the Transit Circle. 3s.
    1853. Refraction Tables. 3s.
    1854. Description of the Zenith Tube. 3s.
         Six Years' Catalogue of Stars, from Observations. 1848 to 1853. 4s.
    1862. Seven Years' Catalogue of Stars, from Observations. 1854 to 1860. 10s.
         Plan of Ground Buildings. 3s.
         Longitude of Valentia (Galvanic). 2s.
    1864. Moon's Semid. from Occultations. 2s.
         Planetary Observations, 1831 to 1835. 2s.
    1868. Corrections of Elements of Jupiter and Saturn. 2s.
         Second Seven Years' Catalogue of 2760 Stars for 1861 to 1867. 4s.
         Description of the Great Equatorial. 3s.
    1856. Descriptive Chronograph. 3s.
    1860. Reduction of Deep Thermometer Observations. 2s.
    1871. History and Description of Water Telescope. 3s.
    Cape of Good Hope Observations (Star Ledgers). 1856 to 1863. 2s.
    ——————————————— 1856. 5s.
    ——————— Astronomical Results. 1857 to 1858. 5s.
    Report on Teneriffe Astronomical Experiment. 1856. 5s.
    Paramatta Catalogue of 7385 Stars. 1822 to 1826. 4s.

ASTRONOMICAL RESULTS. 1847 to 1871. 4to. 3s. each.

MAGNETICAL AND METEOROLOGICAL RESULTS. 1847 to 1871. 4to. 3s. each.

REDUCTION OF THE OBSERVATIONS OF PLANETS. 1750 to 1830. Royal 4to. 20s. each.

———————————————— LUNAR OBSERVATIONS. 1750 to 1830. 2 Vols. Royal 4to. 20s. each.

———————————————— 1831 to 1851. 4to. 10s. each.

BERNOULLI'S SEXCENTENARY TABLE. 1779. 4to. 5s.

BESSEL'S AUXILIARY TABLES FOR HIS METHOD OF CLEARING LUNAR DISTANCES. 8vo. 2s.

ENCKE'S BERLINER JAHRBUCH, for 1830. *Berlin*, 1828. 8vo. 9s.

HANSEN'S TABLES DE LA LUNE. 4to. 20s.

LAX'S TABLES FOR FINDING THE LATITUDE AND LONGITUDE. 1821. 8vo. 10s.

ADMIRALTY PUBLICATIONS—*continued.*

LUNAR OBSERVATIONS at GREENWICH. 1783 to 1819. Compared with the Tables, 1821. 4to. 7s. 6d.

MACLEAR ON LACAILLE'S ARC OF MERIDIAN. 2 Vols. 20s. each.

MAYER'S DISTANCES of the MOON'S CENTRE from the PLANETS. 1822, 3s.; 1823, 4s. 6d. 1824 to 1835. 8vo. 4s. each.

———— TABULÆ MOTUUM SOLIS ET LUNÆ. 1770. 5s.

———— ASTRONOMICAL OBSERVATIONS MADE AT GOTTINGEN, from 1756 to 1761. 1826. Folio. 7s. 6d.

NAUTICAL ALMANACS, from 1767 to 1877. 2s. 6d. each.

———————— SELECTIONS FROM, up to 1812. 8vo. 5s. 1834-54. 5s.

———————— SUPPLEMENTS, 1828 to 1833, 1837 and 1839. 2s. each.

———————— TABLE requisite to be used with the N.A. 1781. 8vo. 5s.

SABINE'S PENDULUM EXPERIMENTS to DETERMINE THE FIGURE OF THE EARTH. 1825. 4to. 40s.

SHEPHERD'S TABLES for CORRECTING LUNAR DISTANCES. 1772. Royal 4to. 21s.

———————— TABLES, GENERAL, of the MOON'S DISTANCE from the SUN, and 10 STARS. 1787. Folio. 5s. 6d.

TAYLOR'S SEXAGESIMAL TABLE. 1780. 4to. 15s.

———————— TABLES OF LOGARITHMS. 4to. 60s.

TIARK'S ASTRONOMICAL OBSERVATIONS for the LONGITUDE of MADEIRA. 1822. 4to. 5s.

———————— CHRONOMETRICAL OBSERVATIONS for DIFFERENCES of LONGITUDE between DOVER, PORTSMOUTH, and FALMOUTH. 1823. 4to. 5s.

VENUS and JUPITER: OBSERVATIONS of, compared with the TABLES. *London*, 1822. 4to. 2s.

WALES' AND BAYLY'S ASTRONOMICAL OBSERVATIONS. 1777. 4to. 21s.

———————— REDUCTION OF ASTRONOMICAL OBSERVATIONS MADE IN THE SOUTHERN HEMISPHERE. 1764—1771. 1788. 4to. 10s. 6d.

BARBAULD'S (MRS.) Hymns in Prose for Children. With Illustrations. Crown 8vo. 5s.

BARROW'S (SIR JOHN) Autobiographical Memoir, from Early Life to Advanced Age. Portrait. 8vo. 16s.

———————— (JOHN) Life, Exploits, and Voyages of Sir Francis Drake. Post 8vo. 2s.

BARRY'S (SIR CHARLES) Life and Works. By CANON BARRY. With Portrait and Illustrations. Medium 8vo. 15s.

BATES' (H. W.) Records of a Naturalist on the River Amazon during eleven years of Adventure and Travel. Illustrations. Post 8vo. 7s. 6d.

BAX'S (CAPTAIN) Russian Tartary, Eastern Siberia, China, Japan, and Formosa. A Narrative of a Cruise in the Eastern Seas. With Map and Illustrations. Crown 8vo. 12s.

BEAUCLERK'S (LADY DIANA) Summer and Winter in Norway. With Illustrations. Small 8vo. 6s.

BELCHER'S (LADY) Account of the Mutineers of the 'Bounty,' and their Descendants; with their Settlements in Pitcairn and Norfolk Islands. With Illustrations. Post 8vo. 12s.

BELL'S (SIR CHAS.) Familiar Letters. Portrait. Post 8vo. 12s.

BELT'S (Thos.) Naturalist in Nicaragua, including a Residence at the Gold Mines of Chontales; with Journeys in the Savannahs
and Forests; and Observations on Animals and Plants. Illustrations.
Post 8vo. 12s.

BERTRAM'S (Jas. G.) Harvest of the Sea: an Account of British
Food Fishes, including sketches of Fisheries and Fisher Folk. With
50 Illustrations. 8vo. 9s.

BIBLE COMMENTARY. Explanatory and Critical. With
a Revision of the Translation. By Bishops and Clergy of the
ANGLICAN CHURCH. Edited by F. C. Cook, M.A., Canon of Exeter.
Medium 8vo. Vol. I., 30s. Vols. II. and III., 36s. Vol. IV, 24s.
Vol. V., 20s.   Vol. VI., 20s.

Vol. I.	Genesis. Exodus. Leviticus. Numbers. Deuteronomy.	Vol. IV.	Job. Psalms. Proverbs. Ecclesiastes. Song of Solomon.
Vols. II. and III.	Joshua, Judges, Ruth, Samuel. Kings, Chronicles, Ez- ra, Nehemiah, Esther.	Vol. V.	Isaiah. Jeremiah. Ezekiel. 	Vol. VI.	Daniel. Minor Prophets.

BIRCH'S (Samuel) History of Ancient Pottery and Porcelain :
Egyptian, Assyrian, Greek, Roman, and Etruscan. With Coloured
Plates and 200 Illustrations. Medium 8vo. 42s.

BIRD'S (Isabella) Hawaiian Archipelago; or Six Months Among
the Palm Groves, Coral Reefs, and Volcanoes of the Sandwich Islands.
With Illustrations. Crown 8vo. 12s.

BISSET'S (Andrew) History of the Commonwealth of England,
from the Death of Charles I. to the Expulsion of the Long Parliament
by Cromwell. Chiefly from the MSS. in the State Paper Office. 2 vols.
8vo. 15s.

———— (General) Sport and War in South Africa from 1834
to 1867, with a Narrative of the Duke of Edinburgh's Visit. With
Map and Illustrations. Crown 8vo. 14s.

BLACKSTONE'S COMMENTARIES; adapted to the Present
State of the Law. By R. Malcolm Kerr. LL.D. Revised Edition,
incorporating all the Recent Changes in the Law. 4 vols. 8vo.

BLUNT'S (Rev. J. J.) Undesigned Coincidences in the Writings of
the Old and New Testaments, an Argument of their Veracity : containing
the Books of Moses, Historical and Prophetical Scriptures, and the
Gospels and Acts. Post 8vo. 6s.

———— History of the Church in the First Three Centuries.
Post 8vo. 6s.

———— Parish Priest; His Duties, Acquirements and Obliga-
tions. Post 8vo. 6s.

———— Lectures on the Right Use of the Early Fathers.
8vo. 9s.

———— University Sermons. Post 8vo. 6s.

———— Plain Sermons. 2 vols. Post 8vo. 12s.

BLOMFIELD'S (Bishop) Memoir, with Selections from his Correspondence. By his Son. Portrait, post 8vo. 12s.

BOSWELL'S (James) Life of Samuel Johnson, LL.D. Including
the Tour to the Hebrides. By Mr. Croker. New Edition. Portraits.
4 vols. 8vo.   [In Preparation.

BRACE'S (C. L.) Manual of Ethnology; or the Races of the Old
World. Post 8vo. 6s.

BOOK OF COMMON PRAYER. Illustrated with Coloured
Borders, Initial Letters, and Woodcuts. 8vo. 18s.

BORROW'S (GEORGE) Bible in Spain; or the Journeys, Adventures, and Imprisonments of an Englishman in an Attempt to circulate the Scriptures in the Peninsula. Post 8vo. 5s.
————— Gypsies of Spain; their Manners, Customs, Religion, and Language. With Portrait. Post 8vo. 5s.
————— Lavengro; The Scholar—The Gypsy—and the Priest. Post 8vo. 5s.
————— Romany Rye—a Sequel to "Lavengro." Post 8vo. 5s.
————— WILD WALES: its People, Language, and Scenery. Post 8vo. 5s.
————— Romano Lavo-Lil; Word-Book of the Romany, or English Gypsy Language; with Specimens of their Poetry, and an account of certain Gypsyries. Post 8vo. 10s. 6d.

BRAY'S (MRS.) Life of Thomas Stothard, R.A. With Portrait and 60 Woodcuts. 4to. 21s.
————— Revolt of the Protestants in the Cevennes. With some Account of the Huguenots in the Seventeenth Century. Post 8vo. 10s. 6d.

BRITISH ASSOCIATION REPORTS. 8vo.

York and Oxford, 1831-32, 13s. 6d.
Cambridge, 1833, 12s.
Edinburgh, 1834, 15s.
Dublin, 1835, 13s. 6d.
Bristol, 1836, 12s.
Liverpool, 1837, 16s. 6d.
Newcastle, 1838, 15s.
Birmingham, 1839, 13s. 6d.
Glasgow, 1840, 15s.
Plymouth, 1841, 13s. 6d.
Manchester, 1842, 10s. 6d.
Cork, 1843, 12s.
York, 1844, 20s.
Cambridge, 1845, 12s.
Southampton, 1846, 15s.
Oxford, 1847, 18s.
Swansea, 1848, 9s.
Birmingham, 1849, 10s.
Edinburgh, 1850, 15s.
Ipswich, 1851, 16s. 6d.
Belfast, 1852, 15s.
Hull, 1853, 10s. 6d.

Liverpool, 1854, 18s.
Glasgow, 1855, 15s.
Cheltenham, 1856, 18s.
Dublin, 1857, 15s.
Leeds, 1858, 20s.
Aberdeen, 1859, 15s.
Oxford, 1860, 25s.
Manchester, 1861, 15s.
Cambridge, 1862, 20s.
Newcastle, 1863, 25s.
Bath, 1864, 18s.
Birmingham, 1865, 25s.
Nottingham, 1866, 24s.
Dundee, 1867, 26s.
Norwich, 1868, 25s.
Exeter, 1869, 22s.
Liverpool, 1870, 18s.
Edinburgh, 1871, 16s.
Brighton, 1872, 24s.
Bradford, 1873, 25s.
Belfast, 1874.

BROUGHTON'S (LORD) Journey through Albania, Turkey in Europe and Asia, to Constantinople. Illustrations. 2 Vols. 8vo. 30s.
————— Visits to Italy. 2 Vols. Post 8vo. 18s.

BROWNLOW'S (LADY) Reminiscences of a Septuagenarian. From the year 1802 to 1815. Post 8vo. 7s. 6d.

BRUGSCH'S (PROFESSOR) History of Ancient Egypt. Derived from Monuments and Inscriptions. *New Edition.* Translated by H. DANBY SEYMOUR. 8vo. [In Preparation.

BUCKLEY'S (ARABELLA B.) Short History of Natural Science, and the Progress of Discovery from the time of the Greeks to the present day, for Schools and young Persons. Illustrations. Post 8vo. 9s.

BURGON'S (REV. J. W.) Christian Gentleman; or, Memoir of Patrick Fraser Tytler. Post 8vo. 9s.
————— Letters from Rome. Post 8vo. 12s.

BURN'S (COL.) Dictionary of Naval and Military Technical Terms, English and French—French and English. Crown 8vo. 15s.

BURROW'S (MONTAGU) Constitutional Progress. A Series of Lectures delivered before the University of Oxford. Post 8vo. 5s.

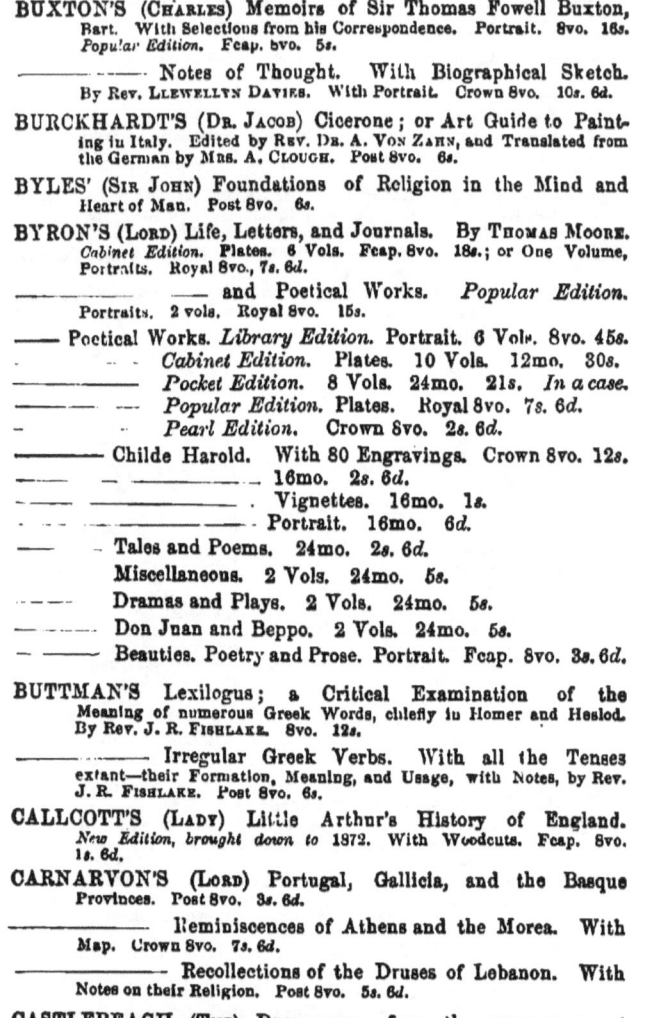

BUXTON'S (CHARLES) Memoirs of Sir Thomas Fowell Buxton, Bart. With Selections from his Correspondence. Portrait. 8vo. 16s. *Popular Edition.* Fcap. 8vo. 5s.

———— ——— Notes of Thought. With Biographical Sketch. By Rev. LLEWELLYN DAVIES. With Portrait. Crown 8vo. 10s. 6d.

BURCKHARDT'S (DR. JACOB) Cicerone; or Art Guide to Painting in Italy. Edited by REV. DR. A. VON ZAHN, and Translated from the German by MRS. A. CLOUGH. Post 8vo. 6s.

BYLES' (SIR JOHN) Foundations of Religion in the Mind and Heart of Man. Post 8vo. 6s.

BYRON'S (LORD) Life, Letters, and Journals. By THOMAS MOORE. *Cabinet Edition.* Plates. 6 Vols. Fcap. 8vo. 18s.; or One Volume, Portraits. Royal 8vo., 7s. 6d.

————— ———— and Poetical Works. *Popular Edition.* Portraits. 2 vols. Royal 8vo. 15s.

———— Poetical Works. *Library Edition.* Portrait. 6 Vols. 8vo. 45s.

      —— —— *Cabinet Edition.* Plates. 10 Vols. 12mo. 30s.

      —— —— *Pocket Edition.* 8 Vols. 24mo. 21s. *In a case.*

———— —— *Popular Edition.* Plates. Royal 8vo. 7s. 6d.

—— —— *Pearl Edition.* Crown 8vo. 2s. 6d.

———— Childe Harold. With 80 Engravings. Crown 8vo. 12s.

—— — ————— 16mo. 2s. 6d.

—— ————— . Vignettes. 16mo. 1s.

— —————— Portrait. 16mo. 6d.

—— — Tales and Poems. 24mo. 2s. 6d.

      Miscellaneous. 2 Vols. 24mo. 5s.

— — — Dramas and Plays. 2 Vols. 24mo. 5s.

— ———— Don Juan and Beppo. 2 Vols. 24mo. 5s.

— ———— Beauties. Poetry and Prose. Portrait. Fcap. 8vo. 3s. 6d.

BUTTMAN'S Lexilogus; a Critical Examination of the Meaning of numerous Greek Words, chiefly in Homer and Hesiod. By Rev. J. R. FISHLAKE. 8vo. 12s.

————— ——— Irregular Greek Verbs. With all the Tenses extant—their Formation, Meaning, and Usage, with Notes, by Rev. J. R. FISHLAKE. Post 8vo. 6s.

CALLCOTT'S (LADY) Little Arthur's History of England. *New Edition, brought down to* 1872. With Woodcuts. Fcap. 8vo. 1s. 6d.

CARNARVON'S (LORD) Portugal, Gallicia, and the Basque Provinces. Post 8vo. 3s. 6d.

————— Reminiscences of Athens and the Morea. With Map. Crown 8vo. 7s. 6d.

————— Recollections of the Druses of Lebanon. With Notes on their Religion. Post 8vo. 5s. 6d.

CASTLEREAGH (THE) DESPATCHES, from the commencement of the official career of Viscount Castlereagh to the close of his life. 12 Vols. 8vo. 14s. each.

CAMPBELL'S (LORD) Lord Chancellors and Keepers of the Great Seal of England. From the Earliest Times to the Death of Lord Eldon in 1838. 10 Vols. Crown 8vo. 6s. each.

——————— Chief Justices of England. From the Norman Conquest to the Death of Lord Tenterden. 4 Vols. Crown 8vo. 6s. each.

——————— Lords Lyndhurst and Brougham. 8vo. 16s.

——————— Shakspeare's Legal Acquirements. 8vo. 5s. 6d.

——————— Lord Bacon. Fcap. 8vo. 2s. 6d.

——————— (SIR NEIL) Account of Napoleon at Fontainebleau and Elba. Being a Journal of Occurrences and Notes of his Conversations, &c. Portrait. 8vo. 15s.

——————— (SIR GEORGE) India as it may be: an Outline of a proposed Government and Policy. 8vo.

——————— (THOS.) Essay on English Poetry. With Short Lives of the British Poets. Post 8vo. 3s. 6d.

CATHCART'S (SIR GEORGE) Commentaries on the War in Russia and Germany, 1812-13. Plans. 8vo. 14s.

CAVALCASELLE AND CROWE'S History of Painting in NORTH ITALY, from the 14th to the 16th Century. With Illustrations. 2 Vols. 8vo. 42s.

——————— Early Flemish Painters, their Lives and Works. Illustrations. Post 8vo. 10s. 6d.; or Large Paper, 8vo. 15s.

CHILD'S (G. CHAPLIN, M.D.) Benedicite; or, Song of the Three Children; being Illustrations of the Power, Beneficence, and Design manifested by the Creator in his works. Post 8vo. 6s.

CHISHOLM'S (Mrs.) Perils of the Polar Seas; True Stories of Arctic Discovery and Adventure. Illustrations. Post 8vo. 6s.

CHURTON'S (ARCHDEACON) Gongora. An Historical Essay on the Age of Philip III. and IV. of Spain. With Translations. Portrait. 2 Vols. Small 8vo. 12s.

——————— Poetical Remains, Translations and Imitations. Portrait. Post 8vo. 7s. 6d.

——————— New Testament. Edited with a Plain Practical Commentary for Families and General Readers. With 100 Panoramic and other Views, from Sketches made on the Spot. 2 vols. 8vo. 2s.

CICERO'S LIFE AND TIMES. His Character as a Statesman, Orator, and Friend, with a Selection from his Correspondence and Orations. By WILLIAM FORSYTH, M.P. With Illustrations. 8vo. 10s. 6d.

CLARK'S (SIR JAMES) Memoir of Dr. John Conolly. Comprising a Sketch of the Treatment of the Insane in Europe and America. With Portrait. Post 8vo. 10s. 6d.

CLIVE'S (LORD) Life. By REV. G. R. GLEIG. Post 8vo. 3s. 6d.

CLODE'S (C. M.) Military Forces of the Crown; their Administration and Government. 2 Vols. 8vo. 21s. each.

——————— Administration of Justice under Military and Martial Law, as applicable to the Army, Navy, Marine, and Auxiliary Forces. 8vo. 12s.

COLCHESTER (THE) Papers. The Diary and Correspondence of Charles Abbott, Lord Colchester, Speaker of the House of Commons, 1802-1817. Portrait. 3 Vols. 8vo. 42s.

CHURCH (THE) & THE AGE. Essays on the Principles and Present Position of the Anglican Church. 2 vols. 8vo. 26s. Contents:—

VOL. I.

Anglican Principles.—Dean Hook.
Modern Religious Thought.—Bishop Ellicott.
State, Church, and Synods.—Rev. Dr. Irons.
Religious Use of Taste.—Rev. R. St. John Tyrwhitt.
Place of the Laity.—Professor Burrows.
Parish Priest.—Rev. Walsham How.
Divines of 16th and 17th Centuries.—Rev. A. W. Haddan.
Liturgies and Ritual, Rev. M. F. Sadler.
Church & Education.—Canon Barry.
Indian Missions.—Sir Bartle Frere.
Church and the People.—Rev. W. D. Maclagan.
Conciliation and Comprehension.—Rev. Dr. Weir.

VOL. II.

Church and Pauperism.—Earl Nelson.
American Church.—Bishop of Western New York.
Church and Science. — Prebendary Clark.
Ecclesiastical Law.—Isambard Brunel.
Church & National Education.—Canon Norris.
Church and Universities.—John G. Talbot.
Toleration.—Dean Cowie.
Eastern Church and Anglican Communion.—Rev. Geo. Williams.
A Disestablished Church.—Dean of Cashel.
Christian Tradition.—Rev. Dr. Irons.
Dogma.—Rev. Dr. Weir.
Parochial Councils. — Archdeacon Chapman.

COLERIDGE'S (SAMUEL TAYLOR) Table-Talk. Portrait. 12mo. 3s. 6d.

COLLINGWOOD'S (CUTHBERT) Rambles of a Naturalist on the Shores and Waters of the China Sea. With Illustrations. 8vo. 16s.

COLONIAL LIBRARY. [See Home and Colonial Library.]

COOK'S (Canon) Sermons Preached at Lincoln's Inn. 8vo. 9s.

COOKE'S (E. W.) Artist's Portfolio. Being Sketches made during Tours in Holland, Germany, Italy, Egypt, &c. 50 Plates. Royal 4to. [In Preparation.

COOKERY (MODERN DOMESTIC). Founded on Principles of Economy and Practical Knowledge. By a Lady. Woodcuts. Fcap. 8vo. 5s.

COOPER'S (T. T.) Travels of a Pioneer of Commerce on an Overland Journey from China towards India. Illustrations. 8vo. 16s.

CORNWALLIS (THE) Papers and Correspondence during the American War,—Administrations in India,—Union with Ireland, and Peace of Amiens. 3 Vols. 8vo. 63s.

COWPER'S (COUNTESS) Diary while Lady of the Bedchamber to Caroline, Princess of Wales, 1714—20. Portrait. 8vo. 10s. 6d.

CRABBE'S (REV. GEORGE) Life and Poetical Works. With Illustrations. Royal 8vo. 7s.

CRAWFORD & BALCARRE'S (Earl of) Etruscan Inscriptions. Analyzed, Translated, and Commented upon. 8vo. 12s.

———————————————————— Argo ; or the Quest of the Golden Fleece. In Ten Books. 8vo.

CROKER'S (J. W.) Progressive Geography for Children. 18mo. 1s. 6d.

————— Stories for Children, Selected from the History of England. Woodcuts. 16mo. 2s. 6d.

————— Boswell's Life of Johnson. Including the Tour to the Hebrides. New Edition. Portraits. 4 vols. 8vo. [In Preparation.

————— Early Period of the French Revolution. 8vo. 15s.

————— Historical Essay on the Guillotine. Fcap. 8vo. 1s.

CUMMING'S (R. GORDON) Five Years of a Hunter's Life in the Far Interior of South Africa. Woodcuts. Post 8vo. 6s.

CROWE'S AND CAVALCASELLE'S Lives of the Early Flemish Painters. Woodcuts. Post 8vo, 10s. 6d.; or Large Paper, 8vo, 15s.

———— History of Painting in North Italy, from 14th to 16th Century. Derived from Researches into the Works of Art in that Country. With Illustrations. 2 Vols. 8vo. 42s.

CUNYNGHAME'S (SIR ARTHUR) Travels in the Eastern Caucasus, on the Caspian, and Black Seas, in Daghestan and the Frontiers of Persia and Turkey. With Map and Illustrations. 8vo. 18s.

CURTIUS' (PROFESSOR) Student's Greek Grammar, for the Upper Forms. Edited by DR. WM. SMITH. Post 8vo. 6s.

———— Elucidations of the above Grammar. Translated by EVELYN ABBOT. Post 8vo. 7s. 6d.

———— Smaller Greek Grammar for the Middle and Lower Forms. Abridged from the larger work. 12mo. 3s. 6d.

———— Accidence of the Greek Language. Extracted from the above work. 12mo. 2s. 6d.

———— Principles of Greek Etymology. Translated by A. S. WILKINS, M.A., and E. B. ENGLAND, B.A. Vol. I. 8vo. 15s.

CURZON'S (HON. ROBERT) ARMENIA AND ERZEROUM. A Year on the Frontiers of Russia, Turkey, and Persia. Woodcuts. Post 8vo. 7s. 6d.

———— Visits to the Monasteries of the Levant. Illustrations. Post 8vo. 7s. 6d.

CUST'S (GENERAL) Warriors of the 17th Century—The Thirty Years' War. 2 Vols. 16s. Civil Wars of France and England. 2 Vols. 16s. Commanders of Fleets and Armies. 2 Vols. 18s.

———— Annals of the Wars—18th & 19th Century, 1700—1815. With Maps. 9 Vols. Post 8vo. 5s. each.

DAVIS'S (NATHAN) Ruined Cities of Numidia and Carthaginia. Illustrations. 8vo. 16s.

DAVY'S (SIR HUMPHRY) Consolations in Travel; or, Last Days of a Philosopher. Woodcuts. Fcap. 8vo. 3s. 6d.

———— Salmonia; or, Days of Fly Fishing. Woodcuts. Fcap. 8vo. 3s. 6d.

DARWIN'S (CHARLES) Journal of a Naturalist during a Voyage round the World. Crown 8vo. 9s.

———— Origin of Species by Means of Natural Selection; or, the Preservation of Favoured Races in the Struggle for Life. Crown 8vo. 7s. 6d.

———— Variation of Animals and Plants under Domestication. With Illustrations. 2 Vols. Crown 8vo. 18s.

———— Descent of Man, and Selection in Relation to Sex. With Illustrations. Crown 8vo. 9s.

———— Expressions of the Emotions in Man and Animals. With Illustrations. Crown 8vo. 12s.

———— Fertilization of Orchids through Insect Agency, and as to the good of Intercrossing. Woodcuts. Post 8vo. 9s.

———— Movements and Habits of Climbing Plants. Woodcuts. Crown 8vo. 6s.

———— Insectivorous Plants. Woodcuts. Crown 8vo. 14s.

———— Fact and Argument for Darwin. By FRITZ MULLER. Translated by W. S. DALLAS. Woodcuts. Post 8vo. 6s.

DELEPIERRE'S (Octave) History of Flemish Literature. 8vo. 9s.

———— Historic Difficulties & Contested Events. Post 8vo. 6s.

DENISON'S (E. B.) Life of Bishop Lonsdale. With Selections from his Writings. With Portrait. Crown 8vo. 10s. 6d.

DERBY'S (Earl of) Iliad of Homer rendered into English Blank Verse. 2 Vols. Post 8vo. 10s.

DE ROS'S (Lord) Young Officer's Companion; or, Essays on Military Duties and Qualities: with Examples and Illustrations from History. Post 8vo. 9s.

DEUTSCH'S (Emanuel) Talmud, Islam, The Targums and other Literary Remains. 8vo. 12s.

DILKE'S (Sir C. W.) Papers of a Critic. Selected from the Writings of the late Chas. Wentworth Dilke. With a Biographical Sketch. 2 Vols. 8vo. 24s.

DOG-BREAKING ; the Most Expeditious, Certain, and Easy Method, whether great excellence or only mediocrity be required. With a Few Hints for those who Love the Dog and the Gun. By Lieut.-Gen. Hutchinson. With 40 Woodcuts. Crown 8vo. 9s.

DOMESTIC MODERN COOKERY. Founded on Principles of Economy and Practical Knowledge, and adapted for Private Families. Woodcuts. Fcap. 8vo. 5s.

DOUGLAS'S (Sir Howard) Life and Adventures. Portrait. 8vo. 15s.

———— Theory and Practice of Gunnery. Plates. 8vo. 21s.

———— Construction of Bridges and the Passage of Rivers, in Military Operations. Plates. 8vo. 21s.

———— (Wm.) Horse-Shoeing; As it Is, and As it Should be. Illustrations. Post 8vo. 7s. 6d.

DRAKE'S (Sir Francis) Life, Voyages, and Exploits, by Sea and Land. By John Barrow. Post 8vo. 2s.

DRINKWATER'S (John) History of the Siege of Gibraltar, 1779-1783. With a Description and Account of that Garrison from the Earliest Periods. Post 8vo. 2s.

DUCANGE'S Mediæval Latin-English Dictionary. Translated by Rev. E. A. Dayman, M.A. Small 4to. [In preparation.

DU CHAILLU'S (Paul B.) Equatorial Africa, with Accounts of the Gorilla, the Nest-building Ape, Chimpanzee, Crocodile, &c. Illustrations. 8vo. 21s.

———— Journey to Ashango Land; and Further Penetration into Equatorial Africa. Illustrations. 8vo. 21s.

DUFFERIN'S (Lord) Letters from High Latitudes; a Yacht Voyage to Iceland, Jan Mayen, and Spitzbergen. Woodcuts. Post 8vo. 7s. 6d.

DUNCAN'S (Major) History of the Royal Artillery. Compiled from the Original Records. With Portraits. 2 Vols. 8vo. 30s.

DYER'S (Thos. H.) History of Modern Europe, from the taking of Constantinople by the Turks to the close of the War in the Crimea. With Index. 4 Vols. 8vo. 42s.

EASTLAKE'S (Sir Charles) Contributions to the Literature of the Fine Arts. With Memoir of the Author, and Selections from his Correspondence. By Lady Eastlake. 2 Vols. 8vo. 24s.

EDWARDS' (W. H.) Voyage up the River Amazons, including a
Visit to Para. Post 8vo. 2s.

EIGHT MONTHS AT ROME, during the Vatican Council, with
a Daily Account of the Proceedings. By POMPONIO LETO. Translated from the Original. 8vo. [*Nearly ready.*

ELDON'S (LORD) Public and Private Life, with Selections from
his Correspondence and Diaries. By HORACE TWISS. Portrait. 2
Vols. Post 8vo. 21s.

ELGIN'S (LORD) Letters and Journals. Edited by THEODORE
WALROND. With Preface by Dean Stanley. 8vo. 14s.

ELLESMERE'S (LORD) Two Sieges of Vienna by the Turks.
Translated from the German. Post 8vo. 2s.

ELLIS'S (W.) Madagascar, including a Journey to the Capital,
with notices of Natural History and the People. Woodcuts. 8vo. 16s.

———————— Madagascar Revisited. Setting forth the Perse-
cutions and Heroic Sufferings of the Native Christians. Illustrations.
8vo. 16s.

———————— Memoir. By HIS SON. With his Character and
Work. By REV. HENRY ALLON, D.D. Portrait. 8vo. 10s. 6d.

———————— (ROBINSON) Poems and Fragments of Catullus. 16mo. 5s.

ELPHINSTONE'S (HON. MOUNTSTUART) History of India—the
Hindoo and Mahomedan Periods. Edited by PROFESSOR COWELL.
Map. 8vo. 18s.

———————— (H. W.) Patterns for Turning; Comprising
Elliptical and other Figures cut on the Lathe without the use of any
Ornamental Chuck. With 70 Illustrations. Small 4to. 16s.

ENGLAND. See CALLCOTT, CROKER, HUME, MARKHAM, SMITH,
and STANHOPE.

ESSAYS ON CATHEDRALS. With an Introduction. By
DEAN HOWSON. 8vo. 12s.

CONTENTS.

Recollections of a Dean.—Bishop of
Carlisle.
Cathedral Canons and their Work.—
Canon Norris.
Cathedrals in Ireland, Past and Fu-
ture.—Dean of Cashel.
Cathedrals in their Missionary Aspect.
—A. J. B. Beresford Hope.
Cathedral Foundations in Relation to
Religious Thought.—Canon West-
cott.

Cathedral Churches of the Old Foun-
dation.—Edward A. Freeman.
Welsh Cathedrals.—Canon Perowne.
Education of Choristers.—Sir F. Gore
Ouseley.
Cathedral Schools.—Canon Durham.
Cathedral Reform.—Chancellor Mas-
singberd.
Relation of the Chapter to the Bishop.
Chancellor Benson.
Architecture of the Cathedral
Churches.—Canon Venables.

ELZE'S (KARL) Life of Lord Byron. With a Critical Essay on
his Place in Literature. Translated from the German. With Portrait.
8vo. 16s.

FARRAR'S (A. S.) Critical History of Free Thought in
reference to the Christian Religion. 8vo. 16s.

FERGUSSON'S (JAMES) History of Architecture in all Countries
from the Earliest Times. With 1,600 Illustrations. 4 Vols. Medium
8vo. 31s. 6d. each.
Vol. I. & II. Ancient and Mediæval.
Vol. III. Indian and Eastern. Vol. IV. Modern.

———————— Rude Stone Monuments in all Countries; their Age
and Uses. With 230 Illustrations. Medium 8vo. 24s.

———————— Holy Sepulchre and the Temple at Jerusalem.
Woodcuts. 8vo. 7s. 6d.

FLEMING'S (Professor) Student's Manual of Moral Philosophy. With Quotations and References. Post 8vo. 7s. 6d.

FLOWER GARDEN. By Rev. Thos. James. Fcap. 8vo. 1s.

FORD'S (Richard) Gatherings from Spain. Post 8vo. 3s. 6d.

FORSYTH'S (William) Life and Times of Cicero. With Selections from his Correspondence and Orations. Illustrations. 8vo. 10s. 6d.

—— ———— Hortensius; an Historical Essay on the Office and Duties of an Advocate. Illustrations. 8vo. 12s.

— ———— History of Ancient Manuscripts. Post 8vo. 2s. 6d.

———————— Novels and Novelists of the 18th Century, in Illustration of the Manners and Morals of the Age. Post 8vo. 10s. 6d.

FORTUNE'S (Robert) Narrative of Two Visits to the Tea Countries of China, 1843-52. Woodcuts. 2 Vols. Post 8vo. 18s.

FORSTER'S (John) Life of Jonathan Swift. Vol. I. 1667-1711. With Portrait. 8vo. 15s.

FOSS' (Edward) Biographia Juridica, or Biographical Dictionary of the Judges of England, from the Conquest to the Present Time, 1066-1870. Medium 8vo. 21s.

———————— Tabulæ Curiales; or, Tables of the Superior Courts of Westminster Hall. Showing the Judges who sat in them from 1066 to 1864. 8vo. 10s. 6d.

FRANCE. *₊* See Markham—Smith—Student's.

FRENCH (The) in Algiers; The Soldier of the Foreign Legion— and the Prisoners of Abd-el-Kadir. Translated by Lady Duff Gordon. Post 8vo. 2s.

FRERE'S (Sir Bartle) Indian Missions. Small 8vo. 2s. 6d.

— ——— Eastern Africa as a field for Missionary Labour. With Map. Crown 8vo. 5s.

———————— Bengal Famine. How it will be Met and How to Prevent Future Famines in India. With Maps. Crown 8vo. 5s.

GALTON'S (Francis) Art of Travel; or, Hints on the Shifts and Contrivances available in Wild Countries. Woodcuts. Post 8vo. 7s. 6d.

GEOGRAPHICAL SOCIETY'S JOURNAL. (*Published Yearly.*)

GEORGE'S (Ernest) Mosel; a Series of Twenty Etchings, with Descriptive Letterpress. Imperial 4to. 42s.

———————— Loire and South of France; a Series of Twenty Etchings, with Descriptive Text. Folio. 42s.

GERMANY (History of). See Markham.

GIBBON'S (Edward) History of the Decline and Fall of the Roman Empire. Edited by Milman and Guizot. Edited, with Notes, by Dr. Wm. Smith. Maps. 8 Vols. 8vo. 60s.

———————— (The Student's Gibbon); Being an Epitome of the above work, incorporating the Researches of Recent Commentators. By Dr. Wm. Smith. Woodcuts. Post 8vo. 7s. 6d.

GIFFARD'S (Edward) Deeds of Naval Daring; or, Anecdotes of the British Navy. Fcap. 8vo. 3s. 6d.

GLADSTONE'S (W. E.) Financial Statements of 1853, 1860, 63–65. 8vo. 12s.

———— Rome and the Newest Fashions in Religion. Three Tracts. *Collected Edition.* With a new Preface. 8vo. 7s. 6d.

GLEIG'S (G. R.) Campaigns of the British Army at Washington and New Orleans. Post 8vo. 2s.

———— Story of the Battle of Waterloo. Post 8vo. 3s. 6d.

———— Narrative of Sale's Brigade in Affghanistan. Post 8vo. 2s.

———— Life of Lord Clive. Post 8vo. 3s. 6d.

———— Sir Thomas Munro. Post 8vo. 3s. 6d.

GOLDSMITH'S (Oliver) Works. Edited with Notes by Peter Cunningham. Vignettes. 4 Vols. 8vo. 30s.

GORDON'S (Sir Alex.) Sketches of German Life, and Scenes from the War of Liberation. Post 8vo. 3s. 6d.

———— (Lady Duff) Amber-Witch: A Trial for Witchcraft. Post 8vo. 2s.

———— French in Algiers. 1. The Soldier of the Foreign Legion. 2. The Prisoners of Abd-el-Kadir. Post 8vo. 2s.

GRAMMARS. See Curtius; Hall; Hutton; King Edward; Matthiæ; Maetzner; Smith.

GREECE. *See* Grote—Smith—Student.

GREY'S (Earl) Correspondence with King William IVth and Sir Herbert Taylor, from 1830 to 1832. 2 Vols. 8vo. 30s.

———— Parliamentary Government and Reform; with Suggestions for the Improvement of our Representative System. *Second Edition.* 8vo.

GUIZOT'S (M.) Meditations on Christianity, and on the Religious Questions of the Day. 3 Vols. Post 8vo.

GROTE'S (George) History of Greece. From the Earliest Times to the close of the generation contemporary with the death of Alexander the Great. *Library Edition.* Portrait, Maps, and Plans. 10 Vols. 8vo. 120s. *Cabinet Edition.* Portrait and Plans. 12 Vols. Post 8vo. 6s. each.

———— Plato, and other Companions of Socrates. 3 Vols. 8vo. 45s.

———— Aristotle. 2 Vols. 8vo. 32s.

- Minor Works. With Critical Remarks on his Intellectual Character, Writings, and Speeches. By Alex.Bain, LL.D. Portrait. 8vo. 14s.

———— Fragments on Ethical Subjects. Being a Selection from his Posthumous Papers. With an Introduction. By Alexander Bain, M.A. 8vo.

———— Personal Life. Compiled from Family Documents, Private Memoranda, and Original Letters to and from Various Friends. By Mrs. Grote. Portrait. 8vo. 12s.

———— (Mrs.) Memoir of Ary Scheffer. Portrait. 8vo. 8s. 6d.

HALL'S (T. D.) School Manual of English Grammar. With Copious Exercises. 12mo. 3s. 6d.

———— Primary English Grammar for Elementary Schools. 16mo. 1s.

———— Child's First Latin Book, including a Systematic Treatment of the New Pronunciation, and a full Praxis of Nouns, Adjectives, and Pronouns. 16mo. 1s. 6d.

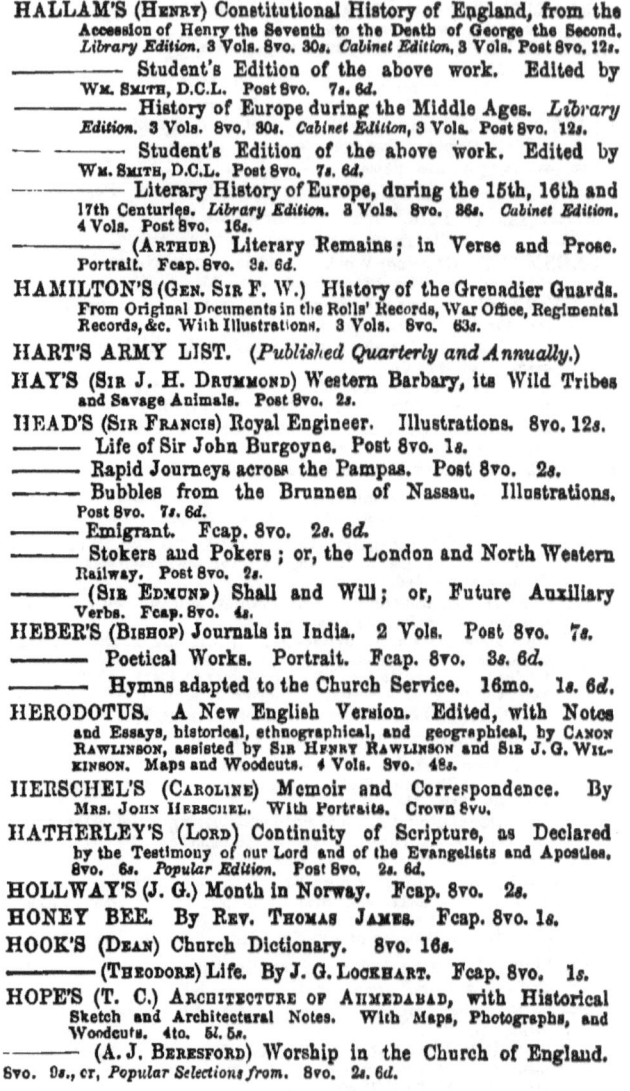

HALLAM'S (Henry) Constitutional History of England, from the Accession of Henry the Seventh to the Death of George the Second. *Library Edition.* 3 Vols. 8vo. 30s. *Cabinet Edition*, 3 Vols. Post 8vo. 12s.

———— Student's Edition of the above work. Edited by Wm. Smith, D.C.L. Post 8vo. 7s. 6d.

———— History of Europe during the Middle Ages. *Library Edition.* 3 Vols. 8vo. 30s. *Cabinet Edition*, 3 Vols. Post 8vo. 12s.

—— ———— Student's Edition of the above work. Edited by Wm. Smith, D.C.L. Post 8vo. 7s. 6d.

———— Literary History of Europe, during the 15th, 16th and 17th Centuries. *Library Edition.* 3 Vols. 8vo. 36s. *Cabinet Edition.* 4 Vols. Post 8vo. 16s.

———— (Arthur) Literary Remains; in Verse and Prose. Portrait. Fcap. 8vo. 3s. 6d.

HAMILTON'S (Gen. Sir F. W.) History of the Grenadier Guards. From Original Documents in the Rolls' Records, War Office, Regimental Records, &c. With Illustrations. 3 Vols. 8vo. 63s.

HART'S ARMY LIST. (*Published Quarterly and Annually.*)

HAY'S (Sir J. H. Drummond) Western Barbary, its Wild Tribes and Savage Animals. Post 8vo. 2s.

HEAD'S (Sir Francis) Royal Engineer. Illustrations. 8vo. 12s.

———— Life of Sir John Burgoyne. Post 8vo. 1s.

———— Rapid Journeys across the Pampas. Post 8vo. 2s.

———— Bubbles from the Brunnen of Nassau. Illustrations. Post 8vo. 7s. 6d.

———— Emigrant. Fcap. 8vo. 2s. 6d.

———— Stokers and Pokers; or, the London and North Western Railway. Post 8vo. 2s.

———— (Sir Edmund) Shall and Will; or, Future Auxiliary Verbs. Fcap. 8vo. 4s.

HEBER'S (Bishop) Journals in India. 2 Vols. Post 8vo. 7s.

———— Poetical Works. Portrait. Fcap. 8vo. 3s. 6d.

———— Hymns adapted to the Church Service. 16mo. 1s. 6d.

HERODOTUS. A New English Version. Edited, with Notes and Essays, historical, ethnographical, and geographical, by Canon Rawlinson, assisted by Sir Henry Rawlinson and Sir J. G. Wilkinson. Maps and Woodcuts. 4 Vols. 8vo. 48s.

HERSCHEL'S (Caroline) Memoir and Correspondence. By Mrs. John Herschel. With Portraits. Crown 8vo.

HATHERLEY'S (Lord) Continuity of Scripture, as Declared by the Testimony of our Lord and of the Evangelists and Apostles. 8vo. 6s. *Popular Edition.* Post 8vo. 2s. 6d.

HOLLWAY'S (J. G.) Month in Norway. Fcap. 8vo. 2s.

HONEY BEE. By Rev. Thomas James. Fcap. 8vo. 1s.

HOOK'S (Dean) Church Dictionary. 8vo. 16s.

———— (Theodore) Life. By J. G. Lockhart. Fcap. 8vo. 1s.

HOPE'S (T. C.) Architecture of Ahmedabad, with Historical Sketch and Architectural Notes. With Maps, Photographs, and Woodcuts. 4to. 5l. 5s.

———— (A. J. Beresford) Worship in the Church of England. 8vo. 9s., cr, *Popular Selections from.* 8vo. 2s. 6d.

FOREIGN HANDBOOKS.

HAND-BOOK—TRAVEL-TALK. English, French, German, and Italian. 18mo. 8s. 6d.

————— HOLLAND,—Belgium, Rhenish Prussia, and the Rhine from Holland to Mayence. Map and Plans. Post 8vo. 6s.

————— NORTH GERMANY,—From the Baltic to the Black Forest, the Hartz, Thüringerwald, Saxon Switzerland, Rügen, the Giant Mountains, Taunus, Odenwald, and the Rhine Countries, from Frankfort to Basle. Map and Plans. Post 8vo. 6s.

————— SOUTH GERMANY,— Wurtemburg, Bavaria, Austria, Styria, Salzburg, the Austrian and Bavarian Alps, Tyrol, Hungary, and the Danube. from Ulm to the Black Sea. Map. Post 8vo. 10s.

————— PAINTING. German, Flemish, and Dutch Schools. Illustrations. 2 Vols. Post 8vo. 24s.

————— LIVES OF EARLY FLEMISH PAINTERS. By Crowe and Cavalcaselle. Illustrations. Post 8vo. 10s. 6d.

————— SWITZERLAND, Alps of Savoy, and Piedmont. Maps. Post 8vo. 9s.

————— FRANCE, Part I. Normandy, Brittany, the French Alps, the Loire, the Seine, the Garonne, and the Pyrenees. Post 8vo. 7s. 6d.

————— Part II. Central France, Auvergne, the Cevennes, Burgundy, the Rhone and Saone, Provence, Nimes, Arles, Marseilles, the French Alps, Alsace, Lorraine, Champagne, &c. Maps. Post 8vo. 7s. 6d.

————— MEDITERRANEAN ISLANDS—Malta, Corsica, Sardinia, and Sicily. Maps. Post 8vo. [In the Press.

————— ALGERIA. Algiers, Constantine, Oran, the Atlas Range. Map. Post 8vo. 9s.

————— PARIS, and its Environs. Map. 16mo. 3s. 6d.
. Murray's Plan of Paris, mounted on canvas. 3s. 6d.

————— SPAIN, Madrid, The Castiles, The Basque Provinces, Leon, The Asturias, Galicia, Estremadura, Andalusia, Ronda, Granada, Murcia, Valencia, Catalonia, Aragon, Navarre, The Balearic Islands, &c. &c. Maps. 2 Vols. Post 8vo. 24s.

————— PORTUGAL, Lisbon, Porto, Cintra, Mafra, &c. Map. Post 8vo. 9s.

————— NORTH ITALY, Turin, Milan, Cremona, the Italian Lakes, Bergamo, Brescia, Verona, Mantua, Vicenza, Padua, Ferrara, Bologna, Ravenna, Rimini, Piacenza, Genoa, the Riviera, Venice, Parma, Modena, and Romagna. Map. Post 8vo. 10s.

————— CENTRAL ITALY, Florence, Lucca, Tuscany, The Marches, Umbria, and the late Patrimony of St. Peter's. Map. Post 8vo. 10s.

————— ROME and its Environs. Map. Post 8vo. 10s.

————— SOUTH ITALY, Two Sicilies, Naples, Pompeii, Herculaneum, and Vesuvius. Map. Post 8vo. 10s.

————— KNAPSACK GUIDE TO ITALY. 16mo.

————— PAINTING. The Italian Schools. Illustrations. 2 Vols. Post 8vo. 30s.

————— LIVES OF ITALIAN PAINTERS, from Cimabue to Bassano. By Mrs. Jameson. Portraits. Post 8vo. 12s.

————— NORWAY, Christiania, Bergen, Trondhjem. The Fjelds and Fjords. Map. Post 8vo. 9s.

————— SWEDEN, Stockholm, Upsala, Gothenburg, the Shores of the Baltic, &c. Post 8vo. 6s.

————— DENMARK, Sleswig, Holstein, Copenhagen, Jutland, Iceland. Map. Post 8vo. 6s.

HAND-BOOK--RUSSIA, St. Petersburg, Moscow, Poland, and
FINLAND. Maps. Post 8vo. 15s.
——————— GREECE, the Ionian Islands, Continental Greece,
Athens, the Peloponnesus, the Islands of the Ægean Sea, Albania,
Thessaly, and Macedonia. Maps. Post 8vo. 15s.
——————— TURKEY IN ASIA—Constantinople, the Bos-
phorus, Dardanelles, Brousa, Plain of Troy, Crete, Cyprus, Smyrna,
Ephesus, the Seven Churches, Coasts of the Black Sea, Armenia,
Mesopotamia, &c. Maps. Post 8vo. 15s.
——————— EGYPT, including Descriptions of the Course of
the Nile through Egypt and Nubia, Alexandria, Cairo, and Thebes, the
Suez Canal, the Pyramids, the Peninsula of Sinai, the Oases, the
Fyoom, &c. Map. Post 8vo. 15s
——————— HOLY LAND—Syria, Palestine, Peninsula of
Sinai, Edom, Syrian Deserts, Petra, Damascus, and Palmyra. Maps.
Post 8vo.
    ₊ Travelling Map of Palestine. In a case. 12s.
——————— INDIA — Bombay and Madras. Map. 2 Vols.
Post 8vo. 12s. each.

ENGLISH HANDBOOKS.

HAND-BOOK—MODERN LONDON. Map. 16mo. 3s. 6d.
——————— EASTERN COUNTIES, Chelmsford, Harwich, Col-
chester, Maldon, Cambridge, Ely, Newmarket, Bury St. Edmunds,
Ipswich, Woodbridge, Felixstowe, Lowestoft, Norwich, Yarmouth,
Cromer, &c. Map and Plans. Post 8vo. 12s.
——————— CATHEDRALS of Oxford, Peterborough, Norwich,
Ely, and Lincoln. With 90 Illustrations. Crown 8vo. 18s.
——————— KENT AND SUSSEX, Canterbury, Dover, Rams-
gate, Sheerness, Rochester, Chatham, Woolwich, Brighton, Chichester,
Worthing, Hastings, Lewes, Arundel, &c. Map. Post 8vo. 10s.
——————— SURREY AND HANTS, Kingston, Croydon, Rei-
gate, Guildford, Dorking, Boxhill, Winchester, Southampton, New
Forest, Portsmouth, and Isle of Wight. Maps. Post 8vo. 10s.
——————— BERKS, BUCKS, AND OXON, Windsor, Eton,
Reading, Aylesbury, Uxbridge, Wycombe, Henley, the City and Uni-
versity of Oxford, Blenheim, and the Descent of the Thames. Map.
Post 8vo. 7s. 6d.
——————— WILTS, DORSET, AND SOMERSET, Salisbury,
Chippenham, Weymouth, Sherborne, Wells, Bath, Bristol, Taunton,
&c. Map. Post 8vo. 10s.
——————— DEVON AND CORNWALL, Exeter, Ilfracombe,
Linton, Sidmouth, Dawlish, Teignmouth, Plymouth, Devonport, Tor-
quay, Launceston, Truro, Penzance, Falmouth, the Lizard, Land's End,
&c. Maps. Post 8vo. 12s.
——————— CATHEDRALS of Winchester, Salisbury, Exeter,
Wells, Chichester, Rochester, Canterbury. With 110 Illustrations.
2 Vols. Crown 8vo 24s.
——————— GLOUCESTER, HEREFORD, and WORCESTER,
Cirencester, Cheltenham. Stroud. Tewkesbury, Leominster, Ross, Mal-
vern, Kidderminster, Dudley, Bromsgrove, Evesham. Map. Post 8vo. 9s.
——————— CATHEDRALS of Bristol, Gloucester, Hereford,
Worcester, and Lichfield With 50 Illustrations. Crown 8vo. 16s.
——————— NORTH WALES, Bangor, Carnarvon, Beaumaris,
Snowdon, Llanberis, Dolgelly, Cader Idris, Conway, &c. Map. Post
8vo. 7s.
——————— SOUTH WALES, Monmouth, Llandaff, Merthyr,
Vale of Neath, Pembroke, Carmarthen, Tenby, Swansea, and The Wye,
&c. Map. Post 8vo. 7s.

HAND-BOOK—CATHEDRALS OF BANGOR, ST. ASAPH, Llaudaff, and St. David's. With Illustrations. Post 8vo. 15s.

———— ———— DERBY, NOTTS, LEICESTER, STAFFORD, Matlock, Bakewell, Chatsworth, The Peak, Buxton, Hardwick, Dove Dale, Ashborne, Southwell, Mansfield, Retford, Burton, Belvoir, Melton Mowbray, Wolverhampton, Lichfield, Walsall, Tamworth. Map. Post 8vo. 9s.

———————— SHROPSHIRE, CHESHIRE AND LANCASHIRE —Shrewsbury, Ludlow, Bridgnorth, Oswestry, Chester, Crewe, Alderley, Stockport, Birkenhead, Warrington, Bury, Manchester, Liverpool, Burnley, Clitheroe, Bolton, Blackburn, Wigan, Preston, Rochdale, Lancaster, Southport, Blackpool, &c. Map. Post 8vo. 10s.

———————— YORKSHIRE, Doncaster, Hull, Selby, Beverley, Scarborough, Whitby, Harrogate, Ripon, Leeds, Wakefield, Bradford, Halifax, Huddersfield, Sheffield. Map and Plans. Post 8vo. 12s.

———————— CATHEDRALS of York, Ripon, Durham, Carlisle, Chester, and Manchester. With 60 Illustrations. 2 Vols. Crown 8vo. 21s.

———————— DURHAM AND NORTHUMBERLAND, New-castle, Darlington, Gateshead, Bishop Auckland, Stockton, Hartlepool, Sunderland, Shields, Berwick-on-Tweed, Morpeth, Tynemouth, Cold-stream, Alnwick, &c. Map. Post 8vo. 9s.

———————— WESTMORLAND AND CUMBERLAND—Lan-caster, Furness Abbey, Ambleside, Kendal, Windermere, Coniston, Keswick, Grasmere, Ulswater, Carlisle, Cockermouth, Penrith, Appleby. Map. Post 8vo. 6s.

₂ MURRAY'S MAP OF THE LAKE DISTRICT, on canvas. 3s. 6d.

———————— SCOTLAND, Edinburgh, Melrose, Kelso, Glasgow, Dumfries, Ayr, Stirling, Arran, The Clyde, Oban, Inverary, Loch Lomond, Loch Katrine and Trossachs, Caledonian Canal, Inverness, Perth, Dundee, Aberdeen, Braemar, Skye, Caithness, Ross, Suther-land, &c. Maps and Plans. Post 8vo. 9s.

———————— IRELAND, Dublin, Belfast, Donegal, Galway, Wexford, Cork, Limerick, Waterford, Killarney, Munster, &c. Maps. Post 8vo. 12s.

HORACE; a New Edition of the Text. Edited by DEAN MILMAN. With 100 Woodcuts. Crown 8vo. 7s. 6d.

———————— Life of. By DEAN MILMAN. Illustrations. 8vo. 9s.

HOUGHTON'S (LORD) Monographs, Vol. I., Personal and Social. With Portraits. Crown 8vo. 10s. 6d.

———————— POETICAL WORKS. *Collected Edition.* With Por-trait 2 Vols Fcap. 8vo. 12s.

HUME'S (The Student's) History of England, from the Inva-sion of Julius Cæsar to the Revolution of 1688. Corrected and con-tinued to 1868. Woodcuts. Post 8vo. 7s. 6d.

HUTCHINSON (GEN.), on the most expeditious, certain, and easy Method of Dog-Breaking. With 40 Illustrations. Crown 8vo. 9s.

HUTTON'S (H. E.) Principia Græca; an Introduction to the Study of Greek. Comprehending Grammar, Delectus, and Exercise-book, with Vocabularies. *Sixth Edition.* 12mo. 3s. 6d.

IRBY AND MANGLES' Travels in Egypt, Nubia, Syria, and the Holy Land. Post 8vo. 2s.

JACOBSON'S (BISHOP) Fragmentary Illustrations of the History of the Book of Common Prayer; from Manuscript Sources (Bishop SANDERSON and Bishop WREN). 8vo. 5s.

JAMES' (REV. THOMAS) Fables of Æsop. A New Translation, with Historical Preface. With 100 Woodcuts by TENNIEL and WOLF. Post 8vo. 2s. 6d.

o

HOME AND COLONIAL LIBRARY.

A Series of Works adapted for all circles and classes of Readers, having been selected for their acknowledged interest, and ability of the Authors. Post 8vo. Published at 2s. and 3s. 6d. each, and arranged under two distinctive heads as follows :—

CLASS A.

HISTORY, BIOGRAPHY, AND HISTORIC TALES.

1. SIEGE OF GIBRALTAR. By JOHN DRINKWATER. 2s.

2. THE AMBER-WITCH. By LADY DUFF GORDON. 2s.

3. CROMWELL AND BUNYAN. By ROBERT SOUTHEY. 2s.

4. LIFE OF SIR FRANCIS DRAKE. By JOHN BARROW. 2s.

5. CAMPAIGNS AT WASHINGTON. By REV. G. R. GLEIG. 2s.

6. THE FRENCH IN ALGIERS. By LADY DUFF GORDON. 2s.

7. THE FALL OF THE JESUITS. 2s.

8. LIVONIAN TALES. 2s.

9. LIFE OF CONDÉ. By LORD MAHON. 3s. 6d.

10. SALE'S BRIGADE. By REV. G. R. GLEIG. 2s.

11. THE SIEGES OF VIENNA. By LORD ELLESMERE. 2s.

12. THE WAYSIDE CROSS. By CAPT. MILMAN. 2s.

13. SKETCHES OF GERMAN LIFE. By SIR A. GORDON. 3s. 6d.

14. THE BATTLE OF WATERLOO. By REV. G. R. GLEIG. 3s. 6d.

15. AUTOBIOGRAPHY OF STEFFENS. 2s.

16. THE BRITISH POETS. By THOMAS CAMPBELL. 3s. 6d.

17. HISTORICAL ESSAYS. By LORD MAHON. 3s. 6d.

18. LIFE OF LORD CLIVE. By REV. G. R. GLEIG. 3s. 6d.

19. NORTH - WESTERN RAILWAY. By SIR F. B. HEAD. 2s.

20. LIFE OF MUNRO. By REV. G. R. GLEIG. 3s. 6d.

CLASS B.

VOYAGES, TRAVELS, AND ADVENTURES.

1. BIBLE IN SPAIN. By GEORGE BORROW. 3s. 6d.

2. GYPSIES OF SPAIN. By GEORGE BORROW. 3s. 6d.

3 & 4. JOURNALS IN INDIA. By BISHOP HEBER. 2 Vols. 7s.

5. TRAVELS IN THE HOLY LAND. By IRBY and MANGLES. 2s.

6. MOROCCO AND THE MOORS. By J. DRUMMOND HAY. 2s.

7. LETTERS FROM THE BALTIC. By a LADY. 2s.

8. NEW SOUTH WALES. By MRS. MEREDITH. 2s.

9. THE WEST INDIES. By M. G. LEWIS. 2s.

10. SKETCHES OF PERSIA. By SIR JOHN MALCOLM. 3s. 6d.

11. MEMOIRS OF FATHER RIPA. 2s.

12 & 13. TYPEE AND OMOO. By HERMANN MELVILLE, 2 Vols. 7s.

14. MISSIONARY LIFE IN CANADA. By REV. J. ABBOTT. 2s.

15. LETTERS FROM MADRAS. By a LADY. 2s.

16. HIGHLAND SPORTS. By CHARLES ST. JOHN. 3s. 6d.

17. PAMPAS JOURNEYS. By SIR F. B. HEAD. 2s.

18. GATHERINGS FROM SPAIN. By RICHARD FORD. 3s. 6d.

19. THE RIVER AMAZON. By W. H. EDWARDS. 2s.

20. MANNERS & CUSTOMS OF INDIA. By REV. C. ACLAND. 2s.

21. ADVENTURES IN MEXICO. By G. F. RUXTON. 3s. 6d.

22. PORTUGAL AND GALLICIA. By LORD CARNARVON. 3s. 6d.

23. BUSH LIFE IN AUSTRALIA. By REV. H. W. HAYGARTH. 2s.

24. THE LIBYAN DESERT. By BAYLE ST. JOHN. 2s.

25. SIERRA LEONE. By A LADY. 3s. 6d.

* Each work may be had separately.

JAMESON'S (Mrs.) Lives of the Early Italian Painters—and the Progress of Painting in Italy—Cimabue to Bassano. With 50 Portraits. Post 8vo. 12s.

JENNINGS' (L. J.) Eighty Years of Republican Government in the United States. Post 8vo. 10s. 6d.

JERVIS'S (Rev. W. H.) Gallican Church, from the Concordat of Bologna, 1516, to the Revolution. With an Introduction. Portraits. 2 Vols. 8vo. 28s.

JESSE'S (Edward) Gleanings in Natural History. Fcp. 8vo. 3s. 6d.

JEX-BLAKE'S (Rev. T. W.) Life in Faith: Sermons Preached at Cheltenham and Rugby. Fcap. 8vo.

JOHNS' (Rev. B. G.) Blind People; their Works and Ways. With Sketches of the Lives of some famous Blind Men. With Illustrations. Post 8vo. 7s. 6d.

JOHNSON'S (Dr. Samuel) Life. By James Boswell. Including the Tour to the Hebrides. Edited by Mr. Croker. *New Edition.* Portraits. 4 Vols. 8vo. [*In Preparation.*

————— Lives of the most eminent English Poets, with Critical Observations on their Works. Edited with Notes, Corrective and Explanatory, by Peter Cunningham. 3 vols. 8vo. 22s. 6d.

JUNIUS' Handwriting Professionally investigated. By Mr. Chabot, Expert. With Preface and Collateral Evidence, by the Hon. Edward Twisleton. With Facsimiles, Woodcuts, &c. 4to. £3 3s.

KEN'S (Bishop) Life. By a Layman. Portrait. 2 Vols. 8vo. 18s.

————— Exposition of the Apostles' Creed. 16mo. 1s. 6d.

KERR'S (Robert) Gentleman's House; or, How to Plan English Residences from the Parsonage to the Palace. With Views and Plans. 8vo. 24s.

————— Small Country House. A Brief Practical Discourse on the Planning of a Residence from 2000l. to 5000l. With Supplementary Estimates to 7000l. Post 8vo. 3s.

————— Ancient Lights; a Book for Architects, Surveyors, Lawyers, and Landlords. 8vo. 5s. 6d.

————— (R. Malcolm) Student's Blackstone. A Systematic Abridgment of the entire Commentaries, adapted to the present state of the law. Post 8vo. 7s. 6d.

KING EDWARD VIth's Latin Grammar. 12mo. 3s. 6d.

————————— First Latin Book. 12mo. 2s 6d.

KING GEORGE IIIrd's Correspondence with Lord North, 1769-82. Edited, with Notes and Introduction, by W. Bodham Donne. 2 vols. 8vo. 32s.

KING'S (R. J.) Archæology, Travel and Art; being Sketches and Studies, Historical and Descriptive. 8vo. 12s.

KIRK'S (J. Foster) History of Charles the Bold, Duke of Burgundy. Portrait. 3 Vols. 8vo. 45s.

KIRKES' Handbook of Physiology. Edited by W. Morrant Baker, F.R.C.S. With 240 Illustrations. Post 8vo. 12s. 6d.

KUGLER'S Handbook of Painting.—The Italian Schools. Revised and Remodelled from the most recent Researches. By Lady Eastlake. With 140 Illustrations. 2 Vols. Crown 8vo. 30s.

————— Handbook of Painting.—The German, Flemish, and Dutch Schools. Revised and in part re-written. By J. A. Crowe. With 60 Illustrations. 2 Vols. Crown 8vo. 24s.

LANE'S (E. W.) Account of the Manners and Customs of Modern Egyptians. With Illustrations. 2 Vols. Post 8vo. 12s

o 2

LAWRENCE'S (Sir Geo.) **Reminiscences of Forty-three Years'** Service in India; including Captivities in Cabul among the Affghans and among the Sikhs, and a Narrative of the Mutiny in Rajputana. Crown 8vo. 10s. 6d.

LAYARD'S (A. H.) **Nineveh and its Remains.** Being a Narrative of Researches and Discoveries amidst the Ruins of Assyria. With an Account of the Chaldean Christians of Kurdistan; the Yezedis, or Devil-worshippers; and an Enquiry into the Manners and Arts of the Ancient Assyrians. Plates and Woodcuts. 2 Vols. 8vo. 36s.
*** A Popular Edition of the above work. With Illustrations. Post 8vo. 7s. 6d.

———— **Nineveh and Babylon;** being the Narrative of Discoveries in the Ruins, with Travels in Armenia, Kurdistan and the Desert, during a Second Expedition to Assyria. With Map and Plates. 8vo. 21s.
*** A Popular Edition of the above work. With Illustrations. Post 8vo. 7s. 6d.

LEATHES' (Stanley) **Practical Hebrew Grammar.** With the Hebrew Text of Genesis i.—vi., and Psalms i.—vi. Grammatical Analysis and Vocabulary. Post 8vo. 7s. 6d.

LENNEP'S (Rev. H. J. Van) **Missionary Travels in Asia Minor.** With Illustrations of Biblical History and Archæology. With Map and Woodcuts. 2 Vols. Post 8vo. 24s.

———— **Modern Customs and Manners of Bible Lands** in Illustration of Scripture. With Coloured Maps and 300 Illustrations. 2 Vols. 8vo. 21s.

LESLIE'S (C. R.) **Handbook for Young Painters.** With Illustrations. Post 8vo. 7s. 6d.

———— **Life and Works of Sir Joshua Reynolds.** Portraits and Illustrations. 2 Vols. 8vo. 42s.

LETTERS From the Baltic. By a Lady. Post 8vo. 2s.

———————— **Madras.** By a Lady. Post 8vo. 2s.

———————— **Sierra Leone.** By a Lady. Post 8vo. 3s. 6d.

LEVI'S (Leone) **History of British Commerce; and of the Economic Progress of the Nation, from 1763 to 1870.** 8vo. 16s.

LIDDELL'S (Dean) **Student's History of Rome, from the earliest Times to the establishment of the Empire.** With Woodcuts. Post 8vo. 7s. 6d.

LLOYD'S (W. Watkiss) **History of Sicily to the Athenian War;** with Elucidations of the Sicilian Odes of Pindar. With Map. 8vo. 14s.

LISPINGS from LOW LATITUDES; or, the Journal of the Hon. Impulsia Gushington. Edited by Lord Dufferin. With 24 Plates. 4to. 21s.

LITTLE ARTHUR'S History of England. By Lady Callcott. New Edition, continued to 1872. With Woodcuts. Fcap. 8vo. 1s. 6d.

LIVINGSTONE'S (Dr.) **Popular Account of his First Expedition to Africa, 1840-56.** Illustrations. Post 8vo. 7s 6d.

———— **Popular Account of his Second Expedition to Africa, 1858-64.** Map and Illustrations. Post 8vo. 7s. 6d.

———— **Last Journals in Central Africa, from 1865 to his Death.** Continued by a Narrative of his last moments and sufferings. By Rev. Horace Waller. Maps and Illustrations. 2 Vols 8vo. 28s.

LIVONIAN TALES. By the Author of "Letters from the Baltic." Post 8vo. 2s.

LOCH'S (H. B.) **Personal Narrative of Events during Lord Elgin's Second Embassy to China.** With Illustrations. Post 8vo. 9s.

LOCKHART'S (J. G.) Ancient Spanish Ballads. Historical and Romantic. Translated, with Notes. With Portrait and Illustrations. Crown 8vo. 5s.

———————— Life of Theodore Hook. Fcap. 8vo. 1s.

LONSDALE'S (Bishop) Life. With Selections from his Writings. By E. B. Denison. With Portrait. Crown 8vo. 10s. 6d.

LOUDON'S (Mrs.) Gardening for Ladies. With Directions and Calendar of Operations for Every Month. Woodcuts. Fcap. 8vo. 3s. 6d.

LUCKNOW: A Lady's Diary of the Siege. Fcap. 8vo. 4s. 6d.

LYELL'S (Sir Charles) Principles of Geology; or, the Modern Changes of the Earth and its Inhabitants considered as illustrative of Geology. With Illustrations. 2 Vols. 8vo. 32s.

———————— Student's Elements of Geology. With Table of British Fossils and 600 Illustrations. Post 8vo. 9s.

———————— Geological Evidences of the Antiquity of Man, including an Outline of Glacial Post-Tertiary Geology, and Remarks on the Origin of Species. Illustrations. 8vo. 14s.

———————— (K. M.) Geographical Handbook of Ferns. With Tables to show their Distribution. Post 8vo. 7s. 6d.

LYTTELTON'S (Lord) Ephemera. 2 Vols. Post 8vo. 19s. 6d.

LYTTON'S (Lord) Memoir of Julian Fane. With Portrait. Post 8vo. 5s.

McCLINTOCK'S (Sir L.) Narrative of the Discovery of the Fate of Sir John Franklin and his Companions in the Arctic Seas. With Illustrations. Post 8vo. 7s. 6d.

MACDOUGALL'S (Col.) Modern Warfare as Influenced by Modern Artillery. With Plans. Post 8vo. 12s.

MACGREGOR'S (J.) Rob Roy on the Jordan, Nile, Red Sea, Gennesareth, &c. A Canoe Cruise in Palestine and Egypt and the Waters of Damascus. With Map and 70 Illustrations. Crown 8vo. 7s. 6d

MACPHERSON'S (Major) Services in India, while Political Agent at Gwalior during the Mutiny. Illustrations. 8vo. 12s.

MAETZNER'S English Grammar. A Methodical, Analytical, and Historical Treatise on the Orthography, Prosody, Inflections, and Syntax of the English Tongue. Translated from the German. By Clair J. Grece, LL.D. 3 Vols. 8vo. 36s.

MAHON (Lord), see Stanhope.

MAINE'S (Sir H. Sumner) Ancient Law: its Connection with the Early History of Society, and its Relation to Modern Ideas. 8vo. 12s.

———————— Village Communities in the East and West. 8vo. 9s.

———————— Early History of Institutions. 8vo. 12s.

MALCOLM'S (Sir John) Sketches of Persia. Post 8vo. 3s. 6d.

MANSEL'S (Dean) Limits of Religious Thought Examined. Post 8vo. 8s. 6d.

———————— Letters, Lectures, and Papers, including the Phrontisterion, or Oxford in the XIXth Century. Edited by H. W. Chandler, M.A. 8vo. 12s.

———————— Gnostic Heresies of the First and Second Centuries. With a sketch of his life and character. By Lord Carnarvon. Edited by Canon Lightfoot. 8vo. 10s. 6d.

MANUAL OF SCIENTIFIC ENQUIRY. For the Use of Travellers. Edited by Rev. R. Main. Post 8vo. 3s. 6d. (Published by order of the Lords of the Admiralty.)

MARCO POLO. The Book of Ser Marco Polo, the Venetian. Concerning the Kingdoms and Marvels of the East. A new English Version. Illustrated by the light of Oriental Writers and Modern Travels. By Col. Henry Yule. Maps and Illustrations. 2 Vols. Medium 8vo. 63s.

MARKHAM'S (Mrs.) History of England. From the First Invasion by the Romans *to* 1867. Woodcuts. 12mo. 3*s.* 6*d.*

———————— History of France. From the Conquest by the Gauls *to* 1861. Woodcuts. 12mo. 3*s.* 6*d.*

———————— History of Germany. From the Invasion by Marius *to* 1867. Woodcuts. 12mo. 3*s.* 6*d.*

MARLBOROUGH'S (Sarah, Duchess of) Letters. Now first published from the Original MSS. at Madresfield Court. With an Introduction. 8vo. 10*s.* 6*d.*

MARRYAT'S (Joseph) History of Modern and Mediæval Pottery and Porcelain. With a Description of the Manufacture. Plates and Woodcuts. 8vo. 42*s.*

MARSH'S (G. P.) Student's Manual of the English Language. Post 8vo. 7*s.* 6*d.*

MATTHIÆ'S Greek Grammar. Abridged by Blomfield. *Revised* by E. S. Crooke. 12mo. 4*s.*

MAUREL'S Character, Actions, and Writings of Wellington. Fcap. 8vo. 1*s.* 6*d.*

MAYNE'S (Capt.) Four Years in British Columbia and Vancouver Island. Illustrations. 8vo. 16*s.*

MEADE'S (Hon. Herbert) Ride through the Disturbed Districts of New Zealand, with a Cruise among the South Sea Islands. With Illustrations. Medium 8vo. 12*s.*

MELVILLE'S (Hermann) Marquesas and South Sea Islands. 2 Vols. Post 8vo. 7*s.*

MEREDITH'S (Mrs. Charles) Notes and Sketches of New South Wales. Post 8vo. 2*s.*

MESSIAH (THE): The Life, Travels, Death, Resurrection, and Ascension of our Blessed Lord. By A Layman. Map. 8vo. 18*s.*

MILLINGTON'S (Rev. T. S.) Signs and Wonders in the Land of Ham, or the Ten Plagues of Egypt, with Ancient and Modern Illustrations. Woodcuts. Post 8vo. 7*s.* 6*d.*

MILMAN'S (Dean) History of the Jews, from the earliest Period down to Modern Times. 3 Vols. Post 8vo. 18*s.*

———————— Early Christianity, from the Birth of Christ to the Abolition of Paganism in the Roman Empire. 3 Vols. Post 8vo. 18*s.*

———————— Latin Christianity, including that of the Popes to the Pontificate of Nicholas V. 9 Vols. Post 8vo. 54*s.*

———————— Annals of St. Paul's Cathedral, from the Romans to the funeral of Wellington. Portrait and Illustrations. 8vo. 18*s.*

———————— Character and Conduct of the Apostles considered as an Evidence of Christianity. 8vo. 10*s.* 6*d.*

———————— Quinti Horatii Flacci Opera. With 100 Woodcuts. Small 8vo. 7*s.* 6*d.*

- Life of Quintus Horatius Flaccus. With Illustrations. 8vo. 9*s.*

———————— Poetical Works. The Fall of Jerusalem—Martyr of Antioch—Balshazzar—Tamor—Anne Boleyn—Fazio, &c. With Portrait and Illustrations. 3 Vols. Fcap. 8vo. 18*s.*

———————— Fall of Jerusalem. Fcap. 8vo. 1*s.*

———————— (Capt. E. A.) Wayside Cross. Post 8vo. 2*s.*

MIVART'S (St. George) Lessons from Nature; as manifested in Mind and Matter. 8vo.

MODERN DOMESTIC COOKERY. Founded on Principles of Economy and Practical Knowledge. *New Edition.* Woodcuts. Fcap. 8vo. 5*s.*

MONGREDIEN'S (Augustus) Trees and Shrubs for English
Plantation. A Selection and Description of the most Ornamental
which will flourish in the open air in our climate. With Classified
Lists. With 30 Illustrations. 8vo. 16s.

MOORE & JACKMAN on the Clematis as a Garden Flower.
Descriptions of the Hardy Species and Varieties, with Directions for
their Cultivation. 8vo. 10s. 6d.

MOORE'S (Thomas) Life and Letters of Lord Byron. *Cabinet
Edition.* With Plates. 6 Vols. Fcap. 8vo. 18s.; *Popular Edition,*
with Portraits. Royal 8vo. 7s. 6d.

MOSSMAN'S (Samuel) New Japan; the Land of the Rising Sun;
its Annals and Progress during the past Twenty Years, recording the
remarkable Progress of the Japanese in Western Civilisation. With
Map. 8vo. 15s.

MOTLEY'S (J. L.) History of the United Netherlands: from the
Death of William the Silent to the Twelve Years' Truce, 1609. *Library
Edition.* Portraits. 4 Vols. 8vo. 60s. *Cabinet Edition.* 4 Vols. Post
8vo. 6s. each.

———— Life and Death of John of Barneveld,
Advocate of Holland. With a View of the Primary Causes and
Movements of the Thirty Years' War. *Library Edition.* Illustrations.
2 Vols. 8vo. 28s. *Cabinet Edition.* 2 vols. Post 8vo. 12s.

MOUHOT'S (Henri) Siam, Cambojia, and Lao; a Narrative of
Travels and Discoveries. Illustrations. 2 Vols. 8vo.

MOZLEY'S (Canon) Treatise on Predestination. 8vo. 14s.

———— Primitive Doctrine of Baptismal Regeneration. 8vo. 7s. 6d.

MUIRHEAD'S (Jas.) Vaux-de-Vire of Maistre Jean Le Houx,
Advocate of Vire. Translated and Edited. With Portrait and Illustrations. 8vo.

MUNRO'S (General) Life and Letters. By Rev. G. R. Gleig.
Post 8vo. 3s. 6d.

MURCHISON'S (Sir Roderick) Siluria; or, a History of the
Oldest rocks containing Organic Remains. Map and Plates. 8vo. 18s.

———— Memoirs. With Notices of his Contemporaries,
and Rise and Progress of Palæozoic Geology. By Archibald Geikie.
Portraits. 2 Vols. 8vo. 30s.

MURRAY'S RAILWAY READING. Containing:—

Wellington. By Lord Ellesmere. 6d.	Mahon's Joan of Arc. 1s.
Nimrod on the Chase. 1s.	Head's Emigrant. 2s. 6d.
Music and Dress. 1s.	Nimrod on the Road. 1s.
Milman's Fall of Jerusalem. 1s.	Croker on the Guillotine. 1s.
Mahon's "Forty-Five." 3s.	Hollway's Norway. 2s.
Life of Theodore Hook. 1s.	Maurel's Wellington. 1s. 6d.
Deeds of Naval Daring. 3s. 6d.	Campbell's Life of Bacon. 2s. 6d.
The Honey Bee. 1s.	The Flower Garden. 1s.
Æsop's Fables. 2s. 6d.	Taylor's Notes from Life. 2s.
Nimrod on the Turf. 1s. 6d.	Rejected Addresses. 1s.
Art of Dining. 1s. 6d.	Penn's Hints on Angling. 1s.

MUSTERS' (Capt.) Patagonians; a Year's Wanderings over
Untrodden Ground from the Straits of Magellan to the Rio Negro.
Illustrations. Post 8vo. 7s. 6d.

NAPIER'S (Sir Chas.) Life, Journals, and Letters. Portraits.
4 Vols. Crown 8vo. 48s.

———— (Sir Wm.) Life and Letters. Portraits. 2 Vols.
Crown 8vo. 28s.

———— English Battles and Sieges of the Peninsular War.
Portrait. Post 8vo. 9s.

NAPOLEON at Fontainebleau and Elba. A Journal of
Occurrences and Notes of Conversations. By Sir Neil Campbell,
C.B. With a Memoir. By Rev. A. N. C. Maclachlan, M.A. Portrait.
8vo. 15s.

NASMYTH and **CARPENTER**. The Moon. Considered as a
Planet, a World, and a Satellite. With Illustrations from Drawings
made with the aid of Powerful Telescopes, Woodcuts, &c. 4to. 30s.

NAUTICAL ALMANAC (THE). (*By Authority.*) 2*s.* 6*d.*

NAVY LIST. (Monthly and Quarterly.) Post 8vo.

NEW TESTAMENT. With Short Explanatory Commentary. By ARCHDEACON CHURTON, M.A., and ARCHDEACON BASIL JONES, M.A. With 110 authentic Views, &c. 2 Vols. Crown 8vo 21*s. bound.*

NEWTH'S (SAMUEL) First Book of Natural Philosophy ; an Introduction to the Study of Statics, Dynamics, Hydrostatics, Optics, and Acoustics, with numerous Examples. Small 8vo. 3*s.* 6*d.*

—————————— Elements of Mechanics, including Hydrostatics, with numerous Examples. Small 8vo. 8*s.* 6*d.*

—————————— Mathematical Examinations. A Graduated Series of Elementary Examples in Arithmetic, Algebra, Logarithms, Trigonometry, and Mechanics. Small 8vo. 8*s.* 6*d.*

NICHOLS' (J. G.) Pilgrimages to Walsingham and Canterbury. By ERASMUS. Translated, with Notes. With Illustrations. Post 8vo. 6*s.*

—————————— (SIR GEORGE) History of the English, Irish and Scotch Poor Laws. 4 Vols. 8vo.

NICOLAS' (SIR HARRIS) Historic Peerage of England. Exhibiting the Origin, Descent, and Present State of every Title of Peerage which has existed in this Country since the Conquest. By WILLIAM COURTHOPE. 8vo. 30*s.*

NIMROD, On the Chace—Turf—and Road. With Portrait and Plates. Crown 8vo. 5*s.* Or with Coloured Plates, 7*s.* 6*d.*

NORDHOFF'S (CHAS.) Communistic Societies of the United States ; including Detailed Accounts of the Shakers, The Amana, Oneida, Bethell, Aurora, Icarian and other existing Societies; with Particulars of their Religious Creeds, Industries, and Present Condition. With 40 Illustrations. 8vo. 15*s.*

OLD LONDON ; Papers read at the Archæological Institute. By various Authors. 8vo. 12*s.*

ORMATHWAITE'S (LORD) Astronomy and Geology—Darwin and Buckle—Progress and Civilisation. Crown 8vo. 6*s.*

OWEN'S (LIEUT.-COL.) Principles and Practice of Modern Artillery, including Artillery Material, Gunnery, and Organisation and Use of Artillery in Warfare. With Illustrations. 8vo. 15*s.*

OXENHAM'S (REV. W.) English Notes for Latin Elegiacs ; designed for early Proficients in the Art of Latin Versification, with Prefatory Rules of Composition in Elegiac Metre. 12mo. 3*s.* 6*d.*

PALGRAVE'S (R. H. I.) Local Taxation of Great Britain and Ireland. 8vo. 5*s.*

—————————— NOTES ON BANKING IN GREAT BRITAIN AND IRELAND, SWEDEN, DENMARK, AND HAMBURG, with some Remarks on the amount of Bills in circulation, both Inland and Foreign. 8vo. 6*s.*

PALLISER'S (MRS.) Brittany and its Byeways, its Inhabitants, and Antiquities. With Illustrations. Post 8vo. 12*s.*

—————————— Mottoes for Monuments, or Epitaphs selected for General Use and Study. With Illustrations. Crown 8vo. 7*s.* 6*d.*

PARIS' (DR.) Philosophy in Sport made Science in Earnest; or, the First Principles of Natural Philosophy inculcated by aid of the Toys and Sports of Youth. Woodcuts. Post 8vo. 7*s.*6*d.*

PARKMAN'S (FRANCIS) Discovery of the Great West ; or, The Valleys of the Mississippi and the Lakes of North America. An Historical Narrative. Map. 8vo. 10*s.* 6*d.*

PARKYNS' (MANSFIELD) Three Years' Residence in Abyssinia : with Travels in that Country. With Illustrations. Post 8vo. 7*s.* 6*d.*

PEEK PRIZE ESSAYS. The Maintenance of the Church of England as an Established Church. By REV. CHARLES HOLE—REV. R. WATSON DIXON—and REV. JULIUS LLOYD. 8vo. 10*s.* 6*d.*

PEEL'S (SIR ROBERT) Memoirs. 2 Vols. Post 8vo. 15*s.*

PENN'S (RICHARD) Maxims and Hints for an Angler and Chess-player. Woodcuts. Fcap. 8vo. 1s.

PERCY'S (JOHN, M.D.) Metallurgy. Vol. I., Part 1. FUEL, Wood, Peat, Coal, Charcoal, Coke, Refractory Materials, Fire-Clays, &c. With Illustrations. 8vo. 30s.

——— Vol. I., Part 2. Copper, Zinc, Brass. With Illustra-tions. 8vo [In the Press.

——— Vol. II. Iron and Steel. With Illustrations. 8vo. [In Preparation.

——— Vol. III. Lead, including part of SILVER. With Illus-trations. 8vo. 30s.

——— Vols. IV. and V. Gold, Silver, and Mercury, Platinum, Tin, Nickel, Cobalt, Antimony, Bismuth, Arsenic, and other Metals. With Illustrations. 8vo. [In Preparation.

PERSIA'S (SHAH OF) Diary during his Tour through Europe in 1873. Translated from the Original. By J. W. REDHOUSE. With Portrait and Coloured Title. Crown 8vo. 12s.

PHILLIPS' (JOHN) Memoirs of William Smith. 8vo. 7s. 6d.

——— Geology of Yorkshire, The Coast, and Limestone District. Plates. 2 Vols. 4to.

——— Rivers, Mountains, and Sea Coast of Yorkshire. With Essays on the Climate, Scenery, and Ancient Inhabitants. Plates. 8vo. 15s.

——— (SAMUEL) Literary Essays from "The Times." With Portrait. 2 Vols. Fcap. 8vo. 7s.

POPE'S (ALEXANDER) Works. With Introductions and Notes, by REV. WHITWELL ELWIN. Vols. I., II., VI., VII., VIII. With Por-traits. 8vo. 10s. 6d. each.

PORTER'S (REV. J. L.) Damascus, Palmyra, and Lebanon. With Travels among the Giant Cities of Bashan and the Hauran. Map and Woodcuts. Post 8vo. 7s. 6d.

PRAYER-BOOK (ILLUSTRATED), with Borders, Initials, Vig-nettes, &c. Edited, with Notes, by REV. THOS. JAMES. Medium 8vo. 18s. cloth ; 31s. 6d. calf ; 36s. morocco.

PRINCESS CHARLOTTE OF WALES. A Brief Memoir. With Selections from her Correspondence and other unpublished Papers. By LADY ROSE WEIGALL. With Portrait. 8vo. 8s. 6d.

PUSS IN BOOTS. With 12 Illustrations. By OTTO SPECKTER. 16mo. 1s. 6d. Or coloured, 2s. 6d.

PRINCIPLES AT STAKE. Essays on Church Questions of the Day. 8vo. 12s. Contents :—

Ritualism and Uniformity.—Benjamin Shaw.	Scripture and Ritual.—Canon Bernard.
The Episcopate.—Bishop of Bath and Wells.	Church in South Africa. — Arthur Mills.
The Priesthood.—Dean of Canterbury.	Schismatical Tendency of Ritualism. —Rev. Dr. Salmon.
National Education.—Rev. Alexander R. Grant.	Revisions of the Liturgy.—Rev. W. G. Humphry.
Doctrine of the Eucharist.—Rev. G. H. Sumner.	Parties and Party Spirit.—Dean of Chester.

PRIVY COUNCIL JUDGMENTS in Ecclesiastical Cases re-lating to Doctrine and Discipline. With Historical Introduction, by G. C. BRODRICK and W. H. FREMANTLE. 8vo. 10s. 6d.

QUARTERLY REVIEW (THE). 8vo. 6s.

RAE'S (EDWARD) Land of the North Wind; or Travels among the Laplanders and Samoyedes, and along the Shores of the White Sea. With Map and Woodcuts. Post 8vo. 10s. 6d.

RAMBLES in the Syrian Deserts. Post 8vo. 10s. 6d.

RANKE'S (LEOPOLD) History of the Popes of Rome during the 16th and 17th Centuries. Translated from the German by SARAH AUSTIN. 3 Vols. 8vo. 30s.

RASSAM'S (HORMUZD) Narrative of the British Mission to Abyssinia. With Notices of the Countries Traversed from Massowah to Magdala. Illustrations. 2 Vols. 8vo. 28s.

RAWLINSON'S (CANON) Herodotus. A New English Version. Edited with Notes and Essays. Maps and Woodcut. 4 Vols. 8vo. 48s.

———————— Five Great Monarchies of Chaldæa, Assyria, Media, Babylonia, and Persia. With Maps and Illustrations. 3 Vols. 8vo. 42s.

———————— (SIR HENRY) England and Russia in the East; a Series of Papers on the Political and Geographical Condition of Central Asia. Map. 8vo. 12s.

REED'S (E. J.) Shipbuilding in Iron and Steel; a Practical Treatise, giving full details of Construction, Processes of Manufacture, and Building Arrangements. With 5 Plans and 250 Woodcuts. 8vo.

———— Iron-Clad Ships; their Qualities, Performances, and Cost. With Chapters on Turret Ships, Iron-Clad Rams, &c. With Illustrations. 8vo. 12s.

REJECTED ADDRESSES (THE). By JAMES AND HORACE SMITH. Woodcuts. Post 8vo. 3s. 6d.; or Popular Edition, Fcap. 8vo. 1s.

RESIDENCE IN BULGARIA; or, Notes on the Resources and Administration of Turkey, &c. By S. G. B. ST.CLAIR and CHARLES A. BROPHY. 8vo. 12s.

REYNOLDS' (SIR JOSHUA) Life and Times. By C. R. LESLIE, R.A. and TOM TAYLOR. Portraits. 2 Vols. 8vo.

RICARDO'S (DAVID) Political Works. With a Notice of his Life and Writings. By J. R. M'CULLOCH. 8vo. 16s.

RIPA'S (FATHER) Thirteen Years' Residence at the Court of Peking. Post 8vo. 2s.

ROBERTSON'S (CANON) History of the Christian Church, from the Apostolic Age to the Reformation, 1517. Library Edition. 4 Vols. 8vo. Cabinet Edition. 8 Vols. Post 8vo. 6s. each.

———————— How shall we Conform to the Liturgy. 12mo. 9s.

ROME. See LIDDELL and SMITH.

ROWLAND'S (DAVID) Manual of the English Constitution. Its Rise, Growth, and Present State. Post 8vo. 10s. 6d.

———————— Laws of Nature the Foundation of Morals. Post 8vo. 6s.

ROBSON'S (E. R.) SCHOOL ARCHITECTURE. Being Practical Remarks on the Planning, Designing, Building, and Furnishing of School-houses. With 300 Illustrations. Medium 8vo. 31s. 6d.

RUNDELL'S (MRS.) Modern Domestic Cookery. Fcap. 8vo. 5s.

RUXTON'S (GEORGE F.) Travels in Mexico; with Adventures among the Wild Tribes and Animals of the Prairies and Rocky Mountains. Post 8vo. 3s. 6d.

ROBINSON'S (REV. DR.) Biblical Researches in Palestine and the Adjacent Regions, 1838—52. Maps. 3 Vols. 8vo. 42s.

———————— Physical Geography of the Holy Land. Post 8vo. 10s. 6d.

———————— (WM.) Alpine Flowers for English Gardens. With 70 Illustrations. Crown 8vo. 12s.

———————— Wild Gardens; or, our Groves and Shrubberies made beautiful by the Naturalization of Hardy Exotic Plants. With Frontispiece. Small 8vo. 6s.

———————— Sub-Tropical Gardens; or, Beauty of Form in the Flower Garden. With Illustrations. Small 8vo. 7s. 6d.

SALE'S (Sir Robert) Brigade in Affghanistan. With an Account of the Defence of Jellalabad. By Rev. G. R. Gleig. Post 8vo. 2s.

SCHLIEMANN'S (Dr. Henry) Troy and Its Remains. A Narrative of Researches and Discoveries made on the Site of Ilium, and in the Trojan Plain. Edited by Philip Smith, B.A. With Maps, Views, and 500 Illustrations. Medium 8vo. 42s.

SCOTT'S (Sir G. G.) Secular and Domestic Architecture, Present and Future. 8vo. 9s.

—— — (Dean) University Sermons. Post 8vo. 8s. 6d.

SHADOWS OF A SICK ROOM. With a Preface by Canon Liddon. 16mo. 2s 6d.

SCROPE'S (G. P.) Geology and Extinct Volcanoes of Central France. Illustrations. Medium 8vo. 30s.

SHAW'S (T. B.) Manual of English Literature. Post 8vo. 7s. 6d.

—— Specimens of English Literature. Selected from the Chief Writers. Post 8vo. 7s. 6d.

—— (Robert) Visit to High Tartary, Yarkand, and Kashgar (formerly Chinese Tartary), and Return Journey over the Karakorum Pass. With Map and Illustrations. 8vo. 16s.

SHIRLEY'S (Evelyn P.) Deer and Deer Parks; or some Account of English Parks, with Notes on the Management of Deer. Illustrations. 4to. 21s.

SIERRA LEONE; Described in Letters to Friends at Home. By A Lady. Post 8vo. 3s. 6d.

SINCLAIR'S (Archdeacon) Old Times and Distant Places. A Series of Sketches. Crown 8vo. 9s.

SMILES' (Samuel) British Engineers; from the Earliest Period to the death of the Stephensons. With Illustrations. 5 Vols. Crown 8vo. 7s. 6d. each.

—— George and Robert Stephenson. Illustrations. Medium 8vo. 21s.

—— Boulton and Watt. Illustrations. Medium 8vo. 21s.

—— Self-Help. With Illustrations of Conduct and Perseverance. Post 8vo. 6s. Or in French, 5s.

—— Character. A Sequel to "Self-Help." Post 8vo. 6s.

—— Thrift. A Companion Volume to " Self-Help " and " Character." Post 8vo. 6s.

—— Boy's Voyage round the World. With Illustrations. Post 8vo. 6s.

STANLEY'S (Dean) Sinai and Palestine, in connexion with their History. 20th Thousand. Map. 8vo. 14s.

—— Bible in the Holy Land; Extracted from the above Work. Second Edition. Woodcuts. Fcap. 8vo. 2s. 6d.

—— Eastern Church. Fourth Edition. Plans. 8vo. 12s.

—— Jewish Church. 1st & 2nd Series. From the Earliest Times to the Captivity 8vo. 24s.

—— Third Series. From the Captivity to the Destruction of Jerusalem. 8vo.

—— Church of Scotland. 8vo. 7s. 6d.

—— Memorials of Canterbury Cathedral. Woodcuts. Post 8vo. 7s. 6d.

—— Westminster Abbey. With Illustrations. 8vo. 21s.

—— Sermons during a Tour in the East. 8vo. 9s.

—— Addresses and Charges of the late Bishop Stanley. With Memoir. 8vo. 10s. 6d.

—— Epistles of St. Paul to the Corinthians. 8vo. 18s.

SMITH'S (Dr. Wm) Dictionary of the Bible; its Antiquities, Biography, Geography, and Natural History. Illustrations. 3 Vols. 8vo. 105s.

———— Concise Bible Dictionary. With 300 Illustrations. Medium 8vo. 21s.

———— Smaller Bible Dictionary. With Illustrations. Post 8vo. 7s. 6d.

———— Christian Antiquities. Comprising the History, Institutions, and Antiquities of the Christian Church. With Illustrations. Vol. I. 8vo. 31s. 6d.

———————— Biography and Doctrines; from the Times of the Apostles to the Age of Charlemagne. 8vo.   [*In Preparation.*

———— Atlas of Ancient Geography—Biblical and Classical. Folio. 6l. 6s.

———— Greek and Roman Antiquities. With 500 Illustrations. Medium 8vo. 28s.

———————— Biography and Mythology. With 600 Illustrations. 3 Vols. Medium 8vo. 4l. 4s.

———————— Geography. 2 Vols. With 500 Illustrations. Medium 8vo. 56s.

———— Classical Dictionary of Mythology, Biography, and Geography. 1 Vol. With 750 Woodcuts. 8vo. 18s.

———— Smaller Classical Dictionary. With 200 Woodcuts. Crown 8vo. 7s. 6d.

———————— Greek and Roman Antiquities. With 200 Woodcuts. Crown 8vo. 7s. 6d.

———— Latin-English Dictionary. With Tables of the Roman Calendar, Measures, Weights, and Money. Medium 8vo. 21s.

———— Smaller Latin-English Dictionary. 12mo. 7s. 6d.

———— English-Latin Dictionary. Medium 8vo. 21s.

———— Smaller English-Latin Dictionary. 12mo. 7s. 6d.

———— School Manual of English Grammar, with Copious Exercises. Post 8vo. 3s. 6d.

———————— Modern Geography. 12mo.
     [*Nearly ready.*

—— ———— Primary English Grammar. 16mo. 1s.

———————— History of Britain. 12mo. 2s. 6d.

———— French Principia. Part I. A First Course, containing a Grammar, Delectus, Exercises, and Vocabularies. 12mo. 3s. 6d.

———————— Part II. A Reading Book, containing Fables, Stories, and Anecdotes, Natural History, and Scenes from the History of France. With Grammatical Questions, Notes and copious Etymological Dictionary. 12mo. 4s. 6d.

———————— Part III. Prose Composition, containing a Systematic Course of Exercises on the Syntax, with the Principal Rules of Syntax. 12mo.   [*In the Press.*

———— German Principia, Part I. A First German Course, containing a Grammar, Delectus, Exercise Book, and Vocabularies. 12mo. 3s. 6d.

———————— Part II. A Reading Book; containing Fables, Stories, and Anecdotes, Natural History, and Scenes from the History of Germany. With Grammatical Questions, Notes, and Dictionary. 12mo. 3s. 6d.

———————— Part III. An Introduction to German Prose Composition; containing a Systematic Course of Exercises on the Syntax, with the Principal Rules of Syntax. 12mo.
     [*In the Press.*

SMITH'S (Dr. Wm.) Principia Latina—Part I. First Latin Course, containing a Grammar, Delectus, and Exercise Book, with Vocabularies. 12mo. 3s. 6d.
In this Edition the Cases of the Nouns, Adjectives, and Pronouns are arranged both as in the ORDINARY GRAMMARS and as in the PUBLIC SCHOOL PRIMER, together with the corresponding Exercises.

———————————— Part II. A Reading-book of Mythology, Geography, Roman Antiquities, and History. With Notes and Dictionary. 12mo. 3s. 6d.

———————————— Part III. A Poetry Book. Hexameters and Pentameters; Eclog. Ovidianæ; Latin Prosody. 12mo. 3s. 6d.

———————————— Part IV. Prose Composition. Rules of Syntax with Examples, Explanations of Synonyms, and Exercises on the Syntax. 12mo. 3s. 6d.

———————————— Part V. Short Tales and Anecdotes for Translation into Latin. 12mo. 3s.

———————— Latin-English Vocabulary and First Latin-English Dictionary for Phædrus, Cornelius Nepos, and Cæsar. 12mo. 3s. 6d.

———————— Student's Latin Grammar. Post 8vo. 6s.

———————— Smaller Latin Grammar. 12mo. 3s. 6d.

———————— Tacitus, Germania, Agricola, &c. With English Notes. 12mo. 3s. 6d.

———————— Initia Græca, Part I. A First Greek Course, containing a Grammar, Delectus, and Exercise-book. With Vocabularies. 12mo. 3s. 6d.

———————————— Part II. A Reading Book. Containing Short Tales, Anecdotes, Fables, Mythology, and Grecian History. 12mo. 3s. 6d.

———————————— Part III. Prose Composition. Containing the Rules of Syntax, with copious Examples and Exercises. 12mo. 3s. 6d.

———————— Student's Greek Grammar. By PROFESSOR CURTIUS. Post 8vo. 6s.

———————— Smaller Greek Grammar. 12mo. 3s. 6d.

———————— Greek Accidence. Extracted from the above work. 12mo. 2s. 6d.

———————— Plato. The Apology of Socrates, the Crito, and Part of the Phædo; with Notes in English from Stallbaum and Schleiermacher's Introductions. 12mo. 3s. 6d.

———————— Smaller Scripture History. Woodcuts. 16mo. 3s. 6d.

———————————— Ancient History. Woodcuts. 16mo. 3s. 6d.

———————————— Geography. Woodcuts. 16mo. 3s. 6d.

———————— Rome. Woodcuts. 16mo. 3s. 6d.

———————— Greece. Woodcuts. 16mo. 3s. 6d.

———————— Classical Mythology. Woodcuts. 16mo. 3s. 6d.

———————— History of England. Woodcuts. 16mo. 3s. 6d.

———————— English Literature. 16mo. 3s. 6d.

———————— Specimens of English Literature. 16mo. 3s. 6d.

———————— (PHILIP) History of the Ancient World, from the Creation to the Fall of the Roman Empire, A.D. 455. *Fourth Edition.* 3 Vols. 8vo. 31s. 6d.

———————— (REV. A. C.) Nile and its Banks. Woodcuts. 2 Vols. Post 8vo. 18s.

SIMMONS' (CAPT.) Constitution and Practice of Courts-Martial. *Seventh Edition.* 8vo. 15s.

STUDENT'S OLD TESTAMENT HISTORY; from the Creation to the Return of the Jews from Captivity. Maps and Woodcuts. Post 8vo. 7s. 6d.

————— NEW TESTAMENT HISTORY. With an Introduction connecting the History of the Old and New Testaments. Maps and Woodcuts. Post 8vo. 7s. 6d.

————— ECCLESIASTICAL HISTORY. A History of the Christian Church from its Foundation to the Eve of the Protestant Reformation. Post 8vo. 7s 6d.

————— ANCIENT HISTORY OF THE EAST; Egypt, Assyria, Babylonia, Media, Persia, Asia Minor, and Phœnicia. Woodcuts. Post 8vo. 7s. 6d.

————— GEOGRAPHY. By Rev. W. L. Bevan. Woodcuts. Post 8vo. 7s. 6d.

————— HISTORY OF GREECE; from the Earliest Times to the Roman Conquest. By Wm. Smith, D.C.L. Woodcuts. Crown 8vo. 7s. 6d.
*** Questions on the above Work, 12mo. 2s.

————— HISTORY OF ROME; from the Earliest Times to the Establishment of the Empire. By Dean Liddell. Woodcuts. Crown 8vo. 7s. 6d.

————— GIBBON'S Decline and Fall of the Roman Empire. Woodcuts. Post 8vo. 7s. 6d.

————— HALLAM'S HISTORY OF EUROPE during the Middle Ages. Post 8vo. 7s. 6d.

————— HALLAM'S HISTORY OF ENGLAND; from the Accession of Henry VII. to the Death of George II. Post 8vo. 7s. 6d.

————— HUME'S History of England from the Invasion of Julius Cæsar to the Revolution in 1688. Continued down to 1863. Woodcuts. Post 8vo. 7s. 6d.
*** Questions on the above Work, 12mo. 2s.

————— HISTORY OF FRANCE; from the Earliest Times to the Establishment of the Second Empire, 1852. By Rev. H. W. Jervis. Woodcuts. Post 8vo. 7s. 6d.

————— ENGLISH LANGUAGE. By Geo. P. Marsh. Post 8vo. 7s. 6d.

————— LITERATURE. By T. B. Shaw, M.A. Post 8vo. 7s. 6d.

————— SPECIMENS of English Literature from the Chief Writers. By T. B. Shaw, Post 8vo. 7s. 6d.

————— MODERN GEOGRAPHY; Mathematical, Physical, and Descriptive. By Rev. W. L. Bevan. Woodcuts. Post 8vo. 7s. 6d.

————— MORAL PHILOSOPHY. By William Fleming, D.D. Post 8vo. 7s. 6d.

————— BLACKSTONE'S Commentaries on the Laws of England. By R. Malcolm Kerr, LL.D. Post 8vo. 7s. 6d.

SPALDING'S (Captain) Tale of Frithiof. Translated from the Swedish of Esias Tegner. Post 8vo. 7s. 6d.

STEPHEN'S (Rev. W. R.) Life and Times of St. Chrysostom. With Portrait. 8vo. 15s.

ST. JAMES (The) LECTURES. Companions for the Devout Life. By the following authors. 8vo. 7s. 6d.
Imitation of Christ. Rev. Dr. Farrar.
Pascal's Pensees. Dean Church.
S. François de Sales. Dean Goulbourn.
Baxter's Saints' Rest. Archbishop Trench.
S. Augustine's Confessions. Bishop Alexander.
Jeremy Taylor's Holy Living and Dying. Rev. Dr Humphry

ST. JOHN'S (CHARLES) Wild Sports and Natural History of the Highlands. Post 8vo. 3s. 6d.

——————— (BAYLE) Adventures in the Libyan Desert. Post 8vo. 2s.

STORIES FOR DARLINGS. With Illustrations. 16mo. 5s.

STREET'S (G. E.) Gothic Architecture in Spain. From Personal Observations made during several Journeys. With Illustrations. Royal 8vo. 30s.

——————————————————— in Italy, chiefly in Brick and Marble. With Notes of Tours in the North of Italy. With 60 Illustrations. Royal 8vo. 26s.

STANHOPE'S (EARL) England during the Reign of Queen Anne, 1701—13. Library Edition. 8vo. 16s. Cabinet Edition. Portrait. 2 Vols. Post 8vo. 10s.

——————————————————— from the Peace of Utrecht to the Peace of Versailles, 1713-81. Library Edition. 7 vols. 8vo. 93s. Cabinet Edition, 7 vols. Post 8vo. 5s. each.

——————— British India, from its Origin to 1783. 8vo. 3s. 6d.

——————— History of "Forty-Five." Post 8vo. 3s.

——————— Historical and Critical Essays. Post 8vo. 3s. 6d.

——————— Life of Belisarius. Post 8vo. 10s. 6d.

——————— Condé. Post 8vo. 3s. 6d.

——————— William Pitt. Portraits. 4 Vols. 8vo. 24s.

——————— Miscellanies. 2 Vols. Post 8vo. 13s.

——————— Story of Joan of Arc. Fcap. 8vo. 1s.

——————— Addresses Delivered on Various Occasions. 16mo. 1s.

STYFFE'S (KNUTT) Strength of Iron and Steel. Plates. 8vo. 12s.

SOMERVILLE'S (MARY) Personal Recollections from Early Life to Old Age. With Selections from her Correspondence. Portrait. Crown 8vo. 12s.

——————— Physical Geography. Portrait. Post 8vo.

——————— Connexion of the Physical Sciences. Portrait. Post 8vo.

——————— Molecular and Microscopic Science. Illustrations. 2 Vols. Post 8vo. 21s.

SOUTHEY'S (ROBERT) Book of the Church. Post 8vo. 7s. 6d.

—— — Lives of Bunyan and Cromwell. Post 8vo. 2s.

SWAINSON'S (CANON) Nicene and Apostles' Creeds; Their Literary History; together with some Account of "The Creed of St. Athanasius." 8vo.

SYBEL'S (VON) History of Europe during the French Revolution, 1789—1795. 4 Vols. 8vo. 48s.

SYMONDS' (REV. W.) Records of the Rocks; or Notes on the Geology, Natural History, and Antiquities of North and South Wales, Siluria, Devon, and Cornwall. With Illustrations. Crown 8vo. 12s.

TAYLOR'S (SIR HENRY) Notes from Life. Fcap. 8vo. 2s.

THIELMAN'S (BARON) Journey through the Caucasus to Tabreez, Kurdistan, down the Tigris and Euphrates to Nineveh and Babylon, and across the Desert to Palmyra. Translated by CHAS. HENEAGE. Illustrations. 2 Vols. Post 8vo. 18s.

THOMS' (W. J.) Longevity of Man; its Facts and its Fiction. Including Observations on the more Remarkable Instances. Post 8vo. 10s. 6d.

THOMSON'S (ARCHBISHOP) Lincoln's Inn Sermons. 8vo. 10s. 6d.

—————— Life in the Light of God's Word. Post 8vo. 5s.

TOCQUEVILLE'S State of Society in France before the Revolution, 1789, and on the Causes which led to that Event. Translated by HENRY REEVE. 8vo. 12s.

TOMLINSON (CHARLES); The Sonnet; Its Origin, Structure, and Place in Poetry. With translations from Dante, Petrarch, &c. Post 8vo. 9s.

TOZER'S (REV. H. F.) Highlands of Turkey, with Visits to Mounts Ida, Athos, Olympus, and Pelion. 2 Vols. Crown 8vo. 24s.

———— Lectures on the Geography of Greece. Map. Post 8vo. 9s.

TRISTRAM'S (CANON) Great Sahara. Illustrations. Crown 8vo. 15s.

———— Land of Moab; Travels and Discoveries on the East Side of the Dead Sea and the Jordan. Illustrations. Crown 8vo. 15s.

TWISLETON (EDWARD). The Tongue not Essential to Speech, with Illustrations of the Power of Speech in the case of the African Confessors. Post 8vo. 6s.

TWISS' (HORACE) Life of Lord Eldon. 2 Vols. Post 8vo. 21s.

TYLOR'S (E. B.) Early History of Mankind, and Development of Civilization. 8vo. 12s.

———— Primitive Culture; the Development of Mythology, Philosophy, Religion, Art, and Custom. 2 Vols. 8vo. 24s.

VAMBERY'S (ARMINIUS) Travels from Teheran across the Turkoman Desert on the Eastern Shore of the Caspian. Illustrations. 8vo. 21s.

VAN LENNEP'S (HENRY J.) Travels in Asia Minor. With Illustrations of Biblical Literature, and Archæology. With Woodcuts. 2 Vols. Post 8vo. 24s.

———— Modern Customs and Manners of Bible Lands, in illustration of Scripture. With Maps and 300 Illustrations. 2 Vols. 8vo. 21s.

WELLINGTON'S Despatches during his Campaigns in India, Denmark, Portugal, Spain, the Low Countries, and France. Edited by COLONEL GURWOOD. 8 Vols. 8vo. 20s. each.

———— Supplementary Despatches, relating to India, Ireland, Denmark, Spanish America, Spain, Portugal, France, Congress of Vienna, Waterloo and Paris. Edited by his SON. 14 Vols. 8vo. 20s. each. ** An Index. 8vo. 20s.

———— Civil and Political Correspondence. Edited by his SON. Vols. I. to V. 8vo. 20s. each.

———— Despatches (Selections from). 8vo. 18s.

———— Speeches in Parliament. 2 Vols. 8vo. 42s.

WHEELER'S (G.) Choice of a Dwelling; a Practical Handbook of Useful Information on Building a House. Plans. Post 8vo. 7s. 6d.

WHYMPER'S (FREDERICK) Travels and Adventures in Alaska. Illustrations. 8vo. 16s.

WILBERFORCE'S (BISHOP) Essays on Various Subjects. 2 vols. 8vo. 21s.

———— Life of William Wilberforce. Portrait. Crown 8vo. 6s.

WILKINSON'S (SIR J. G.) Popular Account of the Ancient Egyptians. With 500 Woodcuts. 2 Vols. Post 8vo. 12s.

WOOD'S (CAPTAIN) Source of the Oxus. With the Geography of the Valley of the Oxus. By COL. YULE. Map. 8vo. 12s.

WORDS OF HUMAN WISDOM. Collected and Arranged by E. S. With a Preface by CANON LIDDON. Fcap. 8vo. 3s. 6d.

WORDSWORTH'S (BISHOP) Athens and Attica. Plates. 8vo. 5s.

———— Greece. With 600 Woodcuts. Royal 8vo.

YULE'S (COLONEL) Book of Marco Polo. Illustrated by the Light of Oriental Writers and Modern Travels. With Maps and 80 Plates. 2 Vols. Medium 8vo. 63s.

www.ingramcontent.com/pod-product-compliance
Lightning Source LLC
Chambersburg PA
CBHW031053110726
47900CB00003B/905